Thunder in May

Thunder in May

Andy Johnson

Spiderwize

Thunder in May

Spiderwize
Office 404, 4th Floor
Albany House
324/326 Regent Street
London
W1B 3HH
UK

www.spiderwize.com

This is a work of fiction. Names, characters and incidents are products of the author's imagination. Any resemblance to persons living or dead is entirely coincidental.

The views expressed in this work are solely those of the author and do not necessarily reflect the views of the publisher, and the publisher hereby disclaims any responsibility for them.

ISBN: 978-1-908128-20-1

This book is dedicated to my friends and comrades who did their duty and paid the ultimate price.

At the going down of the sun, and in the morning, _I will_ remember them.

It is also for my wife, Clare, who always believed.

And for Mac' and Simon – the loyalists.

Contents

Acknowledgments

The author would like to thank Mo Mowbray, Andy Mowbray, Neil Thackeray, Gary Watson, Frank Waite, Graeme Atkinson, Andy Layton, Anne Waite and Victoria Watson of The Frontline Association for their kind assistance in producing the cover photographs.

Cover images are copyright
A Johnson/The Frontline Association.

A percentage of the profit from all of the author's novels is donated annually to various British military charities.

Foreword

As with Seelöwe Nord, this novel is *not* a work of historical reference. It is an adventure story of men at war. Although some forty percent of the characters are historical and almost all of the events are well documented historical fact, I have, as with any work of fiction, dramatised events where I have seen fit and even made a bit of it up! Not that the events of May and June 1940 need any dramatisation of course; they were dramatic enough for those who experienced them.

I first had the idea of this novel more than twenty years ago when, as a wide-eyed recruit, I first learned the story of my regiment's wartime escapades. Over the years I have trawled through the regimental archives to read every bit of detail I could find, but I never felt confident enough to put pen to paper. Partly due to the great reception that Seelöwe Nord has received, and partly because I have stopped worrying about trying to get everything 'watertight' in order to please everyone, I finally decided to get on with this particular story. If nothing else, it gave me the opportunity to revive some of my favourite characters from the first novel.

The problem with writing about military history of course, is that there are so many experts; some highly qualified and well respected, others self appointed. Most of them have their own belief systems about military history and see any deviation from their considered opinion as heresy. I am not a historian and make no pretence to be one. I am, quite simply, a retired soldier with a healthy interest in the history of his profession. As a former soldier with a modest amount of combat experience, the one thing I can do is 'put myself in the shoes' of those soldiers who have gone before.

For me, to walk along the beaches of Bray Dunes and La Panne, or to stand inside the reconstructed barn near Wormhoudt, where the SS Leibstandarte massacred their British prisoners, is a very real, very personal, and very thought provoking experience. I felt the same in those places as I did at Monte Cassino, on Omaha Beach, on the battlefield of Waterloo, and on the plateau at Towton. Whenever I walk the ground where men have fought, I can, as all former soldiers can, feel the tension; identify with the physical and mental strain of the soldiers who fought there, and the commanders who wracked their brains to find the recipe for victory. I know what it is to march twenty miles at night in full kit, deprived of food and sleep, reliant on whispered updates being passed from man to man, with no end in sight. I understand, in short, what von Clausewitz referred to as the 'frictions of war'.

I have no political stand-point and I do not seek to make or break reputations. I make no attempt to re-write history to my own satisfaction. I write this novel, as with my others, to try and help people to understand the 'experience' of war; and to honour the memory of *all* those who fought in the campaigns of 1940, regardless of their nationality. They were, after all, extraordinary people caught up in extraordinary circumstances. Soldiers rarely have a choice about where, when and who they fight, but it is their duty to fight all the same, and to fight well. I also write these novels, so that in some small way, I can do my bit for the servicemen and women of today, by donating a percentage of my profits annually to British military charities.

I hope readers can understand that in war there are rarely such things as incontrovertible facts. Even in the modern world, with the aid of satellite surveillance, extensive battlefield technology and the desire for moral accountability, it is still almost impossible to get the 'exact' story. Perhaps the reason for this is that, ultimately, the experience of battle is different for everybody. No one person remembers a battle quite the same as another. A very competent policeman once told me that you can always tell when there's something not quite right with an investigation when all the witness statements match too closely, for it is human nature to perceive events in our own unique way.

By way of illustration, the last battle in which I took part before retirement lasted three and a half hours and was a fighting withdrawal across two and a quarter miles of complex terrain against a highly mobile enemy. The entire spectrum of infantry weapons was employed, in addition to medium mortars and ground attack aircraft. To this day, I clearly remember the battle consisted of four distinct engagements, whereas several of my comrades insist that there were only three. Other comrades swear blind there were no less than five separate engagements. Many of them talk with animation about the moment 'the enemy blew the bridge on us'. For my part, even with hindsight, I cannot remember the bridge being blown up, or even hearing the massive explosion that undoubtedly occurred. In fact, it was more than an hour after the battle before I found out, by sheer accident, that the bridge in question had been demolished during the fire-fight. During the after action review, the commanders amongst us disagreed on several occasions about which buildings we had been pinned down in. And that is the problem with military history. Sometimes, we may never know quite *how* things happened, only that they *did* happen.

Having said all this, if readers would like to learn more about the *facts* concerning the May and June 1940 campaign in North-West Europe, then there is no shortage of information. There are many readily available memoires now in print along with an endless list of academic works. For the layman, Len Deighton's classic *Blitzkrieg* is a good starting point, and Hugh Sebag-Montefiore's *Dunkirk: Fight to the last man* is compulsive reading. Major General Julian Thompson's incisive *Dunkirk: Retreat to victory* tells the British version of the campaign in precise and analytical detail.

One book, sadly out of print now but available through second hand book dealers, was a wonderful find for me. Though I had already studied the various histories of the Guards regiments from the Dunkirk campaign, I found Dilip Sarkar's outstanding work *Guards VC: Blitzkrieg 1940* to be priceless. This detailed narrative of one British formation's experiences is written with a policeman's eye for chronological and evidential clarity. The book brings all the Guards source material together neatly, adds to it with personal recollections from veterans, sourced by the author, and also brings in the German side of the story to produce a well rounded and thought provoking tribute. Mr Sarkar achieved his aim of honouring the combatants with his excellent academic work. I can only hope that this novel does something similar. I hope you enjoy this novel. I also hope you will remember those who feature in it with the respect their memory deserves.

Andy Johnson
May 2011

PLAN YELLOW - THE GERMAN OFFENSIVE OF MAY 1940

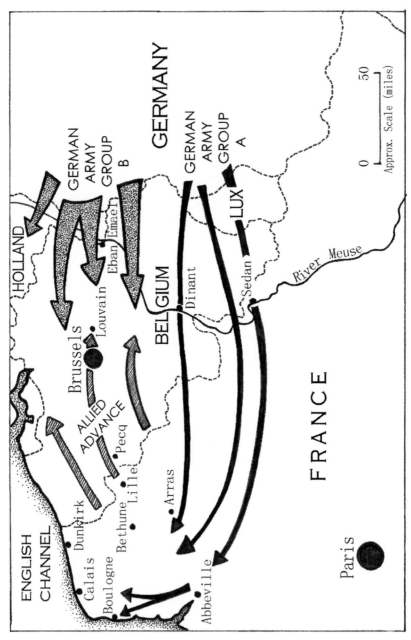

Map produced by Laura Martin of LM-Art

PART ONE

OVERTURE

Thursday 9th May 1940
Approaching Midnight

STORM BATTALION SECRET AIRFIELD – NEAR COLOGNE, GERMANY THURSDAY 9TH MAY 1940 – 2255 HOURS

The air of expectation in the hangar was palpable. The huge building was crammed with the men of the specially trained Storm Battalion, yet there was hardly a murmur from them. Instead, the constant, urgent scratching of pen on paper filled the great space as the paratroopers and assault pioneers wrote out their last letters home, and in some cases, their wills.

"Two minutes, men, then I need the last ones in the sack."

The battalion chief clerk's voice echoed through the hangar, and the assembled troops, already writing at speed, scrawled faster.

Moments later, the side door of the hangar clattered open and a group of unfamiliar staff officers entered, carrying trestle tables and boards covered with dark cloth. Without a word, watched by the now alert storm-troopers, the dozen or so officers began erecting the tables and propping up the boards on top of them. Before they had finished, another group of officers entered the hangar. This time, the men of the Storm Battalion recognised the new-comers. The first was Lieutenant Witzig, the second in command, accompanied by Sergeant Major Linden, and they in turn were followed by Captain Koch, their commanding officer. The three senior ranks of the battalion were accompanied by a colonel they had not seen before.

"Alright, you lot; stop what you're doing and form up in front of the briefing area. Move!" Linden's curt orders echoed inside the huge building.

Instantly, the highly trained storm-troopers scrambled to their feet and began to form orderly lines in front of the boards. Once assembled, Linden ordered them to sit. The sergeant major then nodded to Koch, who came and stood in front of his battalion, surveying the eager, expectant faces.

"Men, tonight is a big night; probably the biggest night of all our lives. We have trained hard these last few months and we've all been bursting to know what it's all been for; me just as much as any of you. Well…now we're going to find out."

He turned towards the colonel who was standing patiently by the covered boards and executed a smart salute.

"The Storm Battalion is ready for your orders, Colonel." Koch snapped, then took his position to one side.

The colonel took a few moments to gaze around the audience and study the rapt faces. Eventually he spoke, his voice clear, sharp and precise.

"Tonight, Germany will launch an offensive which will go down in history. Our plan is to smash the combined armies of Holland, Belgium, France and Britain before they even get out of bed. You, the men of the Storm Battalion, will lead that assault."

The colonel paused slightly, nodding to the group of staff captains. Swiftly, they removed the covers from the boards, revealing a selection of maps and air photographs. Still utterly silent, the men of the battalion strained their eyes to see the detail on the three map boards. The colonel tapped the central board with his riding crop.

"Your target is Fort Eben Emael...in Belgium. You take off at 0300 hours..."

HEADQUARTERS BRITISH 2ND CORPS – PHALEMPIN, NEAR LILLE, FRANCE
THURSDAY 9TH MAY 1940 – 2300 HOURS

Lieutenant General Alan Brooke stared out of the window into the darkness and strained his ears, trying to detect any sound. Nothing. The anti-aircraft battery down the lane had ceased fire several minutes earlier, and the faint sound of the crew commanders giving their orders had faded away. There was no sound of aircraft either; the last German raiders having passed over completely. Brooke wondered where they were heading, and why, but at the same time remained thankful that the enemy was intent on finding another target and not his Corps HQ.

Closing the blackout curtains with care, Brooke returned to his small writing bureau and switched the lamp back on again. He took a seat and returned to his journal. Despite his tiredness, he decided to make sure that his entry for the day was complete before he turned in for the night. He quickly scanned the most recent sentence that referred to his visit to the Cypriot Mule Column, then began scratching away again with his pen.

This evening German planes came over about 10 pm...

He completed the entry, then placed his pen down and removed his glasses, raising his free hand and rubbing his temples with thumb and forefinger. There was still so much to do. The British Expeditionary Force was being pulled in every direction on a daily basis by the meddling amateurs back home, who constantly sent orders for redeployments of brigades and divisions, moving them from one formation to another and generally confusing everybody. As if their predicament wasn't bad enough. In Brooke's opinion, the BEF needed the whole summer to sort itself out, and even then it would still leave a lot to be desired. His men needed to train, some more than others, and many of them were still short of important equipment and weaponry. Still, no use worrying about that now; it could all wait till the morning.

Despite his fatalistic attitude, Brooke was still worried. His son, Tom, a junior officer with the BEF, remained desperately ill in hospital, his life very much in the balance after the appendicitis that had nearly killed him a fortnight earlier. And of course John Dill was gone; returned to England to assume the appointment of Vice Chief of the Imperial General Staff. Dill had been a tower of strength for Brooke over the last few months. As neighbouring corps commanders, the two of them, old friends anyway, had enjoyed a harmonious partnership as they both struggled to get their formations ready for war. Now he was gone however and Brooke felt that intellectually he was very much alone amongst the other senior officers of the BEF. On a more encouraging note, Dill should certainly have a positive effect back in the War Office. Perhaps some of the more pressing issues would finally be resolved with his competent hand at the helm?

Whatever…Brooke needed to sleep. There was no end of things to attend to in the morning, and so with a deep sigh, he rose to his feet and wandered through to his bedroom, unbuckling his Sam Browne as he went.

THE IN-LYING PICQUET, 2ND BATTALION COLDSTREAM GUARDS
PONT-A-MARCQ – JUST SOUTH OF LILLE, FRANCE
THURSDAY 9TH MAY 1940 – 2310 HOURS

"Picquet Officer!"

Sergeant Davey Jackson of No.4 Company, tonight acting as the Sergeant of the Battalion In-lying Picquet, announced the arrival of himself and the Picquet Officer in a loud, business-like voice. In the darkness, he heard the scrabbling of ammunition boots on cobbles and a burst of urgent whispering. He reached the sand-bagged machine-gun position that covered the road eastwards and stepped to one side, allowing the Picquet Officer, his own platoon commander, the newly arrived Mr Dunstable, to step forward and conduct his inspection.

From inside the small redoubt, two dark silhouettes popped up, and a moment later, Jackson heard the familiar 'crunch-crunch' as the two sentries pulled their feet in and adopted the position of attention.

"No.1 Section, Sixteen Platoon, Sir, and all's well." Came the voice with a Yorkshire accent, using the prescribed formula.

Instantly, Jackson recognised the voice and pulled a sour, disapproving face.

"Evening Guardsman Hawkins." Said Dunstable brightly. "Who's that with you?"

"Guardsman Richards, Sir." Came the second voice from within the machine-gun post; a heavy Cockney accent this time.

"How are we all tonight, chaps? Everything alright? A bit boring I imagine?"

Dunstable continued in his bright tone.

Jackson's frown deepened as he found his way to the position's entrance and stepped through. As the two guardsmen continued to engage in small talk with the Picquet Officer, Jackson prowled about the redoubt, checking that everything was just as it should be. After a short while, he interrupted the conversation.

"Where's the barrel bag for the Bren Gun?" He demanded.

The other three men broke off their conversation and, after a short pause, Richards reached down and picked something up from the floor.

"Here, Sergeant." He answered, lifting the webbing valise up where it could be seen.

Jackson was unimpressed.

"Get it on here, next to the Bren. You don't want to be groping around for it in the dark during a barrel change if you've got half the German army coming at you!"

The young guardsman hurriedly placed it on the rampart next to the section's light machine-gun.

"Sorry Sergeant." He mumbled.

Jackson watched him do it, before snapping another question.

"Range card?"

There was another brief pause as Richards and Hawkins looked at each other through the darkness. After a moment, Hawkins fumbled in his trouser pocket and pulled out a piece of folded paper.

"It's here Sergeant." He replied. "I was going to put it out at first light. Not much point having it out in the dark…" His voice trailed off, stopping short of becoming insolent.

There was another brief pause.

"Where are your arc markers, then?" Jackson demanded, his voice low and dangerous.

Silence again. This time, nobody spoke. After long moments, it was Jackson who broke the spell.

"Range cards go away at last light, and arc markers go up, don't they?" He asked in a clipped, rhetorical tone. "If the Jerries come tonight, and you don't have your arc markers up, what's to stop you from swinging too far left and brassing up the nearest platoon from No.3 Company?"

Again, there was no answer.

"Get it sorted, sharpish!" Jackson growled, leaving the sandbagged post.

"Okay, chaps," Dunstable intervened in an uncomfortable voice, "we'll leave you to sort that out."

"May I have your permission for myself and one other guardsman to carry on, Sir, please?"

Hawkins' voice rapped out the required phrase as dictated by regimental custom, at a speed that suggested he was keen to be rid of the Picquet Officer and Picquet Sergeant just as soon as possible.

"Yes, please." Dunstable acknowledged the request. "Oh, and keep your eyes peeled. There's been a bit of a flap on for the last couple of hours. It'll probably all calm down soon enough, but best be on your guard, eh?"

The two guardsmen murmured their affirmation, and Dunstable turned away, followed by a grim looking Jackson.

Together, the officer and his platoon sergeant strode away, their boots ringing on the cobbles of the road as they headed towards the next section's sentry post. When they were out of ear-shot, Dunstable threw a nervous glance at Jackson.

"I get the idea that you don't like Hawkins very much, Sergeant Jackson?"

Jackson gave a low growl, before answering.

"He's a little fucking scrote, Sir, is Hawkins!"

Dunstable raised an eyebrow in mild surprise but had little chance to remark on Jackson's comment, for the senior NCO went on quickly.

"I know his family, Sir. They're from Hull, just down the road from my folks in Goole. Everybody in the East Riding knows the Hawkins clan. A bunch of crooks, every last one of them; never done a days work in their lives, they haven't. Not honest work any road."

Dunstable couldn't help but smile.

"Well, our resident member of the Hawkins family won't have any choice with you as his platoon sergeant, will he?"

Jackson grunted; a strange sound that almost smacked of grudging humour.

"Too right, he won't, Sir! If that little fucker puts one foot wrong while I'm around, I'll be using his bollocks for a game of conkers!"

7TH PANZER DIVISION ASSEMBLY AREA – GERMAN/LUXEMBOURG BORDER THURSDAY 9TH MAY 1940 – 2320 HOURS

Captain Herman Vosse strained his eyes into the pitch dark, using his peripheral vision to try and locate the track ahead; no easy task in a thick forestry block in the dead of night.

"A little further, Bauer." He murmured to the driver over the low hum of the engine.

The corporal, at the wheel of the open topped staff car, gunned the engine a little more and the vehicle lurched forward over the badly churned up track. Vosse hung on tightly, staring over the wind-shield in an attempt to pick out his route, but then ducked suddenly as a branch, covered in long, sharp pine-needles whipped upwards and into his face. The captain stifled a curse as the springy branch caught him sharply on the crown of his head, knocking his service cap off into the rear passenger seat. He cursed slightly louder just a second later as the car came to a sudden stop and he was thrown into the glass wind-shield with a painful thud.

Before the German officer had a chance to ask, his corporal informed him of the reason for the sudden halt.

"Torch." Snapped the driver, in a hushed voice.

Vosse pushed himself upright again and stared beyond the bonnet of the vehicle. There. A flash of a small red torch; then another short flash just a moment later.

"Hold it there." Vosse whispered unnecessarily to his companion, who was staring with bleary eyes towards the flashing torch. They had been driving for several hours and both of them were tired and on edge.

The flashing of the torch ceased and a dark figure emerged from the gloom and came towards them cautiously.

"Who's that?" Came a blunt, German voice that was familiar to both of the men in the car.

"Henschel? Is that you?" Vosse ignored the stranger's question and delivered his own.

There was a slight pause and then the voice came again.

"Yes, it's me. Who's that?"

Vosse let out a small sigh of relief as the military police sergeant who commanded one of the security detachments assigned to the divisional headquarters confirmed his identity.

"It's Captain Vosse." The officer now gave his own identity to the dark figure standing hard by the bonnet of the vehicle. "Where's the divisional commander's Tac' HQ?"

The sergeant raised his arm and pointed further along the dark track towards the seemingly impenetrable woodland.

"Just up there a little way, Captain." He replied, keeping his voice as low as possible. "You'll come to a small clearing on your left. Park the car up there next to the motorcycles, then go into the trees on the right. You'll find the General's vehicles tucked in there with the canvas and cam' nets up."

"Good man." Vosse thanked the helpful sergeant and muttered the command to Bauer to advance again. The dark figure of Sergeant Henschel stepped aside as the car's engine revved gently again and lurched forward over another furrow of earth.

They found the clearing a minute later, just as described. Vosse, having begun to suffer from fatigue and worry earlier that night, felt a sudden wave of relief wash over him. He'd found his way back! These forests were a nightmare for navigation at night, especially under blackout conditions, but now he was here, right where he needed to be, and the first pulse of excitement began to course through his body. Moving as quickly as he dared, being careful not to poke his eyes out on one of the dozen branches that obstructed his path, Vosse pushed through the undergrowth and quickly came up against the collection of command vehicles, parked back to back in a kind of star formation, a large, camouflaged tent filling the space in the centre. He circumnavigated the arrangement of canvas and netting, tripping over several pegs as he did so. Eventually however, he came to the opening and pulled the flap back, just a touch, before stepping carefully inside. As he entered the tent, he registered a constant hubbub of low murmuring, shielded torch-lights, and the pungent smell of hot coffee. His mouth began to water involuntarily.

"Who's that?" One of the dark figures within asked sharply as Vosse stepped amongst the crowd in the headquarters tent.

Instantly, he recognised the voice of the Divisional Commander's aide-de-camp, Lieutenant Most.

"It's me; Captain Vosse. Where's the General?"

There was a brief pause, and then Most's voice sounded again, respectful this time, but also tinged with a sense of expectation.

"He's over here, Captain. Just here, look?"

The lieutenant's dark silhouette moved across the crowded interior of the tent, and Vosse followed him, squeezing past signallers who sat on small camp chairs at collapsible desks, peering at map boards and documents by torch light, headsets clamped firmly over their ears.

Vosse's eyes were starting to adjust to his new surroundings and he could now make out the detail of the packed, and quietly busy, headquarters. There was an air of tension in the place; an electric buzz that one could feel amongst the highly trained command staff. In front of him, Most came to a halt and addressed a figure that sat hunched over a map board.

"Herr General?" Most interrupted the preoccupied looking figure.

The man looked up.

"Captain Vosse has returned, Sir." Most said simply.

The man stood instantly and turned around, spotted Vosse's outline, then stepped forward towards the captain and squinted at him in the darkness. Despite the gloomy interior, the glow from several torches and dials on the radio sets threw a sickly green-yellow glare across the other man's face, and Vosse found himself staring into the shrewd, business-like features of General Erwin Rommel, hero of the First World War, one of Hitler's favourites and commander of the 7th Panzer Division.

Rommel eyed the staff captain for a few seconds then, quietly, asked, "You've come from Corps Headquarters?"

Vosse nodded in acknowledgement.

"Yes, General. I have come directly. Corps insisted that radio silence is maintained and so they sent me personally to give you the message."

Rommel's face was unreadable, yet all around the tent, the murmuring had stopped, and all eyes were focussed on the General and his liaison officer, the sense of expectation obvious in everyone else's body language.

"And the message is?" Rommel enquired mildly.

Vosse opened his mouth to reply but found that he had suddenly gone dry. He caught his breath and swallowed hard, whilst Rommel patiently awaited his answer. Finally he found his voice.

"Danzig, Sir. Codeword Danzig. It's on, General." Croaked Vosse, his pulse racing.

"Definitely?" Rommel queried, his voice still calm and measured. "At the appointed time?"

Vosse nodded eagerly.

"Yes, General." He replied, his voice rising with the release of tension. "Exactly as per the warning order. Plan Yellow is a 'go'."

OFFICE OF THE RIGHT HONOURABLE WINSTON CHURCHILL, MP – LONDON
THURSDAY 9TH MAY 1940 – 2330 HOURS

Churchill swilled the last drop of brandy around his glass and looked up over the rim of his spectacles at the door.

"Yes?" He rumbled in his deep, sonorous voice, in response to the knock.

The door opened and a familiar face appeared; that of Brendan Bracken, Member of Parliament for Paddington North and long time confidant of Churchill.

"Brendan? How very nice to see you, even at this late hour."

Bracken smiled back, revealing bad, unattractive teeth.

"Do you have a moment or two, Winston?"

"For you old friend, all the time in the world." Churchill replied. "Please come in."

Bracken entered the office and quietly clicked the door shut, throwing a characteristically furtive look behind him as he did so. Having shut the door, the tall red-headed politician moved awkwardly across to the centre of the room and gave Churchill a look that spoke of barely suppressed excitement. Churchill continued to regard him with a calm, measured gaze.

"The news isn't good about Norway." Churchill grunted, conversationally.

"No…no, not very." Bracken agreed, shifting from one foot to another.

Churchill smiled.

"But I gather you are not here to simply join me in debating the ills of current military and naval operations?"

Bracken gave a thin-lipped smile which was confirmation enough. At length, he drew breath and spoke.

"I have been keeping my ear to the ground; talking to a few people."

Churchill continued to smile benignly, sensing the game.

"And did you hear anything interesting during your evening of 'listening'?"

Bracken held his breath for a moment, but then it came tumbling out.

"They say Chamberlain will go; tomorrow possibly."

The only reaction that Churchill made that might suggest surprise was the slight raising of one bushy eyebrow.

"He will go sometime, that's for sure. I think he feels that he cannot go on without full support from across the benches. It is really a case of who will follow him? Given the meeting we had today with our friends from The Opposition, I'm not sure they are willing to see Chamberlain continue, even if they were given a place in a coalition government"

Bracken nodded back vigorously.

"Indeed not, Winston. But they would follow you."

Churchill took a deep breath and sat back slightly in his chair.

"What, even after the way I spoke to them in the debate yesterday? Even after I defended Chamberlain? Me? The old 'warmonger' ". He chuckled in amusement.

Bracken nodded once more, firmly.

"Yes they would. Despite their long opposition to your stance, they see now, as everyone does, that you have been right all along. They know you have the measure of the situation."

Churchill continued to regard his friend with mild amusement.

"If I was asked to step up to the wheel, then I would do my duty readily. You know that Brendan. But I have the impression that Chamberlain prefers Halifax."

Bracken shook his head quickly.

"It won't be Halifax." He stated, his tone confident.

Churchill raised both eyebrows now.

"Not Halifax?"

Bracken was barely able to contain himself. He rushed on in a low, urgent voice.

"Halifax will refuse it; I am sure. He believes that it is not appropriate for a member of the Upper House to be Prime Minister and do his business in the Commons. At least that's what he will say in public. Perhaps he just has no intention of accepting a poison chalice? He knows how bad things are. He knows that it will require a miracle to reverse our fortunes now. And he is not a man in favour of war."

Churchill stirred slightly, a rising sense of fate making him fidget in his seat. Was it just Bracken's furtiveness that was catching his imagination, he wondered, or did he detect something more profound here?

"So what is Chamberlain going to do?" Churchill felt the breath catch in his throat even as he asked the question, almost scared of what the answer might be.

Bracken's smile was broadening now, his unsightly teeth plain to see, like filthy piano keys.

"Tomorrow you are meeting with Chamberlain and Halifax?"

Churchill nodded.

"In that meeting, you should remain silent and let things play out. Chamberlain will tell you that The Opposition will not accept his continuance as Prime Minister under any circumstances. Halifax will refuse the position. That leaves only one suitable candidate. The only person that Attlee and Greenwood will accept. That's *you* Winston."

Churchill placed the brandy glass down on the side table with a surprisingly loud bang and closed his eyes, taking a deep breath. In his ears, he felt a rushing of blood, and in his mind he heard every cruel word said about him over the last ten years. Was it possible that he could have come from the political wilderness to this place in time and history? The sound of his detractors' voices clamoured inside his head, so real to his imagination that he barely registered Bracken's next words.

"They want *you* to be Prime Minister."

Friday 10th May 1940
The First Day

THE GARRISON HEADQUARTERS – FORT EBEN EMAEL, BELGIUM
FRIDAY 10TH MAY 1940 – 0120 HOURS

Major Jean Jottrand, Commanding Officer of the garrison of Fort Eben Emael, the linchpin of Belgium's defences along the River Maas, entered his subterranean headquarters deep within the fortress and glanced around the room. Only a small portion of the garrison's officers, those on duty, were present; lounging on the small amount of furniture in a casual, bored manner. Even so, they displayed the courtesy expected by standing when their commander appeared through the doorway.

He gazed at the faces of his subordinates, registering the variety of expressions. Pauwels looked half asleep still, Renard annoyed at being tipped out of bed at such an hour, whilst Dupont looked reasonably alert, if a little full of wine perhaps?

"Gentlemen," he began, deciding to avoid pre-amble, "I have been sent a message by Divisional Headquarters. It arrived just over half an hour ago. Its contents are somewhat unusual, not to mention disturbing."

The assembled officers exchanged puzzled expressions before looking back at their commander. Jottrand quickly unfolded the piece of paper and began to read it. As he recited the message, his subordinates began shuffling uncomfortably. At length, Jottrand looked up from the paper and gazed at each of the officers in turn.

"I repeat," he said bleakly, "this is a *real alert.*"

For a moment, there was absolute silence, but then Dupont, his senior lieutenant, pulled a face and made a reply.

"That cannot be correct Major. Only just two hours ago we received the order that we could increase the men's leave from two days a month to five. Surely we wouldn't receive such a message as this latest one after having been told that?"

The lieutenant looked about him, looking for support.

"We've had this before, remember?" Renard grumbled. "You know? The one when the General got sacked for scaring the King half to death with wild stories about a German attack. This may be another false alarm. I say we treat it with caution until we get confirmation of its authenticity."

Next to Renard, Pauwels stirred.

"But it's an official message, is it not Major? Surely we should take it seriously until told otherwise?"

The room instantly came alive with heated discussion, and Jottrand's own sleep-fuddled mind was finding it hard enough to keep up with the strange sequence of contradictory messages he had received during the previous evening, without the added distraction of the noisy disagreement now taking place in the small room. He was about to call the group to order when another man entered the headquarters. He looked up sharply as the figure entered, then felt his heart lighten slightly as he laid eyes on his second in command, Captain Vermeulen.

The captain looked worried and cast his gaze about the room, trying to make sense of the fraught scene he had happened upon.

"Major?" He gave Jottrand a quizzical look. "What is happening? What's all the excitement about? You can hear it half-way around the fort; the men are getting uneasy."

As he spoke, the remaining officers fell silent and turned toward the newcomer. Jottrand took advantage of the sudden break in the debate to read the message once more. As he did so, he kept his eyes on the captain, gauging his response. That response was pronounced.

Vermeulen's face darkened, and a deep frown spread across his face.

"Then we must move quickly, Sir. Time is vital. There is much to be done. I have not heard the signal-gun fire yet; has the order been given?"

Jottrand glanced quickly towards the group of lieutenants. Before he could speak, Renard answered the query.

"We are still discussing the matter Henri. The word has yet to be sent to the signal-gun crew."

The captain's eyes widened.

"Discussing the matter?" He gasped. "This is a direct order from the High Command! There is nothing to discuss; surely Major?" He turned appealing eyes on Jottrand.

A pang of guilt ran through Jottrand. Vermeulen was right, of course. Jottrand had been reluctant to execute the order in the face of his ambivalent junior officers, but now Vermeulen's robust demeanour was providing the moral lever he needed.

"You are absolutely right, Captain." The Major replied, steeling himself to deliver the final word on the matter. "Although there is a good chance that the message may be a false alarm, for whatever reason, it is still an official instruction and must be obeyed. If we end up spending half the night awake for no good reason then tomorrow we can catch up on our sleep and all will be fine. However, just in case this is not a mistake… Renard; start organising the evacuation of the barracks and headquarters outside the main gate; get all the files and essential equipment inside the fort. Pauwels, go and give the order to the signal-gun crew. Fire the guns and start assembling the garrison. I want every man at his post by dawn."

STORM BATTALION SECRET AIRFIELD – NEAR COLOGNE, GERMANY
FRIDAY 10TH MAY 1940 – 0400 HOURS

Lieutenant Gustav Pilsner drummed his fingers on the desk, glancing up at the clock on the window ledge for the hundredth time that night. The operations room was deathly quiet as he and the duty clerk sat waiting, impatiently, for any news. The special unit, the designation of which he didn't even know, had left the airfield about an hour ago, crammed inside gliders that had been towed by JU52 transport aircraft. The gaggle of senior officers who had appeared just before midnight had crammed themselves into a small room elsewhere in the building and locked the door behind them. It was all very mysterious, but something big was going on; that much was obvious.

He glanced across to the clerk who was reading a book, lost in his own little world.

"Hey, Becker; how about some coffee? Just one more cup to see us through until breakfast, eh?"

The clerk nodded tiredly, his eyes bulging through lack of sleep.

"No problem, Lieutenant." The private replied, placing his book down. "I could do with a break. My eyes are popping out like a racing dog's bollocks!"

Pilsner emitted a grunt of a laugh.

"Mine too. Can't wait until this shift is over. I can hear my bed calling for me."

Becker smiled and wandered through to the back room where the stove was situated.

As the clerk disappeared, the sound of a vehicle engine came to Pilsner. He looked toward the window in mild surprise, even though he could see nothing through the heavy blackout curtains. The sound of the engine grew louder. Whoever was driving round the airfield at this time of the morning was in a hurry. Pilsner stood, intrigued. Even as he was getting to his feet, he heard the vehicle roar up to the building and brake hard. Whilst the brakes were still squealing, he heard the sound of the door being opened, followed a split second later by urgent footsteps. The duty officer began to get a sinking feeling. This wasn't normal.

He began walking to the door but stopped halfway when he heard the door of the building bang open, and the sound of running feet in the corridor. Becker appeared in the doorway of the side room and looked at Pilsner with a puzzled expression.

"I just peeked out the window, Lieutenant. It's one of those paratroopers; he's just jumped out of a civilian car."

Before Pilsner had a chance to digest the information, the door to the office flew open and a lone figure entered.

"Where's the duty officer?" The newcomer demanded, even before he had stepped over the threshold.

Pilsner and Becker stood blinking in surprise as they gawped at the man in the doorway. It was indeed one of the paratroopers who had been based at the airfield; dressed in full jump gear and helmet, and looking very agitated. Pilsner tried to remember the man's name.

"Witzig?" He guessed. "What's the matter?"

Witzig looked directly at him.

"I need a plane; a Junkers. Quickly!"

"What?" Pilsner frowned. "I thought you'd all gone…"

"We did." Witzig snapped, cutting him short. "But the fucking tow-rope on the glider snapped, thanks to the Junkers pilot nearly crashing into another plane and then taking evasive action! We've come down about six kilometres away. I've left my men preparing an improvised airstrip. Get me another Junkers, quickly. I need to get back to the glider and get moving again or else the rest of my company will have to assault the objective on their own."

Pilsner was lost already; the sudden flurry of information too quick for him.

"What objective? What do you mean?"

Witzig's face darkened.

"Just get me a fucking Junkers ready, quick man! Or else you'll have the Fuhrer himself to deal with!"

Pilsner felt his heart lurch. He had no idea what this Witzig or the rest of his unit were up to, but he sensed that whatever it was, they had some very important patrons backing them.

"I… I don't think there are any." He stammered. "Every aircraft is up already…"

"Then get one from somewhere else, man!" Witzig snarled.

The paratrooper was obviously in a state of high emotion.

"I… I can try the airfield at…" Pilsner began.

"Do it." Witzig snapped sharply.

With his mind racing, Pilsner hurried across to the phone and picked up the handset, dialling the military operator with trembling hands.

"Hello? Yes, this is the duty officer at Koln-Ostheim; get me the duty officer at Gutersloh, quickly."

There was a pause while the connection was made.

"Hello? Becker here, from Koln-Ostheim. Listen, I have an urgent problem. I need a Junkers 52 immediately. Have you got one spare?"

Another pause. Pilsner looked up at Witzig as he spoke again.

"I can't give details over the phone; suffice to say that the mission is of personal interest to the Fuhrer himself."

Witzig nodded his approval.

A moment later, a look of relief flooded over Pilsner's face.

"Good. Excellent. How soon can it get here?"

Another pause.

"Okay; we'll be waiting. Thank you."

He slammed the phone down and looked back at the grim faced Fallschirmjager officer.

"They've got one." He breathed with some relief. "It's on its way."

GLIDER 'GRANITE 12' – OVER FORT EBEN EMAEL, BELGIUM
FRIDAY 10TH MAY 1940 – 0425 HOURS

"Brace, brace, brace!"

Corporal Erich Braun pushed his feet against the edge of the seat opposite, and linked arms with the men on either side of him. In the cramped interior of the glider, the other members of his squad did the same.

"What's it looking like Willi?" He shouted to the pilot.

The pilot's voice came back, calm and measured.

"Looks fine; nothing on the roof. Nothing I can see, anyway. No fire coming up at us. These fuckers must be fast asleep!"

"Amen to that." Braun whispered.

Silently, he prayed that the roof of the fort wasn't mined. Perhaps that was why it wasn't wired?

"OK boys, here we go!" The pilot's voice called again. "Twenty seconds to landing, hold onto your wedding tackle!"

The specially trained assault troopers of the Storm Battalion grimaced at each other as they prepared themselves for the impact of touchdown. No matter how many times you practiced, it never got any easier.

Crash!

The glider hit the ground with a bone-juddering bounce that had the occupants jumping madly in the canvas seats. The bounce became a slide and the soldiers fell sideways as they gripped onto each other tightly.

Suddenly the glider seemed to slew to one side, lost speed, then with a final crunch, came to a halt and lolled over to one side, sending the German assault troopers sprawling. After a moment of absolute stillness and silence, the pilot's voice came back once more. "I'd get out the starboard side if you don't want to fall off the edge and break your necks fellas."

Instantly, Braun snapped into action.

"Out!" He roared in his thick Hamburg accent. "Let's go!"

He pushed himself upwards and kicked out the starboard door, leaping into the weak light of the new morning without hesitation.

As his feet hit the ground, he brought his machine-pistol up and looked about him. They had done it! They were on the roof of the great fortress of Eben Emael, although when he glanced to his left he saw that the glider was indeed situated precariously close to the edge of the vast stronghold. Behind him, his men began leaping out after him. He could see small turrets, steel set in concrete, dotted around the vast expanse of turf covered roof, but no gunfire came from them.

"Over there!"

The sound of one of his men shouting the warning made Braun swing around in surprise. As he did so, he caught sight of a lone Belgian soldier running towards the fortress at a fast sprint.

Crack!

The sound of the gunshot from the nearest storm-trooper half deafened the corporal and he twisted his head away.

"Leave him!" He snapped at the private who had taken the pot shot. "Come on, let's go for the nearest turret!"

With that, Braun lurched forward and set off at the double towards the nearest enemy gun turret which was situated about a hundred metres away, followed closely by his seven troopers and the two crewmen from the glider. As they ran, weighed down with explosive charges and grenades, another glider slid down onto the roof of the fort, just off to their right, about fifty metres away. Ignoring the aircraft, Braun and his men pounded onwards towards the enemy position. It was 0425 hours on Friday 10th of May 1940, and the most spectacular feat of German arms in the war so far was well and truly underway... and the defenders of Fort Eben Emael were in for a *very* rude awakening.

THE GARRISON HEADQUARTERS – FORT EBEN EMAEL, BELGIUM
FRIDAY 10TH MAY 1940 – 0430 HOURS

Jottrand hurtled down the steps, hollering at the two tired looking men who emerged from a doorway halfway along the corridor.

"Get up! Everyone! Get to your positions! Man the turrets!"

The two men, a corporal and a private, exchanged puzzled glances then looked back at their commander in bemused silence, their eyes heavy and dark with sleep.

"What's the fuss Major?" The corporal grumbled, sounding slightly upset at the sudden clamour.

Jottrand was level with them now and his eyes bulged in disbelief at the stupidity of the corporal's question.

"What do you think's the bloody matter? The God-damned Boche are here! Get to your bloody positions...*now!*"

From far above there was a muted, but sudden and unmistakeable sound of gunfire. The two soldiers in the doorway looked at each other again then came alive as their tired minds caught up with the reality of the situation.

They bundled back inside the room, lurching for their equipment and shouting to several other unseen occupants of the underground billet. Jottrand turned away and ran on towards the series of rooms that served as the headquarters of the fort. As he rushed along the concrete passageway, yet more voices began shouting to each other from within the maze of tunnels that connected the various positions of the subterranean stronghold. Some of the voices sounded confused; some sounded excited; all of them sounded frightened.

He rounded a corner and ran straight into someone coming the other way. As they bounced back from each other and fell against the wall, Jottrand looked up and instantly recognised Lieutenant Dupont. The lieutenant was full of questions, his face as confused as the two rank and file soldiers further down the corridor.

"Major? What's going on? Why is everyone shouting? Someone said there is shooting going on outside the fort!"

Jottrand fought to keep his voice calm.

"Not just outside. They're on the roof."

"The roof? Who are?" Dupont pulled a face, completely nonplussed.

"The Germans are, you fool!" Jottrand snapped. "Have the garrison stand-to, immediately! They're supposed to be manning the guns already for pity's sake!"

Dupont continued to stare back at him with a puzzled expression.

"Germans? On the roof? Are you sure Major?"

"Of course I'm bloody sure! They've just been shooting at me as I ran inside! They're landing in gliders, right on top of us! Get up to the roof positions and get the turrets into action, straight away!"

As Jottrand was barking out his orders to Dupont, a harassed looking private soldier in shirt sleeves came running along the corridor and squeezed past them. He was carrying two boxes of machine gun ammunition.

"You, man! Where are you going with those?" Jottrand called after him.

The young soldier paused briefly and looked back at the garrison commander.

"Up top, Sir, to Machine-Gun Nest South West; they've asked for spare ammo."

Jottrand flapped his arms in exasperation at the answer, looking first at Dupont and then back to the soldier.

"What the hell have we been doing for the last two hours since the alert was issued?"

Neither the lieutenant nor the private answered him.

"Go, man!" The major jerked his head at the soldier. "Get it up there, now!"

The man turned and disappeared around the bend, his footsteps clattering on the concrete floor. Jottrand regarded his senior lieutenant with a dark expression. When he spoke, his voice was suddenly quieter, calmer, but weighted with gravity.

"Dupont, don't ask me how they've done it, or why they've done it, but the fact is we've got German gliders landing all over the bloody place and German soldiers crawling all over the roof. They've come for us Dupont. It's time to fight. Now get your arse around this fort and get every last man to a fighting position and make it…"

Boom!

The deep, ominous sound echoed through the tunnels of the fort and stopped Jottrand in mid-sentence. At the same time, the solid earth around them seemed to tremble, causing a fine smattering of concrete dust to float gently from the ceiling.

"What the hell was that?" Jottrand murmured, looking up the corridor.

"Sounded like thunder, right over the top of us?" Dupont stared vaguely at the ceiling. Jottrand turned bleak eyes on his subordinate.

"It's the middle of May, Dupont? It *never* thunders in May. Does it?"

Boooooooom!

This time the second and much bigger roar was unmistakable. The two officers staggered as they felt the tremor run through the fort and a moment later clamped their hands to their ears as an ear splitting echo rippled through the narrow tunnels.

"Holy Mother of God!" Dupont cried out as the shock-wave passed down the corridor. "My fucking ears!"

As the din subsided, a pungent, acrid smell reached their nostrils; the familiar smell of burnt explosives. There was lots of shouting now; and screaming. Cautiously, Jottrand began walking back the way he had come until he reached a crossroads in the tunnel system. Dupont followed and together they turned a corner to stare down a smoke shrouded corridor. The bottom end of the long passage was a fog of thick grey smoke, beyond which were the sounds of panic, followed a second later by machine-gun fire. Jottrand drew his pistol from its holster and Dupont followed suit.

Two figures suddenly appeared from the smoke, both of them carrying something between them. The two officers watched in horror as the two figures, both Belgian privates, emerged from the fog and dumped their burden on the floor of the passage. The smoke blackened human figure on the floor, missing an arm and caked in blood, lay moaning pitifully on the concrete as his two helpers turned back into the smoke. Jottrand heard the squeal of heavy metal hinges, and then one of the two uninjured men shouted something.

"Come on, Phillipe, for God's sake; get the damn thing shut! Hurry!"

Jottrand broke into a run, hurrying towards the unfolding drama, followed by Dupont and several more soldiers who had appeared behind them. As Jottrand reached the slowly dissipating smoke cloud, he stared down at the disfigured soldier on the floor and realised with shock that it was the private who had passed him literally a minute or so before, carrying the spare ammunition. He heard the heavy 'clang' of a reinforced steel door closing shut.

"What's going on?" He demanded from the two men who had sealed the corridor.

One of the men, his face smeared with dark grime and his eyes white with fear, turned to his commanding officer and croaked the dreaded news.

"It's an attack, Sir! They've blown open Machine-Gun Nest South West and they're throwing grenades down the shaft! There are Germans inside, Sir; they're *inside* the fort!"

MACHINE-GUN NEST SOUTH WEST – FORT EBEN EMAEL, BELGIUM
FRIDAY 10TH MAY 1940 – 0440 HOURS

"There's no way we're going to get through that bastard!" Braun stared in consternation at the solid looking doorway that barred the corridor at the base of the stairwell.

They had already used their two main charges to blow open the cupola and force entry to the underground labyrinth and even then, the largest of the charges had only blown a hole big enough for one man at a time to crawl through.

"We need some bigger charges." Braun decided out loud. He turned to the five men who had followed him down the stairs. "Stay here, all of you, and keep your eyes on this door. If anybody comes through it, kill them. Then try and keep the door open and shout for support. Witman?" He looked across at one of his most experienced soldiers. "You're in charge for now. I'm going back up top to get hold of some decent sized charges and to find Lieutenant Witzig. Keep this stairwell secure. Understand?"

Witman nodded his understanding and Braun immediately turned back up the stairs.

He climbed the concrete stairs carefully, trying not to slip on the rivulets of blood that caked the concrete steps about halfway up, where two Belgian soldiers lay dead; both of them victims of the grenades that Braun and his men had thrown down after the retreating enemy. He tried not to think of the mangled, shredded remains as having once been living, breathing, human beings. They were dead now; just pieces of meat. He ignored the smell too; the metallic stench of blood which somehow seemed to permeate the air to the point where one could almost taste it.

He was breathing heavily, for the steps were steep and he had spent far too long in a cramped glider until just forty minutes ago. Finally, he reached the interior of the defensive cupola. The mess on the stairs was nothing compared to the carnage inside this room, where the large German charges had blown open the cupola itself and torn apart the occupants within. He nodded at the two men crouching in one corner, both of them trying to stay clear of the blood and bone and flesh that carpeted one side of the room, along with the mangled wreck of the heavy machine gun.

"The corridor's blocked at the bottom by a steel door. I'm going to find Witzig and get some more explosive down there. If we can blow the door through then we'll have the fort to ourselves in no time."

He stepped over the pile of personal equipment that most of them had dumped, having removed it to squeeze through the narrow hole in the fortification, and stuck his head through that very breach to stare out onto the roof once more. The smell of fresh air, tainted by acrid smoke reached his nostrils. There was sporadic gunfire and the sound of shouting. With a heave, he pulled himself through the hole, pushing his machine-pistol through in front of him. As he squirmed through the ragged breach, he caught sight of the glider pilot from Granite Six, squatting nearby.

"Karl." Braun stopped wriggling and called to the man.

The pilot glanced across at him and a flash of recognition crossed his face.

"Erich? How's it going inside?"

"So far, so good." Braun replied. "But we've got a slight hitch. We've got right down the stairs to the bottom of the fort, but there's a steel door blocking the way; a proper big bastard too. We'll need a couple of big cutting charges to get through it. Do me a favour will you? Go and find Witzig and tell him we're inside. Tell him what we need and get it sent over here as soon as you can."

The pilot nodded thoughtfully.

"I'll have a look round and see what I can do, but I don't think I'll find Witzig anywhere. I've been watching the gliders come in and there's no sign of Granite Eleven anywhere. Doesn't look like he's made it. On top of that, we're starting to take sniper fire from positions away from the fort, so it's difficult to move around without getting your turnip blown off."

Braun pulled a face.

"Fuck. Well, never mind that. Just get yourself around and see who's got anything big left. As soon as you find it then get it over here. Find whoever's in charge and tell them; once we're through that door then we've got this place in our pockets."

The pilot nodded in acknowledgement.

"I'm on it, Erich."

With that, he scuttled off across the roof of the fort in a low crouch.

Braun pushed himself back inside the cupola and stood up straight, taking the opportunity to stretch off. As he did so, he gazed down at the bloody mess of bodies in the corner, then looked over at his two link men, still crouching at the other side of the room.

"Tell you what boys," Braun grinned, "I'm fucking starving. I could murder a good breakfast."

The younger of the two crouching soldiers turned suddenly pale and then, with a terrible groan, spewed a huge gush of watery vomit across the blood stained floor.

HURRICANE 'F' FOR FREDDIE – OVER NORTHERN FRANCE
FRIDAY 10TH MAY 1940 – 0445 HOURS

Flight Lieutenant Richard 'Windy' Whittaker rubbed a gloved hand over his face and massaged the corners of his eyes where they met his nose. It had been a late night, followed by a short, poor sleep and an uncivilised reveille. Now he was cruising at 15,000 feet with the rest of A Flight somewhere over northern France, in the vicinity of Vouziers. The cause of their sudden call to action was the unusually heavy enemy air activity of the last five or six hours. Everyone was jumpy, and the word from Ops was that Wing HQ had a big flap on.

Thus far however, Whittaker had seen nothing to justify the big 'flap'. There was thick haze at low-level, which made the ground rather indistinct and featureless, while the early morning sun was making visibility difficult and Whittaker was already fed up with squinting into its bright glare. In addition to all the other frictions, he was feeling distinctly unsettled. Over the last couple of months Whittaker had downed three German aircraft; two

Dorniers and one of the twin-engined Messerschmitt 110's. The last of his actions however, had nearly proved his undoing. Having chased a Dornier 17 down to low level and made the bugger smoke from one engine, he had closed in to about a hundred and fifty yards to finish the bomber off, when quite unexpectedly one of the enemy gunners had put a well aimed burst right into the nose of his Hurricane, causing the engine to cut out.

Consequently, Whittaker had been forced to pull away from his prey and attempt to glide in to a forced landing in a field outside Metz. It had been a near run thing; being at low level anyway. He'd only just managed to clear some tall trees and locate a suitable field when he felt his machine starting to give way to gravity, and the landing that ensued was bumpy in the extreme. The whole experience had left him feeling piqued and more than a little bruised. Now he was keen to redeem himself and get back into action again. It was like riding a horse with the local hunt, he reflected. If you fell off, you had to get back on straight away before your confidence drained away and gave way to fear.

"Turning port. We'll swing north for a few minutes. If we don't spot anything soon we'll head home."

The sound of Squadron Leader 'Jolly' Rogers' voice crackling over the RT made him jump and brought him back to the present. He saw Jolly's Hurricane bank and he conformed to the manoeuvre with the rest of Yellow Section, who were in close echelon starboard of the Squadron Leader's section. With a slight rise to the normal purr of its engine, the Hurricane banked gracefully to port and Whittaker smoothly took station again on his section leader. To his starboard and slightly back, the third member of Yellow Section came into position alongside him.

Together, the six Hurricanes cruised northwards, their observation made easier now thanks to the sun being well over to starboard. Even so, the ground still remained indistinct some 15,000 feet below them. Whittaker checked his fuel gauge and saw that they would be lucky to have more than fifteen minutes left on station before they needed to turn for home. The thought irritated him. He was desperate to have a crack at the Boche again, if only to prove to himself that he still had the nerve for it.

"Bingo!" The sound of Jolly's voice on the RT made him jump. "Three of the buggers, down there; eleven o'clock low! We'll go in with sections echeloned; deflection shoot from this side of them; peeling off now!"

Jolly's aircraft banked and dived with a menacing roar, followed immediately by his two wing men. Whilst Whittaker awaited the order from his own section leader, he strained to spot the enemy aircraft.

There! Barely visible against the backdrop of the dark, haze covered earth; three Dornier 17s, heading east, obviously on their way back from a raid.

"Here we go chaps; peeling now." The section leader's calm voice came over the RT.

Following the other section's lead, Yellow Section banked and dived, swooping down like birds of prey towards the enemy bombers. Whittaker's heart was beating faster now, his throat becoming dry, his mind racing as he concentrated on keeping station whilst focussing on his impending attack run. He had to be careful this time; not get too cocky. Remember that these buggers had their own guns. They weren't completely helpless. Out of habit he glanced up momentarily. He did so for only a second then looked back towards the remainder of the flight as it closed in on the three enemy aircraft which appeared to be blissfully unaware of their attackers' presence thus far.

Suddenly however, Whittaker snapped his head back up in shock, his mind suddenly registering the information that his eyes had sent to it just a split second earlier. Numerous black dots were coming down towards them from ten o'clock high. For a moment he was stunned, his heart lurching with dread, but then he found his voice and called out in alarm over the RT.

"Jerries high left! Jerries high left! Loads of the buggers! Break, break, break!"

Reacting simultaneously, Yellow Section split from each other and began climbing and twisting away, desperately trying to evade the pouncing aircraft.

There were nine of them; Messerschmitt 110s. Theoretically, the Hurricanes should be more than a match for them, but they outnumbered the British fighters and had the drop on them. Not only that, the 110s sported nose-mounted cannon; and that was not something you wanted to be on the wrong end of. As Whittaker twisted frantically away from his previous course, the heavy smack of cannon shells passing nearby came to his ears, even above the noise of his aircraft's groaning engine, and bright blurs raced past his vision, far too close for comfort. Whittaker's prayer for action had finally been answered, and once again. on this beautiful spring morning, he found himself fighting for his life.

THE SUBALTERNS' BILLETS – PONT-A-MARCQ, NEAR LILLE, FRANCE
FRIDAY 10TH MAY 1940 – 0530 HOURS

"Sir! Mr Dunstable, Sir! Wake up, Sir, it's me!"

Dunstable sat up in his bed abruptly at the sudden disturbance. It was past dawn he observed miserably, although the weak light suggested that it was still early. He recognised the voice of Sergeant Jackson instantly. Scrabbling for his watch, Dunstable felt a brief flicker of panic. Surely he hadn't over-slept and missed early-morning rounds? He was sure he had set his alarm clock. Forcing himself upright, the young second lieutenant stumbled across to the doorway in his baggy pyjamas and fumbled for the handle.

Yanking the door open, he indeed found his platoon sergeant standing there and, quite unsurprisingly, the tall, fierce looking Yorkshireman was fully dressed, his uniform immaculate, his jaw-line clean shaven, his eyes fully alert. Did the man ever sleep, Dunstable wondered?

"Sergeant Jackson? What is it?" Dunstable dragged a hand through his fine, sandy hair.

Jackson appeared to be completely unaffected by the rather unmilitary sight presented by his platoon commander. Instead, he threw up a smart salute.

"Morning, Sir. The watchkeeper sends his regards. He has received the order for the Battalion to stand-to, Sir. We're being brought to five hours notice to move. The Duty Drill Sergeant is waking the Captain of the Week and the Adjutant. Can you get the other gentlemen up, Sir, please? I've got to go and tip out the Sarn't Major."

Dunstable blinked rapidly, several times, as he tried to digest the stream of information.

"Five hours notice to move?" He murmured.

"Yes, Sir." Jackson nodded firmly. "And this time it's 'no-duff'. Apparently there's a bloody big flap on; rumours about the Jerries attacking Belgium. Looks like we're going to get ourselves a scrap at long last, Sir, eh?"

"Bloody hell!" Dunstable was suddenly animated.

"I'll leave you to wake the officers, Sir," Jackson went on. "I'll go and tip out the Sergeants in Waiting and the Sarn't Major. The Battalion has to be on parade, ready to move by 0700 hours. I'll see you down on the main street in the usual spot."

Without further explanation, Jackson went to turn away, but then suddenly stopped and looked back at his officer.

"Oh, and Mr Dunstable, Sir?"

"Yes?"

"Wake the other gentlemen first and *then* get dressed."

And with those final words of wisdom, Jackson turned away and stomped off down the stairs. As he did so, the door of the room opposite Dunstable opened and a neat, well groomed looking young man stepped out onto the landing, dressed in a smart bath-robe.

"Morning Harry!" Chirped Lieutenant Jimmy Langley, one of the officers from No.3 Company. "What's all the racket about, old boy?"

"Erm, Battalion stand-to, Jimmy. On parade at 0700 hours ready to go. 'No-duff' apparently. It seems the Jerries are attacking Belgium."

Langley pulled a face that spoke of mild surprise.

"Hmm...well, about bloody time! Fancy starting on a Friday though!" The slightly older and more experienced officer raised his arms and gave a loud yawn as he stretched off. "Righto, then;" He continued, turning back into his room. "better find my revolver I suppose..."

REIMS-CHAMPAGNE AERODROME – NORTHERN FRANCE
FRIDAY 10TH MAY 1940 – 0605 HOURS

Whittaker dropped out of the cockpit, onto the wing, then onto the grass, his heart still in his mouth. He stared around at the concerned faces of his ground crew and took in a huge gulp of air. His momentary relief at being out of immediate danger and back on the ground was tempered by the sight that met him now. The airfield had been bombed heavily, and he'd been forced to swerve around a large crater during landing, narrowly avoiding a nasty pile-in. Smoke drifted across the expanse of grass from the direction of the aerodrome's main buildings, and in one corner of the large base something was burning fiercely.

Surprisingly, his two ground crewmen seemed oblivious to the chaos around them and were focussing their attention on the badly shot up Hurricane.

"Blimey Mr Whittaker, Sir!" Exclaimed Leading Air Craftsman Devine. "What have you done with the poor old girl this time?

The fitter surveyed the series of large gaping holes in the superstructure of the fighter with a hurt look.

"Sorry, chaps." Whittaker shrugged his shoulders in a sheepish manner. "I'm afraid I took a few cannon shells from a 110. Buggers jumped as from above; nine of them. Doesn't seem to have damaged anything vital, thankfully. Still, I managed to give one of them a belly full in return. Sent him running back to Germany with smoke pouring out of his starboard engine. I don't reckon he'll make it all the way back."

Another Hurricane came in to land behind them on the main strip, and the three men paused while it passed by.

"Guns'll be empty then, Sir?" Murmured Senior Air Craftsman McWilliams, climbing onto the port wing and starting to remove the gun panels.

"Almost." Whittaker confirmed. "But it was lack of fuel that made me break off."

He waved a hand vaguely towards the plumes of billowing smoke.

"So what happened here then? Looks like a bad one?" He suggested.

Devine clambered up the wing and dropped into the cockpit to start checking over the controls of the damaged aircraft.

"Oh, aye, Sir." He shouted down. "Jerry bastards came over just after you took off. Surprised you never saw them. Must have been twenty of the buggers in all. They came in bloody low over yonder trees and dropped their eggs right on top of us. There's a load of people hurt; especially amongst the Frogs. Mind you, it's hardly surprising if the balloon really has gone up."

Whittaker raised an eyebrow at the remark.

"What do you mean? *Has* the balloon gone up?"

"So they reckon, Sir. Nothing clear coming through just yet, but I heard one of the sergeants from operations saying that all the airfields here about were getting clobbered, and there's talk of the Jerries having a crack at Holland. All rumours so far though. You know how people like to exaggerate, Sir; especially McWilliams here."

From the wing, McWilliams grunted a profanity in his harsh cockney accent.

Whittaker nodded thoughtfully as he listened to his fitter, but his thoughts were interrupted by a shout from behind him.

"Windy! Windy!"

Whittaker turned at the sound of his name being called and instantly spotted his squadron leader walking quickly towards him, pulling his flying helmet off as he strode purposefully across the field. Behind him, a flight lieutenant from operations was hurrying to catch up with the more senior officer.

"How's your machine, Windy? Is she fit to go again?"

Whittaker looked up at Devine but the airman was busy with his checks.

"I think so." Whittaker ventured. "She's got a couple of holes in, but no serious damage by the looks. I should know in the next few minutes."

Rogers had reached him by now and the squadron leader ran an appraising eye over Whittaker's aircraft as he yanked out a yellow, silk handkerchief from his trouser pocket and dabbed at his sweat-streaked face.

"Okay." Rogers nodded. "If she's good to fly then get her bombed up and refuelled, ready to go. I reckon we'll be up again in no time. Evans here reckons that something big has kicked off. Wing HQ is in a flat spin; even more than usual. Looking at what happened here I'd say the Hun is definitely up to something."

Whittaker let out a long breath.

"I'm with you on that one."

Rogers gave him a shrewd, sideways glance.

"Well done this morning, Windy. Thank God you had your eyes open. If those buggers had come in behind us we'd have been mince-meat. Did you get anything?"

Whittaker shrugged.

"Not sure, Skipper. Chased one off home with his starboard engine pouring smoke, but can't confirm he went down. I had to break off due to lack of fuel."

Rogers grunted an acknowledgement and nodded again, a wry smile on his face.

"I wouldn't worry too much old boy; if this *is* the start of the big show then you'll have plenty more chance to bag another Hun before the sun goes down."

ON THE NORTHERN FRINGE OF THE ARDENNES – LUXEMBOURG
FRIDAY 10TH MAY 1940 – 0610 HOURS

The dawn was over an hour old, but here in the outskirts of the vast forest the murkiness still lingered, aided by the damp, woodland mist. It was clearing steadily however, and the air was fresh, promising a fine, clear day. Vosse stood atop the bonnet of his staff car and surveyed the crossroads in the centre of the tiny hamlet. It wasn't much of a crossroads, nor even much of a hamlet, yet soon it would be like an autobahn with hundreds of vehicles flowing past in an endless stream of military might. Vosse gazed about him at the platoon of military policemen who were standing ready in their allotted positions. Some of them stood by the junction itself, ready to log every vehicle, platoon, company and battalion as it passed through. Others stood guard on a perimeter around the small settlement, ensuring that none of its inhabitants would be able to leave the area and spread word of what was happening here, deep in the forest.

He heard the sudden growl of engines starting up and he glanced off to a flank and saw a small group of motorcycle combinations and armoured cars pull out of the trees and onto the road heading west. Moments later, from one of the side tracks, a small convoy of trucks emerged and joined on the rear of the small reconnaissance force. They were the vehicles from one of the advanced engineer companies, each one laden with essential stores, from humble picks and shovels to the lightweight hollow metal pipe fascines that could be inserted into the smallest of culverts to help support them when the heavy armour began to trundle over.

Barely had the last of the engineer vehicles disappeared, when the sound of yet more engines came to Vosse's ears. This time however, the engines were deeper, heavier, and accompanied by the clatter and squeal of tracks and bogies. He looked back eastwards towards the road that led back into Germany and was rewarded by the sight of the first German armour rumbling towards him. A whole column of Panzer I tanks, followed by a trio of armoured cars came rumbling steadily through the drifting morning mist. The sight and sound of all that armour caused the boyish excitement to rise in Vosse yet again, and a proud smile spread across his face as the first of the vehicles clattered onto the crossroads.

The military police were ready. The lead panzer was flagged down, a hasty conversation was had with the commander, a note was made on a log-sheet and then the vehicles were waved onwards. Off they went, slowly, steadily, inexorably westwards. No less than sixteen of the small light tanks passed by Vosse, and then, right behind them, the three armoured cars rolled onto the junction. Instantly, Vosse recognised the rigid, distinguished profile of the divisional commander, standing upright in the turret of the leading vehicle.

The general caught sight of Vosse standing on his car, and gave him a wave.

"So far, so good, Captain." Rommel shouted across. "Have the recce and engineer units moved on yet?"

Vosse nodded his head vigorously in acknowledgement.

"Yes, General. The advance call-signs moved off half an hour ago, the units who dealt with this section have just left to follow them up. There have been no reports of obstacles or resistance as yet."

Vosse was rewarded with a brief, but very genuine smile from the general.

"Good, Vosse; good. Well done so far. Now, get yourself up the front again and make sure they keep it up. No delays please. No delays at all."

"Yes, Sir." Vosse responded with a smart salute and jumped down into the passenger seat of the car. His driver already had the engine started. The excitement, rather than melting away, was becoming keener and keener inside Vosse. It was like that in the 7th Panzer Division. No man could be around Erwin Rommel and not feel the thrill. His reputation from the last war was well known, and even this early on in the present war, he was gaining a reputation as a ruthless adventurer. To be on the man's staff was electrifying. Here he was, the divisional commander, right behind the leading company of tanks during the advance. The soldiers will do anything for this man, Vosse reflected, and included himself in that mental assertion.

The captain held on tightly as the car lurched over a small pothole on the narrow, poorly maintained excuse for a road, and glanced back once to see Rommel standing high in his vehicle, consulting a map and rapping out short, precise instructions to the battle-captains who accompanied him. With a smile on his face and a fierce sense of joy filling his chest and throat, Vosse looked forwards again and began to hum an old marching tune as his vehicle followed on behind the company of light tanks. As the vehicle bounced and trundled westwards, Vosse hummed a little louder, and next to him his driver began to sing along quietly to the tune.

"…We're marching against Eng-a-land…"

DEPOT, THE 12TH TRANSPORT REGIMENT – NEAR LILLE, FRANCE
FRIDAY 10TH MAY 1940 – 0615 HOURS

"Where the bloody hell have you two been?" Corporal 'Rusty' Barnes hissed at the two private soldiers who had sidled up behind him on the vehicle park.

All around them, engines growled and revved as the company's vehicles were first paraded, the sickly smell of petrol fumes hanging rank in the misty morning air.

Privates Stan Fellows and Micky Moxon grinned amiably back at the red-haired corporal, their hands in their pockets and their side-caps stuffed under the epaulettes of their serge blousons.

"Ease up Rusty!" Soothed Fellows. "What happened mate? Did you get out the wrong side of the bed this morning or what?"

The agitated corporal's cheeks flushed ever so slightly.

"At least I got out of my own bed, regardless of which bloody side it was!" He retorted. "You two should've been back in for midnight. I had to bloody well cover for you again at tattoo. This is going to bloody well stop, let me tell you!"

"Oh, come on Rusty." Moxon smiled disarmingly. "We've two lovely mademoiselles in Lille just pining to see us every night. You wouldn't want us to break their little hearts would you?"

Barnes shook his head impatiently.

"There's plenty of others with good money to spend; your two little French bints won't be short of paying company."

Moxon affected a hurt expression.

"Ooh, Rusty! That was low, mate. You should come with us some time. I bet we could find you a lovely young thing to keep you warm at night; especially on a corporal's pay."

Again the corporal shook his head.

"I don't think so. And I reckon you won't be keeping too warm at nights for a while now, either."

The two privates frowned at that comment and flung dubious looks around the busy vehicle park.

"Why, what's going on Rusty? Is there a scheme on or something?"

The corporal fixed them with a serious look.

"No scheme this time. It's the real thing."

Moxon and Fellows exchanged a surprised look.

"No way!" Moxon frowned. "After all this time? The Jerries have never got off their arses, have they?"

"According to Sergeant Danby, they have." Barnes confirmed. "And we've been told to get ready to go as soon as possible. We've got to be on thirty minutes notice to move by seven, so you two had best get a bloody move on and grab your kit. I've got your vehicles turning over, but you two need to get them seen to, sharpish. If you're not back here and working on those vehicles in the next fifteen minutes, then old Danby is going to smell a rat, and if he does, I'll be pointing out exactly where he can find a couple!"

Moxon looked offended, but before he had the opportunity to reply, a loud, belligerent voice cut through the low grumble of vehicle engines.

"Corporal Barnes! Corporal Barnes!"

Barnes looked over his shoulder in alarm.

"Bollocks! That's Danby now. Get the fuck over to your billet and get your kit; go on!"

Without further prompting, the two private soldiers spun on their heels and hurried off around the rear of the nearest truck. Barely had they gone out of sight when Danby appeared around the front of the vehicle.

"There you are." Snapped the barrel-chested troop sergeant, the corners of his moustache flaring in annoyance. "Where are the drivers for those two trucks over there?"

"Sorry, Sarge." Barnes apologised quickly. "Moxon and Fellows forgot their bloody gas masks; I've sent them back to grab 'em. Forget their bloody heads, those two, if they weren't screwed on!"

The bull-necked sergeant screwed his face up in disdain.

"You aint wrong there, Corporal Barnes. I'm starting to get a bad feeling about that pair. Give the buggers a kick up the bloody arse when they get back, then give 'em another one from me. And you can tell 'em both, if they don't sort themselves out in the very near future I'll be coming down on them like a ton of bloody horse-shit."

"Yes, Sarge; will do."

Danby nodded, grumpily.

"Good. Now keep chasing the rest of them up; everyone's half asleep this morning. The Jerries will be here before we get off the park at this rate!"

And with that parting comment, Danby strode off across the vehicle park, already bawling for another non-commissioned officer to get a grip of his men. Behind him, Barnes gave a relieved sigh.

"Christ all-bloody-mighty," he breathed, "it's going to be one of those days!"

MACHINE-GUN NEST SOUTH WEST – FORT EBEN EMAEL, BELGIUM
FRIDAY 10TH MAY 1940 – 0620 HOURS

"About bloody time!"

Braun looked up as the pilot's head appeared through the hole in the concrete casemate. His look of relief didn't last for long however. The pilot, blinking rapidly as his eyes adjusted to the dim light inside the bunker, caught sight of the corporal and shook his head in resignation.

"Don't wet yourself with excitement just yet Erich." He cautioned. "There isn't any big stuff left; or at least I can't find any left anywhere. Best I could do is a couple of satchel charges and a few more grenades.

"Are you fucking joking?" Braun demanded in consternation.

"Afraid not, mate." The pilot confirmed. "It's chaos up here. Looks as though we've taken care of most of the turrets and casemates, but there's a big one just at the bottom end here with twin turrets, and it's still in action. We can't get near the bastard; not enough blokes around to do anything else other than keep an eye on it. The staff sergeant says two of the gliders are missing and that Witzig is in one of them. On top of that, the Belgiques have just tried a counter-attack on the western edge. The lads over there broke it up though; it wasn't up to much. Oh, and we've managed to seal the main entrance to the fort, so there's no way the garrison can come out and bother us without us brassing the bastards up, big style."

Braun spat onto the concrete floor and grunted acknowledgement.

"Did you tell the staff sergeant we were inside the fort?"

The pilot nodded.

"I did mate. We're not the only ones either. There's two more groups got inside bunkers, but they're in the same boat as us. There's a shortage of explosives all round. They had to use the last of the big stuff to spike the main guns on the canal side."

Braun was nodding, accepting the reality of the situation, despite his frustration.

"Right then, nothing we can do about it other than crack on with what we've got. Shove all of that bangs-kit through and we'll see what we can do with it."

The pilot's head disappeared and moments later the first bag was pushed through the breach in the wall. Together with the two link men, Braun grabbed the satchels of explosive and the spare grenades and began the descent into the belly of the fortress once more.

Arriving at the bottom of the stairwell, the corporal found his men still watching the door, which remained firmly closed; as immovable as ever. Quickly, he briefed the soldiers and after a short debate, they decided to stack the grenades against the door, backed up by the two satchel charges, and then pack the whole pile of explosives in with lumps of concrete and metal brought down from the wrecked turret above them. With desperate urgency, the group did exactly that, whilst one man remained covering the doorway with his machine-pistol. After ten minutes, they were ready to blow.

"Okay," Braun waved his men back up the stairs, "get back up there, right the way to the top, because this is going to make a fucking big bang. And when it does go bang, we get our arses right back down here, ready to go right through that door. Got it?"

His small group nodded back, their faces grim and determined.

"Do you want me to set the fuse, corporal?" Asked one of the young soldiers.

Braun gave a thin smile.

"You're alright thanks, Linneman; I'll do it. Rank has its privileges don't you know? And trying to blow yourself up before breakfast is one of them. Now, everyone, get yourselves up those stairs; move."

Braun waited until the sound of scraping boots on concrete steps had faded and then knelt by the stash of explosives and rubble that had been piled against the huge metal door. He pushed his machine-pistol around his back and took a deep breath.

"Right then, Erich lad," he murmured quietly to himself, "time to set a record for the sprint then…"

He took hold of the grip-switch that was attached to the safety-fuse on one of the satchel charges and gave a short, humourless grunt of laughter.

"…In full kit, in the dark, up a set of endless fucking stairs!"

He rotated the grip-switch and squeezed it shut with the heel of his hand.

Pop. Hssssssss…

Braun ran.

He ran like he had never run before. His thighs protested at the pace and the repeated impact as he bounded upwards, two steps at a time. Half-way up, he stumbled over a dead Belgian soldier, cursed, then forced himself on, his hands scraping against the concrete walls as he sought to propel himself faster. His breathing was coming in harsh, fast gulps, and inside his mind he was silently counting down the fuse. After what seemed like an age he turned one final bend in the stairwell and saw the open space of the casemate in front of him. Pale faces peered around the corner towards him.

"Get down!" He tried to shout, but his voice came out as nothing more than a breathless gasp.

Even so, the faces disappeared, understanding what was coming.

Braun toppled upwards, over the last couple of steps and into the casemate which was now packed with his squad members. He pulled himself across the bloody floor and away from the opening of the stairwell, breathing like an asthmatic.

"Get in against the wall…" He breathed, taking huge gulps of air. "Open your mouths…cover your ears…any moment…"

Boooooom.

The tremor came first; like an earthquake. Then came the unbelievable noise that made every one of the German soldiers cry out as their ear drums rang in protest. All of this was followed by the sudden vacuum that sucked the air out of their lungs, turning them instantly breathless, followed last of all by the shock wave and a thick cloud of smoke that billowed up the stairs and filled the tiny room.

As the echo of the huge explosion faded, the German storm-troopers staggered to their feet, coughing and choking on the dust and smoke.

"Go!" Spluttered Braun. "Go, go go!"

They clattered back down the stairwell, groping their way through the dust cloud, trying not to trip and fall in the gloom and confusion.

Braun, short of breath anyway, could hardly breathe at all now. Never-the-less, he led the way, retracing his steps of just a few moments ago, dragging his machine pistol back to the front of his body as he went.

Suddenly, he was there. The steps came to an end and he was back in the short corridor. Instantly, he brought his weapon up and, in keeping with the endless drills of the preceding few months, fired a long burst of 9mm bullets through the drifting smoke and dust towards where he knew the door had been.

A split second later, he threw himself sideways as the bullets ricocheted off something with a metallic whine and began bouncing around the concrete walls of the corridor. As the bullets spent their energy and the whining stopped, Braun raised his head slightly and stared through the last skeins of smoke to survey the doorway. The large steel door was still there, scorched, dented, the surrounding walls blackened and missing chunks of concrete, but intact. Braun licked his dry, cracked lips and cursed quietly to himself.

"For fuck's sake…"

RUE D'AVELIN, PONT-A-MARCQ – NEAR LILLE, FRANCE
FRIDAY 10TH MAY 1940 – 0700 HOURS

The street was a scene of organised chaos. As Dunstable threaded his way between the mass of men, the harsh, barking voices of the battalion's non-commissioned officers' cut through the air like a pack of angry fox-hounds in full cry. He hurried past the men of No.3 Company as they doubled to and fro, forming up by platoons and being ushered and pushed from one spot to another by their fierce looking platoon sergeants.

"Company Sergeant Majors!" Roared a deep, commanding voice from somewhere nearby. "On me with parade states in five minutes!"

Dunstable looked through the milling crowd and spotted the Regimental Sergeant Major, recognisable by the huge, royal coat-of-arms badge on his blouson sleeve, standing like a rock amongst the ebb and flow of soldiery. The Sergeant Major's shrewd eyes darted left and right, taking in every movement, every word, every action, and storing the information, good or bad, for later attention.

"Morning Sergeant Major." Dunstable said brightly as he hurried past, feeling as always, a little intimidated by the man who was simply referred to by the rank and file as 'The Badge'.

The Sergeant Major swung his gaze onto Dunstable instantly, his dark eyes picking out the young officer much like a bird of prey picks out a small shrew in an open field. After nothing more than a brief hesitation, the tall, imposing warrant officer threw up an immaculate salute.

"Good morning, Mr Dunstable, Sir." He barked as the young second lieutenant hurried past, returning the salute. Then, his eyes still following the junior officer, he called after him. "And would you mind sorting that tie out too, Sir, please?"

Dunstable cringed as the Sergeant Major's polite, yet firm reprimand followed him along the street, and he hurriedly brought his hands up to adjust the offending item. He paused momentarily to check his reflection in a window and saw that the tie was askew and not pulled tightly up to the top button. Quickly, Dunstable finished his adjustments to the tie and then moved on again. After another thirty yards or so, he spotted an island of calm amongst the seething mass of men.

Standing quietly at ease, formed into three ranks, were No.16 Platoon; his platoon. In front of them, Sergeant Jackson stood in similar manner to the Regimental Sergeant Major, calling out short yet detailed instructions to the section commanders.

"Okay, water bottles next." He snapped in a business-like manner.

Immediately, the three lance sergeants commanding the rifle sections began moving down the ranks, inspecting each man's bottle to ensure it was full, and with water at that, rather than anything more intoxicating.

The platoon was conspicuous by its obvious readiness to move, even at such short notice. That was down to Jackson of course. He was absolutely ruthless, even for a member of the Foot Guards, and he ruled the platoon with a rod of iron. As Dunstable looked around at the confusion and fuss that was everywhere about him, he silently thanked his lucky stars that he had been given Jackson as his platoon sergeant. Jackson would see to it that everything was right. There would be no mistakes with him on watch, and Dunstable was more than willing for the highly efficient sergeant to show him how it was done. His first few weeks in the battalion had been confusing enough, without the sudden call to arms adding to it. Here though, in Jackson, there was a rock among the choppy waters of uncertainty.

As Dunstable approached, Jackson spotted him and instantly went into the prescribed regimental custom.

"Stand still!" Barked the tall sergeant in a voice that pierced the hubbub like the crack of a bullet.

Instantly, every member of the platoon went rigid, frozen in position as if by magic. Jackson meanwhile turned to face Dunstable and smartly slammed his feet together, before executing a butt salute.

"Good morning, Sir." Jackson intoned. "With the exception of two men on sentry and one lance corporal sent to recover them, Number Sixteen Platoon is formed up and present, Sir."

Dunstable returned the salute, rather self-consciously, then smiled sheepishly around.

"Thank you, Sergeant Jackson." He replied. "Please, carry on and don't let me interrupt. I can see that you're in mid-flow. Just shout if there's anything you want me to look at."

"Right, Sir." Jackson snapped obediently, as if he were talking to the King himself and not some green second lieutenant straight out of public school. "Carry on." The Sergeant barked at the section commanders, who at once returned to their detailed inspection of water bottles.

"Any more news yet?" Dunstable enquired in a low voice as he came to stand close by Jackson.

"Nothing yet, Sir." The sergeant gave the briefest shake of his head. "Just as well. Look at all this buggering about that's going on. It's the sort of thing you expect from 'line-swine', not from guardsmen. It's all those months sitting around in cosy barns and visiting whores that's done it, Sir. Taken everybody off the boil it has."

Dunstable smiled indulgently at the sergeant's lament.

"I'm sure it'll sort itself out soon enough. And at least our chaps look ready for the off. You've done a top job so far, Sergeant 'J'."

Before the non commissioned officer had a chance to reply, a call went up from the Regimental Sergeant Major.

"Quiet!" Bellowed the senior warrant officer in the battalion. "Shut up! Listen in to the Adjutant."

Dunstable and Jackson turned to see the Adjutant standing hard by the Sergeant Major, dressed immaculately in service dress tunic, riding breeches and boots.

"Alright everyone, time to calm down slightly. Brigade has passed a message from Division. We've been given a 'no move before' time of 1600 hours this afternoon, so there's no mad rush. All Company Commanders are to report to Battalion Headquarters at 0900 hours, straight after breakfast. All

Company Sergeant Majors are to render their parade states to the Sarn't Major by 0745 hours, then get their companies fed. That is all for now."

Without another word, the Adjutant nodded to the Regimental Sergeant Major and turned away, heading for the Field Officers' billets.

Dunstable glanced over at Jackson and offered a lame smile.

"Order, counter-order, disorder?" He suggested.

Jackson, frowning deeply, shook his head.

"Bring on the dancing fucking horses, more like!"

THE ROOF OF FORT EBEN EMAEL – BELGIUM
FRIDAY 10TH MAY 1940 – 0830 HOURS

"D'you hear that Braun?"

The corporal looked up at the sound of his name being called. Amongst the press of men tearing away at the parachute silks, he saw the face of Staff Sergeant Groenig looking straight at him.

"Sorry, Staff Sergeant; I missed that."

The staff sergeant stopped what he was doing and pushed his way through the group of men who were desperately trying to get to the ammunition containers that had just been air-dropped onto the fort by the Luftwaffe. Groenig drew alongside Braun and knelt down.

"That runner's just come from Captain Koch at the bridges. They've got most of them intact, although at least one has been blown by the Belgies. The Captain says he's had radio contact with the ground forces leading the spearhead; they're on time and should be with us in a few hours. We just need to hang on a bit longer."

Braun grunted as he struggled with the catches on the large metal pannier in front of him.

"As long as this bastard is full of ammo then I don't have any problem with that." He replied. "Because I reckon it's only a matter of time before those half-breed Belgies put in a proper counter-attack."

Groenig muttered his agreement.

"Reckon you're right there; can't be long now before they get their act together. Still, we've got the high ground for the time being and our planes are all over the place, so we should be ok for a bit longer. I've put a machine-gun team outside the main exit from the fort, just in case those bastards decide to come up for air."

Braun let out a small roar of triumph as he succeeded in flicking open the pannier. He stared down at the contents; bandoliers of rifle ammunition, belts of ammunition for the MG34 light machine-guns, and no less than 10 stick grenades.

"Well, that's a start…" He nodded in satisfaction. "But we could do with a couple more charges to blow in those big doors down below."

Groenig concurred.

"I'll go and check the other panniers. Some of those might have explosives in."

The NCO made to stand, but a cry of alarm sent him sprawling on the earth, followed by Braun and the other nearby storm troopers.

"Down!" Came an urgent shout. "Glider inbound!"

No sooner had the two NCOs flattened themselves when they heard a loud thump, followed by a screeching, grating sound. They looked sideways and saw one of their own gliders make touchdown on the fort's roof, just metres away from where were laying. The aircraft slid past them in a spurt of soil, the wing tips passing almost close enough to touch.

"Christ on a bike!" Braun swore. "Who's that bloody maniac? Didn't he get out of bed on time or what?"

Groenig studied the glider as its nose dug into the soil and its tail end reared up a little, before settling once more.

"I don't believe it…" The staff sergeant murmured as he studied the gliders identity number.

"What?" Braun was frowning at his fellow NCO.

Before the senior soldier could reply, the door of the glider was kicked open from within and a figure leapt out onto the roof of the fortress. Before the fully equipped soldier had even hit the ground, he was shouting out instructions at the top of his voice.

"Groenig! Boreman! Herschel! All commanders, rally on me!"

"Fuck me!" Exclaimed Braun. "It's Witzig! I thought he was dead!"

Groenig gave a cynical grunt of a laugh.

"Looks like he's risen from the grave then; and still with a mouth the size of the Brandenburg Gate."

"Praise the Lord." Braun commented laconically. "It's a real, live, fucking miracle…"

HEADQUARTERS BRITISH 2ND CORPS – PHALEMPIN, FRANCE
FRIDAY 10TH MAY 1940 – 1240 HOURS

Brooke finished the last crumb of his sandwich, wiped his mouth quickly with the napkin, then walked from the side room back through to his main headquarters. The room was a hive of activity, with half the corps staff poring over maps and charts, telephones glued to their ears, and the other half urgently packing away all unnecessary paperwork and equipment. The headquarters would move forward tomorrow, once the bulk of the fighting elements of his corps had moved across the Belgian border. The tail end of this huge military beast however, would take almost another week to follow them up. By then, Brooke knew, he would already be in contact with the Germans and more than likely fighting hard.

He spotted his Brigadier General Staff and moved around the large central table to speak to him. Brook made a point of walking slowly, hands behind his back, maintaining a calm façade. In truth, there wasn't much to get excited about just yet. The fighting was happening many dozens of miles away and his plan for moving his corps forward was as watertight as possible. He had personally double checked all the movement orders before lunch and, thus far, everything seemed to be working like clockwork. It was understandable that after months of inactivity, the sudden call to arms would bring everyone to a high pitch of excitement, but Brooke knew from experience that it was essential to maintain one's poise, one's balance; one's rationality.

The BGS looked up from his notes as Brooke joined him and gave a curt nod in acknowledgement of his commander's presence.

"All well, BGS?" Asked Brooke, returning the nod. "Any news from 3 Div?"

The staff officer nodded enthusiastically.

"Yes, Sir. The GOC 3 Div telephoned personally a few minutes ago to let us know that his lead elements have moved off. He was in rather a jolly mood, Sir, I have to say; on account of the response from the Belgian authorities."

Brook narrowed his eyes in suspicion.

"Really? And what has their response been?"

"Well, Sir; General Montgomery tells me that his divisional cavalry were asked for their passports when they crossed the border."

The BGS was smiling broadly. Brooke raised one eye-brow in mild surprise.

"Indeed? How absurd. And what did 3 Div do about that then?"

The BGS gave a gruff chuckle.

"I'm led to believe they just crashed through the barriers and drove on, Sir."

This time, even Brooke allowed himself a smile, shaking his head slowly.

"That's Montgomery for you." He sighed. "Thank God he's in my corps. I'm not sure they'd know how to deal with him elsewhere."

He paused for a moment, trying to visualise the long streams of vehicles, tanks and guns that even now would be rumbling eastwards for their appointment with fate. Dismissing the thought, he looked back at the BGS.

"Any news from Headquarters BEF?"

The BGS consulted a scribbled note on his clip-board.

"Not that much, Sir. Just an update on what's been happening in Belgium and Holland. There's talk about the Germans using paratroopers and soldiers in disguise to capture bridges and other key points. The Dutch in particular are claiming that there are large amounts of Fifth Column operating behind their lines and disrupting the defence."

Brooke digested the information quietly, only his eyebrows betraying his surprise.

"Paratroopers, eh?" He murmured with mock nonchalance. "And Fifth Columnists? How very novel."

He thought on it for a moment.

"Once we're in position along the Dyle, the men will need to watch what they're doing. We don't want the enemy infiltrating our lines covertly, but at the same time I don't want unnecessary alarm being spread with stories of enemy soldiers in disguise. We will need to give it some careful thought once we know some more about the enemy's tactics."

He shrugged the thoughts of Fifth Columnists away and regarded his BGS with an enquiring look again.

"Nothing else come through at all?"

"Only that we now have a new Prime Minister, Sir."

Brooke blinked in surprise.

"I beg your pardon?"

"We have a new Prime Minister apparently, Sir. A flash signal came in a short while ago. Mr Chamberlain has resigned and I believe that Mr Churchill is now in office.

The look of surprise on Brooke's face widened.

"Churchill? As in Winston Churchill? Goodness me!"

The general let out a deep sigh and shook his head slightly.

"Well, nothing for us to worry about at the moment, eh? We have more pressing matters."

He glanced at his watch.

"I'm just going to take a short walk in the gardens for ten minutes. I'll be back in at one o'clock and we can go over the logistical plan again while we wait for a situation report from 3 Div."

"Very well, Sir." The BGS acknowledged as Brooke turned away and headed for the doors that led onto the patio at the rear of the large house.

Brooke strolled across the large room, maintaining his outward calm, whilst inside his mind, dozens of pieces of the complex command jigsaw rattled around interminably. He wasn't convinced by the plan they had been ordered to adopt. The BEF, along with the French, had just spent more than six months digging-in and preparing defensive positions all along the border, without having sufficient time to exercise their formations properly. But now they were abandoning all those carefully prepared positions and rushing forwards into Belgium, and into the unknown.

As Brooke emerged onto the patio, a tall, immaculately turned-out sentry in full battle dress sprang to attention, one heavy ammunition boot crashing onto the paving slab like a thunderclap. Within moments, the sentry had brought his rifle to the slope, then, in a flurry of well practiced movements, brought the bayonet-tipped weapon into the present arms stance, his right boot crashing down now, this time a half pace to the rear of the left foot.

"No.5 Post, Sir, and all's well." The sentry rapped out the prescribed phrase in a heavy Welsh accent.

As Brooke saluted the sentry, he ran an appraising eye over the man. A tall, powerfully built guardsman from the Welsh Guards; one of a detachment of Welsh Guardsmen attached to his Corps HQ for defence purposes, and part of the Guards battalion that was responsible for securing the main headquarters of the BEF. For his rank, the soldier was quite old; mid-twenties perhaps, and with the face and cauliflower ears of a rugby player or boxer; possibly both.

Brooke reflected that there were too few units manned by soldiers like this. The pre-war regulars, like this chap, were excellent quality, but too many units of the BEF were Territorial Army outfits; hastily mobilised and full of young, gawky, under-trained amateurs. As he returned the soldier's salute, Brooke silently thanked his lucky stars for having a Guards Brigade embedded in his 3rd Infantry Division. Despite that, as he walked on into the gardens, he agonised that none of the BEF, Regular or Territorial, had been properly tested at formation level yet. And now the time had run out to do so.

The first major test for all of them would be under the gaze of a most unforgiving umpire; that being the German Army.

He was halfway across the lawn now; a wide, lush, well kept blanket of green, surrounded by wonderful shrubs, many of which were in full blossom already. The sun was up in a blue sky and it was comfortably warm. The birdsong from a nearby avenue of trees was music to Brooke's ears. As an avid bird-watcher, he found the whole experience of being in this delightful garden quite uplifting and his thoughts turned naturally to his family. It really was a beautiful day.

As he pondered all these things, the sound of vehicle engines interrupted his thoughts. He looked up and saw a line of large olive green and black painted artillery tractors and trucks rumbling along the nearby lane, heading towards the border. He watched with professional curiosity as the convoy rolled by at a steady, inexorable speed; radio trucks and staff cars first, followed by the tractors themselves, towing some of the excellent and relatively new 25 Pounder field guns. The contrast of the artificial, man-made, drab-painted machinery of war against the beautiful, divinely created back-drop of nature couldn't have been starker.

"What a shame." Brooke murmured to himself as the gun battery rolled by. "What a terrible shame…"

Saturday 11th May 1940
The Second Day

HURRICANE 'F' FOR FREDDIE – OVER NORTHERN FRANCE
SATURDAY 11TH MAY 1940 – 1000 HOURS

"Watch out for those buggers up there Archie!" Whittaker cautioned his wingman as they both watched the Me 110 spin away from them pouring smoke, its tail plane snapping off as it fell. They had run into a whole bunch of the twin engined fighters whilst chasing off a large formation of Heinkels, and on this occasion, they had got the drop on the enemy good and proper. Their whole squadron had ploughed into the 110s from astern before the enemy aircraft had managed to form into one of their defensive circles, a tactic favoured by the twin-engined fighters. Whittaker had already taken one of the Jerries down and so too had Archie Armstrong, on his starboard. Now however, he was watching a trio of the enemy who were climbing desperately away from the fight, presumably so they could wheel round and dive back down onto their British attackers.

"Let's follow them up, Windy." Armstrong's voice crackled over the RT. "Don't want them getting the chance to sort themselves out."

"Roger. I'm with you." Whittaker agreed and brought the nose of his aircraft up, giving her everything the engine had.

Together, Armstrong and Whittaker climbed after the 110s. They were both tired. They had flown three missions and three combats yesterday, risen at 3 am this morning and were now in another huge bust-up. Despite their fatigue, the immediacy of the fight had brought their minds into sharp focus again.

"First one's turning for a dive." Armstrong said. "I'll take him."

Whittaker let him go, catching a brief glimpse of tracer as Armstrong engaged the Jerry with a deflection burst. The remaining two 110s were also turning now, but staying together, and Whittaker easily came round inside their curve and raked the left hand plane with a two second burst. He saw parts of canopy and fuselage erupt from the unfortunate German and several bits bounced off his own aircraft as he passed behind his target. Not hesitating, Whittaker swung hard round again in order to come back onto his target for another burst. He didn't need to however, for the German was already losing height and trailing an ominous amount of dirty black smoke.

Besides that, Whittaker had other things to worry about. Apart from the third German plane that was desperately turning to try and get in behind him, Whittaker saw a further three Germans coming straight up for him, having broken away from the main fight below.

"Bloody hell!" He murmured quietly to himself. "I am proving popular today!"

He had very little time to react, so brought himself square on to the centre aircraft of the newcomers, went for him nose on, squeezed off a short burst, then dropped his nose and went right under the trio, holding his breath as bright blobs of 20mm tracer came whipping back towards him from his opponents.

Yet again, Whittaker swung his plane round in a tight arc, knowing that he would be able to out-turn his less manoeuvrable opponents, but wondering how long he could successfully hold up against four enemy machines at a time. His answer came very quickly.

His sharp turn had, as predicted, brought him into an excellent position to give one of the enemy aircraft a good burst right along his fuselage, however, much to Whittaker's dismay, as he pressed his fire button, the banks of machine-guns gave one small cough and then stopped.

"What the bloody hell-fire…"

Whittaker realised immediately that any chance of continuing the fight was over. His guns were jammed. He was defenceless.

As the enemy aircraft swarmed around him, trying to get into position to give him a burst, Whittaker cursed his armourer, though in truth, the fault was probably beyond the poor fellow's control. Above the roar of the engine, the sound of high pitched cracking sounded close by as more blobs of heavy calibre tracer flew past Whittaker's cockpit from behind. He took violent evasive action; port, starboard, port, then a steep dive to starboard. His machine protested as he hurtled away from his pursuers and Whittaker felt the g-force squeezing at his consciousness.

"McWilliams…" He muttered to himself as he brought the Hurricane out of its dive and twisted off to port again. "If I ever get out of this alive you bloody well owe me a dozen beers!"

HEADQUARTERS BRITISH 2ND CORPS – PHALEMPIN, FRANCE
SATURDAY 11TH MAY 1940 – 1100 HOURS

"Do we know for certain what's happening with the Dutch and Belgians?"

Brooke addressed the question to both men who were sitting opposite him in the leather armchairs.

General, The Lord Gort, Commander in Chief of the British Expeditionary Force and Lieutenant General Henry Pownall, his Chief of Staff, exchanged a sober look. It was Gort who replied.

"Henry has been trying to make sense of all the conflicting information since yesterday. There are all kinds of rumours floating about and mixed messages coming from our allies. In essence, what we know to be a fact is that the Germans have launched a huge offensive into both Belgium and Holland and have thus far made significant progress. There is lots of talk of the Belgians being a bit wobbly, but as yet they seem to be hanging on. Now that your leading divisions are at the Dyle, the Belgians should steady down a bit, knowing that we're right behind them."

Brooke pulled a face.

"I think I'd prefer it if they just stepped to the side and let us get on with it."

Gort gave a slight rumble in his throat.

"Yes…well, we shall see what the Belgians are up to soon enough. I aim to visit General Georges tomorrow at some point to ensure that we are in agreement about how best to cooperate with the Belgian Army. And you will see for yourself how the ground lies with them soon enough."

Brooke nodded curtly.

"Indeed I will. I intend to depart shortly after lunch and get as far forward as possible. If light conditions permit I shall conduct a visit to 3 Div' before nightfall, whilst my headquarters gets itself established."

Gort accepted the comment with his own, approving nod.

"I had heard the Germans have been using gliders and parachutists?" Brooke went on.

Gort shifted uncomfortably in his chair.

"Yes, there has been talk of it, especially from Holland. We have heard that large groups of enemy parachutists have been dropped all over the place, trying to capture strategic targets by storm. There is also talk of bridges being captured by flying boats laden with infantry and enemy spies in all manner of disguises. Regardless of that, the Dutch appear to be having some success and The Hague remains secure at present. The French have already despatched armoured units northwards to assist them. I think that we have quite a good chance of keeping the enemy at bay until we are fully established along the Dyle."

Again, Brooke pulled a face.

"I do hope so. I believe that at the moment, our most dangerous enemy is rumour. What with all this talk of parachutists and what not, there is a possibility our men could end up firing at shadows in their rear. I do not intend to pass on anything to my divisions that isn't established fact. I need them to focus on what's going to appear in their front."

"Quite so." Gort murmured. "Quite so. And you're ready for the off then?"

"I am, Sir." Brooke confirmed.

Gort stood and offered his hand. Pownall jumped to his feet also and Brooke followed suit.

"The very best of luck then, Alan." Gort shook the commander of the 2nd Corps firmly by the hand. "Very shortly we shall be getting to grips with the Germans again, eh? Just like old times."

Brooke smiled weakly at the C-in-C's enthusiasm. Gort was a hero of the First War, a Victoria Cross winner and a real fire-eater. To Brooke's mind however, he was not particularly suited to handling a large formation like the BEF. Gort would much prefer to be leading a raiding party from his old regiment, the Grenadier Guards, against German trenches, rather than wrestling with the complexities of logistics and grand strategy. One had to admire Gort's fighting spirit, but Brooke needed more than that from his commander."

"Thank you, Sir." Brooke replied, formally.

"Righto, then." Gort picked up his cane. "We'll be off and leave you to it. "See you at the sharp end, Alan."

Brooke saluted the C-in-C as, with Pownall in tow, Gort made for the door.

"The great adventure begins…" Gort chuckled as he left the room.

"Great adventure?" Murmured Brooke as the two men disappeared. "Or a damned nightmare?"

DEEP INSIDE FORT EBEN EMAEL – BELGIUM
SATURDAY 11TH MAY 1940 – 1155 HOURS

Jottrand felt utterly washed out. The last thirty six hours had probably been the longest and most frustrating of his life. His garrison had effectively been trapped inside their fortress within an hour of the German assault. Here they had remained, deep underground, stuck behind their steel doors, and without the ability to fight back at their attackers. All the defensive cupolas were out of action, the major gun batteries were unable to operate, having themselves been put out of action by the enemy, whilst beyond the steel doors of the lower levels, German storm-troopers lurked on the stairwells, ready to break-in at any moment.

And that moment couldn't be far away, Jottrand now reasoned with his tired mind. The lack of sleep made it difficult for him to think clearly, and the claustrophobic atmosphere of the fort was beginning to get to him too. He had never been bothered by the confined nature of the fortress before, but now the warren of corridors and rooms seemed oppressive and he longed for fresh air. Despite that, he dreaded to think what lay in wait for them beyond those doors, should they attempt a break-out. Before their last observation cupola had been put out of action, the men there had reported seeing dozens of German aircraft overhead, parachutes descending all around the fort, and there was lots of speculation about whether German tanks had been seen on the distant bridges over the Albert Canal and River Maas.

All in all, it was a miserable state of affairs. He looked around the drawn, weary faces of his junior officers and realised that there was little fight left in them. They were badly shaken, as were the men. Firstly, they had been affected by the terrible wailing of their wounded and dying comrades that they had managed to pull back down from the cupolas to the lower level of the fortress in the wake of that first, overwhelming attack by the German glider troops. Secondly, not a single man had been able to relax for a moment throughout that long day and night, as the enemy continued his attempts to break into their underground lair. The noise of grenades exploding in the ventilation shafts and stairwells at frequent intervals throughout the night had frayed everybody's nerves and now, Jottrand saw, some of them were at breaking point. Despite all this, Jottrand felt that it was his duty to do more. But what? What could he do with a frightened garrison of second rate troops who were scared witless, tired and in shock at the terrible turn of events?

"It is our duty to fight on..." He said, rather feebly to the assembled officers at large. He was rewarded by a mixture of frightened looks and sullen stares.

After a while, it was Renard who finally broke the uncomfortable silence.

"Fight on, Major? With what? How? We cannot even see our enemy, let alone shoot at him. If we so much as stick our heads round the door, we'll get them blown off. We are at the enemy's mercy; trapped, like rats in a barrel..."

The lieutenant tailed off moodily.

"But we have to do something." Jottrand protested, the frustration evident in his voice. "The honour of Belgium is at stake. As long as we can keep the enemy at bay there is a chance..."

Again it was Renard who spoke, but this time more forcefully.

"A chance of what? Breathing fetid air for another day and night? It doesn't matter how long we sit here for, Major; if we can't engage the enemy in any way then what use are we? He could be getting up to all sorts outside this fort at the moment and we have no idea at all what it might be..."

The entire garrison found out what the enemy were up to just a split second later. Barely had Renard uttered his words when the hillside seemed to physically shudder. The vibration gained a sudden momentum and a moment later, the deafening roar ripped through the corridors of the subterranean stronghold like the eruption of a volcano. Boooooooooooom!

The tremor that shook the fort was so violent that Jottrand slipped off the edge of the table he was leaning against. All around him there were cries of alarm from the officers of the garrison. Elsewhere in the fortress, Jottrand could hear his men screaming in terror. In truth, it was only what was left of his personal pride that stopped him from doing the same. Something had exploded not far away in the main ventilation shaft; something very, very big.

As the echoes of the terrible blast subsided and the room stopped shaking, Renard jumped up from his chair, his face contorted with a mixture of anger and despair.

"There, Major; do you see? That's all we've got left if we stay down here! More of that! More explosions, and yet more; until they finally break through or we all choke to death on concrete dust! We're just being killed for nothing; nothing apart from your stupid soldier's pride!"

The man was wild eyed, staring at his commander as a terrified horse stares at its groom when it has a mind to bolt. Jottrand dropped his hand to the pistol holster at his waist but at precisely that point, Captain Vermeulen stepped in front of him.

"Major, might I make a suggestion?"

Jottrand glanced at his second in command, keeping one eye fixed on the hysterical Renard. He nodded to the captain.

"Why don't I go up; with a white flag? Just to speak to them? Find out what's going on; what our position is? I might be able to gain some intelligence of their strength. Who knows, we may yet stand a chance of breaking out? Once I know what is going on up there we can make a proper plan, based on facts. As long as we sit down here blind then we will never know. Perhaps I can even arrange some sort of deal with the Germans?"

Vermeulen was talking in a very reasonable manner, and much of what he said made sense. Jottrand still wasn't keen to just give in without a fight however and he hesitated slightly. The others did not.

"Yes, Captain; that's what you must do!" Renard agreed loudly, and was backed up by a ripple of approving mutters.

"It *does* make sense, Major." Pauwels joined in. "We may as well give it a try. There's nothing else we can do other than sit here and let them bomb the shit out of us."

More rumblings of assent came from the crowd of officers. Jottrand felt the moment slipping away from his grasp. With a sigh, he nodded his head wearily.

"Very well, gentlemen." The major agreed. "Captain Vermeulen will go up top under a flag of truce, on his own; and only to gather facts and see what the Germans are about. The rest of us must be prepared for fast, aggressive action if the situation warrants it."

Jottrand glanced round the room and saw the look of hope appear on all the faces before him. Instead of feeling anything similar, Jottrand felt his heart begin to sink. His eyes flicked back to Vermeulen.

"Find yourself a white handkerchief or a bed sheet, Captain." He grunted.

THE ROOF OF, FORT EBEN EMAEL – BELGIUM
SATURDAY 11TH MAY 1940 – 1215 HOURS

"Woohoo!"

Braun and the men gathered around him gave a collective cheer as the huge hollow-charge they had lowered into the ventilation shaft went up with a thunderous roar. They pressed themselves flat against the cupola that was their shelter and grinned at each other madly. As the debris came pattering down around them, Braun laughed out loud, his exhaustion forgotten for a moment.

"Ha, ha! Wakey, wakey, my little Belgian friends! Time to get up! Uncle Erich wants a word with you!"

Nearby, one of Braun's men shouted through the shattered opening of the ruined cupola that had provided their shelter from the blast.

"Little pig, little pig, please let me in?"

Another soldier responded in a squeaky, comical voice.

"Oh, no, I won't let you in; not by the hair of my chinny, chin, chin!"

His mate responded again, in a gruff imitation of the big, bad wolf of fairy tale.

"Then I'll huff, and I'll puff, and I'll blow your house in!"

The other squad members laughed openly at the childish performance. They were hungry and tired, but knew they had the Belgians at their mercy. The storm troopers knew that their tanks and armoured cars had reached the surviving bridges and that the relief column was streaming up the road to relieve them. The first soldiers from one of the Army's assault pioneer battalions had already linked up with other members of their tiny force and were, even now, escalating the reign of terror against the fort's defenders. It was only a matter of hours at the most before their duty was done now.

"Come on, lads." Braun grunted as he stood upright, stretching his muscles in the warm, midday sun. "Let's go see what the damage is."

The rest of his squad pushed themselves to their feet and, moving in a loose, open formation, they jogged over to the still smouldering ventilation shaft. Gathering around it, the German soldiers knelt down and tried to look into the deep hole, but it continued to pour thick black smoke which made the task impossible. They were however rewarded with the echoes of someone sobbing loudly and uncontrollably far below.

"Poor little darling." One of the privates commented dryly.

"What's he saying? Can you make it out?" Another soldier asked.

"I think he asked for another one…" Braun replied, casually producing a stick-grenade and priming it with a sharp tug on the firing cord.

"Below!" He called out as he dropped the grenade into the smoke filled shaft.

"Fucking hell!" One of his men swore, as he watched the grenade drop.

Laughing like school children, the squad of Germans ducked away from the opening and ran a little distance away. Several seconds later, there was a sharp explosion from deep within the shaft, but after the detonation of the hollow-charge, it sounded like a pop-gun going off.

"Braun! Over here!"

The shouted order brought the squad up short. Braun looked across the roof of the fortress and saw a figure waving at him madly.

"It's Groenig." One of Braun's men observed. "What's he want?"

"The Belgies have opened the door!" Came the NCOs voice again. "Get the fuck over here in case they're after a fight! Come on, move it!"

Neither Braun, nor any of his men needed further prompting. They broke into a run, haring across the fort's roof towards the path that led down to the stronghold's main exit. Accompanying the sound of their heavy breathing and footfalls on the hard packed earth, came the metallic click-clack as, like the true professionals they were, the storm-troopers made a final check of their magazines, ramming home fresh ammunition where required.

They reach the lip of the fort's roof and the staff sergeant beckoned them down the steep slope.

"Spread out here, quickly; covering the door down there." He waved Braun and his men into place, and they slid down the bank into position.

Braun quickly took in the scene. He was side on to the big doors in the wall of the fort. Off to his right, lower down and facing the doors, Witzig was crouching in a small dip in the ground, next to an MG34 team and another officer, who was dressed in Army uniform. All of them were in the prone position and aiming directly towards the doors. The Army officer was shouting something.

"We won't shoot. We can see the white flag. Come out slowly where I can see you and then we can talk."

Braun aimed his machine-pistol towards the area of ground in front of the doorway and tried to slow his breathing down. Groenig's voice came from close behind him, issuing a hushed message to everyone in the squad.

"Do not fire unless I give the word. I repeat; *do not* fire unless I give the word."

Braun kept his trigger finger straight, along the side of the trigger guard and continued to watch the doors. A moment later, a man appeared, side on to Braun, from within the fortress.

He was a man of medium height, slight of build, and dressed in a Belgian uniform; that of an officer. He held a cane, to the end of which was tied a large white cloth. The Belgian officer advanced slowly until he had come about ten steps into the open, then he halted. Braun was barely fifteen metres away and could see every detail of the man's face. He was pale. Pale and nervous. He blinked several times, adjusting his eyes to the brightness of the bright morning light and licked his cracked lips. Braun saw the man swallow hard.

"I have been sent by my commanding officer to talk with the commander of the Germans." The man announced, glancing cautiously to his left, then to his right, staring straight at Braun for a second. Braun watched the man's eyes and saw the look of mild alarm as he realised he was ringed by German soldiers.

"You are talking to him." Witzig's voice floated back. "What do you want?"

Again the officer licked his lips.

"I…I have been asked to see if we might come to an arrangement of some kind; one that might be to our mutual benefit." The Belgian stammered.

As he was talking, more figures appeared from within the fortress and Braun caught his breath, his finger moving to the trigger, ready to fire if necessary. There was no need though, for the figures that emerged were weaponless and had their hands raised high in the air. Three, four, five men, and then more still emerged from within.

"You want to surrender?" Witzig's voice demanded of the Belgian officer.

"I am not necessarily offering an immediate surrender…" The Belgian began, but Witzig's voice cut him short.

"Your men appear to think differently."

The enemy officer blinked a couple of times, not sure if he had understood the German words correctly, but then suddenly turned and looked behind him. His eyes bulged with alarm.

"No! No!" He suddenly blustered in the Belgian dialect that was similar to the German language, and moved back towards the doorway, his arms spread wide as if trying to herd the other Belgian soldiers back inside. "We haven't surrendered! I'm just holding discussions. Back inside, everyone!"

His men ignored him, and side stepped his attempts to direct them back inside. Yet more Belgians appeared in the open with their arms raised and the trickle became a flood.

"No! Please, men? Think of your honour! Think of Belgium!" The officer continued, almost swallowed up by the sudden swarm of dejected looking soldiers.

It was too late.

"Braun!" The staff sergeant's voice barked out suddenly. "Get your squad down there and keep that door open. Get all the bastards out here where we can see them."

Instantly, Braun and his men were on their feet and tumbling down-slope onto the flat patch of gravel in front of the doors.

"Get away from the doors!" Braun shouted. "Move! Get away from the doors; out there into the open! Keep your fucking hands up!"

The big corporal pushed two Belgian soldiers out of the way and strode up to the steel double doors, one of which was well ajar. He raised his machine-pistol high and stepped carefully up to the threshold. To his amazement, there was a long queue of men trailing far back into the dim confines of the underground fort. As soon as they saw his silhouette in the doorway, their arms reached upwards smartly.

"Outside! Quickly!" He barked into the gloom of the interior.

Another man came past him into the daylight. The man was middle-aged and sobbing openly; a pathetic sight. More came, and more yet, a seemingly endless line of ragged, beaten looking men, desperate to be free from their subterranean hideaway.

"Christ on a bike!" Breathed the German corporal to himself as the enemy soldiers kept coming.

Nearby, he could hear the Army officer shouting instructions.

"Get them all over there, out of the way. And get a squad inside the fort quickly. I want every nook and cranny of that place searched."

It was just past midday on the 11th May, and Fort Eben Emael, pride of Belgium, had surrendered.

PART TWO

THUNDER

Whit Sunday 12th May 1940
The Third Day

THE VELDWEZELT BRIDGE – NEAR FORT EBEN EMAEL
WHIT SUNDAY 12TH MAY 1940 – 0920 HOURS

"How did you sleep, Witzig?"

Captain Walter Koch, commander of the Storm Battalion, glanced sideways at the commander of Assault Group Granite, the part of his force that had neutralised and then captured the great fortress of Eben Emael during those first, critical two days of the offensive. The younger man smiled back at him.

"Very well thank you, Captain. And I slept all the better for seeing this lot."

He gestured towards the still intact bridge and the two men paused to gaze at the endless column of vehicles, horses and men that were trundling purposefully over the Albert Canal.

"We did it Witzig. We saved the Army at least a 24 hour delay, maybe 48 hours; probably more. There'll be medals in this, you know? And probably some promotions, too. More importantly, the Belgians will be on the back foot and the Tommies and the Frenchies will be panicking like fuck! They'll be breaking their necks to get up here. Our little bit of theatre should have really got them hopping!"

Witzig chuckled.

"Let 'em come, Sir. If they're anything like the Belgians then we've got nothing to fear."

Koch frowned slightly.

"Mmm…Maybe… But the Tommies have a reputation from the last war for hard fighting. The French can be pretty stubborn too, when they want to be. Look at what happened at Verdun. Still, I reckon they might get a nasty surprise all the same, when they find out what we're really up to."

Before Witzig had an opportunity to comment, the sound of distant but intensive gunfire came floating across the morning air. The sound of machine-guns joined the sudden flurry of noise and as the seconds passed, the gunfire seemed to come closer.

"That doesn't sound like good news…" Koch murmured, throwing his gaze around, trying to locate the direction of the firing.

Witzig strained his eyes to the west.

"Anti-aircraft fire I reckon…" Witzig suggested. "No sign of aircraft though…"

"Coming in low perhaps?" Koch said.

Suddenly, a nearby stand of 20mm flak cannon opened up in a furious barrage and just seconds later, trailing a long plume of black smoke, a single engined aircraft appeared over the trees and roared over the heads of the two Storm Battalion officers, heading straight for the bridge.

"Christ on a fucking bike!" Koch swore.

Instinctively, the two officers threw themselves down on the canal bank. The plane was very, very low indeed; maybe 120 feet at the most, and as it passed overhead, it was followed by streams of tracer. The sound of the bullets passing dangerously close was more than a little disconcerting for Koch and Witzig, who were in danger of getting hit by dozens of spent rounds from their own anti-aircraft units.

"He's low enough to bloody touch!" Witzig shouted as he sprawled face down on the muddy bank.

The two men looked up and watched as the plane went straight on for the bridge. Bits of the aircraft were falling off and splashing down into the water as it roared onwards to its intended target. When it seemed that the plane must slam into the bridge, it suddenly flipped to starboard, gained a little height until it was almost vertical, and then passed over the bridge, before suddenly diving straight down and smashing into the opposite bank of the canal some four hundred metres away with a blinding flash and deafening explosion.

"Fuck me! Poor bastard…" Witzig breathed as the debris from the exploding aircraft began pattering down onto the surface of the water and the troops who were caught in the middle of the bridge.

"I wondered where those bloody Tommies had got to…" Koch shouted as the sound of another aircraft filled the air above them.

"The Tommies are gentlemen aren't they, Captain?" Witzig grinned, shouting over the racket as he watched the troops and vehicles on the bridge hurrying for the relative safety of the banks. "Perhaps they wanted to give us a fighting chance?"

The sound of the enemy aircraft drowned out Koch's response as it screamed overhead, flying straight at the bridge.

The two soldiers gawped in fascination as the aircraft, seemingly at the centre of a dozen converging lines of tracer, brought up its nose at the last moment and passed over the bridge, releasing its bombs. They watched as four black objects fell, almost lazily, toward the bridge.

"Jesus…" Koch gasped as he watched the unfolding drama.

Then, just a moment later, he released his breath as every one of the bombs missed their target by just a whisker and landed in the Albert Canal, sending huge spouts of water into the air.

"That was bloody close!" Koch shouted.

"Don't think he'll get a second chance though." Witzig gestured at the ungainly looking British plane as it started banking to starboard in a wide turn, climbing as it went. The aircraft was on fire, thick black smoke billowing out behind it. The plane was clearly doomed, but even so, the lines of tracer continued to follow the stricken bomber.

"They need to bale out sharpish before the bloody thing explodes…" Koch observed, sounding surprisingly concerned for the enemy bomber's crew.

As they watched, the burning aircraft suddenly came round in a shockingly tight turn, back towards the bridge, and then, to the horror of the two soldiers, the pilot dropped the nose of his plane and dived straight towards it.

"Fuck me…" Koch's jaw dropped open in disbelief.

"Bloody lunatic…" Witzig was equally stunned.

The Tommy aircraft was emitting a high-pitched whine as it came hurtling down towards the Veldwezelt Bridge, and that terrible noise was enhanced by a sudden surge in the anti-aircraft fire as every German gunner tried to deflect the pilot from his intended course of action.

It didn't work. Moments later, the stricken aircraft smashed into the western side of the bridge, exploding in a huge ball of orange flame. From their position on the canal bank some two hundred metres away, Koch and Witzig felt the heat and blast-wave roll over them. They pressed their faces into the dirt as it passed over them, only slowly raising their heads as the sound of the explosion and the anti-aircraft fire subsided. Looking up, they could see that a full third of the bridge's span on the near side was on fire. Bits of plane or bridge, possibly both, were falling into the canal below. Koch looked at Witzig with raised eyebrows.

"Shit the fucking bed…" He breathed.

GENERAL HEADQUARTERS, BELGIAN ARMY – NEAR ANTWERP
WHIT SUNDAY 12TH MAY 1940 – 1030 HOURS

The Belgian King looked worried and, from what Brooke had learned over the course of the last twenty four hours, he had good cause to be. The

Germans had broken through at Maastricht which meant that one of the country's major natural defensive barriers had been compromised. It was now more essential than ever that the Dyle position be prepared for defence before the enemy arrived on the doorstep of Brussels. And that was becoming ever more difficult for a frustrated Brooke to achieve.

His lead division, the 3rd, had arrived on their section of the front yesterday to find it occupied by the 10th Belgian Division. That threw out the whole defensive plan for the BEF, especially as Brooke didn't like what he'd seen of the Belgian Army thus far. He had been given differing bits of advice by his own headquarters, most of it of dubious quality, especially the suggestion that he should try to squeeze his corps in between the Belgians and the British 1st Corps. That particular suggestion was plainly a ridiculous one, and the option of double-banking the Belgians was not much better. The BEF's liaison officer here had done nothing to try and resolve the situation and therefore Brooke had been forced to request an audience with the Belgian King, who was acting as the Commander-in-Chief.

As Brooke presented his case to the monarch, he watched the man's response. The King was as pleasant as his reputation claimed him to be, yet it was obvious to Brooke that he was a man under pressure. As he sat listening in the armchair by the fireplace, the King continually stroked his chin, his eyes darting around the room, as if searching for inspiration. It was obvious that his role of C-in-C was more that of a figurehead than a decisive, professional soldier. That is not to say that King Leopold III knew nothing of war, for as a teenager, and while holding the title of Crown Prince, he had fought in the Great War as a private soldier. For high command however, he appeared to have little talent.

"We do not have sufficient forces to double-bank the front along the River Dyle, Your Majesty..." Brooke continued with his monologue. "I believe it would be best for all concerned if your 10th Division moved to its left, so that it links up with the French 7th Army. That will allow my corps to fall into line alongside the British 1st Corps. That will ensure integrity in command structures and logistical chains. When battle is joined, that will be of vital importance."

Brooke had been speaking in English, something initiated by the King who himself was a fluent English speaker. Now, the King sat there, staring vaguely past Brooke, nodding his head slowly as if digesting the information. Brooke however, wasn't sure how much of the grand-strategy the King understood. Nevertheless, he seemed to be warming to Brooke's entreaty, realising that the British general was a professional soldier of proven ability and that he could be relied upon to advise the King wisely. Just at the point where Leopold looked as if he might agree to the British requests however, there was an interruption from behind Brooke's right shoulder, by somebody speaking in French.

"Your Majesty, it is quite impossible to move the 10th Division. They are well entrenched and the enemy are almost upon us. It would take far too long to move them. Besides, it is for Belgian troops to defend Brussels. The British should hold back to the south of Brussels in reserve, where they can be called on should they be needed."

Brooke looked round in surprise at the speaker who had suddenly interrupted his conversation with the King. He found a pompous looking Belgian officer, his uniform adorned with medals and ribbons and braid, standing close behind him. Without introducing himself, the officer stepped forward, ignoring Brooke, and went on speaking to the King in French.

"The British do not understand the details of the situation adequately, Your Majesty…" The Belgian officer was saying as he advanced on the King, placing himself between his monarch and Brooke.

Recovering from his initial surprise, Brooke cut the officer short, breaking into French himself.

"You are not putting the full facts before the King. There is much that can be done to improve the situation now, before we come into contact with the Germans."

The Belgian officer, presumably a general of some kind, stopped abruptly and turned on Brooke with a raised eyebrow.

"Oh. Do you speak French?"

"I do indeed." Brooke assured him coldly. "I was born in France, in fact."

With that curt reply, Brooke stepped around the mystery Belgian general so that he was able to address the King once more.

"Both the British and French armies have light armoured forces forward of the Dyle as we speak Your Majesty, ready to delay any German advance. And I am sure that your own troops are fighting valiantly to contain the Maastricht bridgeheads. There is still time yet to reposition ourselves in the most advantageous manner. It will require a little staff work; simple enough if it is coordinated properly…"

The Belgian officer stepped forward again and once more positioned himself between Brooke and the King. Brooke gave the man an icy look. The King, obviously feeling uncomfortable at witnessing the confrontation, and faced with conflicting advice, stood and moved across to the window. As he walked across the room, Brooke heard the Belgian sovereign murmur to himself in English.

"It is all so very difficult…"

It was over, Brooke realised. The King had been swung from almost accepting Brooke's advice to hovering now in some no-man's land of indecision thanks to this puffed up peacock of a Belgian general. It would be improper for Brooke to force his presence on the King again and besides, the monarch was now even further from being able to make a balanced decision than he had been previously. The commander of the British 2nd Corps gave the Belgian general, who he assumed must be the Chief of Staff, an icy glare.

"I see I am wasting my time discussing strategy here." He whispered to the Belgian in French. "You will excuse me, Sir; I have a battle to prepare for."

With that departing comment, Brooke turned to the King.

"Your Majesty has been very gracious to hear my concerns. I am sure that our respective headquarters will be able to come to a suitable arrangement in due course. By your leave, Your Majesty, I will rejoin my corps."

King Leopold, looking a little relieved, glanced over his shoulder and gave Brooke a thin, almost sad smile, and nodded. Brooke saluted, then, with one final belligerent glance towards the Belgian general, he left the room. As he closed the door behind him and turned into the hallway, Brooke's Aide-de-Camp jumped to his feet from a nearby chair.

"How did that go, Sir?" The young captain asked brightly.

"Awful." Brooke snapped. "The Belgians haven't got the faintest idea of what needs to be done."

He strode down the hallway, his ADC hurrying after him.

"Mark my words," Brooke grumbled. "This has scope for going horribly wrong."

THE RIVER MEUSE AT HOUX – 3 MILES NORTH OF DINANT, BELGIUM
WHIT SUNDAY 12TH MAY 1940 – 1830 HOURS

With a roar, the BMW motorcycles took the bend in the road as it mirrored the course of the great River Meuse. Behind the two lone outriders, spread out in staggered formation, came two motorcycle combinations, the machine-gunners in the sidecars training their weapons to either side of the road, anticipating trouble at any moment. Behind these machines, Sergeant Roland Gritz of the 5th Panzer Division's Motorcycle Reconnaissance Company followed in his open topped car, his machine-pistol cradled on his lap, along with his map. Behind him, the remainder of his platoon; four more combinations and four more lone riders, followed at spacious intervals.

The warm evening sun was extremely pleasant as it fell on them, and the whole river valley was bathed in a beautiful, warm glow. Unfortunately, Gritz was not in a position to enjoy the scenery; he was far too preoccupied with his mission. Unbelievably, just two days after crossing their start line, the lead elements of their division had reached the River Meuse, the one great obstacle to the German advance. Crossing it would decide the fate of the entire offensive in the west, and thus, finding a way over was critical. Much to the disappointment of his commanders, the enemy, a mixture of Belgians and French it was believed, had managed to destroy the bridge at Yvoir, and so Gritz had been despatched southwards, along the river bank, to try and locate another crossing.

His finger traced his route on the map. Houx; that was the name of the village they had just passed through. No bridge. The next one marked on the map was about three miles to the south, at Dinant, but that was supposedly in 7th Panzer Division's area. He studied the map more closely, trying to focus as the vehicle juddered along. He spotted a dotted line on the map, connecting the river bank with what appeared to be an island in the middle of the river. What was that?

Before he had the chance to ponder any further, the sound of distant shouting came to him above the noise of the engine.

"Sergeant Gritz." The driver shouted over the engine. "Up ahead…the boys have seen something."

Gritz looked up, expecting trouble, and saw the motorcycles and combinations pulling over to the right hand verge, the riders pointing across the river. He quickly followed their indication and spotted the long thin island immediately; the one on the map he realised.

His own driver was slowing to a halt now and pulled in behind the nearest combination.

"What is it?" He demanded, standing upright to peer over the windscreen.

Even as he did so, he spotted it for himself.

"It's a weir, Sergeant. Down there, look; by the southern tip of the island. Looks like it's still intact."

Gritz caught his breath.

"Take me down there." He snapped at his driver. " Quickly…"

Hardly daring to believe his luck, Gritz remained standing as his driver pulled past the motorcycles and sped forwards another couple of hundred metres along the river bank. Behind the car, the motorcycles and combinations followed on. Just a few seconds later, they pulled in again, and Gritz felt a rising sense of excitement.

"It *is* in one piece." He murmured incredulously. "Stupid fucking Belgies! It's still intact!"

He leapt out of the car and turned back to face his motorcyclists.

"Engines off!" He drew his finger across his throat to signal 'cut engines'. "Dismount the guns! Quickly! Everyone off and follow me!"

Within moments, the entire platoon was dismounted and fanning out along the river bank.

"Third Squad, wait here and cover us across. Once we're over, follow on. Leave two men with the machines."

Without pausing any longer, Gritz dropped down the slight embankment and onto the weir. Machine-pistol up at the ready, he stepped from block to block, crossing the river as quickly as he could, keeping one eye on the frothing water below, and another on the tree filled island before him. In less than a minute, he was stepping cautiously onto the island itself.

Pausing for a moment, he knelt by a tree and scanned the woodland. There was no movement apparent within the trees; no sound less the distant background noise of occasional shell and small arms fire. Gritz beckoned the rest of his men forward and they filtered onto the island, automatically fanning out into a defensive perimeter. Gritz waited until the men from Third Squad were halfway across the weir, then stood up and waved the other squads forward.

They advanced in line, cautiously, expecting some kind of sudden attack, but nothing happened. After less than a hundred metres, the trees thinned out and came to an end, and Gritz and his men settled down into kneeling positions once more on the western edge of the island, from where they were able to gaze across the river once more towards the western bank of the Meuse. And there, right in front of Gritz, was the most welcome sight of his life. Another weir, connecting the island with the far bank, ran without break across the river. It had not been destroyed or blocked in any way. It was fully intact.

Gritz murmured to himself in disbelief.

"Are they mad? Leaving this in one piece for us to just walk across?"

The voice of First Squad's commander interrupted his thoughts.

"We going over, Sergeant?"

Gritz gave the corporal a wide grin.

"Fucking right we are. Get your boys together and take a walk over. Have a sniff around on the other bank and push out into a small perimeter. If all seems quiet, we'll take it from there."

The corporal nodded and doubled away to prepare his squad. As he did so, Third Squad came up behind Gritz and he quickly briefed them to fall into the position vacated by First Squad, ready to cover them over.

Within a couple of minutes, the first riflemen of First Squad were stepping deftly across the weir. Gritz began planning the options in his mind. The far bank sported a couple of houses, hard by the river. Beyond the houses open ground rose towards steep, wooded hillsides. His little force wouldn't be able to go too far up that slope on its own. He needed to get the rest of the company up here, and also let his battalion headquarters know. The excitement welling in Gritz's chest was almost unbearable. He wanted to shout out loud with joy. His platoon would be the first German unit across the Meuse. He would go down in military legend for this. And then the first shot rang out.

It seemed almost casual at first. A single, isolated, high-pitched crack; and then the lead rifleman from First Squad simply toppled, without any theatrics, into the river.

"Bollocks!" Gritz swore as he watched the soldier's body splash into the water and disappear.

On the weir itself, the other three members of the squad who had got onto the walk-way paused momentarily, automatically crouching as they hesitated at the sudden development. More shots rang out, cracking past the soldiers and hitting the trees above Gritz's head.

"Get over the fucking river!" Gritz bawled out from his position in the trees, then, turning to the men flanking him on the river bank. "Open fire, for fuck's sake! Aim for the buildings and the tree lines. Give them some fucking cover!"

Instantly, the weapons of Second and Third Squads burst into life. Within moments, the peaceful quiet of the river valley was shattered and chaos ensued.

Rifle and machine-gun bullets cracked this way and that. On the weir, the men from First Squad began dashing forwards, hopping from block to block on the weir. A tracer round came from somewhere high on the wooded hill opposite, followed by several more. One of them hit the water, whilst another ricocheted off the weir with a high pitched whine, just below where the lead man of First Squad was picking his way across. A moment later, the man staggered back a step, holding one arm, letting his rifle drop. He lost his footing and toppled backwards into the water. Behind him the next soldier stopped, dropped into a kneeling position and looked back over his shoulder hesitantly.

More bullets slammed into the weir from the west bank, sending the kneeling soldier skittering backwards. Gritz cursed to himself.

"Get back!" He called out across the river. "Pass it along! Tell First Squad to pull back onto the island! Get them back!"

He heard his orders being relayed along the bank to where the rear men of First Squad were hovering in the tree line by the entry point to the weir. A moment later, the poor soldier crouching on the exposed walkway of the weir looked back towards the island again, heard the shouts from his comrades, and without need for further prompting, jumped to his feet and sprinted back towards the cover of the trees.

Within moments, the survivors of First Squad were back in cover, whilst the remainder of the platoon continued to rake the opposite bank with fire, their rifles and MG34 machine-guns chattering away viciously. Gritz, keeping at a low crouch, moved along the tree line to find the commander of First Squad. He found the corporal busily pushing his men down into fire positions. As Gritz approached, the corporal looked up, his face pale with shock.

"Fuck me! That was close! They caught us right in the middle!"

"I know." Gritz acknowledged. "Bad luck. How many do you reckon there are? I don't think it's that many?"

The corporal nodded back.

"Think you're right. Just a handful of them by the looks; but with a machine-gun. As long as it's daylight, they can hold us here, but I reckon after dark we can get across there if we really go for it."

Gritz pulled his cuff back and checked his watch.

"A couple of hours until last light; three, maybe four until full dark. We can try it again then."

He wracked his brains, thinking through the options quickly, just as he had been trained to do.

"Right…" he looked up at the corporal, having reached his decision, "I want you to send two men back up the road to track down the Company Commander; anyone in fact, as long as they're German. Tell them where we are and tell them that the weir is still intact. Rustle up any support you can and get back here before last light. As soon as it gets dark, we're going over again."

HEADQUARTERS GERMAN 19TH CORPS – NEAR BOUILLON, BELGIUM WHIT SUNDAY 12TH MAY 1940 – 1850 HOURS

General Heinz Guderian swept into his newly established headquarters, his face set in a stern, businesslike manner. It had already been an eventful day for him and it was set to get a whole lot busier. This was his third HQ location of the day, the first two being subjected to enemy bombing, and the first of those bombing raids almost proving fatal for him. Despite the inconvenience, Guderian's corps was almost in position for its attempt on the River Meuse, and that had been the reason for him being summoned to Army HQ earlier that afternoon. The summons had been a slight surprise for him. Only when the Fieseler-Storch courier aircraft had landed in the field next to his own command post had Guderian been given the message that his presence was required by his superiors.

Nevertheless, he had made the journey readily enough as he was keen to ensure that all was set for the big event which must only be 48 hours away at most. The flight to meet with General von Kleist had been short and uneventful, but the subsequent meeting had not been to Guderian's liking. He had been ordered to make an attempt on the Meuse the very next day, before all of his divisions would be up to the river. This did not correspond with Guderian's intention as it was his firm belief that he needed to concentrate maximum, overwhelming force at one point in order to punch across the river. The idea of throwing his forces at the river piece-meal disturbed him somewhat, although on balance, given that the bombing of his HQ indicated the enemy now knew of his approach, Guderian accepted that perhaps, on this occasion, speed and momentum would have to suffice in place of brute force.

This wasn't the only source of friction at the meeting. He had been presented with details of the Luftwaffe support to his crossing and this plan, like the directive for the crossing itself, was not how Guderian had arranged things with the local commander of the Luftwaffe supporting his corps. He had, despite his arguments, been overruled and informed that it was too late to change the orders at Army level. Instead, it was he who must now make last minute changes.

With a pile of new operational staff work to contend with, Guderian had been flown back in the Fieseler-Storch once more, but this time with a different pilot to the young man who had originally collected him. The new pilot had assured Guderian that he knew where he was going, yet after a while, it was clear that the pilot had become hopelessly lost. As the evening sun dropped lower in the sky, the commander of the 19th Army Corps had found himself flying at low level over the enemy held bank of the River Meuse. He had promptly, and rather curtly, ordered his pilot to turn north and keep flying straight on. Mercifully, just a short while later, he had spotted some familiar features and located the landing strip. It could have turned into an absolute disaster at several points in the day, but now Guderian was back on the ground, back with his planning team, and ready to get things moving again.

And the gods only knew, he needed to get moving. He was the spearhead of the southernmost attack column, and commanded the most powerful force in the Army; three full panzer divisions and the elite Gross Deutschland infantry regiment. Above him, to the north, were two other armoured spearheads, like his own, working their way rapidly through the Ardennes to appear by surprise on the Meuse within five days or less from the start of their offensive. If they managed to get there, and then force their way across the river, they would be able to punch deep into the rear of the Allied armies while their attention remained fully focussed on the invasion of northern Belgium and Holland. This operation *had* to work first time. He knew he could do it; just as long as people stopped interfering with his plans.

"Nehring!" Guderian called out in a loud voice as he entered the main operations room of his headquarters.

The colonel of that name, Guderian's chief of staff, looked up from the map table with a look of relief.

"General! Thank God. I was starting to get worried…"

"You have good reason to be." Guderian quipped back. "Grab your notebook and pencil and come with me."

The general stomped through the operations room to where a table and some chairs were positioned in the far corner.

"Coffee." Guderian snapped at his orderly who had suddenly appeared by his shoulder.

Guderian threw his cap onto the table, unfastened his greatcoat and shrugged it onto the back of a chair. He dropped onto the chair and waved his chief of staff into the seat opposite.

"Sit."

Nehring sat, pencil at the ready, a concerned look on his face.

"The plan has changed." Guderian began without preamble. "We cross the Meuse tomorrow, with or without 2nd Panzer Division."

"Tomorrow?" Nehring blinked in surprise.

"Yes; tomorrow. And it gets better…" Guderian quickly explained the new orders from high command, emphasising the complete change in the plan for the Luftwaffe.

"My initial thoughts…" Guderian concluded, is that 2nd Panzer give priority to getting their artillery forward. 1st Panzer, supported by Gross Deutschland will be the point of main effort, so they will need all the artillery they can get. If 2nd Panzer can't reach the Meuse in its entirety, then we'll settle for its guns. Given that the Luftwaffe plan has been messed with, we will need every piece of artillery we can muster to make up for it."

Colonel Nehring leaned back in his chair, releasing a long breath, his brow furrowed, fingers of one hand fiddling with an ear. Guderian watched his chief of staff for moment, knowing that the highly efficient colonel would be turning the problem over in his mind, coming up with solutions and preparing a measured response for his commander. Guderian was not disappointed.

"And you say that zero hour is to be 1600, General?"

Guderian nodded.

"Then I think we may have a simple way of getting the orders out in enough time for the divisions to alter their own plans."

"Which is?"

Nehring leaned forward again and looked his commander squarely in the eye.

"You remember the wargame at Koblenz, General?"

"Koblenz?" Guderian muttered, trying to recall that particular wargame from the many he had taken part in.

"The one where we were given the contingency of having to lose a division as flank guard, or through heavy losses…" Nehring prompted him.

Guderian sat up abruptly.

"I do." He said, suddenly recalling the scenario.

His orderly appeared again, placing two metal mugs of black coffee on the table.

Nehring warmed to his theme.

"We still have drafts of the orders from our wargames in the archive files, General. And the orders we produced at Koblenz were for a scenario virtually identical to the current situation. As I remember it, the only real difference in the situation was that we envisaged our zero hour to be at 1000 hours. If we run a quick check over the orders, I am sure that we will have to do little more than amend the timings and then distribute them to the divisions. We can save several hours that way. The divisions can too; if they adopt the same procedure and dig out their archived orders from the wargames."

Guderian smiled and lifted a mug of steaming coffee.

"Well done, Walther. I knew there was a reason I hadn't sacked you before now." He joked. "That solution will work very nicely under present circumstances."

The general took a sip of the dark, bitter coffee then nodded at his chief of staff.

"Do it."

THE WEIR AT HOUX – 2.5 MILES NORTH OF DINANT, BELGIUM
WHIT SUNDAY 12TH MAY 1940 – 2250 HOURS

"Where the fuck did you get to?" Gritz hissed through the dark at the young soldier from First Squad.

"Sorry, Sergeant. It's absolute chaos back up the road. The division's getting ready for a full assault crossing, and Colonel Werner hasn't got time to fart. Still, he told the Company Commander to get his arse down here sharpish with the rest of the boys to support us. He says that once we're over, we're to try and get up to that big hill there and deny it to the enemy."

Gritz snorted.

"Well, we can't wait around all night. The Belgies, or French, or whoever's at the other side; they'll know we're here now and they'll be bringing their own reserves up. We need to get moving. How long before the rest of the company get here?"

"The Company Commander reckoned within the hour." The soldier answered.

Even as the young rifleman was speaking, the sound of motorcycles driving along the eastern bank sounded clearly through the valley. There were no lights evident; the troops knowing they would be visible to the enemy on the western side of the river.

"That'll be them now." Gritz whispered with a sense of relief. "Get back over to the east bank and guide them in. Once you're back, we'll get cracking.

"Okay." The soldier acknowledged and disappeared off into the darkness again.

Gritz checked his watch. It was just gone ten minutes to eleven. He looked back across the dark water to the western bank which was indistinct in the gloom. All quiet. If they moved quickly, he and his men should be able to storm the far bank without taking too many casualties. With the rest of the company now joining them, they would have much more firepower.

The sergeant waited impatiently for the return of the young rifleman, hopefully with the remainder of their company in tow. After what seemed like an age there was movement in the trees behind Gritz, and he strained his eyes to see who was approaching. He picked out the line of dark figures threading its way towards him. Eventually, two figures came up close to him.

"That you, Gruber?" Gritz whispered.

"Yes, Sergeant. Got someone here who wants to speak to you…"

"Who is it?" Gritz asked, straining to pick out the features of the other man.

"Hello mate. Hans Litteman, Recce Battalion from 7th Panzer." The second figure introduced himself.

"7th Panzer?" Gritz asked, his surprise obvious. "What are you lot doing here?"

"We got sent upriver to find some likely crossing sites." The newcomer answered. "Bumped into your man here and he told us you had yourself a crossing point for the taking. Thought we may as well come and give you a hand; bit of a partnership so to speak."

Gritz weighed up the man's words for a moment.

"How many of you are there?" He asked eventually.

"Thirty two all up; and five machine-guns." Came the reply.

That immediately removed any doubt from Gritz's mind. If they waited for the rest of their company, then the enemy might have time to reinforce their own position. But with another thirty odd men, he could make a rush for the far bank now and seize the initiative.

"OK. Nice to have you on board. Can your boys form a fire base along this tree line and cover my platoon over? Once we're all across, we'll cover you lot over too."

"No problem." Answered Litteman with a grin; his teeth bright in the darkness. "I'll get the boys shaken out now. I'll give you a nod when we're all in."

With that, the NCO from 7th Panzer moved off to organise his men.

Gritz did likewise, peeling his men sideways towards the entry point to the weir. After a few minutes of bustling and urgent whispering, Gritz had his men bunched up in a less than tactical formation ready to go. It wasn't a pretty set up but it would do. A runner from Litteman came across to give the signal that the 7th Panzer boys were all in position, and Gritz checked his watch one last time. One minute to eleven. Time to go.

The First Squad led once more; moving cautiously after the earlier episode. Gritz watched man after man cross the weir and disappear into the dark. He tried to picture the scene. He had studied the short route through his binoculars in the fading light as he waited patiently for support, and for darkness. The weir led to a small concrete pier, beyond which was a lock gate with a walk-way, and that led onto the bank at the far side. He could still hardly believe that the lock had not been blown and the weir demolished. His tenth man stepped onto the weir. The first few men must be right over the other side now. A moment later, a red torch light flashed three times from the far bank. They were over.

Gritz stood and took his first steps towards the weir. He placed his foot onto the first concrete block and stepped onto the structure. He paused for a moment, looking at the rushing water below, then walked onwards, machine-pistol at the ready. He was a third of the way across when there was a loud crack, followed by a thump, somewhere in the darkness. He froze, staring intently at the far bank. Another shot cracked out. Then there was a burst of machine-pistol fire, shouting in German, and a signal flare rose lazily up into the night sky from somewhere up the hill.

"Fuck!" Gritz cursed, then, hollering out loud. "Get moving! 5th Panzer! Get over the river! Everyone get moving!"

Gritz began loping across the weir as fast as he dare. As he did so, the signal flare reached its zenith and plummeted down towards the river. In its glare he saw another three of his men in front of him, strung out along the weir and the lock gate.

"Keep moving!" He screamed at the top of his voice. "Get over the fucking river!"

As he roared his orders, a series of cracks cut through the air in front of him and a tracer round whizzed past his field of vision. Behind him, on the island, the 7th Panzer contingent suddenly opened fire in a thunderous explosion of noise. More and more bullets cracked around him, some coming from the enemy bank, but many more coming from behind him, arcing up the hill towards the hidden enemy positions.

The scene was illuminated by another signal flare and in its glow, Gritz saw the man in front of him suddenly stagger and fall backwards. The man disappeared into the black, frothing water beneath the weir. Gritz felt a heavy sense of dread descend on him. He fought the fear and lurched onwards towards the concrete pier. He was almost there; just a few more metres. A single bullet slammed into the concrete block behind him, causing Gritz to give a startled cry. He missed his footing and slipped, falling forwards.

"Ugh!"

He landed heavily, scraping one knee and one hand on the concrete block, but managing to stop himself from sliding over the edge into the river.

"Fucking hell…" He gasped in shock, pushing himself up.

He felt himself being lifted.

"Are you OK, Sergeant?"

"What? Yes…Thanks."

A soldier from Second Squad was holding him steady as he fought to regain his balance.

"Let's go…" Gritz muttered, recovering from the shock of his fall, and began moving along the weir again.

Moments later he stepped onto the concrete of the long thin pier and, as he did so, realised that the gunfire had subsided slightly. He now moved onto the lock gate and picked his way across the walk-way. There was lots of shouting now, all in German, and the firing had trailed off to just the odd shot. By the time Gritz set foot on the west bank of the River Meuse, the firing had stopped completely.

As he crossed onto the west bank, he took in the scene quickly. The house loomed up before him, dark and menacing. Shadowy figures moved around urgently, either side of it.

"Heigel? Heigel?" Gritz called out as loud as he dare for the commander of First Squad.

"Here!" A voice called from close by and moments later Corporal Heigel was in front of him.

"What's going on?" Gritz demanded.

"Enemy sentries, Sergeant. Not many though. Half a dozen at most. We killed a couple; the rest have fucked off. I think they've gone up that hill there, on the right. There was a machine-gun firing from up there a few moments ago; must be their main position."

Gritz knew his own position was precarious, but now was not the time for caution. As far as he knew, they were the first German soldiers over the Meuse. They had to stay there. He made his decision in less than a second.

"We can't give them time to get organised. Spread everyone out into extended line; sweeping formation. We're going after them."

Monday 13th May 1940
The Fourth Day

BOUVIGNES ON THE MEUSE – ONE MILE NORTH OF DINANT
MONDAY 13TH MAY 1940 – 0535 HOURS

"Watch your footing; loose rocks and scree!" Corporal Richter's voice called from just a few paces in front. "Whoaa!"

Private Franz Middenburg fought to maintain his footing as he began to slide on the loose gravel of the steep slope.

"Careful Franz…" Murmured Private Bern, Middenburg's battle-partner, as he reached out one hand to prevent his friend from going flat on his arse.

"This is fucking madness!" Middenburg swore, steadying himself.

The men, all of them panzer grenadiers from the 6th Rifle Regiment of 7th Panzer Division, were weighed down in the extreme. On their left shoulders they hefted the heavy rubber assault boat, whilst in their right hands every man carried a container of two mortar bombs. All this of course, was in addition to their usual battle equipment and personal weapons which were slung over their shoulders, rattling and bumping off the boat as they stumbled down the steep, wooded slopes of the east bank of the River Meuse.

It was barely dawn, and the division's assault crossing of the River Meuse was just a few minutes old. The enemy, securely entrenched on the other side of the river and the equally steep slopes of the western bank, were not in a mood to make it an easy task. From down below by the water's edge, the sound of frantic shouting and screaming cut through the chill air, mixed with the thunderous roar of incoming artillery and the rattle of small arms fire. Whistles blew their shrill notes and the hollow 'thunk' of friendly mortars being fired joined the cacophony. Middenburg realised that today was not going to be an average day.

Almost without warning the gradient changed from its steep angle to virtually flat and Middenburg saw that they had reached the bottom of the valley. His half-squad burst through the cover of the wooded slope into open ground, and a spiky branch, thick with pine needles, whipped backwards, slapping him in the face.

"Ah! Fucking hell!" Middenburg cursed, spitting pine needles and bark as he emerged into more open ground.

As he cleared his mouth and blinked at the sudden daylight, Middenburg caught his breath. Lines of tracer of various colours flew in both directions across the deep ravine through which the Meuse flowed. He realised that the ground under his feet seemed to be trembling and the rising plumes of dirty grey smoke beyond the next set of trees gave a clue to the source of the tremors. He could hear bullets cracking overhead and bits of spent shrapnel hissed past him, far too close for comfort.

Thunk. Thunk.

He glanced over to his right and saw a line of 8 centimetre mortars going into action. A soldier from the mortar line was running across to them.

"Have you got any bombs?" He was calling above the racket.

"Yeah; where do you want them?" Corporal Richter answered, coming to a sudden stop so that everyone holding the boat bumped into the back of the man in front.

"Just drop 'em there…" The mortarman shouted as he drew closer.

Without need for any further prompting, the four riflemen of their half-squad dropped the heavy plastic containers at their feet, shaking off their arms and flexing their fingers. The only man still with a burden was Lucker, carrying the MG34.

From their rear left another group of men with a boat appeared through the trees.

"Don't stop there!" Someone shouted, and all of them recognised Sergeant Heffner's voice. "Keep fucking going!"

"Just dropping the bombs…" Richter explained, then gave the boat a tug. "Come on lads…"

The five men stumbled forward again, each of them now using both hands to heft the boat. Beside them, the mortarman had already grabbed two containers and was doubling back towards the firing line.

On they staggered with their burden, pushing through the next line of trees. Barely had they emerged onto the river bank proper when there was a sudden explosion not far away to their left. The thunder-clap of the explosion caused Middenburg to wince, and a split second later the shock wave pushed the entire group and their boat over onto the ground.

"Christ on a fucking bike!" Bern called out in terror.

Middenburg raised his head, stunned, and gawped around him.

They were just metres away from the river now. A narrow road cut left to right in front of them, following the course of the Meuse. There was a building nearby that was already on fire, spewing black smoke from its burning roof. The scene on the river bank was one of carnage. Another boat sat just metres away from Middenburg, shredded and deflated. Beneath and around the remnants of the boat, the half-squad that had carried it down the hill lay strewn on the ground in a bloody sprawl.

"Shit!" Middenburg hissed in sudden fear.

"Up!" Richter's voice jerked him back to reality. "On your feet; the boat's still good...let's go!"

Together the five panzer grenadiers staggered to their feet and began hauling the assault boat forward again. They had barely gone a few steps however when a line of tracer seemed to arc down towards them from the opposite hillside. A split second later, a series of small spurts of earth began erupting in front of them; each subsequent bullet impacting closer and closer to the half-squad. They all saw the danger and without any verbal command, they veered naturally off to one side, avoiding the fall of shot, throwing themselves behind the burning building.

Hidden temporarily from the enemy's fire, the half-squad of Germans gathered their wits.

"Fuck me!" Bern shouted above the crackle of flames from above them. "This place is a fucking death trap! We'll be minced before we even get to the water!"

Richter, as shaken as the rest of them, did his best to sound confident.

"I can see boats in the water; First and Second Platoons are nearly half way across."

Jurgens, another of the riflemen, grumbled loudly at the assertion.

"What's left of them..."

As they stood there, catching their breath and trying to summon up courage to emerge into the hail of fire once more, Sergeant Heffner's half-squad appeared through the trees again, stomping across the open ground towards the river. Middenburg watched the faces of his squad mates twist in exhaustion as they forced themselves onwards towards the water's edge, their own rubber boat bouncing about on their shoulders. Heffner caught sight of the other half of his squad cowering behind the burning house and roared at them.

"Get fucking moving you idle fuckers!"

A heartbeat later, he, along with the two men behind him, suddenly collapsed, falling heavily backwards onto each other as a burst of fire sliced through the three of them. The front of the boat dropped and the remaining two soldiers in the half-squad toppled clumsily over the pile of bodies that had suddenly appeared at their feet.

"Oh my fucking God!" Richter gasped in horror.

"Fuck me!" Lucker, the machine-gunner was saying. "They got the lot of 'em!"

He was wrong. The two rear men, having toppled over their three dead comrades, were still alive, if a little stunned. Sprawled out, face down, the two men looked up and gawped around them stupidly.

"Over here!" Richter shouted across at them. "Get over here!"

The two riflemen spotted their squad mates and began crawling on all fours towards them, fear and shock etched thickly on their white faces. An enemy artillery shell exploded not far away, showering them all with mud, but otherwise doing no harm. Moments later, the two survivors from Sergeant Heffner's boat scrambled behind the shelter of the building.

"I'm not going back out there!" One of the men wailed as he pressed himself in against the wall.

It was at that point that another four men appeared from the tree line and advanced directly towards where Heffner and his two dead comrades lay. These newcomers were not carrying a boat, and only one of them was armed with anything more than a pistol. It was clear they were all officers and every man in Richter's squad recognised the figure of their Battalion Commander instantly, striding along with his machine-pistol cradled in both arms. He, like two of the other three unarmed men, was wearing a helmet and standard field dress. The fourth man however, was wearing a greatcoat and an officer's soft, peaked cap. Unbelievably, the party of four advanced without hurry towards them. The man in the cap was looking around with great interest and gesticulating expressively, clearly giving directives and orders, seemingly oblivious to the death and chaos that surrounded him. A pair of binoculars hung around his neck and, with a start, the watching soldiers noticed his badges of rank.

"Fucking hell! It's the Divisonal Commander!" Richter cursed.

Erwin Rommel, commander of the 7th Panzer Division was an old hand at this sort of thing. He might not have been from typical Prussian officer stock, but he was a natural fighter and leader of men who had enjoyed great success in the First War. The sound, sight and smell of battle were all familiar to him, and now he wandered across the bottom of the Meuse valley as if he were simply observing his men whilst on manoeuvres. He walked up to the corner of the house where Richter and his men were sheltering, his attention fixed on the opposite bank. His three companions were too busy listening to his constant stream of instructions to notice the group of panzer grenadiers just a few paces away.

"And that's your first company nearly across, you say?" Rommel was asking.

"Yes, General." The battalion commander confirmed. "And this is the second company trying to get across now, but as you can see, the enemy has finally got his artillery into action and his machine-gunners have woken up too."

"Mmm…" Rommel pulled a thoughtful face and glanced up at the burning roof of the house. "This smoke is helpful though. Shame we haven't got more of it."

He turned northwards and squinted up the river valley. After a couple of moments, his arm shot out, ramrod straight, a finger pointing in imperious command.

"Those houses up there." Rommel snapped. They are up-wind. Have them all set on fire immediately; the whole row. The smoke will drift down here and shield the crossing somewhat. "Most; see to it."

One of the unarmed officers snapped to attention, nodded, and doubled away to make the arrangements.

Rommel had turned his attention to the Battalion Commander again.

"Keep your men going. It will be a sharp, nasty business for the first hour or so, but once you are across you will quickly knock the enemy off balance. It's all about speed and momentum; don't hang around or you'll just make yourselves a target."

The general looked now to the other staff officer.

"Vosse, you have seen the enemy bunkers on the opposite hillside? Get a couple of tank companies up here, and some 88's too. Get them firing directly across at those bunkers on the other side."

A burst of machine-gun fire cracked right past the general and slammed into the ground just a few feet away, kicking up small clods of earth. Rommel didn't even blink.

Suddenly, the weather-beaten general looked directly at the group of panzer grenadiers kneeling behind the house. Still holding their rubber boat, the group of infantrymen stared back at their divisional commander in awe.

"You men." Rommel snapped. "Is that boat in one piece?"

Finding his voice, Richter mumbled an embarrassed reply.

"Yes General… it's fine."

Rommel gave the group an icy stare and addressed them in a calm, school-masterly voice.

"Well… get it on the water then. We haven't got all day and your comrades are waiting for you on the other side. Let's be having you, gentlemen."

Without further prompting, Richter and the survivors of his squad staggered to their feet and stepped out from behind the building once more, breaking into a clumsy run for the water's edge, dragging their boat with them. Rommel watched them go for a moment or two, but then looked away at the sound of his name being called.

"General Rommel!"

He turned to see one of his signallers running across to him.

"General! You are required back at headquarters, Sir. The Corps Commander and Army Commander are here to see you."

Rommel frowned.

"Christ almighty." He cursed quietly to himself, looking away so that the others would not catch his words. "What are they doing here so early? Have they wet their damned beds or what?"

FRENCH SECTOR HEADQUARTERS – NEAR DINANT
MONDAY 13TH MAY 1940 – 0700 HOURS

General Pierre Duval, commanding the French defenders in the Dinant area, was in a bad mood. He had been woken early, given some bad news, which then turned out to be not so bad after all, and now his stomach was rumbling with a desire for breakfast.

"So, we are confident that the crossing attempt has failed?" He fixed the staff officer with a grumpy look.

The major hesitated slightly, but finally settled for a nod of confirmation.

"For the time being, it looks as though the enemy have been held, General. Certainly, they have ceased their attempts to cross it would seem…"

Duval grunted acknowledgement.

"Good. That is very good…" He paused for a moment, turning the recent situation report over in his mind. "Although you can hardly credit the enemy with this. The Germans must be mad; trying to force the river with just their reconnaissance troops. Their main body must be strung out all the way back to the German border."

He looked up at the major from under a furrowed brow.

"It's bad generalship that, Boullon; launching an attack without proper support. Bad generalship, I tell you; typical of the Boche. Still…" He chuckled quietly. "They're making our job easy for us, so who's complaining?" I just wish the commanders at the front would just calm down a bit, instead of sending in all these garbled reports. It's just causing everyone to panic unnecessarily."

Before Duval could go any further, he was interrupted by the ringing of his telephone. He glowered at the device for a long second before reaching out and snatching up the receiver.

"Duval."

He paused a moment as the operator apologised for the early hour and explained that there was a call waiting for the general from one of the frontline commanders.

"What? The 66th? Commandant Boulanger? Yes, alright, put him on."

Duval glanced up at the major and pulled an exasperated face. The major smiled back weakly, remaining tactfully quiet as the general took the call.

"Yes, Boulanger; it's me. What is it?" Duval spoke without preamble as soon the commandant came on the line.

The major from Duval's staff continued to gaze at the general as he listened intently to the voice of Boulanger at the other end of the phone. As the general listened, his face grew darker. He snorted once, then a second time. Boullon could hear the feint sound of the commandant's voice from within the ear piece. The commandant sounded very excited. After a while, the voice ceased, and Duval heaved a great sigh before answering.

"The Heights of Wastia? Are you sure about that? I have just been told that the enemy crossing is being held, so how have the Germans got up to the Heights of Wastia? Have they got wings?"

A pause whilst Commandant Boulanger answered.

"The weir? What weir?" Duval demanded. "The only one I know of is the one near Houx, and that should have been demolished."

Again a pause for Boulanger's explanation. The staff major saw Duval's eyebrows dip in a deep frown.

"What do you mean it's still intact? Why in the name of God hasn't it been blown?"

After another pause, Duval exploded.

"Right, well, get those bloody Germans off that hill and make it quick; that's if they are really there at all and this is not just another random panic attack from some wet behind the ears lieutenant! And then find an engineer and get him to blow up the bloody lock gates, and the weir too if he can manage it. I will organise some support to go up to the Heights to check what's going on and to calm everybody down, but in the meantime, get a grip of the officers on the river line and tell them to calm down and start using their bloody brains!"

The general slammed the phone down.

Duval drummed his fingers on the desk irritably for a few seconds then glanced up at the major, who was still waiting nervously at the other side of the desk.

"Those bloody idiots in the 66th reckon a group of Germans have sneaked over the weir at Houx during the night and got themselves up the hill onto the

Heights of Wastia. Neither the weir, nor the lock has been blown up. Personally, I think that it's just an exaggeration. It's more than likely just another reconnaissance group, so there isn't much of a threat from them. Either way, I want those buffoons in the 66th given a kick up the arse. Get hold of the tank company and tell them to conduct a patrol up to the Heights of Wastia, then to swing south and do a sweep via Bouvignes. If any of the Boche have managed to cross the river, I want them driven back, killed or captured. Then I want the infantry to do what they're supposed to do and stop anymore Germans from crossing. Got all that?"

The major nodded. "Yes, General; perfectly clear."

"Good." Duval grunted, standing suddenly and reaching for his tunic which was laid over the back of his chair. "And prepare a message to go up to the Corps Commander. Tell him that we think a few Germans have managed to get across, but that we're going to deal with them using our tank company. Tell him that we can expect the German main body within the next twenty four hours; a tad earlier than we initially thought. We probably need the reserves up at the river by tonight… Tomorrow morning at the latest."

"Yes, General."

"Now then; as I'm up, I may as well go and have some breakfast."

BOUVIGNES ON THE MEUSE – ONE MILE NORTH OF DINANT
MONDAY 13TH MAY 1940 – 0715 HOURS

"What's going on? What's the hold up? Why isn't anyone moving?"

Rommel strode along the line of trees and bushes that offered the last bit of cover before the water's edge, his face set as hard as stone. Around him, all along the tree line, panzer grenadiers lay flat on their bellies, tucked in against their rubber boats, whilst beyond the trees, littering the east bank of the river, were strewn the casualties and debris of the first assault wave. The panzer grenadiers of the 6th Rifle Regiment had taken heavy casualties forcing their way across the Meuse, but Rommel had stood there on the bank, exhorting them and watching the young soldiers throw themselves desperately over the river through the hail of fire. They had done it. Despite the losses, the 6th Regiment was on the west bank and fighting to expand its little bridgehead. Now however, during Rommel's short visit to his command post, the attack seemed to have stalled, and the 7th Rifle Regiment remained stuck on the east bank, apparently reluctant to run the gauntlet of artillery and machine-gun fire.

Rommel stalked along the tree line, followed by his staff officers, his face grim. He came across one of the battalion commanders, crouching amongst some long grass with his tactical headquarters group.

"Why isn't your battalion moving, Major?" Rommel demanded coldly. "What are you waiting for?"

The major looked up in surprise; stunned to find the divisional commander suddenly bearing down on him.

"Err…we're waiting for a gap in fire before we cross. The enemy are bringing down heavy artillery concentrations on the bank, and they still have machine-guns covering the whole valley."

Rommel was less than impressed.

"Of course they have." He snapped. "Because no-one has seen fit to climb the hillside opposite and stop them!"

A French shell slammed into the river bank less then a hundred metres away and the shrapnel and soil rattled through the branches of the trees above Rommel's head. He didn't even blink.

"The 6th Regiment are fighting to maintain their hold on the far side, but they'd do a whole lot better with the 7th over there to give them a hand."

The major paled under the unspoken accusation.

"Yes, Sir." He mumbled.

"Get your battalion ready." Rommel announced. "We're going over in two minutes. I'm coming with you."

The major blinked repeatedly, then, as if he had been jabbed with a hot poker, he leapt to his feet and began shouting orders along the tree line.

Rommel turned to his staff officers.

"Most? Go find the commander of the 7th. Tell him the 2nd Battalion is going over the river and that I'm going with them. I want his other battalions to follow straight afterwards; and organise the divisional engineers to get a cable ferry set up as soon as the 7th are across. I want some guns on the other side sooner rather than later."

"Yes, General." Most saluted and departed.

"Vosse; you're with me."

"Yes, General." The captain acknowledged.

More artillery shells slammed into the river bank.

Rommel turned to look for the commanding officer of the 2nd Battalion and found him waiting expectantly, nearby.

"Ready?" Rommel raised an enquiring eyebrow.

"Yes, General." The major confirmed, looking suddenly alert and full of energy.

"Good." Rommel said curtly. "Then get on with it. I'll find a boat with one of the companies."

The major nodded obediently and raised a whistle to his lips. He took a huge breath and then blew a long shrill note, followed by two more.

"Go, go, go!" Hollered the major.

All about them, groups of heavily laden soldiers rose from the long grass and undergrowth to the accompaniment of shouting and more whistle blasts. Then, with a low collective growl that swelled into a roar, the 2nd Battalion of the 7th Rifle Regiment broke through the tree line and hurled themselves at the river bank. The grey-clad assault troops surged across the narrow strip of water meadow, over the bodies of fallen comrades, and hurried their boats to the water. Almost instantly, the sound of incoming artillery filled the valley and two simultaneous explosions sent men and boats flying through the air. Above the roar of hundreds of voices and the thunderclap of exploding shells, the crack, crack, crack of a machine-gun punctuated the morning air.

Rommel, accompanied by Vosse, was amongst the panzer grenadiers, doubling forward towards the river, still wearing only his soft cap, but having ditched his greatcoat. A pair of binoculars bumped against his chest and a wicked smile was etched on the general's face. The veteran and hero of the First World War was feeling the adrenalin rush of being in the front line again; that strange combination of fear, excitement and rage that filled one at times of great danger. Vosse glanced left and right and saw that the men around him had seen Rommel's broad grin also. Here was their general, leading them forward in person, into battle, and they loved him for it.

The first boats were in the river now and Rommel was there with them. Vosse saw the general veer left towards a boat packed with machine-gunners, commanded by a young sergeant. The soldiers were piling into the boat, stacking their weapons and ammunition boxes in the centre whilst exchanging them temporarily for paddles. As they settled themselves and prepared to push off, Rommel jumped in amongst them, and Vosse followed suit. The soldiers looked around in surprise at the two unexpected guests.

"Room for a small one?" Rommel asked in a booming voice.

The soldiers grinned stupidly back at him.

"Of course, General. The more, the merrier!"

"In – in – in!" The sergeant's voice began calling the rhythm and the soldiers started digging their paddles deep into the water, propelling the boat forward across the Meuse.

"In – in – in!"

The boat was well into the open water now. Left and right more boats joined them. To their right, a line of tracer arced down from the opposite hillside and stitched a line of splashes across the water in front of a neighbouring boat. One of the soldiers in that boat suddenly gave a surprised grunt and flipped overboard into the water, disappearing into the murky depths of the river.

At the front of their own boat, a single machine-gunner crouched low over the bow and squeezed the trigger of his weapon.

Rat-tat-tat-tat-tat-tat!

Rommel approved. The man was being aggressive. As the hail of bullets flew up towards the steep hillside on the west bank, the general knew that they probably wouldn't hit any enemy soldier. But the noise of the bullets was good. Noise scared people; just as the noise of the French guns scared his own men. So, it was good to give something back.

Rat-tat-tat-tat-tat-tat!

A shell plunged into the river to their left, sending up a huge spout of water that caused Rommel's boat to rise and fall with a gut-wrenching lurch.

"Are you sure this is a good idea, General?"

One of the privates wielding a paddle glanced sideways at Rommel, a grimace of both fear and elation on his young features.

"It's going to be a rough crossing I reckon!"

Rommel grinned back at the panzer-grenadier.

"I'll be fine, thank you; I've seen worse."

The private gave a grunt as he dug his paddle into the water once more then flung Rommel another cheeky grin.

"Perhaps, General; but I'd hate to be accused of getting the Divisional Commander killed! Mind you; we'll probably all die anyway!"

Rommel regarded the soldier with amusement and gave him a knowing wink.

"In which case, young man, I'll see you in Valhalla!"

FRENCH SECTOR HEADQUARTERS – NEAR DINANT
MONDAY 13TH MAY 1940 – 0930 HOURS

"I thought you said we had held the Germans? I thought this was only a reconnaissance? What are you trying to say?"

Duval was in no better a mood than earlier and the unfortunate major from his headquarters staff was on the receiving end of the general's latest tirade, having been yet again the bearer of bad news.

"The enemy has launched more attacks, General," the major gulped uncomfortably, paling under the divisional commander's withering glare, "with stronger forces. And there are small groups of enemy infantry using infiltration tactics. I believe it is time to bring up our reserves, General. I believe that the enemy is further advanced than we have given him credit for. I don't know how they have done it but they seem to be in great strength on the east bank of the Meuse and they seem intent on crossing it today."

Duval snorted angrily and looked out of his window for a moment, drumming his fingers on the highly polished desk in irritation.

"It is impossible." He murmured grumpily. "I have no idea how the enemy could move so quickly. I suspect that our troops are making the situation out to be much worse than it actually is."

He looked back at the major and gave him a meaningful look.

"Either that or they are not attending to their duty as fully as they should."

The general paused and raised a questioning eyebrow at the major.

"Perhaps, General…" Replied the staff officer hesitantly.

Before the general could press him further, he was spared by a knock on the door. Looking around, both Duval and the long suffering staff officer watched as another member of the headquarters entered the large office. A young captain, his face full of worry, advanced cautiously toward the two men clutching a piece of paper; his eyes darting nervously from the major to the general.

"My apologies for interrupting, General, but we have had a telephone call from the unit in the Bouvignes sector; about the tank company…"

"Ah!" Duval brightened suddenly. "They have attacked the Germans then?"

The captain seemed to shrink slightly.

"No, General. That is the problem. They don't seem to have moved off yet. I have sent a despatch rider to find out what's going on. The regimental commander in Bouvignes is asking how long it will be before the tanks can attack the German bridgehead?"

Duval stood up and glared at the captain.

"Why haven't they moved off? Why haven't they attacked?" He demanded. "And what does he mean, 'bridgehead'? How many Germans have got across exactly?"

The captain swallowed nervously again.

"I don't know, Sir. As I said, I have sent a…"

"Get hold of them!" Duval thumped the desk with his fist. "Get hold of them and tell them to get moving. I don't want excuses. I want them to move to the Heights of Wastia immediately and secure that ground. From there, I want them to locate where the enemy has crossed and then I want them to attack and repulse any German on this side of the river."

The captain was nodding repeatedly.

"And get some infantry support organised for them." Duval went on. He glanced at the major and then back to the captain. "Both of you; see to it personally. I want a proper counter-attack organised and I'll give you until one o'clock to get it sorted. I will be in the planning room shortly…"

Duval lifted the receiver of his telephone and took a deep breath.

"Once I have informed the Corps Commander of these latest developments. I think it's time we took some firm action against these German probes. I don't like the sound of any of it. I don't like it at all."

The sector commander put the telephone to his ear and with his free hand, waved at the two staff officers in dismissal.

"Get that attack organised and get those tanks moving. One o'clock; no excuses."

As the two officers backed out of the room, the operator came on the telephone line and the general barked at him.

"Yes, this is General Duval."

The sector commander heaved another deep breath.

"Put me onto Corps Headquarters; immediately. Tell them it is urgent."

BOUVIGNES ON THE MEUSE – ONE MILE NORTH OF DINANT
MONDAY 13TH MAY 1940 – 1135 HOURS

The engineer squad gave one more heave and the raft clunked against the river bank. The moment it did so, Rommel stepped deftly off the metal platform and strode up the small rise onto the level ground, Vosse hurrying behind him. Lieutenant Most was waiting for them.

"Where's the engineer commander?" Rommel asked with his customary briskness.

"I'll go and get him, Sir." Most saluted the general and doubled away to find the officer.

Rommel turned around and looked back across the Meuse at the enemy bank. He had crossed the river with the 7th Panzer Grenadiers in a rubber assault boat. Having got the infantry moving on the western bank and briefed their commanders to start infiltrating into Bouvignes town itself, Rommel had stayed on for a while to supervise the expansion of the bridgehead.

Whilst there, he had seen some enemy tanks in the distance, which could have proved a real problem. Fortunately they didn't seem keen on coming too close. He had ordered the nearby troops to engage them at long range with their machine-guns and even flare pistols. The small show of force seemed to have done the trick and the enemy vehicles had disappeared from view again. Even so, the presence of enemy armour wasn't good. To that end, Rommel had come back over the river courtesy of the engineers, who had managed to get a cable ferry up and running. The general had crossed back over the river once more on an 8 ton platform, once it had off-loaded its anti-tank gun. More of the PAK 36 anti-tank guns were queued up ready to go across and Rommel was pleased at the news that Bouvignes was now completely in the hands of his panzer grenadiers. And so he was back on the east bank again, tireless in his desire to keep things moving and make sure that every part of his division was being pro-active.

"Vosse?"

"Yes, General?"

"I make that eighteen anti-tank guns so far. Agree?"

"Eighteen it is, General."

Rommel nodded curtly.

"That is good. The bridgehead is a little more secure now, should those enemy tanks decide to come back and have a poke at us."

He paused only for a moment, watching as another PAK 36 was wheeled forward onto the ferry, followed by a line of men carrying ammunition boxes.

"But that will only allow us to *defend* our hard-earned ground. We need to exploit. Take yourself on a run, Vosse. I want the first of the light tank companies brought down to the river bank ready to cross. I will make the arrangements with the engineers. Go and see to it straight away."

"Of course, General." Vosse nodded and made to head off on his task.

"Oh, and Vosse?"

"Yes, General?"

"Make sure all the heavy tank companies remain on the edge of the valley on this side of the river. I want them prepared to engage targets over the river with direct fire if needed."

Vosse saluted in acknowledgement and headed off.

As the staff captain jogged away across the water meadows to where the mobile tactical headquarters was parked amongst the trees, an enemy artillery shell whooshed through the air, dropping into the valley. It slammed into the water mid-river sending a spout of water high into the air. As usual, Rommel ignored it. Almost absently, he noted that the enemy artillery fire was slackening. More a harassing fire now rather than a bombardment, he reflected.

"Yes, General?"

The arrival of the major commanding the engineer unit interrupted Rommel's musings. He turned to face the officer. Most was beside the engineer and the two officers saluted their general together. Rommel returned the compliment and then fixed the engineer officer with a hard look.

"Well done, Major." He began. "The ferry is working well. Your men have done a good job."

"Thank you, Sir."

Rommel paused for only a heartbeat.

"We need to send tanks over next."

The engineer major nodded.

"We're working on it now, General." He replied. "We're rigging up more platforms. It will take a little time though, because we need 16 ton units to ferry tanks across."

Rommel nodded his understanding.

"How long?"

The major's mouth twisted slightly as he weighed up the situation, running through a quick time-appreciation in his mind.

"Two hours perhaps, General." He answered after a little thought.

Rommel fixed the major with his flat, grey eyes for a moment before replying.

"I'll give you one hour." He said.

BLOCKHOUSE 75 – SEDAN ON THE RIVER MEUSE
MONDAY 13TH MAY 1940 – 1610 HOURS

While Rommel was forcing a crossing of the Meuse near Dinant, the main act of the great drama was beginning to unfold some forty miles to the south.

Crump, crump, crump!

Despite being shielded by two feet of reinforced concrete, Lieutenant Raoul Blanche of the French 55th Infantry Division cried out in consternation as the latest stick of bombs landed somewhere not far away from his bunker. He and his men were responsible for defending this northern loop of the River Meuse above Sedan, but at the moment, the only thing they were doing was cringing in the corners of their small fortress. The air attack had begun a little over ten minutes ago, but it seemed to him that it had been going on for ten hours. The concussive shock waves from each bomb punched through the firing ports of their blockhouse leaving every man feeling shattered. Physically they were reasonably safe, but the effect on their nerves was mortifying. Blanche hoped that the bombing would prove to be short lived, if only to stop him from having to listen to the terrified cries of his men, who were even more anxious than he was.

"In the name of God, when will it stop?" Private Douet was wailing from a dark corner by the main observation port.

Nobody replied; each man was too lost in his own fear to comment.

As the tremors and vibrations subsided, there followed a few moments of relative quiet, the only sound from outside being the dying echoes of the last explosion and the distant drone of departing aircraft. Blanche lay motionless on the floor, hardly daring to move in case it somehow prompted another whistle of descending bombs. Around the dim interior of the blockhouse, men were whimpering and breathing heavily, as if they had just run a tremendous race and collapsed with exhaustion.

After a few moments, Blanche forced himself to raise his head. The room was full of dust and smoke, and he gave a short bark of a cough as he gaped around his bunker to reassure himself it was still in one piece.

"Holy Mary, Mother of God…" Someone was praying out loud.

It sounded muffled to Blanche however, as if the person uttering the words were doing so from a distance. The lieutenant's ears were ringing with a constant high pitched whine and he realised that the bombs had affected his hearing somewhat. He climbed shakily to his feet and staggered over to the observation port.

"Don't worry, Douet…" He mumbled to the shaking private on the floor. "It's over now. Come on, stand up…get your head to the window and breath in some fresh air."

The private glanced up at the officer with a look that suggested he was not convinced by the wisdom of that instruction. Blanche ignored him and stared out of the gap in front of him. Outside in the morning sunshine, thin grey smoke drifted across the water meadows, partially obscuring the river valley. He stared through the smoke for a while as it began to thin and noticed with relief that the tiny black dots, high up in the blue sky, were moving steadily away from them.

"They've gone." He called back over his shoulder. "I can see them flying eastwards."

He heard the sounds of his men stirring from their hiding places at last.

As his men began to come out of their initial shock, Blanche lifted his binoculars and began to scan the ground beyond the river. There wasn't much to see at first; just the usual, delightful view of the Meuse and its surrounding countryside, and it seemed quite unreal that on this wonderful evening he and his men should have been subjected to such a terrifying attack. As he scanned the ground, he sensed, rather than saw, Private Douet appear next to him.

"All seems quiet now…" Blanche commented, trying to sound casual. It was his job to set an example after all; to calm his men down.

"What's that?" Douet asked in a worried voice.

"I said it all…"

"No." Douet cut Blanche off mid-sentence. "What's *that* over there?"

Blanche took his eyes away from the binoculars and followed the direction of Douet's outstretched arm. The young private was pointing way off to the right, almost beyond their bunker's right of arc; down to where the Meuse twisted southwards towards the city of Sedan. At first, Blanche could see nothing more than the usual vista to which he was accustomed, but then something flashed bright in the morning sun; a reflection on glass or metal. Something was moving. He raised his binoculars and aligned them onto the area he was now focussing on. It took a while for him to settle the image, and for a while, he stared at the patchwork of grassy water meadow, woodland, and river valley. Then he caught his breath. Vehicles; of the German variety…

Across the river, some four hundred metres away, there were several armoured cars nosing their way from one stand of trees to the next. Even more worrying, Blanche could see trucks further back, partially obscured. And there were men, carrying large box like objects towards a factory on the opposite bank.

"My God!" Gasped Blanche. "They're getting ready to cross!"

"What?" Demanded Douet in a voice full of apprehension. "Coming over here?"

Blanche didn't reply. He was already moving across the bunker towards the field telephone. He reached the phone, picked up the handset then wound the call handle furiously. As he placed the telephone to his ear, Blanche threw a look around his bunker.

"On your feet; everybody! Man your positions! The Boche are on their way!"

From around the bunker came the sound of scrabbling feet and the rattle of weapons being loaded.

"Hello? Dallier speaking?"

The sound of Captain Dallier's voice came to Blanche through the receiver.

"Captain, this is Blanche…"

"Blanche? Are you alright? Those bombs were pretty close, eh?"

"Yes…fine." Blanche answered, remembering that Dallier was only a few hundred metres behind him in the village of Glaire. "But Captain…the Germans…they are making ready to cross the river, over by Gaulier."

Silence.

"Captain?"

"Yes…yes, I heard you, Blanche. But you are mistaken. The Germans cannot be getting ready to cross the river yet; they have only just reached Sedan. It will take them time to organise a crossing of the river…"

"No, Captain…" Blanche interrupted him, "I have seen them. There are Germans approaching the edge of the river. They have armoured cars; and there are men on foot too, a couple of dozen of them…"

"Blanche, Blanche, Blanche…" Dallier interjected. "Calm down, my young friend. Of course you can see Germans; they will be conducting reconnaissance before they attempt a crossing. It is likely to go on for several days whilst their columns get through the Ardennes. Our reserve divisions are on their way as we speak. They will be here long before the Germans are anywhere near ready to attack. Trust me, Blanche."

Blanche didn't respond.

"Blanche? Are you there?"

"Yes, Captain." The young lieutenant found his voice. "I'm here. I…I was just wondering; should we shell the opposite bank? Can we call on our artillery to bombard them? I can send you the coordinates…"

Again there was a pause in the conversation until Dallier finally responded.

"Not really, Blanche I'm afraid. The artillery ammunition is rationed. They've got to save it for the main German attack when it comes."

"So what should we do?" Blanche asked in exasperation.

"Well…if they come in range, you may shoot them if you have a clear field of fire. But don't waste too much ammunition on reconnaissance troops; you'll need every round in a day or two. Just keep your eyes on them and let me know if there are any developments…"

Blanche murmured a reply.

"Yes, Captain. We'll watch out for any developments."

He clicked the handset back down. For a moment, the lieutenant just stared at the telephone in stunned silence.

"What did the Captain say then, Lieutenant?"

Corporal Chassespot was standing close by, eyeing his officer warily.

Blanche looked up in surprise.

"He said to keep an eye on the Germans. If they come too close, we are to shoot them. No need to panic though; apparently the main German forces are still moving through the forests to the east. Our own reserves are on the way, however. They'll be here long before the Germans arrive in force. So, get the men to their defence positions. Let's see exactly what those Boche are up to shall we?"

"The planes are coming back!"

The shout of alarm from Douet made Blanche jump.

"What?" The lieutenant demanded as he strode back over to the firing port.

"There look!" Douet was pointing, northwards now, over to the left and almost straight up.

Blanche cocked his head and stared upwards. Sure enough, high above, another swarm of black dots was approaching steadily. This time however, it looked as though they might pass by them, for they were angling off to the north slightly.

"I think they're going past us…" Blanche commented hopefully.

After a while, the black dots went out of sight, flying straight past them, and the French soldiers let out a collective sigh. Blanche was about to speak when a soldier from the rear of the bunker shouted a warning.

"They're turning back this way!"

Blanche exchanged dark looks with Douet and Chassepot.

"They're circling!" The soldier at the rear observation slot shouted another update.

They could hear them now, somewhere high above, droning menacingly as they seemed to hover over the bunker, like a swarm of flies.

"What are they doing?" Chassepot wondered.

"I don't know." Blanche murmured, staring up at the concrete roof of the building as if expecting to see something appear through it at any moment.

"Maybe they're lost? Looking for another target perhaps?"

Then the sound of the aircraft changed suddenly. A horrid, gut-wrenching, whine came plainly though the morning air, along with the sound of protesting engines.

"Holy Mary! What in the name of God is that?" Douet suddenly began jumping around the bunker, as if unsure of where he should take cover.

For a moment, nobody replied. Everyone was rooted to the spot in fear, staring up at the roof of the bunker, their mouths agape. Eventually, as the terrible noise filled the blockhouse, it was the young lieutenant who realised what the awful new noise heralded. Suddenly, he hurled himself into a corner of the bunker, screaming out the warning as he went.

"Dive-bombers!"

GERMAN 19TH CORPS OBSERVATION POST – SEDAN ON THE MEUSE
MONDAY 13TH MAY 1940 – 1615 HOURS

"I don't believe it…"

Guderian kept his binoculars firmly glued to his eyes as he watched the next squadron of Luftwaffe aircraft commence their bombing run on the enemy held bank of the Meuse.

"Would you believe it? After all that angst yesterday and the running around to change all the orders…"

The commander of the 19th Panzer Corps finally lowered his field glasses and shook his head in mild amusement. He glanced at his aide-de-camp with a wry grin.

"They're sticking to the original plan… Our plan."

The young captain from Guderian's staff glanced back up at the sky and, without doubt, the pattern of the Luftwaffe bombing was exactly as requested by Guderian, and not as directed by the Group and Army HQ.

"Perhaps Group HQ finally saw sense, General?" The young officer suggested.

Guderian grunted, good-naturedly.

"Either that or their battle procedure wasn't as slick as ours, eh? Maybe their new plan never even got to the Luftwaffe in time?"

The two men continued to stare skywards where the first two squadrons of Heinkel 111 medium bombers had now been replaced by a steady stream of Ju 87 Stuka dive-bombers. Instead of the huge, intensive, but worryingly short bombing raid that had been directed by his superiors, the Luftwaffe were conforming to the original plan that Guderian had personally agreed upon with the commander of the Luftwaffe group supporting this section of the front. Instead of one overwhelming 'firework display', as Guderian liked to call it, he had insisted that the Luftwaffe attacks came in a long, steady, continuous stream; partly to make up for any deficit in artillery support caused by traffic jams in the Ardennes, but partly to wear down the defenders' will to fight. Guderian wanted them cowering in their bunkers for hours, rather than minutes. And while the enemy was taking cover, his men would be carrying out the highly vulnerable first moves of the crossing operation.

Now, as the panzer general and his small tactical staff watched, the Luftwaffe was giving an outstanding display of fully integrated tactical air support. High up in the relatively cloudless sky, small swarms of fighters circled protectively in wide sweeps, whilst lower down, in several menacing flocks, the Stukas hovered like carrion crows, waiting to dive down and take their pound of flesh. The squat, ugly looking dive-bombers droned endlessly over the western bank of the Meuse, flying in a large, neat circle, whilst one at a time, they took their turn to hurtle earthwards, their sirens shrieking, before pulling up sharply having released their deadly cargo of bombs. Every now and then, one of the aircraft, having already released its payload, would conduct a dummy dive, allowing its sirens to terrify the shocked defenders below in their concrete blockhouses, before pulling away and leaving those frightened enemy soldiers waiting for the inevitable explosions, which subsequently failed to come. The effect on the enemy's nerve must be awful; exactly what Guderian wanted.

For long minutes, the general and his tactical staff watched the awesome spectacle with deep, professional satisfaction until, eventually, the lead aircraft of the nearest squadron of Stukas peeled off from the main group and headed away to the north-east; followed promptly by the remainder. Guderian glanced off to the north and east and saw that the next wave of aircraft was still many miles off; just dark little specs in the vast blue sky. The general suddenly became animated again and turned to the major of artillery who was commanding this forward observation post.

"Now's your time Major Werner. You've got a good five minutes before the next wave is over the target. Get the guns in action again. Don't give those buggers on the far bank a moment of peace. Keep your guns firing until the last safe moment."

The major responded with nothing more than a business-like nod and immediately began rapping out fire-direction orders to his own staff.

Guderian, knowing that the young major understood his general's intent perfectly, turned back to his own small staff.

"Back to the vehicle's everyone; mount up. Let's get over to 1st Panzer and see the assault going in. I want to make sure we get this absolutely right."

BLOCKHOUSE 75 – SEDAN ON THE RIVER MEUSE
MONDAY 13TH MAY 1940 – 1640 HOURS

If the first bombing raid had been bad, the second wave of bombing had been almost unbearable. The combined sound of screaming sirens, explosions and sobbing men had almost driven Blanche mad. Only his officer's pride was holding him together and if he was honest with himself, he wasn't sure how long that pride would hold up. Especially now the artillery bombardment had begun.

Within two minutes of the enemy planes departing, the first shells had come whooshing through the afternoon air, slamming into the water meadows around their bunker, filling the temporary silence left by the dive-bombers as they droned off to the north-east, their work complete. Although the bombardment was not particularly pleasant, it seemed to Blanche, in a crazy kind of way, somewhat more bearable than the heaving of the ground underneath them caused by the aerial bombing. And so, despite the feelings of nausea, shock and fear that currently threatened to overwhelm his senses, the lieutenant propped himself against the parapet of the bunker's window and forced himself to peer out of the aperture across the smoke shrouded panorama of the Meuse.

Whoosh-crump.

Blanche cringed slightly as the latest shell slammed into the ground some thirty metres away from his bunker, just off to his extreme left. Bits of earth and shrapnel flew across his field of vision, followed a few moments later by skeins of black pungent smoke. He grimaced at the acrid smell of explosive which now pervaded every lungful of air he inhaled. Trying to stay calm, he peered across the river to where he'd seen the German troops moving earlier. As he tried to focus on the far bank, Blanche became aware of the sound of small arms fire; quite a lot of it in fact, and not too far away.

The smoke of the last explosion was clearing now and Blanche squinted with concentration as he tried to observe movement on the far bank, amongst the trees and bushes.

"My God…"

He held his breath for a moment and blinked. A moment later, he fumbled for his binoculars and dragged them to his eyes. Quickly adjusting the focus and steadying the glasses, he cursed again.

"Oh, sweet Mary, Mother of God!"

The German troops were still there. More than that, there were more of them than before; lots more of them. And they had boats. There were boats in the water, crammed with men, paddling furiously until they were hidden by the curve in the river. There were men on the far bank; dozens of small groups carrying yet more boats. Behind them, vehicle mounted machine-guns spat tracer across the river, arcing over the heads of the assaulting German infantry.

"Stand to!" Blanche yelled. "Stand to! The Boche are on the river! Dozens of them; over to the south!"

He began waving his arms frantically.

"Chassepot, get the men up! Get them up on the south apertures. Start firing at the enemy on the river. It's long range but put down as much fire as you can…"

The other men in the bunker, Chassepot included, were looking a little stunned, hardly able to believe how much their world could have been turned upside down in less than an hour.

Their tardiness infuriated Blanche and he flew into a rage.

"Come on! Get moving, damn you! What are you waiting for? An order from the President himself? Get up to the parapets and start bloody firing!"

The sudden explosion of anger did the trick and Chassepot started pushing the stunned soldiers towards their positions.

"That side!" Blanche gestured towards the firing ports on the southern side of the blockhouse. "They're crossing further along the river…over there."

The lieutenant grabbed hold of Chassepot and gave him a fierce look.

"I'm ringing the Captain. Get the men into action. Maximum fire on the bend in the river and the far bank. Do it now."

He released the corporal and grabbed for the telephone again, turning the call handle like there was no tomorrow.

There was no answer first time, so Blanche wound the handle again, several times over.

Eventually, the phone clicked and Dallier's voice sounded in the ear piece.

"Hello; Dallier."

"Captain," Blanche shouted down the phone, "they're crossing! The Germans really are crossing! They've got boats in the water to our south; opposite the stretch where there are no bunkers!"

"Wha…are you sure?" Dallier sounded vacant, as if his mind was elsewhere.

"Yes I am sure!" Blanche snapped, too forcefully perhaps for a conversation with a superior officer. "I can see them. There are boats on the river full of Boche, and more Boche soldiers on the opposite bank carrying more boats! We need artillery fire bringing down on targets X170 and X171 immediately!"

There was a pause at the other end.

"Captain?"

"Yes… I heard you…Erm… I will speak to battalion headquarters and try to arrange it… Blanche?"

"Yes"

"You must fire on them with everything you have. Do not let them cross."

Blanche gasped with exasperation. His men were at their posts now, and firing at the rapid rate under Chassepot's direction. Blanche held out the receiver so the sound of small arms fire could be heard by Dallier.

"We are engaging them, Captain." He confirmed after a moment or two. "But they are crossing to our south, on the very edge of our arc of fire. We won't be able to stop them on our own…"

Another shell landed close by, causing the bunker to tremble and filling the strongpoint with foul smelling fumes once more.

"Have the reserves got forward into the trenches along the Gaulier Gap yet?" Blanche demanded when the noise of the explosion had faded.

Again, there was a lengthy delay at the other end.

"Erm… I'm not sure. I will check for you…No, in fact, Blanche…you send someone to check. Get a runner to go take a look to your south and report back to me as soon as possible. And stand by to counter-attack if required."

"Counter-attack?" Blanche asked incredulously as another shell landed not far away.

The line went dead.

"Captain?"

No reply.

"Captain, can you hear me?"

Nothing.

Blanche slammed the phone down angrily and ran up the steps to where Chassepot was shouting orders at the men. As he walked along the firing step, Blanche's feet crunched on the empty cartridge cases that had been ejected from rifles and their one light machine-gun.

"How's it looking?" The lieutenant shouted to the corporal above the racket.

"Bad." The dark eyed corporal responded with a grim look. "They just keep coming. We've only got them in our sights for a few moments, then they're hidden by the bend in the river.

Blanche digested the information wordlessly.

"What did the Captain say?" Chassepot asked hopefully.

Blanche gathered his thoughts for a moment before replying.

"He's organising a bombardment by our own artillery…" He was stretching the truth very thin, he knew. "But we need to know what the situation is further along the bank. He wants us to send a runner to see if the troops covering the gap in the line are holding the enemy or if they need reinforcements. We need to let him know as soon as possible. I need someone reliable…"

The corporal raised a surprised eyebrow at his officer's words and glanced around at the collection of private soldiers who were fully focussed engaging the distant enemy.

"What? From amongst this lot? You've got to be kidding? We're lucky they haven't buggered off home already!"

The grumpy looking NCO fixed his officer with the look of a condemned man and gave a sigh of resignation.

"I'll go." He said.

ABOARD AN ASSAULT BOAT – SEDAN ON THE MEUSE MONDAY 13TH MAY 1940 – 1730 HOURS

The water was covered with boats going in both directions; fully laden going to the western bank, empty as they were tugged back over on a pulley system to the home bank. On the western side, Guderian could see German troops milling around, their officers and NCOs gesturing wildly. The sound of their shouted orders and shrieking whistles filled the evening air between the sporadic shellfire that dropped, from time to time, in a haphazard manner on both banks of the Meuse.

It had been a busy hour for Guderian. Having left the artillery observation post, he had motored with his tactical headquarters to the jump-off points for both the Gross Deutschland Regiment and then the 1st Rifle Regiment of 1st Panzer Division. Everywhere he had been, his soldiers were fully engaged with the crossing operation, pausing only briefly to greet their corps commander with brief salutes and broad, confident grins. It made him proud to see them in action. He had trained these men intensely over recent months, giving them little rest and always driving them on to do better. Now they were being rewarded by success in battle. And they knew they were winning. They were up for it, these men. Whatever the enemy threw at them, they would rise to the challenge and overcome it, regardless of the odds.

There had been casualties of course; that was inevitable. Even with heavy covering fire from artillery and the Luftwaffe, the assault units were always going to be vulnerable as they crossed the open water meadows on the edge of the Meuse. Thankfully however, the French artillery, though accurate, was not concentrating its fire enough to prevent his men getting through the bombardment. Therefore, despite the shredded boats behind him on the home bank, and the groups of dead and wounded panzer grenadiers being tended by medics, the scene that had met Guderian on arrival at the crossing point was one of calm urgency as his men went about their business; coolly, efficiently.

A stream of bullets cracked high overhead from the north and splashed down into the water far over to the left of Guderian's boat and the general peered up the river to try and spot the source of the enemy fire. One of the soldiers paddling the boat saw the general creasing his brow as he searched the distant countryside and chimed in with an explanation.

"Bunker, General; quite a big one. It's up on the bend of the river where it loops to the west. We're bang on its extreme right of arc by the look of it. Thankfully it doesn't have a very clear field of fire, but it's been keeping up a harassing fire on us for the last hour. We'll be alright once we're halfway across. Besides, the boys are spreading out fast from the bridgehead. We'll be giving those French bastards and wake up call any minute now I reckon."

Guderian smiled at the young soldier's brash confidence and turned back to gaze at the enemy bank, which was coming closer with every stroke.

Guderian could make more sense of the mass of soldiery now. A line of soldiers, a full platoon by the look of it, were kneeling down against a row of buildings while a young lieutenant barked out quick battle orders to them. As he watched, Guderian saw the lieutenant wave his hand and turn towards the distant high ground where the French depth positions must be. The officer trotted off like a young deer scampering through a forest and he was followed immediately by his entire platoon in a long single file; their weapons, equipment and ammunition boxes rattling noisily as they doubled after their commander. They looked good; professional, business-like, unbeatable.

He glanced at another group of soldiers by the river bank; a smaller group of men, huddled around a map and gesturing expansively in various directions, mainly back across to the eastern bank. That would be the reconnaissance group from his engineers, preparing their plans for getting a bridge across the river. That was also good. Lots of concurrent activity; just what was needed. He watched with careless interest as a pair of rubber boats, tied together and hooked up to a pulley were hauled past his own boat on their return journey to the eastern bank.

"Ready ashore!"

The call of the young oarsman brought Guderian's attention back to the western bank. They were almost there now.

"Ship oars!" Called the soldier again as the boat glided the last couple of metres to nose against the grassy bank.

A rope was thrown to an engineer waiting on the river bank and within moments the boat was being pulled in sideways against the firm earth. Guderian stood and carefully raised a foot, placing it onto a patch of muddy bank where the grass and reeds had been trampled flat by dozens of boots already. Another engineer came forward and held out his hand to the general.

Guderian grasped the proffered forearm and allowed himself to be pulled up onto the bank.

Finding himself with a better view, Guderian cast his eyes about the surrounding meadow. Barely ten metres away, tucked in against a small clump of bushes, several medics worked with practiced speed on a number of wounded soldiers, all of whom seemed to be bearing their injuries with great fortitude. Off to one side of the group, a line of around half a dozen jack-booted bodies covered with ground-sheets demonstrated that other members of the 1st Rifle Regiment had not been quite so lucky.

Guderian continued to study the various groups of soldiers going about their business and quickly spotted the man he had come to see. Lieutenant Colonel Hermann Balck, commander of the 1st Rifle Regiment, was standing amongst a collection of captains and majors, issuing a string of very firm, and very urgent instructions. Guderian wasn't close enough to hear the detail of what was being said, but moments later the colonel's audience gave a loud, collective bark of understanding and then broke off in various directions at the double.

As the officers dispersed, Balck turned towards the river and spotted his commanding general instantly. To Guderian's surprise, instead of snapping to attention and saluting, Balck roared at him with bold good humour.

"Hey; haven't you heard? Joy riding in canoes on the Meuse is forbidden!"

With a bark of a laugh, Balck strode across to the general and threw up a belated yet impressive salute. Guderian's face creased with a broad grin and he laughed back at the colonel, recognising instantly his own phrase which he had used over and over again during training in order to keep people focussed on the reality of forcing the crossing of a heavily defended river line.

"Your reprimand is accepted with good grace, Colonel!" Guderian greeted the regimental commander, returning the salute and then thrusting out his arm.

The two men shook hands firmly, and laughed together.

"Well done, Hermann! Very well done indeed!" Guderian patted the colonel's arm.

"Thank you, General. But to be honest we couldn't fail; not with such a good plan and such superb training. It was just like an exercise, only an exercise with real casualties!"

Guderian nodded, gazing about him.

"Indeed, it all seems to be ticking along nicely."

"So far, so good…" Balck confirmed, taking Guderian's elbow and gently guiding him along the river bank. "If you don't mind, General, we'll wander in this direction a little. There's a French bunker just across the fields there. If we go too far then we'll walk into their field of fire."

Guderian was still nodding.

"Yes, they put a couple of bursts our way as we crossed."

"They won't be causing trouble for much longer. I've just tasked the Second Battalion to sweep around the curve of the river to our north and clear all those bunkers out."

Guderian came to a halt as he saw a line of about a dozen French prisoners being marched down to the river bank by two panzer grenadiers. The Frenchmen, some of them still wearing greatcoats, looked thoroughly dejected and scared out of their wits.

"How was it along this stretch? Much resistance?"

"Not that bad actually." Balck replied. "Looks like we were right about the gap in their bunker line. There's a couple of trench systems further in, about a hundred metres or so, but they weren't heavily manned so we made short work of them."

Guderian turned to look the colonel in the eyes.

"Well done, Hermann. I mean that. Tell your men how proud I am of what they have achieved. But tell them to keep it up. We need to expand this bridgehead quickly. Push hard, Hermann. Don't give the French a chance to regroup. Just keep pushing and pushing. The harder you push, the more I will send across to back you up."

Balck nodded curtly in response to his general's instructions.

"I will, General. As long as we've got breath in our bodies, we'll keep on pushing."

"Good man." Guderian smiled. "And don't stop for the night. Keep going in the dark. By morning I want us to be right through the main French lines of defence. And then…" He paused and took a deep breath. "And then we're going to drive right up the enemy's backside and give him the shock of his life!"

BLOCKHOUSE 75 – SEDAN ON THE RIVER MEUSE
MONDAY 13TH MAY 1940 – 1735 HOURS

"Keep your eyes peeled!" Blanche shouted; though it felt more like a croak to him, such was the dryness of his throat resulting from the endless dust and smoke.

The bombing had been replaced by shell-fire, and then added to with trench-mortar fire. Whatever the means of projection, the shells were all having the same effect. The blockhouse was essentially isolated. Explosions landed close by and, occasionally, directly on top of the bunker, sending shards of white hot metal shrapnel and clods of earth flying through the gun ports of their concrete fortress. They had become almost comfortable with the constant trembling of the ground beneath their feet, but the smoke and dust was becoming their real enemy. The defenders were literally choking on the stuff; coughing and spluttering as they tried to communicate with each other. More worryingly, they were virtually blind.

"Every time the smoke clears a little, put a couple of bursts in the general direction of the river to the south." Blanche ordered. "You can guarantee that the Boche are still out there somewhere."

He scanned the interior of the bunker and tried to judge the state of his men's resilience. They were not the best the army had to offer in the first place, and lacked proper field training. Their nerves had been shredded by the bombing and shelling, and now they were suffering from the dislocation of not being able to see what was going on around them. Despite that, they were coping with it so far. Just getting them to fire through the dust and smoke in the rough direction of the enemy was helping to steady them; giving them something proactive to do. Blanche couldn't help wondering, however, how long that would last. He knew more than they did; had a better idea of the bigger picture, but even he was starting to feel isolated and vulnerable up here by the loop in the river.

"Someone's coming!"

The shout from a soldier by the rear gun port made Blanche whirl round in alarm.

"Is it a Boche?" Wondered the soldier's neighbour.

"No! Wait...Don't shoot..." The first soldier reached out a restraining arm to his comrade.

Blanche took several hesitant steps towards the two men at the rear of the bunker and was about to ask what was going on, when the first soldier looked over his shoulder, straight towards his officer.

"It's Corporal Chassepot! He's back!"

"Thank God!" Blanche murmured.

He had been thinking that he would never see the corporal alive again. Surely nobody could survive in the open with such a huge bombardment taking place? With a sense of relief, Blanche made for the bunker's doorway. Before he got there, he heard the sound of stumbling feet and a moment later, Corporal Chassepot burst into the blockhouse from behind the blast wall that covered the exit.

The middle-aged NCO stumbled as he entered the dim confines of the bunker and bounced off the rear wall, coming to a halt by one of the concrete ammunition shelves. He grabbed hold of the shelf to steady himself and stared around with wide, excited eyes.

"Chassepot!" Blanche stepped in close and grabbed the corporal by the sleeve of his greatcoat. "Thank God you have returned!"

The corporal was breathing heavily; sucking in air like a drowning man. He stared back at Blanche for a moment, trying to focus on the officer's face in the gloom of the subterranean fortress.

"Lieutenant? You're still here?" The corporal finally managed to gasp.

Blanche did his best to smile.

"Of course we are. We weren't going anywhere without you. Now, tell me; what did you find out. What's happening over there to the south?"

Chassepot took a huge gulp of air and tried to steady his breathing. He slipped a hand under his chinstrap, yanked off his helmet and ran a shaking hand through his dark hair, which was starting to grey at the temples.

"There are Boche everywhere, Lieutenant." He finally managed to say. "Everywhere... as far as I could see to the south. All along the river bank; boat loads of the bastards, moving quickly once they get across this side. They're spreading out fast."

Blanche felt a rising sense of dread.

"What about our men in the trench lines? Are they holding them?"

Chassepot was shaking his head even before the lieutenant had finished talking.

"There are none of *our* men in the trench lines. If they *were* there, then they are dead or prisoners."

"What?" Blanche gasped in horror.

"The Boche are in the trench lines. They're forming up for an advance. I watched them."

Chassepot began to elaborate, but then gave way to a coughing fit.

He quickly dragged his canteen of water from his belt and placed it to his lips, taking a long swig. Having gulped down several large mouthfuls, the corporal pulled the canteen away from his mouth and looked back at his officer, droplets of water falling from his chin.

"I went back to the third line; to where the reserve infantry were supposed to be posted. The trenches were empty. There is no reserve. Not anywhere near here leastways."

The young lieutenant stepped back a pace, shocked by Chassepot's revelation.

"No reserves? Then who..."

The NCO cut him short.

"So I went back to company headquarters in the village; to warn the Captain."

Blanche was blinking repeatedly, trying to register the facts and put them in some kind of order in his brain.

"Well done, Chassepot." He gabbled. "That was good thinking. What did the Captain say? Is he calling the reserves forward? I've been trying to get through to him about getting the artillery…"

Again, Chassepot cut him short.

"You won't get through to the Captain on *that* telephone, Lieutenant." He said, shaking his head; a dark look settling on his features. "Because he's not there. He's gone. The whole headquarters has gone."

Blanche just stared at the corporal for long moments, his features draining of blood until his face was as pale as a ghost.

"Gone?" He asked incredulously. "Gone? How…where…"

He was lost for words. Not that it mattered, for just at that point there was a sudden eruption of gunfire from within the bunker.

The lieutenant whirled about once more to see that the soldiers manning the firing ports on the southern corner of the blockhouse were letting rip with their weapons at a rapid rate at some unseen target.

"Over there, look! A whole load of 'em! By the tree…"

Blanche heard one of the men shouting an indication to the others. Even as the words came to Blanche's ears, another group of his men manning the forward firing ports also went into sudden action, the light-machine gun rattling away noisily.

"Enemy!" Blanche heard Private Douet shout the fateful word. "Enemy! Right by the bank in front of us!"

Then, a moment later, Douet's urgent shout became more of a scream.

"Holy Mother, there's hundreds of them!"

The young man looked away from the firing port towards Blanche.

"The Boche are here, Lieutenant! They're here! They're all around us!"

Blanche simply stood there, gaping back at the young soldier. Chassepot stepped in close beside Blanche and gave him a look of utter resignation.

"Everyone else has gone, Lieutenant. We're the only ones left. And now the Germans are coming for us…"

BY THE CABLE FERRY – BOUVIGNES ON THE MEUSE
MONDAY 13TH MAY 1940 – 1750 HOURS

"This is taking too long; far too long."

Rommel uttered the phrase, not as a frustrated curse, but rather as a simple statement of fact; made in his typically clipped, decisive tone. He turned to his two staff officers.

"This is only the seventh tank to cross; correct?"

Vosse nodded his acknowledgement to the divisional commander.

"Yes, General; along with four armoured cars from the reconnaissance battalion."

Rommel accepted the information with a grunt.

"We need more armour over the river, and fast. The enemy can't remain half asleep forever. We need to break out quickly…"

The general was cut short by a sudden whoosh, followed by an explosion, which caught even him off guard. Despite that, his reaction was characteristically understated; a mere shrug of the soldiers, as if it were nothing more than the sound of a waiter dropping a plate in a restaurant. The sudden bout of panic-stricken voices that followed immediately after the explosion, elicited a more animated reaction however.

Together with Captain Vosse and Lieutenant Most, Rommel whirled around at the sudden commotion and watched with surprise, and a certain amount of horrified fascination, as one of the ferry platforms in the middle of the river, already wreathed in black smoke from the shell strike, began to capsize, aided by the weight of the Panzer Mark 2 that it was carrying. It was a lucky shot for the enemy, firing indirectly at an unseen target. Indeed, the enemy's shells had been dropping into the river and along the banks all afternoon, without achieving very much. This time however, just one shell had wrought havoc.

The ferry platform was now almost vertical as the weight of the sliding tank pushed one end further into the water. The men on the raft who had not been killed or injured in the explosion were all in the water, thrown overboard by the blast and the sudden heave of the raft. Then, with an awful metallic squeal, the tank slid down the upended raft, breaking its steel chain and chocks in the process, and plunged into the river amid a bubbling spout of water. In just a few heartbeats, the tank was gone, leaving nothing but frothing water and an empty raft on the surface of the Meuse.

The group of officers watched in silence as large ripples of water came rushing outwards from the scene of the minor disaster to wash up against the river bank with a slopping noise and causing the other ferry platforms on the river to rise and fall in a manner that alarmed their crews. Around them on the bank, engineer officers and NCOs were shouting at each other frantically, trying to minimise the chaos. Rommel, watching the unfolding drama with a stern frown, turned suddenly and slapped his hand against the hull of his own six-wheeled armoured command vehicle.

"I want this over next. Most; get it organised. The very next ferry takes my vehicle, my Tac' HQ and me."

Most was on his way instantly to make the arrangements. As he doubled off, Rommel heaved a deep breath through his nose, the resulting sound akin to a snort of disgust. He flicked his gaze at Vosse.

"Get me the commander of the engineers." He said quietly.

Vosse snapped up a salute and was off, loping down the bank to find the major in charge of the bridging unit.

He was fast. Within just a couple of minutes, the major of engineers was standing in front of Rommel, red faced from exertion and looking a trifle flustered. Rommel, as ever, wasted no time on pre-amble.

"That was unfortunate, Major; unlucky. My vehicle will go over next. But…" He paused, watching as another shell plummeted out of the sky and plunged into the water, more than a hundred metres from the nearest raft. "This is taking too long. We need to get our tanks over the river faster."

The general paused again and the engineer major looked as though he were about to defend his men's efforts, but Rommel went on, not giving him the opportunity.

"I know that we are still under fire and that conditions are not ideal, however, it is time to get a bridge across the river. It's the only way."

Silence. The major simply stared at Rommel, blinking in surprise. Rommel went on again.

"I want the bridge thrown over the river by 0400 hours tomorrow. I want a company of tanks minimum over this river by dawn."

Rommel fixed the major with a look that indicated he had finished speaking and that the engineer should confirm that he fully understood his orders.

" But, General…" The major began hesitantly. "We can't possibly build a bridge here, now."

Rommel's brow instantly furrowed in a deep frown.

"Why?"

The major glanced briefly towards Captain Vosse, waiting discreetly to one side.

"Because… all the bridging tackle has been used already, General. The ferries have taken up all of our resources, and much of the equipment has been damaged during the operation. There is no way we could put a full bridge together with what is still serviceable; not over such a wide stretch of water. And even if we could, General, we would have to suspend the ferrying operation immediately to recover the equipment and get the bridge built. It would all take time and even if we worked at record speed, the bridge would not be complete before mid-morning tomorrow at the earliest. And between now and then, nothing would cross the river other than infantry boats."

Rommel's eye-brows had risen markedly during the major's explanation, and at this point, he inwardly cursed himself. He had not been commanding panzer troops for very long, and thus he was still getting used to the sheer logistics that went with moving such powerful, but heavy forces. As an infantry soldier, he was used to travelling light and moving fast. His mind worked feverishly, wrestling with the information and formulating a solution. After just a few moments of contemplation, he spoke.

"There is plenty of bridging tackle left, major. I have seen it."

This time it was the major who raised his eyebrows.

"I'm sorry, General. I don't mean to contradict you, but I can assure you, every last piece of bridging equipment that this division carries is already in use. We have nothing left over..." He tailed off, worried his commander might fly into a rage.

Instead, Rommel flung a questioning look at Vosse.

"Vosse? Am I going senile before my time, or did we pass a convoy of bridging equipment not less than an hour ago, and just a couple of kilometres back up the road?"

Vosse thought for a moment, his brow creasing as he struggled to remember.

Suddenly, his face brightened. Then, just as quickly, it dropped again.

"You are partly correct, Sir. We did indeed pass a bridging unit back in the woods, but it does not belong to us. It belongs to 5th Panzer. They have sent their engineer units forward with their advance guard and recce, General, but they are not making a crossing attempt until the bulk of the division has closed on the river."

Rommel suddenly looked as if he had been slapped in the face.

"Then the bridging unit is sitting idle?" He snapped.

"Erm...yes, General. I suppose. But I assume that General von Hartlieb is planning to launch a deliberate..."

Rommel cut him off.

"So, it is idle?" The question this time was rhetorical.

Vosse nodded slowly in acknowledgement at the General's assertion.

Rommel became animated again, as he did when confronted by a challenge and scenting a solution.

"There is no time to waste." He declared. "We must take opportunities as they arise for the good of the whole army. Vosse, go and requisition that bridging unit and bring it here; all of it."

Vosse was stunned.

"Sorry, General…You want me to requisition the 5th Panzer's bridging unit?"

"Immediately." Rommel confirmed.

Vosse continued to stare at his commander in disbelief.

"Will you be arranging it with General von Hartlieb, Sir? Can I tell the commander of the bridging unit that it has been cleared through higher authority?"

Rommel waved his hand dismissively.

"I'll discuss it with von Hartlieb later; he'll understand. Besides, we'll be doing his job for him. He won't have to bother finding a crossing point; he can just follow us over…"

He paused, seeing the hesitancy in Vosse's face.

"Give me your note book, Vosse." Rommel said.

With a jolt, Vosse snapped out of his own private thoughts and hurriedly produced his field notebook and pencil, passing them across to the general.

Rommel snatched the book from him, flicked it open to an empty page and began scribbling furiously. His note was short and peremptory. He finished it and signed the short order with a flourish.

"Here." The general snapped, handing the notebook back to Vosse. "This is a requisition order from me. Give it to the commander of that bridging unit and tell him to follow you back here with every bit of equipment he has. Don't take any nonsense from him, Vosse. The fate of the entire offensive rests on getting this bridge over the river; you understand that?"

This time, there was no hesitancy in Vosse's demeanour. He had the authority he needed and yet again he was astounded, and enthused, by Rommel's decisive and bold method of command.

"Yes, General." He threw up a sharp salute, then turned away and ran off to find a spare vehicle.

Rommel watched him go for a second or two then looked back at the engineer major, who had listened to the entire conversation with a somewhat dumfounded expression on his face. He too was in awe of this dynamic, sharp minded general who didn't allow anything to get in is way.

"You will have an entire bridging unit here within the hour, Major." Rommel informed the engineer in a manner that was almost conversational. "Will that do for you?"

The major's face creased into a childish grin.

"It will indeed, General; thank you. And you shall have your bridge before dawn."

THE HEIGHTS OF WASTIA – ABOVE HOUX ON THE MEUSE
MONDAY 13TH MAY 1940 – 1930 HOURS

"Tanks!"

The sudden shouting woke Gritz with a start.

The sergeant was exhausted. He hadn't slept for two days. Yesterday, he had led his men over the river and fought his way up the slopes during the night, until he had captured these heights that dominated the surrounding countryside and, most importantly, the Meuse valley. But the early elation had turned to disappointment and frustration. Despite sending several messages back to his division, Gritz's little platoon had received no reinforcements from 5th Panzer, other than some more boxes of ammunition brought back by his runners.

They weren't completely on their own of course, for he had been joined in his venture by a platoon of recce troops from 7th Panzer, led by another sergeant, Litteman. Together they mustered around fifty odd men, with no less than ten MG 34 light machine-guns between them. It was in reality though, a tiny force, and they were already over extended. They were up here, on the highest point of the battlefield, yet nobody seemed to care. He had spent much of the morning scaring off the occasional French patrol that had come too close, in between watching the grand spectacle of the 7th Panzer's assault river crossing just a mile or so to the south. But, as the long hot day wore on, and no support came, he found his fatigue catching up with him, to the point where he must have dozed off.

"Tanks! Eight hundred metres to the west!"

Gritz was awake now though, and he quickly absorbed the words that his men were shouting with a certain degree of alarm. Tanks. If they were coming from the west then Gritz seriously doubted that they were German. He felt a cold hand of fear reach into his stomach and clutch it in an icy grip.

"Fuck!"

The sergeant pushed himself upright and doubled forward towards his perimeter posts. He had barely got within ten metres of the edge of the plateau when he heard the engines; deep, powerful sounding engines. He stooped lower as he approached the lip of the hill and veered slightly right towards a group of his men who were positioned in a hastily improvised shell-scrape that they had reinforced with logs and boulders. He dropped in amongst the trio of soldiers and elbowed his way beside the machine-gunner.

"Where are they?" He demanded, fumbling for his binoculars.

"Everywhere…" Came the curt reply. "Look…"

He looked. He didn't need his binoculars. There was no mistaking them. Large, green and brown mottled monsters, spread out in a line below them, trundling steadily up the slope. They were closing at a cautious pace, edging forward through a distant tree-line.

"Bollocks!" Gritz cursed.

He used his binoculars now, scanning from left to right, trying to pick out more detail. He counted eight of the lumbering beasts. No infantry; none that he could see anyway.

"Open up on the centre vehicle." He ordered. "Let's see if we can scare this lot off too; persuade them that we're a bigger force. Aim for the front of their turrets; long bursts."

The gunner obliged without hesitation and pulled his trigger immediately. The light machine-gun burst into life with a deafening chatter.

The sergeant grimaced, but otherwise ignored the noise and pushed himself up. He shouted down at the riflemen as he leapt away towards another of the perimeter posts.

"Keep on engaging! Hold them back for as long as you can!"

With that he lurched off across the ridge line and came to another position with just a couple of riflemen in it.

"Open fire you two! Keep engaging them! If they get too close, lob a couple of grenades!"

He ran on. Fifty metres further along he found three more men in a properly constructed trench; one of those vacated by the enemy during the night. Gritz dropped in amongst them. He instantly recognised Heigel, the commander of First Squad, and Gruber, the young private. He strained to see who the third man was, crouched over the MG 34 and already rattling away at the distant tanks. It was Dolgau; quiet, dour, tough.

"This is all we need, Sergeant!" Heigel greeted his platoon leader, shouting above the noise of the machine-gun.

"What the fuck do we do now?"

Gritz spat a gob of mucus onto the floor of the trench.

"Just keep firing at the fuckers! Try and make them think we're more powerful than we are. If they get brave and come close, we'll have to use grenades."

Heigel grinned at him madly.

"None of our tanks arrived yet then?"

Gritz shook his head.

"Have they fuck-as-like! I've been watching some come over the river on ferries, further south. Think it's the 7th Panzer making a crossing. No word from anyone yet though. I've sent five runners back in total since last night. I just keep getting the same reply. *'Here's some more ammo; hang on; we're coming...'*"

"Sounds like they're palming us off, if you ask me." Heigel observed.

"Sounds like we're getting shafted to be perfectly honest." Gritz commented sourly.

Together, they watched the distant enemy. The line of tanks had come closer now. They were still moving slowly, hesitantly. Whether they were trying to keep their dressing as a line of tanks, or whether they were unsure about where their enemies were, it was hard to tell. Even so, the tanks were now only four to five hundred metres away.

"Looks like they're stopping?" Heigel commented.

"Expended belt!" Dolgau suddenly roared and flung up the top cover of his weapon.

Gruber, the rifleman, instantly slapped a new belt of ammunition onto the machine-gun and held it in place. With practiced ease, Dolgau slammed the top cover back down and gave it a tap to double check it was locked, before hauling back on the cocking handle. Within moments, he had realigned onto his target and the weapon burst into life again. Gruber, his boots crunching on a pile of empty cartridge cases on the floor of the trench, recovered the expended belt and went about the laborious task of refilling it.

Gritz studied the enemy with interest. They had stopped alright. As he squinted towards the enemy, the setting evening sun shining right into his eyes, a loud series of cracks whipped past him, just off to the right.

"Bastards have seen us then!" Heigel cursed. "Thank God they've only got machine-guns."

"They might have something bigger than that." Gritz warned. "Hard to tell from this distance. They're probably saving their big stuff for a more suitable target."

"Oh, well, that's alright then." Heigel joked.

Gritz didn't laugh. He was too busy staring at the nearest enemy tank.

He had been watching the tank closely, trying to gauge what it was doing, what its commander was thinking, when it suddenly emitted a large and distinct cloud of exhaust fumes. A moment later, the tank lurched forward, picking up speed, its engine roaring as it attacked the steep slope of the plateau. Across the frontage of the enemy line, the other tanks followed suit.

"Fuck!" Gritz swore. "They've sussed on! They're coming for us!"

"Oh, shit!" Heigel murmured and brought his rifle up.

He knew it would have no effect on the enemy tanks, but firing it would make him feel better.

"Rapid fire!" Gritz bawled to his left and right.

His men had already made the decision themselves, for the level of outgoing fire was intensifying; streams of tracer whipping downhill to bounce off the metal monsters that were now advancing on them resolutely. The tanks were no more than three hundred metres away now and closing fast. Gritz could hear the constant ping and whine of bullets as they bounced harmlessly off the advancing steel monsters. The enemy seemed to have located the German positions now, for the tanks were forming into pairs, closing up as they bore down on precise points of reference on the crest. Gritz knew his small force was finished.

"Stand by to pull back!" He shouted above the racket. "Heigel; get along the ridge and tell the men to start falling back in short bounds. Not too fast; nice and steady. We need to hold these bastards back as long as we can. If they take the plateau they'll have a proper duck shoot down onto 7th Panzer's crossing point!"

"I'm on it!" Heigel shouted, hauling himself out of the trench and stumbling off to the right at a low crouch.

"Gruber!" Gritz called to the young rifleman. "You and me need to cover Dolgau back! Dolly, get yourself back there about fifty metres and set up the gun again. As soon as you're in position, we'll come back and join you!"

Obediently and wordlessly, Dolgau ceased fire and quickly threw two spare belts of ammunition around his neck. Moments later, he was out of the trench and doubling back across the plateau with his machine-gun.

Gruber was in action with his rifle, working the bolt furiously and loosing off at the nearest tank. Gritz joined him. There were two tanks coming straight for them; both within one hundred and fifty metres now. The movements of Heigel and Dolgau must have been spotted because three bursts of machine-gun fire from the tanks slammed into the ground just a little way in front of the trench, the last sending spurts of soil and grass over the trench and into Gritz's face.

"They've ranged in on us!" Gritz realised. "Get the fuck out! Quickly!"

He and Gruber scrambled out of the trench, one to the left, one to the right, just as a fourth burst of fire straddled the centre of the trench. The young rifleman called out in alarm, more out of fright than through injury.

"Come on! Back!" Gritz yelled and sprinted through the long grass and bushes, then out onto the grassy meadow of the plateau.

As they burst into the open, they spotted Dolgau further back, tucked into a fold in the ground, settling himself behind the machine-gun. Over to their left, other soldiers were running backwards, parallel with them. Gritz was running as fast as his tired legs could carry him now, his breath coming in huge gulps. He could see a figure running towards him from the far side of the plateau, nearest the river. Gritz began waving frantically at the man. He saw the figure slow down and come to a halt. He heard him shout but couldn't make out the words.

"Tanks!" Gritz shouted as loud as he could whilst in mid-sprint. "Enemy fucking tanks!"

The figure must have heard Gritz's warning for he suddenly bolted back the way he had come. The sergeant had no time to worry for just at that point Dolgau fired a long burst from his MG34 and the bullets streaked by Gritz, heading towards an unseen target; the crack of their passing being uncomfortably close for the sergeant's liking. With a moan of relief, Gritz half threw himself and half slid into the small depression in the ground next to Dolgau. Gruber too, dropped in beside him. Even as the sergeant rolled over, he caught sight of the dark silhouette of the enemy tank lurching up over the crest of the plateau, before its weight carried it forward and over the top.

"Fire at the fucker…" He gasped unnecessarily and brought his own rifle up. He brought his eye down to the sight and aimed at the tank. To his alarm, the foresight of his rifle was moving up and down rapidly on the target as a result of his erratic breathing and he forced himself to take a huge gulp of air before holding his breath. For a moment, the sight picture steadied and he squeezed the trigger.

Blam. The bullet whizzed off towards its target and he threw the bolt back. He glanced down and saw that his magazine was empty.

"Magazine!" He called instinctively.

He fumbled with a clip of ammunition in his pouch, freed it, then slid it into the charger guide on his rifle. He pushed the rounds down into the magazine, catching his fingers on the ammunition clip as he did so, drawing blood. Oblivious to the minor cut, he flicked the empty clip away and slammed his rifle bolt shut. When he looked up, he saw that there were now two enemy tanks on the ridgeline and that one of them was raking the plateau with machine gun fire, systematically edging its turret from one side to the other, blazing away with a burst after every movement and correction.

"Dolgau, get back again. Right back to the far side! We'll cover you!"

Once again, the cool, stolid Dolgau was on his feet in an instant and doubling away with his gun and spare belts. Gritz continued to fire. He heard Gruber call out a warning that he too was reloading. Streams of tracer cut in from left and right of Gritz to bounce off the tanks' hulls, evidence that every defender of the plateau had come from their perimeter post to face this new, overwhelming threat to their precarious bridgehead.

"Get ready to move back, Gruber…" The sergeant warned his companion.

Just then however, one of the tanks suddenly revved its engines and Gritz knew what was coming.

"Back!" He yelled desperately, just as the tank lurched forward.

He pushed himself up onto his knees but realised that he was already too late. The tank was on level ground now and it accelerated towards them at a surprising speed. Gritz's heart sank. What now? Just as he contemplated that thought, a movement to his left caught his attention. Young Gruber, the rifleman, was on his feet. He was running forwards towards the tank, and Gritz saw that he was not carrying his rifle. He heard the young man shout something over his shoulder.

"I'll cover you, Sergeant!"

Gritz watched the young man in disbelief.

With both arms pumping, the rifleman sprinted straight at the advancing tank. As he neared the vehicle, Gritz saw Gruber raise one arm and noticed the stick grenade that he held in that same hand. Fifteen metres from the tank, the private hurled the grenade straight at it. The sergeant watched in fascination as the ungainly grenade toppled through the air, hit the front of the turret then bounced sideways off the vehicle.

Crump.

The grenade exploded with a bright flash, followed by a small cloud of dirty grey smoke.

"Gruber!" Gritz shouted out in protest.

It was too late. He watched in horror as the enemy tank, undamaged in the slightest by the blast, ploughed onwards, straight towards Gruber. He was transfixed as he watched the young man face down the tank without a flinch, bravely pulling a second grenade from his belt and priming it, ready to throw. A burst of fire, rounds cracking through the air, Gruber staggering.

"Gruber!" Gritz shouted in despair.

The tank hit the wounded Gruber full on and the brave rifleman crumpled to the ground as the tank drove straight over him, coming straight for Gritz.

Crump!

Gritz ducked as Gruber's second grenade exploded underneath the tank, where its owner's dead body now lay. Again, a dark cloud of smoke billowed out from under the tank, and to Gritz's surprise, the green and brown monster slid to a halt, barely twenty metres in front of him. A deluge of machine-gun bullets, some of them tracer, descended on the enemy vehicle from several directions; the loud, jarring crack of passing bullets filling the air around Gritz. With a jolt, the sergeant came-to from his reverie as a spectator of the horrific confrontation between Gruber and the tank, and he staggered to his feet and began running for his life back across the plateau.

As he ran, the crack of small arms fire filled his mind. It was impossible to hear anything above the cacophony of battle. He could however, see that the eastern crest of the plateau was lined with German troops; the survivors of his ad hoc force, gathering for their last stand against the unstoppable tanks. He ran, and he ran. As he neared the far side of the plateau he could see down into the Meuse valley once more. His heart sank as he realised that his desperate gamble was about to end in abject failure, and almost certainly death, despite everything he'd done. Where were those bloody reinforcements? He cursed every officer whose name he could remember. If 7th Panzer were crossing the Meuse, then why wasn't his own division? And why hadn't the 7th come to his rescue anyway? These heights were as valuable to the 7th as they were to his own division.

As he slid over the edge of the crest, collapsing in exhaustion amongst the ranks of his men, his eyes briefly registered the sight of tanks on ferries, southwards along the river. Soon they would be receiving direct fire from these French tanks and the 7th Panzer Division's crossing would descend into bloody chaos. The end was almost upon them. Gritz flopped onto his side against the slope of the hill and drew in huge lung-fulls of air accompanied by a strange, desperate sobbing noise that he somehow couldn't prevent himself from making. There was a face in front of him; vaguely familiar. Litteman; the sergeant from the 7th.

"Gritzy, we've made up some grenade clusters; I'm going to get in among those tanks and take the bastards out!"

Gritz stared up at his fellow sergeant. The man was dangling a clutch of four stick grenades that appeared to have been tied together with leather straps and bits of string.

"Won't work..." Gritz managed to gasp, his voice barely understandable as he fought for breath.

"It will, mate, I'm telling you..." Litteman was grinning back at him madly. "We're going for the tracks."

Without any further explanation, the other sergeant disappeared off to the left flank, followed by a group of about half a dozen other men. For a moment, Gritz just stared up at the sky, fighting to regain his composure. As he did, he realised that the sky was no longer blue, but grey. He glanced around him and saw that the shadows of the evening sun were gone. It was starting to get dark.

"Sergeant Gritz? Sergeant Gritz?"

The sound of his name made the sergeant sit up. Almost instantly he spotted Heigel, walking at a low crouch just below the crest of the plateau. The corporal was studying the faces of the men that were lining the ridge, searching for his sergeant. The men were all busy engaging the enemy tanks however, so when Gritz suddenly popped his head up, the corporal spotted him instantly.

"Sergeant Gritz? Thank fuck for that! I thought they'd got you at the last minute!"

Gritz just shook his head, still unable to catch his breath.

"Who was that poor fucker under the tank?" Heigel asked.

Gritz fixed him with a sad look, fought to calm his breathing, then replied.

"Gruber." He managed to gasp.

"Brave little fucker." Heigel commented in a surprisingly compassionate voice. "Deserves the Iron Cross for that."

The corporal brightened again quickly.

"Anyway, he did the trick; those tanks have slowed up. Not so confident now. Got no infantry with them at all by the looks."

Gritz turned his head to look back over the plateau and sure enough, he could see at least half a dozen tanks sitting out in the middle of the open ground or back in the bushes near the far crest. They were all either stationary or else trundling very slowly forward, their turrets traversing menacingly, like predatory monsters that suddenly realised they might be in danger themselves.

"Sergeant Litteman wants us to give rapid fire when we see the red flare." Heigel was saying behind Gritz. "We're keeping it steady at the moment. Just trying to keep them distracted."

Even as Heigel elaborated on the plan, Gritz saw a red flare sail lazily across the plateau, right over the top of several enemy tanks.

"That's it!" Heigel also spotted the flare. "Here we go lads, rapid...fire!"

The rate of fire from along the crest suddenly increased, the rifles and machine-guns erupting into violent life. Gritz, recovering now, ordered Heigel to go back along the ridge and control the fire so that their men didn't produce a crescendo of fire that would suddenly leave a complete lull when belts and magazines were expended. Then he began casting his gaze about the plateau, trying to see what Litteman was up to.

He saw the men instantly. A group of four suddenly burst into the open from behind a patch of long grass that edged a small depression and pounded towards one of two enemy tanks that were sitting in the centre of the open ground. Three of the men seemed to veer off and start running round inexplicably, jumping from one dip in the ground to another, before running blatantly across the line of sight of the enemy tanks. The fourth man, carrying something in a bundle, ran straight on for the nearest tank however. At the last moment, the enemy must have realised the intent, and several streams of tracer arced through the evening air to stitch the ground just behind the man with the bundle.

The enemy had realised the danger too late however. With one last burst of energy, the soldier covered the final twenty meters towards the tank and slid onto one knee by the side of vehicle. Gritz watched, hardly daring to breathe as the soldier fiddled with his bundle, then tossed it amongst the running gear of the tank's tracks. Having released his bundle, the soldier leapt up and began running away from the tank. Another burst of fire sliced through the air, narrowly missing him. The crew of the tank he had targeted were suspicious perhaps, for at that point the vehicle began to reverse. Just at that point there was a bright flash and the sound of a strange, almost stuttering explosion; the sound of a grenade detonating other grenades.

The soldier was thrown flat on his face by the blast. A moment later, he scrambled to his feet and began running for cover again. Black, oily smoke billowed out from the side of the tank, which had come to a halt again. After a moment or two, the tank revved its engine and juddered backwards once more. As it did so, it made a high-pitched metal on metal screech and veered awkwardly to one side. Gritz saw something flap wildly at the side of the tank and flop onto the ground. The track. The vehicle came to a halt. He watched to see what would happen next, but nothing did. Around him, his men were still firing at the remaining tanks, although at a more deliberate rate, and some of them gave a tired, ragged cheer as they saw the immobilised tank throw its track. Gritz gave a small sigh. It was a start if nothing else.

The light was fading fast. He checked his watch. It was gone 2030 hours. He was shocked. The battle had seemed to last just a few minutes, yet they had been fighting for over an hour.

"They're withdrawing!"

Gritz looked up sharply at the comment from someone further along the ridge. He squinted into the ever deepening gloom, trying to spot the dark outlines of the tanks against the dark bushes and scrub of the far ridgeline. Above the sound of gunfire he could hear the engines of the enemy tanks. Revving engines. Gritz lifted his binoculars and scanned the plateau. It really was starting to get dark very quickly now.

There.

He saw it. One of the enemy tanks was backing off slowly at the far side of the plateau. Just jockeying for position though, surely?

He saw the front of the tank rise and then slide out of view as it reversed back over the edge of the plateau.

"They're fucking off!"

Gritz heard another soldier voice the unbelievable and he scanned further left. Another enemy tank, the one that had killed Gruber he thought, going backwards. He watched it grind carefully to the rear, its machine-gun spitting out occasional wild bursts of fire. Then, like the other tank, it disappeared back over the ridge from whence it came. Slowly, hardly able to believe his eyes, Gritz lowered his binoculars. Some of his men were laughing now. Gritz shook his head.

"I don't believe it." He murmured, overcome with relief. "I don't fucking believe it…"

HEADQUARTERS GERMAN 19TH CORPS – LA CHAPELLE, 4 MILES NORTH-EAST OF SEDAN MONDAY 13TH MAY 1940 – 2330 HOURS

"Yes, Lorzer, it's me. I'm sorry to bother you so late in the day."

Guderian smiled at the reply from the Luftwaffe commander who was at the other end of the telephone.

"Well, make sure you get some sleep. I know what you air force types are like when you get tired!"

Lorzer made another comment and Guderian laughed.

"Indeed, Lorzer; indeed. Now listen, I won't keep you long. I was just ringing to pass on my thanks for the outstanding job your boys did today. The air support was first class; exactly what I wanted."

Guderian paused while the Luftwaffe officer dismissed the praise modestly.

"Even so, it was absolutely spot-on." Guderian continued. "Please tell your crews; they did a marvellous job. Now, there is just one thing. I was wondering if you were given any instructions by Army HQ that contradicted our original arrangements at all? I was told that the *'powers that be'* had rearranged the air support plan to something radically different from that which you and I agreed on. I have to say how pleased I was that we ended up going for the original plan in the end."

There was a longer pause now while Lorzer made a lengthy reply. Guderian nodded slowly as he digested Lorzer's information. Eventually, the corps commander spoke again.

"I see. Well, I have to say that for once, shortage of time has worked in our favour. You made the right decision and I am most obliged to you for going with the original plan. My thanks again, Lorzer….Yes, good night; and sleep well."

Guderian placed down the telephone and looked up at Nehring who had been hovering close by.

"Well, that explains it…" Guderian said, a tired smile crossing his features. "Lorzer says that he received the new orders for the air support plan, but that they arrived at the last moment. So, rather than cause chaos amongst his command by trying to distribute the new plan at such short notice, he decided to just go with what we had already arranged."

Colonel Nehring gave a sigh of relief and smiled back at his commander.

"Thank God somebody is exercising common sense apart from us then, Sir."

Guderian gave a grunt of a laugh.

"Oh, yes. Thank God indeed. Let's just see how long before the next random order gets thrown our way! Anyway, how are we set? Have the orders for tomorrow been sent out?"

Nehring nodded his affirmation.

"It's done, General, and every division has acknowledged. We've also received word from 1st Panzer that their engineers have worked miracles. They estimate that they will have the bridge over the river by around midnight, providing that they don't hit any unexpected problems."

Guderian beamed with delight.

"Excellent! Excellent! You see, Nehring, what a fine military tool we have crafted with this Panzer Corps? Who can stand against us, eh?"

"Only the enemies of common sense at Army Headquarters, Sir." The colonel replied mischievously.

Guderian groaned.

"Yes, well, God save us all from that breed, eh?"

The general was quiet for a moment. He was thinking back over the recent months, during the planning and training for this offensive. The discussions, heated debates, and in some cases the outright squabbles that had taken place amongst the high command. He remembered the conference in Berlin where the Fuhrer had asked each commander what they intended to do during the coming offensive; how they would achieve their aims. He remembered how Hitler had sat there quietly, listening to everything; watching how the generals argued, without intervening. Above all, he remembered General Busch, who commanded the 16th Army, barking out in contemptuous dismissal when he heard about Guderian's plan for crossing the Meuse and for the exploitation westwards. He could hear the man's words in his mind, even now. *'Ha! Well, I tell you Guderian; I seriously doubt you will even get across the river in the first place!"*

Guderian suddenly looked up at Nehring again, a sparkle in his tired eyes.

"Have all of the staff assemble in the main map room, will you? I would like to thank them all for their outstanding work these last few days. They have achieved a brilliant victory on the Meuse today."

Nehring nodded and made to turn away, but Guderian called him back.

"Oh, and one more thing. Once I have spoken to the staff, I want you to do something for me. I would like you to send a signal to General Busch at Headquarters 16th Army. Please give him my kind regards and tell him that he will be delighted to hear that today the 19th Panzer Corps successfully crossed the River Meuse at Sedan…And that tomorrow we are commencing our drive westwards for the English Channel."

Tuesday 14th May 1940
The Fifth Day

THE COAL YARD – LEEFDAL, BELGIUM
TUESDAY 14TH MAY 1940 – 0630 HOURS

"*We're going to hang out the washing on the Siegfried Line, have you any dirty washing mother dear…"*

Jackson looked up sharply as the truck rumbled past and the sound of high-spirited singing came to his ears.

"We're going to hang out the washing on the Siegfried Line, 'cause the washing day is here…"

As the vehicle passed the gateway of the coal merchant's yard, Jackson caught sight of the troops inside the truck. He glimpsed a shoulder flash. Hambledon and Moorlanders; a territorial unit. He wasn't usually a fan of singing during unit moves, as he considered it un-soldierly, but on this occasion, he couldn't help but raise a smile at the spirit of it all.

After the drudgery of the last few months, digging in and building field defences on the Franco-Belgian border in appalling weather, it felt good to be on the move; going forward. At last, Jackson would have a chance to get at the enemy and prove both himself and his regiment. That said, he worried slightly that the winter months had been wasted. They had done precious few training schemes above company level, and little physical exercise. That had shown on the march into Belgium, for after more than thirty miles on the straight, cobbled roads, Jackson's feet were burning, and running to possible blisters. Now he had blisters on his thumbs too, for having arrived in their final position the night before, the battalion had been ordered to start digging-in again. Yet more defensive positions! Listening to the tired groans of his platoon as they stripped off their equipment, he realised that they too were also feeling the long hours of digging in the dark.

It had been a long and frustrating twenty four hours after the initial alert, back on Friday. Having stood-to, ready to move, their battalion, indeed the whole corps, had been held back while the 2nd Corps led the advance into Belgium. That irked Jackson slightly as it meant that their sister battalion, the 1st, would probably get to grips with the Germans before them. There was always tremendous rivalry between the battalions and this would only serve to fuel the ongoing competition between them. Still, the call had finally come for the 2nd Battalion Coldstream Guards and, for the last few days, at first on vehicles, but then largely on foot, they had been advancing steadily eastwards to meet the enemy.

"Sarn't Jackson…close in on the Company Quarter Master Sergeant. Section commanders… get your men ready for scoff."

The shout from the Company Sergeant Major interrupted Jackson's musings. He glanced across the yard and saw that the team from the company stores were busy unloading dixie-containers from their fifteen hundredweight truck. It was standard practice in the British Army for commanders to personally feed their men, ensuring that they had been taken care of before looking to their own welfare.

"Sergeant Granger," Jackson called to his senior lance sergeant, "get the lads sorted, please? Line 'em up as soon as they're all ready."

Leaving his platoon to sort themselves out, Jackson strode off across the wide yard and was joined en route by Lance Sergeant 'Piggy' Hogson, another of his section commanders.

"Fuck me, Davey," Hogson grunted as they crossed the yard together, "I'm bollocksed. And I'm sick of digging fucking trenches too."

Jackson murmured his agreement.

"Soon be done now, Piggy. Once we're down and the position's been wired, we'll be ready for the Jerries. We'll give 'em what for when they get here?"

"Bloody hope so." Hogson replied. "Don't fancy any more marching; or digging trenches in the dark. I just want a bloody good fight now."

They reached the line of dixies and were greeted by the red-faced and jovial looking Company Quarter Master Sergeant, Tom Colley.

"Ey up, fellas. Usual drill, please." The colour sergeant in charge of the company stores greeted them. "Davey, can you do the scrambled egg, mate? Piggy, you're on corned beef hash. I'll do the porridge."

"No dramas, Sir." Jackson acknowledged, taking the proffered ladle.

He lifted the lid from the dixie and inspected the contents. Inside, he saw a mass of hard, yellow, over-cooked scrambled egg, sitting in a bath of greasy, eggy-fluid. It was the usual fare for a unit in the field, and after a long night of digging Jackson was ready for a mess-tin full of the steaming mixture, regardless of what it looked like.

He stood straight and glanced about him. The platoon commanders were gathered nearby with the Company Commander, chatting quietly whilst they waited for the men to be fed. The officers from the other platoons had hung back whilst their own men had relieved Jackson's platoon on the company defensive position. Jackson now overheard a part of their conversation.

"We got down quite far last night, Charles." Jackson's own platoon commander, Dunstable, was saying excitedly. "We'll soon have the position revetted and wired; then we can get ready for the Hun. We can organise a nice deep dugout for Company Headquarters and make it quite cosy. It'll be just like the last war…"

The Company Commander, a quietly spoken veteran of the previous conflict, gave a deep sigh.

"Good Lord, I hope it won't be anything like the last one…"

"Long night then, Davey?"

The comment from the Company Quarter Master Sergeant focussed Jackson's attention again.

"Eh? Oh…Aye, Sir; bloody long one too, after all that marching over the weekend."

"Not to worry, Davey lad. You should get a few hours gonk before you go back into the line."

Jackson was about to reply, but as he opened his mouth to speak, the sound of distant gunfire made him look away to the east.

Looking up into the sky, Jackson noticed small puffs of black smoke, high up in the air, some distance away. The remainder of the company staff looked up too, following his gaze.

"What's all that about then?" Hogson wondered aloud from nearby.

Colley squinted up into the bright blue morning sky.

"Looks like aircraft. See 'em?"

Jackson could indeed see aircraft; a dozen of them maybe, high up, just above where the small explosions of anti-aircraft fire were punctuating the expanse of clear sky. They were getting closer now, looking as if they were going to pass close by the village of Leefdal.

Nearby, the officers were making their own, excited observations.

"Must be the Jerry air force?" Dunstable was saying.

The noise of the aircraft engines was audible now.

"Wonder where they're heading to?"

"Probably looking for convoys coming up the road from France I reckon." The Company Commander answered.

"Hope our RAF chaps appear and give them a good clobbering..." Another young platoon commander said.

Then the sound of the aircraft engines changed.

As the group of aircraft drew level with the village, one of them peeled off, followed by the others, and began to fly in a wide circle, right above the staring guardsmen. For a moment, everyone was silent, transfixed by the almost beautiful display of formation flying.

"I don't much like the look of that..." The Company Commander observed, his voice suddenly filled with an uncharacteristic tone of concern.

Just then, the leading aircraft suddenly dropped like a stone, straight down towards the collection of guardsmen in the coal yard.

"Ruddy hell!" Dunstable's voice cried out in disbelief. "They're going to bomb us!"

"Take cover!" The Company Sergeant Major's voice roared out across the yard.

"Shit!" Jackson swore under his breath as he watched the small black dot suddenly get larger and larger.

Without further prompting, everyone began scattering in various directions, and Jackson, still clutching his ladle, threw himself flat on the floor behind the dixies. The aircraft, now followed by the others, was coming straight at them; there was nowhere to hide.

Jackson's stomach felt as though it was going to drop right out of his arse; as if a heavy stone had just been dropped right inside his guts. This was his first contact with the enemy, and it was definitely not how he had imagined it would be. He was laying here in the open, armed with nothing more than a ladle, with a dozen or more German dive-bombers coming straight for him. As if that wasn't terrifying enough, the sound of the German planes had transformed from a powerful growl to a high-pitched whine, as if some prehistoric monster was screeching in rage as it dived for its prey.

Next to Jackson, Colley was flat on his face, arms over his head.

"Oh, my fucking God! What the fuck is that?"

Jackson, laid in a similar manner to Colley, squinted at the colour sergeant. The older man was as white as a ghost, his eyes filled with the same terror that was infecting Jackson. Above them, the screaming of the enemy aircraft grew louder and louder, filling Jackson's head and threatening to overwhelm his senses. It seemed to go on forever. Surely the plane would be crashing into the ground any moment if it didn't pull up? The sergeant didn't dare look up to see.

Suddenly, Colley began scrambling to his feet.

"It's going to fucking hit us!" He screamed out as he stood upright and looked about him for somewhere to run.

"Get down, Sir! For fuck's sake..." Jackson shouted at Colley above the deafening screech.

The sound of the aircraft suddenly changed once more, the scream of the siren fading and the roar of the engine becoming more dominant again. And then came the whistling noise...

"Sir! Get down..."

Crack-Crump!

Jackson felt the explosion before he heard it. The tremor began under his stomach and he thought for a moment that his bowels were going to betray him. Then, his whole body seemed to lift up as the ground reared underneath him. At the same time, a terrible thunderclap almost shattered his ear drums. Then, just a split second later, he felt a wave of air slap him like a physical blow, after which his lungs seemed to empty of oxygen in an instant. Next he was dumped face down on the gravel again. As he lay there in shock, something hot and fluid splattered over his back, making him cry out in alarm.

He had no chance to worry any further however, as the air was filled with screeching again, then more whistling, then yet more violent explosions that continued to throw him up and down on the floor of the yard. Jackson's soldierly pride had gone out of the window now. As one huge blast followed another, and bits of God knew what smashed into the floor around him and against the truck, the young sergeant gave small, terrified cries, as he prayed to nobody in particular for the experience to end.

Eventually, after what seemed like a lifetime, the explosions and the screeching stopped abruptly. As his senses returned to normal, all Jackson could hear was the rapidly fading sound of engines. He lay there for a few moments, scared to move, but after a short while, when he realised that he was alive, and that he could still move his arms and legs, he forced himself up onto all fours.

As he gazed about the smoke shrouded yard, nothing seemed to be stirring at first, but then, slowly, heads began to pop up from their various hiding places and the shocked eyes of his fellow guardsmen stared back at him. A whole combination of smells assailed his nostrils, but one of the most pronounced was that of scrambled egg. With surprise, he realised that he was absolutely covered in it. Blobs of sticky egg were covering his hands and arms and his battle-dress was soaked with the greasy egg-water. To his left, the dixie that had once held the food had been torn wide open, allowing its contents to spill out.

Jackson, rather shakily, pushed himself to his feet. He was surprised to see the Company Commander staring back at him, covered in black coal dust but looking remarkably calm. Next to him, the Company Sergeant Major and platoon commanders were also climbing to their feet.

"Company Sergeant Major?" The Company Commander snapped in a steady, yet business like tone. "Get everyone assembled and call the roll, please? Let's see what the damage is."

"Right, Sir." Came the dutiful reply.

At that point, Hogson's voice brought everyone up short.

"Oh, Jesus fucking Christ! The Q-Bloke..."

Jackson looked down and saw, with a renewed sense of horror, that the Company Quarter Master Sergeant was dead. Obviously dead at that, for the poor man's head was missing and there was a lake of thick red blood on the floor in front of Hogson. In fact, Hogson's whole left side was covered in blood too.

This was the first person that Jackson had ever seen killed by enemy action and he was transfixed by the awful sight of the headless corpse.

"Oh, dear me." The Company Commander murmured as he too saw the body.

Still unable to believe his eyes, Jackson took a tentative step forward.

"Fucking hell, Piggy..." He stammered. "You're covered in blood mate."

As Hogson glanced down at his battledress and began to survey the red gore that had covered him, Jackson looked around him and suddenly caught his breath.

He was staring towards one of the dixies containing his platoon's breakfast. Beyond the container filled with corned beef hash was a third container filled with porridge. Amongst the thick grey goo, sat what was left of the Company Quarter Master Sergeant's head. The blood had mingled with the porridge and in a terrible way, made it look as though someone had just dropped a giant blob of jam into the mixture. With surprising and unexpected force, Jackson's stomach heaved and he felt the 'all-in stew' of last night's meal start to regurgitate. He turned away from the macabre scene quickly, just as the first wave of vomit burst out of his mouth and splashed up the side of the stores truck.

TACTICAL HQ 7TH PANZER DIVISION – BY DINANT ON THE MEUSE
TUESDAY 14TH MAY 1940 – 0645 HOURS

Rommel chomped on the hunk of bread as he listened to Lieutenant Most reading the various situation reports aloud. As he listened and ate, the general nodded his head repeatedly, acknowledging certain points in each of the reports and grunting with satisfaction. It was all good; very good indeed. His motorcycle troops and those of 5th Panzer still held the Heights of Wastia and his rifle regiments would soon be relieving them, along with some anti-tank guns that would make the vantage point much more secure. The French had begun counter-attacking those heights late the previous evening and they were still at it, but Rommel was pretty sure that his men could hold on there long enough for the important move of the day to take effect. And of course, he had his bridge. Even as he spoke, yet more tanks were rumbling slowly across it in the growing light of what promised to be another glorious spring day.

Having finished the bread, Rommel grabbed the mug of bitter, black coffee from the front fender of his command vehicle and began swigging the steaming, dark liquid as fast as he dared. Most continued with the reports, before ending with the updated intelligence assessment for the next 24 hours. As the young lieutenant finished speaking, he looked up at his general for a response. Rommel swilled the last mouthful of coffee around his cheeks thoughtfully for a moment before finally swallowing it.

"So, the enemy are trying to make a stand at Onhaye, then?"

"That's correct, General. They are holding the village in strength it seems."

Rommel nodded repeatedly, turning the situation reports over in his mind. At length he spoke again.

"These heights up here, the Heights of Wastia; they are useful, but not the key to victory…"

He pointed in the general direction of the road to Onahye.

"Victory lies in the west. We need complete breakthrough. Our infantry and support troops are now spreading out steadily and will be able to secure the river line and this crossing point in short order. The threat, gentlemen…"

And at this, Rommel cast a meaningful look around the faces of his staff.

"The threat, gentlemen, lies in the west. We have achieved surprise and gained a foothold; made a small hole in the enemy front. Now what we must do is tear that hole wide open and punch hard, fast and deep through the enemy's depth positions and into his rear."

He put the mug down on the vehicle's fender with a metallic clang.

"Vosse? Find me a tank, please; a Mark 3. I will go forward with the lead tank company and the recce units. Every tank that is across the river is to advance to Onhaye immediately. As every subsequent tank comes over, it is to move immediately towards Onhaye and attach itself to the forces there. This is our main effort for the morning; breakthrough at Onhaye then start driving westwards. Every bit of combat power we have is to be thrown into the battle immediately it is available. Understand?"

"Yes, General. I'll sort the tank immediately."

The captain sped off and Rommel turned his attention to Most now.

"Most? Ensure my intentions have been relayed back to Divisional Main Headquarters. I want you to remain here and brief every commander who comes over that bridge, personally. Every tank is to move directly to Onhaye. Every single one. Do not worry about what's happening to the flanks; the rifle regiments know what they're doing with that business. Once Main Headquarters crosses the bridge, hand over to the Chief of Staff and then follow me up in our wireless vehicle."

The lieutenant nodded his acknowledgement.

"Yes, General. That is clear."

As the young lieutenant was replying, one of the signallers in the wireless truck leaned down and passed him a note.

Most took the piece of paper and scanned it quickly, before glancing back up at his commander with a worried look. Rommel spotted the discomfort in the man's eyes.

"What is it, Most?" He asked.

The young lieutenant cleared his throat then replied.

"It is a signal from 5th Panzer, Sir…From General von Hartlieb. It is a complaint, Sir. He protests most strongly about our seizing his bridging unit. It says he is reporting the matter to Corps Headquarters…"

Rommel held out a hand.

"Let me see?"

The general quickly scanned the document, gave a small grunt and passed it back to Most.

"Get your notebook out, Most, and take this message down. It is to be sent by flash signal to Army Headquarters immediately."

Most, fumbling for his notebook, shot a surprised look at his commander.

"*Army* Headquarters, Sir?"

"Yes." Rommel confirmed. "You can copy it to Corps Headquarters, too... after you've sent it to Army."

Trying not to look surprised at the blatant breaking of the chain of command system, Most stood ready with his pencil and notebook. Rommel began to dictate.

"From Commander 7th Panzer to Commander 4th Army. Urgent. I must protest strongly at the slow progress of 5th Panzer and their consistent failure to utilize resources to best effect. Successful breakthrough has been achieved by 7th Panzer at Dinant on the Meuse and this must be exploited immediately. Failure by 5th Panzer to keep up with the advance will expose 7th Panzer's flanks dangerously..."

Most's mouth dropped open as he copied the words down. Again, Rommel noted the surprise on the young officer's face.

"Have you got all that, Most? Not going too fast am I?"

"Erm, no, General." Was all Most could say.

"Good." Rommel quipped, and continued dictating. "I request that pressure is placed on 5th Panzer to increase their tempo of operations with immediate effect..."

BRIDGE OVER THE MEUSE – GLAIRE, 1 MILE NORTH OF SEDAN
TUESDAY 14TH MAY 1940 – 1130 HOURS

Guderian watched the French bomber plummet straight down, trailing black smoke, before smashing into the distant fields with a loud 'crump' and orange flash. Moments later, a cloud of dark smoke rose from the scene, as if to act as a warning to all other enemy aircraft of the fate that awaited them. The first wave of enemy aircraft had come in an hour ago and been met by a deadly hail of fire from the combination of anti-aircraft units that now ringed this vital bridge over the river. Guderian had been too busy up to now to worry about the air raid, although he reckoned he must have counted at least nine enemy bombers going down in flames as he had gone about his morning's business. Now, standing by the western end of 1st Panzer's bridge, he had a grandstand view of the air battle as it continued to rage. The air above was filled with the small, dirty grey clouds of exploding anti-aircraft shells whilst streams of tracer snaked upwards between them to chase the incoming bombers.

He watched as yet more tanks from the second tank brigade of 1st Panzer rumbled off the bridge and were directed to their assembly area by the field police. Beyond the bridge, set back from the river a couple of hundred metres, was a vast sea of people. Dressed in drab khaki greatcoats and trousers with their strange, green helmets, they were the prisoners of war taken so far during the course of the crossing and the subsequent night battles. The general ran his eye over the scene for a few moments, trying to estimate how many prisoners must be there, sitting in huge groups in the water meadows and cringing in fear as each new wave of their own aircraft came diving in to attack. At some point, Guderian would need to get them shifted out of the way. No time now though; getting his tanks moving was the important thing. He took one last look at the mass of men and decided that there must be a couple of thousand Frenchmen there, at least.

Guderian turned his attention back to the bridge. Another tank company was trundling across, the big Mk 4 tanks coming over one at a time, not wanting to put excessive stress on the delicate bridge. As he watched the armour come across, he allowed his mind to wander slightly, going back over the events of the morning thus far. It was going well. 2nd Panzer Division was now over the river at Donchery and 10th Panzer was expanding its small bridgehead too. The 1st Panzer meanwhile, along with the Gross Deutschland Regiment, had expanded this bridgehead considerably during the night and was chomping at the bit to breakout.

Indeed, he had visited the orders group of the divisional commander as objectives for the day were being given out. During that orders session, information had come in that the French were forming up tanks and infantry for a counter attack near Stonne. Without hesitation, the divisional commander had ordered his own tanks, every one that was available, to advance immediately on Stonne and destroy the enemy force in a spoiling attack. This was how Guderian had trained his men to be; decisive, aggressive, never allowing the enemy to take the advantage.

Next though, he must turn his attention to the bigger picture. It was now almost time to make a momentous decision; a decision on which he had been given no direction by higher formation to date. The decision would be where he was going to go next. Did he drift south-west, anticipating an attack by a strong French reserve, or did he carry out his desired option; to strike due west, in order to punch deep into the enemy's rear, before wheeling northwards and ripping the enemy's guts out from behind. His musings were interrupted by a shout from his staff officer.

"General! The Army Group Commander is here! Colonel-General von Rundstedt, Sir... Look!"

Guderian, surprised yet delighted at the announcement, threw his gaze across the river. The tanks had come to a halt in order to let a wheeled, armoured command vehicle onto the bridge. Even at this distance, Guderian recognised the figure standing upright in the vehicle, and the identity flash on the front bumper confirmed that they were indeed witnessing the arrival of the man charged with the main thrust of the whole offensive. Guderian stepped out onto the pontoon bridge and began striding across, back towards the eastern bank, as the command vehicle began rolling towards him.

Vehicle and pedestrian met in the very middle of the bridge. As they did so, three bombers came swooping in, flying straight up the valley from the south. A fierce barrage of anti-aircraft fire erupted around Guderian as every gun along the Meuse was turned on the three aircraft. Before they even reached the bridge, one of the bombers burst into flames and heeled over to its starboard, plunging into the ground on the eastern bank and exploding. In the split second it took to crash, Guderian briefly caught sight of the markings on the aircraft undercarriage. British, he noted. Looked as though the Allies were throwing everything they could find at them today.

The remaining two bombers roared over Guderian's head at just a few hundred feet. He heard the briefest whistle of bombs descending, and then the water on either side of the bridge erupted in huge geysers as the deadly explosives missed their target and splashed harmlessly into the river. Droplets of water pattered down onto Guderian and, ignoring the departing bombers, he squinted up at the figure looking down on him from the armoured car.

"Morning, Heinz!" Shouted von Rundstedt above the noise of gunfire and aircraft engines.

The commander of the 19th Corps snapped to attention and saluted.

"Good morning, Sir. How very nice to see you."

The Army Group Commander returned the salute and grinned down at him.

"And how very nice to see this bridge over the river! You've done a marvellous job Heinz; absolutely marvellous! Well done."

"Thank you, General."

Just at that point, one of the two surviving British bombers exploded in mid air; it's fuselage and wings enveloped by flames. The two generals paused momentarily and watched as the burning debris pattered down onto the surface of the river. After a moment or two, von Rundstedt looked back down at the corps commander.

"Bit of a noisy party you're throwing, Heinz!" He observed. "Hope you didn't go to the trouble of laying it on just for me! Is it always like this around here?"

Guderian laughed.

"Pretty much, General. Pretty much…"

PART THREE

LIGHTNING

Wednesday 15th May 1940
The Sixth Day

Churchill, still in his pyjamas, bathrobe and slippers, waddled across the darkened library with a scowl on his face. The library was lit only by a small lamp and one of his minor aides was holding the telephone and staring at him apologetically.

"I am told it is urgent?" Churchill rumbled, his mind still groggy with sleep.

The aide gave a weak smile and placed his hand over the telephone's mouth-piece.

"It is the French President on the line for you Prime Minister; Monsieur Reynaud. He's in a bit of a state…"

Churchill stopped dead and frowned at the aide.

"Monsieur Reynaud?"

The aide simply nodded confirmation.

Suddenly awake, and alert to the fact that something didn't feel right about receiving such an early morning call from the French President himself, Churchill moved quickly across to the chair by his writing desk and dropped into it. He took a deep breath, nodded to the aide, then held out his hand and took the telephone.

"Monsieur President." Churchill began in his school-boy French. "Good morning to you. My apologies for keeping you waiting."

Churchill had attempted to sound as bright as he possibly could, not wanting to appear disconcerted at being woken so early by the call of Prime Ministerial duty. The President's reply however, turned Churchill's blood cold. The colour drained from his face and his eyebrows, arched through habit as he attempted to sound perky, suddenly dropped to accentuate the deep worried frown that appeared on those craggy features. For a moment, his mind didn't register the despairing words of the French President as they were literally sobbed down the phone. After a moment however, the import of those words hit home.

"We are beaten…We have lost the battle!"

For a while, Churchill couldn't speak; his mind not able to compute the meaning of such a sweeping statement. After a while however, the Prime Minister found his voice.

"Monsieur President, whatever do you mean?"

At the other end of the telephone, Reynaud began talking. Quickly, endlessly, without pause, the normally optimistic President of France began to pour out his fears and concerns to Churchill. The Germans were across the Meuse. They had broken through at Sedan, Dinant, Montherme and were brushing aside his divisions. There were reports of thousands of German tanks heading south and west; for Paris, for Amiens, and who knew where else. The French generals were telling the President that it was nothing more than a 'bulge' and that they had sealed it off, but he didn't trust them. The enemy had outflanked the Maginot Line at its northern extremity and broken through the defences there. The reports were confusing, said the President, and often contradictory, but the one thing that was clear was that the Germans were over the Meuse. The one great obstacle that was key to the defence of Belgium and France was breached.

It took Churchill a while to calm the French President, even as he himself tried to digest the whirlwind of information; some of which was seriously bad news, and some of which was a mixture of speculation and dire prophecy. Churchill would fly to France the very next day to meet the President and his commanders, he promised him. The President must not worry himself. In war, the advantage often swung backwards and forwards between combatants. This set-back could be reversed, Churchill assured the leader of the French, providing the allies could co-ordinate their action properly. He would come to Paris and see to it personally. Tomorrow; a promise.

Eventually, having calmed the President somewhat, Churchill placed the telephone down. He sat for a moment, brooding, then took a deep breath and glared up at the aide who remained in the office, waiting patiently for instructions.

"Get hold of the Secretary of State for me…" Churchill growled, his face set. "And the Chief of the Imperial General Staff too. Tell them I want to see them immediately; within the hour. Earlier if possible…"

REIMS-CHAMPAGNE AERODROME – NORTHERN FRANCE
WEDNESDAY 15TH MAY 1940 – 0800 HOURS

Whittaker sat up, blinking stupidly in the early morning sun as his greatcoat dropped from his face. He stared around with a lost expression, not quite sure where, or who he was. He gawped at the Hurricane parked nearby, at McWilliams kneeling on its port wing, carrying out his pre-flight checks on the guns, then directly at Devine who was standing over him.

"Mr Whittaker, Sir?"

With a sudden jolt, Whittaker remembered everything.

He struggled to his feet, his mind slowly picking up speed now that he was awake. It had been an unbelievable five days since the German offensive had begun. Whittaker had lost count of the sorties he had flown; fifteen at least he reckoned, probably more. That was a punishing schedule anyway, even worse considering the several near misses he had suffered during the furious aerial combat of the past week. In that time, he had managed to down no less than five enemy aircraft with a sixth possible, but any euphoria he had felt during those initial kills had long since faded thanks to the endless, exhausting drudgery of mission after mission.

The Germans it seemed, had no limit to the aircraft they could put into the sky, and his squadron had been at it from the very crack of dawn until the last chink of daylight had faded, every day since the balloon had gone up. Whittaker, like everyone else in the squadron, was shattered. He was so tired that he was functioning more out of habit than conscious thought, and he knew that it was a dangerous state to be in when taking part in a dog fight. It was only a matter of time he reckoned, before his dulled senses were his undoing whilst confronting a fresher, more alert enemy pilot. Still, that was his job he supposed. And now, it seemed that duty was about to call once more. He stared at Devine through bloodshot, sunken eyes.

"The Squadron Leader has asked to speak to everyone at the dispersal tent, Sir. He says it's important news; something about a move."

Whittaker frowned and ran a hand through his unkempt hair.

"A move? What kind of move?"

"Not sure, Sir." The mechanic shrugged back. "But there's talk of the Jerries breaking through at Sedan, Sir. I've heard tell they've got tanks charging like hell across half of France."

Whittaker's frown turned to a scowl.

"Germans at Sedan? I find that hard to believe. It's not even fifty miles away. I could drive there in an hour or so."

The pilot struggled into his greatcoat as the morning chill got to him.

"If I was you, I'd ignore all those rumours. It just gets everyone jumpy for no reason."

Feeling decidedly grumpy, Whittaker began shuffling away from his dispersal position at the edge of the airfield and across the wide expanse of grass towards the distant tents. As he went, he glanced up at McWilliams, who was still busy with the guns in the port wing.

"Make sure those guns are in good order, McWilliams." He grunted. "Don't want to find myself in any more pickles like the other day."

The armourer didn't even look at his pilot.

"Try to avoid getting your wings shot through by cannon shells then, Sir; I find it tends to help…"

Neither Whittaker's or McWilliams' words were delivered with any conviction; for it was a ritual they had begun after Whittaker's guns had jammed during an air battle some days before. Having returned to the airfield, Whittaker had gone into a rant about his guns not working properly. Only after he had lambasted his crew for several minutes had McWilliams and Devine both pointed out that the Hurricane was riddled with bullet holes from large calibre guns, and in particular, both wings had been absolutely peppered, damaging the firing mechanism for both port and starboard batteries of machine-guns. Since then, it had been something of a standing joke between them all. After days and nights of little sleep however, they were all finding it hard to smile, let alone laugh anymore.

Whittaker left his crew to their ministrations, and ambled casually across the field. He had barely gone twenty yards when the sound of aircraft engines came to him. He glanced up, worried that he might have missed an order to scramble, but his eyes fell on a fairly sedentary picture. The other aircraft of the squadron remained stationary across the span of the airfield, crews and pilots strolling unhurriedly about their business. Then he heard someone shout. Then someone else shouted too. Then the anti-aircraft guns on the perimeter of the airfield opened up with an urgent rattle.

He saw people at the other side of the field begin running, and just then, the sound of the aircraft engines suddenly increased in volume to a deafening roar. Whittaker whirled round and froze, his eyes bulging and his mouth dropping open in surprise. The Messerschmitt was coming straight for him…

A twin-engined 110, his arch-nemesis, was screaming towards him across the flat meadow, flying at barely tree-top height. All Whittaker could see was the awful, deadly snub-nose of the aircraft where it sported its quadruple 20mm cannons. He threw himself flat as the plane passed right over him. Even as he thumped painfully to the floor, face down in the dew-soaked grass, he heard the thunder of the aircraft's cannons as they barked into life.

The air above him was filled with noise; the throaty roar of powerful engines and the chatter of heavy calibre machine-guns.

After a few seconds, Whittaker glanced up. He instantly regretted the decision. Another 110 was coming straight for him, lower than the other one, and already firing. Clods of earth flew up in great spurts as the cannon shells ripped into the ground directly to Whittaker's front, perhaps fifty yards at the most. There was nowhere to run, and no time, so Whittaker simply pushed his face into the dirt and covered his head with his arms, expecting his life to end any second now. Instead he felt himself being showered with dirt, and then, a few moments later, as the second aircraft roared past him, something heavy thumped him on the back.

For a moment or two he laid there, terrified, expecting that his entire back had been ripped open by a cannon shell. But that didn't make sense. Why wasn't he dead? Come to think of it, the impact wasn't that painful. He moved his legs and was surprised to find that they worked. He risked another peek from beneath his arms. More enemy planes were swooping across the airfield now, in various directions, and he could hear explosions in the distance. He suddenly noticed something glinting in the grass, just an arm's length away. Without thinking, he reached out, grabbed it, then held it up.

Still warm, it was an empty 20mm shell case. With a flood of realisation and relief, Whittaker rolled over. As he did so, another of the spent shell cases rolled off his back and into the grass behind him. The cylindrical brass cases were all around him, lying where they had fallen from the passing Messerschmitt. Rather inappropriately, Whittaker began to laugh. He rolled back onto his front, tossing away the shell case, and gazed out across the airfield.

The enemy aircraft were still making passes. He saw several Hurricanes on the ground, burning brightly; thick black smoke pouring from the ruined machines. To Whittaker's satisfaction, he saw one of the enemy aircraft streak across the airfield from right to left, trailing a stream of dark smoke itself. At least the Jerries weren't getting away with it completely unscathed. It was just at that point, as Whittaker decided that he really, really detested Messerschmitt 110s, and that he would dedicate himself to knocking as many of them out of the sky in future as he could, that he remembered his own crew.

With a small gasp of alarm, Whittaker twisted round to look back the way he had come. He saw the Hurricane, the 'F' for Freddie symbol clearly visible on its upended fuselage, burning furiously at the edge of the field. The flames were all over the front of the aircraft by the cockpit and wings; angry orange flames licking wickedly at the rapidly disintegrating frame, whilst oily black smoke billowed out to mark his beloved aircraft's funeral pyre. Through the smoke, he spotted two figures in blue overalls lying face down, close by the aircraft.

His heart sinking, Whittaker gave an involuntary moan.

"Mac! Charley!" His voice croaked the words through a suddenly dry throat.

"Lads!"

The raid was still in full swing, and yet another flight of enemy aircraft swooped across the aerodrome looking for targets, their deadly cannon hammering out a relentless tune of destruction. Despite the obvious danger, Whittaker picked himself up and began staggering back towards his burning aircraft and its prone crew.

"Chaps, are you ok?"

Neither of the figures moved or made any kind or response. Whittaker's awkward stumble turned into a run.

"Lads..? Lads!"

VANGUARD 5TH PANZER DIVISION – FLAVION, 8 MILES WEST OF DINANT ON THE MEUSE WEDNESDAY 15TH MAY 1940 – 0900 HOURS

"What's this next place called then?" Asked the gunner, sounding as if he wasn't particularly bothered about getting an answer.

"Flavion." Replied the commander of the Panzer Mk 3, Corporal Max Weimer. "Just a small place; much like the last one."

The gunner grunted acknowledgement.

"What's the drill when we get there?"

"Same as usual, I suppose." Replied Weimer. "Check if there's any fuel in the place. Food too. If so, take what's useful and move on. If any Frenchies get in the way; we just blast through the fuckers."

The gunner gave him a sideways glance.

"We expecting trouble then? I thought we'd broken through their lines?"

Weimer pulled a non-committal face.

"Maybe we'll bump into some of their reserves. There was talk at the orders group of some French tanks and trucks moving our way. Apparently 7th Panzer bumped into a load earlier on. If it's right then it's probably the enemy getting organised for a counter attack. Not that it's a problem of course. From what I've seen of the Belgies and the Frenchies so far, we'll knock them off their feet before they even realise what's happening. I imagine that 7th Panzer gave them a good seeing to already."

As Weimer was speaking with his gunner, the tank began to slow. Weimer ducked his head low in the turret and shouted down to the driver.

"What's going on? Why are you slowing up?"

He heard the driver shout something back up, but it was unintelligible. It fell to the loader to repeat the driver's message.

"Platoon Commander has stopped, Sir, apparently."

Weimer stuck his head out of the cupola and scanned the countryside ahead.

Their company was moving in open, staggered formation, with Weimer's tank on the rear left. Sure enough, up in front and way over to the right, all the tanks in the leading wave had slowed to a halt, just as they reached the boundary of the large field they were crossing. Directly to the front of Weimer's tank, on the company's left flank, was a small copse on the ridge where the field boundary lay. Being so far back, Weimer could see nothing beyond the ridge. As he watched the other tanks for some kind of indication of what might be happening, the radio crackled into life.

"All Leopold callsigns, this is Leopold Zero; we've got enemy tanks approaching us head on from the valley floor beyond. Looks like a large force; couple of companies maybe? They're fanning out from the village. All callsigns move into extended line on the ridge, level with me, and adopt firing positions. Stay hidden and try to get into hull-down positions where you can. Prepare to fire on my order; not before. I say again, only fire on my order."

The radio operator relayed the order to his commander, word for word.

Weimer needed no further prompting.

"Forwards! Straight into that copse from the rear."

The loader shouted the order down to the driver and a moment later, the big tank lurched forward and picked up speed, aiming directly for the small clump of trees. To the right, another tank, that of Sergeant Holbier, was angling across towards the copse too.

"Give this other tank room on our right as we go in." Weimer sent the order down to the driver.

Moments later, they were on the edge of the copse. The trees were almost in full leaf and so the wooded area offered good cover. To Weimer's delight, he saw too that the trees were growing from within a slight depression.

"Okay, take it steady here." He called down. "Nudge your way in gently and try not to bring any trees down. Just get us forward nice and steady to the forward edge…just between those two trees there, look. "

The driver did as instructed and nosed the heavy tank carefully forward, the twenty three ton monster dropping down into the slight dip, before trundling onwards a few more metres towards the forward edge of the tree line.

Weimer shouted several more minor adjustments until he was happy with his final position. It wasn't bad at all. Most of the hull was in the dip and the tank itself was a few metres back from the very edge of the tree line, taking advantage of the shadow.

"Traverse the gun and check your arcs." Weimer instructed his gunner. "Make sure we've got armour piercing up the spout."

As the turret crew went about their business, Weimer used his binoculars to scan the open ground beyond.

He could see the roofs of the village in the shallow valley beyond, maybe eight hundred metres away, but the gradient of the slope to his front was slightly convex so his full range of vision was perhaps three hundred metres at most; not as good as he would have liked. Beside him, about fifteen metres to his right, Holbier's tank nosed its way into the copse and adopted a similar position to his own. Out beyond the copse, extending for hundreds of metres to his right, the remainder of his company were lined up behind the tree-studded hedgerow of the field, their stubby 37mm guns poking menacingly through the foliage.

"The Company Commander reminds us to hold our fire until he gives the signal, Corporal."

The radio operator's voice came up through the turret.

"Got it." Weimer acknowledged.

He ducked his head inside the turret and addressed the gun crew.

"You two ready?"

Neither the gunner or loader looked up, they were poised over their weapon, ready to engage as soon as the word was given and a target presented itself. Both men, their faces serious, gave curt nods.

"The slope works against us here, so we won't get much warning when they appear. It's going to be a close up business this time."

Weimer looked up again and gazed across the open fields beyond. The sun was shining and the green and brown patchwork was bathed in glorious light, and the scene was really quite delightful. It would be a shame to spoil such a perfect morning, he reflected. But then, instantly, the beauty of the countryside became an irrelevance as the first enemy tank rolled into view. It was over to the right, about five hundred metres away, on the shallower part of the slope, and so Weimer had a perfect view of the vehicle as it was followed moments later by several others, and together they rumbled upwards toward where the bulk of Weimer's company were lined along the hedgerow.

"Fuck me!" Weimer breathed when he saw the tanks.

"What's that, Corporal?" The gunner's voice came from within the turret.

Weimer didn't reply for a moment as he took in the size of the powerful looking French tanks. Even from this distance, it was obvious they were heavy tanks; very heavy tanks indeed. Eventually, he found his voice.

"They're fucking huge!" He called down.

Weimer ducked down inside the tank.

"They're heavy tanks!" He told the crew. "And I mean *very*, fucking heavy. Make sure you're bang on with your shooting or we're toast!"

As he was briefing the turret crew, he heard the first angry bark from over to the right, followed instantly by several more. Weimer put his head out of the cupola once more as the radio operator shouted up.

"Company Commander says open fire!"

"Got it." Weimer responded. "Stand by; they'll be appearing over our part of the ridge any moment. Make sure you're fucking quick with that traverse gear boys!"

Weimer had one eye on the slope to his front and one eye on the engagement that had begun over to the right. The entire company was blazing away from the ridge line now and it seemed that the French tanks had come to a halt, or at least slowed considerably. He watched in anticipation, expecting to see the flash of an exploding vehicle or thick black smoke pouring from a tank that had been mortally struck. For the moment however, there was lots of firing and not much in the way of burning tanks. He caught sight of something small and bright flash through the air, heading down-slope towards the leading French tank. His eye tracked the bright blur of the armour piercing round as it flashed towards the great metal beast and hit it square on... then bounced off.

"Bollocks..." Weimer murmured to himself, amazed that the shell had failed to do any damage to the enemy vehicle. He watched as the same enemy tank was hit by a second shell. This time there was an explosive flash and a small cloud of smoke, but despite that, the enemy vehicle didn't so much as shudder under the impact. Then, like a mighty beast stirring itself from slumber, the French tank opened fire with not just one gun, mounted in its turret, but another, larger gun, mounted in the hull. Then, belching a cloud of exhaust fumes, the lead enemy tank lurched forward again, heading straight for the ridgeline.

"Oh fuck..." Weimer exclaimed as a sinking feeling descended on his guts.

At that point, his contemplation of the strength of the enemy tanks was interrupted by the cry of alarm from his own turret crew.

"Enemy tank! Stand by!"

The corporal whipped his head back round to stare straight forwards across his own field of fire. His eyes widened as he saw the silhouette of the huge metal beast growing ever larger, directly to his front, as it crawled up the steep slope and came straight on towards the copse.

"Aim for its…" Weimer began to shout as he dropped down into the turret and pulled the hatch shut behind him, but before he could finish, his own vehicle rocked back on its suspension and above the thunderous roar of the 37mm gun, he heard his gunner screaming out the prescribed commands of the gunnery drill.

"Firing now!"

Whoomph.

"Reload…"

LEAD COMPANY, FRENCH 1ST ARMOURED DIVISION – NEAR FLAVION
WEDNESDAY 15TH MAY 1940 – 0910 HOURS

Clang!

"Stop!" Yelled Lieutenant Maurice Lubec, commander of the 3rd Platoon of the tank company. "We just got hit! Where did that come from?"

He desperately tried to search the ridge line through his periscope. The battle was joined over on his left; that much he knew. But where was *he* being engaged from? He had barely crested this, the steepest part of the ridge when the shell had hit them. He shouted down to the radio operator.

"Duvall, tell the rest of the platoon to stop level with us. There are enemy guns somewhere nearby."

The operator acknowledged and began relaying the message. Frantically, Lubec began traversing his turret, scanning the ridge line in an effort to find the enemy gun. As he did so, he saw that they were facing frontally towards a copse. At first there was nothing much to be seen, but then, from the left of the copse, a sudden flash caught his eye.

"Incom…" He began to shout, but his cry was then drowned out by the terrific crash as the enemy shell hit their tank and exploded.

The noise was terrific and even though Lubec instinctively opened his mouth to protect his ear drums, he cried out in protest at the deafening crash of the impact.

As the noise subsided, he shouted down to the crew.

"Everyone ok?"

The men chorused back up that they were fine except for ringing ears.

"I've spotted them, they're in the copse, slightly to the left!" Lubec warned them. "I'm going to engage. Duvall? Tell the platoon to come to our right and get behind that copse. The enemy guns are in there."

As the operator acknowledged and began passing the orders using Morse Code, Lubec focussed his eyes through the gun-sight. It was difficult, for the morning sun was right above the copse, but nevertheless, he managed to traverse the gun onto the rough spot where he had seen the muzzle flash.

"Come on…" He murmured as he pressed his eye to the rubber sight hood. "Where are you, you Boche scu…"

Lubec went silent and caught his breath. He saw movement, almost directly in front of his aiming mark. A large, dark silhouette within the copse's shady confines suddenly moved forwards with a jerk. Lubec saw the spout of exhaust fumes drift out of the tree line on the fresh morning air, a moment later, he spotted the snout of the high mounted gun.

"It's a tank!" Lubec shouted to nobody in particular, and quickly turned the fine deflection and elevation drums on his gun.

"Tanks everybody!" He was shouting excitedly. "More tanks! Just like the ones from earlier! Standby…"

The lieutenant locked his firing gears then placed a hand on the firing bar. His 47mm gun was already loaded with armour piercing ammunition.

"Firing now…"

Whoomph!

The heavy Char B1 tank rocked slightly as the gun launched its deadly missile towards the target in the wood. Lubec saw the cross hairs in the gun-sight rise and fall slightly, settling back onto the original target, and he knew his aim was good. It was a difficult job this, cramped in the confines of a tiny turret, having to command the vehicle, load, lay and operate the gun on his own, whilst also trying to control his platoon. Even that was a difficult process as his orders had to be sent by Morse Code through his operator. Other armoured divisions had taken on new radio sets that allowed the passage of verbal instructions, but his own division had retained the telegraphic sets, claiming that voice radio was useless due to the engine noise in the tanks. Lubec had never been convinced of that argument.

He had no time to worry on that particular matter as, just a split second after firing, he saw his shell hit the dark silhouette within the copse. The shell slammed into the target with a bright orange flash and even from a distance of some two hundred metres he heard the 'crump' of the impact. Then, a moment later, there was a bigger, larger explosion that blew bits of tree and undergrowth out into the field, along with what appeared to be bits of scrap metal. Almost immediately afterwards, a large cloud of black smoke billowed out of the clump of trees.

"Holy Mother!" Lubec whistled. "We got him. We blew him to bits."

There was a small cheer from below.

"Well done, Lieutenant." He heard the radio operator shouting.

"Let's go round the back of the copse and see if there are any more of them…" Lubec began, but just at that point, he was thrown against the side of his turret by a violent impact.

Clang-boom!

The noise of the shell strike was even worse than before and Lubec watched in fear as the side of his turret, low down by the turret ring, suddenly turned a bright orange-red colour. The acrid smell of burnt explosive came to his nostrils and for just a second, he had the awful feeling that the enemy shell was about to penetrate the turret and vaporise him in the blink of an eye. To his relief, the orange glow on the inside of the turret faded as the armour held. There was a pain in his right ear, and when Lubec went to lick his dry lips, he tasted something wet and metallic. He wiped his hand across his mouth and nose and it came away streaked with blood.

"Jesus…" He murmured, half relieved and half terrified.

His men were shouting urgently below him, but he couldn't make sense of it.

"What's that?" He yelled down at them. "I can't hear you?"

"There's another tank in the copse!" He heard the loader on the 75mm howitzer shout. "To the right of the one we just killed… He just fired at us. Can you see him, Lieutenant?"

Lubec's mind caught up again.

"Hold on, I'll traverse onto him."

The Lieutenant pulled on the breech handle and with a metallic clunk, the breech block slid open and spat the empty shell case half to the rear. He flipped it out and let it fall onto the turret's floor whilst at the same time, reaching for another shell. He slid the shell home into the gun's breech and pushed the bar. The breech block slid over and locked once more. Having reloaded, Lubec began to turn the traverse gear. Or at least he tried to turn it. The handle moved just a centimetre or two then jammed. Irritated, the tank commander reversed his movement a little then tried again. Once more the gear jammed. He gave a curse and tried reversing the turret anti-clockwise. It went a few centimetres then stopped dead. Lubec's heart sank.

"I can't traverse!" He cried out in alarm. "The turret's jammed! Prioux, use the howitzer!"

There was a sudden commotion down below as Prioux, the driver, who was also responsible for aiming the 75mm hull-mounted howitzer, went into frantic action. The vehicle rocked slightly as Prioux carried out a neutral turn to align the big gun roughly onto target. The vehicle settled as the driver used his fine adjustment gear.

"Come on, Prioux; quickly!" Lubec shouted down. "Before he gets another shot at us!"

Again, Lubec heard the driver shout something unintelligible.

Whoomph.

The howitzer roared, causing the tank to rock back on its suspension.

"Did you hit him, Prioux?" Lubec demanded almost as soon as the gun was fired. "Did you hit him?"

"Not sure, Sir." He heard the voice drift up. "Maybe? Hard to tell…"

"Go right, then." Lubec ordered. "Go forwards and right. Get us around the back of that copse. We're a sitting duck out here!"

The driver must have heard him for the tank lurched forwards almost instantly and began jerking its way off to one side. Lubec remembered the rest of his platoon suddenly and shouted down to Duvall.

"Tell the platoon to go to the right of the copse, then drive along the ridge line to the left. The enemy are all along the trees and hedges."

The lieutenant clung on as his tank manoeuvred its way across the ploughed field and towards the copse. He tried to use the periscopes to get an idea of what was happening outside. It was difficult, for the tank was moving and the world went by in a blur of jolting images. He saw trees, the copse, and a hedgerow, then just sky, then more trees. He saw a fleeting image of a field dotted with tanks. Flames from one of them; lots of smoke drifting across the landscape. If only he had a hatch in his turret, he could have opened up to get himself properly orientated. The sense of displacement was exacerbated by the fact that his turret was jammed at an angle from the frontal axis of his tank. Lubec suddenly realised how hot he was. His shirt was soaked with sweat beneath his tunic, and rivulets of moisture were running down his forehead into his eyes. He wiped the sweat away with his blood smeared hand, and took another look through the periscope.

Before he had placed his eyes to the viewer however, he was thrown backwards as the vehicle shuddered violently. He banged the back of his head off another periscope viewer and cursed foully. As he rubbed at his head and winced at the painful cut that was already sticky with blood, Lubec realised that the tank had stopped.

"What's going on?" He shouted. "Why have we stopped?"

A muffled reply from the driver.

"What?"

"He says we've been hit, Sir." Duvall called up. "Looks like the track on our left side has been taken off."

Again, Lubec uttered a profanity that would have shamed his mother.

Panting now, partly from the heat inside the tight confines of the turret, and partly from the adrenalin that coursed through his body, Lubec tried desperately to see what was happening outside the vehicle. He jammed his eye to a periscope and scanned desperately through the viewer. All he could see was trees and sky.

"Prioux, try again... Try and reverse..." He shouted down.

The vehicle juddered slightly a moment later and Lubec heard the engine rev. He heard the sound of a metallic grinding noise, and then the engine fell away as Prioux reduced the revs.

"It's not working, Sir. We're stuck where we are..."

Any further explanation was drowned out by the sudden impact of another shell, this time on the left hand side of the tank. Once more, Lubec was thrown violently against the side of the turret, but more worryingly, the vehicle began to fill with grey smoke. It was slight at first, like the hit they had received against the turret ring, but after a moment or two, instead of dissipating, the smoke began to thicken and turn oily black.

"We're on fire! We're on fire!" Duvall's sudden cry of alarm hit Lubec like a slap in the face.

"Oh, my good God!" He whispered in a voice filled with dread.

The tank was filling with smoke rapidly and now the entire crew were screaming in alarm. Lubec heard Duvall scrambling down the tunnel for the hatch in the hull.

"We're on fire! Bale out! Bale out!"

VANGUARD 5TH PANZER DIVISION – THE COPSE BY FLAVION
WEDNESDAY 15TH MAY 1940 – 0910 HOURS

"Reload! Quickly!" Weimer was screaming at his gun crew.

"I don't fucking believe it." The gunner was cursing as he went through the drill. "Both shells just fucking bounced off it!"

Weimer realised that they were in a tight spot. Their first shell had hit the enemy tank square on the front of its hull and ricocheted off without even exploding. The shell fired by Sergeant Holbier's tank to their right had hit the side of the enemy vehicle, making a bright flash and a 'crump', but otherwise having no apparent effect.

Now, Weimer's mind was racing as he desperately tried to think of a way of defeating the steel giant that was sitting menacingly to his front, barely two hundred yards away. Even worse, he could see more tanks coming forwards to support it.

"Fuck me, we're dead men..." He whispered to himself, one eye on his gun crew and one eye looking through the periscope.

As he watched, he saw the small turret on the enemy vehicle traverse away from their position. The turret moved back and forth a couple of times, as if searching for them. Only then did Weimer realise that the enemy couldn't see them under the shadow of the trees. Of course! The sun was behind them in the east. The shadows were in their favour.

"Reloaded!" The gunner called out.

As Weimer's own gunner announced his readiness to fire, the enemy vehicle spotted Holbier's tank. Weimer saw the slim gun in the small turret of the French tank spit out a small dart of light. Even before Weimer was able to get his eyes to the next periscope along, he heard the shell hit Holbier's tank. It was a loud, sharp 'crump', followed almost instantly by a much louder, more violent explosion.

"Shit!" Weimer cursed as his own vehicle was battered by debris.

A small tree toppled across the front deck of Weimer's tank and unseen objects clanged off the side of the turret.

Weimer finally got his eyes to the periscope and gawped through the viewer at the awful sight. Perhaps his theory about the enemy being blinded was incorrect then?

Over to the right, just fifteen metres away, sat the ruins of Holbier's tank. The Panzer was engulfed in flames and smoke, but it was clear from the unnatural angle of the displaced turret and gun, that the vehicle had been blown apart by a secondary explosion.

"Fuck me!" Weimer gasped.

He turned to his gunner.

"Aim for the turret! Not the hull; the turret. Where it joins the hull... Quickly!"

He leaned down and shouted through to the forward compartment.

"Driver; be prepared to reverse out of here at speed if I give the word!"

"On!"

The gunner's call brought Weimer back upright. He jammed his eyes to the front periscope.

"Go on!" He snapped.

"Firing now!"

The vehicle lurched as the gun roared, spitting its 37mm armour piercing shell at the French tank. Weimer sat glued to his viewer, desperate to see the result and preparing for a hasty retreat.

"Target!" He cried out automatically as the shell slammed straight into the turret of the enemy tank, just where he'd ordered the gunner to aim for.

"Reload!" The crew went into their usual drill.

Weimer kept his eyes fixed on the enemy vehicle. The turret didn't move. A small cloud of grey smoke hung around the base of the turret where the shell had struck it.

"Loaded!" The gunner called, then, in a quieter voice. "Is it dead?"

Weimer frowned into his periscope.

"Not sure…" He began.

Just then, a bright flash from low on the front of the tank's hull made the corporal duck instinctively.

"No…" He managed to shout, just before the large explosion rocked their Panzer.

"Fuck me! That was a big one! Are we hit?"

The gunner was looking worriedly round the turret of the vehicle as the tremor of the huge explosion subsided.

Weimer looked at the man with wide eyes.

"No. Don't think so. Bloody near miss though! The bastard's got a secondary gun in his hull. Aim low and take it out."

The gunner nodded and pressed his eyes to the gun-sight.

"He's moving!"

Weimer looked back through the periscope. Sure enough, the French tank was now trundling forwards and wheeling to its right, Weimer's left. The small turret on the enemy vehicle was still offset to one side.

"They're trying to get round our flank!" Weimer realised out loud. "Engage him side on…"

The gunner quickly released the traverse locking lever and began rotating the turret, tracking the enemy vehicle. He brought the gun onto line using the predictive aiming mark and locked off the gears.

"Stand by…" He murmured as he waited for the tank to cut the predictive aiming point.

"Firing now!"

Whoomph.

The shot was even better than Weimer could have hoped for. It hit the vehicle square on, but missed the turret and caught the top of the hull. As the flash and the smoke subsided, the corporal saw the French tank slow to a halt, it tracks flailing wildly.

"You've crippled him!" Weimer shouted excitedly. "Reload and fire again!"

Beside him, the gunner and loader worked quietly and efficiently at the gun.

"There's some kind of grill on the side of the hull, look. You can't miss it. Try and put one right through it."

Within seconds, the gunner was locked on and once more, the 37mm gun lurched as it spat another deadly shell at the French armoured leviathan.

"Target!" Weimer yelled as he saw the shell slam home exactly where he wanted it. "Well done that man!" He reached out and slapped the gunner on the shoulder.

Moments later, Weimer was shrieking with delight.

"You did it! He's on fire!"

The gunner simply grinned and shrugged.

"French fuckers." He murmured nonchalantly.

"Get on the radio." Weimer shouted to the operator. "Pass the word to engage the enemy from their left hand side and aim for the big square filters on the hulls."

"I'm on it…" The radio operator instantly began relaying the advice.

"Driver; stand-by to go straight back. I can see more tanks cutting across our front. I think they're trying to outflank us…"

Weimer studied the scene through his periscope a moment longer. The French tank was burning fiercely now, obscuring the view somewhat, but Weimer was sure that the enemy was trying to filter around his flank.

"Ok driver, let's go. Straight back until we're out of the copse; then we'll go left and try to catch them in the flank before they do the same to us. Reverse."

The Panzer's engines gave a throaty roar, and then it gave a jolt as it lurched backwards through the copse. Moments later, Weimer felt the vehicle begin to reverse up the slight slope of the depression. He turned around to look through the rear periscope and as he got his eyes to the viewer, suddenly called out a warning.

"Stop!"

Too late. With a crash, the Panzer smashed straight into the French tank that was sitting side onto them at the rear of the copse, throwing the turret crew around like a trio of rag dolls.

"What the fuck was that!" The driver bawled in a shocked voice.

"Enemy tank!" Weimer screamed. "Right behind us! We just drove into it!"

"Shit." The gunner commented in his understated fashion.

"Forwards!" Weimer yelled down to the driver. "Quickly, before he swings his gun onto us! Straight forwards!"

"Then what?" The driver yelled back as he threw the vehicle into forward motion again.

"Straight through the front of the copse, out onto the field." Weimer ordered.

Next to him, the gunner gave the corporal a sidelong glance.

"Out there? Into the open?"

Weimer gave the gunner a demented grin.

"You once told me you wanted to go out in a blaze of glory? Die like a hero?"

The gunner pulled a face.

"I do… just not today."

HEADQUARTERS GERMAN 19TH CORPS – 6 MILES WEST OF SEDAN
WEDNESDAY 15TH MAY 1940 – 2300 HOURS

Guderian nodded at his staff officers and they saluted together, before turning on their heels and heading off to relay their corps commander's orders to the various formations in the field. As they dispersed, the general stretched out his legs and sat back in the camp chair, removing his cap and rubbing the bridge of his nose between thumb and forefinger. He was tired, but pleased. It had been another very long day, yet a satisfactory one. The French had, as expected, attempted several counter attacks, and the fighting around the village of Stonne had been particularly intense. The Gross Deutschland Regiment had been hard at it for forty eight hours, and when Guderian had visited them earlier that afternoon, he had seen for himself how desperate the struggle was on that particular sector of the front.

He had been present in the village when a French attack had come in and he had been unable to talk to the commander of the regiment, as every available man was in the frontline, getting to grips with the enemy. There had been a real air of desperation in Stonne for a short while, but eventually, the Gross Deutschland had prevailed, and the position was held. And it was essential that the southern flank *was* held, Guderian reflected, for it was his intention to make a start on his drive westwards the next day, slicing deep into the enemy's rear. For the time being, that drive would have to be conducted by just the 1st and 2nd Panzer Divisions on their own, whilst 10th Panzer and Gross Deutschland held that southern blocking position along the Ardennes Canal.

Not for long though. He had spent much of the day with von Wietersheim, making arrangements for his troops to be relieved in place by the follow-up echelons. Even now, the lead elements of a motorised infantry division, the 29th, were filtering into the bridgehead to begin that process. Another twenty four hours or so, and he would have his full strength available once more. Then, Guderian reflected, the *real* drive west could begin. He smiled in anticipation of the next day's events. It would see another leap forward; not too big, but enough to lay the foundations for the day after. The decisive moment was coming; he could feel it.

Guderian's musings were interrupted by the arrival of Colonel Nehring, who approached him in an urgent manner, a piece of paper clamped firmly in his hand. Guderian could see, even by the dim light of the hooded lanterns that hung in the command tent, that Nehring's expression was one of consternation. Guderian sat up, sensing a problem.

"Walther?" He raised a questioning eyebrow as the chief of staff halted in front of him. "You don't look happy?"

The colonel offered the sheet of paper to his commander.

"I don't think you'll be happy with this either, Sir…"

Perplexed, Guderian took the paper and held it up to the light. He studied the message carefully, and as he did so, his mouth dropped open in surprise.

"What?" He murmured. "They want us to…"

Guderian stood suddenly, his face like thunder.

"They want us to stop?" He almost shrieked the question. "Are they mad?"

He looked at the despatch again, running his eyes over the text, hoping to find that he had misread it. He hadn't.

"Stop? Now?" He gawped at Nehring incredulously. "After achieving such a magnificent victory, they will have us throw it all away while we wait for the infantry to catch up?"

Nehring grimaced.

"I know, General. It's madness."

"Madness it is!" Guderian ranted. "Absolute madness of the highest order! I will not have it! I will not waste the sacrifice of our troops by allowing the enemy to regain the advantage!"

Guderian's eyebrows knotted for a moment or two as he studied the note once more. After a couple of seconds, he looked back up at Nehring, his face set hard.

"Walther, get the Panzer Group Headquarters on the line for me please…*immediately.*"

Thursday 16th May 1940
The Seventh Day

2ND BATTALION COLDSTREAM GUARDS – THE RIVER DYLE, BELGIUM
THURSDAY 16TH MAY 1940 – 1430 HOURS

"With the greatest of respect, Sir, are you having a laugh, or what?" Jackson stared up from the trench in astonishment.

The young second lieutenant grinned sheepishly and shook his head.

"No, I'm afraid not, Sergeant J; wish I was. We've got to start pulling pack at 2200 hours."

Jackson was incredulous.

"But we've only been here a couple of days, Sir! And the Jerries haven't managed to get anywhere yet. We can stand here and hold 'em off till hell freezes over at this rate. Why on earth have we got to pull back?"

Dunstable settled himself into the prone position on the edge of the trench, resting on one elbow so that he was at the same level as his platoon sergeant.

"I'm afraid it doesn't seem to make sense to us at all, does it? But the fact is the decision has been made because of what's happening elsewhere; not because of how things are going on our stretch of the front."

Jackson wrinkled his brow suspiciously.

"How do you mean, Sir?"

Dunstable removed his helmet and ran his hand through his thick, golden-blonde hair.

"It's the French, I'm led to believe."

"The French?" Jackson's tone suddenly hardened.

Dunstable gave a sigh.

"Yes. It seems that the Jerries have broken through the French, way off to our south, somewhere towards Sedan on the River Meuse."

Jackson knew little about the geography of France but he understood roughly where he was in relationship to the French in the south. He frowned as he tried to picture a basic map of France in his mind.

"There's all manner of rumours, but the reality is that the French have been pushed back, so it's important that the whole frontline is straightened out, in order to stop the Germans from breaking through and outflanking us.

The second lieutenant noted the look of concentration on Jackson's face and quickly delved into his pocket.

"Here, look at it on the map."

The officer produced a pocket sized road map of France. It was quite small scale, but enough to show what he wanted.

"Don't let on to anyone else that I've got this by the way…" Dunstable lowered his voice and grinned at Jackson. "Maps are in short supply and somebody will want it off me. It's my own map from home. I came on a driving holiday to Europe with my father just before the war."

Jackson simply grunted and peered at the pages, covered as they were in coloured lines and symbols.

Quickly, using a blade of grass as a pointer, Dunstable explained the strategic situation as he understood it to Jackson once more. The sergeant, seeing the explanation superimposed on the map, quickly saw the logic of it. He was no general, but even Jackson could see that if the Germans had managed to push forward to the south, then the whole of the Allied line was under threat. He summed up his feelings about the nature of the situation in two words.

"Useless sods." He quipped.

Dunstable smiled at that. Life was simple in Jackson's world. You did as you were told and you did it well. If you stuck to that, then you were alright. If you did it wrong and failed in your task, you were a 'shit fucker'; simple as that.

Somewhere, far off to their north, the sound of artillery and distant small arms fire could be heard. At the moment however, everything remained quiet in front of the 2nd Battalion Coldstream Guards. Jackson took a deep breath.

"Suppose there's no option then, eh, Sir? Tell you what though; I'm fed up with all this marching, digging, marching and then more bloody digging. I just want to get my hands on some Jerries and teach 'em a lesson. Give 'em a good hiding and pay 'em back for what they did to the Q Bloke."

To the north, the sound of the distant gunfire increased in tempo. Dunstable glanced briefly in that direction. Somebody was having a hot time of it. He looked back at Jackson.

"Yes, well, I'm sure we'll get our chance soon enough."

FRENCH MINISTRY OF FOREIGN AFFAIRS – PARIS
THURSDAY 16TH MAY 1940 – 1730 HOURS

They were all there; the big three. Reynaud, the President, stood looking around at the other men in the room, his face lined with worry. Daladier, the Prime Minister, was in much the same state. Gamelin, the French Commander in Chief, stood between them, looking completely and utterly deflated, as if he had lost the will to live. At the other side of the room, General Sir John Dill, the quiet, calculating Vice Chief of the Imperial General Staff, accompanied by General Ismay, stood watching the three Frenchmen; just as Churchill was watching them.

Churchill was also on his feet, striding up and down the room, subjecting those in attendance at this emergency meeting to a relentless barrage of his gruff, accented French.

"I hear your request for more fighters, General." Churchill growled towards Gamelin. "And I will speak with the marshal who commands our fighter squadrons. I have in fact, already held preliminary discussions with him. He tells me that he needs at least twenty five squadrons retained in England for the defence of our factories and ports. Therefore I would tentatively suggest that we might be able to stretch to a further reinforcement of ten squadrons of Hurricane fighters…"

Churchill stopped pacing for a moment and threw a look at the three Frenchmen.

"That is not a promise, gentlemen, but I shall do my very best."

He began pacing again, taking a puff on his cigar. The meeting had begun badly. The French President and his Prime Minister were rattled. As soon as General Gamelin had started speaking, Churchill could see why. The man was as good as beaten. That surprised him, for his experience of the French from the last war was that they were determined, aggressive people, with the ability for both tenacious defence and spirited attack. He saw little of either in Gamelin at the moment. Churchill turned at the end of his small beat on the carpet and paused again, looking straight at Gamelin.

"We must not lose sight of the vital point though, General. Although the air battle is important, it is the troops on the ground that will bring victory. It is they who must fight the decisive battle. It is the mighty French Army, with its long and illustrious history, that must bring the invader to a halt and give him a mauling that he will never forget…"

Gamelin looked up at Churchill through tired, sunken eyes.

"We are trying…" He said weakly. "But the Boche have crossed the Meuse in strength. They have hundreds of tanks. It is so… difficult…" He trailed off.

Churchill eyed him for a moment, then turned toward the nearby window and walked across to it. As he went, the British Prime Minister continued to speak.

"We must consolidate, General." Churchill said, reaching the window and turning back to face the men at the table. "We must create a solid front on both flanks of this German…" He paused, trying to find the right word in French. He gestured at the map with its curious depiction of the front-line. "…This German *bulge.*"

He fixed Gamelin with a stern look and then went on.

"Then you must take your strategic reserve and strike hard and fast. You must take it and cut the head off this German serpent!"

Churchill was deliberately using his most animated form of address, in order to try and put some fire in the belly of the French leadership. Gamelin however, remained downcast and could not hold Churchill's gaze. The General had a hunted look about him and looked sheepishly from the President to the Prime Minister, and finally down at the floor.

Sir John Dill threw a look at Churchill that showed how unimpressed he was with the French attitude. Sighing deeply, Churchill turned his head away and looked out of the window. He frowned. Down on the grass lawn outside the building, large numbers of officials were stacking up piles of paper and cardboard files in half a dozen separate little bonfires. Two of those little heaps of paper were already alight and more harassed looking civil servants were carrying yet more bundles to add to the blaze.

Churchill suddenly turned back to face the other men and fixed Gamelin with another hard stare.

"General Gamelin," he rumbled, "where currently, is your strategic reserve?"

The French General almost jumped with alarm at the sudden question. He shot another hopeless glance at his President then looked back up at Churchill. With a sigh of resignation, he shrugged his shoulders.

"There isn't one."

For the first time in his life, Churchill was utterly speechless.

VANGUARD 7TH PANZER DIVISION – 5 MILES INSIDE FRANCE
THURSDAY 16TH MAY 1940 – 2140 HOURS

Rommel was on top of the world. It might be dark, and it had certainly been an exhausting day, but the commander of 7th Panzer Division was in no mood for rest. Just hours earlier, his leading panzer battalion, supported by assault pioneers and a half battalion of panzer grenadiers, had punched its way through the French frontier defences, having raced across Belgium after leaving 5th Panzer Division to finish off the enemy armour around Flavion. The enemy had been taken completely by surprise at the lightning fast strike. Rommel had been there with his vanguard, urging the commanders on; telling them not to look over their shoulders but to just drive straight on for Landrecies.

The much vaunted Maginot Line, Rommel reflected, hadn't been anywhere near as formidable as he had anticipated. To be honest, Rommel suspected that the legendary defence line wasn't even fully complete. Whatever; he was through it, and now racing headlong into the heart of France, brushing all resistance aside; and the general was in his element. He felt the same exhilarating sense of achievement now, as he had done whilst commanding a battalion in the First War. Only now, that exhilaration was at a pitch that was hard to control. Rommel could scent victory. It was his for the taking. Now was the time for the glorious breakthrough that had been denied them back in 1914.

He mused for a moment on the scenes of the early evening as his tanks, his own included, had rumbled inexorably up the highway after the breakthrough, firing their guns on the move; raking hedgerows and houses with machine-gun fire and putting the odd high explosive shell into copses and tree lines. It had created sheer panic amongst the terrified Frenchmen, both soldier and civilian. The enemy had helplessly watched them drive by, throwing their weapons down in despair, defeat stamped firmly across their faces. Victory felt good to Rommel. It felt very good.

Now though, it was time for another push. Never mind the darkness; night would be their ally. By daybreak he wanted to be at Landrecies, but first he needed to clear out the village of Avesnes, just a few miles up the road. He glanced at his watch. Five more minutes and they would move out. He had reluctantly allowed his vanguard thirty minutes to reorganise and restock the ready-to-use racks in the panzers; allow his grenadiers time to refill ammunition belts and refuel vehicles from the spare fuel cans.

"General?"

The radio operator's voice made Rommel jump.

"A message from Divisional Headquarters, Sir."

"What is it?"

"They say that an order has arrived from Corps Headquarters. We have been ordered to halt. We are not to attack Avesnes before 0700 hours tomorrow morning. The Corps is closing up behind us in order to secure our flanks, therefore we are not to advance before the time stated."

Rommel almost swore out loud, such was his shock. His mouth dropped open and he felt, for just a moment, a stinging touch of disappointment. He was glad it was dark and that the crew of his borrowed tank couldn't see the shock that was evident on his face. Stop? Now? When ultimate victory was within his grasp?

Just as quickly, Rommel gathered himself. He set his jaw once more and his quick mind made the decision that he knew to be the right one. He leaned down into the turret and spoke to the radio operator.

"Have you acknowledged that radio message yet?"

"Not yet, Sir."

"Good. Tell Divisional Headquarters that they are breaking up and that you did not get their last message. Ask them to send it again. Have you got that?"

"…Yes, Sir." Came the radio operator's hesitant reply.

"Then," Rommel continued, "when they repeat the message, tell them they are unworkable. Then do not acknowledge any more messages from anybody until I tell you to do so. Understand?"

There was a long pause.

"Understand?" Rommel snapped again.

"Yes, General."

Rommel smiled in the darkness.

"Good. Once you've done that, get on the battalion radio net and tell the vanguard that we're going to move off again in two minutes."

1ST BATTALION COLDSTREAM GUARDS – HERENT, NEAR LOUVAIN ON THE RIVER DYLE
THURSDAY 16TH MAY 1940 – 2210 HOURS

Much like Sergeant Jackson and the other members of their sister battalion, the 2nd, who were somewhere to the south on the Dyle defensive line, the men of 1st Battalion Coldstream Guards had been pretty fed up at the prospect of having to withdraw when the news first broke. Now however, they couldn't wait to get moving. As the extreme left battalion of the British Expeditionary Force, they had been put in a very tight spot when, early that afternoon, the Belgian Army to their left had suddenly disappeared. It transpired that the Belgians had received orders that required them to withdraw at midday, instead of the 2200 hours 'no move before time' that all other Allied units were working on.

Regardless of how the confusion had arisen, the result had been predictable. The Germans had, with aggressive confidence, followed up the Belgian withdrawal immediately and fallen onto the open Coldstream flank. The afternoon had turned into a desperate struggle as the reserve companies had been forced to establish a hard-shoulder on the rear left of the battalion's position, whilst a machine-gun battalion from the Middlesex Regiment had been hastily re-positioned to give the Coldstreamers even more depth to this particular flank. The full weight of the divisional artillery too, had been thrown into the contest to try and hold back the German infiltration. It had worked; just. Even so, the remainder of the daylight hours had proved very uncomfortable for the guardsmen, now fighting on two sides; both front and flank.

Movement around the position had become almost impossible, with streams of deadly machine-gun fire zipping through the air above the open, water meadows on the banks of the River Dyle. Guardsman Ted Davis of No.1 Company, now squatting in the dark by a low hedge, was feeling particularly glad that at last it was their time to pull back. As the Company Sergeant Major's runner, he had been sent out on numerous occasions that afternoon to carry out a variety of tasks, and consequently, he had felt as though every soldier in the German Army was out to get *him*, personally. Lines of tracer had chased him constantly, as he scurried from trench to trench, from platoon to platoon, to battalion headquarters and back. He might have protested at the danger had it not been for the fact that he was working under the personal direction of Company Sergeant Major Gallows, or, as the guardsmen had predictably nicknamed him, *'The Hangman'*.

At six feet and eight inches, huge even for a guardsman, The Hangman was an old, weather-beaten, foul-mouthed warrant officer of the kind that everyone dreaded. Generally a quiet man, when he did speak, The Hangman's voice was like acid; his sharp East London accent laced with venom and profanities. Built like a gorilla, with arms that resembled steam-driven industrial hammers, the warrant officer had become something of a living legend within the battalion. It was often told that he had once been jumped by a dozen market boys one night in Caterham, whilst out drinking. When the police had arrived at the pub where the altercation occurred, it had merely been a case of carrying out the casualties for the waiting ambulances. The Hangman had been sent quietly on his way by an uncomfortable looking Bobby who had readily accepted his explanation of 'self-defence'.

So, regardless of the threat from the Germans, Davis was not about to question anything he was told to do by his immediate superior. Besides, it had its advantages being The Hangman's runner. He looked after Davis; made sure he wasn't taken for too many casual fatigues, and never for guards. Apart from that, Davis reckoned, as long as he stuck close to The Hangman then there was no way any Jerry would get too close to *him*.

The sound of Gallows' harsh voice, albeit subdued, brought Davis from his reverie.

"'Undred and ten, 'undred and eleven. That's it."

Davis looked up at the silhouette of the huge warrant officer, as he counted each member of the company through the checkpoint. He saw the dark figure turn and look round at him through the darkness.

"What do you make it, Davis lad?"

"Hundred and eleven too, Sir."

"'Undred and thirteen with us two, then. Less the casualties from earlier, that means we've got everyone."

The Hangman's voice was heavy with concentration. For all his physical talents, arithmetic was not one of his strongest subjects. Having convinced himself of the maths, the warrant officer growled down at Davis.

"Come on then, conker-bollocks, let's get after 'em."

Davis stood, hefting his rifle, his thighs protesting at the stretch after so long in the squatting position, and set off after the last man of No.3 Platoon. Behind him, he heard the heavy footfalls as the Company Sergeant Major followed on behind.

It was far from quiet. There was artillery fire all along the line of the River Dyle to the south and, over to the north, the divisional artillery was still going at it hammer and tong. Every now and then, enemy shells would come whooshing overhead and fall uncomfortably close. Davis would be very glad indeed to get out of here. He didn't like the idea of having Jerries sitting on their flank one little bit.

They were moving quickly, heading for the company rendezvous, hoping to break clean from their position before the Germans got wind of what they were up to. Davis kept his eyes fixed on the dark outline of the man in front, keeping just a few yards back from him. They were out of the fields now and onto a dirt track that ran alongside an orchard or copse or such like, and the column seemed to be moving even faster. Terrified that he would lose sight of the man in front, Davis jogged several steps to close up the distance a little.

"Stop fucking running."

He heard Gallows comment from behind.

The pace remained brisk, until suddenly Davis found himself staring at a small-pack from very close range.

"Umph!"

Davis walked straight into the back of the man to his front before he realised he had even stopped. The individual turned and whispered something.

"Open your fucking eyes, lad! Watch where you're going!"

Davis recognised the sound of Sergeant Jessop's voice immediately.

He saw everybody kneel down to his front and followed suit. As he did so, Gallows came past him.

"Stay here, Davis." He ordered, and strode off up the line of guardsmen, towards the head of the column.

Davis heard the occasional 'clunk' of a helmet being tapped with a rifle butt as the Company Sergeant Major passed up the line and found fault with various individuals, rapping their helmets and delivering a sharp, succinct instruction. After a while, the young runner heard whispering; a message being passed down the line. Eventually, Sergeant Jessop turned to him and repeated the message.

"This is the Company RV. We're moving off to the Battalion Checkpoint in a couple of minutes."

Barely had the words been uttered, when the sound of scuffing and shuffling told Davis that the company was already on the move again. Once more he stood and followed on after the man in front. He had gone perhaps a hundred yards when he passed the unmistakable figure of Gallows, looming out of the darkness by the side of a low cottage.

"That you, Davis, you Geordie maggot?" The warrant officer's voice sounded laconically from the shadows.

"Aye, Sir."

"Good. We're moving up to the Battalion Checkpoint now. About another mile they reckon, just on the outskirts of the town.

Davis acknowledged and kept moving as Gallows fell in behind him.

They continued to march at a fast pace, the sound of their studded boots ringing on cobbles now as the column turned onto a metalled road. Up ahead, some way off, Davis could see buildings; a small town or village of some kind. Judging by the brightness of the sky directly above it, he assumed that something was on fire. Off to his right, away to the north, artillery shells continued to explode and the sound of the occasional machine-gun punctuated the dull, continuous cacophony. Perhaps he was just nervous, but it sounded to Davis as if the barrage was increasing in its tempo perhaps?

They were very close to the built-up area now, and the flames from a burning building were bathing the column of guardsmen in a sickly yellow half-light. The pace was relentless and Davis was sweating profusely under his battledress. Even though he was wearing only fighting order with small-pack, he was also carrying some of the company's reserve ammunition; namely six canvas bandoliers of .303 inch ammunition and six 2 inch mortar bombs. He couldn't really complain; The Hangman was carrying twice that amount.

Suddenly, the air above them came alive with a deep sigh that turned into an ominous 'whoosh'.

Crump, crump, crump!

The salvo of artillery shells slammed into the village in front of them, and the impact caused a tremor to run through the ground beneath Davis' feet.

"Christ! They're a bit close." He murmured.

"Right in the village too." Gallows' voice came from behind. "We've got to go through there."

"Through *there*, Sir?" Davis asked worriedly.

"Yeah," Gallows replied, "the Battalion Checkpoint's at this side of it and the RV is at the other side. We're meant to be getting picked up by lorry once we get there."

The sound of more shells passed overhead and then an even bigger series of explosions rocked the village. Silently, Davis said a quick prayer. As he moved his lips soundlessly and focussed on keeping his station on the man in front, the sound of machine-gun fire suddenly cut in on the chaos of noise around him. Not the distant, sporadic machine-gun fire that he had become used to, but a sudden, urgent, and very nearby eruption of small arms fire. Davis glanced up towards the buildings which were looming closer now, and saw lines of tracer arcing through the sky in several directions. He could also hear the bark of individual rifles being fired. Well off to the north edge of the village, a green flare sailed lazily into the night sky and then, reaching its zenith, suddenly plunged down towards a burning building.

That was when the shouting started. Distant shouting, accompanied by the frenzied shrill of whistles. The column suddenly halted again and there was urgent shouting somewhere up at the front of the line. In front of him, Davis saw men dropping down into the cover of the grass verge to the left of the road.

"Stay here, Davis." He heard Gallows bark again.

The Company Sergeant Major went up the column once more, this time at a steady trot, his Lee-Enfield rifle at the short trail. Davis realised that his heart was beating like a bass drum during a warm-up on the drill square, and it was nothing to do with the speed march they had just conducted. He had a sinking feeling that something wasn't quite right. For what seemed like hours, he sat there in the long grass of the verge, staring towards the burning village and watching the display of tracer, desperately trying to make sense of the deadly symphony of battle that was being played out just across the fields in the built-up area.

Eventually, the hulking figure of The Hangman came loping back down the line. Davis heard his voice calling out the orders as he approached, the warrant officer's voice now filled with the loud, decisive snap of authority that he usually reserved for the parade square.

"On your feet Number One Company! One your feet!"

Davis scrambled into a standing position as Gallows slowed to a walk and began stalking up and down the centre of the company column, calling out a string of instructions, his voice deep and clear above the noise of battle.

"Alright, listen in. The Jerries have got round the battalion's flank and they've got into the village up in front. At the moment, they're blocking our withdrawal route. Battalion Headquarters and Number Four Company are just about holding them but the Commanding Officer wants us to go and turf the sausage-munching fuckers out of the place!"

The big company sergeant major paused for just a second whilst his words sank in.

"The Company Commander is going to lead us off to the forming up point in a minute or two. One Platoon is to shake out as left assault, Two Platoon right assault; both in extended line. Three Platoon in staggered file behind the Company Commander as reserve. Any questions?"

There were none. Davis felt his stomach sink. He suddenly needed a piss.

The voice of Company Sergeant Major Gallows cut through the night once more.

"Number One Company will fix bayonets..." He roared as if on Horse Guards Parade in London.

"Oh, shit..." Davis murmured as he fumbled for the hilt of his own bayonet.

"Fix..." Hollered Gallows.

Davis drew his bayonet almost fully out, automatically leaving the tip of the blade hovering by the scabbard's lip, as if he were executing the movement on a Queen's Guard Mount.

"Bayonets!" Gallows thundered.

"Oh, shit…" Davis muttered again.

With an ominous, metallic rattle, a hundred bayonets glittered in the night…

12TH TRANSPORT REGIMENT – SOMEWHERE IN HERENT THURSDAY 16TH MAY 1940 – 2215 HOURS

"This has got to be Herent." Sergeant Danby stated, scratching his chin thoughtfully and looking about him at the blazing buildings with concern. "We can't have gone that far off course, and we're obviously pretty close to the front line."

He continued to look about him, doing a bad job of masking his concern. The three other men could sense his uncertainty.

Their four vehicles had been separated from the remainder of their transport company just thirty minutes earlier, during the final stages of their move to a rendezvous with one of the battalions from 7th Guards Brigade, who they were due to lift and transport back to the Divisional RV. They had lost sight of the trucks in front for just a few moments, but it was enough to split the column. Moxon, driving the truck that had lost sight of the one in front, had taken a guess at which junction to take when he had come around a bend and found himself confronted with a Y-junction, and after a while, it had become clear that he had made the wrong choice. Moxon had been forced to stop and tell Danby the bad news and, after delivering a profanity-strewn reprimand, the sergeant had taken over the lead. Assuming that the distant, burning village was probably somewhere near their final destination, Danby had led the four lorries through narrow back roads until they had nosed their way, cautiously, in amongst the deserted, burning buildings.

They had come to a halt in what looked like some kind of village green or square. There was little sign of life, and many buildings that bordered the square, including the church, were burning furiously. The heat was intense and the flames lit up the village like a scene from hell.

"Should we take a look around and see if we can find anyone?" Moxon suggested, feeling slightly guilty that it was his fault they had become separated from the rest of the convoy in the first place and keen to make amends.

"Not sure that's a good idea really…" Private Fellows commented next to him.

"Looks like whoever was here is already gone…" Corporal Barnes added.

Danby looked grim.

"We're supposed to be picking up the Coldstream Guards. We probably *should* have a quick check round, just in case. There are definitely still troops in the area because you can hear the…"

His words were cut short by the strange sound of something hurtling past above their heads. All four men glanced up at the sound, which was similar to that made by an express train passing through a station at high speed, displacing the air as it went.

Whoosh – crump!

"Bloody hell!"

The soldiers gave a collective cry of alarm as a shell slammed into a terrace of houses at the far side of the square and exploded with a sharp bang. The blast was enough to make them all stagger, Fellows stumbling backwards and falling over onto his backside.

Whoosh – crump! Whoosh – crump!

Two more shells slammed into buildings on the same side of the square as the first one, sending bits of glass, brick and other detritus flying through the air. Moxon and Barnes threw themselves down beside Fellows and the three men pushed their faces into the cobbles, covering their heads with their arms.

As the echo and shockwave of the blast subsided, the three men lifted their heads together, hesitantly.

"Not been funny, Sarge," Barnes began in a shaky voice, "but I reckon we need to get the fuck of here sharpish; it's not a healthy place to be."

There was no reply, and the three men realised that Danby wasn't on the floor beside them. They rolled onto their sides and looked behind, to find Danby standing over them. They fully expected him to shout some kind of obscenity at them for being so cowardly under the shell fire, but instead, the burly sergeant simply stared down at them, wordlessly. Then, for no apparent reason, the sergeant's mouth sagged open. As his eyes rolled back in their sockets, a wave of thick, dark blood, poured out of his open mouth and down the front of his battledress. Then he fell.

He toppled straight forwards, collapsing onto Barnes' legs, his blood splattering the brown serge of the corporal's trousers. The three drivers looked on horrified at the huge, messy, bloody hole in Danby's back. Barnes, suddenly aware of the sergeant's blood soaking his legs, gave a terrified cry.

"Ah!"

The red-headed corporal shuffled backwards on his hands, desperately kicking his legs free of the cadaver, his eyes bulging with shock.

"Jesus Christ!" Barnes swore. "I'm not staying here!"

And with that, the corporal rose to his feet and ran for his vehicle.

Fellows stared at the sergeant's dead body, then at the figure of Barnes, struggling to get into his cab, then to his pal, Moxon. Moxon, to his own surprise, gently rolled Danby's body over and stared down at the man's dead features.

"Bloody hell!" He breathed. "We can't just leave him here…"

He looked towards Barnes who was in the process of starting his vehicle.

"Rusty! Rusty! Hold up, mate! We've got to take him with us!"

Barnes wasn't listening. The engine of his truck revved and a moment later, it began to trundle backwards as the terrified corporal prepared to pull away from behind Fellows' truck.

"Rusty!" Moxon shouted again, standing up and waving at the corporal.

Then he heard it.

"Down!" Moxon shouted, almost to himself, as the whine of the incoming shell pierced the night air once more.

He threw himself flat on the cobbles again as another series of deafening explosions rocked the square, this time falling much closer than the previous salvo. Moxon heard Fellows cry out in terror as the ground lurched beneath them. He heard the shattering of glass, the rending of metal, and the patter of debris hitting the floor. He felt an intense wave of heat across one side of his body, and felt himself being lifted up into the air as if the ground beneath him were alive. Then, with a sense of disorientation that left him feeling sick, he was dumped back down onto the ground again, a strange, continuous, high-pitched whine sounding in his ears.

It was several moments before he could muster both the strength and courage to lift his head. He gawped up stupidly through a haze of smoke. An odour came to him that was oily and unpleasant. As he blinked the dust from his eyes, his mind suddenly registered the scene of devastation around him. Of Barnes' truck, there was little left bar twisted metal and burning canvas. A wheel lay nearby, the rubber tyre burning angrily and pouring out thick black smoke. The other trucks, although still more or less in one piece, were obviously write-offs. The cabs were devoid of glass, the metal bodies ripped open with great gashes as if they had been attacked by giant can-openers. The canopies were torn and shredded and at least one of the vehicles appeared to be sitting back on its haunches where its rear axle had been snapped clean in half.

"Help!"

The muffled cry found its way to Moxon's stunned brain.

"Mickey! Help! I'm blind! I'm buried alive! Oh Jesus Christ…please…"

With a jolt, Moxon's mind caught up. He pushed himself up on his elbows and looked around at the carpet of debris and junk that now littered the whole square. He saw something moving and squinted at it in confusion, then after a moment, realised that it was Fellows, trapped under a heavy tarpaulin sheet that had been blown onto him. Gingerly, Moxon pushed himself upright and staggered over to the writhing mass of canvas.

"Stan! You're alright; I'm here. It's just a canopy sheet; hold still mate."

With an effort, Moxon dragged the heavy tarpaulin away, and a moment later, Fellows appeared from beneath it, his arms swishing about in panic.

"Oh, God! Get this fucking thing off me!"

The driver was in a blind panic.

"Stan…" Moxon stumbled over to him and placed a hand on his shoulder.

The other driver continued to thrash about, swearing and cursing and appealing to every saint and god that he could think of.

"Stan!" Moxon shouted in his ear, pressing down on both of his shoulders. "You're alright; calm down, mate!"

The other man's arms stopped waving and his body suddenly sagged with relief.

"Oh, Jesus…" He murmured as he stared about him at the scene of destruction.

Moxon shuffled round so that he could look his mate directly in the eye. He saw that Fellows was in a state of considerable shock.

"Stan, listen to me mate. We need to get away from here. The vehicles have been hit and they're on fire. Any minute now the petrol tanks could go up. We need to get moving. Let's go over by the church, mate."

Fellows nodded at him dumbly and allowed his friend to assist him to his feet. Together, leaning on each other for support, not trusting their shaking legs to carry them without assistance, the two men tumbled through the rubble and debris towards the huge edifice of the church, which itself was burning merrily.

They were barely halfway across the square when they heard the sound of the whistles. They stopped and cocked their ears to one side. Gunfire too; small arms rather than artillery, and nearby at that. More whistles, then shouting. Completely lost amongst the tumult of the noise of battle, the two drivers stared about them as they tried to fathom exactly what they had got themselves into. Then the first rifle shot whipped past them, like the crack of a whip. They both cried out in alarm at the sudden noise.

Suddenly, all about them, the square was filled with people. Dark figures in helmets with excited, aggressive looking faces were swarming all about them. Many of the figures raced straight past them in the garish light of the flames, their uniforms unfamiliar, their weapons even more so. More figures appeared and surrounded them, staring at them with hard, ruthless expressions. Moxon and Fellows gawped back at them, taking in the strange shaped helmets, the small cylindrical cases slung over their backs, the knee high boots and the eagle badges. With a surge of dread, Moxon realised he had just come face to face with the Nazi war machine.

"Hands up!" One of the figures shouted at the two drivers in heavily accented English.

For a moment, the two men stared at the German stupidly, but he jerked his rifle barrel upwards several times and took a threatening step forward.

"Come on, Tommy; hands up!"

Fellows and Moxon, still completely at a loss with their sudden predicament, slowly raised their arms above their heads.

No.1 COMPANY FORMING UP POINT – HERENT
THURSDAY 16TH MAY 1940 – 2250 HOURS

Davis licked his lips and wondered if he had enough time for a swig of water from his canteen. Probably not. He looked left. In the flickering light of the burning village he could see the silhouettes of his fellow guardsmen, those from No.1 Platoon. Looking right he saw the men of No.2 Platoon in a mirror image. Kneeling amongst the bushes that bordered the half destroyed village, the men of No.1 Company were now in their FUP, sword bayonets fixed to the ends of their rifles, awaiting the signal to attack. In front of him, just a few yards away, the Company Commander was kneeling beside Gallows, discussing the final plan.

Davis had picked up most of it already, being as he was, close to the Company Sergeant Major as a matter of routine. Battalion Headquarters and No.4 Company had, it seemed, been pushed back to the road. They still held it but were pinned down and no one could pass along the highway until the enemy were pushed back out of the northern side of the village. So here they were, No.1 Company, the tallest men in the battalion, lined out in assault formation on the eastern edge of the village, bordering the open pastures and staring intently at the fiery scene of hell on earth before them. Perhaps the Germans would just bugger off before H-Hour, Davis thought to himself hopefully. He had practiced plenty of bayonet charges in training, but now the thought of doing it for real was making him think twice. Could he really stick his bayonet in another human being?

There was a chance he would find out soon enough. He saw the Company Commander check his watch and then nod to Gallows. The Company Sergeant Major rose to his feet like a gigantic monster stirring from its lair.

His deep, harsh voice brayed out above the background crackle of gunfire and flames.

"Number One Company; stand-up!"

All around him, Davis saw the dark figures of his fellow guardsmen emerge from cover, the bayonet tipped rifles and Bren Guns distinct in the light of the burning houses.

"Oh, God; here we go…" Davis murmured to himself.

"At the walk…" Gallows called out. "By the centre…advance!"

The line moved forward, briskly, the men half crouching as they filtered through the hedgerow and into the village. The wave of men distorted as it negotiated the first buildings, only to fall back into place as the guardsmen emerged beyond the cluster of houses onto a wide avenue. Gallows had dropped back a pace, to walk alongside Davis.

"Alright, Davis?"

"Aye, Sir; right as rain…" The guardsman lied.

"Good lad." The big warrant officer murmured.

Just then, Davis heard someone call out a warning.

"Enemy front!"

"Where?"

"Small house with the barn attached, not on fire, fifty yards…"

Davis was searching for the building indicated. Even before he saw it, he spotted the enemy. Several figures, just dark shapes outlined against flames, threading their way across the company's front from right to left.

"Seen!" Called the Company Commander.

As he did so, one of the distant figures suddenly stopped and turned to look towards the line of advancing Coldstreamers. Davis heard a shout of alarm in a strange, guttural language. A rifle shot cracked past them, and then the Company Commander was shouting at the top of his voice, calm and business like, his upper class accent sounding almost conversational.

"Alright, Number One Company; chins up, here we go…Charge!"

Davis flinched as Gallows blew a deafening blast on his whistle, right beside him, and then felt his heart lurch with exhilaration as he heard a hundred Coldstream voices roar in defiance as the company broke into a headlong run, their bayonet tipped rifles dropping from the high-port to the charge. The whistle blast ceased as Gallows spat the whistle from between his lips, allowing it to dangle from its leather strap.

"Come on, Davis." He growled. "Let's go stick some fucking Huns!"

With that, the warrant officer launched himself after the rest of the company, screaming like a madman, and Davis found himself going along with him.

"Charge!"

The long line of guardsmen surged forward, flowing around the various obstacles in their path; perambulators, an abandoned car, what looked like a pile of suitcases, their contents spilled out on the cobbles. Bullets cracked towards them as they came; a handful at first, but then longer, concentrated bursts of fire, coming from the array of buildings before them, which included a burning church. Davis heard a grunt to his left and saw a guardsman from No.1 Platoon simply stop abruptly and crumple to the floor. A line of tracer snaked out from deep within the village and sliced through the centre of No.2 Platoon, sending a pair of soldiers tumbling to the ground.

The Hangman was screaming like a madman and, with his huge stride, was beginning to overtake the main line of guardsmen and the Company Commander. Davis felt a sudden urge to be near the big warrant officer, believing his safety depended on it. He put on a spurt, pumping his arms and his rifle madly as he struggled forward to keep up with the Company Sergeant Major. The ammunition bandoliers and mortar bomb satchels bounced against his hips awkwardly, but Davis ignored the discomfort and focussed all his energy on keeping up with his superior.

"Come on you fuckers!" The Hangman was screaming.

Something tumbled through the air in a high arc from the side of the church, and Davis watched the small, dark object bounce on the cobbles over to his right amongst No.2 Platoon. Grenade! A second after he realised the danger, the grenade exploded with a short, sharp crump, and sent another guardsman tumbling over.

Davis ignored the blast and looked forward again. To his surprise he was just yards from the corner of the church. He saw a figure step out from the cover of the burning building, aim a weapon in his direction, then fire. He heard the crack as the bullet whipped past him, and watched as the figure suddenly turned about and ran backwards.

"Yaaagh!" The Hangman was screaming, and then he, Davis, the Company Commander and half a dozen others were bursting around the corner of the church with a war cry to curdle the blood of the most hardened enemy soldier.

Another figure loomed up in front of them and before anyone else could react, The Hangman had impaled the German on his bayonet and slammed the unfortunate man back against the wall of the church. The enemy soldier gave a high pitched scream as he was pinned against the bricks, but The Hangman simply screamed back at him, jammed a heavy ammunition boot into the man's crotch and withdrew his bayonet, before stabbing him again, this time through the chest. The German's terrible cry was cut off abruptly and Gallows yanked out the blade once more then ran on.

Davis went with him and, from out of nowhere, behind what appeared to be the remains of a vehicle, a head appeared. The young guardsman's blade was already past the figure and so, reacting instinctively, Davis simply stopped dead and back-swung the heavy, brass butt-plate of his rifle into the man's face. There was the sound of splintering bone and then the German thudded back down behind the pile of wreckage with a grunt. Davis made to turn around and finish the man with his bayonet, but the Company Commander was already pushing his way past. With casual ease, the officer pointed his revolver down at the German and fired once. The enemy soldier jerked briefly then went still.

Davis looked about him and saw one of the lance sergeants from No.1 Platoon charging through the half open door of the church, followed by the rest of his section. He searched franticly for The Hangman, then spotted him crouching over a body on the floor. The huge warrant officer had reversed his rifle and was pounding the prostrate figure with the butt of his Lee-Enfield. As Davis watched the ferocious struggle going on around him, a group of figures broke cover from behind the church and began fleeing across the open square beyond, towards the buildings at the far side of the open area that the Coldstreamers now found themselves in.

"There they go!" The Company Commander called out, and Davis watched the major extend an arm, take careful aim and fire a single shot at the retreating enemy. The nearest German suddenly hit the cobbles, face down, and Davis heard the Company Commander grunt with satisfaction.

"Give 'em a good lead before you shoot…" The major shouted to nobody in particular, as if giving advice during a day's rough shooting for pheasants.

The guardsmen were in no mood for shooting though, and as the last defenders of the church were finished off, and their comrades beat a hasty retreat back across the village square, the Coldstreamers surged after them, baying for blood, bayonets at the charge. The Hangman was leading that wild, blood thirsty charge, giving free rein to the fury that seethed inside him. Davis, appalled yet at the same time intoxicated by the terrible thrill of the battle, lurched after his Company Sergeant Major. The chase was on, his tail was up, and there were Germans to kill.

THE VILLAGE SQUARE – HERENT
THURSDAY 16TH MAY 1940 – 2300 HOURS

"Jesus Christ!" Fellows sobbed. "What have we got ourselves into?"

He was laying face down, his arms covering his head, staring with fear into the flaring light of the burning village. Next to him Moxon did likewise. Several yards away, a lone German soldier sat against the wall of the cottage, his rifle pointing towards them. Beneath his helmet, the enemy soldier looked to be even younger than the two British drivers, and his smooth features were streaked with dirty sweat; his eyes wide and nervous looking. He was just as scared as his two prisoners.

Moxon and Fellows had been swept up in the German assault and without even realising what was going on they had been bundled away to the far side of the square, opposite the church, and pushed into an alleyway between two smaller buildings. A group of Germans had searched them, roughly, before pushing them down to the floor and using hand signals to indicate that they should stay on the floor or else risk getting shot. Then, leaving just one man to guard them, the enemy soldiers had moved on.

More had come. Long lines of enemy infantry, festooned with belts and boxes of ammunition, rifles and machine-guns, and every accoutrement of war. It was soon apparent that the two drivers and their now deceased NCOs had driven right into the middle of somebody's battle. Only now, as the two men laid there on the cold cobbles, were their minds finally beginning to appreciate the enormity of their predicament. They were prisoners of war. A war that, less than a week ago, had seemed like nothing more than a fairy story. Now they were in the middle of something that resembled Dante's Inferno and they were at the mercy of the German Army.

Just as the two drivers began to come out of their state of shock at the sudden, tumultuous turn of events, the world seemed to go mad again. Around them, the sound of small arms fire and shouting, already a relentless background noise, seemed to intensify to an even higher degree. The shouting of their captors, harsh, urgent and guttural, became laced with the unmistakeable sound of fear, and then the crack of bullets filled the air out in the village square. Then, out of the night, audible above the cacophony of battle, came a roar of voices that reminded Moxon of a crowd at a football match, yelling their defiance at the other team's supporters as their own team scored a blinder of a goal. And then the screaming began.

It was a sound that turned Moxon's blood cold. It was the sound of death. More precisely, it was the sound of bloody murder. As the awful shriek of dying men filled their senses, the two British prisoners saw their guard suddenly stir himself and run to the corner of the alley. The young German peered round the corner of the cottage and, immediately, Moxon and Fellows heard his exclamation of fear. His words they did not understand, but the tone of them was clear. Unable to do anything other than gawp at the unfolding nightmare, Moxon and Fellows watched the German raise his rifle and fire a shot at some unseen target. They heard him work the bolt of his rifle and fire again. Then, with a yelp of utter terror, the young man turned back towards them and began running away.

He clattered past them at full tilt then passed out of sight. They heard his footfalls as he pounded down the cobbles, panting heavily. Moxon and Fellows glanced at each other worriedly for a moment then jumped in alarm as several dark figures appeared in the gap at the end of the alley. Illuminated against the flames of the church at the far side of the square, the newcomers looked like giants and Moxon felt his breath catch in his throat. One of the figures held a pistol and the other two brandished rifles with long, wicked looking bayonets attached. The man with the pistol raised his weapon and fired a single shot down the alley at the retreating German.

The shot, deafening in the confines of the alley, made Fellows cry out. The three figures above them reacted with sudden alarm. Moxon saw the rifles swing down, the deadly blades reaching for them, whilst the man with the pistol dropped his aim towards where they lay.

"On the floor!" They heard one of the men call out the warning.

"Don't shoot! We're British!" Moxon somehow managed to blurt out. "Don't shoot! Please! We're British soldiers!"

The three dark figures went perfectly still. Their weapons were still poised, aiming directly at Moxon and Fellows, and for a heartbeat, nobody spoke. After a moment, an upper-class voice gave an order.

"Get on your feet. Keep your arms up where we can see them."

Slowly, carefully, the two drivers did as they were told. As they struggled to their feet, the man with the posh voice spoke again.

"Come out here; where we can see you."

Hesitantly, Moxon and Fellows stumbled out of the alley.

As they emerged into the flickering light of the flames, the two drivers were able to take in the scene around them. The square was filled with men once more, but this time they were all dressed in khaki and wore the familiar British pattern steel helmets and battledress. And they were all huge. Moxon was not a short man, yet even so, the British soldiers that now watched him with grim eyes were a tall bunch of mean looking bastards to be sure. He flicked his eyes over the three men who had found them in the alley and saw that one of them was a major. The officer was watching them with interest, and after a couple of moments, he lowered his revolver. Next to him, the two soldiers with rifles relaxed their stance a little.

"I'm the Company Commander of No.1 Company, 1st Battalion Coldstream Guards." Said the officer. "Who, pray tell, are you?"

Moxon felt a surge of relief flood through his body, and next to him, Fellows gave a sigh that indicated he might just feint at any moment.

"Coldstream Guards?" Moxon breathed. "Thank God for that…"

"We're from the RASC; 12th Transport Regiment. We've been looking for you lot all night."

The Coldstream Guards major raised an eyebrow then turned to one of the riflemen.

"Davis…" He murmured to the man, "go and get the Company Sergeant Major will you, please?"

"Right, Sir." The soldier snapped obediently and raced off.

Moxon watched him go for a moment.

"What are you doing here?" The major asked suddenly. "This is no place for Lines of Communication troops."

"We were looking for your mob…" Moxon explained. "To pick you up. We had orders to move you back to…"

A sudden scream of rage cut Moxon dead. With a startled gasp he looked to his left, and then cringed as he saw a huge, khaki monster approaching him. By his side, Moxon heard Fellows groan in fear.

Coming across the rubble and body strewn square was a monster of a man. Taller than any of the other guardsmen, this particular creature wore the crown of a warrant officer class two on his sleeve and his pig-ugly face was contorted into a ferocious mask of rage. For a tiny moment, Moxon thought his bowels would fail him.

"Fucking well stand to attention!" The big warrant officer was screaming at them. "You two, stand to fucking attention!"

The two drivers realised he was talking to them and braced up immediately, in a way they had never reacted for poor old Sergeant Danby.

They stared in terror as the warrant officer bore down on them, his eyes bulging like a lunatic as he spat out a string of expletives at a faster rate than a machine-gun.

"Where the fucking hell do you think you are? Who the fucking hell are you? And where the shagging hell are your helmets?"

The huge warrant officer stopped, just inches away, and leered over them, his mouth throwing out spittle as he continued to rage.

"Ain't you ever seen an officer before? Sort yourselves out you fucking little shit monkeys! Who are you? Well? Who are you?"

Completely taken aback, neither Moxon nor Fellows could find the words.

"I gather they're from some transport unit that's supposed to be picking us up, Company Sergeant Major." The officer interjected as he casually began reloading his revolver.

The warrant officer glanced at the major then back at the two drivers, baring his teeth like a dog straining at its leash.

"Oh, really?"

His voice suddenly dropped from its hysterical ranting to a low, menacing growl.

"Fucking Chippies, eh?"

"It would seem so." The officer spoke again. "We found them in the alley there. Looks like the Jerries had them."

"That's right, Sir." Fellows bleated suddenly. "Took us prisoner, Sir, they did."

The monstrous warrant officer just stared at the pair of drivers, his eyes narrowing now as he weighed them up. Moxon couldn't look the man in the eyes and so he dropped his gaze. As he did so, he saw that the bayonet on the Company Sergeant Major's rifle was thick with blood. He gulped at the sight and suddenly wished he was still a prisoner of war.

"Where are your rifles?" The warrant officer asked suddenly in dangerous voice.

Moxon glanced up again.

"We lost 'em, Sir...In the vehicles..."

"Lost 'em, did you?" Snapped the big Coldstreamer.

Before Moxon could reply, another soldier appeared next to the group and slammed his feet in on the cobbles in a fashion that was more usually seen on the drill square. The young soldier had his rifle at the slope and slapped the wooden butt with his free hand in salute.

"Excuse me, Sir." The soldier began as the major returned the compliment. "The Commanding Officer sends his regards and says once you've driven the Jerries back out, could you please reform your company and pull back through Number Four Company? As quick as possible if you could, Sir, please?"

The major nodded his understanding.

"No problem at all. Tell the Commanding Officer we're on our way. We'll be coming through in the next few minutes."

The young man nodded back.

"May I have your permission to carry on, Sir, please?"

"Yes, please."

As the guardsman slapped his rifle once more and executed an immaculate right turn at the halt, Moxon and Fellows exchanged worried looks.

"Righto..." The major said, turning back to them. "No time to hang around here. Looks like you two are with us for the time being until we've broken contact with Jerry. Company Sergeant Major, can you bring them along with you, please? I'll get the platoon commanders together and then we can get moving."

Without further ado, the major turned away, leaving Moxon and Fellows to the mercy of the vicious looking warrant officer.

The Company Sergeant Major sized the two drivers up with dark, malevolent eyes.

"My name is Company Sergeant Major Gallows." He began. "Behind my back, the blokes call me 'The Hangman'."

Moxon felt his bowels loosen again.

"Davis," The Hangman snarled to one of the riflemen nearby. "Find this pair of Chippies a rifle each and keep 'em close to you."

He looked back at the two quaking drivers.

"Congratulations; you just joined the Guards!"

HEADQUARTERS GERMAN 19TH CORPS – MONTCORNET, 40 MILES WEST OF SEDAN THURSDAY 16TH MAY 1940 – 2330 HOURS

"Believe me, Walther, if anybody deserves the Knight's Cross, it's that man."

Guderian shook his head slowly in admiration.

"You should have seen him. I've never seen a man so utterly exhausted, yet still so full of fighting spirit. There is no wonder his men had no choice but to follow him. I believe he really would have taken that village on his own if his men had not responded to his exhortations."

The general was talking about Lieutenant Colonel Hermann Balck, commander of the 1st Rifle Regiment in 1st Panzer Division. His unit had been in non-stop action for six days now and the last thirty six hours had seen some of the most difficult fighting yet. At one point, by all accounts, the weary panzer grenadiers had begun to flag, and when ordered to capture the next objective, a small village called Bouvellemont, their officers had complained to the regimental commander that their troops were in no fit state to continue the advance. In typical Balck style, he had simply replied that he would attack the village on his own in that case, and begun to walk towards the distant buildings. After a while, Balck had been rewarded by the sight of his panzer grenadiers emerging from their shell-scrapes and stumbling along with him towards the objective.

The village was now in German hands after a long and bitter contest against one of the better French units and, that morning, Guderian had found Balck in the main street of the village, phlegmatically going about the business of mopping up the last pockets of enemy resistance. The colonel had appeared to be physically shattered, yet still he had raised a smile for his general, explained the situation diligently and clearly, and expressed his desire to press on with the advance yet further. If anything, it had reaffirmed Guderian's belief that now was the time to move on with even greater tempo, rather than stop.

Indeed, Guderian had spent long enough on the telephone the night before, arguing against the order to stop that had been received from Headquarters Panzer Group Kleist. At first, he had remonstrated with the chief of staff at the headquarters, but then, getting no joy, he had spoken to General von Kleist personally. There had followed a heated debate between the two, where Guderian had thrown historical precedent in his superior's direction in order to reinforce his case for continuing the advance. After a lengthy, and at times, painful conversation, von Kleist had reluctantly agreed to let Guderian expand his bridgehead.

And that was exactly what his corps had been doing all day. The lead elements of his forces were now some 55 miles from their crossing point at Sedan on the Meuse. The tipping point was fast approaching; Guderian could feel it. Today his men had rounded up hundreds of demoralised prisoners, here in this town, along with a dozen abandoned tanks. Just one more push and he felt sure that the enemy would finally collapse, despite the fierce resistance they had offered over the last day or two. Reinhardt's corps was now immediately to his right, the 6th Panzer Division of that corps actually brushing into the town where Guderian's own headquarters were now established. And tomorrow, Guderian would finally have 10th Panzer and the Gross Deutschland Regiment back under commander, released at last from their flank guard duties. Now was the time, he judged. The critical moment of this whole war was upon him. Any hour now and he would have his freedom, despite the nervousness of the panzer group's staff.

"Are we all set for the morning then?" He glanced up at Nehring, who had been listening patiently to his tales of adventure.

"Yes, general." His chief of staff replied. "The warning orders are being transmitted as we speak."

"Good." Guderian nodded, tiredly. "And we have informed Panzer Group Headquarters of our progress today?"

"We have, Sir, yes. We are also in the final stages of taking 10th Panzer back on strength…"

The chief of staff broke off in mid-sentence as the clatter of urgent footsteps sounded on the stairs. A moment later a staff captain appeared in the doorway, absently knocking on the door and entering the room without waiting for permission. Hurriedly, he approached the chief of staff and thrust his hand out, brandishing a piece of paper.

"Colonel; General; my apologies, but I think you need to see this immediately."

Nehring took the sheet of paper and rapidly scanned the text. Guderian saw the look of disapproval on the colonel's face.

"I suspect that we have yet another batch of bad news, Walther?" Guderian ventured, his stomach suddenly knotting with apprehension.

Nehring looked up from the document.

"It is from General von Kleist, Sir. It is an order, stating that with immediate effect, our corps is to freeze all movement. It forbids us, under any circumstances, to exploit any further, in any direction. All troops are to adopt defensive posture until further notice. Furthermore, General von Kleist will visit this headquarters tomorrow morning at 0700 hours. He will arrive by plane and requires you to be at the airstrip to meet him, Sir."

Guderian bit back a waspish remark, and settled for a dark scowl instead. He took a deep breath before finally passing comment.

"Oh, dear. How very inconvenient…"

Friday 17th May 1940
The Eighth Day

THE AIRSTRIP – MONTCORNET, 40 MILES WEST OF SEDAN
FRIDAY 17TH MAY 1940 – 0700 HOURS

The Fieseler Storch aircraft droned down towards the field and made a short, tidy landing on the grassy meadow. It required little in the way of taxiing before it rolled to a halt and, as soon as it did so, the engine coughed once then cut out. Standing by the hedgerow, wrapped in his greatcoat against the chill morning mist, Guderian watched as the pilot quickly dismounted and then assisted his lone passenger out of the aircraft. Leaving his staff by the hedge, Guderian walked forwards to greet the commander of the panzer group.

He paused, several metres back from the plane, whilst von Kleist disembarked. As soon as the general was on the ground, he turned and spotted Guderian. Without any greeting, his face stern, the general simply jerked his head, indicating that Guderian should join him, and then began walking across the field, away from where Guderian's staff waited. The corps commander followed after his superior, striding to catch up. Eventually von Kleist came to a halt some hundred and fifty metres away from the aircraft and Guderian's staff, the line of sight to the group blocked by the aeroplane. Guderian slowed to a halt beside the panzer group commander. Without warning, von Kleist turned on him.

"How dare you?" The general's top lip wobbled in barely suppressed rage.

Guderian was stunned.

"How dare you disobey my direct orders? How dare you?"

Guderian simply stared at his superior, taken aback by the unexpected vehemence of von Kleist's opening remarks.

"Do you think you are excused from taking orders? Do you think you can do whatever you want? Just ignore instructions at whim?"

Guderian managed to find some words at last.

"But General, we agreed that the bridgehead could be expanded..."

"Expand!" von Kleist suddenly snapped, giving way to his temper. "Expand! Move sideways, get some elbow room, make space for the follow up divisions! Not attack! Not advance! Not race off thirty miles into the sunset! Thirty miles into enemy held territory against God knows what!"

Guderian was shocked to the core. Not frightened or ashamed in any way, just shocked.

"General..." He began, "we merely took advantage..."

"That is exactly your problem, Guderian! You always take advantage!"

The group commander was red in the face now.

"I listened to your arguments last night and on the basis of that I gave you permission to make small adjustments to your bridgehead in order to allow the follow up troops to deploy, but instead of accepting that, you just took advantage! You leave the whole of the ground gained floating in the air, and disappear off on another mad dash westwards, without proper support, without flank protection, and without permission!"

Guderian, far from being cowed, felt his belligerence rising at the accusations.

"I did what was necessary to prevent an enemy counter-attack from developing into a major offensive." He retorted. "I seized the initiative and took the battle to the enemy. I dislocated him and defeated him. And now he is on his knees and it is time to strike the decisive blow. This is not the time to stop; this is the time to attack. Attack, attack, attack; whilst he is weak. Defeat him now. Finish the business…"

Guderian tailed off as he realised that he was beginning to shout at his superior, who was only becoming more indignant by the moment.

"The high command will decide how to finish this business off, Guderian." Von Kleist scowled. "You are just a corps commander, and you will do as you are ordered. And your orders are to stop. Stop and remain where you are until you receive further, specific orders to advance."

Guderian stared back at his superior defiantly.

"Those are my orders?"

"They are." Von Kleist snapped coldly.

Guderian remained silent for a moment.

"It is the duty of a commander to follow his orders obediently." He stated curtly.

"It is." Agreed von Kleist, detecting that he had brought the corps commander to heel.

Guderian shook his head suddenly.

"My conscience will not allow me to follow orders such as these, therefore I cannot be in command." He said firmly.

Von Kleist frowned.

"I resign." Guderian stated flatly.

It was the turn of von Kleist to be taken aback. For a moment, he looked as if he had just been slapped across the face. The look of shock turned to one of annoyance. It was clear that a range of emotions were bombarding the group commander and he was finding it difficult to cope with Guderian's shock announcement. Eventually, von Kleist's face settled into a cold, emotionless mask.

"Very well." He quipped. "If that is your decision… Who is the next senior general in your corps?"

"General Veiel."

"Then you are to make the arrangements immediately and wait at your headquarters. You will receive further instructions in due course."

Without another word, von Kleist brushed past Guderian and strode off towards his waiting aircraft. Guderian watched him go, his fists clenched tightly behind his back, and the bitter taste of injustice on his tongue…"

SOMEWHERE JUST SOUTH OF BRUSSELS
FRIDAY 17TH MAY 1940 – 0710 HOURS

Jackson was in a foul mood. They were on the move again. They had started nine hours ago, pulling out of the line on the River Dyle without a hitch. Yet more abandoned trenches, given up without a contest, he reflected. They had marched all night; stopping and starting, speeding up and slowing down, moving along tracks and roads in what soldiers referred to as a 'battalion snake'. Now the sun was up and Jackson's stomach was roaring with hunger. They were not far from their destination, so he had been told at the last halt. The battalion was being put into a defensive line, a temporary one mind you, along the Brussels – Charleroi Canal, so that the 3rd Battalion of the Grenadier Guards, currently the brigade's rear guard, could fall back through them.

It was the classic leap-frog system of withdrawal that the British Army had always practiced. Despite the familiarity of the tactic, it gave Jackson no comfort at all. Withdrawals meant more digging and more marching. More importantly, withdrawal meant you were losing.

He clumped along the cobbled road, passing an old Belgian man and his wife. They had a look of resignation on their faces as they shambled down the road in the same direction as the British, two small, battered looking suitcases between them. The old couple looked as if they had seen it all before. Given their age, Jackson realised, they probably had. He looked to his front again and studied the backs of the men in his platoon. Spread out in two single files on both sides of the road, his men were crunching along the cobbles at a steady pace now the sun was up. Several hundred yards in front of them, he could see the distant khaki blobs of the leading platoon, leading the company towards its next rendezvous. Between the two platoons, there ambled a constant stream of local civilians of all ages. They knew that the Germans were coming and didn't want to be around when they got here. Jackson understood that, but all the same, these bloody civilians didn't half get in the way when you were trying to move an army around.

He allowed his mind to wander as he marched at the rear of his platoon; thinking of the poor old Company Quarter Master Sergeant who had been killed in that first, shattering air raid. The thought of the man's head sitting amongst the food made his stomach turn, as it did every time he thought about it. For a second he remembered the cold fear he had felt at the sound of the enemy dive-bombers, and the memory of it made him angry. If only he could finally get to grips with Jerry; then he would show them.

They were entering a stretch of road bordered by avenues of tall, elegant poplar trees now, and for a moment, despite his tiredness and blistered feet, the sergeant thought how pleasant the surrounding countryside was on such a lovely morning. He looked up the road again and saw that the platoon had almost caught up with the next batch of civilians. He could see a score of them; some walking, several on a horse drawn cart, one pushing a bicycle with flat tyres. He was so busy staring up ahead with absent minded curiosity that he didn't register the noise of the aircraft until the last moment.

It was the sound of the distant shouting from No.17 Platoon, far behind them, that first alerted him. He turned about to see the khaki clad guardsmen throwing themselves into the ditches at either side of the road, a couple of hundred yards back. Then he heard the engine and his heart leapt in terror. He suddenly caught sight of the aircraft, coming straight towards him along the line of the road, flying just above the height of the tree tops it seemed. Then he heard the crack of the bullets.

"Take cover!" He yelled, throwing himself sideways into the nearest ditch and pressing himself into the soil.

All around him, he heard the shouting of his men as they too realised the danger and hurled themselves into cover. The sound of the machine-gun fire was getting louder now, but even above the racket, Jackson could hear the desperate screams of women and the terrified whinny of horses. He winced and pushed his head down further as bullets cracked past him, whining menacingly as they ricocheted off the cobbles. Then, just a moment later, the ground lurched beneath him in a horribly familiar fashion, and it was followed almost instantly by the deafening 'crump' of an exploding bomb. There was nothing the sergeant could do other then press himself further into the dirt and hope that the nightmare would pass him by.

Surprisingly, that's exactly what happened. As quickly as the attack started, it finished. There had only been one plane, and now its engine was just a distant drone as it flew off into the cloudless morning sky. All around Jackson, there were long moments of deathly silence. Then the sobbing began.

With an effort, he pushed himself up from the ditch and took a deep breath, preparing himself for what he might see. Thin skeins of grey, pungent smoke drifted past him and he looked up the road to see a large, smouldering crater in the highway, just beyond the front of the platoon, and right where the clump of civilians had been shambling along just moments before. With a sense of dread rising inside him, Jackson stepped up from the ditch and onto the cobbles once more. With his rifle at the trail, he jogged up the road towards the head of his platoon.

"Section commanders! Head check your men, quick as you can! Two minutes, then into me with casualty states!"

At the sound of Jackson's voice, heads began popping up from the ditches at either side of the road; the stunned guardsmen blinking in surprise from beneath the rims of their steel helmets.

"Come on!" Jackson bawled, feeling instantly better at the sight of so many familiar faces obviously still full of life. "On your feet! No time to hang around!"

He was almost at the front of the platoon now and Jackson spotted the figure of his platoon commander scrambling back up onto the road.

The young lieutenant straightened his gas mask satchel and his helmet briefly, as if preening himself prior to dinner, then looked at Jackson and blew out his cheeks.

"Crikey, Sergeant J; that was another ruddy close one!"

"You alright, Mr Dunstable, Sir?" Jackson enquired, slowing to a walk as he approached.

"Yes, fine thank you…" Replied the young man, brushing a spec of soil from his sleeve. "Not sure about this bunch though…"

The officer nodded at the scene of carnage just a little way ahead.

The cart was on its side, one horse laying dead in its traces, the second horse thrashing noisily on the floor beside it. Two dead bodies lay face down in the road, the whole of which was covered by a dark red lake of blood.

"Jesus!" Jackson breathed as he surveyed the destruction.

A woman's voice moaned pitifully from somewhere.

"Better take a look and see what we can do…" Dunstable suggested.

Together, the two men began walking cautiously forward.

As they went, civilians began to emerge from the ditches. Some were crying, some shaking in abject terror. Some were simply too stunned to react and went through the motions of movement as if in a dream. They watched a middle-aged, well dressed man, pick up his buckled and completely useless bicycle, and begin wheeling it along the road, his eyes vacant and devoid of expression. Of the passengers on the cart, there were no survivors, and even the dead bodies were largely unrecognisable as human beings. The mortally wounded horse was making a dreadful commotion, its hind quarters torn right open to the bone. Feeling suddenly queasy, Jackson strode around the wreckage, careful not to step in the ever widening pool of blood, and raised his rifle. The horse turned its terrified eyes to him, and without a moment of hesitation, Jackson pulled the trigger.

Blam!

The horse's head dropped to the cobbles immediately, its cries cut off abruptly. Trying not to think about the look in the horse's eyes in the last moment of its life, the sergeant walked back round to Dunstable. The officer had moved on however, and Jackson saw him standing in the ditch at the far side of the road, staring down intently at something. He walked over to the verge and looked down at where his officer was standing. He caught his breath.

In the bottom of the ditch, flat on her back, her once pretty face shredded by cuts and abrasions, lay a girl; maybe fifteen or sixteen years old at the most. It wasn't the terrible, bloody lacerations on the girl's face that brought Jackson up sharp, but the fact that both of the girls legs were missing, just two bloody stumps remaining from what had once been her thighs. With her femoral arteries severed, the ditch was filled with blood. Even worse, she was still alive.

Jackson clamped his teeth together and watched with ever growing distress as Dunstable knelt down beside the girl and gently stroked her hair away from her face, speaking in quiet, soft French as he did so. The maimed girl gave a low, pathetic sob, and murmured something. Dunstable stroked the child's face again.

"She's Belgian." Dunstable said, his voice taught. "I think she said she wants her mother…"

"Oh, Christ…" Jackson gulped, trying to hold himself together.

He gulped again, surveying the shattered mess of the girl's lower limbs.

"If she was on the cart then her family are all dead." Jackson blurted. Then, forcing himself to calm down… "She's dying too, Sir."

Dunstable didn't reply for a moment.

"I know." He said finally.

Jackson watched as the young man stroked the girl's face over and over again, murmuring something to her in French; his voice soft, soothing, calm.

"We can't do anything for her…" Jackson said, trying to find more appropriate words, but failing.

Dunstable simply nodded and continued to soothe the girl.

"Sergeant Jackson?"

The NCO turned at the sound of his name and saw one of his section commanders coming over. Hurriedly, Jackson moved towards him, stopping the lance sergeant short of the ditch.

"What's the damage?" He demanded.

"You ain't gonna believe it, but nobody's got so-much as a scratch! God knows how!"

A momentary sense of relief flooded through Jackson.

"Thank fuck for that." He swore, his voice thick with emotion. "Get everyone on their feet and ready to move. We'll be on our way again in a minute."

As the section commander rushed off to pass the message, Jackson gave an involuntary jump at the sound of a gunshot, right behind him. He turned and saw Dunstable, still crouching in the ditch, his head bowed. The young officer's lips were moving silently, as if in prayer, and then a moment later he saw the lieutenant make the sign of the cross. Then, with a jerk, the officer stood and stepped back up onto the road without looking behind him. Jackson saw the revolver in his hand and swallowed hard.

"Alright, Sir?" The sergeant asked as the officer walked casually back over towards him.

The young ensign gave him a brief, sad smile as he fumbled with his holster, pushing his revolver back inside it. Having fastened the buckle, Dunstable looked at Jackson with a distant expression.

"Okay, Sergeant Jackson." He said, his voice breaking slightly. "Let's get moving again, shall we?"

HEADQUARTERS GERMAN 19TH CORPS – MONTCORNET FRIDAY 17TH MAY 1940 – 1320 HOURS

Colonel-General Siegmund Wilhelm List slammed the door behind him, swept across the room and removed his cap, throwing it onto the nearby dressing table. He turned towards Guderian, his round little face, drooping moustache and searching dark eyes all too familiar to the corps commander.

"Go on then." He said without preamble. "Tell me what the bloody hell is going on, Guderian?"

The commander of the 19th Corps, if that is what Guderian still was, took a deep breath as he considered his answer.

He had expected a response of some kind when he had signalled his resignation and the change of command arrangements through to higher formation, but he had not expected that response to be so swift, or result in the arrival of the Commander of the 12th Army within just a matter of hours. He eyed the army commander briefly and noted, with some relief, that despite his gruff tone, List appeared to be entirely calm and unlikely to explode in a sudden rage. So he began.

He told List about the misunderstanding over the direction he had been given the previous night and, seeing that List remained calm, went further and explained his belief that the moment to break through had arrived, and that any failure to seize the initiative now would have catastrophic results. He added that if the order to halt must be obeyed, then he felt he could not retain his position as corps commander and follow through an instruction that was, in his opinion, quite obviously a mistake.

Once he had finished, Guderian watched the army commander for a reaction. List gave a low, throaty rumble as he plonked himself down on the edge of the dresser and fixed Guderian with a hard stare.

"Do you think von Kleist was wrong to pass on the Fuhrer's order?" He asked suddenly.

Guderian blinked.

"The Fuhrer's order?"

"Yes." List replied crisply. "What? Did you think that von Kleist had suddenly woken up with cold feet and decided to put the brakes on everything? This order has come direct from Hitler himself. We're not having some petty squabble over a wargame here, Guderian. This is a Fuhrer directive. And as you know, *everybody* must obey the Fuhrer... Even you."

Guderian felt his spine go cold.

"I have spoken with von Rundstedt." List went on without pause. "You are ordered to remain in command. You *will not* resign; understand?"

Guderian attempted to speak, but List cut him short.

"*Understand?*"

"Yes, General." Guderian replied.

"Good." List stood up and began pacing the room. "As for the halt order, it remains in force." He stopped for a moment and gave Guderian a hard stare. "However..." He began pacing again. "I have discussed the matter with von Rundstedt in detail, and you raise a valid point about retaining the initiative."

The army commander turned to face Guderian again.

"There is a dire need to bring up our reserves as quickly as possible to fill the huge void that you have left in the wake of your advance; if only to ensure your southern flank remains secure. The Fuhrer is terrified that the French have got some nasty surprise waiting for us in the south..."

He stretched an eyebrow in Guderian's direction.

"*Terrified*, Guderian. The Fuhrer is truly taken aback by your...*catastrophic success*."

Guderian couldn't help smiling at the term.

"Therefore, Guderian, your headquarters will remain here; at Montcornet. It will not move any further forward just yet; that way you can be easily reached." List was pacing again now, talking quickly. "It will remain here until the reserve divisions have been brought forward, and the southern flank properly secured. However…"

Once more, the army commander stopped and turned to fix Guderian with that shrewd stare.

"Your divisions may conduct… *reconnaissance in force*."

Guderian fought to maintain his composure as his heart suddenly leapt with joy.

List was holding his gaze now, the expression on his face full of meaning.

"The corps stays here, Guderian. Here." List stamped his heel on the floor. "But your divisions may get on with their reconnaissance…"

He gave Guderian the briefest of smiles.

"…in force."

PART FOUR

RIPOSTE

Monday 20th May 1940
The Eleventh Day

THE DEMOLITION GUARD – PECQ BRIDGE OVER THE RIVER ESCAUT, 12 MILES EAST OF LILLE
MONDAY 20TH MAY 1940 – 0115 HOURS

"How long now, Sir? Any word from the Sappers?"
Jackson peered intently at Dunstable's face in the darkness.

"Their officer reckons they should be good to go in about fifteen or twenty minutes. We're just waiting for the thumbs up from Brigade Headquarters to blow. As soon as that comes through, we can let the Engineers crack on and pull back to rejoin the rest of the company."

The night was eerily quiet. It had been three long days and nights since their withdrawal from the River Dyle, through a series of stop lines, until finally arriving here on the River Escaut, almost back to the French border once more. Now, it was hoped, the BEF had withdrawn far enough to straighten the line and they could finally turn and get to grips with the enemy. For Jackson, who had marched into Belgium with such determination and sense of purpose just ten days ago, this war was something of a disappointment so far. He hadn't fired his weapon in anger once, but he had been bombed and strafed by German aircraft on four separate occasions, been shelled twice, dug and then subsequently abandoned three trenches, and marched God only knew how many miles, backwards and forwards across Belgium.

"So do you reckon that's it then, Sir? Will this be our final position?"

He could see Dunstable pulling a thoughtful face in the gloom.

"I hope so. There's talk of it. We're definitely staying in the town tonight. I believe we're due to get orders from Brigade first thing tomorrow. If nothing else, we might just get some sleep tonight."

Jackson gave a low rumble in his throat.

"I just want to give those Jerry bastards a lesson or two."

"Yes…" Dunstable didn't sound quite as belligerent as his platoon sergeant. "Well, it would be nice to have a real job to get stuck into, instead of just marching and digging all the time; especially with all these refugees on the…"

The young lieutenant stopped abruptly as Jackson heard the sound of raw emotion creep into the officer's voice. The poor bastard was still remembering that girl by the side of the road from the other day. The memory was still fresh in the young man's mind. Such a terrible thing. To be truthful, Jackson didn't like thinking about it too much either, and it wasn't even him who had pulled the trigger.

They were both saved from the awkwardness of the moment by the unexpected sound of engines. Jackson's head whipped round, his eyes turning eastwards.

"Vehicles." He stated flatly, suspicion in his voice.

"There, look." Dunstable pointed at several pin pricks of light that suddenly appeared in the distance, back towards where the Germans were advancing from.

"Headlights?" Jackson marvelled. "Are they fucking stupid?"

"Quite possibly…" Dunstable murmured. "Question is; who the bloody hell are they? All of our boys should be back over the river by now."

"Surely the Jerries can't be that full of themselves?" Jackson wondered aloud as he watched the lights get brighter.

"Well they're definitely coming right for us." Dunstable commented, a tone of worry creeping into his voice.

"Go speak to the Engineers, Sir; just in case it is the Jerries. Make sure they're ready to blow. I'll go up to the forward section and keep an eye on things."

"Okay." Dunstable agreed. "But if it *is* the Jerries, don't hang around too long. Just give them a good volley or two then get everybody back over the bridge as fast as you can. We don't want to blow it and leave half the platoon on this side."

Murmuring his understanding, Jackson doubled forward along the cobbles until he saw the dim shapes of No.1 Section huddled on the grass verges inside their hastily dug shell-scrapes. He dropped down on one knee behind the right hand position and hissed for the section commander.

"Piggy? Piggy?"

A bulky figure shuffled backwards out of the shell-scrape and came up close to Jackson's face.

"Is that you, Davey?"

"Yeah; make sure you and the lads are ready to fire if these buggers try and drive through without stopping or if they try any funny business. I'll take one of your riflemen and go on the road to stop them. Looks like there's two or three of 'em."

"Right you are; no dramas." Replied the lance sergeant. "Just watch yourself though, Davey. Don't reckon there's any of our lot left this side. They've *got* to be Jerries."

"Hmm." Jackson grunted. "We'll see soon enough."

The vehicles were just a couple of hundred yards away now and the noise of their engines was deep and powerful; obviously the sound of large trucks. Jackson grabbed the nearest rifleman from the shallow pit and pulled him up into the road.

"Come with me, big lad." Jackson said. "And keep your rifle trained on the cab window when I approach the driver's side. First hint of trouble; just shoot the driver and anyone else in the cab."

"Ok, Sergeant." Murmured the guardsman.

With a slight sense of disappointment, Jackson realised he had picked Hawkins, perhaps his least favourite member of the platoon. It was too late to worry however, because the lead vehicle was less than a hundred yards away and they could hear the driver gunning the engine. Whoever the driver was, he was in a hurry, pushing the vehicle along at some speed.

"Here we go…" Jackson called out loudly to the men around him as he stepped out onto the road, followed by Hawkins.

The headlights were dazzling as they illuminated the two soldiers standing on the cobbles, and Jackson made a point of keeping his right eye closed in order not to completely lose his night vision. He began waving his arms above his head, signalling for the vehicle to slow down. At first there was no response, and he saw Hawkins raise his rifle into the shoulder.

"Fucker's not going to stop…" The young guardsman muttered.

Jackson thought he was probably right and prepared to throw himself sideways and give the order to fire.

Suddenly however, the sound of squealing brakes cut through the noise of the engine and the lead vehicle of the three began to slow rapidly. Realising that the driver had at last seen them, Jackson began flapping one arm authoritatively, signalling the driver to halt completely. He watched as the large truck squealed to a halt several yards in front of him, still squinting as the lights on the vehicle blinded his open eye. As he heard the unmistakable noise of the handbrake being applied, Jackson stepped forward and round to the side of the vehicle by the driver's door. Even before he got level with the door, a harsh, angry sounding English voice called out to him.

"What the fuck do you think you're doing, you maniac! What're you doing standing in the middle of the bloody road!"

Instantly, Jackson's temper, which was already fraying, frayed a little more.

"Shut up." He snapped. "And turn your headlamps off."

There was a moment of silence as the unseen occupants of the cab registered his words.

"You what?" Came an outraged voice.

"I said turn your fucking lights off, before my Bren Gunner riddles you with bloody bullets!" Jackson snarled, his patience wearing thin.

Again, there was stunned silence, but then the truck's lights suddenly went out.

"Hawkins?" Jackson snapped over his shoulder. "Go and tell those other trucks to kill the lights."

As the guardsman moved off to carry out Jackson's instructions, the sergeant stepped up onto the mounting plate next to the door of the truck and heaved himself up so that he was level with the driver's open window. As he pulled himself up, Jackson saw two faces in the gloom. The driver, nearest, was leaning back in his seat, and beside him the passenger was leaning across the man to get his face as close to Jackson's as possible.

"Who the fucking hell are you?" Snarled the passenger, his voice betraying a South Yorkshire accent.

"*My* name is Sergeant Jackson of the Coldstream Guards, and I'm the second in command of the Demolition Guard here. More importantly, *who the fuck are you*?"

Jackson heard a sharp intake of breath, and realised he must be talking to somebody of rank.

"My name's Captain Tobin, Quartermaster of the 3rd Hallamshire Rifles and you need to watch your bloody mouth, Sergeant! I thought a wooden-top would have known better."

Had that comment come from anyone else, Jackson would be happily dragging them out of the vehicle cab by their throat now. Instead, he forced himself to remain calm.

"Identity papers." He said firmly.

"What?" The shadowy figure of Tobin asked incredulously.

"Identity papers." Jackson demanded again, his voice cold and business-like. "You could be anyone for all I know."

"You cheeky fucking bastard!" Swore Tobin. "I'll have you fucking bust to…"

"You've got ten seconds to produce your papers or I'll order my Bren Gunners to shoot this cab to 'kingdom come'."

Once more, there was a long silence, and even in the darkness Jackson could see the look of shock that was etched on the obnoxious captain's face.

"Sergeant Jackson, is that you?"

The big sergeant turned and looked down at the sound of his name. He recognised the voice of the dark figure standing below him on the cobbles. It was Captain Pilkington, the Acting Company Commander.

"It is, Sir, yes." Jackson answered.

"Is there a problem?"

Jackson hastily dropped onto the cobbles so he could speak to the Company Commander face to face.

"There's a Captain Quartermaster from the Hallamshires in the cab, Sir; being a bit shirty with me. I was just asking to see his papers…"

"Hmm…" Murmured Pilkington. "More waifs and strays, eh? Well, they've only just got here in time because we've just been told to blow the bridge. I'll deal with this."

Immediately, Pilkington clambered up to the position that Jackson had just abandoned.

"Who's in charge?" He demanded.

"I am…" Jackson hard Tobin begin to speak, but the Company Commander cut him dead.

"Right, well, listen carefully. My name is Pilkington and I'm responsible for this bridge you're about to cross. First of all, don't let me catch you with your headlights on again or I'll have you all shot. Secondly, consider yourselves lucky because this bridge is getting blown in the next couple of minutes. Now, get over the bridge, keep your lights off and try not to squash any of my men in the process. Drive straight on into the town of Pecq and then straight out the other side. Our battalion is preparing it for defence and there's going to be a battle, so take your trucks and go find your own unit. No hanging around; understand?"

Jackson was smiling in the darkness as he heard a chastened reply from within the cab.

"Good; now get off with you…" Pilkington snapped at Tobin before clambering down.

Without wasting time, the truck began trundling forwards and Pilkington stepped back a pace, waving at the other two trucks to follow it. Together, he and Jackson watched the three vehicles disappear into the darkness towards the bridge. Once they were out of sight and the sound of their engines fading, Pilkington looked at Jackson through the gloom and pulled a wry face.

"Bloody Line-Swine! No discipline, Sergeant J; no discipline at all. Now then, get yourself back along the road. I've just told Mr Dunstable to start forming the platoon up. We need to get back over to the other bank sharpish because Brigade's just told us to blow. I'll come along with you. The Engineer firing party is with No.3 Company so as we pass through, we'll let them know it's all clear."

Jackson acknowledged and, calling Hawkins back in, started moving back towards the bridge. Within a couple of minutes they found the remainder of the platoon forming up, ready for the off.

"Alright, Harry." Pilkington greeted Dunstable. "I've got Sergeant Jackson and the other chap here. Get your boys moving and I'll bring up the rear with them."

With nervous urgency, the platoon began filing off after the young second lieutenant, the sound of their studded boots scraping on the cobbles in the darkness.

"Reckon this'll make a bloody big bang when it goes up." Pilkington observed casually to Jackson as they followed the platoon back down the road.

"Reckon so, Sir."

They were crossing the bridge now, the still water beneath them looking dark and uninviting.

"Are we stopping here to fight then, Sir?" Jackson ventured as he walked, side by side with the captain.

"I bloody hope so…" Pilkington said. "Don't know about you Sergeant J, but I've had enough of running away from the Hun."

"Aye, me too, Sir."

They passed by a small group of figures, huddled behind a pile of logs at the road side.

"That's all of us through, Angus." Pilkington called as they clumped past. "Last man of Number Four Company."

"Thanks, old boy." Came the voice of No.3 Company's commander. "We'll give you two or three minutes to get clear before we blow."

"Much obliged." Pilkington responded cheerfully.

For the first time in days, Jackson was starting to feel a little brighter. The cool, calm behaviour of the battalion's senior officers was reassuring. Despite all the rumour, the endless columns of refugees, the ill-disciplined flotsam of the army as it withdrew, and the repeated air attacks, Jackson knew that as long as he was with his battalion all would be well. And hopefully, tomorrow, the battalion would get its first proper scrap.

Boom!

The thunderclap of the explosion rocked the night, just as Jackson and his platoon began entering the town of Pecq. The night lit up momentarily as the bridge was blown to pieces by the carefully placed charges, the echo of the blast rolling across the water meadows of the River Escaut and off into the distance. As the initial crack of the explosion passed, the tinkling sound of glass came to Jackson's ears as every window in the town shattered under the shock wave. Beside him, Captain Pilkington sucked on his teeth.

"I hope those were all windows and not mirrors…" He commented laconically. "We don't need any more bad luck, do we?"

HURRICANE 'L' FOR LEATHER – OVER ST QUENTIN, FRANCE
MONDAY 20TH MAY 1940 – 0930 HOURS

Something didn't feel right. After ten gruelling days of air combat, airfield moves, enemy air raids, rumour and counter-rumour, Whittaker was feeling more than a little jumpy. Perhaps he was still upset that Devine, his aircraft's mechanic had been killed by shrapnel during the air raid a few days earlier, whilst McWilliams, his armourer, had been left heavily shell-shocked and almost incapable of doing anything remotely useful for more than forty eight hours after the event? They had been together as a crew for a good while when all was said and done, and it hadn't been a pleasant way of losing the old, trusted team. Perhaps it was even worse that his beloved Hurricane, 'F' for Freddie, had been completely destroyed on the ground during the same raid?

Perhaps this borrowed machine, another identical Hurricane, yet not *quite* the same as old 'Freddie' was the reason for his discomfort? After all, one became used to the tiny, almost intangible but unique quirks of one's own machine. Theoretically, this plane was exactly the same as his old one, yet for some reason it just *wasn't* the same. Perhaps of course, the reason for his uneasiness was the sheer fatigue that now enveloped him every minute of the day, along with the realisation that four of the squadron's original fourteen pilots had been killed or were missing as a result of the combats over the last ten days? Or perhaps it was due to this latest, and very cryptic, mission on which he was now engaged?

It had been rumoured that today might be the squadron's last day on operations. A warning order of sorts, not quite official but more substantive than rumour, had come in from Wing HQ, suggesting that the squadron might be pulled out of the line; maybe even back to England at some point over the next twenty four hours. In the meantime, six of the squadron's eight serviceable machines had been ordered to an airfield outside Amiens for a 'special op', and Whittaker was one of those who had volunteered to go. It was a strange task; very mysterious. Nobody knew quite what their job would be on arrival, but they reckoned it must be something important as it was a long flight to make, almost at extreme range for them, and there was a chance that they might not even make it without refuelling en route.

There had been talk of a co-ordinated British air offensive against the German spearheads that had apparently driven deep into the French lines, and one of the theories was that the squadron was being sent to act as top cover for a large bomber force being concentrated in the Amiens area. If that turned out to be true, then it would be nice for both the British fighter and bomber units to be working in concert at last.

As Whittaker considered all this, he was aware of the squadron leader speaking to the others in turn, checking their fuel states. It looked as though he was considering a refuelling stop after all. A sudden explosion nearby shook Whittaker's thoughts away from the technical problems associated with this mission and brought him back to more immediate matters. He veered to port slightly, startled by the sudden pop of anti-aircraft fire, and saw that more little black puffs were appearing in the air around him. A line of small calibre tracer ammunition also curved up from below, snaking past one of the Hurricanes to his forward right.

"Ruddy hell!" The metallic voice of Squadron Leader Rogers came across the air waves. "Where did that come from?"

"Bloody Frogs again!" Commented one of the other pilots sourly. "Shooting at anything that flies, as usual!"

"Doesn't look like French ack-ack to me…". Said another. "They're not usually that accurate, or that lively!"

"Wing didn't say anything about the Hun being in the area. If they are then that's bloody worrying, because we're just passing St Quentin. If that's Jerry gunfire then it means the buggers are less than eighty miles from the sea!"

Regardless of who was responsible for the fire, and without specific instruction, the squadron automatically began taking evasive action, whilst still keeping together as a loose formation. It was something they had become accustomed to during the last fortnight. This kind of drill was instinctive now; every pilot knew the score and the requirement for orders was minimal. The pilots followed the lead of Rogers as he led them slightly higher and away from the barrage of ground fire.

Just as they were settling down again, and starting to tighten up their formation once more, the cry of alarm came from the aircraft immediately to Whittaker's starboard.

"Behind us! Behind us! Watch out!"

The pilot's words were drowned out by the sudden crack of bullets slicing through the squadron of Hurricanes from their rear starboard side. Whittaker didn't need to look to realise what had happened. They were being bounced from above and behind by German fighters coming out of the morning sun and, with a practiced hand, he flicked the machine over in a tight roll to port and then dropped away from the formation.

The Hurricane responded as it should do; not as good as old Freddie of course, but well enough. Whittaker brought the nose up again after just a few seconds into the dive and conducted a sharp turn to starboard. More bullets streaked past his field of vision in a bright blur, the high pitched 'clack-clack-clack' of their passing audible above the roar of engines. And then he caught a brief glimpse of one of his attackers and his heart sank. 109s.

They had encountered relatively few of the deadly little single-seat Messerschmitt fighters thus far in the campaign, but from their few brushes with them, the British pilots knew how dangerous these aircraft could be. Fighting to gain height, Whittaker threw his aircraft over repeatedly, making himself a difficult target, before suddenly hauling on the steering column and bringing the Hurricane around in an acute turn upwards. It was a dangerous manoeuvre to try with an unknown quantity of enemy aircraft behind you, but he needed to get a look at what he was up against and perhaps the unexpected turn might throw the enemy off.

As the engine of the Hurricane protested, he glanced up through the canopy and caught his breath. The air was full of 109s; more than a dozen of the bastards, easily. Two were coming straight at him and he instinctively pressed the fire button on his control, letting rip with a wild, one second burst, before dropping his nose and diving straight underneath the two Germans.

Even as the shadows of the aircraft passed over him, Whittaker began to bring his machine around again in another tight turn to port. As he did so, he saw, with great satisfaction, that one of the enemy pilots had made the fatal mistake of trying to turn back on him. The 109 was trying to come round tightly, the same as Whittaker, but the British pilot had a two second lead on his opponent, and as the Messerschmitt was still coming out of its turn, Whittaker was able to bring his gun-sight over the aircraft and let go with a long, two second burst.

The two aircraft passed each other, just yards between them, and Whittaker caught a whiff of something burning. He didn't dare turn back to look but he was positive he had finished the Hun with his burst. There was no time to worry though because the second Messerschmitt had now managed to manoeuvre itself round and was coming in at him from his port side. He flipped to port and dived again, before rolling back over and throwing the plane around in a series of gut wrenching moves.

As he finally came up, thinking that the immediate danger had passed, two separate bursts of tracer came past him from behind, only just missing his plane.

"Bugger!" He cursed, realising he had another pair on his tail.

Whittaker was about to manoeuvre again when he spotted yet another pair of 109s coming for him from his forward right.

"Jesus!" He blasphemed once more as he realised that the odds were just too high on this occasion.

There was nothing he could do but run for it and save his remaining ammunition for any opportunity targets that arose as he made his escape. He might be able to take on a pair of Jerries, but not four. He dropped his nose again and put on a spurt, heading now for tree-top height as he fought to outrun his pursuers.

The next few minutes seemed like hours as he raced above the green fields of Northern France, twisting constantly as his attackers followed him with dogged persistence. Every now and then, a burst fire would come after him, reminding him that they were still there. He dared not turn or even make his evasive action too pronounced lest it give his enemy the chance to close up. With a sudden lurch of his heart, Whittaker remembered his fuel gauge and, glancing down, saw that he was extremely low. Much longer and he would be flying on fumes. He wracked his brain for an answer as he continued to weave across the countryside.

An unusually long pause in gunfire made him dare to hope that his pursuers had given up, but deep inside, he also feared they might be teasing him; daring him to turn his machine for a look back, at which point they would pounce on him, making the extra distance and catching him in mid-manoeuvre. He flew on, flat out, until eventually his sixth sense told him that the immediate danger was over. With great concentration, he executed a broad twist to starboard and then back to port, flinging a searching glance around him as he did so. He saw nothing.

He did it again, only this time for longer, allowing himself a more detailed scan of the scene to his rear. He saw them; just four black specs against the morning sky, heading back to where the battle had started, the chase abandoned. With a sigh of relief, he eased off on the throttle and wiped the sweat from his face, which was now pouring out of him by the bucket load. His shirt was soaked and his head was throbbing like a boiler, fit to burst. Steadying his breathing, Whittaker looked around and tried to get his bearings. He had been over St Quentin when they had been jumped, and looking at the sun he was obviously flying almost due north at the moment. Not having any maps, he had no idea where he might be, but he reckoned that north of St Quentin must be safe enough. After all, the BEF were to the north somewhere. He would need to look for an airfield; there were sure to be some in the area. And then his aircraft gave a cough.

At least it sounded like a cough. Then it turned into a splutter. Then the engine cut out completely.

"Shit!"

There was little time to worry about the detail. He was at about a thousand feet and somewhere just a few miles ahead he could see a major town or city. The countryside around him was largely flat and green, the broad fields lined with tall, elegant poplar trees, whilst beyond the town he could see a long, thickly wooded ridge.

With tremendous difficulty, Whittaker tried to bring the plane down in a gentle glide. He was doing fine until he was just a hundred feet off the ground, when suddenly it felt as if the air beneath the Hurricane had just disappeared. The aircraft began to drop in a much steeper dive than he had planned and he worked the controls like a man possessed in order to prevent the machine from hitting the ground nose first. He was over the last line of trees and staring at a field of half grown, yellow crops when he felt the unmistakable pull of gravity. He struggled to keep the nose up, desperately using all his skill and experience as the ground rushed towards him.

With a horrendous thud, the Hurricane thumped down into the corn field. The world became a blur of yellow, blue and green for several seconds, as Whittaker was jolted backwards and forwards and side to side. He heard the rending sound of metal being twisted and torn, and the metallic crunch of machinery being smashed until, after a few terrifying moments, the aircraft came to a stop. It was a sudden stop at that, which caused Whittaker to bang his head off the canopy and almost wrench one of his arms from the socket. But he was down.

For long moments he sat there, wincing at the pain in his head and arm, staring out at the expanse of crops around him. He was panting like a dog, his body completely soaked with sweat, his pulse racing like that of an Olympic sprinter. And then he let out a sob. Then another. And for a minute or so, he allowed the days of fear and exhaustion, of exhilaration and tragedy, to overtake him. He cried for the loss of Devine, and for the loss of his fellow pilots. He cried in relief at being spared yet again, in another one-sided combat. And he cried because he was tired. So very tired. He stopped sobbing when he heard the voices. English voices.

Whittaker looked up sharply and saw the three men wading through the waist high corn towards him; all of them dressed in khaki and one of them carrying a Lee-Enfield rifle. Wearily, Whittaker reached up and pushed his canopy back. He looked down at the three curious faces of the soldiers.

"Morning chaps. Thank God I've landed amongst friends!" He smiled weakly.

One of the soldiers, wearing the single stripe of a lance corporal, surveyed Whittaker and his machine with deep interest.

"Only just, matey..." He replied. "If you'd come down a couple of miles further back you'd have been right on top of Jerry."

The NCO was gesturing vaguely off into the distance.

"Really?" Whittaker asked. "I thought I'd come quite far north. Wasn't expecting to see Germans this far over. Where are we?"

The army corporal jerked his thumb over his shoulder.

"Arras is a mile or so that way."

"Arras?" Whittaker demanded, taken aback. "Arras? What are the bloody Germans doing near Arras? Are you sure about that? If the Jerries are near Arras then something's gone horribly wrong."

The lance corporal regarded him with a pitying glance. One of the other soldiers whispered something under his breath which Whittaker only just caught.

"Ruddy hell! What planet has this fellah been on?"

The corporal shot the man a warning glance, then looked back up at Whittaker.

"You'd best get yourself down from there and I'll fill you in on the details. Something's gone wrong alright, and believe me, you don't know the bloody half of it..."

THE TANNERY – PECQ ON THE RIVER ESCAUT
MONDAY 20TH MAY 1940 – 1030 HOURS

Jackson lifted the barrel of the Bren Gun up to the light and stared through it with his right eye, closing the left; scanning every twist of the rifling for evidence of dirt or rust. He found none and opened his left eye, using it to glare, firstly at Guardsman Richards, then at Guardsman Hawkins.

"That'll do." The sergeant murmured, before lowering the barrel and handing it back to a nervous looking Richards.

Next to him, Dunstable was placing the breech block and piston for the weapon back onto the towel where the remainder of the gun's working parts were laid out for inspection.

"Well done, Richards. Well done, Hawkins." Dunstable commented, rubbing his hands together.

"Leave the oil off until after the inspection next time though, alright?"

"Yes, Sir." Hawkins nodded obediently, as if receiving the wisdom of the Gods.

"You should know better, Hawkins." Jackson growled as he and the platoon commander moved off. "You too, Richards."

There was a crunch of boots as the attendant section commander slammed his feet together behind them.

"May I have your permission to carry on, Sir, please?"

"Yes, please." Dunstable responded, throwing up a salute in acknowledgement as he and Jackson sauntered away from the platoon.

As they went, the sound of metal on metal rang through the expanse of the tannery as the platoon slid the bolts back into their rifles and reassembled the Bren Guns.

It had been a standard morning for No.16 Platoon; stand-to just before dawn until the sun was up, then stand-down, wash, shave, breakfast and weapon cleaning. It was the way things were done in the Guards; no room for error. Everything as it should be. If these guardsmen had to fight the Germans today, they would do it with serviceable weapons and clean boots. It was called discipline and the Guards insisted on it by the cart load.

"Perhaps you should give young Hawkins a breather?" Dunstable suggested quietly as he wandered towards a window with his platoon sergeant by his side.

Several weeks ago, Dunstable would never have made such a comment to Jackson, but over the course of the last ten days, the two of them had become much more comfortable with each other; the shared stress of running the platoon in demanding circumstances bringing them together in a way that wouldn't happen during peace time.

Jackson gave a rumble in his throat.

"Perhaps..." He agreed reluctantly. "He's done alright these last few days; not dropped any major bollocks. Maybe he's actually starting to learn? It'd be the first time for a member of that bloody family, mind you."

Dunstable smiled. It was as close as Jackson could get to giving the unfortunate Guardsman Hawkins a compliment. Hawkins was a rogue of course. Even Dunstable, with his privileged, public school background could see that. But, he suspected, Hawkins was the kind of rogue who might come good in a crisis. And he looked like a fighter; as Jackson did. Perhaps that was the problem? Perhaps the two men were just too similar.

Neither Jackson nor Hawkins threw their weight around as such, and both men were relatively quiet when compared against their peers, yet there was something very unsettling about both men; a kind of fierce presence that suggested a store of submerged fury just waiting to burst to the surface. A silent, unintended menace. He dismissed the thought as he came to the window and gazed out across a dazzling sea of green and yellow fields, bounded by elegant rows of tall trees, with the canalised River Escaut flowing peacefully through the middle of the whole panorama.

"Lovely day." He murmured.

To his surprise, Jackson let out a long, wistful, sigh.

"It's actually quite beautiful isn't it, Sir?"

Dunstable glanced sideways at his platoon sergeant in mild astonishment. The tall NCO was staring out the window across the endless fields, his face no longer full of resolve or ferocity, or any of his usual emotions. Instead, he wore a look of deep sadness.

"Reminds me of the East Riding, this does." The sergeant commented in an unusually mellow voice. "Between Goole and the Wolds... Good farmland. Peaceful."

Dunstable hid a smile and looked back out at the countryside beyond.

"Yes, it is rather beautiful."

They stood there for a long while, gazing at the scenery, a comfortable silence between them. After a while, Dunstable looked at his watch.

"Ten thirty. I wonder if the Jerries will come today?"

Next to him, Jackson let out another deep sigh.

"I hope not."

"Really?" Dunstable looked at his platoon sergeant again with renewed surprise. "I thought you couldn't wait to get your hands on them?"

Jackson grunted.

"I can't." He said, his voice thick with uncharacteristic emotion. "But it's far too nice a day for dying..."

Dunstable had been unprepared for the comment; so alien was it coming from a man who was nothing short of a military drill manual in human guise. He felt a lump rise in his throat and the face of the injured girl by the roadside came back into his mind again.

"Yes..." Dunstable murmured, looking away as he felt a tear prick at the corner of his eye. "You're right there. Far too nice a day..."

"Ah, Harry! Just the man!"

The sound of the Company Commander's voice snapped the two men out of their melancholy. They turned to see Captain Pilkington approaching them from across the big warehouse.

"Good news, gentlemen; good news…" He boomed out as he stomped towards them. "I've just come back from a Battalion O'Group. You'll be delighted to hear that we're not going anywhere today. We're going to start digging in. This time however, it's for real. We're going to stand and fight the buggers!"

THE ASSEMBLY AREA – VIMY RIDGE, JUST NORTH OF ARRAS
MONDAY 20TH MAY 1940 – 1900 HOURS

It was a spooky place to be. Corporal Stan Claxton of the 7th Battalion, Royal Tank Regiment pulled his greatcoat tightly around him as he listened to the Company Commander run through the plan once more. It was getting dark early, here amongst the trees. That, combined with the fact that they were sitting amongst the preserved First World War trenches of the Canadian Army, and the war graves that went with them, was giving the young tank commander the creeps. He knew that this was to be the eve of his first battle and it felt as if the ghosts of a thousand long dead souls were watching him; half amused, half pitying.

He gave a small shudder and tried to shrug off the thought, turning his attention back to the Company Commander. The major who commanded his infantry tank company was briefing every single tank commander, together in one go, rather than feeding the orders via platoon commanders, as was the usual form. There was one main reason for this and it was quite simply that there was only one map of the area amongst the whole company. Not an auspicious start to the battle, Claxton reflected, but then again this was real war, and one should expect a certain amount of confusion during wartime.

He comforted himself with the fact that his company was one of the better equipped, his own platoon boasting no less than three of the big, well armed Mark II tanks, affectionately known as Matildas. It was a slow, solid, powerful looking vehicle, and Claxton had grown more than fond of his own machine. He was looking forward to finally getting it into action tomorrow. It would be nice to give the Germans a taste of British tanks, he reckoned, after all the talk he was hearing about how the German Panzers were 'everywhere'.

"So, just to recap…" The Company Commander was saying. "We'll have a screen of motorcyclists from the Royal Northumberland Fusiliers moving ahead of us by about a mile or so. They should be able to scoot back and give us early warning of any enemy presence in the area so that we can shake out into the required formation. No.5 Platoon? As you have the most Mk II tanks then you will take the centre with company headquarters directly behind you. No.4 Platoon will take the left and No.6 Platoon the right. When we move off, I want the Mk IIs to watch their speed so we don't leave the Mk Is behind."

And so he went on.

The plan was simple it seemed. The Germans had passed by to the south of Arras somewhere, but it was believed to be only a small vanguard and consequently the enemy had left a long and unguarded line of communication in their wake. To that end, 7th RTR, along with their sister battalion, 4th RTR, the Northumberland Fusiliers and two battalions from the Durham Light Infantry, were to conduct a two pronged clearance operation of the area to the south of Arras by sweeping around its western edge, and then swinging east, thereby severing the German lines of communication. There was talk of this being co-ordinated with a sally by the Arras garrison and an attack by some French units to the east and west of Arras, but there was no detail on that. Claxton was happy enough. Follow the rest of the company and shoot at anything German; nothing difficult about that. He liked simplicity.

The Company Commander was finishing off now.

"Any questions gentlemen?"

There was a moment of silence as the assembled officers and non-commissioned officers considered the plan. After a couple of seconds, one of the young second lieutenants put his hand up.

"Is there any supporting artillery, Sir?"

The look on the Company Commander's face suggested that it was not the sort of question he had hoped for.

"I'm afraid there won't be any on this occasion Jeremy, but to be honest, I'm not sure that it would be of much use as we are planning to make quite a rapid advance. I doubt we will come across any fixed or deeply entrenched targets that would be suitable for artillery. We are most likely going to encounter opportunity targets that will be dealt with best by our speed and manoeuvrability."

There were a couple more questions concerning minor detail, but nothing of any great consequence. On the whole, everybody was feeling pretty positive and ready for the off.

"Right then, gentlemen." The Company Commander said brightly. "We're all set to give Jerry a good kick in the pants tomorrow. H-Hour will be at 1400 hours, so let's synchronise watches. In two minutes it will be 1907 hours exactly…"

Claxton pulled back his cuff and began adjusting his watch. As he waited for the Company Commander to mark the time, he glanced sideways. In the gathering gloom of the trees he could see a distant memorial to the fallen of the last war, standing tall, pale and ghostly among the trees. He fancied he could see the ghosts of the dead lingering amongst the shadows; watching, waiting, expectant.

"Don't worry, lads…" He murmured under his breath. "Tomorrow we'll give the Jerries and damn good thrashing and pay them back for you; good and proper."

"What's that, mate?"

Claxton jumped slightly as, to his left, Corporal Ronnie Peters from No.4 Platoon leaned in close.

"Did you say something?"

Claxton smiled sheepishly back.

"Nothing important, mate; just talking to myself. First sign of madness that is…"

HEADQUARTERS GERMAN 19TH CORPS – QUERRIEU, NEAR AMIENS
MONDAY 20TH MAY 1940 – 2030 HOURS

Guderian looked at the two Luftwaffe pilots with the kind of stern glare that a schoolmaster would reserve for a pupil who had underperformed but was capable of much better. The young lieutenant and his sergeant were standing before him looking extremely shamefaced. They were lucky not to be dead however. Just half an hour earlier, in one of those unfortunate occurrences that were so common in battle, the two men, in their Messerschmitt 110 fighter-bomber, along with two other aircraft, had mistakenly attacked Guderian's Headquarters, thinking that they had caught a British or French formation unprepared in the last few minutes of daylight. Although on a reconnaissance mission, they had decided that the target was too good an opportunity to miss.

Unfortunately for these two, they had learned the hard way exactly how effective their own flak could be. Their machine had been shot down in short order, whilst the other two planes had veered away from the firestorm of anti-aircraft fire. It was only when the two crewmen had floated to earth by parachute and were subsequently 'captured' by German soldiers that they had realised, with horror, that they had just strafed their own troops.

"You should know better, gentlemen!" Guderian snapped at them. "We have procedures in place to stop this kind of thing happening. It's just as well that nobody was killed during the whole damn business. There would have been some interesting letters to write home to wives and mothers then, wouldn't there? *I'm sorry madam, but the Luftwaffe has killed your husband by mistake...*"

He left the potential consequences hanging in the air as the crew of the 110 looked at their boots, their faces going redder than they already were. Guderian was not finished yet, however.

"To be honest with you though, it's not that possibility that annoys me the most. It's the fact that we've just had to destroy one of our own aircraft! Aircraft which cost a lot of money and which are already in short supply! What an unnecessary waste of a plane..."

He treated them to another indignant scowl. After a while, his face relaxed slightly.

"However, this *is* war...And as von Clausewitz tells us, war is laced with friction. The easiest of things in peacetime become most difficult under the pressure of war..."

Guderian tailed off. The two airmen looked up a little, sensing that their rebuke was coming to an end.

"You look tired." The general said, changing tack suddenly. "How many missions have you flown today?"

"This was our third sortie, General." The lieutenant replied.

Guderian nodded acknowledgement.

"A punishing schedule then, gentlemen?"

He glanced off to one side and saw that his orderly was waiting with three glasses of Champagne. Guderian had ordered the drinks to be brought in earlier, before he had confronted the two pilots, knowing that his audience with them was always going to be a small piece of theatre. He beckoned the orderly over.

"Gentlemen, grab yourselves a glass. Let us drink to the *'frictions of war'*."

The two Luftwaffe crewmen blinked in surprise as the orderly appeared and offered the tray to them. A look of relief began to flood across their young features as they realised that this Army general was not such a bad old stick after all. They reached for the glasses, mumbling their thanks.

"I too have had my fair share of frictions these last few days." Guderian commented, and quickly reflected on the rapid chain of events of the past week. His resignation, immediate reinstatement, his authority to conduct reconnaissance in force, followed by the eventual cancellation of the halt order, had all put their own particular pressure on him. It was the way of war.

Guderian took the third glass and was about to raise it in toast when the dependable Colonel Nehring came bustling into the map room from the communications area. Guderian paused, glancing across at his chief of staff. The colonel was flushed, excited, and it was clear he was finding it difficult to restrain himself, though not in any bad way. The sparkle in the colonel's eyes said it all.

"General…" Nehring interrupted the little gathering without apology. "2nd Panzer Division has just signalled us. Their lead panzer battalion has taken Abbeville."

At last, the colonel could restrain himself no longer and his face broke into a wide grin. The staff officer's tired face lit up like a beacon, such was his excitement.

"We have reached the sea, General!"

Guderian felt his own heart flutter with delight at the news. They had done it. Against all the odds, all the pressures, all the doubters, they had done it. They had reached the French coast and now the main Allied armies, including the British, were surrounded. With a broad smile, Guderian looked back at the two aviators.

"To the frictions of war, gentlemen…" He said raising his glass. "And to victory!"

Tuesday 21st May 1940
The Twelfth Day – Morning

WEST BANK OF THE RIVER ESCAUT – NEAR PECQ
TUESDAY 21ST MAY 1940 – 0300 HOURS

Jackson paused where the bushes came to an end in the stream bed. He signalled the halt and dropped to one knee. Behind him the men of No.3 Section did the same. They had been on patrol for about an hour now, having been tasked by company headquarters at the last minute. The reason, apparently, was that a gap had been identified between the right hand positions of their own battalion and the left hand positions of the 3rd Battalion Grenadiers Guards; their neighbours. It shouldn't have happened, given that accepted military thought understood that boundaries between units were particularly vulnerable to attack, and therefore should be adequately covered.

On this occasion there had been an oversight and there was a gap of several hundred yards between the inner-flank positions of the two Guards battalions. Jackson was led to believe that the gap had been discovered by an officer from their own battalion who, having reported the matter, had tried to fill the gap with some of his own men before being accidentally shot dead by a friendly sentry. It didn't sound like a very good start to the impending confrontation with the Germans, but that was war for you. Jackson was now beginning to understand the reality of it. He had started out some ten days before thinking that the campaign would unfold as clearly and logically as a Queen's Birthday Parade. Only now did he realise how confusing war could be. The contradictory reports and rumours, the silly little mistakes by men who hadn't slept for days, they all added to the melting pot of chaos.

Still, this was more like it. Jackson was now engaged on a task that carried a certain amount of familiarity. Accepting that the oversight had been made, his small standing patrol had been hurriedly despatched to cover the gap during the hours of darkness. By first light, they would be back at the tannery, manning the positions they had built up the day before, awaiting the arrival of the Germans. He scanned the open fields across to his right and saw the pale expanse of corn fields rising up slightly to what looked like a small wood or tree-line. The Grenadiers were over there somewhere. He looked back towards where the river should be, picking out the dim silhouettes of well-spaced trees that lined it on this bank. He reckoned it would make sense to follow this stream right down to the river, then handrail the bank southwards until he was in a decent position to cover the whole stretch.

Signalling to the men behind him, Jackson stood, and with his rifle in the ready-alert position, began walking carefully along the edge of the small brook in the direction of the river. The night was dark and clear, myriad stars twinkling in the black expanse of space. Consequently, it was also cold. There were tiny wisps of mist drifting across the fields around him, and Jackson reckoned that come morning there would be a thick ground mist covering the whole area. He was an East Yorkshireman and this ground reminded him so much of home. He could easily tell what the morning would bring, weather-wise. Even so, he mused as he trod carefully along the edge of the stream, the misty start would probably give way to another lovely warm day.

He was almost at the tree-lined bank now, and he dropped to one knee again. Once more, his patrol followed suit behind him. The sergeant knelt there for a while, searching the darkness ahead. He could see the surface of the river through the tree-line, calm and black. Apart from the odd, very distant rumble of artillery fire or rifle shot, the night was silent. No owls hooting, no voices, no vehicles, no dogs barking; not even the sound of fish jumping. Reassured, Jackson moved on once more, signalling the others to follow.

He led them along the bank of the Escaut, moving from tree to tree, slowly heading south. As they moved cautiously onwards, Jackson scanned the opposite side of the river. It was all quiet there, too. Eerily quiet. A little way further on, he noted the dark outline of bushes in the field next to the river. Perhaps that would do as a nice spot for the patrol to lie-up and watch the bank? He was still considering this when, as he stepped toward one of the trees, he noticed a figure crouching by its trunk.

Jackson froze instantly. There was no mistaking the outline of the human figure, crouching in the shadow of the tree and gazing out across the river. As if sensing Jackson's presence, the person by the tree half turned their body and the Coldstream sergeant saw the pale blob of their face as they stared up at him. He heard the rustle and scrape of the person's kit as they adjusted their position. Somewhat surprised to have come across someone on the bank, Jackson hissed at them.

"Are you a Coldstreamer or a Grenadier?"

There was a moment of silence, the sound of a surprised gasp, then the unmistakeable sound of a foul curse in a foreign language.

"Fuck…" Jackson suddenly blurted out loud, forgetting to keep his voice to a whisper.

He took an involuntary step back as he automatically brought his rifle to bear on the figure, and that single movement probably saved his life.

At precisely that moment, the night was shattered by the thunderous chatter of machine-gun fire and a series of bright muzzle flashes erupted from the base of the tree. A whole burst of bullets cracked upwards, past Jackson's face, and into the branches of the tree behind him as he jumped backwards yet another pace in shock. The sergeant fancied he could almost feel the wind on his face as the bullets streaked past him.

Without thinking, and as shocked as he was by the sudden eruption of gunfire, he leapt forwards at the figure as the machine-gun went silent for a moment. Being tall, it took Jackson just two long strides before he was right up to the figure by the tree trunk and taking a swing with his right leg, as if taking a penalty at a football match. His heavy ammunition boot connected with something hard that made a crunching noise and he heard his enemy give a painful grunt. The resistance against his foot gave way and the dark figure fell backwards onto the open riverbank. As the man toppled back, his weapon clattered to the earth and Jackson stepped after him, remembering his own rifle and bringing it into a position to fire.

Before Jackson had the chance to fire however, and much to his surprise, the man on the floor simply rolled over onto one knee and launched himself at the big Coldstreamer in a lightning-fast response. Now it was Jackson's turn to grunt as the man slammed into him, pushing him back against the tree trunk with a thud. He heard the man snarl something in his foreign language and Jackson suddenly felt the rage swell within him. He growled, and locked his left leg around the other man's right, and leaned forward with all his weight.

With a sickening crash, the two men toppled over onto the ground, nothing more than a rifle between them. As they struggled on the floor, Jackson's rifle was pushed aside. In truth, he had forgotten his weapon, his mind reverting to the days when he used to mix it with the big-time dockers from Goole on a Saturday night. The two men were snarling at each other now and Jackson could smell the other man's breath; the bitter smell of coffee and something spicy assailing the sergeant's senses. The German was trying to knee Jackson in his crotch whilst simultaneously throwing punch after punch into his ribs on the right side.

"Yaagh!" Jackson snarled, partly in pain and partly in anger, pummelling the man back in similar fashion.

Without warning, the German changed tactics and clutched a big, meaty hand around Jackson's throat. The Coldstreamer gasped as strong fingers dug into his flesh, seeking out his windpipe. The sergeant's mind was racing now. He could hear voices shouting but couldn't understand a word that was being said, and he could swear he heard more gunshots. This was crazy; war wasn't supposed to be like this! He was struggling now, even though he was on top of the German. The enemy soldier was squeezing harder on Jackson's throat and his other hand was scrabbling for the same spot too.

The Coldstreamer decided he'd had just about enough of this and opted for one of his favourite tricks. Quickly, he worked his mouth and his tongue, trying to summon saliva. Then, with an effort, he hawked and spat right into his enemy's face. For just a moment, the German cried out in disgusted alarm and his grip on Jackson's throat relaxed. It was all the big man needed and with tremendous force he smashed his head down towards his opponent's, driving his steel helmet into the man's face.

Jackson heard another crunch and the man gave a stunned grunt. He felt the German's body relax even more, so he repeated the action. This time the man gave a sickly gurgle.

The blood was rushing through Jackson's ears now, as if he were trapped in a storm drain that was suffering a flash flood. He felt a hand on his shoulder and was about to react, thinking that his enemy wasn't yet finished. As he made to respond, a vaguely familiar voice registered in his mind.

"Sergeant Jackson! Get out of the fucking way!"

Something clicked in his mind, and Jackson allowed himself to be pushed sideways, falling to his left. As he half rolled, half fell, Jackson saw the long stubby snout of a Lee-Enfield rifle slide past him, and then a split second later there was a tremendous bang and a bright flash.

The sergeant fell onto his elbows and stared dumbly ahead as his eyes adjusted to the dark again after the sudden flash of light from the weapon, drinking in huge lung-fulls of air as he did so. As his vision returned to normal he saw the body of his opponent lying motionless beside him, his arms flung loosely off to the sides. A hand grabbed Jackson's shoulder again and then another face was close to his.

"Are you alright, Sergeant?"

Jackson recognised the voice. Guardsman Hawkins; the little bastard.

"Fine..." Jackson blurted, scrabbling to find his rifle.

All around him there was gunfire, the bullets travelling in all directions. His senses were recovering now, his stunned mind catching up with reality.

"Jacko? Jacko?"

The sound of another familiar voice calling him. Piggy Hogson.

"He's here Sergeant!" Hawkins called out to the section commander.

A moment later, the stocky lance sergeant slid down on one knee next to Jackson and the young guardsman.

"What's everyone shooting at?" Jackson demanded, still shaken.

"Jerries along the bank, Davey!" Hogson replied. "Right down by the water's edge..."

The unmistakable sound of the section's Bren Gun cut through the night.

"Twenty five yards at the most..." Hogson went on over the noise.

Crump!

"Aagh!"

A blinding flash, a sickening tremor and shock wave; the sound of one of their own men screaming in pain.

"Grenade!" Jackson realised out loud.

"Fucking arseholes!" Hawkins swore and let off a rifle shot in the direction of the enemy.

"Throw one back, Hawkins!" Jackson snapped. "Grenade the fuckers!"

The sergeant turned to Hogson.

"Piggy, shake the boys out and give rapid fire at the bastards. I'll put up a Very Light and see what we've got."

"Someone's been hit…" The section commander began.

"Leave 'em." Jackson snarled. "Kill the fucking Germans first!"

Hogson turned away and began screaming out orders to the section. Meanwhile, Jackson fumbled for the Very Pistol and cartridges that he was carrying in his side pack. With trembling fingers, he fumbled a small cartridge into the pistol and snapped it shut. The gunfire from his own men was deafening now, but the crack of enemy bullets coming back at them seemed to have tailed off.

Rolling onto his stomach Jackson raised his arm and aimed the pistol upwards, away from the tree's branches and out over the river.

Pop.

There was a shower of sparks and the flare sailed lazily upwards over the river.

"Jesus!" Hawkins swore as the flare missed his ear by a matter of inches.

Instantly, the dark banks and murky water of the river were bathed in a sickly yellow light and everything became suddenly clear.

"There they are!" Someone yelled.

"They're trying to get away!" Hawkins grunted.

Jackson squinted at the illuminated scene and quickly took in the detail. Two rubber dinghies, one against this bank, the other a few yards into the river. A press of men was trying to get into one, whilst the boat on the water was being paddled furiously by several others. For a brief second, Jackson gawped at the sight of them, absorbing the most trivial of details. The strange shaped German helmets, rifles and machine-pistols slung across backs alongside cylindrical cases and assorted bags and pouches; paddles rising and falling.

"Open fire!" Jackson bawled. "Kill 'em all!"

The gunfire from his section swung immediately out from the bank towards the water and Hawkins swung his arm like a cricketer as he lobbed his grenade down the bank towards the enemy crowding around the nearest boat. As the light from the flare began to fade, Jackson saw the splashes on the water around the furthest dinghy as bullets sliced through the night. One of the Germans suddenly toppled sideways off the boat and into the dark water with a loud 'kersplosh', his paddle flopping uselessly onto the surface. The light faded abruptly as the flare died, but a moment later there was another 'crump' as Hawkins' grenade exploded by the waterline.

There were more screams, and the sound of urgent shouting; this time in German.

"We've got the bastards!" Hawkins yelled triumphantly.

"Keep firing!" Jackson roared as he ejected the spent cartridge from the Very Pistol and fumbled for another.

Before he had the chance to reload, an unbelievably loud clatter of incoming bullets slashed past his head, the tracer rounds in the burst whizzing past in a bright blur.

"Get down, Hawkins!" Jackson warned.

The young man needed no encouragement as another long burst streaked above them. There was more fire now, coming from the opposite bank. Jackson could see the flashes. Machine-guns. Big ones, and lots of them. One of the bursts was more accurate and slammed into the bank just an arm's length away. Jackson and Hawkins pressed themselves flat as spurts of mud and grass showered them.

"Get back!" Jackson ordered above the racket. "Get back from the bank! Drop into the furrows in the field!"

He followed his own advice, scurrying as fast as possible behind the tree-line and into the cornfield, keeping himself pressed flat against the earth all the way.

The enemy machine-guns were laying down a terrific rate of fire now, far outstripping anything Jackson's men could attempt with their single Bren Gun. As the sergeant, accompanied by Hawkins, elbowed themselves down into the ruts of the corn field, they could see the other members of the patrol clustered along its border.

"Piggy! Piggy!" Jackson called out.

"Here!"

"Get the lads moving; back along the field towards the stream bed, and keep low."

"Richards has been hit!" Hogson's voice came back. "He's bleeding like fuck!"

"Drag him!" Jackson shouted. "We'll patch him up when we're back in the stream bed!"

As Jackson uttered the words, he was aware of a not so distant rumble. He cocked his head to one side, registering the unusual sound above the noise of machine-guns. Hogson was shouting something back, but Jackson wasn't listening to the reply. He could still hear the strange rumbling. Then he heard something else which turned his blood cold.

Whoosh...

"Incoming!" Jackson managed to scream, just as the first shell slammed into the field, some thirty metres away.

The ground underneath him suddenly lurched and Jackson winced as shell after shell followed the first, exploding in an ear shattering series of blasts all around them. Then, even worse, several more shells exploded in mid air and Jackson heard the unmistakable hiss of shrapnel flying through the dark night. He turned his head sideways, panting with fear and found himself looking straight into the face of Guardsman Hawkins.

"Fucking hell, Sergeant!" The young soldier laughed nervously. "This is turning into a right old punch-up!"

GERMAN FORMING UP POINT – EAST BANK OF THE RIVER ESCAUT
TUESDAY 21ST MAY 1940 – 0710 HOURS

Captain Siegfried Dullman thrust out his hand and beamed confidently at the smaller man who had turned to face him.

"Morning my friend. Name's Dullman. Siegfried Dullman, 2nd Battalion, 82nd Infantry Regiment. My company's on the left as we go over, so I reckon that makes us neighbours."

The diminutive captain he was addressing smiled back, accepting Dullman's hand and shaking it firmly.

"Lothar Ambrosius." He introduced himself. "2nd Battalion, 12th Infantry. We're the right assault battalion, so neighbours we are, then."

"You all set for it?" Dullman asked.

The smaller man nodded, taking a deep breath.

"We are indeed. Seems like we've been punching at ghosts for the last few days. Every time we go to attack the British, they've pulled back and disappeared off the face of the earth. Maybe today they might give us a fight, eh?"

Dullman nodded his agreement.

"I reckon you could be right there, Lothar. Our regiment put some recce patrols across last night and they got into a bit of trouble. They reckon the Tommies have dug in on the other bank, ready for a fight. One of the patrols got completely minced as it was pulling back."

Ambrosius winced.

"Many casualties?"

"Half a dozen dead and missing." Dullman sighed. "Most of the others wounded. Got caught on the water as they paddled back apparently."

Ambrosius shook his head in dismay.

"Well, if the Tommies are still there, it's probably going to be an even bloodier day."

"This mist should help us though." Dullman said brightly, looking about him. "Just hope it stays like this until we're across."

Ambrosius sucked his teeth.

"I reckon when our artillery starts coming down it could break the mist up a bit mind you. Still, the observers have got a good view from up on the high ground at Mont St Aubert. They should be able to give us a good show."

He fumbled for his map suddenly.

"I suppose we'd better de-conflict our boundaries quickly..."

"Hmm, better had; especially if this mist does stay down." Dullman agreed.

The two captains peered down at the map and Ambrosius used his pencil to indicate various points of interest.

"My left assault company is heading for this small hamlet here, Esquelmes I believe it's called. The right assault company are going for this piece of high ground here; it's a ridge that runs up to the main north-south road. You can't miss it because it's covered with tall Poplars and it dominates the whole area."

Dullman nodded and jabbed his little finger at the map.

"That works nicely. Our battalion's been tasked with capturing the town of Pecq, just to your north. The commanding officer wants me to try and break into the village from the south, so I was going to try and hit the opposite bank about here. There's a stream bed, thick with undergrowth, that runs towards the road at the southern end of the village. I'd like to follow it along and get right in behind them if I can."

Ambrosius grunted his approval of Dullman's intent.

"That'll work nicely; we shouldn't get in each other's way. Besides, once I'm up on that high ground my machine-guns can cover your flank and rear across these open fields."

Dullman grinned at his opposite number.

"Sounds like a plan to me."

At that point, there was a tremendous rumble of heavy gun fire from behind them, some distance away. The two men turned and stared into the mist. Within a moment or two, the air above them was filled with the sound of artillery shells streaking overhead towards their targets. A thrill of anticipation ran through both men as the ground beneath them suddenly shuddered. Somewhere in the distance, at the British side of the river, the first shells began to explode with an ominous 'crump'.

"That's the preliminary bombardment going in." Ambrosius murmured. "Ten minutes to Zero Hour."

Dullman glanced at his watch.

"Fuck! Where did the time go? I'd best get back over to my boys."

He flung his hand out once more.

"The best of luck to you, Lothar."

Ambrosius shook hands with the other captain a second time.

"And to you, Siegfried. Give the Tommies hell, eh?"

"Oh, I will, my friend; don't you worry. I certainly will."

With that, Dullman turned way and doubled off into the mist, as yet more heavy artillery shells screamed through the morning mist towards the west bank of the River Escaut. It was time for battle to commence.

FORWARD POSITIONS, 3RD BATTALION GRENADIER GUARDS – ON THE ESCAUT, 800 YARDS SOUTH-EAST OF PECQ
TUESDAY 21ST MAY 1940 – 0710 HOURS

Crack-crump! Crack-crump! Crack-crump!

"Jesus Christ!"

Guardsman 'Jack' Dawes jumped in alarm as the first salvo of air-burst artillery shells exploded above his platoon's positions along the western bank of the river. The ear shattering cracks were followed instantly by the evil hiss of red hot shrapnel slicing through the air, searching for the soft, vulnerable flesh of the men who occupied the open trenches.

"Fucking Germans!" Lance Corporal Dixon grunted as he threw himself flat against the side of their trench.

Dawes, following the non-commissioned officer's example, flung his mess tin with its half-eaten corned beef hash to one side and pressed himself in against the wall of their hastily prepared defensive position.

Crack-crump! Crack-crump! Crack-crump!

Another salvo shattered the morning air above them, and instantly a nerve shattering scream of agony cut through the noise of the explosions.

Dawes glanced sideways and saw Dixon twist away from him, collapsing face down on the floor of the trench.

"Aagh! Fucking hell!"

With wide eyes, Dawes watched as a six inch long red gash opened up along Dixon's right shoulder blade, from which emerged an unbelievable wave of blood.

"Oh, my God!" The guardsman breathed, shocked at the terrible sight.

The lance corporal was writhing on the bottom of the trench, sobbing with pain.

"Corporal Dixon, lay still..." Dawes called out to the injured man, dropping to his knees at the same time and crawling along the trench towards him.

"Jack! What's happened?"

The voice of Guardsman Dave Hastings, the section Bren Gunner and the third occupant of their trench, sounded above the thunder of the bombardment. Dawes looked back over his shoulder at his comrade who was huddled against the far end of the position.

"Dicko's been hit! Throw me the shell-dressings over!"

Hastings grabbed for the small web-satchel and threw it along the bottom of the trench.

"Cheers!" Dawes grabbed the bag and turned back towards Dixon who continued to writhe on the earthen floor.

"Oh, Christ! I've lost my arm! I can't feel it!"

The corporal was going into shock quickly.

"Dicko, you're alright, mate; don't worry!" Dawes shouted above the racket of incoming artillery. "You've copped some shrapnel in your shoulder; lay still mate and I'll get it bandaged for you! We'll get you back to the company aid post in a mo'."

He fumbled with the straps of the satchel and finally managed to open one of them. Rummaging inside the bag he dragged out a shell dressing and began, with trembling fingers, to rip open the canvas wrapping.

Whoosh-crump!

The sound of the artillery changed and the ground shook even more, the earth heaving beneath the soldiers in the trench. Lumps of soil came away from the side of the trench and fell onto Dawes, finding its way under the collar of his battle dress. The enemy had switched the fuses on their shells to explode on impact. Two more shells slammed into the ground nearby, and Dawes dug his fingers into the ground, as if trying to hold onto a narrow mountain ledge. The earth was trembling continuously. Beneath Dawes, his section second in command continued to scream in agony.

Dawes could feel his heart thumping inside his chest, and his stomach felt suddenly heavy, which in turn gave him the sensation of needing a shit. Fighting to control his breathing, Dawes ripped the dressing fully open, turned it inside out and then pressed it down over the gaping wound in Dixon's shoulder.

"Aagh!" The corporal screamed even louder as Dawes pressed firmly down with the pad of the dressing.

Was that a good sign? If Dixon could feel pain when Dawes pressed the dressing on then surely he must still have sensation in that part of his body?

Dawes pressed harder and began fumbling with the bandage's loose end, trying to fathom how best to tie it off around the man's shoulder. His mind racing, Dawes suddenly thought that it would be better if he could get rid of the corporal's webbing straps first. He was still wrestling with the practical problem of how best to achieve that when he realised that his hands were wet. Looking down, Dawes saw that the dressing pad was already saturated with blood and that he was going to need more than one.

"Bloody hell..." He cursed. "Dave? Get me another shell dressing out, quick..."

Whoosh-crump!

The explosion was close. Very close. So close that the force of it pushed Dawes flat on top of the wounded Dixon and sucked the air from his lungs. His ears hurt like hell from the thunderclap of the blast and he was sure he could smell the awful scent of singed hair.

The corporal screamed again at the additional pressure, whilst something heavy thumped Dawes on top of his helmet, then bounced painfully onto his back. At the same time, the sides of the trench shuddered and huge lumps of soil dropped over the pair of prostrate soldiers. Somewhere above the noise, and despite his ringing ears, Dawes heard the splintering of wood and the whipping noise of branches as a nearby tree toppled over.

"Fucking hell! This is getting far too close for comfort!"

He pushed himself up again and the heavy object on his back fell off, landing beside him and Dixon on the floor of the trench. The guardsman blinked in surprise as he saw it was the Bren Gun which had been resting on the parapet.

"Dave? Get this ruddy Bren Gun out of the way, will you? Dave?"

Dawes tried to pull the light machine-gun out of the way, looking around for Hastings as he did so.

"Dave..."

The guardsman blinked in surprise to find the space behind him empty. Empty of sorts. The end of the trench where Hastings had been was partially collapsed. Of the said guardsman there was no sign although, rather curiously, one of his ammunition boots sat atop a pile of loosened soil.

Dawes stared at the lone boot with a dumbfounded expression on his face. As his mind attempted to make sense of this sudden chaos around him, he vaguely registered the sound of incoming artillery, followed by a loud 'kersplosh'. A moment or two elapsed, after which Dawes was suddenly drenched by a sheet of water that dropped down on him from above. The unexpected shower brought him to, and without a word, he returned to the difficult job of trying to stem the flow of blood from Dixon's gaping shoulder wound. He shut his mind off from everything else and applied every inch of his concentration to the task in hand.

Quickly, ignoring Dixon's sobbing, Dawes managed to tie the first dressing in position. Having done so, he fumbled inside the satchel for another dressing and repeated the process, trying his best to seal the huge gash. As he fumbled with a third dressing, the young guardsman noticed that the shelling seemed to be less intense now, as if the enemy fire was being directed slightly further away of a sudden. In addition, Dixon was making a lot less fuss. That was probably a bad sign, Dawes thought. Probably the loss of blood was starting to have an effect.

A shadow appeared over the trench.

"Who's that down there?"

Dawes looked up at the sound of the well-spoken voice and instantly recognised the face of Lieutenant Boyd staring down at him.

"Guardsman Dawes, Sir." He replied. "Corporal Dixon's copped some shrapnel; he's lost a lot of blood. I don't know where Hastings has gone…"

"Never mind that now…" Boyd cut him short. "The Jerries are coming. Get that Bren Gun up here and stand-to. As soon as you see the buggers come into range, let them have it. Understand?"

Dawes blinked in surprise, his mind racing.

"Sir." He blurted the standard response.

Boyd nodded his satisfaction with the reply then disappeared from view.

"Dicko; on your feet mate. Come on; let me give you a hand up…"

With an effort, Dawes began levering Dixon up, first onto his knees, then onto his feet. The lance corporal was now emitting a continuous, quiet moan, the loss of blood beginning to affect his senses. After several attempts, Dawes finally got the big corporal propped up against the end of the trench.

"Dicko, you need to get back to the company aid post mate. You'll have to go on your own; I've got to stay here and man the Bren. You got that mate?"

The corporal nodded dumbly.

"I'll give you a leg up." Dawes continued. "Use your good arm to pull yourself over when I push."

Without pausing to confirm that the corporal was ready, Dawes squatted down, grabbed hold of one of Dixon's feet with both hands, pushed his shoulder under the other man's buttocks, then heaved with all his might. The corporal let out a loud, unintelligible, pain-filled curse as Dawes pushed him upwards. The young guardsman snarled with the effort of lifting the heavy non-commissioned officer, but after just a couple of moments struggling, he felt the burden lessen as Dixon used his good arm to drag himself over the rear lip of the trench.

Standing fully upright now, Dawes pushed Dixon's legs, rather unceremoniously, after the rest of his body. Face down on the ground behind the trench, Dixon was panting heavily. Dawes noticed that the corporal's face was as white as a sheet.

"Get yourself back to the aid post, mate; quick as you can. Keep low."

Leaving Dixon to fend for himself now, Dawes reverted to his orders from Boyd. He stooped down, grabbed the Bren Gun, then hauled it up onto the front parapet. Unfolding the bipod legs, he set the gun up, digging the legs into the spoil and turf.

He looked round for the gun's spare magazines but could see only one of them on the floor on the trench, which he swiftly recovered from the churned up soil by his feet. He scanned round in vain for the others but couldn't see any. Where were they? Then he realised that they were in Hasting's ammunition pouches, wherever he had got to. On impulse he glanced back down at Hasting's lone boot and froze in shock as he noticed that the bloody stump of a foot was still inside it. For a long moment, Dawes stared at the severed foot in the boot with horrid fascination, the realisation of Hasting's fate suddenly occurring in his mind.

He didn't have much time to think on it however, for somewhere to his right he heard the sudden bark of rifle fire, then just a second later, the steady chug of another Bren Gun firing in short bursts. Dawes flicked his gaze back over the front of the trench and caught his breath. His view along the river bank to his right was blocked by a fallen tree, whilst long grass and undergrowth to his left blocked his line of sight after jut a few yards in that direction. Across the narrow river and beyond it however, he had a perfect view. The water of the canalised river was relatively calm, and beyond it, the early morning ground mist was rolling back steadily to give him visibility of more than three hundred yards across the flat, green water meadows and thriving cornfields. And coming out of that mist were figures.

Dozens of them, like grey phantoms in the morning light, flitting through the corn. He could see that some of them were carrying huge, dark, indistinct burdens above their heads. Others ran on alone, waving their arms. He could hear whistles and shouting. The Bren Gun and rifles off to his right burst into life again. Suddenly Dawes understood what he was seeing.

"Christ!" He swore quietly under his breath. "Here we bloody go!"

He yanked back on the cocking handle of the light machine-gun but felt no resistance. The weapon was already cocked and ready to fire. His hand fumbled for the change lever, flicking the weapon from safe, through single shot, then onto automatic. Next he pulled the butt of the gun back into his shoulder and brought his eye up to the rear sight. He paused slightly, remembering to twist the sight drum, making sure the sights were set on three hundred yards. Satisfied, Dawes lined the gun up on a clump of the distant yet rapidly advancing figures.

He took a deep breath.

"Right then, Jerry…" He murmured. "Let's be having you…"

And at that point he squeezed the trigger, and the Bren Gun burst into deadly life.

SECOND FLOOR OF THE TANNERY – PECQ ON THE RIVER ESCAUT
TUESDAY 21ST MAY 1940 – 0715 HOURS

"Is that all his ammunition?" Jackson demanded.

"Yes, Sergeant." Replied the stretcher bearer, an older guardsman who had rejoined from the reserve list at the outbreak of war.

Jackson hoisted the set of webbing over one shoulder and took the proffered bandolier in his left hand.

"Right, get him away to the clearing station."

Without hesitation, the two burly guardsmen lifted their stretcher, along with its occupant, and staggered off towards the stair-well.

Guardsman Wilkinson had been the first casualty from Jackson's platoon during this latest bombardment; badly cut up and knocked unconscious by falling masonry from a direct hit on the floor above. How many more would there be before the day was out, Jackson wondered. He turned away and began striding back along the wall of the big room. The factory stank of piss, or something very like it, and the pungent aroma did little to improve Jackson's temper. He was tired and exhausted from the patrol action of just a few hours earlier, but the last thing he wanted now was sleep. He was after revenge.

Guardsman Richards, wounded in last night's action, had died very shortly after being brought back through the friendly sentries, whilst Lance Corporal Jarvis had been badly wounded by shrapnel in his right knee during the nightmare withdrawal from the river bank under continuous barrage. The medics reckoned the corporal might lose his leg below the knee as it was badly shredded. And of course, Jackson wasn't forgetting the Company Quarter Master Sergeant, killed so pointlessly while serving breakfast just days after the balloon had gone up. Somewhere in the back of his mind too, in a place he didn't like to go, he remembered the young girl bleeding to death by the side of the road just a couple of days back. As tired as he was,

Jackson was glad that it was time to stand and fight at last; it was payback time for the Germans.

He strode quickly along, stepping over the prone soldiers who lay ready in their stand-to positions along the wall. At first, the natural intention of everyone had been to use the windows as firing ports. No way. Not in Jackson's platoon. The windows were huge; obvious targets. They might afford useful vantage points but they would also be the focus for every bit of enemy small arms fire that came back at them. Instead he had made his platoon chip away at the mortar in the brickwork so that they could remove individual bricks, close to floor level, thus providing small but useful loopholes. A laborious task perhaps, but in Jackson's mind, entirely vindicated already, judging by the amount of shrapnel that had come whistling through the windows thus far.

Outside, the bombardment seemed to be easing; moving deeper into the town, away from the river itself. The tall sergeant bent low as he passed one of the big windows then paused briefly by two riflemen lying ready at a loophole.

"Keep your eyes peeled lads; sounds like the barrage is moving away from us."

The two serious faced guardsmen simply nodded and continued to stare through their tiny apertures. Jackson moved on. A little further along, he came up against a small improvised barricade against one of the smaller windows. This position he had no say over, for it belonged to the forward observation officer of a Royal Artillery battery. The captain, along with his small team, were comfortably ensconced inside their mini-bunker, constructed from bits of furniture, machinery and sandbags; surrounded by maps, manuals, a radio and a field telephone, from which a thin land-line ran across the floor of the room and out of the window, opposite.

As Jackson negotiated the small observation post, he caught the eye of the Royal Artillery captain, who nodded in greeting and gave him a confident smile.

"Won't be long now, Sergeant..." The officer beamed. "They've switched from air-burst to impact fuse and lifted their range by a couple of hundred yards. That suggests to me that they don't want to hurt anybody who's too close to the river... or *on* it!"

Jackson nodded curt acknowledgement.

"Let the bastards come, Sir."

The Captain laughed.

"Indeed Sergeant. Let them come. Hope you have a good shoot."

Jackson couldn't resist a smile at the officer's boyish anticipation of action. He moved on.

The next person he came to was Hawkins. For the last few months, ever since Jackson had become the platoon sergeant, he had disliked this man. He knew the Hawkins family from back home, and he knew that they were the most crooked and immoral bunch of rascals that ever set foot in the East Riding of Yorkshire. Needless to say, Jackson had imagined that this particular member of the family would be no different. Since last night however, Jackson was reluctantly starting to revise his opinion. It was Hawkins who had come to Jackson's assistance during the tussle with the German on the riverbank. It was Hawkins who had so enthusiastically engaged the enemy with rifle and grenade, and Hawkins who had almost single-handedly dragged and carried the stricken Guardsman Richards all the way back to their own lines. Perhaps this member of the Hawkins family was good for something, after all?

"You okay, Hawkins?" Jackson grunted, dropping to one knee beside him.

The guardsman looked up from behind his Bren Gun, the weapon he had inherited from the unfortunate Guardsman Richards.

"I will be when the Jerries appear, Sergeant. I've got a score to settle with the bastards!"

Jackson nodded grimly.

"You and me both, Hawkins, lad. You and me both."

He switched his glance to the other guardsman who had stepped up as the No.2 on the gun.

"You know what you're doing, big lad? Don't worry about your rifle for now; just make sure that Hawkins gets one full magazine after another, and get the barrel changed every two hundred rounds, alright?"

The guardsman nodded, his face set and determined.

"Where's that Jerry Tommy Gun you pilfered last night?" Jackson asked, switching his gaze back to Hawkins.

"Over there, next to the spare ammo, Sergeant."

Jackson spotted the weapon, a finely made, skeletal looking, all-metal affair, fitted with a long, thin magazine. It looked deadly.

"Did you manage to pick up any spare ammunition for it?"

Hawkins nodded again.

"Aye, Sergeant, I pulled that dead Jerry's entire belt kit off. It's behind the ammo box. There's another three magazines in the pouches."

Jackson resisted a smile. Perhaps this member of the Hawkins family *had* inherited some of his wider family's traits after all?

"Well done, Hawkins." Jackson grunted, and was rewarded by a flicker of surprise in the guardsman's eyes. "Well done for last night, big lad. And thanks for getting that fucking Jerry off me."

He saw Hawkins' face register mild shock at the unexpected compliment.

"Now, keep your eyes peeled over that river. That gunner officer reckons…"

"Here they come!"

The sudden shout of alarm cut Jackson dead. Everyone in the room looked up, surprised by the shout. It was Dunstable's voice, coming from somewhere above them. He had gone up to the top floor where No.17 Platoon was positioned, in order to get himself a better view of the countryside.

Contrary to his own direction, and for want of a loophole, Jackson moved quickly across to the nearest window and peered around the corner. Below them, beyond the thin ribbon of dark water where the river passed by the outer edge of the town, the green and yellow patchwork of fields were slowly being revealed as the morning mist cleared, aided presumably by the effects of the bombardment. At first, Jackson stared with a bemused face at the scene in front of him. Across those distant fields, emerging from the mist was an army of what appeared to be giant, black beetles. He frowned, trying to understand the image that was being presented to him. Then it clicked.

Boats! They weren't beetles at all, but big, rubber, assault boats. The dozens of tiny legs protruding from beneath them were the legs of the boat crews as they doubled clumsily forward through the corn and the grass towards the river. Further along the river, towards the Grenadiers' sector, Jackson heard the first sounds of small arms fire. This was it. At last the Germans were making a general assault.

"Hello Charley One Two, this is Charley One Two Able, fire mission over…"

The sound of the gunner captain's calm, precise voice echoed through the big work-room.

"Fire mission. Target, Baker One Zero Seven. Large concentration of infantry in open ground. Five rounds fire for effect, on my order…"

The young captain's voice was unbelievably calm and steady, as if he were merely going about his business on a training scheme. Jackson's heart was pounding now. The prospect of impending action set his pulse racing. His mouth was suddenly dry. He heard the clatter of hobnailed boots on stairs and a moment later Dunstable appeared inside the room.

"Sixteen Platoon, stand-by! Jerries approaching the river. Pick your targets carefully. Stand-by to engage with rapid fire on my order…"

Jackson gawped back out of the window. There must have been several dozen boats he reckoned. The meadows now were covered with masses of enemy infantry, all of them lugging their assault craft along with obvious urgency.

A new sound cut through the air; a soft whisper, followed instantly by a dull 'crump'.

"Trench mortar!" Jackson called out. "Keep your heads down!"

More of the smaller explosions occurred in the grounds of the tannery yard and the surrounding fields. Here and there, a long, thin, stream of smoke emitted from the seat of several explosions. Smoke bombs.

"They're almost on the reference point, Sir."

Jackson heard one of the Royal Artillery boys murmur the warning to the captain. A moment later, the officer's voice sounded clear and calm again as he spoke into the field telephone.

"Charley One Two this is Charley One Two Able, Target, Baker One Zero Seven, fire now, fire now…"

A few moments elapsed and then from somewhere in the distance, a distinct rumble joined the background noise of artillery fire. There was another brief pause, and then the scream of artillery shells sounded loud overhead. Then, in the middle distance amongst the swarms of enemy infantry and boat crews, the first, bright explosions of British 25 Pounder shells punctuated the dim morning light. It was 0720 hours, and the battle for the River Escaut had begun.

THE ESCAUT CROSSING – 800 YARDS SOUTH-EAST OF PECQ
TUESDAY 21ST MAY 1940 – 0725 HOURS

"That way! That way!"

Ambrosius physically put his hands up against the rubber boat and began pushing it, and its crew, over to the right.

"You're veering too far left! Keep right! Aim for those trees on the hill in the distance!"

The boat, carried by an entire squad from Ambrosius' right hand company, swung away in the correct direction. He stood and watched for a moment as the squad staggered like drunken men, moving steadily toward their objective. Content they were now following the axis, he ran onwards, falling in alongside a group of machine-gunners.

"Come on! Faster!" The acting battalion commander yelled at the gun teams. "Get up to the bank and start suppressing those Tommy positions!"

The gunners and their partners put a spurt on, their faces already purple with exertion as they pounded over the rough ground towards the river, their spare barrel boxes, personal equipment and ammunition rattling madly as they went. Ambrosius spotted one of his officers amongst the crowd of men.

"Lieutenant Michael! Get up to the bank and start getting those boats in the water! Get them moving!"

The first lieutenant gave a wave of acknowledgement and sprinted off towards the crossing point.

Ambrosius looked around again. All across the field to his rear were the crumpled shapes of fallen soldiers and abandoned boats. Despite the preliminary bombardment and the follow-up barrage by mortars, the Tommies were far from being neutralised. In fact, it was very apparent that they were still in the mood for a fight and not going anywhere in a hurry. The deadly slugs from countless rifles and machine-guns snapped through the air in all directions, taking an odd man down here, a complete squad with their boat there. They needed to get moving if they were to succeed. If they didn't get off these bare-arsed fields quickly, they would all be dead.

A strange groaning noise sounded overhead and then a moment later a shell exploded in mid-air, about a hundred metres to the left of Ambrosius. He saw an entire boat crew and several machine-gunners simply flop down, face first in the dirt, as if swept off their feet by an invisible hand.

"Bollocks!" He cursed. "Tommy artillery!"

Ducking his head, he ran on with even greater urgency. He saw a group of men going to ground in front of him, lining up close together, and was about to shout a reprimand when he realised they were at the river's edge. The men concerned were yet more machine-gunners. Swiftly they threw themselves down and began setting up their guns in the light role. Seconds later, the first bursts of automatic fire were spitting across the water towards the hidden Tommy positions. Ambrosius spotted a staff sergeant and roared at him.

"Take charge of these guns and keep that bank suppressed until we're across!"

The non-commissioned officer shouted his understanding above the clatter of small arms fire and began bellowing fire control orders at the machine-gunners.

Hard by Ambrosius, the No.2 on the nearest MG34 sat upright as he struggled to change the belt on his partner's gun. With distracted fascination, Ambrosius saw the young soldier's head jerk sharply, after which a great spurt of dark liquid burst out from within his helmet, covering his features instantly, and then the man simply toppled sideways and lay still.

"Christ almighty!" Ambrosius muttered under his breath.

He ran to his right, along the bank, to where he could see the assault teams man-handling their boats over the bank and into the water. As he sprinted towards the crossing point he could hear Lieutenant Michael's voice roaring out orders above the cacophony of artillery and small arms fire.

A ground-burst shell exploded back in the field, off to his right, and the shock of the blast sent Ambrosius staggering to his left so that he almost fell down the bank and into the water. Steadying himself, he bent lower and ran on. He could see Michael now, standing upright on the bank some thirty metres ahead, gesturing forcefully to each successive boat crew as they reached the waterline.

"There!" He was shouting, chopping with his hand to a point on the bank. "Get your boat in there and get paddling! Come on! Faster!"

There were boats on the river now. Ambrosius could see them pushing out from the bank, the paddles rising and falling. From inside one of the boats, someone was firing their MP40 machine-pistol wildly towards the opposite bank. Another airburst shell exploded with a bright flash nearby and the shockwave pushed Ambrosius down onto his knees.

"Jesus!" He swore, shocked by the pain in his ears.

He looked up, amazed to find that he was unhurt, but quickly saw a pile of bodies just metres away; those who had not been lucky enough to avoid the lethal shrapnel. The captain staggered to his feet and ran over to where Michael was still throwing boat crews into their launch positions.

"Michael, well done! Stay here and keep throwing them across! I'm going over; you follow on with the last platoon from your company!"

"Yes, Captain!" The lieutenant snapped as he beckoned to another boat-laded assault squad.

Even as he was acknowledging his battalion commander, the lieutenant gave a sudden yelp and span around, collapsing onto his knees.

"Michael!" Ambrosius called out in sudden alarm and stepped in close to the young company commander.

As he did so, the lieutenant looked up, a grimace of pain on his face. His right hand was clamped over his left shoulder and blood was pouring through his fingers. The lieutenant caught his commander's eye.

"I'm alright, Captain..." He blurted. "Just a nick, that's all. Get yourself over..."

Michael gestured awkwardly across the river. Ambrosius nodded.

"Get that shoulder dressed, Lieutenant." The captain snapped as he turned away and dropped down the side of the bank.

There were two boats launching nearby and Ambrosius chose the left hand one of the two. He threw himself amongst the men inside the crowded dinghy as they pushed off from the bank.

"Well done, men!" Ambrosius called. "We'll soon be there; then we'll give the Tommies a good hiding they'll never forget! Now, paddle!"

The soldiers dug their paddles in the water as a corporal called out the rhythm.

"Stroke! Stroke! Stroke!"

There was little Ambrosius could do but catch his breath and study the opposite bank. It was not a wide river in reality, but every second on the water felt like an age. The sound of machine-gun bullets cracking past made the captain jump for a moment, but then he realised that if he could hear the bullets passing then he was safe enough.

The boat to his right was not so lucky. He heard the shouts of alarm, pain and distress as the bullets ripped through the occupants of the boat. There were two loud splashes as men fell overboard and he glimpsed a pair of thrashing legs amidst the remaining men on the boat. A shrill, spine-chilling screaming came from amongst the press of men in the craft.

"Stroke! Stroke! Stroke!" The corporal was chanting relentlessly.

The bank was getting tantalisingly close now. Ambrosius could see at least two other boats already nudging the far bank.

"Stand-by!" He called out to the men around him. "Corporal Heyderich, send the boat back over with two men; everyone else with me. No hesitation on the bank; we go straight into the tree line."

"Here we go!" The corporal's voice shouted above the noise of battle. "One last stroke…"

The boat bounced against the side of the enemy bank and instantly the soldier at the front slid over the edge of the boat, sinking up to his thighs in water. He dragged the boat in against the bank with one hand, his other clutching at the thick stalk of some riverside weed. Another man jumped out and did the same, steadying the small craft. Ambrosius was already on his feet, readying himself to leap onto the firm ground of the river bank. He gathered himself and lurched forwards and up. The bank was steep, but not too high and he found himself sprawling forwards over the edge of it within just a heartbeat. Drawing a huge breath, he rolled onto one arm and looked back down at the men in the boat.

"Alright then, Second Battalion; let's go!"

THE ESCAUT CROSSING – 350 YARDS SOUTH-EAST OF PECQ
TUESDAY 21ST MAY 1940 – 0730 HOURS

"Give me your hand, Captain!"

Dullman heard the words and caught a glimpse of the outstretched arm, just as his head went below the surface of the water. As he kicked furiously with his feet, trying to establish a firm foothold on the small muddy ledge that lay just below the surface at the water's edge, the company commander threw his own free hand upwards and towards the proffered hand. His head fully below the surface now, Dullman tried not to panic as he felt his uniform filling with water, threatening to drag him down.

With a profound sense of relief, he felt a strong hand grab his forearm, and he scrabbled desperately with his fingers to grab hold of his rescuer's jacket sleeve. For a moment, nothing happened; he neither sank any further, nor was able to get his head back above water. Just as he thought his lungs would burst however, he felt another pair of hands grab his equipment straps, and then suddenly he was being hauled upwards with tremendous force.

The captain emerged into the daylight again, the muffled noise of the battle returning sharply back to its full volume and intensity. As the water poured from under his helmet and down his face, Dullman vaguely registered the sight of the two soldiers on the river bank, both of them grimacing with the effort of hauling their sodden company commander out of the water. His mouth opened automatically and he emitted a strange sob as his protesting lungs drew in a huge gulp of air. As he was dragged over the edge of the bank like a landed fish, Dullman felt completely limp, as if his uniform were suddenly made of lead and his body was unable to support itself. With a final growl of effort, the two soldiers fell backwards as their officer flopped onto his side on the muddy grass bank. For a moment the two men lay there, fighting for their own breath, whilst Dullman lay there gulping in one mouthful of air after another.

The company commander didn't move for long moments. Completely drained of energy, Dullman lay watching the remains of his bullet-riddled assault boat sinking in the river just a couple of metres away; the dead body of his company runner still within the deflated remnants of the rubber craft, the lifeless arms flopping gently on the water as the boat wrapped itself around him like a shroud. Dullman was shaking all over. Partly from the cold water, partly from physical exhaustion, but mainly from the pure shock and fear of almost drowning in what was, to be honest, a relatively shallow river.

"You alright, Sir?"

The soldier's query brought Dullman to his senses. With an effort, he pushed himself up into a sitting position; dirty, foul-smelling river water pouring out of his uniform with every movement. He twisted around to face the men.

"Yes... thank you..."

One of the soldiers was Sergeant Hartzer; the other a young private who's name he couldn't remember.

"How many have we got across?" Dullman panted, his breathing still ragged.

The sergeant shook his head, his expression serious.

"Not many, Captain. My squad complete, although two of the boys have been winged in the arm, then a handful of men from different squads in Nine Platoon. Maybe twenty of us in all..."

Dullman absorbed the information quietly, his heart sinking as fast as his boat had.

"Any officers?"

Sergeant Hartzer hesitated for a moment before replying.

"Just Lieutenant Gruber, Sir; but he's dying."

"Dying?"

Hartzer nodded.

"Got one through the side of the head just as we got on the bank. He's still got a pulse...just. His head's in a proper fucking mess, though. Poor little bastard won't last much longer."

Again, Dullman digested the information in silence.

After a moment of contemplation, the captain threw his gaze around.

"Is this the stream bed?"

Hartzer nodded.

"Looks like it, Sir. Quite a wide and deep drainage channel. It goes directly across the fields, off to the side of the town and towards the road. Quite a bit of undergrowth further along it; no sign of Tommies nearby."

Dullman grunted in cynical amusement.

"That's because they're all sat up in those factory windows shooting the fuck out of us on the river!"

He turned and looked back across the water.

It was a massacre. There weren't many other ways to describe it. Despite their own covering bombardment, the German infantrymen of the assault wave had been caught by the British artillery as they had struggled across the wide, open fields towards the river, lugging their assault boats with them. The deadly combination of air and ground-burst shells had wrought havoc amongst the small groups of German soldiers clustered around their rubber dinghies. Then, as Dullman and his men had reached the river, the enemy infantry had revealed themselves. Dullman had expected the Tommies to be waiting, and also that they would put up a fight, but he had not expected the weight of concentrated, accurate, small-arms fire that had swept the banks and surface of the Escaut, chopping down man after man, and ripping the flimsy boats to pieces.

Dullman could hear the Tommy machine-guns now; distinctive from any other weapon by their slow, almost casual 'chug-chug-chug'. It was almost as if those Tommy machine-guns were taunting their enemies. 'Come on,' they were saying, 'we're in no rush. We can sit here all day.' The thought angered Dullman, as did the scene of carnage before him. There were at least half a dozen ruined boats adrift or sinking on the surface of the narrow river. Bodies bobbed amongst the debris of the boats, and on the opposite bank he could see yet more abandoned dinghies, surrounded by heaps of dead soldiers. His soldiers.

With a silent curse, Dullman turned back to Hartzer. His strength was returning now; his resolve stiffening.

"Well; we've got what we've got, and we're here now. We may as well do what we came here for."

Hartzer regarded his company commander with a cautious look.

"What *are* we going to do, Captain?"

Dullman pushed himself up onto his knees and gave his machine-pistol a shake, trying to clear it of water.

"The rest of the battalion won't get across this river until something gets done about those Tommy positions in the big buildings."

He looked and Hartzer and gave him a reassuring grin.

"We're going to attack…"

FORWARD POSITIONS, 3RD BATTALION GRENADIER GUARDS – ON THE ESCAUT, JUST SOUTH OF PECQ TUESDAY 21ST MAY 1940 – 0735 HOURS

Rat-tat-tat-tat-tat! Rat-tat-tat-tat-tat!

In between each burst, Dawes jerked his eye away from the rear sight a little and observed his fall of shot. He was rewarded with the image of German soldiers tumbling sideways, down onto the grass, or else tumbling forwards over the edge of the bank into the river. The Bren Gun had a reputation for accuracy, but at this short range it was just impossible to miss. Without realising it, Dawes had given way to the relentless training that was the haul-mark of the professional, regular British Army, and in particular of the Guards. Forgetting the missing Hastings and the wounded Dixon now, the young Grenadier Guardsman had assumed the duty of Bren Gunner readily enough, and from the moment he had first squeezed the trigger, he had slipped into the oft practiced routine. Now, he was dealing death to the Germans in as casual a manner as though he were taking his annual weapon test on the ranges at Bisley, firing steadily in tight, controlled bursts of three to five rounds.

Rat-tat-tat-tat-tat! Rat-tat-tat-click!

"Magazine..." Dawes murmured to himself automatically as the breech block slammed shut on an empty chamber.

Quickly, Dawes went into the drill for changing magazines, but then stopped abruptly.

"Shit!"

He had emptied both of the magazines he had to hand. The unfortunate Hastings had been carrying the remaining spare magazines, and with Corporal Dixon crawling away towards the company aid post, there was no one to refill the empty magazines for Dawes. The guardsman looked back across the river. Despite the numerous German bodies that lay all along the opposite bank, there were already German boats on the water; boats filled with yet more enemy infantrymen.

"Shit, shit, shit!"

Dawes pushed the Bren Gun over to one side and grabbed for his Lee-Enfield.

As he ducked down to seize the weapon from where it lay on the bottom of the trench, an ear-shattering serres of cracks sounded right over his head, making him wince, and he was showered with dirt and clumps of grass. His fingers closed around the stock of his rifle and he looked up at the top of the trench, just as more enemy bullets slammed into the parapet and sent yet more dirt tumbling down into his face.

"Oh Christ, they've spotted me!" He breathed nervously to himself.

Carefully, keeping low, he moved as far along the trench as he could go. Just a couple of yards, but that would have to do.

The young guardsman brought his rifle up, readying himself. He noticed that his rifle was still made safe, the hammer on the rear of the bolt being fully forward. Using his thumb, he flicked the safety catch forward and then dragged the bolt open. The magazine was full of the big, shiny .303 inch rounds, so he slid the bolt forward once more, feeding a round into the breech and then locking the bolt shut. The Grenadier took one more deep breath and then stood upright, sliding the muzzle of his rifle over the parapet as he did so. The enemy were that close now that he could use the battle-sight on the weapon, and when it came to targets, there was no shortage. Initially, he went to line up on some enemy across the river, but then movement in his peripheral vision made him look left.

"Ruddy hell!" He cursed as he saw the boat full of enemy that was just yards away from the near bank, a little way off to the left of his position.

Quickly swivelling his rifle to the left, he leaned into it and took aim at the crowded boat.

Blam!

The powerful rifle jerked violently in his shoulder, and as soon as the barrel settled, Dawes was working the bolt, ejecting the empty cartridge case and feeding another round into the chamber. He barely noticed the German soldier in the target boat who suddenly flopped sideways into the river, disappearing beneath the dark, murky water of the Escaut.

He was about to fire when the enemy machine-gunner put another burst into the parapet of the trench, the nearest bullet landing just inches away from Dawes' right arm. The guardsman jerked backwards in shock and dropped his head as low as he could get it, whilst still looking over the lip of the trench.

"Where the fuck is that coming from?" He asked himself in frustration.

He had no idea, but the enemy gunner could obviously see him though.

Carefully, keeping a low profile, he slid his rifle forward again, ready to fire at the enemy boat. Once in position, he froze. The boat had gone. He scanned the water but couldn't see any sign of the craft. Surely it couldn't have been hit and sunk without a trace in just a few seconds? He eyed the bank on his side of the river, about twenty five yards away. They must have got across. If that was the case, then the enemy would be appearing over the bank any moment now. Dawes looked across the river. There were more boats on the river, and more enemy running about on the far bank. Easy targets, but he couldn't afford to start wasting his ammunition on them, not with the possibility of enemy soldiers appearing right in front of him on the home bank any moment now.

The enemy removed any doubt from his mind just a moment later. In almost exactly the same spot he had been observing just a heartbeat before, a group of five grey-clad figures suddenly loomed up on the edge of the bank. Dawes' heart began thumping even faster now.

"Oh, Jesus! Oh, Jesus!"

The young Grenadier kept repeating the whispered prayer to himself over and over again as he took aim on the leading German soldier. What chance did he have? Five against one? The enemy looked cautious. They moved away from the water's edge a couple of yards, then dropped down onto one knee, their nervous, energised faces scanning the undergrowth and trees for signs of the British defenders. Dawes noted the man with a black, inverted triangle badge on his sleeve, who was snapping orders to the others and pointing.

"Make this count, Jack, lad…" Dawes whispered as he squinted through the battle-sight.

As he aimed the rifle, the mantra of the four marksmanship principals crept back into his mind like a ghost. How many times had he been made to repeat those principals by his skill-at-arms instructor during basic training? He steadied his breathing, watching the foresight blade settle on the German giving the orders. As Dawes held his breath momentarily, the last marksmanship principal echoed through his mind.

'The shot must be released and followed through without disturbing the position…'

Blam!

The Lee-Enfield barked angrily, leapt in his hands, but Dawes grasped the weapon firmly, still holding his breath, and waited for the foresight blade to settle again. Even as it did, he saw the German flip backwards. Dawes worked the bolt madly as the other Germans looked at their dead comrade in shock, but even as he slammed the bolt shut again, Dawes saw the remaining enemy throw themselves flat on the ground. They fired.

It wasn't particularly accurate, and they probably didn't know exactly where Dawes was, allowing for the undergrowth between their position and his trench, but even so, the sound of the bullets cracking overhead was disconcerting to say the least. Dawes fired again, but he didn't think he found his mark. As he re-cocked his weapon, the Grenadier Guardsman knew that if they charged him he was a dead man. Beyond the four prone Germans, he glimpsed more helmeted heads bobbing up from the river bank.

"Time to go…" Dawes muttered to himself as he locked the bolt down once more.

He placed his rifle down and scrabbled in his right hand pouch for his hand grenade. With trembling fingers he dragged the grenade out and grasped it firmly in his right hand, pushing the fly-off lever into the web between his thumb and forefinger.

Again, Dawes took a deep breath then slid his left forefinger through the safety pin of the grenade and dragged it clear. A streak of tracer blurred past his eyes with a menacing snap, but he ignored the burst of fire and drew his arm back, preparing for the throw of his life. With a heave, he swung his arm overhead and released the grenade. Without pause, Dawes grabbed his rifle and threw himself up and over the rear lip of the trench. Above the crack of gunfire he heard nearby voices, shouting with alarm in a strange language. He began crawling on his belly through the tree-line, towards the cornfield that lay a few yards to his rear behind the bushes.

Crump!

His grenade detonated with a hollow thump, and Dawes felt the vibrations in the ground beneath him. He kept crawling. In the aftermath of the explosion there seemed to be a pause of a few seconds when nobody was shooting at anyone, but then, with a renewed frenzy, more bullets cracked through the air nearby. Fortunately, none of those bullets appeared to be going too near Dawes, and he kept on moving. As he dragged himself along the ground with his arms and pushed himself on with his feet, the young guardsman's heavy steel helmet slopped left and right on his head, uncomfortably, but he ignored the awkwardness of his equipment and pushed himself on desperately.

He paused for a heartbeat to get his bearings and was pleased to see that he was just a couple of yards away from the waist high corn. With a final effort, he propelled himself forwards and broke his way through the golden curtain of half-grown crops. Understanding that corn was far from bullet-proof, Dawes kept going, pushing his way through the tough stalks, his head down to avoid being poked in the eyes. After a few more yards, Dawes suddenly came up against something. He stopped, gasping for breath, and looked up. He found himself staring at the sole of a British Army ammunition boot, the thirteen studs laid out neatly in the prescribed pattern.

"Who's that?" He whispered hoarsely.

There was no answer.

Moving carefully forward, Dawes worked himself up alongside the prone figure, and as he brushed a swathe of corn aside, he caught sight of the boot's owner. It was Dixon; and he was dead. The corporal was laying face down, his arms and legs animated in a fashion that suggested he had still been trying to drag himself forwards when unconsciousness finally claimed him. Half-heartedly, Dawes pushed his fingers into the man's neck to feel for a pulse, but he knew that it was pointless. The pallid nature of the NCO's skin and the blueness around his eyes and lips, told the story that he had lost far too much blood. If that wasn't evidence enough, the gaping wound on his back confirmed it. The terrible injury had been uncovered once more, the dressings pulled out of place with all Dixon's crawling, and the whole of the poor man's back was soaked in dark, sticky red gore.

Dawes let out a hopeless sigh. Poor old Dicko. He hadn't been a bad lad really, compared to some corporals. The young guardsman sat there for a moment or two, catching his breath, trying to decide what he should do next. Then he heard the sharp blast of a whistle nearby, followed by the rattle of equipment and the 'clump, clump, clump' of heavy footfalls on soil. The hackles on Dawes' neck stood up and he cocked his head to one side. Then he heard the German voices. Close. Very close indeed. He didn't understand German but he recognised the nature of the curt, decisive words that were being spoken. It was an officer or an NCO, giving orders. And whistles meant only one thing. The enemy was rallying and forming up for an attack, and it looked as though Dawes was going to be right in the middle of it. Slowly, as quietly as he possibly could, Dawes hefted his rifle across his legs then reached down to his left hip and fumbled for his bayonet.

GERMAN BRIDGHEAD – 850 YARDS SOUTH-EAST OF PECQ
TUESDAY 21ST MAY 1940 – 0845 HOURS

Crump! Crump!
    The ground shook as the two stick grenades exploded in rapid succession.
    "Go, go, go!"
Ambrosius heard the frantic orders of the NCO in charge as the ad hoc platoon launched itself through the latest line of trees and undergrowth and towards the barn. From his position amongst the crops, the infantry captain saw more than a dozen men spring up from the corn and leap forwards, charging headlong into the enemy held position. From one flank, he heard one of his MG34 teams rattling away as they covered the final bound of the attack.
    Ambrosius glanced to his right and briefly surveyed the dead German soldier next to him; the poor man's features now a mass of bloody pulp where he had been hit squarely in the face by a British bullet. The unfortunate German corpse was just one of many however, and the assault was barely an hour old. The enemy were holding out with unbelievable determination; quite unlike anything Ambrosius had yet experienced, either during this or the Polish campaign. His battalion had been shredded by artillery as it forced its way over the river, and cut down in large numbers by the Tommy machine-gunners and marksmen in their hidden positions. Now those same Tommies were fighting tooth and nail for every metre of ground.
    Forgetting the corpse, Ambrosius leapt up and doubled forward, close behind the assaulting troops. He heard a couple of bursts from an MP40,

several rifle shots, and then lots of shouting in a curious mix of German and English.

"Hands up, Tommy! Hands up! Quickly; hands up!"

Ambrosius veered towards the shouting. As he did so, the barn that had been held by the enemy came into full view. It was surprisingly large, its outer walls pock-marked with bullet holes. He glanced down briefly as he passed a shallow trench with a dead British soldier laid face down in it.

"I think that's them all…" Another German voice was calling.

The gunfire was subsiding as his men secured the area. Arriving in a small clearing between the tree line and the barn, Ambrosius found half a dozen of his men milling around a pair of Tommy soldiers. He slowed to a halt and surveyed the confused scene.

Another shallow trench was situated off to one side; quite a large one. Within the trench were three Tommies; two obviously dead and another groaning in pain, holding his ribs as blood seeped between his fingers. Two more British soldiers, both looking dazed by the recent grenade explosions, were being dragged to their feet and disarmed. The captain took a good look at the two men as they staggered to their feet unsteadily, raising their arms as they did so. One of them had blood smeared across his face.

The first thing that struck Ambrosius was how tall the two prisoners were. Ambrosius himself was of smallish stature, but even against some of his taller men, these two British soldiers looked huge. He glanced at the injured man and the two British corpses. They too were obviously tall men. At this point, his train of thought was disturbed by the sudden roar of an engine close by. He whipped his head round to look towards the barn as the sound of the revving engine was joined by urgent shouting in German. There was a sharp bang, a squeal of hinges, and then a heartbeat later a Tommy truck burst through the double doors of the barn and veered straight in front of Ambrosius.

"Stop that fucking truck!" Ambrosius yelled, bringing his own machine-pistol up into the aim. He checked himself from firing as some of his own men appeared from behind trees and undergrowth in the immediate path of the truck. As he cursed silently, the roar of another engine made him whip his head off to the right. Ambrosius caught sight of another British truck roaring off in the opposite direction. The two vehicles had obviously been parked inside the barn, their drivers waiting for the right moment.

He looked back towards the first truck and saw his men scattering as the vehicle drove straight through them in a cloud of dust. Eventually, the first of his men began to fire at the truck and Ambrosius heard the clang of bullets hitting metal. Another sound kicked in; the slower, repetitive chug of a

Tommy machine-gun, and a split second later several enemy bullets cracked dangerously low through the trees that surrounded the barn.

In seconds, it was all over. Both of the trucks and their occupants were disappearing over a slight ridge towards the Poplar wood that was the axis of advance for Ambrosius and his men; just a few desultory shots chasing the vehicles as they sped out of sight.

"Check that barn!" Ambrosius hollered to the soldiers left standing around in the settling dust. "And sweep the ditches and the edge of the corn field; we don't want any more surprises!"

He turned back to stare at the two unwounded British prisoners. The two big men were staring down at their captors now, not with fear, but with a surly look of resentment. Ambrosius took a couple of steps closer to them as his own men began searching their prisoners' equipment and pockets. He circled around them, catching a glimpse of a red flash sewn onto their upper sleeves. Unable to read the white writing that was stitched into the flash, the young German officer walked up to one of the British prisoners and grabbed hold of the man's sleeve, twisting the material so he could read the wording properly. The Tommy gave Ambrosius a defiant glare, and although the captain avoided the man's gaze, he couldn't help feeling uncomfortable under the big man's scrutiny.

Ambrosius read the words on the red flash. *Grenadier Guards*. He felt his stomach go suddenly heavy. So that was it? This explained why he and his men were experiencing so tough a contest. They were up against the personal bodyguard regiments of the British King. Renown for their excellence on ceremonial duties, these men were obviously as skilful on the field of battle as they were on the parade ground. He took a step back from the man.

"Keep your eyes on these two." He ordered the nearest German guard. "They're from the British Guards, which means they are dangerous people. Keep them busy, looking after their own wounded."

The German private nodded his understanding.

"Captain?"

The familiar voice sounded behind Ambrosius, and he turned to see Lieutenant Schlinke running across to him.

"Schlinke? Thank the gods you're alive! How many men have you got?"

The lieutenant slowed to a halt in front of Ambrosius.

"Not many, Captain; maybe twenty or so, with just one machine-gun. We got shot to pieces on the way across…"

The lieutenant was panting heavily. Ambrosius nodded, acknowledging the officer's brief report.

"Us too." He replied. "In fact the whole battalion has been cut up quite badly."

"What are your orders, Captain?" Schlinke enquired, catching his breath.

Ambrosius didn't hesitate for a moment. He turned slightly and shot his arm out in the direction taken by the first of the British trucks.

"We're going up there," He said, his finger extended like a spear point, "towards that small strip wood. It dominates the surrounding area and is close to the main road."

He glanced back at Schlinke.

"Shake your men out on the right, Schlinke. We're going to take the high ground."

HEADQUARTERS, 1ST BATTALION COLDSTREAM GUARDS – 2 MILES NORTH OF PECQ ON THE ESCAUT. TUESDAY 21ST MAY 1940 – 0850 HOURS

"This is the place; turn in here."

Brooke gave his driver the order and the big staff car swung into the gateway of the old farm. There was no mistaking the place. By the side of the gateway was a small wooden sign, its background consisting of three horizontal bars of equal proportion in the colours of the Guards; blue, red and blue. In the centre of the red bar was painted a Coldstream Capstar, whilst around the regimental badge was painted the legend, *Battalion Headquarters, 1st Battalion Coldstream Guards.*

As they turned into the lane that led to the farmyard, a tall soldier, dressed in full battle-dress and helmet and carrying a bayonet tipped rifle, stepped out from behind a barricade on the verge and held up his hand. Brooke's driver slowed to a halt as the soldier approached them warily. Brooke noticed that another soldier had remained behind the barricade and was covering them with his own rifle, the man's tired face looking serious and uncompromising.

Brooke wound the window down as the first soldier approached. The man had a brass drum badge on his right sleeve. A member of the battalion's Corps of Drums then, pressed into service for the defence of their battalion's HQ. As soon as the soldier spotted Brooke, he snapped to attention and threw his rifle into the slope, before executing an immaculate butt salute.

"Good morning, Sir. Battalion Headquarters is just along the lane. The Regimental Police will show you where to go, Sir."

"Thank you." Brooke returned the man's salute.

His driver gunned the engine slightly and the staff car drove forward again, trundling carefully down the pot-holed track.

"They look bushed, Sir." Brooke's ADC commented as they passed the Coldstream drummer.

"Bushed, yet still efficient as ever." Brooke murmured. "They've done some hard fighting and hard marching, these chaps."

Indeed, the Coldstream drummer and his companion behind the barricade, despite being evidently tired and covered in the dust and dirt of ten days constant campaigning, were both cleanly shaven, wearing their full equipment, and most definitely on their toes.

This particular battalion had suffered badly during the withdrawal from the Dyle, having to bear the brunt of the German attempt to get between the BEF and the Belgian Army. They had done their bit though and held the Germans off, turfing the enemy out of Herent at the point of the bayonet. A good battalion, in a good brigade, in a good division. If only the BEF had more like it. The car had now reached the muddy yard of a modest farm and, as promised, another tall Coldstreamer was waiting to direct them. A corporal indicated where they should park and Brooke caught sight of the man's wrist band, bearing the letters *RP* in red, marking him as a member of the battalion's own Regimental Police detachment.

"You may as well stay here." Brooke told his ADC. "I won't be long. I just want to have a quick chat with Cazenove; see how his chaps are doing after that business near Louvain the other day."

He jumped out of the car as the driver pulled the door open and was immediately greeted by the Coldstream corporal who slammed his feet together as if he were on Horse Guards Parade in London.

"Good morning, Sir; 1st Battalion Coldstream Guards, Battalion Headquarters." The corporal threw a salute up. "The Commanding Officer's in the cottage over there, Sir."

Again, Brooke thanked the corporal and returned the salute, then set off across the farmyard. As he went, he took a quick look around. In the fields and hedgerows that surrounded the farm, he could see more guardsmen, hurriedly digging trenches or constructing barricades. The place was a hive of quiet, efficient activity. He paused slightly and looked southwards. There was a ferocious bombardment in progress a couple of miles to the south, and lots of gunfire. He should go there next and speak to Alexander, commanding the 1st Division. It seemed that the Germans had selected that particular sector for their first push against the Escaut line.

Brooke turned back and strode over to the farmhouse door. Another drummer was standing guard outside, and the man promptly executed a general salute, present arms, when he recognised the Corps Commander. Brooke turned the handle and entered. As he stepped over the threshold, he paused momentarily, allowing his eyes to adjust to the light in the big room with its low ceiling. There was a smell of wood smoke, cigarettes and fried corned beef, and as Brooke scanned the dim interior, he saw that almost a dozen men occupied the space.

He saw a group of men huddled around a table in one corner, talking quietly as they pored over a map. Other men, signallers by the look, sat hunched over radio sets and field telephones to one side of the room by a window.

"Room!"

The sudden, terrifying shout from somewhere off to Brooke's right made him jump. He shot a look into the dark corner, blinking stupidly towards the giant, fierce looking warrant officer standing to attention in the shadows. A brief glimpse at the enormous royal coat of arms badge on the man's sleeve told Brooke that this must be the Regimental Sergeant Major of the battalion.

Brooke looked back towards the others around the table. Every man there had stood up straight, their bodies rigid in the position of attention. Even the signallers, squatting by the window had braced up. Brooke recognised the face of Lieutenant Colonel Cazenove, the Commanding Officer. The colonel blinked towards Brooke a couple of times, then recognised his visitor.

"Good morning, Sir." Cazenove greeted him with a pleasant smile, his voice smooth and urbane. "1st Battalion Coldstream Guards, and all's well."

Brooke acknowledged with a salute, trying not to smile at the inbred formality and custom that was the trademark of all Guards battalions.

"Thank you." He replied. "Stand easy, gentlemen. Please, relax."

Instantly, the occupants of the room began to move. The huddle of officers around the table turned to face their Corps Commander whilst Cazenove advanced on him, his tired face breaking into a broad smile.

"How very nice to see you, Sir. Are you well?"

Brooke was instantly disarmed. Here they were in the middle of a war, having been through ten days of hell, and he was being asked about his health as if he had bumped into an old friend in St James' Park.

"Fine, thank you, Cazenove." Brooke replied, allowing his own veil of formality to slip a touch. "Just thought I'd pop in and see how you're all doing. You've had a busy few days."

"Always good to be busy, Sir." Cazenove beamed. "You know what they say… *'The Devil finds work for idle hands'*…"

Brooke couldn't help emitting a small chuckle at the colonel's optimistic comments. A man appeared at Brooke's side; a captain wearing jodhpurs, brown riding boots and a service dress jacket. It was the battalion's adjutant.

"Can I take your hat and cane, Sir?" The captain asked politely and took them from Brooke without waiting for a reply.

A moment later, and much to Brooke's surprise, a guardsman appeared and offered him a drink of tea. It was an absurd sight; the tea contained in a white, enamel mug, perched awkwardly on a small, chipped, china plate. At the side of the plate, bizarrely, sat a hard, brown, army biscuit. Even in wartime, the Guards were unbelievably gracious hosts.

Having thanked the young orderly and accepted the hot brew, Brooke looked back at the assembled officers in the room.

"I just wanted to say well done to you all, gentlemen, for your outstanding performance the other day on the flank, not just of this corps, but of the entire BEF. Had you not held on so gallantly and kept your heads under such trying circumstances, I dread to think what would have happened. It was sterling work and you should be rightly proud of yourselves. Make sure your guardsmen know that too."

He glanced at Cazenove and inclined his head towards the door.

"Can we go for a short walk?"

"Of course, Sir." Cazenove smiled, understanding the form, and reaching for the door handle.

Together, the two men stepped back out into the sunlight and began strolling around the side of the cottage towards the small vegetable garden. For a while, they kept a companionable silence, content to listen to the distant sound of heavy gunfire.

"Sounds like the 1st Division have got a right old battle on their hands, Sir?" Cazenove ventured. "Looks like our 2nd Battalion will be having its share of the action today."

Brooke nodded.

"Yes…I was forgetting, they're just down the road from here, aren't they? In Pecq? It certainly sounds like they're up against it this morning. I'm going along to see General Alexander after this; find out what's going on."

Cazenove brightened instantly.

"Oh, you must pass on my regards to General Alex', Sir. And tell him to keep his eyes on our 2nd Battalion; they're a bunch of slackers, you know?"

The two officers laughed.

Reaching the vegetable patch, Brooke suddenly stopped and looked sideways at Cazenove.

"How many did you lose the other day? A hundred and twenty was it?"

Cazenove's face went serious for a moment and he gave an involuntary grimace.

"A hundred and sixty altogether, Sir; including five officers."

Brooke absorbed the information, watching the colonel closely. Cazenove brightened again.

"Still, the Hun got a good taste of cold steel from us! He came off just as badly if not worse…"

Brooke took a sip of his tea. It was surprisingly good.

"How is everybody?" He asked after a moment.

"Oh, you know, Sir…" Cazenove smiled, the fatigue evident in his face. "A bit on the tired side and footsore with it, but pleased to be standing and fighting again at long last. We'll give Jerry an even tougher lesson this time round."

Brooke glanced southwards, observing the rising plumes of smoke from burning buildings. He suddenly noticed two soldiers digging a trench in a nearby field. To his mild surprise, he noted that they were members of the RASC rather than guardsmen. For a moment, he wondered why two RASC privates would be digging trenches amongst a Guards battalion, but then focussed back on the colonel.

"Well, it sounds as if the party's already started…"

Cazenove followed his general's gaze to the south.

"This is *it*, Sir isn't it? We are *staying* here this time? To stand and fight?"

Brooke took another thoughtful sip of his tea.

"We have been told to hold the river line for at least forty eight hours, so you will indeed get another chance to teach the enemy a lesson or two. That will give some of our other divisions in the south, along with the French, time to try and punch into the side of the German thrust. If it's successful, then we may just stabilise the situation."

The Coldstream colonel gave Brooke a deep, searching look.

"And if the attack in the south doesn't work, Sir?"

Brooke took a deep breath, before answering in a clear voice.

"Then I think we might find ourselves in a bit of a pickle, Cazenove; which means I will need you and your battalion more than ever…"

THE TANNERY – PECQ ON THE ESCAUT
TUESDAY 21ST MAY 1940 – 0900 HOURS

Jackson squinted through the sights of his Lee-Enfield, lining up the rifle on the latest group of Germans who were struggling to get their boat in the water at the far side of the river.

Blam!

He worked the bolt quickly, realigned and fired again.

Blam!

He let loose every round in his magazine before pausing to check his fall of shot.

He smiled in triumph as he saw bodies draped over the river bank, the rubber boat laying abandoned next to the corpses, and the sight of the remaining enemy scuttling back into the cover of the corn.

"Take that, you bastards!" He grunted as he delved in his pouch for two fresh clips of ammunition.

"Barrel!"

The shout from his left caught Jackson's attention. He glanced in that direction as the No.2 on Hawkins' Bren Gun jerked the steaming barrel forwards and upwards, removing it from its housing. As he did so, Hawkins changed the empty magazine on the gun for a full one.

"You alright there, lads?" Jackson hollered across to them.

He had to shout at the top of his voice above the thunderous noise that filled the factory around him. The sound of his own platoon's weapons, the enemy mortars, the friendly artillery passing overhead, along with the constant flow of shouted orders, all combined to produce a deafening cacophony. Hawkins pushed a fresh magazine down into the magazine housing and glanced briefly in Jackson's direction.

"Fine, Sergeant. Getting a bit low on ammo though."

A pang of guilt cut through Jackson. He had been enjoying himself immensely, shooting at the Germans as they offered themselves up as prize targets on the river bank, but he had been neglecting his duties as the man responsible for ammunition resupply and casualty evacuation.

As he watched the other guardsman slam the fresh barrel into place on Hawkins' gun, Jackson slammed the bolt of his own rifle forward, feeding one of the fresh rounds into the chamber. With reluctance, he realised that he would have to stop playing soldiers for a moment and start behaving like a platoon sergeant. To that end, he scrambled to his feet, keeping clear of the window, and ran across to the two men behind the Bren. He paused over them, wrestling his spare bandolier of fifty rounds over his head then dropped it onto the concrete floor beside the No.2.

"There you go. Start bombing those spare magazines up; I'll go and get some more."

He turned and ran across the big room, exited onto the stair-well then clattered down the steps to where the Company Sergeant Major was manning the company's command post in the cellars. He squeezed past a pair of stretcher bearers who were struggling up the stairs.

"Where you two going?" He demanded.

"Top floor, Sergeant; Seventeen Platoon have taken another mortar bomb, right through the roof."

"Okay." He dismissed them and tumbled on down towards the cellar.

He turned the corner of the stairwell sharply and threw himself down the stairs into the cellar. As he reached the central corridor in the subterranean level, Jackson slowed, searching ahead through the gloom for his destination. As his eyes finally adjusted, he stomped along the central corridor with increasing speed, aiming for the side room where the Company Sergeant Major's group was located. He passed a door to his right and heard the sobbing of wounded men and the urgent murmuring of medical orderlies. Ignoring the company aid post, the sergeant walked on and turned into the next doorway on the right. This room was a little brighter, with a small hurricane lamp in one corner throwing out a degree of illumination.

Jackson gazed around the room, surprised to find it packed with men. In addition to the Company Sergeant Major who was scribbling away in his notebook, the room was filled by several runners, along with the Company Commander and Jackson's own officer, Dunstable. As he entered the room, both Pilkington and Dunstable looked up.

"Ah, just the man!" Pilkington said without pause. "The runner found you, then?"

Jackson was just about to ask 'what runner?' when Pilkington beckoned him over and continued talking, addressing his comments to both Jackson and Dunstable together.

"Right, gentlemen; I've got a job for your platoon. The Commanding Officer has just popped over to let me know what's going on and we have a bit of a problem that needs addressing…"

Jackson glanced at the Company Sergeant Major who was still busy writing, and the young sergeant wondered if he really had time to listen to this briefing before his men started to run out of ammunition. He looked back at Pilkington as the captain went on however, realising that he couldn't interrupt him in mid-flow.

"So far we're holding our own pretty much. I think you'll agree that we've given Jerry a bloody good punch on the nose this morning, and it looks like his attack might be stalling. However…"

Pilkington took a deep breath.

"The Germans have made two small incursions on this side of the river. There's a few got over in No.1 Company's area, to our forward left; but they're being held just about. More worrying is a group that have got across to our forward right, smack bang between us and the Grenadiers."

Pilkington paused so that Dunstable and Jackson could nod their understanding thus far. Once happy that they were with him, he went on.

"The reason I've called for you two is because the Jerries on the right seem to have got themselves ensconced in that stream bed that your patrol used last night, Sergeant Jackson. They've managed to work their way up the battalion's right flank and they're pouring fire into the town from that side. If they manage to reinforce their chaps who have got into that stream bed then they may even launch an attack against the town itself. Now, No.2 Company has formed a defensive flank to hold them for the time being, but we need to get into that stream bed and clear those buggers out. That's where your platoon comes in. You know that area well…"

Pilkington nodded at Jackson.

"And so do some of your men, so it makes sense that I use your platoon to counter-attack. Your mission is quite simple, gentlemen. Take your entire platoon to the southern edge of the village, form up there then drive the enemy out of that stream bed. Once you've done it, send word back to No.2 Company who'll be giving you covering fire. They've been ordered to put together a composite platoon to relieve you once you've cleared the enemy out. Once that's complete, bring yourselves back here straight away. Any questions?"

Jackson looked at Dunstable, then both of them looked back at Pilkington.

"No, Sir." They chorused together.

"Good."

Pilkington grinned at the two men.

"Then I look forward to hearing your tales of daring-do on return! I need you to launch your counter-attack no later than 0930 hours. Off you go then."

Jackson turned away, planning to speak to the Company Sergeant Major, but was surprised to find that the warrant officer was already standing next to him, his arms outstretched. Perhaps nine or ten ammunition bandoliers containing the much needed .303 inch ammunition dangled from the Company Sergeant Major's clenched fists.

The warrant officer winked at Jackson.

"Here you go, Sergeant Jackson. If you're going off for your own private war then you'll probably need some of these."

THE STREAM BED – 300 YARDS SOUTH OF PECQ
TUESDAY 21ST MAY 1940 – 0925 HOURS

"Fucking hell, this is shit!"

Dullman cursed angrily and kicked a nearby bush.

"We're only a couple of hundred metres from the main road; we're right on the edge of the village, perfectly situated for a flank attack to roll up the entire Tommy line, but we don't have the men or the ammo to do anything about it!"

He looked around at the small group of NCOs who had managed to survive the crossing of the river, hoping for inspiration, but instead the three men simply stared back at him, as frustrated by their position as their commander.

"Where's the rest of the fucking battalion?" Dullman snarled suddenly, kicking at the bush again in frustration. "All we need is a couple more machine-guns and just one light mortar and we could really give those Tommy bastards a run for their money!"

He glowered at the murky water in the stream bed for long moments as he contemplated their predicament. It had been a difficult fight, getting away from the river bank and along this stream, the enemy raking them with fire all the way. Mortars, machine-guns, well aimed rifle fire; it had all taken its toll on Dullman's tiny force. Now, running short of ammunition, he and his men had essentially become pinned down, just on the outskirts of the town where the stream bed came closest. The Tommies had seen the danger and pulled their flank in sharply, bringing every spare weapon to bear in the process. Dullman needed more ammo, more men and heavier weapons, and he needed them quickly. As the morning wore on however, his chances of being reinforced seemed to be getting less and less.

Suddenly, he turned to one of the corporals.

"Heyderich? I want you to go back down the stream to the river bank. See if you can find anyone else. If there's anyone on the far bank, tell them that we are within a gnat's knacker of busting open the Tommy flank, and that they need to start feeding more men across. Take a man with you too, and search every dead body for ammunition; collect every last round you can find then get it back up here. Understand?"

"Yes, Captain." The corporal snapped obediently and made to turn away.

"And keep low!" Dullman reminded him.

The corporal smiled and was about to say something in reply, but an urgent shout caught everyone's attention.

"The Tommies are up to something, Captain!"

Dullman looked up the stream bed towards the man who had shouted.

"What do you mean?" He demanded.

"Not sure, Sir; but the fuckers are scurrying about all over the place. They're definitely up to something."

"Go find that ammo, Heyderich!" Dullman snapped at the corporal, then splashed through the calf-deep water towards where the young rifleman lay against the side of the bank.

Crawling up beside the soldier, Dullman pulled out his binoculars.

"Where? What's going on? Show me?"

"There, Captain; up towards the corner of that field, behind that row of cottages."

Dullman raised the field glasses to his eyes and scanned the area, keeping as low as possible. A single bullet cracked low overhead, but he ignored it. He scanned for a while, seeing just the corn, the fences and hedgerows, the steeple of the church, the big house, and the...

"Seen!" Dullman chimed suddenly.

And he had seen them indeed. One after another, the khaki figures were shaking out along the garden fences behind the line of cottages. He could see them darting out from an alley of some kind and throwing themselves down into cover at the rear of the buildings. He could see for himself what was going on. They were forming up for an attack. His heart picked up a beat, his mind working quickly. These bastards weren't in the mood to let him and his men sit here all day. These Tommies were up for a fight; that was for sure. Something passed through the air above him, almost lazily, making a soft sigh as it went.

Crump!

The mortar bomb exploded just twenty metres away, back towards where he had just been briefing his NCOs.

"Fuck!" Dullman swore, pushing his face down into the grass as bits of soil and undergrowth showered down around him. "Bastards have got some light mortars in action!"

There was another soft sigh, then another. Crump! A bit of a pause, then...Crump!

"Keep low!" Dullman ordered. "Make sure you've got full magazines on!"

A small mortar bomb plonked down right in front of Dullman, about ten metres away in the cornfield. He winced and ducked his head, expecting to feel the force from the blast, but nothing happened and after a couple of moments he glanced up. And caught his breath...

The latest bomb was emitting smoke; thick, white, pungent smoke, which billowed up from the corn to drift on the slight morning breeze, obscuring his immediate view of the town beyond. Another smoke bomb landed right inside the stream bed just a couple of seconds later, off to his right, instantly filling the sheltered gulley with clouds of artificial smog. From beyond the smoke screen, a fresh upsurge in Tommy machine-gun fire brought burst after burst of powerful slugs cracking over the heads of the handful of Germans in the stream. Then, audible even above the crack of machine-gun fire, he heard the loud, determined British voices of NCOs and officers directing their men.

"Stand-to!" Dullman yelled along the smoke filled ditch. "Stand-to!"

He grabbed his own machine-pistol and brought it into his shoulder, ready to go. Dullman's throat was parched. It was hot, it was noisy, and it was chaotic; and now, the British were coming...

No.16 PLATOON FORMING UP POINT – SOUTH EDGE OF PECQ
TUESDAY 21ST MAY 1940 – 0925 HOURS

"That's the last one, Sergeant."

Guardsman Edwards turned and nodded at Jackson as the last of the smoke bombs from the platoon's 2 inch mortar streaked upwards into the hazy morning air above the cornfield.

Jackson squinted across the field to where the bank of artificial fog was beginning to thicken up nicely, obscuring a hundred yard stretch of the stream bed. He emitted a grunt of satisfaction.

"Well done, Edwards, lad; that was spot on. Now get that mortar slung and prepare to move off when I tell you."

The soldier instantly began to dismount the small mortar, as Jackson doubled along the fence line towards his platoon commander. Spotting the young second lieutenant, Jackson slid down into the kneeling position beside him.

"Right, Sir; that's all mortar bombs gone. I reckon we've got a minute and a half tops before that smoke clears. I'm moving along the track now to get into the top end of that stream bed. Soon as you hear us open fire, you charge in there. Happy?"

Dunstable nodded his understanding, comfortable with sharing the command arrangements with his platoon sergeant. Jackson's eyes were alive with the thrill of the chase now, and he pushed himself upright, patting Dunstable on the arm.

"Get going then, Sir. Give the bastards hell and I'll see you in the stream bed!"

The sergeant sped off back towards his ad hoc fire support section, leaving Dunstable to take a deep breath.

The young lieutenant adopted a low crouch.

"Alright, Number Sixteen Platoon; stand-up!"

To Dunstable's right and left, the riflemen from all three sections rose to their feet, their bayonet tipped weapons at the high port.

The young officer glanced in either direction quickly to ascertain that everybody was ready then gave the order.

"At the walk, by the centre...advance!"

Jackson was already at the end of the line when he heard Dunstable give the order to advance. As he sprinted up the fence line, he could see the eager faces of his own group turned towards him, waiting for their own instructions. Jackson had stripped the three Bren teams from the rifle sections and attached them to his two man mortar crew in order to form a fire support section. Now, having laid down a short bombardment and smoke screen with the mortar, it was time for his hastily assembled force to play their next part.

"On your feet, men! Follow me!" Jackson snapped, rounding the corner of the fence and onto the track without pausing.

In his wake, the three Bren gunners, their No.2s and the two guardsmen who crewed the light mortar, struggled to their feet and followed on behind the platoon sergeant. They followed him down the narrow track that ran alongside the cornfield which the remainder of their platoon was now crossing. After no more than thirty yards, Jackson turned and used his hand to point, with a chopping motion, at the grass verge.

"Down here, Three Section's Bren. Start firing straight away. As soon as the platoon blocks your arc, follow us along the track."

Obediently, the first Bren team dropped into position and hurriedly set up whilst the others ran on. A moment later, the light-machine gun burst into life, spitting its deadly bullets diagonally across the cornfield towards the still obscured stream bed. Jackson and the others ran on; another forty yards or so, perhaps.

"Two Section's gun down here..." The sergeant ordered again. "Same detail..."

On he ran, just his own mortarmen and the remaining Bren team with him now. Although Jackson might deny the fact later, it was no coincidence that the last gunner to remain with him was Guardsman Hawkins.

As soon as the second Bren team was in action, Jackson moved off again. The line of the stream was only fifty or sixty yards away now, the head of it being cut by the track along which the five Coldstreamers now ran. When they were still some thirty yards from that point, Jackson slowed to a halt and dropped to his knees, beckoning the others to close up behind him. The four guardsmen huddled up next to their platoon sergeant and leaned in close to hear his low, urgent voice.

"Right then, lads; any moment now that smoke is going to fade, so we need to move quick. We're going into the stream bed up here where it meets the track. Hawkins and me will lead with the automatic weapons…"

At this point, he hefted the captured German machine-pistol and gave it a shake.

"You two…" He pointed at his mortarmen. "One either side, on the bank. Get ready to shoot anything that breaks out of the stream bed; just like taking rabbits down when you're cutting the corn at harvest time."

The two soldiers nodded their understanding.

"You…" He pointed at the No.2 on the Bren. "Follow us down the stream, right in the middle, and keep feeding Hawkins those spare magazines. Make sense?"

The guardsmen murmured their agreement, their pulses racing, fighting spirit roused by the obvious excitement in their platoon sergeant's face. Jackson grinned back.

"Right, let's do it…"

Quickly, he fumbled inside his right ammunition pouch and pulled out a hand grenade. Having grasped it firmly in his left hand, he jumped up and began moving at a fast pace, bending low, along the lane towards the stream. He glanced left and saw that the smoke screen was only seconds away from clearing. Just at that point, a shot cracked past Jackson's face, missing him by inches, and as he threw himself down against the verge once more, he caught sight of the enemy rifleman in the stream.

"Get ready to charge into the stream…" He gasped, dropping the German machine-pistol momentarily so that he could grip the grenade in his right hand.

Sliding his left forefinger through the safety pin, Jackson drew back his right arm and pulled the pin free. With a huge effort, he lobbed the grenade over-arm towards the ditch. It was a long throw, possibly twenty five yards, but the grenade fell just a foot away from the lip of the stream. *In* the stream would have been better, but he knew his throw would suffice. He heard a shout of alarm in a foreign voice.

Crump!

"Go!" Jackson yelled above the noise of the exploding grenade, and he grabbed for the machine-pistol and launched himself forwards.

The five men sprinted as they had never sprinted before, veering left, off the track and through a few stalks of trampled corn so that they ran straight over the smoking seat of the grenade explosion and on into the stream bed. As Jackson hurled himself through the smoke and into the little gulley, he glimpsed a German soldier in the grass of the bank to his left. Barely had he spotted the man when he saw Hawkins appear on the bank right next to him and deliver a terrible penalty kick to the German's head.

As Jackson lost his footing and slid down the bank, he saw the unfortunate German flip backwards and down into the filthy water in the bed of the drainage ditch. As soon as he came to a juddering halt at the bottom of the ditch, Jackson twisted the captured machine-pistol on the floundering German and pressed the trigger. The all metal weapon lurched violently in Jackson's hands and the water and soil around the German erupted in a series of violent spurts. The enemy soldier gave a wild jerk and then flopped limply back into the water as another burst of fire sounded nearby.

It was Hawkins. Standing halfway up the bank, just above Jackson, the guardsman had dug his heels into the incline of the bank, and was now firing several long bursts along the length of the ditch.

"Come on!" Jackson gasped the words as he struggled to his feet. "Keep going down."

He pushed himself upright and stumbled onto the right hand bank, bringing his machine-pistol up into the aim. Across the stream bed, Hawkins was advancing carefully along the bank with Bren tucked in hard against his right hip, the weapon's sling wrapped firmly around his upper arm and shoulder.

Along the ditch, Jackson saw a sudden flurry of activity. Heads began popping up from behind tufts of grass and bushes, and he heard yet more urgent shouting in German. A bullet cracked between him and Hawkins, and the young Bren gunner responded with two defiant bursts.

"Bloody hell, Hawkins! There's loads of the bastards down there!" The sergeant cursed as he saw the movement of several enemy soldiers some thirty yards further down.

"Let's go get 'em then, Sergeant..." Hawkins grunted as he advanced cautiously along the incline and fired another burst into the thickening undergrowth of the stream bed.

Just at that point, above the noise of gunfire and shouting, the clear, shrill, blast of a whistle rang out from not far away. It was followed almost instantly by one of the most spine-tingling sounds that Jackson had ever heard. It was the sound of No.16 Platoon, *his platoon*, screaming their defiance at the German Army as they levelled their bayonets and broke into a charge through the dissipating smoke screen and onwards into the stream bed. There was a sudden increase in gunfire from further along the water-course and the urgent shouting in German turned to frantic yelling.

As a German soldier exposed himself unintentionally just up ahead, and both Jackson and Hawkins sprayed the man with automatic fire, a wave of terrifying, khaki-clad demons came howling over the left hand lip of the stream and down amongst the Germans in the bed of it. At last, after eleven days of war, Jackson and his men had finally got the battle they wanted.

THE STREAM BED – 300 YARDS SOUTH OF PECQ
TUESDAY 21ST MAY 1940 – 0935 HOURS

"Enemy left! Enemy left!"

Dullman screamed out the alarm at the top of his voice.

"They're coming down the fucking stream! Face left! Face left!"

He grabbed the nearest private and physically pulled him around to face up the stream bed. Inwardly, Dullman was cursing himself. It had been a classic deception plan; laying a false smoke screen then coming in from his left. He cursed himself for not seeing it earlier.

"Rautzen!" He hollered through the last skeins of drifting smoke. "Get everyone facing up stream, now!"

Around him, men began dropping back from the lip of the stream's bank where they had been covering across towards the town, and started splashing through the mud and water towards the nearby clump of bushes so that they could form a protective fire-base against the incursion further upstream. Once again, Dullman cursed his own stupidity. He should have put some more men further up the stream to guard against a flank attack. He hadn't realised how aggressively the British would defend this river after they had pulled back from so many before without really making a stand.

Rautzen appeared before him, a look of near panic on his face. Dullman gave the corporal a hard stare.

"Rautzen; get everyone in this stretch to put fire down along the stream bed! I'll get the remaining men from further down and bring them up to your squad. We're going to have to clear those bastards out with grenades! Start getting it organised!"

The corporal nodded his understanding and turned away, barking orders as he went. Dullman turned in the opposite direction and splashed along the stream looking for more of his men. A burst of fire cracked past his right elbow and he saw two spurts of earth rear up on the bank just a few metres further on.

"Jesus!" He muttered quietly as he struggled through the churned up stream bed.

Looking up, he saw Heyderich splashing back towards him, carrying two sets of belt equipment and a belt of machine-gun ammunition.

"I've left someone to bring the rest, Captain." He shouted as he approached, pushing past some reeds. "I heard the firing. What's going on?"

Dullman stumbled to a halt as the corporal reached him.

"The bastards came from the left instead!" He growled. "They've got in the top end of this ditch so watch yourself because…"

Crack-crack-crack!

The bullets hammered past Dullman and sliced straight through Heyderich's chest leaving a ragged pattern of neat red holes in the front of his tunic. Without a word, and like a tree that had just been felled, the corporal simply toppled backwards and landed with a splash in the stream, the ammunition belts falling from between his lifeless fingers as he did so.

"Shit!" Dullman twisted sideways and threw himself flat against the bank.

He looked up to see several more of his men splashing towards him.

"Stay down!" He yelled at them. "Keep into the sides! The Tommies are firing down the fucking stream!"

His own words were suddenly drowned out by a terrible roar of voices nearby, accompanied by the shrieking blasts of a whistle. The captain whirled round to see what the latest addition to the cacophony of battle would bring, and as he did so, his heart sank. Further up the stream, where Rautzen and his cobbled together squad were trying to make a stand, a wave of Tommy infantry suddenly appeared on the top of the right hand bank. They seemed to pause there for a heart beat, their long, deadly looking bayonets glinting in the weak morning sunlight, and then they suddenly descended like a pack of howling wolves into the gulley itself, falling upon Rautzen's men like avenging angels.

Dullman pushed himself upright and stumbled towards the German soldiers coming in his direction.

"Go back!" He waved at the three men desperately. "All the way to the river bank! Get fucking back!"

POPLAR RIDGE – 1,000 YARDS SOUTH OF PECQ
TUESDAY 21ST MAY 1940 – 1030 HOURS

Ambrosius scanned the tired, yet determined faces that peered back at him beneath the shade of the big trees. The stress and terror of the battle had aged the handful of officers in just a couple of short hours, yet despite that, their eyes still glistened with that old eagerness, bred into them through months of relentless training. They were still up for the fight.

"Right then, gentlemen…" Ambrosius began, "well done so far. It's been a damn hard battle but we've reached our first objective. It is obvious however that the battalion has paid a heavy price for it."

He paused and looked at his Adjutant, Lieutenant Engel, who was quickly calculating the manpower returns from the assembled officers.

"What is the final figure?"

Engel looked up from his note pad, his face serious.

"Just seventy two of us left, including yourself, Captain."

Ambrosius struggled to keep his face impassive.

"And there will be more men still down near the river bank that have lost their way, or those dealing with prisoners and the like. As the time goes by we will get more and more men trickling up here to join us…"

Ambrosius sounded more confident than he felt. He knew how badly his battalion had been cut up during the river crossing and ensuing battle to secure the bank, and he knew that on their current performance, the British were unlikely to let him sit up on this hill without dispute. Wanting to reassure his few surviving commanders however, Ambrosius rattled out a string of instructions.

"Engel, I want you to get back down the hill and start directing any waifs and strays up here towards us. This will be the battalion rendezvous point. I also want you to get a message back to Regimental Headquarters. Tell them that we have reached our first objective, but we have taken significant casualties and will need reinforcement within the next couple of hours, along with more ammunition too. Tell them that I will attempt to advance beyond the main north-south road this afternoon once we have reorganised the battalion and topped up our ammunition. Got all that?"

Engel, who had been scribbling away furiously, nodded his understanding.

"I'll get on it straight away, Captain."

The captain looked back at the other officers who knelt close by.

"Barthels? I want you to distribute your surviving machine-guns around the perimeter so that we've got every avenue covered. The main threat is from due west so ensure you have got your fields of fire inter-locked in that direction. Once you've done that, I want you to take over what's left of Fifth Company for the time being. Start fanning them out from the tip of this wood, around to the right, covering northwards towards Pecq. Hasselmann; you take what's left of your boys and fan them out on the left here. Essentially, I want the battalion in all round defence centred on this wood. As our stragglers start to come in, we can reorganise as required."

The officers nodded silently as Ambrosius outlined the new dispositions. As the captain paused for breath, Lieutenant Hasselmann, commanding Sixth Company took the opportunity to speak.

"Once we've shaken out, Captain, what then?"

Ambrosius considered his answer for a moment.

"Well…" He began, thoughtfully. "We can't go any further without reinforcements, or without at least scraping the battalion back into some kind of shape again. And I don't think the Tommies will be happy about having us sat up here in this wood, not judging by the reception they've given us so far. It's only a matter of time before they try and push us off here, so we need to prepare against counter-attack with urgency. We *must* hold this bridgehead at all costs until the rest of the regiment can follow us over."

He sucked his teeth for moment.

"So, tell your men to start digging in. Tell them to dig for all they're worth."

GRENADIER GUARDS FORMING UP POINT – 300 YARDS SOUTH WEST OF POPLAR RIDGE
TUESDAY 21ST MAY 1940 – 1125 HOURS

"Spread out, lads; push along the tree line and get down."

The platoon sergeant's voice carried loud and steady above the noise of exploding shells and mortar bombs. For Guardsman Tony Slingsby of No.3 Company, 3rd Battalion Grenadier Guards, it was all very disconcerting. His company had been brought up from reserve on the orders of the Commanding Officer. It was a matter of urgency it seemed, because Captain Starkey, the Company Commander, had taken the unusual step of gathering the whole company in a tight huddle, giving out a short, to the point set of orders, before leading them off towards their forming up point near the main road that ran south out of Pecq.

The reason for Captain Starkey dispensing with normal battle procedure soon became evident enough. In his short brief, he had told his men that the news was bad. The Jerries were over the river and they had smashed their way through No.4 Company who had fought on, virtually to the last man. Now the Germans had set themselves up on a wooded ridge overlooking the road and surrounding area.

"So we're going to knock the buggers off their hill and send them back over the Escaut." Starkey had told them "Then we're going to link up with the Coldstreamers in Pecq and restore the situation all along the river line."

And so it was that Slingsby now found himself squatting in the shallow ditch, just back from the road, beyond which lay their objective. Shells exploded at random around them every twenty seconds or so, and the young guardsman had no idea whether those shells were German or British. They had been promised a preliminary bombardment by their own mortars, and he hoped to God that the current shower of explosives was not one of their own making.

He looked left and saw his section's second in command, Lance Corporal Harry Nicholls, chatting nonchalantly with Percy Nash, another guardsman in their section. Nicholls was carrying the Bren Gun; not the normal form for a Lance Corporal, but when the original gunner had been wounded several days ago, Nicholls had assumed ownership of the weapon. He was real fire-breather, Corporal Nicholls was. A battalion boxer, who knew how to take and give a punch, he was really up for a scrap with the Jerries. Now it seemed he would get his wish. Slingsby took comfort from the fact that if he was to go into battle next to anyone, there was no better candidate than Harry Nicholls.

A squeal of metal made Slingsby twist round to look behind him. He was comforted to see a trio of Bren Carriers trundling into position amongst the strung out line of infantrymen. That was good, Slingsby thought; *'Harry Nicholls on my left and three armoured carriers on my right.'*

There was a sudden 'whoosh' in the air above, and then the ground began to shake as a series of explosions rocked the distant wooded ridge-line, which lay partially obscured by the line of trees just in front of the forming up point. And that was even better, Slingsby reasoned. British bombs and shells dropping right on top of the enemy.

"Here we go, men!" An officer's voice sounded from along the line.

A moment later, the unmistakeable sound of the Company Sergeant Major's voice rose above the noise of the bombardment.

"Number Three Company will fix bayonets…Fix…Bayonets!"

Slingsby drew the long blade from the scabbard at his side and clicked it into place on the end of his rifle. He watched the morning sun reflecting of the sharpened point and lower edge. How many times had he practiced this in peace time?

Crump!

"Aagh! Bollocks!"

Slingsby ducked involuntarily as the enemy shell landed no more than twenty yards away, and looked left at the sound of exclamation from Nicholls.

He saw the big corporal shaking his arm in irritation. Not in panic mind you, and with no sign of fear; but more like the action of somebody who had just nettled their hand.

"Are you alright, Corporal Nicholls?" Slingsby heard Nash enquire.

"Yeah, fine…" Nicholls growled. "Just a splinter from that last shell. Bastards! That's another thing they've got to pay for now!"

"Stand up!" The voice of the Company Sergeant Major roared.

They stood, including Nicholls who was ignoring the small blood stain that had begun to spread on his sleeve. Slingsby felt his pulse begin to quicken.

"At the walk, by the centre…advance!"

They stepped up and out of the ditch and began to walk forward, their feet crunching on stalks of corn and rough grass. Slingsby heard the revving of the carriers' engines as they began trundling forward with the rifle company, bolstering their line. They pushed through the tree-line and then, like a theatre curtain being pulled back, the whole panorama of the battlefield opened up before them.

Up on the ridge, the long strip wood of tall Poplar trees stood silhouetted like the wall of a mighty fortress. Before them, for perhaps two hundred yards, the wide, open field was filled with ripening corn, like a golden lake lapping against the wooded ridge.

"Remember what the Captain told us…" Nicholls was calling. "Watch out for any of the Four Company boys who might be trapped in the corn. If anyone pops their head up, check who it is before you blow their turnip off!"

The Poplar trees were shaking and swaying as shell after shell dropped amongst them. So far, so good. This all seemed pretty organised; pretty straight forward. The Germans would probably run when they saw the carriers. At least, that's what Slingsby hoped. The explosions in the Poplar wood began to lessen, and then, almost as suddenly as it had begun, the British bombardment ended. Slingsby frowned. They were still a couple of hundred yards from the wood line. Surely they could have kept shelling the enemy a bit longer?

Then he saw the first tracer rounds whip across the field like some kind of luminous snake. A heartbeat later, the terrible, high-pitched crack-crack-crack of the enemy machine-gun assailed his ear drums, making him jump.

"Bloody hell! How fast are those guns firing?" He murmured to himself.

Glancing left and right he saw that the company was advancing without pause. Another burst of machine-gun fire rattled across the top of the corn, followed immediately by another from a different angle, and Slingsby heard the first cry of shock and pain from somewhere off to his right.

"Christ almighty!" Slingsby whispered with horrid realisation. "We're going to get slaughtered!"

As that thought crossed his mind, the nearest carrier revved its engine once more and accelerated forwards, leaving the line of infantrymen behind as it put a spurt on, charging towards the enemy held ridge. As it did so, a lone whistle blew shrill above the noise of engines and machine-gun fire. More whistles took up the cry, so that it sounded like a football match was in progress with far too many referees on the pitch. Then, starting as a low murmur and transforming itself into a collective roar, the sound of one hundred deep male voices split the morning air in a savage war cry. To his surprise, Slingsby realised that one of those voices was his own. He was running now, crashing through the corn, his rifle and bayonet levelled, his lungs bursting as he repeated the mantra over and over; the years of training taking control.

"Chaaaaarge!"

POPLAR RIDGE – THE GERMAN POSITIONS
TUESDAY 21ST MAY 1940 – 1130 HOURS

"What the fuck is that?"

Ambrosius flicked his head up from the scene of devastation around him as he heard the ominous roar of dozens of voices, sounding clear across the morning air and breaking the sudden hush that followed the end of the bombardment. That bombardment had been short, yet intense; a mixture of artillery and mortars that had sent mind-numbing shock waves through the interior of the wood, bringing branches down on top of the defenders as they cowered in their hastily dug shell-scrapes.

Ambrosius listened intently with a rising sense of dread. That terrible cheer seemed to go on forever, backed by the screeching of whistles. Amongst the din, the captain thought he heard another sound; the sound of engines? Next to him, one of his sergeants cursed endlessly as a private struggled to bandage the NCOs shattered left arm; the result of the deadly shrapnel that had ripped through trees in the wake of every shell burst. Then, a German voice just a few metres away called out in alarm.

"Tanks!"

Ambrosius felt his blood run instantly cold. Tanks! The voice was joined by several others, creating a collective symphony of alarm.

"Tanks! Stand-to! Tanks and infantry coming from the south-west!"

The young battalion commander jumped to his feet, snapping instructions to the private who was still busy administering first aid to the sergeant.

"Leave that! Get on the wood-line!"

Leaving the private to comply, Ambrosius sprinted between the tall, thin tree trunks like a startled gazelle. As he ran, he heard the sound of his own machine-guns opening fire.

Reaching the edge of the wood he threw himself down behind a tree trunk, directly behind a shell-scrape containing two riflemen. His first instinct was to reach for his binoculars, but he checked himself. There was no need. All across his frontage, the situation was clear to see. His heart lurched as he saw the seemingly endless line of khaki-clad men, their strange shaped green helmets bobbing up and down as they trampled through the corn towards him. Even more noticeable, was the glint of sunlight on bayonets. And then he saw the vehicles. Three of them, spaced twenty metres apart and bouncing across the field at a fair speed, smashing down great swathes of corn as they advanced. He could feel his blood pumping madly through his veins, but he forced himself to stay calm. He could see heads popping up from within the vehicles... They were open topped!

"All machine-guns aim at the vehicles!" Roared Ambrosius; first one way, then the other. "Stand-by with your grenades if they come too close! Don't panic! They're open-topped. Stay calm and grenade the bastards!"

He ran down the line, repeating the orders at the top of his voice. In front, he saw Schlinke with one of the MG34 teams.

"Schlinke! Take out those fucking armoured cars!"

The lieutenant glanced towards Ambrosius and merely nodded before returning his attention to the gun crew. They were already engaging the lead vehicle, knowing they had to stop it before it reached their forward positions.

Ambrosius hurtled past Schlinke's gun crew, leaping over the young soldier at the rear of the gun who was busy slotting fresh rounds into an expended belt. He passed another two riflemen, before coming to the second MG34 team on this side of the wood. He yelled the same orders at them, but the crew were already rattling away with everything they had. The captain turned back towards the field to observe the progress of the enemy. The carriers were less than a hundred metres away now, and the closest one was being hit from several directions by masses of small-arms fire. Brightly coloured tracer bullets bounced off the green metal hull of the vehicle in all directions, emitting high-pitched whines as they did so. Behind the armoured vehicles, still perhaps a hundred and twenty metres away, Ambrosius saw the line of infantry begin to falter. The weight of defensive fire from his men was starting to have an effect. Every German at this side of the wood was letting rip with every weapon available.

Ambrosius saw khaki figures go down all along the line, some throwing their hands up before dropping; others simply ducking out of sight. Then, almost on some unseen signal, the whole line of enemy infantry seemed to disappear into the corn. He switched his gaze back to the leading carrier as he saw it come to a sudden halt; rocking forward on its drive wheels, before settling back on its rear idlers. A khaki body lay draped over the side of the vehicle and the engine noise had settled to a steady, idle hum.

"That's it; well done!" Ambrosius yelled above the noise of machine-gun fire. "Now do the same to the others!"

He broke into a run again, back up the slope, towards the first machine-gun crew. As he ran, he saw the two surviving enemy vehicles suddenly lurch forward with renewed vigour and charge headlong at the tree line, right where it crested the ridge line. They were veering away from the machine-guns, aiming for the weakest point of the German line.

"On your feet!" Ambrosius roared. "On your feet, riflemen! Grenade those Tommy tanks! Come on! Stop the bloody things!"

The captain was purple with exertion now, as he threw himself along the wood-line towards where the enemy vehicles were hardly fifteen metres from the trees. He raised his machine-pistol as he went and let off a wild burst towards the nearest carrier. He had no idea where his bullets went, but didn't have time to fire a second burst because, suddenly, his own riflemen were springing up in front of him, emerging from their shell-scrapes to confront the metal monsters.

"Grenade them!" Ambrosius screamed, over and over again.

He saw his men moving forwards into the corn as the enemy vehicles slowed, their crews perhaps unsure of what awaited them in the trees, perhaps wondering what had happened to their supporting infantry? Whatever the reason, their speed suddenly eased off, and the Germans took full advantage. Driven on by their battalion commander, the German soldiers fired at the low silhouettes of the Tommies who were crouched inside the strange little vehicles and, much to the relief of Ambrosius, the first stick grenade went sailing through the air. He watched it drop into the corn, just short of a vehicle, where it exploded with a sharp 'crump'.

Another two grenades followed it, one aimed at each carrier. Both failed to land inside the vehicles but got dangerously close, rocking the vehicles with their deafening blast. The two Tommy carriers appeared to be confused about what to do next. They turned sharply away from their original course and began manoeuvring around with no obvious purpose in front of the wood-line, their small caterpillar tracks lurching over the deep earthen ruts of the field.

"That's it!" Ambrosius yelled at his men, encouraging them. "Drive the bastards off!"

He ran further up the wood-line, his men gathering about him, and as a group they fired as they ran, not giving the vehicle crews a moment to gather their wits. From inside the wood, the sergeant with the wounded left arm suddenly appeared right in front of Ambrosius.

In his right hand he held a stick grenade, the cord and ball-weight hanging loosely from within the handle. With a look of defiance, the sergeant raised the grenade to his face, gripped the ball and cord between his teeth, then yanked the grenade upwards sharply with his good arm; thus initiating the short fuse. Ambrosius held his breath as the sergeant spat the cord from between his lips, drew his arm back, then hurled the grenade as far as he could, emitting a snarl of pain-filled effort as he did so. Ambrosius watched the stick grenade sail through the air towards the nearest enemy vehicle. It looked as if it might even drop right inside it.

Crump! The grenade exploded in mid-air, just a second before it would have dropped onto its target. Never-the-less, the air-burst was enough. The carrier jerked to a halt. Nobody got up or tried to escape from within the small armoured box. With bullets still whining off the sides of its armoured hide, the third enemy carrier turned away from the wood and began lurching back across the cornfield, away from the German positions.

"Well done, men! Bloody well done!" Ambrosius hollered, feeling the pride swell within him.

His men had fought hard to get here. There was no way the Tommies were going to shift them off this hill.

"Captain? Captain Ambrosius?"

He turned at the sound of his name being called. For a moment or two he could see nobody, but then, flitting between the trees, the figure of Lieutenant Engel appeared, calling out for his commander.

"Where's the battalion commander? Has anybody seen him?"

"Engel! Over here!" Ambrosius waved frantically towards him and broke into a jog, threading his way through the trees towards his chief staff officer. "What's the matter, Engel?"

The lieutenant spotted Ambrosius and began running up the wooded slope towards him. As they neared each other, Engel slowed to a halt, his breathing laboured.

"Captain..." He panted. "I've managed to round up another thirty men from the river bank. They're in the cornfield at the back of the wood. Where do you want them?"

Ambrosius felt his spirits lift even further.

"Well done, Engel! Bring them all up here, quickly. I want them to man this side of the wood. There's a Tommy company somewhere out there in that..."

Crack.

The sound of the single bullet passed very close by, cutting off Ambrosius in mid-sentence and making him jump slightly.

He saw Engel stagger back a step, and watched in disbelief as red liquid sprayed out from the side of the man's head. For a long, terrible moment, the young lieutenant just hovered there, staring back at his commander as blood poured down the side of his head from within his helmet, and then he just dropped.

"Engel!" Ambrosius called out in shock as his adjutant's dead body thudded to the floor like a weighted sack.

The captain walked quickly over and stared down at Engel's body. The poor man had been shot straight through the head.

"Oh, my God..." Ambrosius gasped.

There was a sudden eruption of machine-gun fire, back down the wood-line, and the sound of yet more frantic shouting.

"Take the bastards out!" Someone was shouting. "They're a bunch of fucking mad-men!"

Forgetting his dead friend, Ambrosius ran directly to the edge of the trees and threw his gaze down the wood-line. His jaw dropped open in amazement. Of the Tommy infantry company there was little obvious sign, but barely thirty metres from the wood-line, three very tall, khaki-clad figures were forcing their way through the corn in a flat sprint. Two of the figures, both with bayonet tipped rifles, were slightly behind a third man, who wore huge white chevrons on his tunic sleeve and carried one of the big Tommy light-machine guns with its strange, curved magazine.

"Bloody hell!" Ambrosius swore, in a mixture of shock and admiration.

Tracer rounds zipped left and right and between the group of three Tommies, but they didn't seem to notice the hail of German fire. Instead, they trampled through the corn, roaring their defiance at the enemy as they attacked straight towards the wood. Three lone Tommies against a composite company of Germans. It was sheer madness. But charge they did; and they were charging straight for Ambrosius' own machine-guns.

POPLAR RIDGE – THE CORNFIELD, 120 YARDS FROM THE TREES
TUESDAY 21ST MAY 1940 – 1135 HOURS

"Ruddy hell!" Slingsby cried out as he crouched on all fours, deep within the cover of the waist high crops. "What kind of bloody machine-guns have the Jerries got up there?"

His question had been rhetorical; uttered simply for his own benefit as he recovered from the shock of watching half his section being bowled over like skittles by the lengthy burst of automatic fire that had zipped towards them like a luminous snake.

"Ones that fire bloody fast!"

Slingsby heard the deep, East Midlands accent of Corporal Nicholls nearby, making an unexpected reply to his desperate query.

Relieved to hear the voice of somebody who was obviously still alive, Slingsby crawled quickly along the earthen floor, pushing the thick stalks of corn aside. After just a couple of yards, he was greeted by the sight of Nicholls, crouching in the corn, still gripping the Bren Gun, the battledress sleeve of his injured arm covered in blood. Just beyond him, Slingsby spotted Percy Nash peering through the corn. Both men wore a look of consternation.

"Corporal Nicholls…" Slingsby gasped. "I think that burst just took out the whole rifle group from our section, and I saw loads more blokes from the platoon go down further along."

The big corporal grunted.

"Those Jerries have got every inch of this field covered by those bloody machine-guns. We need to do something about it…"

He left the suggestion hanging in the air.

"I just saw one of the carriers go up in smoke a moment ago." Slingsby went on. I think it's been taken out… The others too, by the looks of it."

Beyond Nicholls, Nash was shaking his head, a dark look on his features.

"What are we going to do, Corporal?" Slingsby asked, hoping that the NCO would have a sensible plan.

For a moment, Nicholls made no reply. He simply shook his head, an angry, frustrated look etched on his weather-beaten face. All around them, bullets snapped angrily above the corn, and more explosions sounded nearby. From somewhere very close, the sound of agonised sobbing came drifting through the background noise. Nicholls gave an angry rumble within his throat, setting his face in a determined grimace.

"I'm not having this." He growled. And with that, he pushed himself upright, pulling the Bren Gun firmly in against his hip once more. He glanced down at Nash, and then at Slingsby.

"Come on you two, follow me…"

With no more explanation than that, the tall Grenadier corporal lurched forward once more, flattening the corn as he burst through the half-grown crops towards the enemy in the trees. Shocked by the sudden development, the two guardsmen merely blinked at each other in surprise for a split second, then leapt up and followed him.

Nicholls was a couple of yards in front of them, heading straight for the trees. He fired on the run, the big machine-gun jerking wildly by his side as he sprayed the distant wood-line with fire. Slingsby glanced to the right and left briefly and saw that the three of them were alone; he couldn't see anyone else from the company. The only friendly troops in sight were the motionless green and black hulks of the three Bren Gun Carriers, all of which had a disturbing, lifeless look about them. One was just a few yards away and, as they passed it, Slingsby noted with a sinking heart that a khaki body lay flopped over the side of the vehicle. The two remaining carriers were much closer to the wood, and one of them was on fire and belching dark smoke. The desperate nature of their situation suddenly hit the young guardsman and he felt his legs begin to turn to jelly.

"Down!"

The sound of Nicholls' sharp command drew his eyes back to the front and Slingsby saw the corporal duck into the corn again, having made a dash of about twenty or thirty yards. Slingsby and Nash followed suit, sinking to their knees in the thick crops by the side of Nicholls, just as a burst of deadly machine-gun fire cracked past them.

"Give me another magazine, Nash." Nicholls panted, cocking the Bren sharply and yanking off the empty magazine.

Beside him, Nash passed another of the heavy curved magazines across and stuffed the empty one away in his pouches. Nicholls threw a quick glance at both of his companions in turn.

"Short rushes, lads. Keep zig-zagging as you run. We're going to get that Hun machine-gun right in front of us…"

Slingsby felt his stomach lurch in apprehension once more, but Nash growled his approval of the instructions and Slingsby saw that the other guardsman had caught the same fighting spirit that had infected Nicholls.

"We'll teach these bastards to mess with the Grenadiers!" The corporal muttered as he drew back the cocking handle on the gun once more; the fresh magazine in place. "Right then… Let's go!"

Once more, Nicholls burst upwards and out from the cover of the crops. Once more, Nash and Slingsby went with him.

They ran like they had never run before; despite the resistance of the corn, despite the uneven footing of the ploughed earth beneath them, despite the thump of their equipment and ammunition bandoliers against their hips, and despite the terrifying crack of bullets that seemed to be coming at them with increasing tempo now. Nicholls was firing from the hip again; a difficult practice even when standing still. The tall, lithe battalion boxer made it look easy however, and never faltered a step as they advanced. They had gone maybe forty yards or more this time when Nicholls finally gave the order.

"Down!"

Down they went, and once more Nash fed a new magazine to Nicholls who swiftly changed it for the empty one. Slingsby was panting heavily now, knowing that their next rush would take them right up to the wood-line. He noticed that Nicholls was muttering to himself as he went through the re-loading drill on the Bren, and he leaned in a touch to hear what he was saying. It came as something of a shock to Slingsby when he realised the corporal was singing.

"Some talk of Alexander, some talk of Hercules; of Hector and Lysander, and such great names as these…"

Slingsby looked at Nicholls with a sudden jolt; utterly amazed. The NCO's breathing was ragged, his words coming in a tuneless tumble, but the words were unmistakable. He was singing the regimental quick march.

Slingsby watched in awe as the corporal rammed home the new magazine and re-cocked the gun yet again. Nicholls was still singing.

"But of all the world's great heroes, there's none that can compare…"

Slingsby shook his head in wonder.

"With a tow-row-row-row-row-row, to the British Grenadiers…"

Nicholls looked directly at Slingsby and grinned; a devilish, wicked grin at that.

"Come on, then. Let's go and do this bloody machine-gun!"

They burst out of the corn once more, and this time they were screaming. Screaming defiance at the enemy who were slaughtering their comrades; at the enemy who had stopped and destroyed their carriers; at the enemy who had dared to cross the river in front of the 3rd Battalion Grenadier Guards. Vaguely, Slingsby registered the urgent shouting in a foreign accent; the unmistakable sound of harassed commanders giving desperate orders. Bullets cracked past the three Grenadiers in a constant rattle of defensive fire now. They ignored it, and Slingsby, caught up in the madness of it all, gave a renewed scream of rage as he saw the cloud of smoke rise from the wood-line and veered towards it. It was the enemy machine-gun. No mistake. Just twenty yards away now, tucked right on the edge of the Poplars.

"Uurgh!"

Nicholls suddenly staggered.

"Corporal?" Slingsby heard Nash call out in alarm.

"Keep going!" Nicholls roared, throwing himself forward again. "Yaaaagh!"

The big NCO charged home against the wood-line with the two guardsmen right behind him, and suddenly, they were out of the corn. Right in front of them, a crew of three very surprised Germans looked up in sudden terror as the trio of Grenadiers burst out of the crops, directly in front of them.

The German machine-gun was mounted on a tripod, which in turn was situated in a shallow scrape on the wood-line. The grass and trampled corn in front of the scrape was black with the residue from thousands of expended rounds. The floor of the scrape and the surrounding area was littered with shiny, expended, brass cartridge cases. Seconds later, the bodies of the machine-gun crew joined the detritus of battle.

"Yaaaagh!"

Nicholls screamed out his unintelligible war-cry as he stood in front of the enemy position, legs braced apart, and emptied his entire magazine into the German machine-gunners before him.

As the crew fell dead around the gun, Nicholls strode forward and kicked the gun viciously, tipping it over onto its side. Even before it was settled, Nicholls was bending over the weapon, slamming the brass butt-plate of his own Bren down onto the enemy machine-gun, smashing the sights, and doing his best to smash the rest of it. Without even pausing in his destructive rage against the dreaded enemy weapon, Nicholls yelled at Nash.

"Nash! Magazine…"

Immediately, the young guardsman fed the NCO another full load of ammunition.

Slingsby meanwhile had run around the side of the scrape and come to a stand-still, quickly trying to orientate himself inside the wood. As he stood there, chest heaving, there was sudden movement from behind a tree, close by. He glanced to his forward left, bringing his rifle up, just in time to see a fourth German soldier leap up from behind a Poplar trunk and make a break for it. As Slingsby brought the butt of his rifle into his shoulder, he noted, absently, that the enemy soldier was carrying a half-filled ammunition belt in his hand.

It wasn't ideal; a shot from the standing position at a moving target after completing a hundred yard dash. Never-the-less, it was close range and Slingsby brought his foresight blade down through the centre of the enemy soldier's field grey outline, allowing it to settle low down, near the base of his spine, in order to compensate for the recoil.

Blam!

Holding his breathing steady for a second, Slingsby fired, and was rewarded by the sight of the enemy soldier somersaulting forwards across the rough ground before flopping to a halt; lifeless.

"This way!" Nicholls' ordered. "There's another machine-gun down there..."

He jerked his head along the tree-line.

On they ran; threading their way through the tall trees, keeping the cornfield to their right. The wood was alive with noise. Slingsby could hear the German voices echoing through trees, the alarm clearly evident in their urgent tones. Something moved up ahead, right on the wood-line, and Slingsby caught a bright muzzle flash in his peripheral vision as the crack of the bullet passed just inches away. Nicholls was on it like a flash. He swung his Bren half-left and let rip with a good ten round burst.

A body, dressed in the field-grey of the German Army, toppled sideways amongst the trees, thumping to the ground. A second German suddenly came into view, his rifle up in the aim. There was a loud bark as Nash fired his own Lee-Enfield and the enemy soldier appeared to be thrown backwards by some invisible force.

"Keep going!" Nicholls was shouting.

They did as he ordered, and moments later they came upon the second machine-gun nest.

The gun position was similar to the first, although this one had been camouflaged with underbrush, and as the three Grenadier Guardsmen burst upon it, they found the crew desperately trying to pull the gun from its tripod in order to use it more flexibly against the threat from within the wood. They were too late. Once more, Nicholls delivered a long, sweeping burst from the hip that cut down every member of the crew in a heart beat. Even before the echo of the gunfire had faded, Nicholls was barking out more orders.

"Slingsby... smash this fucking gun! Nash... Magazine..."

It was Slingsby's task to damage the enemy gun beyond repair now. Following his corporal's earlier example, he smashed his rifle butt down against the vulnerable parts, hearing the satisfied crack of the sight unit breaking off. He smashed his butt against several pins and catches, the function of which were a mystery to him, but they looked important all the same. As he completed the task by removing the gun's barrel and lobbing it out into the corn, he looked up at his companions, his breathing ragged, sweat pouring down his face. He took one look at Nicholls and caught his breath. The corporal's battledress jacket was soaked with blood. There was so much blood in fact that Slingsby couldn't even work out where the corporal had been hit.

"Jesus!" Slingsby gasped. "Are you sure you're alright, Corporal?"

"I'm fine…" Nicholls spat a great gob of mucus onto the ground and hitched his reloaded Bren back into position. "Come on. We're going through the wood, into that other field. We came here to drive these bastards back over the river. Let's go and do it!"

He turned and began jogging through the trees towards the other side of the strip wood. Slingsby and Nash, like faithful hounds, went with him.

They were cutting through the bottom corner of the wood now, at an angle, heading down slope, and as they went, shots came after them from their rear left. Slingsby stopped and turned, looking back through the wood, and cursed as he saw a number of dim figures coming through the trees after them. The enemy pursuers were maybe a hundred yards away through the trees, but moving quickly. Reacting instantly, Slingsby brought his Lee-Enfield up into the aim. The weight of his bayonet caused the muzzle to sag slightly and with a supreme effort he kept it up.

Blam!

He worked the bolt and fired again; then again. Up slope, the enemy soldiers suddenly went to ground as his rifle bullets streaked between the trees in rapid succession.

"Come on, Slingsby!" He heard Nicholls shouting, and turning again, he hurried after his companions.

Presently, they came to the opposite side of the wood. Slingsby had expected Nicholls to slow his pace slightly and display some caution at this point, but instead the corporal lowered his head and pushed his way through the last of the trees and into the field beyond.

"There's the river!" Slingsby heard him shout. "Come on!"

Nash and Slingsby followed him, the latter pushing a fresh five round clip of ammunition into his rifle as he went to top it up. He was still closing the bolt as he emerged into daylight again and was presented with the scene before him.

The field beyond the wood swept gently down to the river's edge, and on that river, beyond the lines of trees, he could clearly make out the shape of small boats on the water, with yet more grey-clad figures milling around on the bank. Even more alarming however, was the large gaggle of German soldiers who were kneeling down in a long single file, just a matter of yards away on a narrow track, by the edge of the Poplars.

For long seconds, the three Grenadiers simply stared at the German column in surprise. There must have been two dozen of them at least. For their part, the Germans looked back at the three khaki figures, blinking with equal surprise at their sudden appearance.

"Yaaaagh!"

It was Nicholls who broke the spell. He let out another ferocious war-cry and opened up on the enemy with a long burst. Several Germans flopped backwards against the low hedge, whilst the others suddenly scattered, some throwing themselves flat, whilst others jumped to their feet and leapt out of the way of the hail of bullets.

Blam!

Nash was firing his rifle too, and Slingsby did the same.

Rat-tat-tat-tat-tat!

Nicholls fired another burst and more Germans collapsed to the floor. Then he charged.

It was almost farcical. The Germans could have easily taken Nicholls and his two companions down in seconds, but instead, shocked by the sudden onslaught, the remaining enemy turned and fled. They pelted back down the track towards the river, moving as if the devil himself were after them. Slingsby followed after Nicholls, and Nash was there too. They pushed off the track and into the corn, taking the direct route to the river bank. Down on that river bank, nervous German faces were turning to look up the hill towards the wood. When they looked, they saw German soldiers pelting back towards them in headlong retreat. They also saw a number of men in British uniform charging through the crops towards them, whilst the crack of bullets filled the morning air. And so the Germans on the bank panicked too.

Men began throwing themselves back into boats. One or two jumped into the water and began to swim. Others, the older soldiers, the officers and the NCOs, dropped to their bellies and prepared to defend the river bank. Meanwhile, up in the cornfield, the Grenadiers charged onwards. Slingsby stumbled to a halt whilst Nash and Nicholls went through another magazine change, and stared at the scene before him in disbelief. A sudden feeling of exultation washed over him. They were going to do it! He raised his rifle and took a shot at one of the boats on the distant river.

"Chaaarge!"

Nicholls was off again.

Crack! Crack! Crack!

The bullets whizzed past Slingsby from behind. He whirled around. There were Germans behind them, on the edge of the wood-line. Their pursuers had continued after them it seemed. More bullets cracked past and Slingsby raised his rifle into the shoulder once more, his face twisting in a grimace of defiance.

"We've beaten you!" He screamed at the not too distant German soldiers. "We've beaten you, you German bastards! Get back over the fucking river!"

Blam!

He fired without realising what he was doing; his body functioning automatically now. He never even noticed the German who suddenly jerked backwards, grabbing his shoulder with one hand.

"You're bloody-well beaten!" Slingsby croaked, his throat dry, his lips cracked. "Beaten…"

Blam!

He fired again, but he was exhausted and the shot was wild.

"Uurgh!"

For a moment he didn't realise he had been hit and couldn't understand why the world was spinning all around him. Then he felt the terrible wrench in his knee cap where the enemy bullet had gone straight through it and he felt that awful dread of realisation.

"Umph!"

He hit the ground with a thud that winded him terribly.

"Lads!" Slingsby tried to shout, but his voice seemed ridiculously frail. "Corporal Nicholls? Percy? Harry?"

There was no answer, but he could hear the 'chug-chug-chug' of the Bren Gun still.

"Lads…"

Slingsby felt sick. The world hadn't stopped spinning even though he was flat on his back. It was like being drunk, only worse. He squinted as the sun's bright rays blinded him, and the dim silhouettes of heads wearing funny shaped helmets came into view above him.

"Oh, Jesus…" He gasped, exhaustion overtaking him. "I'm going to puke…"

Then, like a blessed relief, he feinted.

POPLAR RIDGE – THE GERMAN POSITIONS
TUESDAY 21ST MAY 1940 – 1140 HOURS

"Stop them!" Ambrosius screamed the orders at the top of his voice, feeling as though he would tear his vocal chords in half with the effort. "Stop those fucking Tommies!"

He stared with wide eyes down the length of the wood-line to where the Tommies had reached the safety of the trees, and the unusually slow sound of the enemy machine-gun told him that he now had a big problem on his hands. Swinging around, he shouted at the nearest soldiers; those who had only just been involved with the destruction of the British carriers.

"You!" He jabbed a finger towards a private. "And you! And you! You too!"

He rounded up a small group of perhaps half a dozen men, all of them with rifles less a sergeant with a machine-pistol.

"Come with me! We've got Tommies inside the wood!"

Without further explanation, Ambrosius began loping down through the trees, followed by his ad hoc squad.

"Spread out!" He heard the sergeant enforcing the usual battle-discipline on the men. "Into line! Sweep formation!"

They ploughed on, as fast as they dared, weapons at the ready. The sound of gunfire rang through the lower part of the wood.

They had gone about forty metres when they came upon the first gun position. The crew were laid dead around the weapon, which lay on its side; the sight unit smashed off, the top cover hanging uselessly by one retaining bolt. Another soldier was laid dead a few metres away, a half filled ammunition belt still gripped between his lifeless fingers.

"Keep moving!" Ambrosius ordered, and they continued their advance.

The noise of gunfire from within the wood was getting closer now, and over to the left, one of the men shouted that they were passing a rifle pit with two dead men in it; both German.

Suddenly, Ambrosius saw them. About a hundred metres away, through the trees, he could see the khaki figures moving diagonally across his front, as if they intended to go right through the trees and down to the river.

"Enemy front!" One of his men shouted, and a single shot cracked down slope towards the fleeting enemy figures.

Almost instantly, a rifle bullet cracked back upslope towards them, followed rapidly by two more. The shooting was surprisingly accurate, one of the bullets passing close by the captain. Ambrosius threw himself into the cover of a Poplar trunk, and the others around him followed suit. They paused there for a heartbeat, but no more shots came.

"Come on!" Ordered Ambrosius, and they set off again, heading towards where they had last seen the enemy.

The squad of German soldiers had gone perhaps another forty metres when they heard the sudden eruption of gunfire at the very bottom edge of the wood.

"Shit!" Ambrosius cursed. "At the double! Let's go!"

He upped the pace, lurching down the slope, avoiding exposed roots and fallen branches, his arms pumping madly as he raced for the distant wood-line. Surely the Tommies had been stopped now? The reserves that Engel had brought up should be just down here somewhere; a full platoons-worth.

Together, the line of Germans burst through the trees, weapons at the ready. Ambrosius came to a sudden halt and gaped incredulously at the scene of chaos around him. Around half a dozen German corpses lay sprawled along a nearby track, whilst two other German soldiers sat clamping their hands over bullet wounds to their upper limbs in the hedgerow beside it. Across the field to his front he could see dozens of German soldiers, running back towards the river. On the bank itself he could see signs of panic amongst the remainder of his battalion who had been slowly struggling across the shell-raked ground to link up with their unit. In the middle of all this, wading through the corn directly in front of him, were the three Tommy soldiers. It defied belief.

"Shoot those bloody Tommies!" He yelled at his men. "Take them down!"

He knew that if he fired there was a danger that his bullets would miss and streak past the British soldiers and on towards his own men on the river bank. There was no time to worry however. The situation was critical and these three enemy soldiers were creating chaos and panic amongst his men, and Ambrosius needed to end this madness now. He raised his own machine-pistol, aimed towards the three Tommies, and squeezed the trigger.

Rat-tat-tat-tat-tat-tat-tat!

The weapon lurched violently in his hands as he heard the men either side of him open fire too.

The Tommy closest to them suddenly turned around and stared right at him. Calmly, with unbelievable courage, the Tommy yelled something at him, raised his own weapon then fired. With a grunt, the man to the right of Ambrosius staggered back a pace and grabbed at his shoulder.

"Aagh; fuck!" The man cursed, wincing in pain.

The remaining Germans opened fire with another volley and the brave Tommy seemed to spin around like a ballet dancer before plunging into the corn.

"Take the others down!" Ambrosius yelled again, driving his men on.

The two surviving Tommies were almost at the river now, and Ambrosius could see that the bigger of the two men, the one with the machine-gun, was aiming for the rubber pontoons on the water. The captain raised his MP40 again and let rip with another burst. He kept on firing. One of the Tommies went down, out of sight, but the gunner, despite staggering as if he'd been hit, kept on firing.

"Come on! Get the last one!" Ambrosius was screaming like a madman now as he fumbled for a fresh magazine for his own weapon.

Just at that point, the big British soldier with the machine-gun suddenly fell sideways into the corn; right in the middle of the field. Just as quickly, the firing petered out around the edge of the meadow. A strange kind of hush seemed to envelop Ambrosius after the last few minutes of intense activity and the constant angry clatter of small arms fire. The captain was breathing like a marathon runner on the home straight. Down on the river bank, he could see an officer gesticulating in animated fashion at the soldiers around him, and a moment later the distant sound of his harsh voice floated across the field as he began restoring order amongst the men there. Completely stunned by the sudden turn of events, Ambrosius looked towards the men who had followed him out of the wood.

"Come on..." He panted. "Back up onto the ridge. This battle isn't over yet..."

Tuesday 21st May 1940
The Twelfth Day – Afternoon

NEAR WAGONLIEU – 2.5 MILES WEST OF ARRAS
TUESDAY 21ST MAY 1940 – 1430 HOURS

"Are we going the right way?" Jones, the gunner, looked sideways at Claxton with an enquiring look?

The tank commander frowned and gaped through the rear periscope of the Matilda Mk II.

"I think we must be…" He said, not sounding too confident. "There's a whole load of other tanks following us."

"Can you see the Platoon Commander?" Jones asked, sensing his corporal's uncertainty.

"No…" Claxton murmured after a while. "They're all Mk Is. I've got no idea where the boss has got to."

There was a shout from the driver's compartment.

"Well this must be the right way, because somebody's been here before us, look…"

The three men in the turret pressed their eyes against the forward periscopes and gun-sight in order to get a decent view of the way ahead.

"Blimey!" The gunner whistled in awe. "Look at that!"

They were advancing down a narrow track that ran across a ploughed field. Running left to right, directly in front of them along an intersecting track, was a row of trucks; quite obviously German, and quite obviously on fire.

Thick black smoke billowed from the shattered remains of the vehicles where petrol tanks had set alight, and all around the trucks lay over a dozen bodies; all of them motionless; all of them dressed in German field-grey.

"You little dancer!" Horner, the loader chirped happily. "Somebody's given them a pretty thorough seeing-to, haven't they Corp'?"

Claxton murmured agreement, a rising sense of discomfort taking hold of him.

The orders had seemed simple enough, but in practice, carrying out those orders was proving much more difficult. It had been a long, tiring and confusing morning, moving down from Vimy Ridge towards the start line. Even before reaching the start line however, the lead elements of the battalion had run into Germans in a village, somewhere back down the road. Having no map, Claxton had no idea of what the village was called. Suffice to say there had followed a confused and rather untidy scrap, during which he had trundled around behind his company, waiting for orders that never came. One of the other companies appeared to have got stuck-in, along with some French troops apparently, and Claxton had seen some of their own infantry moving around, along with some of the motorcyclist outriders who were meant to be scouting ahead.

After following his Platoon Commander's tank through a small wooded area, Claxton had found himself on this track, having crossed a fairly major road that looked suspiciously like it was meant to be their original start line. Of his Platoon Commander's tank however, there was no sign. He must have turned off somewhere in the wood without Claxton seeing the change of direction. Now, with half a dozen Mk I tanks trundling along behind him, it seemed that he had become the leader of his own little group of tanks. If only he knew where he was! This was, he reflected, nothing short of chaos.

They pushed through the burning remnants of the convoy and to Claxton's surprise, he found himself driving onto a metalled road, and a narrow one at that.

"Motorcyclists!" The driver's voice hollered up.

Claxton had already spotted the vehicle through the periscope.

"Hold it there!" He ordered, and the tank shuddered to a halt.

The approaching vehicle was actually a motorcycle combination. Painted olive green, the curious vehicle was one of those from the Northumberland Fusiliers that had been roaring to and fro' throughout the day thus far. Claxton saw the Bren Gun mounted on the sidecar, and the goggle-wearing crew in their khaki uniforms, and thus re-assured, he reached up, turned the hatch lever, and opened up the turret hatch.

He popped his head up and was about to ask if the motorcycle crew knew where they were, but the rider of the machine, having squealed to a halt beside them, gave the corporal no opportunity to speak.

"Thank God! You've got here just in time! That village is bloody-well full of Jerries!"

Claxton blinked in surprise.

"What village?"

"That one!" The rider shot his arm out, pointing back up the road from whence they had just come. "Less than a mile up there; quite a small place. We think it's called Wagonlieu."

"Wagonlieu?" Claxton tried the name on his tongue. It sounded familiar.

"It's full of Germans, man." The motorcyclist continued in his Geordie accent. "Just sitting round in lorries and that... Calm as you like; as if they're enjoying the sun down on the beach at Whitley Bay..."

Claxton blinked again, trying to catch what the man was saying despite his strong, north-eastern twang.

"Howay, man! Get in there, before the bastards wake up! They're sitting there like rats in a barrel!"

Claxton nodded curtly, needing no further encouragement. He didn't know where he was, and he had no idea how many tanks were behind him. And, for all he knew, half the German Army could be sitting up around the bend waiting for him. However, he had been sent here to clear out the Germans around Arras, so that's what he was going to do.

"Tell the others as they come past." He shouted down to the Geordie motorcyclists then dropped back down into the turret, closing the hatch behind him.

"Straight ahead; up this road." He shouted down to the driver. "Apparently there's a village up ahead that's full of Jerries. Less than a mile away they reckon; and the Jerries are supposed to be half asleep according to those fellas."

He looked sideways and down, at the gunner and loader.

"You two ready for it?" He asked.

The two privates looked back at him with apprehensive faces, nodding their acknowledgement silently.

"Alright…" Claxton took a deep breath. "Let's go and have ourselves a fight, shall we?"

THE MAIN STREET – WAGONLIEU, NEAR ARRAS
TUESDAY 21ST MAY 1940 – 1440 HOURS

Hauptsturmfuhrer Josef Merkal, commanding a company of motorised troops from the SS Division Totenkopf, frowned at the map that lay on the dashboard of his staff car. It was not a good map, he decided, feeling his frustration rise. It was nowhere near detailed enough. He looked up and scowled along the lengthy village street towards where several junctions joined it at intervals. He was looking at the village of Beaumetz-les-Loges on his map, but the symbols that adorned the map didn't suggest that the village street should be as long as this, or with as many exits.

As the flank guard of the division, his company had been tasked to cover the northern flank of the advance, with their right boundary running through Beaumetz village, rubbing up alongside the 7th Panzer Division, but without getting in their way. That particular armoured unit was in the process of trying to outflank the city of Arras and force its way across a line of canals and the Totenkopf Division were being held as a second echelon, should their infantry be needed. That in itself annoyed Merkal. He was, apart from being a fervent National Socialist, a man of jealous disposition. He didn't like the way the regular army officers, bunch of aristocratic morons that they were, looked down their noses at their SS counter-parts.

Neither was he happy that his division had been kept in strategic reserve for almost a week after the start of the campaign. Merkal was desperate to prove that the SS could match anything that the army could do, and he was especially keen to earn himself not just an Iron Cross, but one of the newer, much sought after Knights Crosses. The chances to do so were few and far between at the moment however. Somewhere over to the north and west could be heard the sound of heavy fighting; 7th Panzer trying to grab all the glory no doubt? Merkal meanwhile, was getting fed up with driving around endless narrow country lanes and only coming upon dead enemy soldiers and burning enemy vehicles. Other people were taking his share of the action and he didn't like it one bit.

He twisted round in his seat as he heard the growl of powerful engines behind him, his frown turning instantly to a scowl as he saw a column of half-tracks edging past his own company's lorries. The big armoured troop carriers came clattering up the village street, with dust covered, weary looking panzer grenadiers crammed inside them. As the half-tracks trundled past the stationary SS vehicles, the soldiers stared with casual interest at the SS men crowded in the back of the trucks. For their part, the SS men stared back, their own faces betraying a certain amount of jealousy at the modern vehicles and equipment of the new arrivals.

The leading half-track pulled up next to Merkal's car and he stared up at the crew compartment of the armoured vehicle. A moment later, a head popped over the side of the vehicle and stared down at the SS company commander. Merkal quickly took in the army officer's badge of rank. A first lieutenant. Technically, that meant that Merkal outranked him.

"Hello there…" The regular officer greeted Merkal, a perplexed expression on his weather-beaten features. "What brings you up this way?"

Merkal railed instantly at the lack of respect for his rank, not to mention the blunt, some would say rude questioning.

"My name is Hauptsturmfuhrer Merkal…" He responded in a haughty voice, making sure that the little oik understood which of them was the senior. "And we are the flank guard of the SS Totenkopf."

Much to Merkal's annoyance, the lieutenant didn't look remotely impressed.

"Oh, right…Well, aren't you a bit far north?"

Merkal bridled at the comment.

"No…" He snorted. "This is exactly where we are supposed to be!"

The army lieutenant frowned and lifted a folded map of his own up onto the side of the half-track's hull.

"Oh…" The lieutenant paused again briefly, studying the map. "I thought your boundary ran through Beaumetz?"

He glanced back at Merkal.

The SS officer felt a sudden chill run through him.

"Beaumetz?" He snapped, trying to hide the uncertainty in his voice.

"Yes; from what we were told, you boys weren't going to come any further north than Beaumetz. What brings you up here to Wagonlieu?"

Wagonlieu! The name cut through Merkal like a knife. Trying not to make it obvious, he picked up his own map, running his eye over the detail quickly. There...he saw the name; Wagonlieu. A village marked on the map, some two or three kilometres north-east of Beaumetz. Shit. Merkal was in the wrong place. With a dread sense of realisation, Merkal swallowed hard, his mind working quickly.

"Yes...well..." Merkal thought of an excuse as fast as he could. "We heard all the gunfire up this way and thought you might have run into trouble with the Tommies. We thought we'd better move up ready to support you, just in case. I know how strung out you are..."

The lieutenant took the words in silently, his face impassive for a moment. Had Merkal fooled him?

"Well, your man Rommel *has* sent the tanks off on another dash again; that's true..."

The lieutenant cocked his ear to the wind for a moment.

"That sounds to me like the rest of our regiment just pushing their way across the canals, closer in to the city. I'm sure that our colonel will shout for help if he needs any."

Merkal felt the tension ease slightly. The idiot had swallowed his story. That was good.

"Well..." The SS officer forced a friendly smile. "I thought we would sit here for a while just in case. We can't hang on too long though. We need to get back over onto our axis in case the division gets called forward again."

The lieutenant nodded his understanding.

"No problem. If I were you though, I'd keep my eyes peeled. We've just heard reports of Tommy..."

"Tanks!" The shout of alarm from the machine-gunner in the lieutenant's half-track brought everybody's attention to the junction that was just thirty metres back down the street.

Merkal whipped his head around, as did the army lieutenant, to stare back down the long road between the two rows of houses. Merkal couldn't see much due to the column of trucks and half-tracks that were jamming the road behind him, so he stood upright in the car, placed a foot on top of his door then pulled himself up using the side of the half-track so that he could get a better view. Even as he did so he could hear the urgent shouts of alarm from back along the two columns of vehicles.

"Shit!"

He heard the lieutenant gasp, the man's mouth dropping open in shock.

"Fuck!" Merkal commented himself as he suddenly found himself staring at a Tommy tank, barely a stones throw away.

The solid looking armoured vehicle had appeared out of a side road and come to a sudden stop, having found its way blocked by the packed German vehicles. There was a sudden clatter of machine-gun fire as a panzer grenadier in the half-track nearest to the enemy vehicle opened up on it with a pintle-mounted MG34. The 7.92mm bullets ricocheted off the solid hull of the tank with a tortured whining sound, bouncing off the armour in various directions. Then, with a horrendous boom that echoed down the packed street, the Tommy tank fired its main armament straight into the half-track to its front.

The distance between the two vehicles couldn't have been more than twenty metres and the tank shell ripped through the side of the half-track as if it were made of cardboard. The troop carrier exploded in a bright flash and a black cloud of smoke, and Merkal saw bits of body flying through the air. And then it turned into absolute chaos.

"Drive, drive, drive!" The lieutenant was shouting into the cab of his own vehicle, and without any need for further prompting, his driver did as he was told and the half-track sprang forwards.

Merkal let go of the half-track's hull, surprised by the sudden movement and finding himself having to balance on the rim of his own car door.

His arms flapped ridiculously for a moment, and then the SS officer lost his balance and fell backwards into the car, sprawling over the back seat.

"What's happening, Sir?" Merkal's driver demanded in alarm.

"Just get the fuck out of here!" Merkal blurted out, trying to recover from the shock.

The sound of automatic fire, shouting, screaming and roaring engines filled the tightly packed street now, and petrol and diesel fumes permeated the warm afternoon air. A second half-track clattered past Merkal's car, following the lieutenant's, and Merkal's driver put his foot down as it did so, following immediately on behind it.

Merkal struggled upright and looked back over the rear of the car. He could see the first truck in his column following on behind him, whilst another half-track clattered alongside it. Further down the road however, everything appeared to be chaos. He could see dense black smoke filling the street, flames from a burning vehicle, and bodies lying on the paved roadway.

"Which way, Sir?" The driver shouted.

"Just get out the fucking village!" Was Merkal's response.

Already, Merkal felt that uncomfortable feeling rising inside him again. Having discovered that he had led his company well off course, he had managed to hide the fact nicely, and had dared to hope that he could move back onto his proper axis of advance before anyone from his own division noticed. There was absolutely no chance of that now, however. In fact, there was a good chance that he might never get back to his own division at all.

"Shit!"

Merkal heard the driver curse, felt the sudden application of brakes on the car, and then he was being thrown between the seats of the vehicle as it screeched to a halt at an angle across the road.

"What the fuck?" The driver was shouting at the half-track in front, which had also come to a sudden halt.

"What the fuck are you doing?" Merkal swore angrily as he struggled upright again, reaching for his cap that had fallen into the foot-well.

"They've stopped…" The driver muttered, his voice full of confusion.

Merkal was up on his knees now, staring over the windscreen of the staff car. It took him a couple of seconds to realise what was going on, but when he did, he felt as if he would void his bowels right there and then. Up ahead, about twenty metres or so, the lieutenant's half-track was reversing towards them at speed. Beyond the retreating personnel carrier, small, squat, ugly, green, and very British looking, another tank was turning onto the main street towards them from yet another junction; and its machine-gun was chattering death at them.

Seized by panic, Merkal looked to his right and spotted a narrow lane that ran off the main road through the village.

"Down there!" He yelled, his arm streaking out. "Quickly! Turn down this alley-way!"

The driver was already moving, swinging the vehicle round sharply and into the narrow, cobbled back-street. As the private threw the vehicle into gear and turned off the main road, Merkal beckoned frantically to the truck from his own company that had been following him. As he did so, he threw a final glance to his right and saw that the half-track belonging to the company commander of the panzer grenadiers had come to a halt; limp, lifeless bodies hanging over its side. Even as Merkal looked on in horror, the first of the Tommy tanks came pushing its way past the disabled vehicle, looking for more targets.

And then all Merkal could see was the narrow alley down which his vehicle was driving. Tall, shuttered houses rose up either side of the tight little street as his car roared down it at top speed, the driver desperate to escape the carnage on the main road. The SS officer wracked his brains as he tried to think of what he should do next. Nothing came to him. How could he fight against tanks with an infantry company and a few trucks? He slid down into the passenger seat next to the driver.

"Turn right at the end…" Merkal ordered him. "Then find a way out of the village and head east. Don't stop until I tell you…"

CORPORAL CLAXTON'S MATILDA MK II – WAGONLIEU HIGH STREET
TUESDAY 21ST MAY 1940 – 1450 HOURS

"Whoaaa!"

The three men in the turret and fighting compartment of the tank threw up their hands to protect themselves as they were thrown against the sharp edges of the gun and the turret fittings. With the driver applying the brakes as sharply as possible, the Matilda rocked forward on its suspension, before bouncing back down again with a sickening lurch.

"Bloody hell, Corp'!" They heard the driver shout. "There's hundreds of the buggers!"

Claxton and his gunner stared, open-mouthed, at the endless queue of vehicles that ran up and down the length of the street onto which they'd just emerged.

"What the hell do we do now?" The gunner breathed, his face pressed against the gun-sight.

"Just shoot the fuckers!" Claxton spluttered.

He saw the gunner's hand curl around the firing bar.

"No… I meant…"

Boom!

The vehicle reared as the powerful 2 Pounder gun spat its deadly shell towards the enemy vehicles at point blank range.

There was no apparent gap between the report of the 2 Pounder firing and the explosion that ripped the first enemy vehicle to pieces before their eyes.

"Reload!" The gunner's voice snapped automatically as he went into the oft-practiced drill.

"No!" Claxton yelled at him, thumping the private on the arm. "Not with the main armament! The co-ax!"

Clink. The breech of the 2 Pounder locked shut over a fresh armour piercing shell as the gunner glanced at Claxton in confusion.

"The co-ax?"

"Use the fucking machine-gun!" The corporal screamed at him.

A flood of realisation washed over the gunner's face and he threw himself behind the co-axially mounted Besa machine-gun which, unusually for British weapons, did not use the standard .303 inch round but the same 7.92mm round as German weapons.

"Forward driver!" Claxton yelled down. "And hard left."

He nudged the gunner again.

"Rake the column all the way along; start with the trucks!"

"Got it!"

The gunner crouched over the machine-gun as the vehicle swung left with a judder and a squeal of tracks.

"Bloody hell! Where do I start?" The gunner breathed as he looked through the gun sight.

Normally, engaging targets with the machine-gun was a difficult business and not always the most accurate, however, on this occasion the gunner just couldn't miss. They were looking along a line of enemy vehicles, parked almost bumper to bumper, all of them at point blank range.

"Just bloody fire!" Claxton swore.

Rat-tat-tat-tat-tat-tat-tat-tat-tat!

The first, lengthy burst peppered the side of a truck that was packed with enemy soldiers. With barely a second's pause after the first burst, the gunner fired again.

Rat-tat-tat-tat-tat-tat-tat-tat-tat-tat-tat!

An even longer burst this time, some of which sliced into the cab of the truck as the Matilda began to grind forwards alongside the stalled enemy column. Claxton began rotating the turret half-right as the tank straightened up.

"That's it, just keep on firing!" The corporal yelled at his gunner. Then, raising his voice and hollering down to the driver. "Nice and steady, driver! Not too fast!"

The heavy British tank rumbled along the main street of Wagonlieu, its machine-gun spitting out deadly bursts, one after the other. As it progressed, so the chaos and panic escalated amongst the German columns. Several trucks were already on fire, men hanging dead over the sides. More bodies had fallen to the tarmac, and another truck collided with a half-track as both tried to pull away at the same time, causing a minor obstruction across the street.

"Stand-by for a bump!" The driver shouted up. "We've got vehicles blocking the road!"

"Go for the truck!" Claxton ordered. "Put your foot down and go right through it!"

The driver upped the revs and the Matilda gathered speed, aiming for the nose of the lorry where it was entangled with the front bumper of the enemy armoured carrier. Inside that enemy carrier, a machine-gunner was rattling away at the British tank with his own light-machine gun, and the metallic patter of ricocheting bullets sounded constantly in the background as the British crew got stuck into their grim business.

"Brace yourselves!" Came the driver's voice.

With a sickening thump, the tank slammed into the nose of the truck and there was a high pitched metallic squeal as the Matilda ground down the side of the half-track whilst pushing the lorry over to one side at the same time.

"That's it, keep going!" Claxton chivvied the driver.

"The others are behind us…" The loader said, his eyes glued to the rear periscope.

Claxton took a quick look behind him to see for himself. Sure enough, two of the Mark I tanks were following in their wake, adding their own machine-guns to the chaos. Behind the pair of smaller tanks, he could see a third British tank turning in the opposite direction, driving towards the rear of the column. The details were largely obscured by the flames and belching black smoke coming from burning German vehicles, but it was clear enough that the Germans had been caught fully unprepared and were now suffering the consequences.

"We're through!" The driver called out, and the Matildas surged forward with renewed momentum once more.

Rat-tat-tat-tat-tat!

The gunner was firing again.

"Looks like some of our boys have come in at the other side of the village, Corp'…" The gunner shouted above the clatter of his machine gun. "There's some kind of scrap going on up the top end of the street; more vehicles on fire too."

Claxton jammed his eyes back against the forward periscope again. As he did so, an enemy soldier ran onto the road about fifty yards in front of them and stood facing them defiantly.

"What's this bloody fool up to?" The gunner wondered aloud.

Claxton frowned at the man through the periscope. The German wore the standard grey trousers and helmet that was the haul-mark of their army, along with the jackboots, but his tunic was rather unusual. Instead of the typical grey field jacket, the German was garbed in some kind of baggy smock that was coloured in a mixture of grey, green, yellow and brown; the mottled camouflage effect thus produced looking highly unusual.

"Looks like this bastard's been sick on his jacket!" The gunner observed, reading Claxton's mind.

"Grenade!" Warned the driver.

Claxton and the gunner saw the lone German swing his arm and release something, but the object soon went out of their vision. Several seconds later there was a small explosion right in front of the vehicle, but other than momentarily blinding the crew, it did no damage. The Matilda rumbled through the black smoke and Claxton spotted the German again, still standing there, about thirty yards distant now. The courageous enemy soldier was fiddling with another of the long-handled grenades, determined to make a stand against the great steel monster that advanced upon him.

Rat-tat-tat-tat-tat!

The gunner fired a short burst at maximum depression, before the tank got too close to the man. Small sparks and wisps of dust erupted on the cobbles around the German in the camouflage smock, just as he raised his arm once more. The soldier staggered backwards, a look of shock on his face, and then he dropped like a stone to the tarmac, the primed grenade falling beside him.

"Keep going!" Claxton urged.

The fallen soldier disappeared from the crews' field of vision as they drove straight towards him. As the tank passed over the man's body there was a loud 'crump' beneath the tank which caused it to shudder momentarily. Then the tremor passed and they were rolling forward again, the way ahead clear except for two burning half-tracks.

Coming towards them was a pair of their own Mark I tanks.

"What now, Corporal?" The driver shouted up.

Claxton spotted the alley on their right at the last minute.

"Hard right! Hard right! Into this side street! Let's see if it takes us through the other side of the village? We've got the Jerries on the run now, so let's make sure they *keep* running!"

The driver swung the big metal beast round into the narrow side street and began to rattle along the cobbles between the two rows of high sided buildings. Behind Claxton, another half dozen smaller British tanks followed his lead, leaving behind a street full of burning German vehicles and dead enemy soldiers. The British counter-stroke at Arras had begun in earnest, and the Germans were paying a high-price.

WAGONLIEU TO WAILLY ROAD – 2.5 MILES SOUTH-WEST OF ARRAS
TUESDAY 21ST MAY 1940 – 1510 HOURS

Merkal's mind was racing. What the hell was he going to do now? He had been lucky that the alleyway into which he had turned had not only helped him escape from the main street, but also spat him out onto the main road out of the village. Followed by four of his company's trucks, the SS officer had roared southwards away from the tiny village where the sound of machine-guns and explosions still filled the air behind him.

For just a few moments, after that stupid army lieutenant had swallowed his story, Merkal had thought he would get away with his navigational error. Having been told where he really was by the unwitting lieutenant, all Merkal had to do was turn his company round and head back towards where his axis of advance was supposed to be. Hopefully, nobody would have noticed his absence, being as he was in a relatively independent role on his division's flank. Even if his absence had been noted, he could have explained it away, just as he had to the lieutenant in command of the panzer grenadiers. But all that was ruined now, thanks to the pig-dog Englanders. How was he supposed to explain that half of his company were missing or dead to his commanding officer?

Merkal was still wrestling with that problem when the road suddenly brought them onto the fringes of another village. The bulk of the houses stretched away to Merkal's left, towards Arras, with just a few small cottages and a couple of farms on the periphery of the built-up area.

"Sounds like there's trouble here too?" The driver suddenly suggested, yelling over the noise of the engine.

Merkal cocked his head to one side and sure enough, he heard the constant, angry rattle of machine-gun fire, no more than several hundred metres away.

"Keep going!" He ordered. "Straight through!"

They passed a junction on their left and the Hauptsturmfuhrer glanced down it. With a jolt of fear, he spotted two burning trucks at the far end of the long village street; thick black smoke obscuring the scene beyond it. Then the image was gone and they were racing past the junction, followed by the surviving lorries of the company. The road veered around a bend a little way ahead, and as the staff car rounded the curve, a column of oncoming vehicles suddenly presented itself, just a hundred metres ahead. The driver instantly slammed on the brakes and the car screeched to a halt a few metres in front of the leading half-track. Silently, Merkal cursed.

The half-track at the front of the column trundled right up Merkal's car, edging its way past. As the SS officer glared up at the vehicle, he suddenly noticed that it was towing an anti-tank gun.

"Stop!" Merkal yelled, and began struggling to his feet. "Pull over!"

The head of the vehicle commander was peering over the side at him now, and Merkal heard the engine ease off as the armoured vehicle came to a halt.

"What's the matter?" The vehicle commander shouted over the noise of the engine.

Merkal, despite being riled by the lack of deference, gestured vaguely behind him.

"Enemy tanks!" He shouted back. "Tommy ones I think; dozens of them back there."

The commander in the half-track raised himself a bit higher, resting his arms on the side of his vehicle and Merkal saw once again that this man was a first lieutenant. The army officer looked worried.

"Tommy tanks? We heard there was some kind of British attack taking place west of Arras at this side of the canal. Where did you see them?"

"Just a couple of kilometres up the road..." Merkal replied. "... not even that. There are dozens of the bastards! They just shot up one of your rifle companies and they're coming this way. By the sounds of that gunfire I reckon they've already reached the other side of this village. You need to get those guns of yours deployed and into action quickly; they'll be here any moment!"

The officer in the half-track simply nodded, his face grim, and without another word to Merkal he turned to look back down his column of vehicles and began to wave his hand in a series of deployment signals. Moments later, the lead half-track began pulling off the road and into the open field to the west. As the vehicle executed its manoeuvre, the lieutenant swung back round to look in Merkal's direction and shouted over to him.

"Get your trucks out of the way! Give us a clear field of fire!"

Merkal bit back a retort. Who did the jumped up little bastard think he was giving orders to? Still, Merkal didn't have time to waste, and he had no intention whatsoever of hanging around when there was a pack of British tanks on his heels.

With a deep scowl etched on his face, the SS officer dropped back down in his seat and pointed over the bonnet of the car.

"Forwards." He snapped.

Instantly, the driver was off again, this time moving at a steadier pace as he edged past the big half-tracks on the confines of the narrow road. All in all, Merkal counted six guns in the column; the small 37mm PAK 36 models.

He hoped it would be enough to deal with the Tommies. Either way, he wasn't hanging around to find out; his only objective now was to swing wide and find a way of rejoining his own division. As the car passed the last half-track and picked up speed, Merkal consulted his map once more. He reckoned that he had just passed by the western edge of Dainville, heading for Wailly. All being well, once he got to that village he could turn right and just follow the road all the way to...!

"Police!"

The driver's comment and the sudden slowing of the vehicle made him look up sharply. They were approaching a level crossing over a railway line, and standing in the middle of that crossing was a small group of military policemen. A staff car similar to Merkal's and two motorcycle combinations were parked in the shade of the trees next to the crossing. Merkal's driver slowed to a halt as the big man in the middle of the group flagged them down. Armed with a machine-pistol, and with a military police gorget hanging from his neck by a chain, the big man walked up to the car. Merkal noted the sergeant's badge of rank on his sleeve.

"I haven't got time to waste! Merkal snapped at the NCO. "Let us through!"

The sergeant, a big, ugly looking brute with hard, grey eyes, simply gave the SS officer a blank stare.

"Really, Hauptsturmfuhrer?" The MP replied laconically. "And what's the big hurry?"

Merkal exploded.

"Because there's half a fucking regiment of British tanks coming up that road behind us you big oaf!"

"Tommy tanks?" The sergeant frowned, more mystified by the claim than taken aback by Merkal's anger.

"Yes, Tommy tanks; and I've been sent back to locate as many artillery units as I can find, before they roll us all the way back to the River Meuse!"

Merkal told the lie easily and it had the desired effect.

"How far back are they?" The NCO demanded, looking suddenly alarmed.

"Two kilometres at the most and following on fast..."

Merkal got no further with the sentence because just then, from a few hundred yards back up the road, came the unmistakable sound of anti-tank guns going into action. Within seconds, their sharp, deadly report was answered with the rattle of machine-gun fire. The sergeant became animated.

"Get going, Sir..." He stepped aside and waved Merkal's convoy on.

Then without waiting to discuss the matter further, the sergeant turned his back on the SS officer and began yelling orders to his own squad.

"Get that car pulled over the road as soon as these vehicles have gone through, and get the MG34 set up in the ditch! We've got Tommy tanks approaching! Everyone into cover!"

Merkal needed no further prompting. He merely slapped the dashboard and the driver responded. Once again, the SS convoy pulled away, trying its best to outrun the pursuing British tanks. The vehicles bumped clumsily over the level crossing as the harassed looking MPs began adopting hasty defensive positions in the vicinity. Once over, the driver upped the revs and the car picked up speed again, followed more slowly by the rest of the company in the trucks.

"Arseholes!" Merkal cursed softly to himself as he thought about how little respect these 7th Panzer people were showing him.

"What's that, Sir?" The driver asked, leaning towards him.

"Nothing; just drive."

They drove; but only another couple of hundred metres. This time, after negotiating two small, connected bends, Merkal found his way blocked by three more friendly vehicles.

"Fucking hell!" He swore. "What now?"

Again, his car slowed to a halt. As it did so, Merkal saw that the first vehicle was a tank; a big one. Behind it was a pair of command variant half-tracks. For the first time that afternoon, he felt a mild sense of relief.

"One of our tanks! Thank fuck for that! About bloody time too!"

A man was standing on the front decks of the panzer, next to the stubby looking gun, and as Merkal's car slowed to a halt in front of the armoured vehicle, the figure jumped down onto the tarmac and approached them.

Merkal was just telling himself that he was not going to let any more of these army idiots speak to him in anything less than a respectful tone, when a jolt of recognition went through him like a bolt of electricity. The man who had dismounted from the tank was walking towards him now, his badges of rank clearly visible on his tunic jacket. Merkal saw the goggles pushed up on the front of his cap, the binoculars hanging against his chest, and the Iron Cross First Class with the Pour le Mérite that sat prominently fastened to the collar of his shirt. The Pour le Mérite, or 'Blue Max' as it was often called, had long been defunct as a decoration, but on this occasion, its presence clearly identified its wearer to Merkal. His bronzed, weather-beaten face covered in a layer of dust, Major General Erwin Rommel, commander of the 7th Panzer Division, walked up to the side of Merkal's car and stared down at him with his piercing blue eyes.

"Heil Hitler…" Merkal stammered, streaking his arm upwards so that it was ramrod straight in an immaculate Nazi salute.

The general was clutching a folded map and he casually raised it and touched his cap by way of acknowledgement.

"Who are you?" Rommel demanded of him, his voice calm and businesslike, but not wasting anything on preamble.

"Hauptsturmfuhrer Merkal, General; from SS Totenkopf."

Rommel's eyebrows knitted together.

"And what brings into my divisional area, Hauptsturmfuhrer?"

Merkal thought quickly.

"We were on northern flank guard for our division, General, when we noticed heavy fighting taking place on the forward left of your division's front. I made the decision to come across and support a company from one of your rifle regiments, but the British attacked with a large force of tanks and we were overrun."

The general stared back at him for long moments, his face unreadable. The wily old fox was analysing every word of Merkal's; the SS officer could sense it.

"British tanks? Where?"

"Back up the road, General; about two kilometres, in the village of Wagonlieu."

Rommel continued to stare at the SS officer, his mind working silently behind the impassive mask.

"Wagonlieu? That's not good. What about Dainville? Did you see anything in Dainville?"

"I saw trucks on fire, General…" Merkal floundered slightly. "There was heavy fighting at the north-eastern edge of the place by the sounds…" He thought of a life-line and went for it. "I was busy putting an anti-tank screen in place. I came across a platoon of PAK 36s and had the commander deploy them to the south of Dainville as a delaying force, along with a squad of military police."

The divisional commander was listening to Merkal's every word with interest.

"Really?" He murmured after a while. "And what are you doing now?"

Merkal felt the panic rise inside of him. Think! He glanced over Rommel's shoulder and noticed the tree-lined ridge behind him, about four hundred metres distant.

"I'm heading there, General…" Merkal pointed suddenly, seeing his opportunity to explain his way out of this latest situation.

"...To that ridge. I think it lies on the British axis of advance and it looks like the perfect place to dig in and hold them. We'll have good fields of fire from up there. I've got one of my officers detailed off to go and find some more anti-tank guns..."

He tailed off, hoping it had been enough to convince the General.

Rommel turned and squinted up at the ridge behind him. He stared towards it for a couple of seconds, before turning back to look at Merkal, his face still impassive.

"I think you're right, Hauptsturmfuhrer. It's a good place to deploy in a blocking position."

Merkal felt his heart flutter with relief. The general was swallowing it.

The divisional commander turned away again and shouted up to the man in the turret of the Panzer III.

"Sergeant Rolf, there are enemy tanks coming along this road from the north. Take your panzer up the road until you come across a unit of MPs and an anti-tank screen from our division. Position yourself there and give them support. If any Tommy tanks come down that road... destroy them."

"Yes, General." The tank commander shouted back down in acknowledgement, before sliding out of sight into the turret. Moments later, the big tank ejected a stream of fumes from its engine louvers, gave a deep growl, then began creeping forwards past Merkal's car.

Rommel had turned towards the command vehicles now.

"Vosse? Most? On me!"

He emphasised the order by spreading his hand on the top of his cap using the standard infantry field signal for 'close-in on me'.

Two more officers now appeared, dismounting from the command vehicles and running across to come and stand beside the general. Merkal quickly took in the two staff officers; a lieutenant and a captain.

"Right then, Gentlemen; we have some clarity at last it seems." Rommel began. "The Hauptsturmfuhrer here tells me that the British armour is up that road about two kilometres, advancing on an axis Wagonlieu-Dainville-Wailly."

He paused a moment, allowing the two officers to nod their understanding.

"It appears that they've already overrun some of our troops from the rifle regiments and we have a small screen of light anti-tank guns in place just up ahead. However, judging by all the reports we're getting, and the Hauptsturmfuhrer's own experience so far, I doubt that it will be suffice to stop them. It sounds as if the British are throwing in a major force against us."

The two officers were nodding continuously now, Merkal observed, like a pair of faithful gundogs, waiting on their master's every word.

"To that end, Most…" The lieutenant straightened slightly at the general's words. "Get yourself back towards Wailly and round up everything you can find; every gun, every tank, every anti-aircraft unit, every infantry company. Get them all up here on this ridge as quick as you can. This will become our blocking position. Get on the radio to our Divisional Main HQ; tell them what I've told you. Get everything up here now. And tell them to send a signal to Corps HQ. Tell them we are under attack from a large enemy force; at least one British division, maybe more. Understand?"

"Yes, General."

Rommel nodded in dismissal.

"Go now."

Rommel flicked his gaze to the captain.

"Vosse; you get yourself up to that ridge. I will join you there shortly. Get in the car with the Hauptsturmfuhrer and lead him up onto the high ground…"

At this, Merkal suddenly sat bolt upright. The general was too busy talking to his staff captain to notice the SS officer's discomfort however.

"That unit of 88mm anti-aircraft guns we just passed?"

The captain called Vosse nodded.

"Tell them to come into action, lined up along that ridge. Tell them to load up with anti-tank ammunition and engage all enemy vehicles over open sights. They'll have a good shoot from up there."

At this point, Rommel turned and gestured casually at Merkal. "Once you've done that, take the Hauptsturmfuhrer here and show him where to position his company. I want then strung out all along the ridge protecting the guns. Got all that?"

The captain was nodding, whilst Merkal suddenly felt events spinning out of his control yet again. He had hoped to get away from the general very shortly and continue his circuitous route back to his own division. Instead, Rommel was hijacking him and his company to fight a battle against tanks! As the horrid reality of the situation dawned on Merkal, the general looked down at him, and for the first time in the conversation, his face creased into a smile.

"Right then, Hauptsturmfuhrer; get yourself up on the hill there with young Vosse and start digging. Today you will fight with 7th Panzer…"

Then Rommel clapped Merkal on the shoulder.

"I'm sure General Eicke will approve…"

WAGONLIEU TO WAILLY ROAD – NEAR DAINVILLE
TUESDAY 21ST MAY 1940 – 1540 HOURS

"Woohoo!" The driver was whooping with delight as he watched the half-track go up in flames.

Clink.

The breech locked shut over the fresh 2 Pounder shell.

"Reloaded!" The loader confirmed.

"Good shooting, Baxter!" Claxton called excitedly, his face pressed to the periscope. "Now let's see if we can find some more of those buggers. They must be the waifs and strays from that column we just shot up in the village back there…"

The gunner grunted his approval as he scanned his arcs through the gun sight.

"Certainly feels good to be giving the Jerries what for, eh, Corp'?"

"It does that, Baxter; it does that."

The last hour had seemed to fly past in a matter of minutes. After entering the village, Claxton, followed by a host of Mk Is, had run amok through the snarled up German columns in the narrow streets. Although some of the Germans had tried to make brave, but hopeless stands against the oncoming tanks, the British armour had systematically decimated the enemy transport and the milling infantry as both men and vehicles desperately tried to escape the death-trap. Now they were out of the village and advancing again, and two more Mk I tanks had joined Claxton's little group. Nobody was talking on the radio or trying to take charge; instead, the smaller Matilda's were simply trundling on behind their bigger brother and joining in the fight as they went along.

By Claxton's reckoning, they must have gone a mile south of the village now, and another village was over to their immediate left. His first thought was to go into the built-up area, but the smoke that billowed above the rooftops suggested that somebody had already been through the place, and the loader assured him that he had just spotted a couple more Matilda IIs over to their left, well beyond this latest village. With that assurance, Claxton had elected to plough straight on along the road, and his entourage of smaller tanks were with him as he rolled on.

As the turret crew scanned their arcs, the driver's voice suddenly called out in warning.

"Muzzle flash!"

Clang!

Almost as soon as the driver uttered the words, the enemy shell hit the Matilda with a loud metallic thump and a sharp, but not especially loud explosion.

"What was that?" Claxton demanded. "Where did it come from?"

"Half right!" The driver shouted up. "I saw the flash from that low hedgerow about three hundred yards ahead. Not sure what it was."

"Traversing right!" The gunner was already moving the turret.

"Still!" Claxton ordered when he judged the turret was far enough over. Together, gunner and commander pressed their eyes to the periscopes.

They saw it. First one flash, then another to its left. Claxton had a mind to give an order to the driver, but the young soldier was already swinging the vehicle wildly to one side.

Crump!

A shell struck the side of the road, just in front of them, exploding harmlessly in a small grey-black cloud.

Clang!

The second shell hit them, skidding across the back decks of the tank by the sound of it.

"Seen the bastards!" Claxton thumped the side of the turret. "In the hedgerow, strung out in a line!"

"What are they firing?" The gunner commented. "Fucking pea-shooters?"

"Hard right, driver!" Claxton ordered. "Come off the road! Straight across the field at them; full tilt. Let's go!"

Without further prompting, the driver swung the big tank off the paved road and onto the field with its knee high crops creating a smooth green carpet, across which the Matilda II left huge gouges as it progressed. Claxton was convinced that his radio wasn't working properly, but he sent the message anyway.

"Hello all George callsigns, this is Galahad; we've got anti-tank guns in the hedgerow forward right, range three hundred. Attacking now. Out."

Rat-tat-tat-tat-tat!

The gunner opened up with the Besa. Claxton watched the fall of shot and saw a tracer streak over the top of the low hedge.

"Drop it slightly, Baxter; you're a bit high." He corrected.

Rat-tat-tat-tat-tat!

This time the tracer landed just in front of the hedge, almost at its base.

"That'll do; shoot 'em up Baxter! Traverse along the hedge!"

"Are we going straight through 'em Corp'?" Came the driver's voice.

"Yeah; straight through, run right over the buggers. It'll save us some ammo!"

A thought suddenly occurred to Claxton.

"How much ammo have we got left?"

The gunner glanced down at the ready-to-use rack then threw his answer across to Claxton.

"Loads of main armament!" He shouted above the rattle of the Besa. "But only about four hundred for the co-ax after this belt."

"Okay!" Claxton acknowledged, his eyes still pressed to the periscope.

They were close to the hedge now, and he could clearly identify at least three enemy guns, their crews working franticly away.

Clang-boom!

Another shell hit them, but with no visible effect yet again. Claxton grimaced. Just one hundred yards to go.

"Stop firing, Baxter!" He thumped the gunner's shoulder. "Save your ammo. Driver? Give her everything she's got and squash me one of those ruddy guns!"

The Matilda II roared and Claxton felt the heavy tank pick up a fraction more speed. Then, through the periscope, he saw figures in grey uniforms suddenly spring up from behind the nearest gun and start running.

"Ha, ha! Go on you bastards! Get fucking running!" He laughed out loud and the gunner joined in.

"Here we go; stand by for the bump!" Warned the driver.

The tank suddenly lurched. There was a loud thump, a clatter of tracks trying to grip something, followed by an ear splitting squeal of metal on metal, and then the Matilda was rearing upwards, over the top of the enemy gun, before crashing back down as the weapon's gun-trails broke and the whole thing collapsed into ruin under the immense weight of the British vehicle.

Rat-tat-tat-tat-tat!

Baxter let off a burst at the retreating enemy gunners.

"Leave them!" Claxton warned, mindful of the ammunition state.

"The others are with us!" The loader shouted. "There's a Mark I on the left of us; it's just driven right over another gun. These Jerry bastards don't realise how tough the old Matilda is, eh, Corporal?"

"We'll see…" Claxton was non-committal. "Keep going forward, driver. Hand-rail the road."

They were through the screen of anti-tank guns now and ploughing on at a pace, the burning village to their left falling out of sight. Claxton was scanning the countryside ahead. In the distance he could see a wooded ridge; perhaps a mile away, maybe closer. Then he spotted the slight embankment that seemed to rise up from the field on the left and run across his frontage, way off into the distance on the right.

"What's that then?" He murmured to himself.

"Looks like a railway line to me…" The gunner offered.

"I think you're right…"

"Tank!"

The loader's shout of alarm made Claxton jump.

"Where?"

"Half left! Range one-fifty!" The loader blurted. "Under that tree by the road!"

"Stop the vehicle!" Claxton shouted. "Gunner; traverse left!"

Baxter swung the traverse gear round with fresh urgency and, seconds later, through the gun-sight, Claxton spotted the squat grey monster sitting menacingly under the tree by what appeared to be a level crossing.

"Shit! He's a big bastard!" The loader swore.

"Lay on, Baxter; sharpish!" Claxton said, wiping the sweat from his forehead as he did so.

The gunner was already moving the adjustment gears, needing no prompting, but for the corporal it seemed like hours before the gunner was ready.

"He's seen us Baxter…" Claxton hurried him. "He's laying on…"

"Nearly there…" Murmured the gunner.

"Shit!" Claxton said as he saw the gout of smoke and flame.

There was no interval between the sight of the gun firing and the sudden, deafening crash that rocked the Matilda from side to side.

"Fucking hell!" The loader cried out, holding his ears.

"Bastard!" The gunner yelled as the echo of the explosion rang in the crews' ears. "On! Stand-by…firing…now!"

Whoomph!

The 2 Pounder barked once more, and even before the gunner had opened the breech to release the spent shell case, Claxton saw their own shell hit the enemy panzer squarely under its gun. He saw the flash of the explosion, the cloud of black smoke, and then the secondary explosion that seemed to lift the enemy tank off the ground momentarily, before dumping it back down in the same spot, smoke and flames belching out of every small opening.

"Jesus Christ!" Claxton whispered in awe as he gawped at the burning panzer. "It went right through the bugger!"

"German fuckers!" Baxter growled as the loader slid a fresh round into the chamber.

Claxton suddenly felt a strange overwhelming sense of invincibility. They had taken numerous hits from various German weapons and nothing had penetrated yet. Their armour seemed impervious to everything the Jerries threw at them, yet their own 2 pounder was making short work of everything it hit. A wave of euphoria surged through Claxton's veins.

"Driver; straight on. Head for that ridge. We've got these bastards on the run! And now we're going to chase them all the way back to Berlin!"

ROMMEL'S RIDGE – JUST NORTH OF WAILLY
TUESDAY 21ST MAY 1940 – 1730 HOURS

"Fire!"

The No.1 on the gun yanked on the firing lever and the big 88mm gun roared in defiance, the long slender barrel sliding back on its recoil buffers as the muzzle spat the deadly shell on its way to the target at more than two and a half thousand feet per second.

To one side of the gun, blatantly standing upright in full view of the enemy onslaught, Rommel watched the results through his binoculars. He saw the bright flash against the British tank, the sudden cloud of smoke, and then the sight of the vehicle coming to a dead stop.

"Bang on!" Rommel yelled encouragement at the gun crew. "And again! Keep it going!"

He lowered his binoculars and ran across to the next 88mm gun. It was no more than thirty metres away, having been sited hurriedly on open ground between two wooded areas. Nearby, a smaller anti-aircraft gun was also in action in the ground role.

"Put another round into that one!" He shouted at the crew of the 88, waving his arm at the vehicle which had just been hit. "It's not dead yet. Make sure of it now it's come to a halt!"

Obediently, the layers began adjusting the aim of the big gun.

"We don't have many armour-piercing rounds left, General..." The sergeant commanding the gun warned him.

"No matter." Rommel snapped. "Once it's gone, just keep firing with anything you've got. I'll get more ammunition called forward."

With that, he turned back to face the enemy vehicles and raised his field glasses to his eyes once more.

The last two hours had been desperate. Rommel had only just managed to get the Totenkopf soldiers and the 88mm battery deployed along the very slight ridge that sat astride the road to Wailly before the first Tommy tanks had appeared. He had been mortified by the sight of them. A large group of more than nine had come straight at them, using the road as an axis. Another group of half a dozen had come at their right flank, whilst another smaller group of three or four had appeared over at the far left of the German blocking position. Rommel had been running from gun to gun, allocating targets in an effort to stop his flanks being turned, whilst also trying to stem the attack taking place directly to his front. Thankfully, the big 88s seemed to be up to the job and they had quickly knocked out several of the smaller enemy tanks. The bigger ones though were a different matter.

Rommel had watched in amazement as one of the four heavy British tanks that he could see took no less than three direct hits from the 88s without any apparent effect. It was only when a fourth and fifth round had slammed into the tank in rapid succession that the monster had finally ground to a halt, burning fiercely. Its brave crew had been machine-gunned by the Totenkopf soldiers as they tried to escape. Slightly unnecessary, Rommel thought, but this was a desperate fight and nobody was in the mood for compromise. A battery of lighter, 20mm anti-aircraft guns had arrived at Rommel's position just then, and without pause he had thrown them into position next to the 88s and ordered them into action.

After a nerve-wracking and exhausting twenty minute stand, good old Most had appeared on the ridge, leading a battery of howitzers. Understanding the urgency of the situation, the young lieutenant had pushed them along the ridge and deployed them on the right where they had immediately gone into a crash action, engaging the enemy vehicles over open sights. The howitzers were crude weapons, designed to lob heavy shells over long ranges and down onto the enemy, so against tanks their penetrating power was dubious. However, what they lacked in velocity they made up for in size and rate of fire. Their 105mm shells had quickly begun to saturate the enemy formation coming around the north-eastern flank, slowing the tanks down and making them easier targets for the 88s.

Then, minutes later, yet more 88s arrived on the position and these too were thrown into the fray without pause. Now, looking out from this elevated position, Rommel was feeling somewhat calmer than before. From left to right, some 500 metres distant and spread across an arc spanning several kilometres, was a tide mark of burning enemy armoured vehicles. Most of them were the smaller types, alongside the heavy tank that had taken five rounds to destroy. Now there were just a handful of enemy vehicles left on the field. Instead of coming on at the Germans directly, the slow moving enemy tanks were threading their way carefully from one piece of cover to the next, taking opportunity shots at the German anti-tank screen on the ridge.

It had been a close business thus far and, having received reports from other units nearby, Rommel was sure that his men were facing a major enemy attack in at least corps strength. One of his panzer regiments had been in a sharp, vicious fight a few kilometres away; this time with French tanks it was claimed. Reports stated that the Germans were managing to stave off the enemy, but at high cost. And there were reports too, that the neighbouring SS Totenkopf Division had also been hit hard by a large scale assault. All in all, it was a desperate day; but one that was starting to turn in his favour.

It had been costly of course. Even before he began to count the wider cost to his division, his scratch force here on the ridge had suffered enough. Forced to deploy along the length of the ridge due to the breadth of the enemy push, there had been no choice but for some guns to be sited in the open. Around several guns, crew members lay dead, dying and wounded. At least one of the 88s was nothing more than a mangled wreck; its crew mown down by machine-gun fire and the gun itself warped beyond use after taking a direct hit from a high explosive shell.

"Fire!"

The gun commander's order brought Rommel back to the present. He heard the thunderclap of the shell being launched from the gun then saw the stalled enemy tank rear up as the armour piercing round hit it squarely in the side, just below its turret. As the initial cloud of smoke cleared, Rommel saw the hungry orange flames licking up the side of the vehicle. Nobody tried to get out of it.

"General!"

Rommel turned and saw Most running towards him. Good old Most. The staff officer had been with him all the way, running along the ridge, backwards and forwards, directing the battle with him in order to fend off the relentless British attack. Now the young lieutenant was sprinting along the dusty track towards him.

"General…" Most panted as he stumbled to a halt. "We think we've almost stopped them on the right."

Most took a huge gulp of air, gathering himself.

"We've destroyed nine or ten of their smaller tanks and another heavy, well over to the right. That original group was joined by another handful coming out of Achicourt…"

Rommel creased his brow, picturing the map of the surrounding area in his mind.

"Then the attack has been extremely widespread!" He exclaimed.

"It seems so, General…" Most nodded. "But we've stopped them all… except two."

He pointed vaguely back over to the right.

"There are still two of their heavies on the move over there. They've been playing cat and mouse with us. Every time we get a bead on them they dodge back into cover or speed off. I don't know what they're trying to do but they seem to be driving around in circles shooting up anything of ours they can find. They've done for a couple of our light tanks between here and Mercatel."

The general's face hardened.

"They need to be stopped Most! Immediately! All guns need to be brought into action against them!"

"We're doing that, General. Captain Vosse has gone to bring up a platoon of our own heavy tanks to cut the Tommies off. We're going to herd them back into our main killing area and finish them off…"

Rommel was nodding his approval when another sudden shout snapped his attention back to the battle going on not very far away.

"There he is!" One of the 88s crew was yelling. "It's the big bastard! Half-left, behind that embankment! Lay onto him, quickly!"

Rommel snapped his head round to follow the target indication. Even before he had spotted the enemy vehicle, the big 88mm fired. He watched the shell streak down into the shallow valley, and then he suddenly spotted the British tank, just as the shell slammed into it.

"We hit!" The No.1 on the 88 shouted triumphantly.

"He's still moving!" Another crew member replied.

"Reload!"

With shrewd, professional eyes, Rommel watched the enemy tank suddenly surge forward out of cover.

"Fire again!" He roared at the gun crew. "Stop him dead!"

Even as he was uttering the words, the enemy tank let out a rattle of machine-gun fire. The first bullets cracked overhead, close enough to make the general wince, but not close enough to make anyone duck. Another burst came at them a split second later. The rapid crack-crack-crack of the passing bullets was louder and sharper this time; much closer. Rommel forced himself to stand perfectly still, whilst members of the gun crew suddenly ducked behind their gun in surprise.

"Get on with it!" Rommel yelled at the crew. "Kill the damn thing!"

He watched impatiently as a new shell was slid into the breech of the big gun. Nearby, a smaller 20mm anti-aircraft gun from another battery opened up on the lone British vehicle, joining in the attempt to finish off this last defiant tank.

"Most?" Rommel snapped, turning back to his aide. "Go back over to…"

He stopped in mid-sentence. Lieutenant Most was on the floor, flat on his back, arms and legs flung wide, a look of utter surprise on his young features. Two small, almost insignificant red holes punctuated his field-grey tunic.

Rommel gawped at the fallen staff officer in shock.

"Most?" He said again, stepping towards the young man.

The lieutenant gave a cough at that point, a wave of blood spewing from his mouth. His body jerked twice, and then the officer's eyes rolled back in his sockets and he died.

Rommel, for the first time in the campaign, felt a sudden surge of emotion; a combination of horror, loss, pity and despair. Poor, faithful, courageous Most.

As quickly as the feeling came, Rommel shook it away. Turning sharply, he began running along the ridgeline, screaming out fresh orders.

"All guns engage that tank! Aim for that heavy! Kill that bloody tank, now!"

Tuesday 21st May 1940
The Twelfth Day – Evening

THE GERMAN POSITIONS – POPLAR RIDGE, SOUTH OF PECQ
TUESDAY 21ST MAY 1940 – 1800 HOURS

"What?"

Ambrosius stared back at the lieutenant as if he were mad.

"They still want us to withdraw back over the river?"

Lieutenant Kuthe, the bearer of bad news, nodded his head sagely.

Ambrosius was astounded; so much so that he could hardly find words.

"Did you tell them what I said?" He demanded.

Kuthe nodded his head faster, trying to placate the irate captain.

"I did, Captain; I did. But Regimental Headquarters are insistent. We are the only regiment to have forced a successful crossing. Most other regiments never even got over the river, and those that did have been repulsed with heavy losses."

Ambrosius grunted.

"Heavy losses? Tell me about heavy losses! The battalion was shredded trying to get over that river! Only ninety of us made it here to this wood; now there are barely forty of us left! Have we made all that sacrifice for nothing?"

Kuthe let the captain finish, before continuing in a calm, soothing voice.

"It has been a worthy exploit, Sir, but I am told it is out of the regiment's hands now. The Divisonal and Corps Commanders are in agreement; we must pull back over the river. The bridgehead is too small and far from secure. Besides, the latest reports from the Luftwaffe spotters say that there are two strong columns of armour and infantry approaching this location from the south-west. You only just held the last attack. I doubt you could hold off anything bigger…"

He tailed off, letting his words sink in.

After a while, Ambrosius spoke.

"So, even though the Tommies have not shifted us yet, we will still withdraw, rather than reinforce this bridgehead?"

Kuthe nodded.

"Those are the orders, Sir. From the Corps Commander himself."

Ambrosius looked away, gritting his teeth and trying to keep his temper in check. He was tired; physically and mentally. He had given this attack everything, and so had his men. How could such sacrifice end like this? Running away with their tails between their legs, just because other units had not achieved their own missions?

After a moment or two of silent fuming, Ambrosius looked back at Kuthe.

"It will take a short while to organise." The captain said in a clipped voice. "I will not leave any wounded or equipment behind. We will go back in good order. We won here today, Kuthe. Do you hear me? We won. I will not run away like a scared child. We shall go back in a proper manner."

Kuthe nodded his understanding.

"That is fine, Captain; as long as you have withdrawn by nightfall."

Ambrosius gave the officer from Regimental Headquarters a curt nod then glanced to his left where his acting-adjutant waited for instructions.

"Haersler…" Ambrosius began, his voice tight with barely suppressed frustration. "Get the warning order round to all commanders. Prepare to move by 1830 hours. We're pulling out…"

THE TANNERY – PECQ ON THE ESCAUT
TUESDAY 21ST MAY 1940 – 1810 HOURS

"Get back to your stand-to positions." Jackson rattled out the orders to the line of tired soldiers. "The Platoon Commander will be round in ten minutes to check that we're all set up and ready for the night. Section 2 i/c's, make sure you've got a full ammo state ready for when we get to you; and have a working party of two men ready to go, on call. Section commanders, once you're back in position, get your men working in pairs to clean weapons.

One man cleans while his mucker covers his arcs. I want us ready to fight again as soon as possible."

There was a murmur of acknowledgement from amongst the platoon of weary guardsmen, and under the direction of the NCOs, they began to file back up the steps of the factory to where they had started the morning's battle.

"Well done, gentlemen." Dunstable called out to them as they filed past.

Jackson nodded his head in agreement at the officer's words.

"Here, here." He commented. "Fucking well done in fact."

Guardsman Hawkins, covered in dust and still carrying his Bren Gun, shuffled past his officer and sergeant, glancing up as he did so and offering them a tired smile. Without thinking, Jackson smiled back.

"Well done, Hawkins..." He growled at the soldier, his voice tinged with a mix of pride and humour. "...you big, dozy fucker!"

At the unexpected words of praise, Hawkins' face split into a broad grin.

"Cheers, Sergeant Jackson. All in a day's work..." He chuckled as he climbed the concrete stairs.

Next to Jackson, Dunstable gave the sergeant a sideways glance.

"Don't tell me you're developing a soft spot for Guardsman Hawkins?" He smiled.

"Me, Sir? Going soft?" Jackson smiled back. "Don't be so bloody daft!"

They laughed quietly together for a moment.

It had been an eventful day. Their counter-attack against the enemy had been entirely successful. It had been costly though. Despite Jackson's carefully arranged smoke screen and diversion, the rest of the platoon had not escaped without casualties. Even though the Germans in the stream itself had been taken by surprise, Dunstable and the line of riflemen had taken heavy machine-gun fire from across the river during the last few yards of their dash through the corn. Three men had gone down in that hail of fire. Two of them, one of whom was Lance Sergeant Hogson, had been wounded and had managed to crawl after their comrades to reach shelter in the ditch. Of the third man, Guardsman Mason, there was no sign. He was missing, presumed killed, and the heavy fire that the Germans had continued to bring down on the cornfield had prevented a lengthy search for the missing soldier. Fortunately, neither Hogson or the other guardsman were badly hurt and would fight again.

The fight in the stream had been short, but savage, and at the end of it all, no less than nine dead Germans were counted, whilst another four enemy soldiers, all of them wounded, had been taken prisoner. It was a further two hours after turfing the enemy out however, before Jackson's platoon had been relieved by a platoon from No.2 Company. As midday approached, the jubilant platoon, full of their own success, had begun retracing their steps, very carefully, back towards the tannery in Pecq village. Before they even got near their old positions however, they had been pulled up short by the Commanding Officer.

The Germans, it seemed, had also managed to get men across the river in No.1 Company's sector, at the other side of the village. Although the enemy bridgehead wasn't very big, it had penetrated as far as a factory that dominated much of the northern suburbs. No.1 Company had held their reserve line but needed support in order to launch a successful counter-attack. To that end, after a hasty conference with the Commanding Officer and the No.1 Company Commander, Dunstable and Jackson had once more led their platoon into the assault. This time however, it was a very different kind of assault.

Instead of launching an old fashioned, sweeping attack across open ground, No.16 Platoon had been launched through the outbuildings and stockyard of the factory, negotiating the perilous maze of alleyways before finally getting into a position to assault the main factory building. It had been a tough fight, with the Germans contesting every room and stairwell with grenades and sub-machine guns. Two more men had been hit during the struggle, both of them killed outright during the bitter room to room fighting.

Eventually, after a long hour of exhausting combat, the surviving Germans had abandoned their toe hold in No.1 Company's area and pulled back from the factory, disappearing back across the river under cover of a fresh bombardment. Once again, it had taken several hours before the platoon was relieved and sent back off to its own company. Now, tired but victorious, the men of No.16 Platoon trudged back to their original positions, having fought the enemy tooth and nail throughout the long hours of daylight.

Dunstable and Jackson watched them go. There were only seventy five percent of them left out of those who began the campaign, just eleven days ago.

"I'm parched." Dunstable said as he watched the last of the men disappear around the bend in the stairs.

"Me too." Jackson agreed. "I'll go see if Company Headquarters have got a dixie of tea we can pinch. I could murder a brew."

"I think we earned it today, Sergeant Jackson." Dunstable wiped a tired hand over his face.

Jackson gave a small grunt.

"I reckon you're right there."

He paused for a moment then spoke again, more hesitantly this time.

"We won today, Sir, didn't we? We beat those Jerries hands down?"

Dunstable nodded, a strange melancholy smile settling on his features.

"We did that, Sergeant J… We certainly did that…"

7TH ROYAL TANK REGIMENT RENDEZVOUS – JUST WEST OF ARRAS
TUESDAY 21ST MAY 1940 – 2030 HOURS

"Six… seven … eight… Ruddy hell! Look at the size of this bugger!"

Claxton stood shaking his head in disbelief as he surveyed the huge gouge in the side armour of his tank's turret. Baxter came and stood next to him, emitting a soft whistle.

"Blimey! What do you reckon that was then?"

"Something big." Claxton muttered. "No wonder it nearly deafened us…"

He glanced sideways at Baxter and noted that the gunner still had dry, crusted blood plastered across his top lip; the result of the nose bleed caused by the huge explosion that had rocked their tank in the dying minutes of the battle. Miraculously, the round had not penetrated the thick armour and the Matilda had somehow managed to rumble onwards, despite the fact that the entire crew had gone temporarily deaf.

"There's another three hits on the other side, and two graze marks across the top decks; one at the front and one at the back."

Baxter gave his own count of strike-marks to his vehicle commander.

"So… thirteen hits in total?" Claxton totted up the count in his head.

"She's a tough old bird!" The loader commented as he wandered over to join the two other members of the turret crew.

"Thank God for that!" Claxton replied. "Else we might not be here…"

He tailed off and all three men went silent. They were thinking of the fate that had befallen most of their comrades in the other tanks; the smaller Mark Is. After the exhilarating charge through the village and down the road, shooting up trucks, personnel carriers, infantry and anti-tank guns, along with an enemy panzer, Claxton and the other vehicles in his group had crossed a railway line and driven straight into a storm of much heavier fire from a low ridge to their front. With the bit between their teeth, the tanks had rumbled forward, machine-gunning the fleeting figures up on the distant ridge. But then the first big shells had started coming their way.

Claxton had no idea what calibre of guns were up on that ridge, but what he did know was that they were lethal. For two hours or more, he had enjoyed a game of hide and seek with his enemy, dodging in and out of cover, gaining ground with every new dash and closing the range. All the time, they took pot shots at the enemy they saw and, every time they made a move, a fresh enemy shell would come flying back at them. Some of those shells would miss, others would hit; none of them had stopped their tank. For a while, Claxton and his crew had begun to feel invincible in their tough little Matilda, but when the loader had brought their attention to the scene behind them, that illusion had been shattered.

Looking through the rear periscopes of the turret, Claxton and his two man gun crew had witnessed the tragic sight of burning Mark I tanks littering the fields behind them. Every vehicle that had followed them on this escapade now sat burning and smouldering in the dying evening sunlight. Claxton had tried the radio to see if anybody would answer, but nobody had. Then the enemy had turned their full attention onto Claxton's lone tank. Every time the Matilda moved, half a dozen shells at a time had come streaking towards it, and to be honest, it was a miracle the tank hadn't received more hits. With both ammunition and fuel starting to run low, Claxton and his crew had realised that their adventure was almost over. With one final act of defiance the Matilda had broken cover, expended the last of its machine-gun ammunition towards several enemy guns on the high ground, before turning away sharply and heading, at best speed, back the way it had come.

Enemy shells chased Claxton's tank all the way, and the driver had swerved left and right continuously in order to present a more difficult target to the German guns. Eventually, they had broken contact with the enemy gun-line, although they had one more short engagement left to contend with. Ploughing back down the road, past the outskirts of a village that was littered with burning trucks and dead bodies, Claxton and his men had happened upon a pair of small German tanks, sitting astride a crossroads. With twelve rounds of 2 Pounder ammunition remaining, Claxton and his crew were in no mood to make a detour.

The Germans were obviously not expecting the Matilda's sudden appearance and when Baxter put a 2 Pounder shell straight through the right hand tank of the pair, the crew of the second tank had bailed out hurriedly. With no co-axial ammunition left, Baxter was unable to give the scuttling German soldiers a burst, and so the driver had simply squeezed every bit of power from the Matilda's engine that he could muster, and roared over the junction, leaving the burning panzer behind in a cloud of dust and exhaust fumes.

As the shadows lengthened and Claxton's tank re-crossed their start-line of earlier that day, a motorcyclist from the Northumberland Fusiliers had appeared; directing them back to this place, their unit rendezvous. The attack, the Fusilier had told them, had ground to a halt, and all units had been ordered to regroup.

"We're going to have to split the track on the far side."

The driver's voice snapped Claxton out of his private thoughts.

"What's the problem?" He demanded.

"Looks like we've taken a hit on our running gear, Corporal. The side-skirt's taken most of the blast by the looks, but two of the links are almost hanging off. I'm surprised the track hasn't gone yet. We won't get much further without changing the links."

Claxton pondered the problem for a moment and looked around the village street, where the shadows were deepening by the minute. Two Mark I Tanks were parked up, further down the cobbled street, the crews surveying the damage to their own vehicles. It didn't look like much of the battalion had arrived back at the rendezvous just yet, and in his mind's eye, Claxton once more saw the image of all those burning tanks in the open fields.

"Don't split the track just yet." He told the driver. "We need to find out how long we're going to be here. I'll go see if I can find an officer or someone from Battalion Headquarters."

With that, Claxton set off up the street towards the pair of Matilda Is. He needed to find somebody with rank who could tell him what was supposed to happen next, but as he walked through the ominously quiet village, he began to seriously doubt whether there was anyone left who could give him orders of any kind at all."

THE CORNFIELD BY POPLAR RIDGE – JUST SOUTH OF PECQ
TUESDAY 21ST MAY 1940 – 2200 HOURS

"Who the fuck's that?" The harsh voice demanded.

Despite the hard tone in the man's voice, Dawes breathed a sigh of relief.

"Thank Christ for that! I'm British, don't worry... Guardsman Dawes, No.4 Company. Who's that?"

"It's the Company Sergeant Major of No.3 Company." The voice snapped back through the darkness. "You're lucky we didn't blow your fucking head off! What are you doing out here?"

The dark figure of the warrant officer waded through the corn and came to stand right in front of Dawes, who was shaking from head to foot, partly with the sudden evening chill, and partly with relief.

"I got cut off this morning, Sir..." Dawes explained. "When the Jerries overran our position. Corporal Dixon's dead. I've been sniping at the Jerries all day whenever it was safe to pop my head up, but I couldn't get back to the battalion though; the bastards are everywhere. There's loads of 'em up in those woods on the ridge, Sir, so we'd best be careful..."

Dawes heard the Company Sergeant Major grunt.

"They *were* up there, earlier." The warrant officer said. "We put a big attack in against them and got cut up pretty badly by their bloody machine-guns. We lost over half the company..."

Dawes thought he heard the warrant officer's voice crack slightly with emotion.

"Bloody hell, Sir... Sorry about that. I think most of my company are done for too."

"We've got a load of your lot attached to us; about a platoon's worth. You can slot into one of our sections for now. The battalion's formed into two composite companies for the time being. We're going to re-occupy the river bank and then reorganise the companies again in the morning, once we've rounded up all the stragglers."

Dawes caught his breath.

"Back to the river bank? But what about those Jerries up in the wood, Sir?"

Even through the darkness, Dawes saw the warrant officer shaking his head from side to side.

"The only Jerries left up there are dead ones, big lad. They've pulled back over the river by the looks of it. All the Jerries have gone."

Dawes heard the old soldier give a deep sigh before he spoke again.

"Looks like we beat the bastards after all..."

PART FIVE

DISASTER

Saturday 25th May 1940
The Sixteenth Day

GARRISON HEADQUARTERS – CALAIS
SATURDAY 25TH MAY 1940 – 1515 HOURS

Brigadier Claude Nicholson, commander of the British Garrison at Calais, looked up at the German officer and took in the man's haughty, confident expression. The bastards. They knew it was only a matter of time. The German armoured thrust that had burst through the French on the River Meuse had cut straight through Northern France, reaching the coast at Abbeville on the 20th of this month, effectively surrounding the British Expeditionary Force and the neighbouring French and Belgian Armies. And now the German pincers were closing in on the Allies in their small, and ever shrinking 'pocket'. Here at Calais, on the extreme western edge of that pocket, Nicholson, with the men of the Rifle Brigade and 3rd Royal Tank Regiment, were experiencing the nip of those pincers. More than that, those pincers were squeezing ever tighter with each passing hour.

Just along the coast, Nicholson knew, a scratch force of two Guards battalions had been thrown into Boulogne with less than twenty four hours to spare; their orders to hold off the German advance as long as possible so that several thousand rear echelon troops could be evacuated through that port. He very much doubted whether that particular garrison would manage to hold out for long, and he was starting to have serious concerns about his own ability to fight on. But fight on he must.

He glanced down at the piece of paper in his hand; a scrap from a note book, on which a message had been scrawled in neat block capitals by one of his signallers. The message had come directly from the Secretary of State for War. He already knew what the message said, for he had read it through a dozen times in the hour since its receipt. Silently, he read it again anyway.

"Defence of Calais to the utmost is of the highest importance to our country as symbolising our continuing cooperation with France. The eyes of the Empire are upon the defence of Calais, and HM Government are confident you and your gallant regiments will perform an exploit worthy of the British name."

Nicholson smiled. The message was a wonderful, inspirational piece of rhetoric that had followed on from the stark, yet explicit signal he had received last night from Whitehall, by hand, via Admiral Somerville. He certainly didn't need to re-read *that* message. It was ingrained in his memory and would remain so for the rest of his life.

"...no, repeat no, evacuation... comply for sake of Allied solidarity..."

The brigadier put the piece of paper down next to a crudely typed handbill, one of thousands that had been dropped on the city by German aircraft, encouraging the defenders to give up. He thought about that for a moment. Why are they so desperate to avoid a fight? Why try so hard to force us to surrender when they could, supposedly, take us to pieces in short order? In addition to the leaflet drop, he had been offered a chance to surrender once already, earlier that day; the German ultimatum brought to him by the Mayor of Calais. Nicholson's reply had been blunt and to the point...

"Tell the Germans that if they want Calais, they will have to fight for it!"

Taking a deep breath, Nicholson turned back to face the German officer. He looked him squarely in the eye, making sure that the man could see the look of resolve on the brigadier's face.

"With regard to your demand for our surrender, the answer is no."

He spoke slowly, clearly; ensuring the German officer would not misunderstand him.

"It is the British Army's duty to fight, as much as it is the German's."

He saw the enemy officer take a sharp intake of breath; amazed that the British would still not yield.

"I have nothing more to say on the matter." Nicholson finished. "You may go now..."

HEADQUARTERS BRITISH EXPEDITIONARY FORCE – NEAR LILLE
SATURDAY 25TH MAY 1940 – 1750 HOURS

General the Viscount Lord Gort sat back in the chair and closed his eyes. His mind had been so full of detail these past two weeks it was sometimes impossible to make sense of it all. Now though, here in this room, as he sat in solitary contemplation, it was all starting to become horribly clear. He had been sitting here alone for perhaps half an hour, allowing his mind to forget the trivia and concentrate on the key facts. Now, he was getting close to his decision. He listened to the clock, ticking steadily in the corner of the room, reminding him every second that time was marching on, and so were the Germans. Once more, he went through the situation as it was now apparent to him.

Four days ago, the BEF had fought a desperate, gallant, and successful defensive battle on the Escaut; proving that given a fair wind, the British Army could match the Germans. But the wind wasn't blowing fair this week, and events elsewhere had meant that the small victory on the Escaut had done nothing more than buy Gort some additional time; time which was now running out.

On the same day as the action on the Escaut, a small British and French clearance operation, sweeping around the south of Arras, had caught the Germans on the back foot for a while and made some good initial headway. Once again however, the enemy had proved his ability to assess, decide and react with overwhelming force at the critical point, at the critical time, and with breath-taking speed. Thus, the action at Arras had been rebuffed, achieving nothing more than a brief delay on the enemy. Enough time to avert disaster for the Allies, but not enough time to deliver victory for them; not even a partial one.

Since the failure of the Arras operation, things had worsened. The enemy had reached the coast behind the BEF, cutting them off from their supply bases. The entire BEF, along with the best part of two French armies and the Belgian Army were now caught in a sack; one which was full of holes and one that the Germans were squeezing tighter by the hour. To the east, a large German army group was being held at bay by the main British force, the Belgians and the French. To the west, the Germans were pushing hard towards Dunkirk, the only serviceable port left open to the trapped Allied armies. Boulogne had fallen yesterday, the scratch Guards Brigade defending the port having had to fight their way back to the remaining destroyers once all other personnel had been evacuated. Calais, likewise, was under attack, and even though the garrison there had been ordered to fight to the last man and the last round, Gort doubted it could last much more than another twenty four hours.

The Belgian Army, holding the critical left flank of the BEF's line, was shaky; very shaky. Brooke, commanding the BEF's 2nd Corps, believed the Belgians were on their last legs, and Gort agreed. They weren't going to last much longer. They were almost spent. If they broke, the Germans would get in behind the BEF's rear-left and the campaign would be over; a defeat. A disaster. And as for the long promised French counter-attack from the south, designed to link up with another attack by the BEF's dwindling reserves punching from the north? Well, that was almost laughable. Only Gort wasn't in the mood for laughter.

Time and again, the French high command had promised a counter-offensive from the south to cut the German spearhead in half. Time and again they had postponed, or failed to deliver. A shame that, for those French troops who were trapped with the BEF were fighting hard; fighting well. Good Frenchmen; good soldiers. But their higher command structure? Gort had lost all faith in them. He had wanted to believe in their ability to orchestrate the much discussed offensive; wanted to believe in them so badly. His latest direction from the British Government was that he should still believe in them, and launch his last two reserve formations, the 5th and 50th Divisions, southwards to achieve the desired link-up.

But that wasn't going to happen. Gort could see that now. For better or for worse, the campaign in France was drawing to an end for the BEF. It was merely a case of whether the BEF was destroyed entirely, or whether some part of the force might be recovered back to Britain where it could reconstitute and form the nucleus of a future army. The entire course of the war would rest on Gort's decision in the next few minutes.

It was a terrible decision to make, and Gort knew it. On one hand, he could follow his orders and attack southwards again, with little chance of success. And if, whilst he was doing so, the Belgians gave way, then all would be lost. If, on the other hand, he abandoned the plan to attack southwards, and sent his reserves to bolster the Belgians, then he might just manage to pull his force back to the coast in one piece and extricate a useful portion of it. It could very well end his career, and no doubt there would be generations of historians yet to come who would complain bitterly that he had abandoned the French. But Gort was British; and he had been entrusted with her army. He would not see that army destroyed piecemeal or thrown into captivity. He knew his duty, and that duty was far more important than his ego or reputation.

He sighed deeply, opened his eyes, and rose from the chair. He stood there for a moment and composed himself. He must appear totally calm; totally unflustered. Straightening his tunic, he walked to the door and opened it. In the next room, his operations staff were busy with their many and varied tasks and he watched, quietly proud of how phlegmatically they continued with their work, despite being more than aware of how perilous the situation was.

Sensing the sudden scrutiny, the staff of his General Headquarters stopped, one by one, and looked across at him. Henry Pownall, Gort's Chief of Staff, looked up from the report he was reading. Without speaking, Gort walked calmly across to Pownall, and in a quiet, almost casual voice, he gave his momentous order.

"Henry, get hold of the 5th Division please, and send them over to Brookie on the left. Once you've got them moving, do the same with the 50th. Then we need to prepare some notes for this evening's conference with the corps commanders. I have decided that the BEF will begin operating towards the coast."

Sunday 26th May 1940
The Seventeenth Day

HEADQUARTERS GERMAN 19TH CORPS – CHATAEU COLEMBERT, 13 MILES SOUTH OF CALAIS SUNDAY 26TH MAY 1940 – 1615 HOURS

Guderian gawped at the figure in the doorway, looked across at von Wietersheim, the commander of 14th Army Corps, then back at the man in the doorway. Suddenly, simultaneously, the two German generals exploded into fits of laughter. In the doorway, covered from head to toe in dried mud, the stocky, bull-like figure of SS Obergruppenfuhrer Sepp Dietrich, thrust out his arm in the Nazi salute.

"Good afternoon, General; my apologies for the delay."

He stood there, rigidly to attention, doing his best to maintain his dignity in the face of the generals' unbridled amusement. His face was brown, his hands were brown, his entire uniform, normally the drab SS grey, was caked in the same brown sewage.

"Sepp!" Guderian welcomed him, managing to calm his laughter. "I'm glad you were able to get here safely in the end."

Wietersheim was still chuckling.

"I've heard of *'dropping yourself in the shit'*, Sepp, but you have taken it to a new extreme!"

The SS Obergruppenfuhrer realised that he had earned a place as a fair target for the generals' humour and relaxed, an embarrassed smile crossing his mud caked face.

"Fucking Tommy stragglers!" He cursed, removing his cap. "Shot my bloody car up and set it on fire. Me and my driver nearly got toasted when the petrol tank went up! We had to crawl into a culvert and roll ourselves in the shit to save us being cooked alive!"

Guderian tried to regain his composure, feeling suddenly guilty for finding such amusement in the SS commander's predicament.

"Thank goodness we were able to extricate you in one piece, then. I was just telling General von Wietersheim what good work you've been doing down at Watten, on the canal."

Dietrich glanced at the commander of 14th Army Corps inquisitively. Guderian explained.

"14th Corps will be replacing my corps along this stretch of line shortly. The 20th Motorised Division will be their lead formation and will be under my command until the balance of the corps can be brought forward. I'm going to put them in the line next to the Leibstandarte, so for the time being your regiment, along with Infantry Regiment Gross Deutschland, will be under their command. We just wanted to go through the details of it all with you face to face."

He gave the commander of the Leibstandarte Adolf Hitler an apologetic look.

"I'm sorry it's turned into a bit of an unwanted adventure for you…"

Dietrich ambled forward into the room, his rough, common voice booming in the confines of the small study.

"I tell you what, General. If you give me some coffee and a decent meal then I'll forgive you for endangering the life of the Fuhrer's chosen man."

Guderian and von Wietersheim grinned at the former sergeant major's brash cheek.

"Of course, Sepp." Guderian replied. "It is the least I can do."

"Anyway, General, I'm not in any particular rush to get back." Dietrich threw his cap down on a nearby desk and began scratching flakes of mud from his face. "As long as this *'halt order'* is in place there is very little for us to do other than scowl at the Tommies in the distance and watch our air force fly round in circles!"

Guderian set his face in a wry smile. How true that was. For two full days now, Guderian's corps had been halted once more; forbidden to advance any further east towards Dunkirk and squeeze the Allied pocket out of existence. This, he suspected, was the result of a certain amount of alarm caused by a sharp British counter-attack that had, for a short while, sent 7th Panzer Division reeling, several days ago near Arras. Although 7th Panzer had blocked the British move and launched a fierce response of their own, the fighting had renewed fears amongst the high command that their panzer formations were dangerously over extended. Consequently, just as final victory had been within Guderian's grasp, his forces had been stopped in their tracks once more.

Instead of closing on Dunkirk, he'd been forced to sit on the Aa canal whilst two of his divisions attempted to snuff out the final resistance at Boulogne and Calais. Boulogne had fallen and, he was promised by the divisional commander responsible, Calais would soon be in German hands too. The British garrison in the port had refused two offers of surrender, and it was clear that Guderian's troops would have to make a final, overwhelming assault to secure the port.

Whilst all this went on and the high command prevaricated, Guderian had been forced to watch a steady stream of British ships sailing past Calais on their way to Dunkirk. Whether they were bringing reinforcements and supplies or evacuating Allied troops, Guderian wasn't sure, but his instinct told him that the advantage was being lost and that the Allies were getting away with something. He felt the frustration rising inside once more. He was about to respond to Dietrich's comment when Nehring, Guderian's trusted chief of staff, appeared in the doorway.

The colonel strode into the room, his face flushed with excitement, and addressed his comments directly to Guderian.

"General, we have just received a flash message from Army Headquarters…"

Guderian, Wietersheim and Dietrich all focussed their attention on the chief of staff, scenting impending action.

"The halt order has been cancelled, General." Nehring announced. "The advance on Dunkirk is to resume immediately…"

ESPLANADE DE LA CITADEL – CALAIS
SUNDAY 26TH MAY 1940 – 1745 HOURS

Corporal Sam Digby of the King's Royal Rifle Corps, one of the battalions that constituted the Rifle Brigade holding Calais, ran like he'd never run before. His studded ammunition boots slid on the cobbled street as he, accompanied by two private soldiers from his section, spurted for cover on the right hand side of the wide avenue. They weren't going far mind you; and they'd only been forced back from their barricade by the bridge when it had been crashed by an enemy tank, which in turn had been followed by a mass of infantry. All this of course, had happened under cover of the dreaded German mortars.

The situation was desperate, but Sam Digby wasn't a quitter, and he had no intention of letting the Jerries just capture the Old Town of Calais without a fight.

"In here!" He yelled at his two companions, veering suddenly towards a doorway that was missing its door.

Together they bolted up the three stone steps and into the tall, terraced building, as bullets smacked into the plaster of the house's façade behind them.

"Upstairs!" He ordered without looking back.

Their breathing was ragged, their muscles screaming out in protest at the headlong dash up two flights of stairs, but up they went. They were the Rifle Brigade, and the Rifle Brigade were fighters; and Sam Digby and his comrades still had plenty of fight left in them. Coming to the first floor, Digby spotted the large wooden cupboard positioned on the landing.

"Here..." He pulled up sharply. "Push this over and block the stairs!"

Together the men heaved at the huge piece of furniture.

"Jesus Christ! This thing weighs a bloody ton!" Private Chandler swore as he struggled to tip the big cupboard.

"Exactly..." Digby snarled through gritted teeth, his face going purple as his fingers struggled to get a firm hold on the solid base. "Get the fucking thing over! They won't get past this in a hurry!"

The second private, Wilkinson, somehow managed to get his bayonet under the cupboard, levering it high enough to get the toe of his boot under. Seeing the gap appear, Digby's fingers grappled for it in desperately.

"Don't drop the bastard back down..." The corporal warned. "Now... heave!"

"Yaaaagh!" Chandler cried out with the effort as they brought the cupboard up to reach its tipping point.

"She's going... stand clear!" Digby gasped as he felt the weight of the cupboard give way to gravity.

The solid oak wardrobe toppled over, hitting the landing floor with a deafening crash, effectively blocking access to the stairs down to the ground floor.

"Come on, let's go!" Digby gasped as he straightened up, and made for the next set of stairs, grabbing his rifle as he went.

Up they went, right to the top floor, kicking open doors until they found the room they were after; the one that looked back out on the esplanade.

"Here it is!" Digby called to his men. "Knock out the windows..."

Quickly, using a technique perfected over the last several days, the three soldiers reversed their rifle butts and began hammering out the pains of glass in the big double windows.

"They're in the trees already, Sam!" Chandler warned the corporal as he smashed out the last pains of glass.

"Start firing; pick the bastards off!" Digby ordered, glancing down at the wide avenue below.

Sure enough, the Germans were infiltrating rapidly over the captured bridge. In his heart of hearts, Digby knew that the end was near, but he was determined to go on as long as he could and make the Germans pay for their prize.

Blam!

Chandler fired his first shot, followed shortly afterwards by Wilkinson. Below on the street, crouching behind the trees and bushes that lined the esplanade, the German troops ducked into cover as the bullets began to smack into the ground nearby. Seconds later, German bullets were streaking back up towards the windows on the top floor of the row of houses.

"Watch out!" Digby warned the other two, pushing them away from the window. Chandler and Wilkinson stepped aside as the corporal pulled a grenade out from his ammunition pouch.

"Let's give the Jerries something bigger to dodge!"

Yanking the safety pin out of the grenade, Digby lobbed the small explosive device sideways out of the window, in a similar manner to a child trying to skim a stone off water. The grenade arced through the air then dropped with sudden speed. The small, green egg-shaped device fell like a stone amongst the line of trees, and exploded in a ball of black smoke just before it hit the ground.

Far below, the sound of screaming and frantic shouting in German told Digby that his aim had been true.

"Take that, you bastards!" He shouted triumphantly.

Chandler stepped forward and fired another shot down amongst the trees.

"Tank!" He called out, stepping back into cover, working the bolt of his Lee-Enfield.

Digby glanced down and saw the tank instantly. He wasn't sure if it was the same one that had forced the barricade at the bridge, but it was trundling purposefully along the road now, its turret offset at an angle so that the coaxially mounted machine-gun could rake the ground-floor windows of the buildings as it passed.

Moving quickly, Digby produced his second, and last, grenade. He watched as the enemy tank rumbled closer. As the big, ugly vehicle progressed, more and more German infantrymen appeared from out of cover and fell in behind it.

"They're going for the Citadel!" Digby observed.

Waiting until the tank was almost directly below, he pulled the pin from the grenade and simply dropped it out of the window.

The grenade dropped quickly, just missing the tank, thudding against the cobbles behind it a second before detonating.

Crump!

The grenade went up, bowling over several German soldiers following on behind.

The sound of shouting resumed, and this time, the German voices were echoing in the hallway of the house, far below. A moment later, the sound of boots on wooden steps sounded loud and ominously downstairs.

"Here they come!" Wilkinson shouted the unnecessary warning.

"Cover the stairs Wilko!" Digby nodded to the doorway of the room. "I'll come and give you a hand in a minute…"

Blam!

Chandler was taking another shot at the enemy below.

"Let's show these buggers how the Rifle Brigade fight, boys!" Digby called as he reloaded his own rifle. "We can hold out here all day!"

"Why don't we go on the roof, Sam? See if we can get into the next house?"

Wilkinson's suggestion came from where he stood ready, out on the landing.

"Sam! Look at this!"

Chandler's voice took Digby's attention away from Wilkinson's proposal. He stepped across to where Chandler was and followed his gaze along the esplanade to where the Citadel gates lay set back from the main road. At first, Digby couldn't understand what he was seeing. There were two other German tanks at that end of the esplanade, their short, stubby guns pointing straight at the gateway. A mass of figures swarmed around the gateway, some in the distinctive field grey of the German Army, others in the khaki colour typical of the British and French defenders. It was hard to understand what was happening as the various figures mingled with each other, their actions seeming much less animated than one would expect from enemies locked in hand to hand combat.

And then Digby spotted the improvised white flag; then another.

"Shit…" The corporal swore bitterly, his heart sinking.

It was over. No matter how hard they fought, the outcome was already decided now. The Citadel's garrison had finally been overrun. Calais had fallen.

OPERATIONS CENTRE DOVER COMMAND – DOVER CASTLE TUNNELS
SUNDAY 26TH MAY 1940 – 1857 HOURS

Vice Admiral Bertram Ramsay paced slowly around the newly equipped annex to his operations centre. The large room had formerly housed the large electric generators that powered the whole complex, but they had been replaced by newer generators in a separate location, leaving this cavernous room vacant. It was just as well because, if the operation that was looming was formally approved, then he was going to need a suitable command and support facility in order to give it the best chance of success.

The room was almost ready. Maps and charts now lined the walls and covered desks, whilst roster boards had been hung, shipping and force lists hanging side by side with them. Telephones had been run into the room, connected and tested, whilst desks, typewriters and all the paraphernalia of a headquarters was being arranged by the small army of Naval officers and ratings who had been relieved of their usual tasks and brought here to form an ad hoc operations staff. As Ramsay surveyed the room, running a critical eye over the layout, and silently imagining how this headquarters would need to operate, he listened absently to the Chief Petty Officer responsible for collating statistics, reports and returns, as he briefed the staff of all departments on the correct logging and reporting procedure.

They were almost ready to go. The room was already functioning at a lower level due to the recent need to evacuate troops from Boulogne and extricate all unnecessary troops and wounded through Dunkirk. He was also standing-by in case the Government changed its mind about the Calais Garrison, although something deep inside told him that such a change of heart was unlikely. Besides, if the planned operation did get the go ahead, Calais would be the last of Ramsay's worries. The prospect of what now faced Ramsay's rapidly burgeoning command and the British Expeditionary Force was enough to make any man balk at the challenge. But that wasn't an option; not if Britain was to stave off a defeat of unbelievable proportions and stay in the war.

He stopped in front of the chart that showed the minefields and clear lanes in the English Channel. This was just one of the many difficulties that would face Ramsay; the need to clear and keep open mine-free lanes between Dover and Dunkirk in order to ensure that the shipping could make best speed and evacuate as many men as possible should the need arise. The mine-fields of course had been laid by his own command as a protective measure; now they had become a potential obstacle to success if the worst came to the worst. He should get the clearance of a new lane underway now perhaps; just in case the situation in France couldn't be stabilised?

The sound of footsteps echoing along the corridor made Ramsay look towards the doorway. The footsteps were fast, urgent, ominous. A moment later, a lieutenant-commander from the main operations staff entered the room, coming to a standstill just through the door and casting his gaze around the room.

"Looking for me?" Ramsay addressed the officer.

The lieutenant-commander looked across to where Ramsay hovered in a corner of the room.

"Yes, Sir." The officer replied in a business-like tone. "There's a 'Priority' signal from the Admiralty just come in."

He held up his hand and gave the small piece of notepaper a quick wave.

Around the room, all other conversation stopped and the various groups of officers and ratings looked across at the lieutenant-commander.

"Read it out loud, please?" Ramsay said, keeping his hands clasped firmly behind his back.

The officer gave the piece of paper the briefest glance.

"It's quite short and to the point, Sir." He began. "It just says *'Operation Dynamo is to commence'.*"

Ramsay felt his pulse quicken. He had to use all of his self-control to prevent a visible reaction to the news.

Having ensured he was in control of himself, Ramsay simply nodded, then turned to face the rest of the audience.

"Alright then, ladies and gentlemen, you know what to do. All department heads to the map table for initial orders; remainder... let's get things moving shall we?"

Monday 27th May 1940
The Eighteenth Day

HMS WOLFHOUND – APPROACHING DUNKIRK HARBOUR
MONDAY 27TH MAY 1940 – 0750 HOURS

C aptain William Tennant, Royal Navy, gazed out from the bridge of the destroyer as it edged its way towards the harbour. This wasn't his ship of course. He and his Naval Shore Party were just passengers. Tennant had been filling the appointment of Chief Staff Officer to the First Sea Lord at the Admiralty until just a few days ago. When the evacuation of the BEF became more than just a possibility, Tennant had volunteered to assist with the practical aspects of the operation. The First Sea Lord and Admiral Ramsay knew that an experienced Naval hand would be essential on the ground at Dunkirk and thus it was that Tennant now stared out on the scene of destruction in his new capacity as Senior Naval Officer Ashore at Dunkirk.

The scene was hard to believe. He had been watching the huge palls of oily black smoke since dawn had broken, and that in itself had told him the basics of the story at Dunkirk. Now he was looking at the awful reality. The harbour, almost in its entirety, was on fire. Boats, warehouses, machinery; you name it, it was burning. Far above the ruined town, well above the thick grey cloud from which the rain drizzled incessantly, German bombers cruised invisibly past, releasing deadly cargoes of bombs that tumbled down, like dots of tiny black confetti, before erupting in great orange and yellow explosions that added yet more smoke and flame to the inferno.

Small black clouds appeared momentarily in the sky above Dunkirk then disappeared, but they were hopelessly low, well below the cloud base, presenting little danger to the swarms of German aircraft. It was like a scene from hell, and Tennant wondered how anything could possibly survive in that place, never mind succeed in boarding a ship for evacuation. God help them all if the weather cleared and the Luftwaffe were actually able to see what they were doing. Aware from the outset that his task of organising the evacuation of a quarter of a million men was already the tallest of orders, Tennant now saw the stark reality of what faced him. He glanced down the length of the coastline to the east of the town, seeing the pale white ribbon of the expansive beaches clearly in the morning light.

In happier times, they would have been crowded with holiday makers on sunny days. Now they sat deserted. He glanced down at the signal that had arrived from General Adam, the Army officer ashore who had been tasked with the defence of Dunkirk and the initial arrangements for evacuation. The message had not been intended for Tennant specifically but he had received a copy of it as an interested party. The message was blunt and to the point. Tennant scanned the critical sentence.

...Complete fighter protection now essential if serious disaster is to be avoided...

He stared back towards the burning port of Dunkirk as the destroyer edged closer. There was no disputing the accuracy of that analysis. Tennant glanced eastwards again, studying the endless beaches. After a moment or two, he spoke to the commander who was acting as his second in command.

"Just confirm for me... The Army is still holding a perimeter in that direction as far as Nieuport?"

"That's correct, Sir." The commander confirmed.

Tennant nodded silently at the officer's response. He drummed his fingers on the top of the bridge's shield for a moment then threw a look at his second in command.

"Make a signal to Flag Officer Dover at once..." He snapped. "Message is to read... *Please send every available craft to beaches east of Dunkirk immediately. Evacuation tomorrow night problematical.*"

DURIEZ FARM, LE PARADIS – 33 MILES SOUTH OF DUNKIRK
MONDAY 27TH MAY 1940 – 1400 HOURS

"Outside! Everyone who isn't needed! Man the farmyard perimeter!"

The voice of the Acting Commanding Officer resonated through the farmhouse.

"The forward companies have been over-run! It'll be our turn next! Let's be ready for it because we're not going back! We must hold the Jerries for as long as possible!"

Private Albert Middleton, a signaller in the 2nd Battalion of the Royal Norfolk Regiment, threw down his logbook and pencil and left his post by the field telephone. There was no point manning it anymore; the men at the other end of it were either dead or prisoners of war.

"Middleton; with me…" The voice of his detachment commander came from behind him.

Grabbing his rifle, Middleton turned and saw Corporal Riley standing at the foot of the stairs.

"We'll go out by the orchard; there's a long ditch there, by the hedgerow."

Wordlessly, Middleton followed the corporal at the double.

They were joined by another private, an orderly from the Officers' Mess by the name of Bentley. A jovial, slightly overweight soldier from Thetford, Bentley also had a reputation for being one of the best marksmen in the battalion. How he had ended up as an officer's orderly was a mystery. Now however, the pudgy faced man was pulling on his helmet and carrying his Lee-Enfield at the short trail, his face a mask of grim determination. Together they ran across the rear garden of the farmhouse and towards the edge of the orchard. A sergeant was ordering people into position, splitting the headquarters staff into pairs or threesomes and directing them towards outbuildings and dung heaps.

"Down here…" Riley called back over his shoulder, and Middleton saw the NCO drop down into a long, shallow, and mercifully dry ditch that bordered the orchard on the inside of its hedge. "We'll cover the right flank."

Middleton was disorientated. Having spent hours manning the field telephone inside the farmhouse, he had lost all sense of direction. Not too far away, the sound of sporadic gunfire grew louder, seeming to come from several directions. They were, he assumed, surrounded.

He dropped into position beside Riley, Bentley thumping down heavily next to him.

"Where are they coming from then, Corporal?" Middleton asked, sliding his rifle through the gap in the hedge and shrugging off a bandolier of spare ammunition at the same time.

"God knows!" The corporal grunted. "Everywhere probably. The Jerries are well over the canal by now, so they'll be spread out everywhere. Just keep your eyes peeled and shoot anything that doesn't look British!"

Several bursts of machine-gun fire sounded off to their left, further down the road in the tiny village. For a second, the three soldiers paused, cocking their ears to the wind and listening intently.

"They're nearly here…" Riley murmured ominously.

Bentley hawked and spat.

"Be nice to have a bit of practice with the old Lee-Enfield again." He observed phlegmatically.

Blam! Blam! Rat-tat-tat, blam!

The sudden eruption of gunfire from the far side of the farm made the trio jump.

"Keep down. Cover your arcs…" Riley pushed himself flat against the slope of the ditch and pulled his rifle butt into his shoulder. Middleton and Bentley followed suit. For long minutes, the three men listened to the fierce battle that was developing at the other side of the smallholding.

"Do you think we might be in the wrong place?" Bentley grunted. "Sounds like all the action is over that side."

"Be patient." Riley answered, curtly.

They continued to lay there, nerves on edge, wincing at every sudden flurry of gunfire.

"Why don't we just pull back, anyway?" Middleton asked after a while. "If our rifle companies can't hold 'em, what chance have we got?"

Riley gave the two privates a stern look.

"Because the whole BEF is trying to sort its bloody self out; that's why! Someone's got to hold these buggers up whilst our boys get a new defence line sorted out, Our orders are to hold out at all costs; to the last round…"

He tailed off for a moment, lost in his own thoughts. Suddenly, he looked up again.

"Anyway; can't be helped, can it? We're here; simple as that. We stand and fight."

Middleton experienced a sinking feeling in his gut.

"Ey up! Here they come!"

Bentley's warning snapped the other two men out of their private thoughts. Together, they threw a look across the wide field beyond the orchard. There they were; more than a dozen grey figures, blundering along the hedgerow at the far side of the meadow, as if trying to come in behind the farm complex. Unfortunately for them, they were walking straight into the field of fire of the three men from the Royal Norfolks. Riley bent his head to squint through his rifle sights.

"Bentley, you start from the front; I'll start from the rear. Middleton; you take the buggers in the centre. Ready?"

Bentley and Middleton grunted their acknowledgement. Riley didn't hesitate.

"Fire."

The first shots rang out from the ditch, and at the far side of the meadow, two of the enemy soldiers crashed down into the corn. The others, shocked by the sudden volley, froze in position, coming to a halt but neglecting to take cover.

Blam!

Bentley had already re-cocked his weapon and fired again. A third German soldier spun round and toppled over. The shot seemed to break the spell and the remaining Germans ducked into cover at the edge of the field.

"Just fire into the hedgerow where they went to ground!" Riley shouted as he fired another shot.

Middleton did as he was ordered, every nerve in his body alive with the thrill of the action. Working the bolt of his rifle like a man possessed, the young signaller emptied his entire magazine into the area where the Germans had taken cover.

"Reloading!" He warned, fumbling in his pouch for two more clips of ammunition.

Crack.

The first German bullet snapped through the branches above the heads of the three British infantrymen.

Crack-crack-crack-crack-crack!

A burst of automatic fire came their way.

"There's more of the bastards!" Bentley shouted.

Middleton slammed the bolt closed on his rifle and locked it, then slid the weapon forward again, adopting a fire position once more. He saw the new enemy threat immediately and caught his breath.

"Bloody hell! They must be ruddy mad!" Middleton cursed.

"Just shoot the fuckers!" Riley snarled.

Middleton stared in disbelief at another group of maybe twenty enemy soldiers who had pushed their way through the far hedgerow, and, rather than going to ground with their comrades, were now sprinting along the edge of the field towards the British held farm.

Blam. Blam.

Riley and Bentley fired. One of the running Germans dropped. Middleton pushed his eye up to the rear sight of his rifle and settled the foresight blade on the centre of the group, tracking their movement down the field.

Blam.

The sturdy Lee-Enfield lurched in his grip as it spat its deadly .303 inch bullet towards the advancing enemy. Middleton had no time to think now; the enemy weren't allowing him that luxury. The Germans were coming and Middleton had been ordered to fight to the last round. Working the bolt again, he fed a fresh round into the chamber of the rifle and prepared to do exactly that.

MAIN STREET, LE PARADIS – 33 MILES SOUTH OF DUNKIRK
MONDAY 27TH MAY 1940 – 1700 HOURS

"What the fuck's the hold up now?"

Merkal growled rhetorically as his car slowed, coming to a halt at the rear of the long convoy of trucks.

"Looks like Third Company's trucks, Hauptsturmfuhrer?" His driver suggested as he applied the hand-break.

"Fucking hell!" The SS company commander swore. "At some stage I would actually like to get to the front line. We've been sitting in reserve all pissing day!"

Merkal was in a foul mood, even by his own standards.

He was seething for numerous reasons. Firstly, his company, due to the heavy casualties it had suffered several days back near Arras, were being held back as the battalion reserve. To that end, Merkal had spent a long, miserable day, trundling along behind the spearhead companies of his battalion, covering no more than a couple of hundred metres an hour. He was desperate to see some action; lead his men in a glorious assault in order to prove himself. Instead he had been held back repeatedly from the fighting. And that fighting had been intense.

All day, the entire division had been forcing its way forward, over the La Bassee Canal and onwards, through one small farming village after another, raked all the way by constant gunfire which streaked across the flat, open fields, making progress both slow and deadly. In just the last hour, Merkal had come across numerous khaki clad bodies in the hedgerows and behind improvised barricades; but wherever he found a British corpse, he also found two or three dead SS men. And that fired his anger and frustration even more.

And of course, he was still smarting over the Arras incident. Every time he thought about the debacle, he rewrote the script in his own mind; justifying his own actions to himself. After the battle, when he had rejoined his battalion, he had delivered the news to his battalion commander that his company had suffered twenty seven men killed or missing and a further nineteen wounded. Expecting to be reprimanded for straying into another division's area and getting his company shot to pieces, Merkal had rehearsed his defence. It hadn't been necessary.

The remainder of his division had also been hit hard by an Allied counter-attack, which had inflicted a number of casualties and sent a shock wave of panic throughout the Totenkopf. Some said the enemy tanks had been

French, others claimed them to be British; either way, Merkal had found his own battalion commander rather shaken up. Thus, Merkal had been able to explain his own encounter in much more heroic terms than he had intended, claiming to have gone to the aid of 7th Panzer and standing shoulder to shoulder with them in order to prevent the divisional flank being turned. It had been a fortuitous break for Merkal; convenient to say the least, and had even earned him a brief *'well-done'* from the battalion commander.

Merkal still wasn't happy though. Every time he thought of those big British tanks chasing after him down the packed village street, a shiver of dread ran through him. And then there was that Army general. What was his name again? Rommel? That was it. Merkal remembered the shrewd, searching look that Rommel had given him, as if he could somehow read Merkal's thoughts and sense the lies that the SS officer was telling him. It had discomfited Merkal. And then of course, he had been bossed about by some jumped up captain on Rommel's staff; his company made to act as a defensive screen for the 7th Panzer Division's gun-line. The sheer cheek of it! All in all, it had been an inglorious start to Merkal's quest for an Iron Cross, and ultimately, a Knight's Cross. He looked at the stationary line of vehicles ahead and kicked the foot-well of his car in exasperation. On current form, he was unlikely to get the opportunity to win either of those decorations in the near future.

"Wait here." Merkal suddenly snapped at his driver. "I'll go and see what the fuck's going on..."

And with that, the hauptsturmfuhrer jumped out of the car and began stalking up the road towards the nearest truck. As he neared the rear vehicle, Merkal could see that the line of trucks stretched at least a hundred metres in front of him, right into the next village. Several SS men, presumably the drivers, stood around chatting by the cab of the second vehicle along.

"What's the hold up here?" Merkal snapped at the trio as he approached.

Turning at the sound of the officer's voice, the three men braced up in the position of attention and shot their arms out in salute.

"What's going on?" Merkal demanded again, not bothering to return the salutes. "Why aren't you moving?"

The three drivers exchanged worried looks, sensing the hauptsturmfuhrer's bad temper, and wondering which one of them would take the lead in replying. After a moment or two, the centre man cleared his throat and spoke.

"We've been ordered to wait here, Sir; by Hauptsturmfuhrer Knochlein. The companies are clearing out the last Tommies from the farm at the end of the village. The bastards held on until the very last moment."

Merkal frowned at the explanation.

"So, have the Tommies given up then, or what?"

The centre man nodded, his face serious.

"Yes, Sir; *eventually*. The boys had a hard fight though; from right back at the canal to this place. It looks like that was the last of the Tommies in the big farmhouse. The prisoners are just being rounded up now."

Merkal pulled a face.

"Prisoners? What the fuck are we wasting our time on prisoners for?"

He didn't give the soldier time to comment.

"Where's the battalion commander?" He snapped, changing the subject quickly.

The driver's face seemed to brighten, as if that were a question he was able to answer with ease.

"Oh, he's gone off in his car, Sir. He's been summoned to Regimental Headquarters for orders."

Merkal shook his head.

"So, who's in charge of this gang-fuck?" He waved his hand vaguely at the long column of parked lorries.

Again, the driver's face brightened and he pointed to a field, a little further up the road.

"All the other company commanders are up there, Sir; by the prisoner collection point. They're having a conference."

"Are they, by fuck?" Merkal muttered, and pushed past the three men; heading for the field in question.

He walked another hundred metres up the road, past several more vehicles, until he came to a gateway in the cattle fence that lined the highway. He glanced across the field and instantly recognised the figures of his fellow company commanders, standing in the centre of the meadow. From this distance, it appeared that the three men were holding a very animated conversation. Beyond them, he could see a crowd of SS men in the next field, the sound of bad-tempered shouting carrying across the evening air. Merkal stepped through the gateway and began walking towards his fellow officers. As he did so, he glanced to the right and frowned as he spotted the bodies of three dead SS men lying against the hedgerow.

Merkal stalked across the grass. As he neared the trio of officers, he took in the scene with interest. Knochlein, the hauptsturmfuhrer commanding Third Company, was looking angry, and kept waving his arms in the direction of the adjacent field. Next to him, Hauptsturmfuhrer Kaltofen, who commanded the First Company, was glaring at the third man, Obersturmfuhrer Loew, a junior officer to the others who had stepped up to command Second Company.

"What's going on, gentlemen?" Merkal announced his arrival loudly while he was still several paces away.

The three officers looked round at him as if surprised at being interrupted. When Knochlein saw Merkal, he relaxed slightly. Loew however, took a deep breath and looked away; a grimace on his face.

"Ah, Josef…" Knochlein greeted him. "Glad you've arrived. Perhaps you can help us to get Loew here to see sense?"

Merkal glanced at Loew who avoided his gaze, then looked back at Knochlein.

"Why? What's the matter?"

Instead of replying directly to the question, Knochlein fielded one of his own.

"How many men did you lose at Arras, to those Tommy tanks? The ones that gunned you down without giving you a chance to defend yourselves?"

Merkal felt his ego prickle with discomfort at the question, but he answered with a grunt regardless.

"Nearly thirty dead; total of fifty with the wounded… Tommy bastards!"

Knochlein turned his eyes back to Loew.

"Exactly. And we all took casualties ourselves. Admittedly, they weren't as bad as poor Josef's company, but today we have suffered our own share of heavy losses. The Tommies should have given up a long time ago when they realised they were beaten, instead of playing games with us…"

Loew glared up at Knochlein and the others.

"They were doing their duty, Hauptsturmfuhrer." He said through gritted teeth. "They were fighting as soldiers are expected to."

Kaltofen, standing silently to one side, looked away at Loew's comment, shaking his head. Knochlein exploded.

"For fuck's sake, man! These bastards deserve to be shot! In fact, shooting's too good for them! They've been using dum-dum bullets…"

"How do you know that?" Loew shouted back at the senior officer, his own anger surfacing now. "Where's your proof?"

"And they used a white flag illegally!" Knochlein screamed back at him.

"I've only seen one white flag!" Loew responded. "And that was back at the farm when the survivors surrendered to us!"

The two SS officers stood glaring at each other for a long moment, whilst Merkal and Kaltofen watched with grim fascination. After a moment, Knochlein leaned forward and sneered at the junior officer, his voice dropping to a low, venomous hiss.

"Loew, stop being such a fucking scared little rabbit."

For a second, it looked as if the obersturmfuhrer was going to launch himself at the senior officer, his fists suddenly clenching into tight balls of white-knuckled fury. Quickly however, Merkal stepped between them and put a restraining hand on Loew's chest. The young officer looked up at Merkal, his eyes betraying cold, uncompromising hatred.

"Go back to your company, Obersturmfuhrer." Merkal snapped; his voice as cold as the other man's gaze. "You are no longer required. We'll take care of this business."

For several heartbeats, Loew held Merkal's gaze then, slowly, he took a cautious step backwards. He switched his eyes back to Knochlein, then Kaltofen, then back to Merkal. The young man's face betrayed a look of utter disgust.

"Fine." He said tightly through clenched teeth, still fighting to control his anger. "So be it. I joined the SS to be a soldier. I won't be a part of this…"

And with that, the obersturmfuhrer turned on his heel and stalked away. As he stomped off, Knochlein hawked and spat on the grass.

"Fucking jumped up little shit! Who does he think he is?"

Merkal turned to face his fellow company commander.

"Never mind that spoilt brat now." He said. "Where are these Tommy prisoners?"

Knochlein nodded to the adjacent field.

"Just over there. They're being stripped of their kit and searched."

Merkal looked across to the field and suddenly noticed that beyond the swarms of SS men, there were knots of dishevelled looking men in khaki being pushed and herded into position. The ground all about them was strewn with the funny shaped Tommy helmets and beige coloured packs and pouches. His mind worked quickly. Suddenly, he visualised the long brick barn that was situated by the road where he had left his own car. He flung a look at Knochlein.

"Right then, let's get this sorted, shall we? Fritz, get your men to bring the Tommies onto the road here. Bring them down the road until you reach the front of my company's vehicles. You'll see a gateway into a meadow, with a brick-built barn inside it. Direct the prisoners in there and get them to line up along the wall of the barn; then keep your men well back."

Knochlein stared back at Merkal thoughtfully, understanding what it was that his fellow officer was suggesting they do.

"No problem." Knochlein replied calmly.

"I'll go and get things organised at my end." Merkal said. "Get them moving, Fritz; as quick as you can. Let's get this over with."

And with that, Merkal turned and began moving at speed back the way he had come. As he reached the road, he shouted at the waiting drivers of the stationary vehicles. "Get these trucks out of the way! Clear the road! If you can't go forward then pull the vehicle's over onto the verge. Come on, move it!"

As the drivers ran to their vehicles to comply with the orders, Merkal began jogging back down the road towards his own car, a sense of wicked excitement rising inside him. As he neared the front of his own company column, he saw one of his officers talking to his staff car driver.

"Lodzen!" He called out to the man. "Get me two machine-gun teams up here, now! And a couple of NCOs with machine-pistols too!"

The officer stared back at Merkal for a moment, then turned and ran back towards the nearest truck, shouting instructions as he went.

"What's going on, Hauptsturmfuhrer?" His driver asked, looking perplexed as Merkal leaned into the car and retrieved the MP40 machine-pistol that lay on the back seat.

"Nothing much." Merkal quipped, checking the magazine on the machine-pistol then cocking it sharply, ready to fire. "Just a bit of tidying up to do and then we can get back to the war…"

With that cryptic explanation, Merkal walked around the car and headed for the gateway into the nearby field. As he strode through the gateway, the first machine-gun team came doubling up to him, their weapons and ammunition boxes rattling as they clattered along the cobbles.

"Where do you want us, Hauptsturmfuhrer?"

Merkal walked into the field and waved to the far side of the meadow.

"Set up over there, pointing directly at this barn. Shortly you will have a target to fire at. It will be right in front of the barn. Open fire when I tell you."

Needing no further explanation, the gun team doubled off across the field to take up position. As they did so, two junior NCOs and another gun team came running up behind him. Without fuss, Merkal issued them similar orders and dispersed them to various spots in the field. Having made sure they were all in the right place, the hauptsturmfuhrer strolled back across to the gate. Moments later, Knochlein and his men arrived with the Tommy prisoners.

Merkal surveyed the column as it shambled towards them. There must have been almost a hundred Tommy prisoners; a curious mixture of younger and older soldiers, dark and fair complexions, tall and short, fat and thin. A collection of mongrels when compared against the tall, well built, Aryan looking SS guards that escorted them, Merkal thought. Pathetic in fact,

Merkal revised his opinion. Many of them were hobbling like old men, or holding injured limbs. Several had bloodstained bandages around their heads and none of them wore helmets. Merkal watched nervous looking prisoners being herded like sheep towards him. So this was the much vaunted British Army, was it? He felt his anger surface as he realised that it was a ragged collection of individuals like this who had inflicted so many casualties on his own, elite unit of the Waffen SS.

"Into the field! Keep walking!"

The leading SS guards, shouting in a mixture of German and English, were pushing the Tommies at the front of the column into the field, directing them along the side of the barn wall. Merkal saw Knochlein appear at his side. The two men exchanged a brief look, nodding wordlessly to each other as the Tommies were ushered through the gateway.

At the rear of the column, one of the Tommy soldiers, looking terrified, suddenly came to a standstill. He muttered something in English and then turned back towards the road, as if he was going to make a break for freedom. Merkal jerked his own machine-pistol up in case the Tommy ran, but there was no need. One of Knochlein's men strode over to the man, levelling his rifle, and poked the man in his stomach with the muzzle of the weapon.

"Get in the field you Tommy shit!" The SS guard snarled at him.

With a look of hopelessness, the Tommy turned back again and followed his comrades into the field.

The last of the Tommies were in the meadow now, arrayed in two long lines as they shambled alongside the barn. At the front of the column, Merkal saw the first signs of alarm amongst the British prisoners as they realised that the field appeared to have no other exit. Then several of the prisoners spotted the two machine-guns that were trained on them and a small ripple of panic began to spread through the khaki-clad ranks.

"Oh, sweet Jesus, no…"

"Our Father, who art in heaven…"

"German bastards…"

Merkal didn't speak much English. He had no idea what the prisoners were calling out. To be honest, he didn't even care. He turned to face his men at the other side of the small meadow and waved his hand at them, calling out as he did so.

"Okay Fourth Company… Fire!"

The peace and quiet of the warm spring evening was suddenly shattered as the deadly rattle of machine-gun fire split the air… and the screaming began.

2ND BATTALION COLDSTREAM GUARDS – SOMEWHERE NORTH-WEST OF LILLE
MONDAY 27TH MAY 1940 – 1950 HOURS

"I'm sorry, Sir, but this is fucking bollocks!"

Jackson, squatting next to Dunstable by the side of the road, could barely suppress his anger and frustration. Less than a week ago, Jackson and Dunstable's platoon had helped to repulse two German incursions across the River Escaut, and, as far as Jackson knew, the story had been the same all the way along the BEF's front; the Germans had been pushed back with heavy losses. It had therefore been hugely depressing when the orders came through on the evening of the next day that the BEF was withdrawing again, this time back to the original defences on the Franco-Belgian border that the British Army had spent all winter digging.

Several more days had passed on that latest defence line, known as the Gort Line to the British, fending off yet more German attacks once the enemy had finally caught up with the BEF once more. Now however, even that defence line was being given up and the men of the 1st Guards Brigade were on the move once again. All of this, combined with the wet weather of the last couple of days, had turned Jackson's temperament to the acidic side of sour.

"How is it that every time we give the Jerries a good pasting, it's us that has to withdraw? I don't get it! What the fuck is General Headquarters playing at?"

Dunstable tried to empathise with the irate sergeant. In truth, he too was beginning to wonder what on earth was going on. The orders that filtered down from above were often very short and to the point. It had been just such an order that had resulted in Dunstable's platoon being moved to their present location. Told only that they were withdrawing, with no definite destination, nor any time frames or distances mentioned, the platoon, and indeed the whole battalion, had been marching since early evening to this rendezvous point. Now they sat by the side of the road, spread along it in two long, staggered khaki lines, awaiting their next instructions.

In the field to one side of the road, there was a sudden eruption of noise. Both Dunstable and Jackson glanced up as a battery of 25 Pounder field guns roared defiantly, dirty grey smoke spewing from their muzzles. The barrels of the guns were elevated to an extreme angle, which suggested that they were engaging the enemy at maximum range; covering the withdrawal of the infantry units. Behind the guns, efficient looking gunners knelt or stood rigidly to attention, moving only on the orders barked out by the NCOs in charge, flipping out expended shell cases and ramming home fresh ones. The sight was somewhat reassuring to the watching guardsmen. Here was evidence that at least one other unit was still operating properly, with discipline, as it should be.

"Look on the bright side." Dunstable said in a soothing voice, turning his attention back to Jackson. "At least we managed to have a decent rest while we were in the last position. I know we had a few more scraps but nothing as big as the Escaut. I reckon I've managed to catch a good eight or nine hours sleep over the last couple of days. Shame about the rations being cut down though..."

Jackson simply made a growling noise in his throat. Producing his battered little tourist map, Dunstable opened the document to where Lille was marked.

"Here, look..." He showed the map to Jackson. "Let's see if we can work out what's going on.

Together, the two men peered down at the map.

"This is where we made our stand at the Dyle; then at the Dendre, then the Escaut..."

The lieutenant pointed sequentially at the series of defensive positions they had occupied over the last two and a half weeks.

"And then we were there, just in front of Lille. So now we must be back up here somewhere..."

Jackson was frowning.

"You said the other day that the Germans were making headway to the south though... So, if that's the case, why aren't we heading that way... towards Paris; attacking them? Looks to me like we're starting to peel back towards the sea?"

"That is *exactly* what we are doing."

The sound of Captain Pilkington's voice behind them made both men jump. They jerked their heads up to see the Company Commander's face peering down between them at their map.

"Never told me you had a map of your own Harry..."

Dunstable went red.

"Just an old road map my father lent me..." He muttered sheepishly.

"Right, well..." Pilkington groaned tiredly as he knelt down between Dunstable and Jackson. "Let me show you what I *think* is going on, shall I?"

The Captain reached in his pocket and produced the worn stub of a pencil.

"Christ almighty, my knees are bloody killing me. Must be getting old, eh?" The captain grumbled as he fished the pencil out.

He took hold of Dunstable's map at one edge.

"Put your hand under it Harry and hold it steady."

Dunstable did as he was told.

"Alright, gentlemen… you mentioned our defensive lines…" Pilkington said, drawing several straight, bold pencil marks down the map, roughly over the series of rivers that Dunstable had just pointed out seconds earlier.

"Now, the reason we've had to do that is because the Jerries have broken through right down here…" His pencil dropped well down the map to a place where a city called Sedan was marked. "And they've driven a wedge right through the French and British armies like this…" Pilkington drew a long, sweeping arrow right across the bottom of the map and kept on going, angling upwards until the point of the pencil reached the coast.

"That's where the Germans are now apparently."

He tapped his pencil just over where the town of Boulogne was marked on the north coast of France. Jackson let out a gasp.

"Fucking hell…" His frustration had been replaced by dread realisation.

"My thoughts exactly, Sergeant J; my thoughts exactly. Not a good situation at all is it?"

He looked from Jackson to Dunstable, then began to draw little arrows coming off the big, curved one, all of them turning inwards towards the pocket-shaped bit of map that it encompassed. The little arrows were pointing at places like Lille, Bethune and Hazebrouck.

"And it's getting worse. We're completely surrounded. Our ammunition, food and fuel are all running out, and the Jerries have got hundreds of tanks, so I'm told. I haven't seen one of our own tanks yet, however; don't know about you chaps? In short, we're pretty much buggered. So we've been ordered back. I've just received the word from Battalion Headquarters. We're moving off again in ten minutes. This time we're marching all the way back to Dunkirk; here on the coast."

Pilkington used his pencil to draw a small ellipse around the port of Dunkirk which showed on the map as being the last major place on the French coast before the Belgian border.

"So…what's the plan when we get there, Sir?" Jackson asked, his eyes still glued to the symbols that the captain had drawn on the map.

"Well…" Pilkington began, letting out a tired sigh, "it seems that we either catch a boat back to England… or we go down fighting."

THE EAST MOLE – DUNKIRK HARBOUR
MONDAY 27TH MAY 1940 – 2200 HOURS

It was dark; just. The raids had gone on all day, and the result was, quite simply, that Dunkirk Harbour was beyond use as an embarkation point. The entire place was a burning, rubble strewn mess. That said, the decision to use the beaches that day had not proved to be much of a better solution. The beaches here on this part of the coast shelved gently away, so even the smaller boats from the evacuation force were having to hold off some hundred yards or more from the shore itself, meaning that the troops were having to wade out, and in some cases swim, to the boats; the small lighters, patrol boats or life boats from destroyers and passenger ferries. Then of course, the troops had to get into those boats, something easier said than done. Even in a gentle swell, it was a real danger that the smaller boats would be swamped or capsized as they tried to haul men aboard.

All in all, it had been a slow day for the evacuation; painfully slow. Tennant's staff estimated that the number of troops who had got off today wasn't much more than eight or nine thousand. It was nowhere near enough. Not when the BEF numbered a quarter of a million men, all of whom would be busy fighting their way back to Dunkirk, expecting to find salvation when they arrived. And of course, there were the depressing estimates from certain military sources who reckoned that the Germans could be at the beaches within the next day and a half if the BEF and their French allies were unable to slow them down considerably. And that was why right now, as darkness fell, giving them some degree of cover, Tennant and his staff were about to conduct an experiment, the results of which could mean either disaster or salvation for the BEF.

He stared along the East Mole, out towards the Channel. Despite the darkness, he could see, with his peripheral vision, that a large, bulky, black silhouette was filling the water towards the end of the East Mole.

"Here she comes…" Tennant mumbled to himself.

"Do you want me to release the troops, Sir?"

Tennant glanced at the sub-lieutenant standing next to him by the door of his command post. He thought for a moment. Time was of the essence.

"Yes, set them off; but make sure you've got a Petty Officer and a couple of ratings at the front to keep them in order and make sure they don't swamp the berthing party before everything is ready to go. Let's keep it all calm, eh?"

"Aye, aye, Sir." The sub-lieutenant saluted and turned away, moving off to where a column of tired, nervous, and thoroughly demoralised soldiers waited on the edge of the main harbour wall.

The plan was simple enough, if it worked. The East Mole was not a structure designed for ships to berth against. It was, more or less, just a long break-water made from huge piles of stone that extended out from the main harbour wall. Usefully however, the rough line of the mole was provided with a narrow wooden walk-way that was elevated above the mole itself. If it was possible to get the larger ships alongside the mole, and hold them steady, then there was a possibility of speeding up the rate of embarkation dramatically. *If* it was possible.

To that end, Tennant had ordered the first vessel available to come into the harbour as soon as it was dark and attempt to manoeuvre itself up against the mole. That ship was now just minutes away from establishing whether the plan was going to work or not, and the name of that ship was Queen of the Channel, one of the modern ferries. As he stood there in the dark, listening to the noise of hundreds of hob-nailed boots clattering on wooden planks, Tennant shifted from foot to foot, wracking his brains. What if this didn't work? What then? What other options were there?

"That's them on their way, Sir."

The sub-lieutenant was back, confirming that the column of troops had begun to move along the East Mole.

"Thank you." Tennant acknowledged. "We'll know soon enough, then."

"There's a land-line down, Sir. We've run it along to the berthing point at the far end. They'll ring through once they've got an answer."

Tennant took a deep breath and sank back into his private thoughts.

He lost track of the time. Everything faded to background noise. The distant shellfire of the battles being fought to the west of Dunkirk, the sound of the passing soldiers, and the quiet, urgent conversations of his command post staff as they calmly went about their business. Tennant lost himself in the hundreds of minor details that affected his ability to rise to the task he had been set. Admiral Ramsay in Dover would do everything he could for him, of that he was sure. But how to make it all work, here on the ground in Dunkirk? That was the issue. He thought about the tides, and the time it took for a full round-trip by each ship going from Dover, to Dunkirk, and back to Dover. He thought of the average troop carrying capacities of each type of vessel, from the destroyers who could lift a few hundred, to the big ferries and personnel ships who could take a thousand or more. And of course, he thought of the Luftwaffe; and how kind the weather would be, or otherwise.

Brrrrrrrrrr.

After what seemed a life-time, the distinctive vibration of the field telephone snapped him out of his thoughts. Tennant glanced through the darkness to see the sub-lieutenant reach across for the handset.

"Command post." The young man's voice quipped in business-like fashion.

A pause.

"Okay; well done. I'll brief the Senior Naval Officer and get back to you."

Click. The handset went down on the cradle again. Tennant held his breath. He watched as the pale blob of the lieutenant's face turned towards him.

"Captain Tennant, Sir? That was the berthing party…"

Tennant fought to keep his voice calm.

"Yes?"

"They say that the Queen of the Channel has successfully come alongside the East Mole. They're securing her with lines now and they estimate they'll be ready to start boarding troops within ten minutes. Apparently there's a bit of a drop onto the deck from the gangway so they're going to lash ladders and planks from the mole down to the ship."

Tennant felt the adrenalin race through his veins. It was going to work.

"Good." He snapped. "Let me know as soon as the troops are starting to board. I want them counted as they embark and I want the speed of embarkation timed. Meanwhile, signal to all destroyers and personnel ships currently off Dunkirk. Tell them to pair up and prepare to dock against the East Mole on orders. As soon as the Queen of the Channel has backed out, I want the next two ships coming in."

Tennant looked off into the darkness where he knew hundreds of men were poised to start clambering down from the mole and onto the waiting ship. It was going to work, by God; it was going to work.

Tuesday 28th May 1940
The Nineteenth Day

THE OPEN FLANK – NIEUPORT, BELGIUM, 17 MILES EAST OF DUNKIRK
TUESDAY 28TH MAY 1940 – 1100 HOURS

Lieutenant Jeremy Cummings of the 12th Royal Lancers had a bad feeling. He couldn't explain it, but something wasn't right. His unit had been sent to Nieuport in order to guard this flank of the Dunkirk perimeter and prepare it for occupation by units from the 2nd Corps of the British

Expeditionary Force. Originally, it seemed, there had been an assumption that the Belgian Army would be covering this particular end of the pocket, the small port being just across the Belgian border. However, over the last twenty four hours, there had been rumour upon rumour about the Belgians. Some said that the Belgians were on their last legs. Others said that they were still fighting but that they were incapable of holding the Germans back. At least one report suggested that the Belgian Army had already surrendered and that it was only a matter of hours before the Germans arrived at Dunkirk.

That particular thought alarmed Cummings. His unit was an armoured car regiment. They were not tanks, being thinly armoured and equipped only with light machine guns and the odd Boys Rifle. Their job was reconnaissance and mobile flank protection. Conducting positional defence was not what their Morris armoured cars were best suited for, especially against the might of the seemingly unstoppable German Army. What if the Belgians had given in? By Cummings' reckoning there would be nothing between the Germans and Dunkirk apart from him and his much depleted regiment.

The subaltern raised his binoculars, resting his elbows on the bonnet of his armoured car and scanned the distant fields and roads across the canal. He started from the left, where a small force of Royal Engineers were urgently preparing the demolition charges on the nearest bridge, whilst simultaneously trying to control the constant flow of refugees coming back across the water feature. In truth though, the flow of civilians had become nothing more than a trickle. Even the civilian population, without any understanding of Allied strategy, could see that Dunkirk would soon become a tiny pocket of resistance against which the full weight of the German Army and Luftwaffe would be thrown. Most of them by now, realised that they were better off trying to let the German advance wash over them, rather than fall back in time with it and be caught in the middle of someone else's battle.

He scanned to the right, past an old warehouse and a small set of storage tanks. Beyond the suburbs of Nieuport, the flat green fields of Flanders ran endlessly into the distance. Far away behind Cummings, towards Dunkirk, the sound of bombing and shelling continued unabated. To the east however, all was quite still. Ominously quiet. No Belgian Army on the move towards Dunkirk. No sound of battle in the far distance. Cummings glanced at his watch. If only the infantry units from 2nd Corps would arrive, he would feel much better. Something caught his eye.

A flash of some kind; the reflection of light on metal or glass? He peered even more intently through the binoculars, studying the area of his vision where he had seen the sudden glint. He could see the tree lined avenues of the long, narrow roads, the flat landscape, the small, coloured blobs of civilians ambling along those roads…

"Bugger!"

Cummings held his breath, blinked once, then looked again. No mistake. Heads wearing helmets… Men who were travelling either in several cars or on motorbikes; hard to tell which. Moving fast; coming towards the bridge.

"Start her up!" Cummings shouted to his driver and snatched the binoculars away from his eyes.

He grabbed hold of the vehicle's hull and began hauling himself up the side. As he did so, he shouted back over his shoulder.

"Corporal Sykes! Stand-to! Mount up and cover the bridge from here. I'm going forward onto the bridge to speak to the Sappers."

He dropped into the turret of the vehicle, pointing vaguely across the canal.

"Vehicles approaching from the east at speed! Keep your eyes on them!"

He snapped out his orders to his driver.

"Forward. Onto the bridge; quick as you like. Jones?" He flung a look at the gunner. "Get that gun ready to go; we might have a problem…"

With a healthy roar, the armoured car pulled forwards and began rolling along the street towards the canal bridge. As it did so, the armoured car commanded by Corporal Sykes trundled forwards to occupy the position vacated by his officer.

With increasing speed, the Morris armoured car made for the bridge just two hundred yards away, the driver gunning the engine. In the turret, Sykes struggled to pull the chin strap of his helmet down over his face, whilst throwing a worried glance across the waterway to check on the progress of the approaching vehicles. His heart lurched. The approaching vehicles were probably only three hundred yards from the bridge now and Cummings could see that the two leading machines were definitely both motorcycle combinations. Behind them, a big, open topped car followed. They didn't look Belgian to him, and they were certainly not British.

"Take us right onto the bridge!" He shouted to the driver over the growl of the engine.

His armoured car was about seventy five yards from the bridge now. On the bridge itself, Cummings saw the heads of the Royal Engineers look up at the sound of his revving engine. Some of them knelt there for a while, detonation cord in hand, gawping at him as he began waving frantically with his hands. At the far side, a small knot of Sappers acting as sentries were looking backwards and forwards between Cummings' vehicle and the other machines that were approaching from the east.

"Stand-to!" Cummings shouted the old military term, reasoning that it was a phrase impossible to misinterpret. "Stand-to! I think they're Jerries!"

It was a handful of civilians who first understood what was about to happen. As the Morris armoured car slowed, ready for the turn onto the bridge, Cummings saw the group of refugees suddenly break into a frantic run for the west bank, and the sound of terrified female screams came to him over the noise of his vehicle's engine.

The 4 ton armoured car swung unsteadily round the corner and onto the canal bridge. As it did so, Cummings glanced down and saw two more Sappers manning a barricade constructed from an old cart and various items of furniture taken from nearby houses.

"Stand-to!" Cummings shouted down to them as his vehicle angled past them. "Looks like Jerry's here!"

He caught a brief glimpse of the shocked looks on the faces of the two soldiers, but then he was hanging onto the side of the turret as the armoured car swung onto the bridge itself.

The driver had to put the brakes on almost immediately as they found themselves confronted by a dozen or so civilians coming straight towards them, right in the centre of the carriageway.

"Get out of the way!" Cummings yelled. "Get out of the way! Move over!"

The driver gunned the engine once more and nudged the vehicle forward a few yards as the cluster of refugees split and began to filter to the sides of the bridge.

"What's going on?" A worried looking Royal Engineer sergeant came running across to them from where he had been supervising a demolition party.

"I think we've got Jerries coming up the road..." Cummings warned him. "Any moment now! Get your men back over this side and stand-by to blow the bridge!"

The sergeant swore, his face betraying alarm.

"Shit! We're not ready to blow yet!"

Cummings felt his stomach go suddenly heavy, and a terrible, sinking feeling seemed to swallow him up. Just at that point, the Sapper guards at the far side of the bridge let out a cry of alarm and one of them brought up his rifle and fired at a target that was still out of view beyond the warehouse. There was a sudden 'crack-crack-crack' of automatic fire and the Sapper who had fired suddenly dropped to the floor like a stone. The two other men who had been standing with man suddenly turned and ran back onto the bridge, a look of terror obvious on their faces.

"Get it sorted!" Cummings blurted to the sergeant then slapped his driver on the shoulder hard. "Forward!"

The armoured car purred as the driver threw it in gear and drove it onwards, over the bridge. Even as the vehicle began to pull forward however, the Germans appeared in front of them. The motorcycle combination roared onto the bridge from the road behind the warehouse, hardly bothering to reduce speed, and the rider was forced to make a severe correction in order not to lose control. In the sidecar, his passenger opened fire with the light machine-gun that was mounted on its front. It was a wild burst, fired instinctively, and Cummings heard the sharp crack of the bullets flying wildly past.

The Germans were, perhaps, just as surprised as the British, and Cummings watched with a certain sense of satisfaction as the rider on the motorcycle slammed on his breaks and brought the bike to a halt, skidding to one side as he did so.

"Ram the bastard!" Cummings heard himself saying as he fumbled for the revolver in his holster. As he dragged the .38 inch service revolver from its place at his waist, the gunner let out a snort.

"We're too close to 'em; I can't bring the gun to bear..."

Crunch.

The armoured car smashed into the stalled motorcycle combination with a sickening thud, pushing it to the left and toppling it over. Cummings heard the crew screaming in terror as the heavy British armoured car hit them with brutal force.

At that point, another German motorcycle combination appeared from behind the warehouse, this one moving with more caution and slowing to a controlled halt at the approach to the bridge.

"Kill *those* buggers, then Jones!" Cummings shouted at the gunner, and a split second later the machine-gun hammered into life.

Cummings didn't bother to watch. He leaned out of his turret and pointed his revolver down at the wreckage of the first motorcycle combination, where its crew members were desperately struggling to scramble clear of the ruined machine.

Blam! Blam, blam! Blam!

Cummings emptied his revolver at the two men, shooting until the pistol was empty and both Germans flopped lifelessly on the tarmac.

Rat-tat-tat-tat-tat!

Cummings pulled himself back inside the turret as Jones let loose with another burst. The lieutenant flicked his gaze to the eastern end of the bridge once more and was surprised to see the German motorcycle pulling away in a tight circle as it attempted to get back behind the cover of the warehouse. As the rider brought the machine around, its exhaust blowing grey-blue smoke, Cummings noticed the man in the sidecar was hanging limply over the side, his grey tunic stained a dark red.

Beneath Cummings' feet, he felt the roar of his own vehicle's engine and the armoured car suddenly lurched forward in pursuit, pushing aside the last bits of wreckage from the first motorcycle combination.

"Stop!" The officer slapped the driver's shoulder again. "Reverse back; slowly. Very slowly."

The driver did as he was ordered and threw the vehicle into reverse.

"Jones, keep your eyes peeled on that end of the bridge!" Cummings snapped as he flung his gaze behind him.

Back along the canal, Cummings could see tracer from Sykes' armoured car streaking across the water and towards more targets, back beyond the warehouse. Behind Sykes' vehicle, on the friendly bank, another armoured car poked its nose out of a side street, alerted by the gunfire.

At the friendly side of the canal, the Sappers were gathering behind the barricade, preparing to make a stand behind the flimsy obstacle, whilst kneeling in the middle of the bridge still, was the sergeant and one of his men.

"How long before you're ready to blow?"

Cummings yelled down at the NCO as his vehicle juddered rearwards.

The man glanced up from his work only briefly.

"Five minutes? You sure we're okay to blow this? Have we got any of our blokes still on the other side?"

Cummings grimaced.

"If they *are* on that side then they're already prisoners! And God only knows what's happened to the Belgians! Just get that done as quickly as you can. We'll stop here and give you some cover. As soon as you're ready, let's blow this bridge to 'kingdom come'!"

TENNANT'S COMMAND POST – DUNKIRK HARBOUR TUESDAY 28TH MAY 1940 – 1430 HOURS

Tennant was used to the smell of burning oil now. After thirty-six hours it was just a natural part of his environment. And after ten hours of constant rain, the slate grey clouds and incessant drizzle was becoming just as much a part of the Dunkirk experience for him. That said, he resented neither. Far from it; he welcomed the bad weather. The troops might be getting cold and wet as they waited for evacuation, and the sea might be a shade more choppy, but the combination of heavy cloud, rain and plumes of burning fuel meant that the Luftwaffe were largely unable to interfere with Tennant's operation. And that was important, because following last night's successful trial with the East Mole, the pace of the evacuation had picked up dramatically. Yesterday they had managed to get away just short of eight thousand men according to a signal from Dover Command. Today he reckoned they could double that at least.

But still it needed to be faster. The liaison officer from the BEF's Rear HQ had informed him that the first echelons of the fighting divisions were starting to reach their fall-back positions to the south of Dunkirk. Before long, there would be almost a quarter of a million men squeezing into the perimeter, followed hotly by the entire German Army. Speed was vital now. He needed the weather to stay bad, and the ships to come round faster. Day time trips via Route Z had been suspended, as that took ships directly under the guns of the German artillery based on the coastline at Calais. Route Y, the safest route, was also the longest way by far, thus making it a lengthy round trip for the ships involved.

As he considered this, Tennant looked across at the sub-lieutenant acting as watchkeeper in this, his small command post, based in one of the purpose made bunkers on the fortified harbour.

"Mr Drake? Please remind me? What was the estimate from Dover Command on getting Route X cleared?"

The young officer looked up.

"They said it should be clear by mid-afternoon tomorrow, Sir; all being well."

"All being well..." Tennant murmured, considering the answer.

Another twenty four hours. The Germans could be here by then.

"What's the latest Met' Report telling us?" He changed the subject effortlessly, his agile mind working overtime.

"Much the same for the next twelve hours or so; clearing by tomorrow, Sir. There's a possibility of thunderstorms during this afternoon apparently."

"That's good." Tennant snapped, his face becoming animated for a few brief moments. "That's very good."

"Indeed, Sir." The sub-lieutenant agreed. "Unusual though, don't you think? Thunder in May? Not what you'd expect really; a tad unseasonal."

"It can be as unseasonal as it wants to be Mr Drake; rain and thunder all week for all I care. Anything that keeps the Luftwaffe away and slows the Germans down, I'll take it."

Beside the two officers, a figure in khaki suddenly appeared in the doorway of the small bunker. Turning to view the new arrival, Tennant saw that it was the Army lieutenant colonel from the BEF's Rear Headquarters at La Panne, where the military side of the operation was being conducted.

"Ah, Robert!" Tennant greeted the soldier. "Lovely weather we're having, eh? Just perfect! And you've got the message about the East Mole? We need to keep feeding troops in this direction. We'll still continue to lift from the beaches too, and I've asked Dover Command for more small craft, but the East Mole is the key to everything. We've moved thousands already since last night, and as long as we keep the pump primed, we'll get thousands more away by the end of the day."

The lieutenant colonel removed his helmet and wiped his rain spattered face with a handkerchief.

"That's great news, Bill; absolutely brilliant... and not a moment too soon. We need to get the pace of the evacuation stepped up as quickly as we can."

The officer paused for a moment and gave Tennant a serious look.

"The Germans are in Nieuport."

Tennant stared back at the soldier wordlessly. After a while, he found his voice.

"Nieuport?"

"Yes, I'm afraid so." Bridgeman sighed. "As soon as the Belgians surrendered this morning, the Germans came tearing through their lines towards us. Fortunately we've only seen their advanced reconnaissance units at the moment. We're holding them; just. We're hoping to have our first full fighting division in the perimeter by nightfall and we'll throw them straight in there to hold that flank up."

Tennant's mind began whirring again. It seemed as if every time he solved one problem, two more appeared.

"*Can* you hold them?" He asked the colonel.

"I think so. We should just do it. We're going to have a desperate battle but I'm sure we can hold them off. Although it's not the Germans in Nieuport that are going to be the problem of course..."

Tennant frowned.

"How do you mean?"

The colonel shook his head.

"Holding Nieuport is vital, obviously, but the very fact that the Germans have advanced that far means that even if we hold out, they will still be able to bring their artillery within range of the beaches. By this time tomorrow, it won't just be the Luftwaffe that's the problem. The troops on the beaches will be under shell-fire too."

Tennant heaved a deep sigh, sucked his teeth for a moment then turned to the first-lieutenant.

"Mr Drake, start drafting a signal to Dover Command. Tell them that time is running out. Tell them I need Route X cleared with all speed. And tell them I need every single boat they can spare. Anything that floats, I need it here at Dunkirk, and I need it now…"

Wednesday 29th May 1940
The Twentieth Day

THE DUNKIRK PERIMETER – 6 MILES SOUTH EAST OF DUNKIRK
WEDNESDAY 29TH MAY 1940 – 1200 HOURS

"**B**loody hell, Harry! Have you ever seen anything like it?"

Pilkington, standing beside the young platoon commander, shook his head in disbelief. The flotsam and jetsam of several retreating armies was streaming over the bridge, and clogging the roads as far back as the eye could see. The 1st Guards Brigade, of which 2nd Battalion Coldstream Guards was a part, had arrived here late the previous evening and now they had been ordered to hold the stretch of the Dunkirk perimeter, just south of a village called Uxem.

Based on a wide canal-line, the perimeter had been carefully sited. Many of the surrounding fields, being low lying, had been flooded as an extra defensive measure All in all, the Germans, when they finally appeared, would find themselves faced with a significant obstacle to overcome. That said, the openness of the ground also meant that once battle was joined, the men of the 1st Guards Brigade would have little opportunity of getting away when the time came, unless they were able to move during the hours of darkness.

Beside the Company Commander, Dunstable shook his head, mimicking the older officer.

"It's awful, Sir. It really is. Quite sickening…"

"Yes… I know what you mean."

Together, the two Coldstream officers watched the constant stream of retreating soldiers. They were a mix of French and British; on the whole looking tired, sullen and frightened. The French particularly were in a bad mood, and didn't resemble much of a fighting force. They were getting especially hot under the collar when they were ordered to turn their vehicles around and dump them back down the road, well south of the canal. Such instructions, when given by the Coldstreamers, were usually greeted with a stream of French obscenities, followed by accusations of 'treachery'.

There were exceptions of course. One French unit, perhaps a slightly under-strength company of grim, yet determined looking infantry, had arrived at the bridge, still in possession of their packs, helmets and weapons. Their officer; a shrewd, tough looking captain, announced that he had been tasked to retire to the Dunkirk 'fortress' and adopt a defensive position to the west of Bergues. Pilkington and Dunstable, using the latter's tourist map, happily directed the captain and his men along the canal road towards their intended destination, and offered their best wishes for the impending battle. With a brief word of thanks and a smart salute, the dour French captain had marched his troops off, their cohesive appearance all the more striking against the background of chaos that surrounded them.

The British, on the whole, were a little more disciplined than the French, though not all of them by any means. And, like the French, many of the British arrived at the bridge either as individuals or in small disparate groups, devoid of any leadership. When these military refugees arrived with no apparent organisation, they were systematically stripped of their ammunition, Bren Guns and Boys Rifles, before being sent on towards the beaches east of Dunkirk. The formed bodies were allowed to proceed through to the Brigade Control Point, where liaison officers directed those more cohesive groups to where their parent units were beginning to occupy their own defensive positions around the perimeter.

The most refreshing tonic of the day was the sight of a platoon of Welsh Guardsmen, marching back in formed body, all in step, weapons and equipment carried or worn in the regulation manner, and exuding an air of professional calm. Their dirty, stained battle-dress and weary eyes however showed that these troops had done their own share of fighting and marching. They were not fresh troops, they were just well disciplined.

"We're pretty well stocked up now, Sir."

The sound of Sergeant Jackson's voice snapped the attention of the two officers away from the mass of men shuffling across the bridge.

"We've got enough ammunition to last us a year, Sir, to be honest..." The sergeant assured Pilkington. "And we've got a Bren Gun for every three men in our platoon. The Company Sergeant Major reckons the others are pretty much the same.

"Good." Pilkington nodded his approval. "Well, I suppose if they want us to hold out here for a while then we've got just about everything we need. I'd better go and see the Commanding Officer; see if we've had any clarification of what's going."

He turned back to Dunstable briefly.

"Alright, Harry; I'll leave you to it for a while. Remember, don't take any rubbish from anyone. No vehicles except armour, artillery and signals; and keep directing the French to the west."

"Right-ho, Sir." Dunstable saluted as the captain turned away again.

Jackson braced up into the position of attention as the Company Commander walked off, then sidled over to stand beside his platoon commander.

"Miserable fucking day, Sir…"

Dunstable smiled and gazed up at the dark clouds, from which rain still drizzled endlessly.

"It is that, Sergeant J; in more ways than one. Hard to believe it's all come to this, eh?"

The sergeant grunted moodily.

"It's a fucking disgrace, Sir. Look at them…"

He waved his arm at the soldiers straggling past them.

"Bimbling along with their chins on the floor and their tails between their legs, all feeling sorry for themselves. Makes me bloody steam, Sir, let me tell you."

The sergeant glared at a scruffy trio of Royal Army Service Corps privates who came ambling past, weaponless and smoking.

"Well, if nothing else…" He growled, "there's nowhere left to go except England and I reckon there'll be a bit of a queue for that. So at least this time when Jerry turns up we can stay and fight the buggers to a standstill."

Dunstable didn't have the opportunity to answer, because both men's attention was drawn to the tooting of a vehicle horn nearby. Looking down the road, southwards, the two men spotted a pair of lorries forcing their way through the press of men, coming towards the bridge.

"Here we go again…" Dunstable sighed.

Together, he and Jackson began walking against the flow of men, intending to stop the vehicles short of the bridge. They had perhaps moved twenty yards when the lorries met them. Jackson and Dunstable stood, slightly apart, directly in front of the leading truck, and the lieutenant raised his hand, signalling the vehicle to stop.

The truck slowed to a halt, and moments later, an angry, red face appeared from out of the passenger window of the cab.

"Get out of the bloody way!" The moustachioed man swore at them.

Jackson ran his eyes over him. An officer. A captain. He saw the flash on the sleeve of the man's battledress. Hallamshire Rifles.

"Come on, move, man!" The angry captain shouted again.

There was something about the voice that jerked a memory in Jackson's mind, and he narrowed his eyes as he studied the officer in closer detail. He had met this man before, he was sure. Unfortunately, Jackson's tired brain wouldn't allow him to recall the memory in full.

"Wait here, Sergeant J." Dunstable murmured and sauntered around to the side of the cab, where he looked up at the irate captain.

"I'm afraid the perimeter is out of bounds to all vehicles, unless you're armoured of course, or towing a gun."

Dunstable spoke calmly; politely.

"Don't order me around, young fellah." The captain snapped back in an accent that suggested he had once been a ranker like Jackson. "I had all that shit from the redcaps back there. I've got my battalion's kits on the back here, and I'm not carrying the bloody things to Dunkirk!"

"You won't need to." Dunstable responded, still calm. "You need to reverse these trucks back at least six hundred yards and drive them into a field. Once you've done that you need to immobilise the vehicles and destroy anything of value. If need be, set the things on fire."

The officer in the vehicle, whose pudgy face was already flushed, went almost purple.

"Don't get cocky with me, lieutenant..."

The officer began a retort, but was suddenly cut dead by a totally unexpected explosion of temper from Dunstable.

"Shut up, you bloody great fool!" The young second lieutenant roared, taking both the captain, and Jackson, by surprise. "And don't answer me back! My name is Second Lieutenant Harry Dunstable of the Coldstream Guards, and this is *my* bridge. You *will not* cross it in these vehicles. My orders come direct from the commander of 1st Guards Brigade, so if you have any problem with them, you can get your fat arse out of that cab and walk up to Uxem and question the Brigade Commander directly. Alternatively, you can stand here and continue blocking the road; in which case I will shoot you where you sit, then burn the vehicles anyway. Now, stop behaving like a spoilt brat and get your vehicles back down the road before I get my sergeant here to place you under arrest and convene an emergency courts martial!"

The captain was speechless. So was Jackson. He had no idea that his young officer was capable of such open fury as he now displayed.

"You... you can't do that..." The captain stammered from the cab, his facing turning from purple to deathly white in a moment.

Dunstable reached down to his waist and dragged his service revolver from its web holster. Shaking the lanyard free, Dunstable extended his arm, aiming the pistol directly at the captain's head. Jackson gawped at the scene before him. Around the vehicles, terrified looking soldiers on foot scuttled around the unfolding drama, giving the pistol wielding officer a wide berth.

"Fuck me..." Jackson whispered to himself, hardly daring to breath.

"Alright, alright!" The captain leaned backwards in his cab and began opening the door. "Calm down, lad. No need for that, is there?"

His voice was shaky. Unsurprising really, because the look in Dunstable's eye suggested he was deadly serious about his threat.

"Let me just brief these drivers, then I'll get them sent back..." The captain continued to gabble, his voice having dropped to a conciliatory tone.

Dunstable kept his pistol aimed at the captain's back until he had given instructions to both drivers to start reversing the trucks back down the road. Only when both vehicles began trundling slowly rearwards, did Dunstable finally lower his pistol. As he did so, Jackson noticed that the young man's hand was shaking badly.

The sergeant approached his officer cautiously.

"Well done, Sir." That sorted out that little problem easily enough.

Dunstable himself had gone deathly pale now.

"Bloody fool. Why can't people just do as they're told?"

Jackson grimaced.

"Because he's a Chippy bastard, Sir; that's why."

Dunstable laughed. It was almost a sob; the release of tension palpable in his voice.

"Of course he his, Sergeant J; I was forgetting..."

Together, they walked back to their position by the bridge. As they went, Jackson gave his platoon commander a sideways glance.

"Would you have done it, Sir; really?"

Dunstable gave Jackson a deadpan look.

"I've killed better people these last three weeks."

Jackson felt a cold chill touch him as he remembered the dying girl by the roadside. That was a fact, and no mistake, he thought.

They waited by the bridge for perhaps thirty minutes or more before they noticed the captain, accompanied by two privates and a corporal, shambling past with the crowd. As the group drew level with the two Coldstreamers, the officer from the Hallamshires avoided their gaze. As he passed however, he made a comment to his three men.

"Come on, fellahs. Let's go find someone who knows what they're doing. There's too many toy soldiers around here for my liking."

Dunstable and Jackson both heard the comment and swapped a brief look of annoyance. It was Jackson this time who gave vent to his spleen.

"Fucking line-swine!" He sneered.

The captain suddenly stopped dead and threw a poisonous look at Jackson.

"Did you say something, Sergeant?" He demanded, his eyes filled with hatred.

Jackson's tired mind worked as quickly as it could.

"Yes, Sir... I said *'have a nice time'*..."

The captain held his gaze, knowing it was a lie.

"Yes..." Dunstable interrupted. "Do have a nice time, won't you? When you get back to England, I mean. Have a beer for us, will you? We'll probably still be here... fighting."

The captain switched his furious gaze from Jackson to Dunstable, then back again. He said nothing; knowing it was pointless to force another showdown. Jackson and Dunstable stared back at the man, their sunken eyes regarding him with cold, unimpressed expressions.

After several moments of unspoken hatred passing silently between the men, the officer from the Hallamshires turned away abruptly and began stalking off across the canal bridge. Within just a few heartbeats, he was swallowed up by the mass of soldiery as it passed inside the Dunkirk perimeter and headed for the coast.

HMS GRENADE – THE EAST MOLE, DUNKIRK
WEDNESDAY 29TH MAY 1940 – 1750 HOURS

HMS Grenade was an unlucky ship; everyone knew it. Taken into service just four years ago, Grenade was one of the newest, fastest ships in the Royal Navy and her crew were rightly proud of her. But Christ Almighty, she was unlucky. In four years, she had collided with three other ships, the latest incident occurring just two weeks ago. With repairs completed just three days since at Harwich, Grenade had been thrown straight into the evacuation operation at Dunkirk. And Able Seaman Frank McIntosh didn't like it one bit.

He was probably the newest member of the ship's crew, having joined her as her repairs were completed and she was despatched to Dunkirk. Just one week ago, McIntosh had been filling a fairly comfortable clerical job at a shore base in Chatham, a post he had been filling for almost twelve months. Then, out of the blue, his Chief Petty Officer had appeared with a very attractive young woman from the Women's Royal Naval Service in tow and announced that she was to assume McIntosh's duties with immediate effect, and that he was to report for gunnery training.

Before McIntosh had found time to ask what on earth was going on, he had found himself on a firing range at Purfleet being shown how to load and fire an old fashioned Lewis machine-gun, along with a couple of dozen other ratings who, like himself, had been dragged out of desk jobs from all across the south-east of England. Thus it was that McIntosh now found himself manning a pintle-mounted Lewis Gun on the port-stern of the destroyer with the inauspicious reputation. Beside him stood Able Seaman Walter Gardner, a man he had known for just five days, having come across him on that dreary firing range at Purfleet.

Together, the two men glanced at the crowded spectacle of the East Mole as their ship warped alongside it. They were putting the destroyer in on the harbour side of the mole, closest to the smouldering ruins of the original port, with every other available bit of space already filled by an assortment of craft. Directly adjacent to Grenade's berthing point was an entire flotilla of armed trawlers, whilst other destroyers and larger troop carriers were tied up further along the structure on the seaward side. The long, skeletal structure of the mole itself was jam-packed with troops, so much so that they resembled a huge, khaki snake.

On their approach to Dunkirk, some hours earlier, McIntosh and Gardner had been at first horrified by the rumours of the air attacks and scale of destruction likely to be found at the French port, but then reassured when the word went round that the bad weather was persisting and that subsequently, the enemy's air activity had been drastically curtailed. But HMS Grenade wasn't a lucky ship, and by the time she had arrived off Dunkirk, the sky was much clearer, the remaining cloud well broken up. Word had it that there had been two large air-raids already, and that Grenade was to go into the harbour to lift troops during the lull.

Given the circumstances, McIntosh was happy with that, as he and Gardner, along with their elderly Lewis Gun, formed part of the ship's anti-aircraft defences, along with the two, purpose-built, quadruple 0.5 inch machine-gun batteries. Now, instead of keeping their eyes fixed on the pale blue sky beyond the thinning cloud, the two reluctant gunners gawped incredulously at the scenes on the mole.

"Jesus wept, Frank. What a sight…"

McIntosh couldn't find the words to reply. He was completely overawed by the picture of organised chaos before him.

The mole must have been packed with several thousand men, all squeezing past one another, moving in separate queues to board various ships. Some were fully equipped, wearing helmets and carrying rifles over their shoulders, whilst others were weaponless, tired and sullen looking, unshaven and dirty. Some men were wounded, dirty bloodstained bandages wrapped haphazardly around heads, arms and hands. Amongst the press of khaki, naval ratings and officers in their royal-blue uniforms moved continuously, directing, informing, cajoling, and in some cases, threatening the men who shuffled along the narrow walkway. Some of the naval officers used megaphones to call out their instructions, while standing precariously on the rail of the gangway.

"It's going to take a month of Sundays to get all this lot back to Blighty!"

Gardner shook his head, watching as the destroyer was secured against the mole by ratings from the shore party, whilst others began lowering ladders and planks from the mole to the deck of the ship; doing their best to lash them in place. The embarkation was going to be a precarious one at best. Still, reflected McIntosh as he looked on silently, it would certainly be quicker than doing a run in to the beaches. The ship was now secure, and the shore party were putting the finishing touches to the embarkation planks when the klaxons began to sound.

"What the hell's that?" Gardner jumped at the sudden noise.

"Here comes Jerry!" A voice shouted from the mole.

"Air raid, red! Air raid, red!" Another voice on board was yelling out from the direction of the bridge.

"Oh, my good God! Will you take a look at that Frank?"

McIntosh jerked his eyes skyward, automatically shading them with his hand, following Gardner's outstretched arm. He caught his breath and instantly, a terrible, deep, sinking feeling ran through his body, settling in his stomach and bowels. In the sky above them, small black puffs of cloud were beginning to puncture the air, whilst far above the curtain on anti-aircraft fire, McIntosh spotted the swarm of aircraft, cruising steadily towards them from the east.

"Bloody hell! Please tell me they're ours?" He breathed.

Less than a second later, any hopes he had were dashed.

"Stukas!" Someone called out on the mole.

A moment later, a corporate murmur of fear ran through the cohorts on the long, vulnerable jetty.

"Looks like we're on, Frank!" Gardner said darkly, stepping up to the gun-mount.

McIntosh couldn't speak. He was a man of few words at the best of times, and now, his desire for conversation had dried up entirely. He followed Gardner's lead and stepped up to the gun, taking hold of the weapon and drawing back the cocking handle. All the while, he kept his eyes fixed on the vast array of aircraft that were slowly but surely getting closer to the mass of docked vessels by the East Mole.

All around them, the klaxons on other ships were blaring the warning and in the distance, McIntosh vaguely registered the firing of heavy guns.

The first wave of aircraft were above them now and, like vultures from some 'Wild West' film, they began to circle, at what seemed a leisurely pace, directly above the harbour.

"What are they doing?" McIntosh heard himself asking.

"Don't know, mate…" Gardner replied. "Are Stukas the ones that they call dive-bombers?"

Gardner's question was answered for him by the enemy, just a heart beat later. With a little waggle of its wings, one of the aircraft suddenly heeled over on its side and began dropping like a stone, straight down towards the ships tied up against the mole.

"Cripes!" Gardner gasped.

A moment later, the sound of the screeching came to them. It was a terrible sound; quite like anything either man had heard before. A high-pitched scream, so dreadful that it cut through ones soul, clutching at the heart with an icy grip of fear. McIntosh found himself wincing at the sound and his knees suddenly felt as if they might give way any second.

"Lord God Almighty…" He muttered as the aircraft descended on them, screaming like a Harpy from Greek legend.

On the mole, the murmur of fear coming from the troops had transformed into a roar of terror. Behind the two seamen, there was a sudden eruption of automatic fire as the quad-mounted batteries opened up.

"Fire!" Gardner suddenly spluttered.

Mortified with fear and completely unused to the chaos of battle, McIntosh allowed his knees to sag and brought the barrel of his gun to the near vertical. He didn't bother to use the sights. Instead, he simply looked along the fat barrel of the weapon as if it were a shotgun and pressed the trigger. The gun lurched into life, and McIntosh, transfixed by the ever growing image of the diving Stuka and shocked to the core by its unholy scream, kept his finger firmly depressed on the trigger as he pumped round after round skywards.

Click.

The gun fell silent abruptly as the entire magazine was expended.

McIntosh blinked in surprise, then realised what had happened.

"New magazine, Wally!"

Beside him, Gardner scrabbled to remove the big drum magazine off the weapon. As he did so, both he and McIntosh heard the sound of the aircraft's engine change. The scream of the engine went from a whine to a growl as the pilot began to pull the machine out of its unbelievably steep dive. And then they heard the whistle of the bombs.

Both seamen ducked instinctively as at least two bombs hit the water just yards away from the ship, showering them in a wave of cold, salty, sea water. As the sheet of water splashed over them, both men heard the unmistakable thunderclap of an exploding bomb.

There were sounds of screaming from somewhere behind them, presumably on the mole, but neither sailor had time to worry about that.

"Okay, it's on!" Gardner was shouting above the racket as he slammed a fresh magazine onto the loading-post and rotated it clockwise until it locked.

McIntosh automatically dragged back the cocking handle and began looking up once more, searching for the next attacker.

He didn't have to search very long. The aircraft was already coming at them, its sirens howling like a Banshee as it hurtled down towards the exposed ships in the harbour. McIntosh repeated his drill, still ignoring the weapon's sights and aiming instinctively.

Rat-tat-tat-tat-tat-tat-tat-tat-tat!

His burst was a bit shorter this time, the panic starting to subside; being replaced by his recent training. Just as well, for the enemy dive-bomber was already pulling out of its dive; manoeuvring so tightly that it defied belief.

McIntosh followed the aircraft, standing straight and bringing the gun's barrel down. He followed the big, dark aircraft with its crooked wings as it banked to starboard and pulled up across the middle of the harbour.

Rat-tat-tat-tat-tat-tat-tat-tat-tat!

He loosed off another burst. The plane banked again, and up it went now, climbing rapidly with every ounce of power it had. McIntosh swung the gun up again, determined to chase the monster all the way back to its eyrie above the remnants of the cloud.

Rat-tat-tat-tat-tat-tat-tat-tat-tat-click!

Boooooooom!

The explosion, deafening as it seemed, was not the same sharp thunder-clap as before. This time the detonation was a deeper, hollow-sounding eruption that shook the little ship in the water, throwing both Gardner and McIntosh to the floor.

"Bloody hell! What was that?" Gardner breathed, his voice thoroughly shocked.

McIntosh rolled over onto all fours, stunned by the violent tremor.

"God knows…" He blurted. "I think we got hit…"

Booom – Whoosh!

The ship rocked violently once more, and this time the noise of the explosion was followed by a wall of heat. Both men were thrown sideways onto the deck once more.

"Oh, my God! Oh, my God!"

Gardner was rambling as he pushed himself up into a sitting position. McIntosh struggled up beside him. He was looking straight across the deck towards the mole. The mass of men there were pushing each other in panic, trying to head back down the structure towards the harbour and the beach. They were like rats in a barrel. They were sitting ducks on the mole, and sitting ducks if they boarded the ships. This was sheer murder, thought McIntosh; nothing less than sheer bloody murder.

"We're on fire!" Gardner's voice snapped McIntosh's attention away from the scenes of panic on the mole.

He looked along the side of the ship, towards her bow, and spotted instantly the angry orange flames that licked at the foredeck, not to mention the clouds of bilious, dark smoke that was gushing out of the ship's bowels. McIntosh caught the sickly odour of burning oil.

"Jesus! They've hit the ruddy fuel tanks!" He gasped.

McIntosh sat there agape, hardly capable of taking in the horror that surrounded him. HMS Grenade, just three days out of the repair yard, was not a lucky ship. And now, rocked by two explosions and billowing smoke and fire, her unlucky streak had taken an even bigger turn for the worse.

THE DUNKIRK PERIMETER – 6 MILES SOUTH EAST OF DUNKIRK
WEDNESDAY 29TH MAY 1940 – 1800 HOURS

Whittaker grimaced as he stared into the distance. He was nearly there; he was sure of it. The pyres of dark smoke and the unmistakable swarm of little black dots in the sky told him that he had almost reached Dunkirk. Dunkirk, the place name that, in recent days, had taken on an almost religious significance; the name breathed by soldiers with reverence as if it were another name for heaven. Dunkirk; a place of safety where one could escape from the hellish arena of the war. A kind of Jerusalem for the weary pilgrims of the British Expeditionary Force, and all who were swept up with it.

For Whittaker, the last nine days had been the longest of his life. After being forced to ditch his Hurricane, he had tried to organise some sort of recovery for his aircraft and attempted to seek out an airfield, be it one manned by the French or the British, in order to begin the process of rejoining his squadron. He had realised early on that this was not going to happen. Firstly, just about everyone he spoke to was more concerned about the German armoured units that were reported, in earnest fashion, as being *'somewhere to the south'*. At first, Whittaker believed that the Army chaps were being a little jumpy, until he found himself as a spectator on the edge of a huge battle, right on the doorstep of Arras.

He had then decided that it would be best if he tried to make for Paris. That was foolish, according to the Army types, because the Germans were *'everywhere'* between Arras and the sea. Besides, they told him, everyone knew that the Royal Air Force had pulled out; gone home to Blighty. There wasn't any point in even looking for them. Whittaker's best bet, they said, was to go north. More jumpiness, Whittaker had decided, and set out with a French family in their car to make the journey south to Paris by a circuitous route. And that was when the trouble started.

He and his French companions had spent two days trying to find a way around the German held areas. Eventually, after they had run out of petrol anyway, they had all been forced to admit that the rumours were true. There would be no way out to Paris. The Germans really had cut-off the northern part of France from the interior. And so, the French family had announced their intention of heading towards St Omer where they had relatives. Whittaker however, had no choice but to follow the repeated advice of every soldier he came across. Go north; due north, nowhere else. Eventually that advice had become simpler. Dunkirk. Salvation lay at Dunkirk; it was the only way out. So here he was, perhaps six or seven miles from that promised land, wet through and shivering from the forty-eight hour soaking he had just endured, with feet so badly blistered he was almost tip-toeing along with the host of exhausted, hungry, and terrified men.

Whittaker had never felt so alone in all his life. Although he was surrounded by Britons of every variety, few were in the mood to talk, and none were interested in giving help or advice to a 'fly-boy'. In fact, the only advice he had received of late was to ditch his RAF tunic and find something khaki if he *'didn't want to get strung up'*. At first, Whittaker had been stunned by the angry, resentful attitude of the soldiers he had come across on the long slog back to the coast, but soon enough he understood the reason for it.

"Where the bloody hell is the RAF?" One soldier had asked.

"The only planes we see in the sky are Jerry ones!" Another had commented sourly.

And the worst thing was, it was almost impossible to deny these allegations. Whittaker knew how busy he and his fellow airmen had been these last two weeks. He knew how many sorties they had flown; how many German aircraft they had downed. But even he had to admit that from the ground, it was hard to understand any of that. The simple ground-truth was that, when you saw a plane appear in the sky, you took cover, because invariably it was a Jerry.

Tottering along, Whittaker leaned out slightly, looking down the side of the endless stream of humanity. The fields either side were a foot or two underwater; deliberately flooded by the looks, and burnt out and abandoned vehicles created a wide, stark avenue along which the column of men struggled.

"Bridge up ahead..." He heard somebody say a few yards in front. "Looks like the canal they were on about. We should be safe enough once we're over..."

The information was passed back in fragments, from man to man, down the column. A couple of yards in front of Whittaker, a soldier wearing the single chevron of a lance corporal shambled along with a group of three privates. All wore helmets but, like many of the men on the road, their web equipment and weapons were long gone. Whittaker saw the man glance backwards, as if to pass on the news that salvation was just a little way ahead.

Suddenly, the man stopped dead. Whittaker, seeing the man's sudden change of expression, stopped dead too. The lance corporal was staring at him with fierce, sunken eyes, his face covered in several days of stubble, much like Whittaker's. The pilot felt a feeling of unease take hold of him.

"Well, fuck me!" Snarled the NCO. "So that's what an RAF uniform looks like! Can't say I've seen that many recently; never mind any fucking planes!"

The man's companions stopped and turned at the sound of the corporal's outburst. They regarded Whittaker with contemptuous eyes.

"Shit." Mumbled the young RAF officer under his breath. "This could go very badly wrong..."

The lance corporal suddenly began moving towards Whittaker, his face a mask of unpleasantness. The pilot was rooted to the spot. He had fought duels in the air on many occasions, risking his life on a daily basis without thinking, but this sudden verbal assault from a British soldier, a supposed ally, shocked him to the core. The unexpected confrontation was even more worrying because this man was a mere lance corporal, whereas Whittaker was a commissioned officer in the RAF. He was still wearing his tunic so surely this man could see his bars of rank? Surely this irate soldier understood the basics of the RAF rank structure? How could discipline in the British Army have broken down so badly?

Whittaker was still struggling to comprehend all this when the man came to a halt, barely a pace in front of him, pushing his ugly, rat-like face close to the pilot's. Instantly, Whittaker caught the whiff of alcohol. The man was drunk. Shit. Carefully, as unobtrusively as possible, the pilot allowed his hand to drift under the hem of his tunic, to where he carried his service revolver, salvaged from the cockpit of his aircraft.

"What's the matter, fly-boy?" The drunken soldier raged at him, breathing his stale, fetid breath over Whittaker. "Are the RAF not talking, as well as not flying?"

Whittaker was aware of the soldier's companions closing in on either side of him now, and beyond them, he saw other soldiers slowing down to watch the spectacle, although worryingly, none of them appeared concerned enough to intervene.

"Actually, old chap, the RAF *are* flying. Most pilots are doing three and even four sorties a…"

"Old chap!" The soldier suddenly roared. "I'll fucking 'old chap' you!"

And with that, the drunken corporal suddenly pressed both his hands on Whittaker's chest and pushed him backwards violently. Taken completely by surprise at the sudden assault, Whittaker staggered backwards, waving his arms as he fought for balance. As he steadied himself, his mind began to whirl. The soldier was advancing on him again, his companions alongside. All around him were grim, dirty faces and khaki uniforms. Whittaker was hemmed in and his mind couldn't understand how this could be happening to him.

"Who do you think you're talking to, you toffee-nosed bastard!" The NCO snarled at him in a voice slurred by too much looted wine. "We're the people who have to pay for your fuck-ups, you stuck-up little wanker!"

There was jeering now, and the odd call of encouragement from amongst the thickening crowd. It was going from bad to worse and there was no way Whittaker was going to be able to just walk away from this one. His hand fumbled for his revolver again as the soldier once more thrust his head forward, the veins in his neck standing out like taught rope.

"Problem with you lot is you think you're above the likes of us…"

Just as Whittaker decided that he had no choice but to pull out his pistol and shoot someone, a khaki clad arm suddenly appeared in front of his face. It happened so fast that he barely realised what was happening. One moment, the drunken soldier was leering at him aggressively, the next, his eyes were bulging out of their sockets and he was being lifted clean off the floor by a big hand that was clamped firmly around his throat. In an instant, the tight little arena seemed to open up as the watching soldiers stepped backwards hurriedly. Another soldier stepped in front of Whittaker; a huge soldier, the owner of the arm and hand that was now shaking the drunken corporal by the throat as if he was nothing more than a rag doll.

Then the newcomer began to shout. It was a shout like Whittaker had rarely heard before. Not just an angry cry, but a high-pitched, almost demonic howl of rage, that cut through the air like the crack of a whip.

"Who the fucking hell do you think you are, you little bastard!" The tall soldier screamed into the face of the suspended corporal. "How fucking dare you!"

Whittaker was now looking straight at the back of the man who had intervened and every second or so, caught a glimpse of the corporal's face as the newcomer shook him from side to side.

With what appeared to be a simple, almost casual flick of the wrist, the big stranger released his grip on the corporal, who's face by now was going a purple colour, and flung him contemptuously back down. The NCO landed amongst his companions, almost toppling over from the shock and the impact, drawing in a huge gulp of air as he did so and emitting a great sob. There was a brief, angry growl from the corporal's friends, but it stopped abruptly when suddenly, from Whittaker's left, three or four bayonet-tipped rifles came swinging down to the horizontal and pointed directly at the group of dishevelled men.

It had all happened so quickly that only now did Whittaker have time to register what was happening. He looked at the men with rifles. They were all as tall as the man who had just been strangling the corporal and, like the big man, they were all fully dressed in fighting-order and helmets. Whittaker glanced at the big man and spotted the three chevrons of a sergeant. Then he noticed the curved red flashes embroidered with white letters that the newcomers all wore at the top of their battledress sleeves. He read the words. Coldstream Guards. In an instant, a wave of utter relief swept over Whittaker.

"You dirty, scruffy, insubordinate, Chippy bastard! Look at you!" The big Coldstream Guards sergeant was still screaming at the stunned corporal, as the other soldiers shrank back, appalled by the unbelievable fury of the guardsman. "Look at the state of you. No webbing, no rifle, no discipline…" The sergeant's voice was rising to a crescendo. "And you haven't even had a fucking shave!"

The last sentence was hurled at the disorientated corporal in a manner that indicated the crime of being unshaven was on a par with murder or high treason.

"Call yourself a soldier? You're a fucking disgrace to your regiment! Look at you! I ought to break your fucking legs and leave you here for the Germans!"

The corporal was backing away from the sergeant now, his face having gone from deep purple to palest white in a matter of seconds. The big Coldstreamer advanced on the plainly terrified corporal like a wild beast that had cornered its prey.

"How dare you lay your hands on a commissioned officer, you stinking fucking peasant?" The sergeant, with obvious skill born of much practice, suddenly dropped the volume, pitch and tone of his voice to a medium level snap, like the angry crack of a machine-gun. And like a machine-gun, the sergeant's verbal reprimand went on mercilessly.

"That's a shooting offence, Corporal. If it wasn't for the fact that I've got a battle to fight and I need every single round of ammunition, then I'd stand you against that tree there and fucking well shoot you myself, right here and now!"

With that comment, the sergeant suddenly shot a look around the mass of soldiery who were standing now at a good distance, looking on with a mixture of fear and guilt as the sergeant tore into the NCO.

"And as for you lot!" The Coldstreamer barked. "You can take a fucking note, too. Standing there, looking all sorry for yourselves! No wonder the Jerries are fucking beating us, you pathetic fuckers!"

He raised one arm, thrusting it out with a chopping motion.

"Dunkirk is that way. Go over the bridge and keep going for about six miles. Once you get there you'll probably find some nice, kind Navy bloke who'll take you back to England. Now get moving and get off my fucking battlefield; I've got some Germans to fight."

Everyone had heard enough. The mass of soldiers, including the corporal and his companions, began scurrying away from where the sergeant stood like the Rock of Gibraltar, glaring at anyone who dared to look in his direction. As the column of soldiers began to move rapidly onwards, the guardsmen who had been supporting their sergeant began to relax, their rifles flicking back up to the high-port position. Fighting to control his breathing, the sergeant turned away from his dwindling audience and looked directly at

Whittaker. For a brief second, the pilot felt a thrill of fear run through him. Although the sergeant from the Guards was relatively young, his face was a hard, ruthless mask of grim determination. It was the face of a fighting man, and not the kind of face Whittaker would ever want to be on the wrong end of on the battlefield.

Briefly, Whittaker saw the spark of fury in the sergeant's eyes, but then, like the flick of a light switch, the tall NCO suddenly smiled, and his expression changed to one that bordered on sheepish.

"Sorry about that, Sir." The sergeant murmured apologetically. "I'm afraid there's a few people starting to lose their nerve a bit. We've got all sorts of odds and sods coming through here. We're trying to sort them out at the other side of the bridge and put as many units back together as we can, but it's like pushing water uphill."

After the tension of the last few minutes, the sergeant's sudden change of temper and his black humour were thoroughly disarming, and Whittaker let out a small, nervous laugh.

"It's alright, Sarge; I understand…"

The NCO winced visibly.

"Please don't call me that, Sir? I'm a guardsman. Sergeant will do fine, but never *Sarge*."

"Oh, sorry…" Whittaker blinked. "Sergeant it is then, Sergeant… Sorry, I don't know your name…"

"Jackson, Sir. Sergeant Jackson, 2nd Battalion Coldstream Guards. We're manning the defence line up here on the canal. Come on, Sir; we'll escort you over the bridge. I'm afraid I can't spare anyone to escort you as far as the beaches, so you really will have to watch yourself."

Whittaker hobbled forward, falling in beside Jackson and his men.

"Actually, Sergeant Jackson, if you don't mind, I might hang on with you chaps for a bit?"

The NCO looked down at Whittaker thoughtfully.

"Well, I'm sure Mr Dunstable and the Company Commander would make you welcome enough, Sir, but I don't think you'll want to hang around for too long. Rumour has it we're going to form the Rear Guard, and in the not too distant future we're going to have half the German Army descending on us."

Whittaker ran a hand through his hair and gave a heavy sigh.

"At the moment Sergeant, I think I'd rather face half the German Army than share a beach with the BEF!"

PART SIX

DELIVERANCE

Thursday 30th May 1940
The Twenty First Day

TENNANT'S COMMAND POST – DUNKIRK HARBOUR
THURSDAY 30TH MAY 1940 – 1200 HOURS

In war, things rarely went all one way, or all the other. This was the reality that Tennant pondered as he paced up and down outside his command post not far from the ruined harbour of Dunkirk, sipping at his tea as he went. Things had improved from his first day at Dunkirk. According to his staff, yesterday had been a vast improvement on the numbers being evacuated; over forty five thousand men if the figures were right. Tennant was pretty sure the figures weren't far off because there was no doubt that the East Mole had seen constant traffic throughout the morning and afternoon, with often up to ten ships at a time coming alongside.

Then of course there was the great news that Route X had finally been cleared. Not only would it halve the time it took ships to do the round trip from Dunkirk to Dover and back again, it also meant there was no longer a need to risk ships by sailing them past the enemy held coastline at Calais. In addition, new radios had arrived during the night, which appeared to be working so far and had resulted in the confusion caused by yesterday's air raids being resolved, slowly but surely. Those radios had arrived with Rear Admiral Wake-Walker, newly appointed to co-ordinate the Royal Navy's efforts off-shore, which was a blessed relief for Tennant. With the title of Rear Admiral Dover, Wake-Walker was now able to control the flow of ships more effectively for the Shore Party. Perhaps, best of all however, the weather had once more come to Tennant's aid. Thick fog and sea mist blanketed the harbour and the coastline. Thus, Tennant had yet to hear an enemy bomb drop on the harbour today.

That was the good news. The bad news however, made for grim contemplation. The evacuation of so many men yesterday had been at the cost of no less than 27 craft of all types; several of them being valuable destroyers including the bigger, faster, modern types. Not only had the Luftwaffe finally appeared with a vengeance the previous afternoon, but reports stated that several vessels had been ambushed by German patrol boats on their way across the channel, adding to the carnage on the water. As a result of all this, orders from the very top had apparently forbidden Admiral Ramsay from using any of the modern destroyers for operations off Dunkirk.

Tennant understood why. Every available destroyer would subsequently be needed for the endless convoy duty in the North Atlantic; something that was just as vital to national survival as rescuing Britain's army. Even so, the loss of the five perfectly serviceable destroyers from the evacuation force still hurt.

All things even, Tennant felt that he was just about holding his own. The harbour, though now filled with sunken ships, was still clear enough to allow access to the East Mole. Due partly to the lack of visibility, and partly to the maze of submerged wreckage in the harbour, ships were being called into the mole one at a time. It was frustrating but unavoidable, and it was still faster than the operations on the beaches. Each ship leaving from the mole was taking a minimum of four hundred men at a time. Tennant knew they had to keep going.

There was progress on the beaches of course. Not much, but progress all the same. His Shore Party had been expanded somewhat and so he was now able to allocate a reasonable sized group to co-ordinate the haphazard arrangements currently in place down the coast at La Panne and Bray Dunes. Between his own command post and the BEF Rear HQ, there had been an arrangement to construct makeshift piers on the beaches using otherwise useless vehicles. Ammunition lorries, unnecessary artillery tractors, and God knew what else was, even now, being driven onto the beach where, under supervision of the Royal Engineers, they were parked end to end before having their fuel tanks drained. The vehicles were then being lashed together, boards, doors, planks and vehicle panels being laid across their tops to provide an ad hoc jetty, whilst their cabs and engine sumps were filled with sand and rocks. It was a hasty bit of improvisation, but it would do. It would have to do. All Tennant needed now was a fleet of smaller craft that could properly work the gap between the improvised jetties and the bigger ships that sat further out. Ramsay was on the case; he knew that. Everybody was working flat out. As had become his habit, he checked his watch yet again.

As he looked up, he saw Drake walking back along the quayside towards him. The young sub-lieutenant was returning from his stint on the mole, commanding a berthing party.

"Mr Drake, how goes it on the mole?"

Drake pulled a non-committal face and shook his head.

"Slow, Sir. Slow but steady. I reckon we've maybe got nine or ten thousand off so far."

Tennant winced at the low figure. They were taking a backward step here.

"There's a French destroyer been in earlier, Sir, and another one has just appeared; so we've called forward some of the French troops. I reckon about a thousand of them have gone off so far."

Tennant nodded pensively.

"It's not enough though, Mr Drake. It's just not enough. We need to pick the pace up again while this weather lasts. We'll get more men off the beaches today than previously, but we can't waste this opportunity with the mole."

He sucked his teeth for a moment or two then looked up at the young officer. The boy was clearly tired.

"Thank you, Mr Drake; and well done this morning. Go and get yourself a brew; the Chief's just boiled some water up. Before you do that however, can you do me one quick favour?"

"Of course, Sir." Drake smiled. "Anything…"

Tennant thought for a moment, formulating the words in his mind before speaking.

"Could you draft a signal to Rear Admiral Dover please? Tell him that the improvised piers on the beaches have been constructed and that given more small craft, we can dramatically increase the numbers we lift from those points today. Also, remind him yet again that the harbour is open; I repeat, the harbour *is* open, and that the weather is currently preventing interference from German aircraft…"

Tennant paused slightly.

"Therefore, I request… no, *I beg,* the C-in-C Home Fleet to return those five big destroyers. Time is not on our side, but for just a few hours the weather is. To that end, we must make best use of it, otherwise…"

He drew a deep breath.

"Otherwise I fear that the greater part of the BEF will be lost."

1ST BATTALION COLDSTREAM GUARDS – NEAR FURNES ON THE DUNKIRK PERIMETER
THURSDAY 30TH MAY 1940 – 1400 HOURS

"Alright you two, there's no point in you boys hanging around any more. We ain't got no more driving for you to do, so you may as well get yourselves off to the beaches."

The Hangman gave the two RASC men their new instructions with what probably constituted his friendliest growl.

Standing to attention in front of the warrant officer, and still wearing their borrowed webbing and carrying a rifle each, Moxon and Fellows glanced at each other in surprise.

"Are you sure you don't need us here, Sir?" Moxon asked, looking back at the big man.

The two men had been with the 1st Battalion of the Coldstream Guards for two weeks now. Having been rescued by them amongst the blazing ruins of Herent on the River Dyle, the two drivers, separated from their unit in the chaos, had been 'adopted' by Company Sergeant Major Gallows as part of his small headquarters group. The intention had been to return them to their transport unit at the first opportunity, but unfortunately, the enemy had prevented that from becoming a reality. For more than fourteen days, the two RASC privates had marched and fought alongside the guardsmen of the 1st Coldstream, in turns being terrified by their curious customs and their ruthless implementation of discipline, whilst at the same time being filled with admiration at the fortitude, good humour and fighting spirit that had been evident throughout the long, confusing withdrawal from Belgium. Now, after all of their shared adventures with these men, Moxon and Fellows felt somewhat reluctant to leave them.

The Hangman shook his head.

"Thanks for the offer, lads, but very soon it's going to get nasty around here. You've done alright these last two weeks for a couple of Chippies, but it looks like this is going to be a fight to the finish for us. So, you two highly trained drivers need to get yourselves back to the beaches and find a boat back to England. But…"

And with that the Hangman pointed his finger in warning at the two men.

"Don't you two go falling back into any of them dirty Chippy habits of yours! You keep hold of your rifles and webbing and make sure you keep them clean. And make sure you stay clean shaven, mind you. Just remember that you're British soldiers, so you go and set the example to those other fuckers now. I don't blame them Chippies for anything, of course; they don't know any better. But you boys have spent a couple of weeks with the Coldstream so you *do* know better. Now… off you go, and remember what the Hangman's taught you."

Again Moxon and Fellows exchanged glances, but after a moment, they looked back at the warrant officer.

"May I have your permission for myself and one other private soldier to carry on, Sir, please?"

A small grimace of approval ran over the Company Sergeant Major's face.

"Yes, please." He growled back.

"Up." Moxon muttered the prescribed signal that had been hammered into them during their time with the battalion, and together they executed a right turn in dismissal.

"Don't bend at the waist when you turn, fellahs." The Hangman commented without any particular vehemence.

The two soldiers grinned at each other as they walked away. After just a couple of paces, Moxon suddenly came to a standstill and turned back, calling after the warrant officer.

"Excuse me, Sir?" He said. "Why do you keep calling us 'Chippies'?"

The warrant officer considered the question for a moment before replying.

"It's short for *'fish and chips'* of course. All the mobs in the British Army apart from the Guards are like Fish and Chip Shops. You can find a Chippy on any old street corner. It's not the same with a Guards battalion. You can't just pick one of them up anywhere, can you? Quality costs boys; quality costs."

The big, ugly warrant officer winked at them mischievously then turned away and headed back towards the company's headquarters.

"You know what, Mickey?" Fellows muttered as they watched the Hangman disappear inside the building. "I reckon I'm going to miss those bloody nutters!"

Moxon nodded his head slowly.

"Yeah, I'm with you on that one, Stan. I reckon I am too."

HEADQUARTERS BEF – LA PANNE, 9 MILES EAST OF DUNKIRK
THURSDAY 30TH MAY 1940 – 1820 HOURS

"My best wishes for a successful conclusion."

Brooke clasped hands with Gort and the two men shook firmly.

"Thank you for all you've done, Alan." The commander of the BEF replied with genuine feeling. "Hope you have a decent trip back; and the best of luck with whatever they've got lined up for you."

Brooke nodded his thanks and moved on, shaking hands with the other men in the room.

The end was near, and Brooke, along with Ronald Adam from the virtually defunct 3rd Corps, was one of the first of the big formation commanders to be recalled back to England. Adam, having successfully organised the defence of the Dunkirk perimeter and the initial embarkation plan, had already departed. Brooke should have gone yesterday, but he had managed to sway the War Office and hold on for another twenty four hours so that he could ensure his entire corps was safely in the perimeter and properly deployed before handing over the reins to his replacement.

He came to Michael Barker, his opposite number who commanded 1st Corps. The poor man could barely look Brooke in the eye and, Brooke suspected, he was probably close to tears. He looked quite done in. Brooke had watched his fellow corps commander become more and more stressed as the long, confusing withdrawal had progressed, becoming almost completely overwhelmed by events. In Brooke's personal opinion, Barker wouldn't take much more. In fact, he was somewhat surprised that he had lasted this long. Perhaps that was unfair? Unfortunately war left no room for sensibilities, Brooke reflected. You could either handle it or you couldn't. The two men shook hands. It was a brief, limp affair.

Last of all, Brooke came to Bernard Montgomery, the commander of one of Brooke's own divisions; the 3rd. During this campaign, 'Monty' had been a rock. Regardless of the chaos that had enveloped the BEF, Montgomery, of all Brooke's commanders, had carried on calmly and diligently throughout, tackling every new task and unexpected development with professional skill and determination. Thus it was only natural that Brooke should have selected Montgomery to step-up as the acting corps commander for him, now that he had been ordered home. Brooke suddenly remembered the incident of a few months earlier, where Montgomery had upset the Chaplain General by publishing an order about the use of contraception and other matters of sexual health. The order had outraged the clergyman and the matter had gone right to the top of the Army, before rolling back down the chain of command again. More than one person had been demanding Montgomery's head, but it was Brooke who had stood by him, recognising the divisional commander's many real strengths. As Brooke shook Montgomery's hand firmly and the two men exchanged a look of absolute mutual confidence and respect, Brooke was extremely glad that he *had* stood by this man. He was not sure that the corps would have managed quite so well without this shrewd, sharp featured general in charge of its 3rd Division.

"Well done, Monty; and good luck. Make sure you look after the corps for me, won't you?"

Montgomery smiled.

"I will indeed. And thank you for all of your support, Sir… in everything. It has been a pleasure working with you."

The two men held each others gaze for a moment and, just before they released their grip, almost instinctively, they both flicked their gaze towards

Barker for the briefest of moments. An unspoken thought was passed between the two men. They understood each other completely.

"Well then, everybody…" Brooke stepped away and took in the entire assembly. "I will leave you to it. My thoughts and my prayers are with you all for a successful outcome."

And with those brief, parting words, Lieutenant General Alan Brooke, erstwhile commander of the British 2nd Corps, left the room. For several long moments after the door had closed, nobody spoke. Eventually, Gort let out his breath.

"Right, gentlemen. We should try to come up with a firm plan of action here."

He picked up a message from the nearby desk; a message which had already been read out to his audience.

"Can I just remind you of the clear directions given in the latest signal from London?"

He raised the piece of paper and began to read, slowly and with emphasis.

"Continue to defend the present perimeter to the utmost to cover maximum evacuation now proceeding well. Report every three hours through La Panne. If we can still communicate we shall send you an order to return to England with such officers as you may choose at the moment when we deem your command so reduced that it can be handed over to a corps commander. *You should now nominate that corps commander…"*

Gort continued to read the message to the end. Having finished, he looked up and scanned the faces in the room. Half a dozen men were there, including the two commanders of the two remaining corps and their Brigadiers General Staff.

Gort placed the message down again and took a deep breath.

"It is clear in my mind from that message that the Rear Guard and its commander will almost certainly be lost…"

He turned sad eyes towards Barker.

"I'm afraid, Michael, that given our current dispositions and the need for us to draw-in the perimeter towards Dunkirk, this onerous task is probably going to fall to you."

Montgomery, watching Barker across the room, saw the general flinch as if he had been physically slapped. Gort went on.

"I think 2nd Corps must be pulled in and evacuated, and I think you and your corps must stay and fight on alongside the French. I'm sorry that it has to be you…"

Barker had paled visibly and behind him, his BGS looked similarly aghast. Gort too, was plainly not enjoying the moment, but he went on.

"I think therefore that we must now start laying the plans accordingly. 2nd Corps probably has another twenty four hours of service to give before we are able to pull them out and get them away, whilst 1st Corps must dig in deep and put down roots. We cannot afford to give the enemy one more yard of ground, gentlemen. We must hold on now to the very last, in order to get as many people away as possible. I think it best if you all get back to your commands and ensure that our perimeter is watertight and ready for the day ahead. I suspect the enemy will press us hard tomorrow. Meanwhile, my staff and I will settle the final details of everything and call for you in due course. Thank you, gentlemen."

The conference broke up. The officers began to leave and, surprisingly, Barker seemed to brighten somewhat, smiling nervously at Gort as he made to go.

"Oh, well; there we are, Sir. At least we know for definite now. Makes it all a lot easier…"

Montgomery decided to hold back and sent his own BGS on his way. As the room cleared, Gort saw the acting corps commander hovering at the back, and came over to him.

"Monty? Is there something you need, old boy?"

Montgomery, ever a plain speaker, didn't hesitate.

"I was just thinking, Sir, that the situation is not yet as desperate as everyone seems to think. I am of the opinion that it isn't a foregone conclusion that the 1st Corps will be lost, or that there is any need to deliberately sacrifice it. The loss of the 1st Corps is *not* a certainty, Sir… unless of course Michael Barker remains in command, in which case it is an *absolute* certainty."

Gort, regarding Montgomery with a steady gaze, showed no sign of surprise at the major-general's words.

"He isn't for it anymore, Sir." Montgomery continued in his quiet, precise voice. "The next two days will be critical. They will be chaotic and dangerous. But I am sure there is still a chance we can get the 1st Corps away too… if you put General Alexander in command."

"Alex'?" Gort wondered aloud, referring to the commander of the 1st Division by his nick-name.

"Yes, Sir. You know Alex' as well as me. The man is unflappable. He is a solid, dependable officer. Alexander is the man. If I were in your shoes, Sir, Alex' would be commanding my Rear Guard."

Gort continued to hold Montgomery's gaze, his mind working quickly, evaluating the suggestion.

"Alex'?" He wondered aloud once more.

Major General, The Honourable Harold Alexander was a man that you couldn't help but admire. To those of noble birth he was a wonderful, amiable companion, and to those of lower birth, he was the very best type of gentleman. Wounded and highly decorated in the Great War, the former Irish Guardsman was loved by his officers and men. Most importantly of all however, Alexander, the youngest general officer in the British Army, had nerves of steel. The debonair officer was always immaculately turned out, even in the field, and he regarded the background noise and chaos of battle as one would regard a brass band and May Day crowd in a London Park. Indeed, it was a standing joke in GHQ that you could always tell when Alexander was worried, because he would raise one eyebrow. If he was in a panic, people claimed, he would raise both.

Gort couldn't stop a feint smile from breaking out on his tired features.

"Young Harry Alexander, eh?"

He gave a small, curt nod to Montgomery.

"Thank you for your suggestion, Bernard. I will give it some thought."

1ST BATTALION COLDSTREAM GUARDS – 1 MILE NORTH EAST OF FURNES
THURSDAY 30TH MAY 1940 – 2315 HOURS

"Where's the fucking Company Commander?" The Hangman roared into the darkness.

At first, nobody answered. Unsurprising really, as the Hangman's voice was lost amongst the deafening chaos of the close quarter night battle.

"Grenade!"

Crump! Rat-tat-tat-tat-tat! Blam!

The noise of the battle was intense and the sound of men shouting in German and English, combined with the screaming of the wounded and dying only added to the maelstrom of noise. The fact that it was pitch black completed the disorientation for the men of 1st Battalion Coldstream Guards as they pushed on with their counter-attack against an enemy force who had managed to force their way over the canal on the boundary between the 2nd Battalion of the Grenadiers and 4th Battalion of the Royal Berkshires.

"He's dead, Sir!" A voice came out of the darkness.

"What?" The Hangman demanded of the invisible soldier.

"He's dead, Sir! The Company Commander's gone down!"

Company Sergeant Major Gallows ran at a low crouch across the flat meadow towards the voice, cursing as he suddenly fell into a deep, unseen drainage ditch.

"Fucking hell!"

He splashed down into the muddy water face first, cursing and swearing as he fell. As he pushed himself back up, a shadow loomed in the darkness.

"Who's that?" The dark figure demanded.

"It's me!" The Hangman snapped un-usefully, his voice full of irritation. "Who the fuck's that?"

"Lance Corporal Sheldon, Sir; No.3 Platoon."

Gallows struggled to his feet.

"The Company Commander's dead, Sir. He caught one when we came across the field. The Jerries have got a machine-gun in that farm in front and they shot us up pretty badly as we came over. The Platoon Sarn't Major's copped one too, Sir."

"Where's the Platoon Sergeant?" Gallows demanded.

"Along here, Sir. He's sorting out the sections in the ditch..."

The Hangman didn't reply, he pushed past the shadowy figure of the guardsman and splashed along the water filled ditch. As he went, he passed a number of other soldiers crouching in the ditch.

"Sergeant Malone? Sergeant Malone?"

"Here, Sir!"

The voice of No.3 Platoon's sergeant came to the Hangman's ears from a little way in front.

"What's going on? How many men have you got?"

"The Company Commander's dead, Sir..." The sergeant began.

"I know that." The Hangman cut him off. "I want to know how many men you've got left?"

"Fifteen, Sir." The sergeant replied promptly. "There might be more but there's only fifteen made it this far."

Gallows grunted.

"That'll do. Number Two Platoon is back across the field by that hedgerow..."

He pointed into the darkness at the unseen feature.

"Send a runner across there and find Number Two Platoon's commander. Tell him to stay firm and cover the far side of the hedge, right across to the river bank. We're going to attack that farm with your platoon. This is the plan..."

The warrant officer quickly outlined his idea to Malone. It wasn't a complicated plan, but in complete darkness and with confusion reigning, simple was good.

"I want two Bren teams here, giving fire support. When I give the word I want them to put down everything they've got and make lots of fucking noise. Leave any wounded with them; they can use their rifles or load magazines."

The Hangman then gestured across the darkened field to their front, where the farmhouse sat like a squat, dark fortress just fifty yards away. Stabs of light punctuated the farm as its German defenders raked their attackers with fire.

"Once that's happening, and while the Jerries home in on the gun teams, you and me and every rifleman you've got are going to sprint across that field and get into the farm from the far corner. Every man needs a grenade ready in his hand. Got that?"

"Yes, Sir."

"Good. Get it organised. You've got three minutes."

The surviving members of No.3 Platoon went into a flurry of activity. Gallows stalked back down the ditch to where he was planning to launch his assault from. For miles around, the dark night was being lit up every few seconds for just a heartbeat by explosions, gun fire and the odd Very Light. The Germans were making a push on the whole perimeter; no doubt about that. The Hangman was not a sophisticated man, but the Company Commander's explanation of the situation earlier on had been simple enough. The BEF was surrounded at Dunkirk. Their battalion was due to evacuate tomorrow, but until then, the enemy must be held at the other side of the canal-line. If the Germans got across the canal in force, then it was all over. And now the Germans were over the canal and the Company Commander was dead. You didn't need the brains of an Arch Bishop to work out what needed to happen. The Germans had to be pushed back, else killed in situ. There was no question of just sitting here. It was nice and simple; just how Gallows liked it. It was time to fight.

"Company Sarn't Major, Sir?"

Malone's voice, accompanied by the sound of splashing water, came to the Hangman.

"Here."

"We're ready to go, Sir. There's ten of us; eleven with you, Sir."

"Good lad. Shake your men out either side of me."

Quickly, Malone did as he was ordered. Once everyone was settled, The Hangman called out to his small assault group.

"Everyone got their bayonet's fixed?"

"Yes, Sir." The voices chorused around him.

"Make sure you've got your grenades handy. Don't throw them until I tell you. When we start moving; no shouting at all. Keep your mouths shut until we're at the farm. Got it?"

Again the men chorused acknowledgement.

Gallows raised his voice and bawled down the trench.

"Number Three Platoon gun teams; rapid.....*fire!*"

Thirty yards away to the left, the fire support group's weapons suddenly exploded into life with a defiant crackle. Almost instantly, numerous weapons in the farm flashed brightly in the night, spitting their own deadly hail of bullets back towards the Bren teams.

"Okay Three Platoon; forward!"

The Hangman barked the command, his voice calm, yet determined. Wordlessly, the assault group clambered over the edge of the ditch and began leaping across the ploughed field towards the dim outline of the farm. For long moments, the line of guardsmen stumbled forward in the darkness at best speed, the only noise from them being the ragged sound of their breathing and the clump of their boots on the earth.

The sound of gunfire from the Brens tailed off as the first of the three weapons ran out of ammunition. Then another fell silent. Gallows kept running, leading the way. The fence line of the farmyard, studded with bushes, was just yards away from him now. Suddenly, out of the darkness, just behind one of those bushes, came a startled shout in German. Several bright flashes rang out and Gallows heard the crack of a bullet go past his ear, followed by a grunt of surprise to his right as a guardsman went down.

"Fire!"

Almost instantly their was a ripple of rifle fire around him as the men of No.3 Platoon opened up on the hedge at point blank range. There was a yell of shock from behind the foliage and a dark shape fell over onto the ground. Two other dark figures suddenly leapt up from the edge of the farmyard and began running back towards the buildings.

"Down by the fence!" The Hangman roared. "Down!"

He slid down onto his knees by the sparse hedge and the picket fence.

"Grenades!" He roared another order. "Everyone, grenade the fuckers now!"

Dropping his rifle in his lap, Gallows thrust his hand in his trouser pocket and withdrew the pre-positioned grenade. Quickly, he changed grip and dragged the safety pin clear.

"Grenade!" He called as he lobbed the small explosive towards the wall of the farmhouse.

More calls from the other guardsmen came through the night as they too released their grenades, and the Hangman ducked low against the fence.

Crump! Crump! Crump!

One after the other, the grenades detonated at random across the farmyard and against the walls, windows and doors of the farmhouse itself and the nearby brick barn. Gallows lost count after the fifth explosion, but he waited for several more detonations then bawled out his next order into the darkness.

"On your feet! Over the fence! Those on my left into the house; those on the right take the barn!"

He dragged himself up using the fence for support and vaulted the flimsy obstacle comfortably. As he did so, another grenade exploded in the farm yard. He felt the concussive shock wave and heard the hiss of passing shrapnel but ignored it. Landing heavily, he steadied himself and then broke left, heading for the back door of the farm house. Several guardsmen were by the wall already, hesitating; not sure what to do next. Another was pumping round after round through one of the windows, working the bolt of his Lee-Enfield franticly.

"Get fucking in there!" The Hangman screamed, sprinting past the dallying guardsmen and kicking open the door of the farmhouse. As the door flew inwards, Gallows checked himself and stepped back a pace. As he did so there was bright flash from the hallway and a bullet cracked past him.

In the blink of an eye, Gallows was through the door. He saw the dim silhouette of the man who had fired, heard the rattle of the man's rifle bolt, and registered the pale blob of the man's face.

"Yaaaagh!" The Hangman snarled as he thrust his bayonet-tipped rifle forward at chest height.

He felt the blade hit something, encounter resistance, and then slide smoothly into the man's body, grating on bone as it went. The German let out an unholy scream of agony as the bayonet pierced his chest. The hangman screamed back at him, pushing him down on the floor and placing a boot on his chest, withdrawing his bayonet for another thrust.

Behind Gallows, the other guardsmen were pushing in behind him.

"Get in there!" He shouted above the screams of the dying German. "Clear every room! Kill every fucker! Kill them all!"

And as the Coldstream riflemen pushed past him, he raised his rifle vertically and drove it down once again.

Friday 31st May 1940
The Twenty Second Day

THE BEACH AT LA PANNE – 9 MILES EAST OF DUNKIRK
FRIDAY 31ST MAY 1940 – 1410 HOURS

Major General Bernard Law Montgomery surveyed the scene on the wide expanse of beach. It would have been, for anyone else, a worrying sight, but not for him. Possessed of supreme self confidence and great ambition, he knew what needed to be done, and each fresh obstacle or problem was just another puzzle for him to solve. Nothing was impossible.

He watched as the surf broke alongside the new, improvised pier which was now almost complete. Produced by his engineers in just five hours, it was a longer, sturdier example of the ad hoc efforts that had been tried already. Just as well, for there had been a stiff breeze in the morning which in turn had whipped up the surf, making the operations of the little boats even more hazardous than usual. Thankfully, with the breeze calming and the completion of his makeshift pier, the evacuation of the non-combat elements of his corps was now starting to take place.

That final evacuation of his fighting troops would not take place until later tonight of course, when his last battalions pulled out of Nieuport and Furnes, abandoning them to the enemy and leaving 1st Corps to hold the shortened line. It was a good job that his men were pulling back tonight, he decided, for they had been fighting almost non-stop since the previous evening. The Germans had begun an almost constant bombardment of the Dunkirk pocket and started to launch strong attacks across the canal. Only by outstanding feats of arms had his corps held its positions last night, counter-attacking enemy bridgeheads and fighting the Germans house by house in the blazing ruins of Nieuport and Furnes. The 151st Brigade and the 7th Guards Brigade in particular had been hard at it. But soon, all would be done.

He glanced up, watching another wave of German aircraft appear overhead. Medium bombers, not Stukas, he noted; but deadly enough. He had done everything he could in preparation for the embarkation. Routes were marked, checkpoints were established, control points were manned; and every last artillery round would be fired at the enemy before the guns were spiked and their crews departed. His corps would hold out now until nightfall, he was sure. They were a good formation, with good divisions and good commanders. He glanced out onto the shining surface of the English

Channel and surveyed the worryingly small array of ships that sat offshore. That was the only thing he couldn't control of course. He could make everything work like clockwork here on land, as was his way; but it would all count for nought if there weren't enough ships to pick them up.

"Excuse me, Sir. The divisional commanders have arrived for orders. They're all ready when you are."

The voice of the young staff captain from Corps Headquarters snapped Montgomery from his scrutiny of the beach, with its improvised pier and long lines of men waiting patiently for the promised boats. He turned and gave the captain a confident smile.

"Thank you, Simon. Let's go and get this sorted then, shall we?"

HEADQUARTERS GERMAN 18TH ARMY – NORTHERN FRANCE
FRIDAY 31ST MAY 1940 – 1430 HOURS

If the Allied armies were suffering a catastrophic defeat, then the Germans had, for several days at least, been suffering as a result of catastrophic success. Even in their wildest dreams, the German high command had never expected to win so complete a victory over the best trained and best equipped of the Allied armies. Thus, for nearly three days, various German formations had been making uncoordinated and somewhat haphazard attacks against the Dunkirk pocket, with nobody really in control. None of it had been helped by the vague assurances from head of the Luftwaffe, Herman Goring, that his air fleets could destroy what was left of the French and British armies as they sat trapped against the coast. The constant flow of ships to and fro' Dunkirk however, suggested that the boast was at the very least, a little over ambitious.

Now however, the high command had realised that they were about to let a crushing victory slip from within their grasp and produced a more swept up plan for the capture of the remaining British troops left in France and the thousands of French troops who had joined them in the fortified port of Dunkirk. That plan had involved the removal from the German equation of the panzer divisions. Unsuited to this modern version of siege warfare, these powerful and highly mobile divisions had been turned south and west, ready to punch deep into the heart of France where they expected to find the remainder of the French armies. For the panzers, there was still a lengthy and bloody campaign to fight. Here at Dunkirk, Case Yellow, the German plan for this phase of operations, was reaching its culminating point.

Standing in his temporary headquarters in a requisitioned chateau somewhere north-west of Lille, General Georg von Kuchler, commander of the German 18th Army, was getting stuck into the business of reducing the fortress of Dunkirk and sealing the German victory in Northern France. An artilleryman by trade, a former member of the General Staff, a professional and diligent organiser, and most recently a holder of the coveted Knights Cross, Kuchler was perfectly suited to deal with a task such as this. Methodical and determined, with an eye for detail, the commander of 18th Army was already in full swing, having been given his new responsibility less than twenty four hours ago. He stood facing his map board, studying the detailed dispositions that had been marked upon it, whilst at the same time dictating to one of his staff captains.

"The enemy, both French and British, have proved to be extremely stubborn in the defence of the Dunkirk perimeter. The British soldier in particular, is tenacious in defence and, when assaulted, will launch immediate and ferocious counter-attacks. The British soldier will not yield ground without a fight and will often fight on even when his ammunition is spent…"

Kuchler paused.

"Got all that, Huber?"

"Yes, General." The captain acknowledged.

"Good. New paragraph then… Initial attempts to force the enemy perimeter defences by storm have met with little success, virtually all of them being repulsed by the enemy with great vigour. Therefore it is the intention of 18th Army to conduct a detailed reduction of the enemy defences using all means available before launching renewed infantry assaults. This will involve the integration of all assets, from medium mortars to corps and army heavy artillery, and the continued support of the Luftwaffe. The Army intends to launch major infantry assaults against the southern and western sections of the enemy perimeter once the artillery preparation is complete…"

Again, Kuchler paused whilst the captain finished.

Whilst the young officer's pen scratched away in the Army's war diary, Kuchler frowned in concentration as he considered the current positions and target responsibilities of the many artillery units that he had now brought right up to the Dunkirk pocket. The biggest guns had been brought up to the River Yser, which meant, as Kuchler noted from the templates that had been traced onto the map, that they would be able to cover the entire beach and harbour. In fact, there wasn't a square meter of the enemy pocket that wasn't now covered by German artillery. In addition to that, many of his artillery units on the western and eastern flanks of the pocket would be able to reach the enemy's ships as they waited offshore.

He was still considering his Army's artillery dispositions when another staff captain entered the room.

"Excuse me, General, but the daily update from the Luftwaffe has arrived. I thought you would like to see it immediately?"

Kuchler never took his eyes away from the map board.

"Thank you, Muller." He murmured, holding a hand out.

The captain walked over to the Army Commander and handed him the piece of paper. After a few more moments of study, Kuchler stood straight and glanced down at the report. His eyes scanned the document quickly.

"No Stukas?" He commented suddenly in mild surprise.

"No. General." The captain confirmed. "They have been withdrawn for immediate use in support of Case Red. I am led to believe that the panzer divisions will be rolling southwards within the next few days. We still have Luftwaffe support, as you can see from the update, General; but they're all medium bomber squadrons."

Kuchler studied the document a moment longer.

"Pity." He grunted at last. "Stukas are useful. Still…" he brightened, "the operational ceiling for the Luftwaffe will be much higher, so that means we do not need to worry about the trajectory of our guns. We can blast away all day and just let the Luftwaffe get on with its own business. If nothing else, it makes things simpler."

Kuchler handed the report back to the captain.

"Are all our guns now in position?"

"They are, Sir. All corps have reported their guns as being in action. I don't think I'd like to be standing on the beach at Dunkirk today, if I was a Tommy."

Kuchler looked sideways again at the template traces that overlapped and interlocked each other on the map.

"No," he grimaced, "me neither…"

THE DUNES – LA PANNE BEACH, EAST OF DUNKIRK
FRIDAY 31ST MAY 1940 – 1950 HOURS

Crump… Crump…

Two more of the big German shells slammed into the dunes, close enough to make the ground beneath them shudder, but far enough away not to worry the two soldiers where they lay, side by side, in their snug little dug-out in the side of the dunes. Every time a shell landed, a small shower of loose sand would patter down on Moxon and Fellows, but other than that, the two men were reasonably comfortable.

They had been here on the beach for over a day now. The previous day had been sheer hell. The boats had been few and far between, and the two soldiers had spent most of the day, and much of the night, standing at the back of a queue of soldiers that never seemed to move. In the end, cold, tired and hungry, the two drivers from the Royal Army Service Corps had stumbled into the dunes and found a small hole in which to shelter. Swaddled in several groundsheets and rain capes they had found, the two men had passed a tolerable night in their little snug. The morning however, had brought another day of apparent despair.

A lively breeze had arrived, which blew fine sand into a man's eyes if he stood around on the beach too long; not that many men were queuing on the beach today of course. The enemy shell fire had increased dramatically since first-light, and so both Moxon and Fellows had come to the conclusion that unless there was a pressing need, they would stay in their little hideaway. At least in the dunes, the impact of the enemy shelling didn't seem to be too bad, as if the deep, soft sand was absorbing much of the shock from the huge explosions.

In addition to all of this, the water appeared to be only sparsely populated by boats, so there didn't seem much point in standing out on the beach in harm's way for nothing. The sea was rough too, and Moxon didn't like the idea of standing waist high in water for hours on end as the waves rolled over his head. All in all, the situation seemed pretty hopeless to the two drivers. There was talk that lots of people had got away via the harbour in Dunkirk itself. Apparently, down at far end of the beach, there was a long queue of troops filtering into the harbour where, in due course, they were being loaded by the hundreds into Royal Navy destroyers and evacuated. Moxon and Fellows had stared down the endless beach towards where the great pall of black smoke hung heavy in the air over the burning town of Dunkirk.

"Looks like a bloody long walk, Mickey." Fellows had commented.

"Hmm…" Was Moxon's uncertain response. "Perhaps we should wait round here during daylight and see if there's any improvement? If there's no sign of boats at this end by nightfall, then I say we start walking down the beach and join this queue for the harbour that they're all talking about."

Having decided on this as their plan of action, the two soldiers had endured several tedious hours of waiting around, their stomachs groaning with hunger. The boredom had been relieved for an hour or so mid-morning, when a sudden flurry of activity had begun along their stretch of beach. A large and highly organised body of Royal Engineers had appeared on the beach, followed by a steady stream of transport, which had been duly manoeuvred into place during low tide to form a makeshift pier. Unlike the several, smaller attempts to construct these improvised jetties further down the sand, this latest effort appeared much more deliberate. Along with the Sappers and their transport, more troops for evacuation had also appeared, but most of these were in formed groups and properly led. Military Policemen had appeared too, commanded by staff officers who began the process of bringing a certain degree of order to the chaos.

All in all, the activity exuded an air of professional competence and it proved to be something of a tonic for Moxon and Fellows, both of whom were beginning to miss the ruthless order and discipline of their erstwhile companions in the 1st Battalion Coldstream Guards. But, after a good while of watching the activity, Moxon and Fellows realised that for all the apparent sense of purpose that had infected the troops on the beaches, the reality was that there were precious few boats out there on the water, and many of those that did come into the shore were foundering in the turbulent surf.

"Come on." Moxon had said eventually. "Let's get back in our hole and keep out of the way. There's nothing we can do here."

And so here they sat, tucked up together, shoulder to shoulder, smoking endless cigarettes and trying to find things to talk about in order to pass the time, becoming so used to the crash of incoming artillery fire that they no longer flinched when the shells landed. Fellows shivered.

"Christ, Mickey; it's getting a bit nippy now, even though that wind's died down."

"Wha…"

Moxon blinked his eyes open. He looked around the small dug-out in surprise for a moment.

"Oh, sorry; must have dozed off."

Fellows shifted his position and pulled the ground sheet around him a bit tighter.

"I was just saying, it's getting a bit chilly now, mate. Think it must be getting late. Won't be too long before nightfall, I reckon…"

Moxon grunted.

"Wish my watch was still working."

"I wouldn't worry, Mickey; we'll know soon enough when the sun starts to drop."

He glanced at his friend.

"I was just thinking... Perhaps we should start walking along the beach now; towards the harbour? Make a start of it before it gets dark? Don't want to miss the chance of getting off tonight..."

Moxon frowned tiredly as he considered the suggestion.

"Suppose we could... Don't fancy being on the end of the Jerry planes mind you. How busy are they today?"

"Not that bad, I don't think."

Crump.

Another shell landed somewhere along the beach.

"Jerry's still shelling the fuck out of the beach mind you." Fellows grumbled.

"Mmmm." Moxon stifled a yawn. "Sounds a bit fucking dangerous to me, mate."

"We should risk it though, Mickey." Fellows pressed. "I'd rather be taking my chances while there's still a bit of light, rather than stumbling along in the dark."

Moxon looked round at his friend, detecting a note of desperation in the man's voice.

"You alright, Stan?"

Fellows took a deep breath.

"I've had enough of all this sitting around, mate." He blurted. "At least when we were stuck with the Guards I didn't have any time to think on things. Now we're just sat here, my mind keeps turning over. It's killing me, Mickey, all this waiting round; not knowing what's going to happen next. I'd rather be doing something than just waiting round with no idea how I'm going to get home."

Moxon regarded his friend with pity. The poor chap was near the end of his tether.

"I know mate; I know. But it won't be long now and we'll be off."

Fellows looked away and Moxon saw that his friend was desperately trying to control himself. The man's lips were clamped firmly shut, but even so, his whole face was trembling.

"I don't want to be a bloody prisoner, Mickey." Fellows blurted suddenly. "I just want to go back to England..."

Moxon pushed himself upright and straightened his helmet. Fellows wasn't far off breaking point, he realised. He needed something to keep him going.

"Tell you what then mate. Why don't we get our kit together? We'll have a look round and see if there's any scoff lying about that we can nick; then we'll start walking along the beach a bit, eh. Like you say; won't hurt to get a couple of miles in before the sun goes down."

Fellows nodded his head sharply, but didn't speak or look at his friend. Moxon suspected he was crying.

"Come on then, Stan." Moxon groaned, sliding himself sideways out of the little shelter. "Let's get organised, mate."

"Alright, next group move up onto the jetty. Keep it tight. Once you're on there, keep it nice and calm. No pushing or shoving; take your turn for the boats and keep it nice and orderly."

The sound of the unknown voice came drifting down to Moxon as he scrambled out of the dug-out. The voice was followed by the sound of tramping feet, the footsteps muffled in the deep sand. Moxon, blinking in the sunlight, glanced up at the top of the dune. To his surprise, he saw a Military Police sergeant standing atop the dune, one arm pointing imperiously towards the beach which lay hidden beyond.

Filing past the MP in an orderly column of twos, was a large group of approximately fifty men. As Moxon studied the group closely he spotted the Royal Artillery insignia and noticed that several men were carrying what looked like sight units, whilst others stumbled along with heavy looking lumps of metal; breech blocks from abandoned guns. Moxon stood and, stretching his legs, struggled up the dune to stand beside the sergeant. As he stepped up beside the NCO, Moxon took in the sight below him on the beach. He was so surprised by what he saw that he took a pace back and nearly toppled backwards down the dune again.

Below him on the beach, hundreds, if not thousands of men, were queued along the now finished jetty. The sea, calmer than before, but still lively, had come up the beach to surround the improvised causeway, the waves rolling gently against its sides in a tumble of white froth. And further along the jetty, several hundred yards out into the grey swell of the English Channel, a whole fleet of small boats littered the water.

There were small craft of every description. Good sized sailing boats, motor launches, a small fishing trawler, and what looked like a Thames pleasure boat. These were just the vessels that rose and fell alongside the ad hoc pier as soldiers clambered down into them, one at a time. Further out, and all along the horizon to the west, more of these little ships could be seen. Beyond them, well out from the shallow waters, sat the destroyers and larger passenger ships. Unbeknown to Moxon, he was witnessing the arrival of the 'little ships'; the hastily requisitioned fleet of civilian and merchant vessels assembled by Admiral Ramsay's Dynamo team. Having been warned by naval and military sources alike that there was little time left to rescue the remaining troops, Ramsay was throwing everything he could muster at the evacuation. In addition to the flow of destroyers and passenger ships heading for the battered harbour and mole, and directed by the newly arrived Admiral Wake-Walker from his floating command post, Ramsay's fleet of small craft were now making an all-out effort to lift troops from the beaches.

As Moxon surveyed the unbelievable scene before him, two German shells slammed into the sea between a group of the small boats, sending two huge spouts of water into the air. The boats in the vicinity rose and fell on the swell of the displaced water, but on they sailed; slowly, steadily, coming in against the line of assembled vehicles.

"Bloody hell!" Moxon gasped.

As the last pair of Gunners tramped past, the sergeant from the MPs turned to look at Moxon.

"Are you part of this group, sonny?"

Moxon blinked at the NCO.

"Er, yes… Yes, Sergeant."

The MP jerked his head towards the pier.

"Get a bloody move on then. We haven't got all day."

And with that, the sergeant stomped off after the line of artillerymen headed for the jetty.

"Stan?" Moxon cried out, his voice cracking with elation. "Stan? Get your kit on mate; quickly…"

Fellows shoved his head out of the dug out and stared up at Moxon with red-rimmed eyes.

"What's up?"

Moxon could barely get his words out, so overcome was he with relief.

"Get your kit on, Stan…" He blurted again. "We're going home!"

FRENCH HEADQUARTERS – BASTION 32, DUNKIRK
FRIDAY 31ST MAY 1940 – 2310 HOURS

Major General, The Honourable Harold Alexander found that the mood at the French Headquarters was not much improved from his earlier visit that day. It had been a little after 1300 hours that afternoon when Lord Gort had sprung the news on Alexander that he was to assume command of 1st Corps and fight the rear guard action for the BEF. Having been in plenty of tight spots before, Alexander had taken the news in his stride. In response to Gort's assertion that there was a good chance that the entire corps, and indeed Alexander himself, would end up *'going into the bag'*, Alexander had merely nodded and calmly announced his intention to save every last man that could be saved before the Germans closed in. Gort, without any real conviction, had told him that he might have some difficulties with the French, but as Alexander was now in charge of what was left of the BEF, he must therefore use his own discretion in regard to surrendering the Rear Guard or evacuating it.

Following that discussion, Alexander had come here to the French Headquarters in the centre of the old fortress town, accompanied by Tennant, the Royal Navy officer who was doing such sterling work in masterminding the evacuation. What followed was an uncomfortable hour where various French commanders had vented their spleen on Alexander when they learned he intended to evacuate his remaining forces. They had been given assurances by Gort, they claimed, that the remaining British troops would go down fighting with their French allies. Alexander, remaining calm, had explained that he saw no reason to sacrifice perfectly good soldiers that could fight again another day and that he was duty-bound to do his best for his men.

That had provoked a flurry of barely concealed contempt from the Frenchmen. Whilst Vice-Admiral Jean Abrial, French commander of the Channel coast garrisons, had remained silent, his chief-of-staff had launched a vitriolic attack on Alexander and Gort, accusing one or the other of lying, and trying to abandon the French to their fate. Fagalde, the senior French military commander present, who was actually an old friend of the British from the Great War, had read out a letter from Gort explaining that Alexander was to cooperate with Fagalde in the defence of Dunkirk. Altmayer, a French corps commander, had weighed in, pleading for the British to stay.

Despite the barrage of protest, Alexander had maintained a firm position. His duty was to evacuate the remainder of the BEF. He would of course, cooperate willingly with the French in defence of the port, but only long enough to ensure the escape of the troops who were trapped there. Furthermore, he encouraged the French to do likewise. It was clear however, that the French had given up on the idea of evacuation. They were almost beaten. Instead of thinking practically, all the assembled French officers could talk about was 'honour' and the need to satisfy it. They used that same word to prick Alexander's conscience too; enquiring about the honour of the British Army.

All said, it had been a thoroughly unpleasant hour. Alexander though, was not a man for argument and bad blood. He had left that first meeting having assured his French allies that he would seek clarification from the British

Secretary of State for War as to what he was expected to do. Abrial, desperate to preserve Allied solidarity, had encouraged him to do just that, in order to 'clear up the confusion'. Now, after a busy afternoon and evening, Alexander was back at French headquarters with the answer. And they didn't like it.

Alexander stood there now, in a headquarters that was less busy than earlier. Of the irate chief of staff, there was no sign. Fagalde and Altmayer too were otherwise engaged. Thus it was with some relief that Alexander found himself speaking one to one with Abrial. Even so, the conversation was still difficult.

"But what about this, General Alexander?" Abrial waved the piece of paper at him. "Will you go against the words of your own Prime Minister, who just this afternoon made this decision in Paris at a meeting of the highest level?"

Alexander eyed the piece of paper impassively as it fluttered between Abrial's fingers. He knew what the message said. It was, quite simply, a vague directive from the joint leadership of France and Britain that was open to interpretation.

The admiral had read it to Alexander not just once, but twice. It said that the remaining British troops were under Abrial's command and that the designated British commander should make decisions about the conduct of the defence in conjunction with his French allies. As far as Alexander was concerned, that's exactly what he was doing now. He gathered himself then spoke.

"Admiral, as the senior British officer left at Dunkirk, I am required to follow the direct orders as issued to me by the Secretary of State for War, with who I am in direct contact. As much as I am sure our leaders have tried their best to make an informed decision at their Paris meeting, the fact is that the Secretary of State directs me from London, and in the absence of the Prime Minister he has made his decision based on the most up to date knowledge of the situation available to him. To that end, he has ordered me to hold on until the night of the 1st and 2nd of June, by which time I should have attempted to embark what remains of the British Expeditionary Force. Furthermore, I have been tasked with ensuring that French soldiers are also evacuated alongside the British, at a ratio of one to one."

Abrial lowered his hand; the one clutching the message from Paris. The fire in the admiral's eyes was going out and he regarded Alexander with a look of resignation.

"You will disobey this instruction?" He asked quietly. "You will dishonour your nation?"

Alexander didn't flinch. He faced the admiral quite calmly, knowing that the worst was over and that it was time to finish the business.

"I will obey my direct orders from the Secretary of State for War." The British general said in an even voice. "I will continue the evacuation throughout tomorrow, which will include the evacuation of French troops. My 1st Corps will hold their sector of the perimeter throughout that period, including the shortened flank we now have since our 2nd Corps began to pull out. We will continue to hold until 2359 hours tomorrow evening. At that point, my remaining troops will abandon their positions and withdraw to the coast."

Abrial said nothing. He simply stared at Alexander for several moments. Then, like a man bearing a terrible burden, he turned away and walked quietly from the room.

Saturday 1st June 1940
The Twenty Third Day

THE REAR GUARD – BERGUES-FURNES CANAL, 6 MILES SOUTH-EAST OF DUNKIRK
SATURDAY 1ST JUNE 1940 – 0600 HOURS

"That looks like it hurts… a lot."

Whittaker grimaced as he watched Jackson drag the razor across his chin. The big sergeant was squatting in the bottom of the hastily dug trench, carefully using his razor and mirror to remove any offending remnant of stubble. Due to the lack of water, there was no more than a drop of moisture on the blade, and given the time of morning, Jackson's flesh must be freezing. To shave under such circumstances seemed like an act of torture that no ordinary person would inflict on themselves. But there again, neither Jackson nor the men in his platoon were ordinary in the slightest, Whittaker reflected. They were guardsmen.

The tall sergeant flicked his gaze at Whittaker and grinned.

"You're not wrong there, Sir." He confirmed. "Still, it has to be done. Especially after the battle we had yesterday. Reckon we'll be in for it again today. What would happen if I got shot before I'd had a shave? Christ, old George Monck would be waiting for me at the Pearly Gates to put me on restriction of privileges before I even set foot in Heaven!"

Whittaker gave a grunt of a laugh.

"Who on earth is George Monck?"

Jackson winced as his blade dragged out a particularly stubborn whisker.

"George Monck, Sir, was the 1st Duke of Albemarle, Lord High Admiral, the man who restored the Monarchy to the throne, first Colonel of the Coldstream Guards, and an all round good bloke."

"Ah..." Whittaker murmured, pretending that he understood what the sergeant was talking about. "And do you think the Lord God Almighty takes guardsmen into Heaven then?"

Jackson wiped his razor on the small towel laid across his knee, regarding the pilot with a serious look.

"Of course he does, Sir. God himself is an honorary Coldstreamer. Why else do you think the place is kept so clean?"

Whittaker grinned.

"I doubt he'll have any of you air force types, though..." Jackson went on. "He's only choosey about who he lets in the place... So the padre tells me, anyway."

That made the pilot laugh.

"Sure you don't want to borrow this, Sir?"

Jackson held the razor up.

"No, thank you." Whittaker shook his head and ran a hand self consciously over his beard which was now eleven days old. "I think I'll need some scissors before I try the razor."

The sergeant shrugged and began packing his washing and shaving kit neatly away. As he did so, Whittaker glanced along the trench with a fresh sense of admiration. These men were the most phlegmatic, business-like people he had ever come across. Just yesterday, they had been fighting for their lives against ferocious German attacks, whilst dodging the endless artillery shells that the enemy was throwing into the Dunkirk pocket, doing their best to grind the defenders down.

Despite the relentless battering, these men from the 2nd Battalion of the Coldstream Guards just continued with their duty regardless, as if it were all in a day's work for them. Already, at this early point in the morning, every man in the trench had managed to scrape his face with a razor. Beyond Jackson, another soldier was busy applying polish to his boots. Behind Whittaker, another guardsman was cleaning his rifle. They were tired; dog tired. But they were still defiant; as solid as the Rock of Gibraltar. Whittaker was glad he'd decided to stay with them.

He'd spent the day before filling Bren Gun magazines. Over and over again, the empty magazines had come sliding down the side of the trench into his lap as the gunner and his companion had rattled away furiously at the attacking Germans. With fingers covered in cuts, and small blisters on his thumbs, the RAF officer had shoved round after round into the empty magazines, replenishing them as rapidly as possible. It was surprisingly hard work, especially once you'd done a dozen or more without a break. But still the Germans attacked, so still the Bren Gun spat its deadly bullets towards them, emptying one magazine after another.

Strangely, despite the ferocity of the attacks, Whittaker had not felt the slightest inclination to leave his new found friends. In the absence of his squadron, the young pilot had come across this thoroughly charming bunch of people in the most unlikely circumstances. It was clear that the standards of discipline in this unit were harsh, yet at the same time there was a calm, familiar comradeship amongst the men who shared this long trench. Despite the foul language and black humour, Whittaker was quite taken at how wonderful the manners were of this battered group of infantrymen. They had served him a supper of sliced corned beef and hard biscuits in a mess tin, with all the formality and ceremony of a five course meal at a well-to-do London restaurant, and provided him with a ground-sheet, blanket and steel helmet in the same way that a valet would offer a selection of ties to his master when dressing him in the morning.

Whoosh-crump! Whoosh-crump!

The two shells slammed into the field behind, causing the ground to tremble around them.

"Looks like it's our turn again then?" Jackson commented nonchalantly as he fastened up his small pack, ensuring that his ground sheet was folded under the flap in a manner that was just-so.

The sergeant looked up at Whittaker again.

"Are you sure you won't get off to the beach, Sir? You really don't need to hang around you know? As much as we appreciate your company *and* your help..."

The sergeant gave him a searching look.

"I'm sure they could do with you back in England. I don't suppose fighter pilots grow on trees..."

Whittaker smiled his appreciation.

"Perhaps later..." He replied. "When the shelling has died down a bit."

In his mind, Whittaker didn't like the idea of what he might find if he went to the beach. His experience of two days before was still at the forefront of his mind and it still caused him distress to remember it. The truth was that despite the Germans and despite the shelling, Whittaker felt safe here.

Whoosh-crump! Whoosh-crump!

More shells exploded with a sickening crash nearby and a shower of earth rained down into the trench.

"Looks like the buggers mean business..." Jackson commented sourly, looking up at the sky as if he were assessing the weather rather than enemy artillery fire.

He glanced across at the man behind the Bren Gun.

"Bet you wish you were back home in Hull with your folks, eh, Hawkins?"

The young guardsman looked back over his shoulder.

"You must be joking, Sergeant? I was glad to get away from the place."

Jackson frowned.

"Really?"

"Aye." Hawkins nodded, a sad look crossing his face. "If I'd stayed in Hull I'd only be helping my old man and my brothers to rob scrap metal from decent hardworking folk. Either that or I'd be on some fishing trawler. Can't say it was a way of life that appealed to me."

The guardsman spat over the lip of the trench.

"No. I'm more than happy being here, Sergeant. Joining up was the best thing I could have done. I'm going to make something of myself in this world. I promised myself that, years ago."

Jackson regarded Hawkins thoughtfully.

"Well, I reckon you've done that already, Hawkins lad." He murmured.

"Jerries!"

The calm, yet urgent voice of the guardsman on sentry duty made everyone in the trench look up.

"How many?" Jackson demanded. "Where?"

"About four hundred yards out, Sergeant." The soldier stated. "Must be a couple of dozen of 'em at least' using the drainage ditches to get up to those burnt out trucks. I reckon they're going to set up machine-guns or something. They're coming out of the ditch now... running for the trucks."

"Here they come..." Jackson called to everyone in the trench. "Stand-to!"

The trench came alive. Whittaker heard the man behind him slide his rifle bolt back into its housing. Along the trench, the Bren Gunner called Hawkins and several other riflemen began sliding their weapons up onto the parapet. As the guardsmen began preparing for action, there was the sound of splashing from the nearby drainage ditch. Whittaker and Jackson looked up at the crawl trench which led from their own position back into the ditch. A moment later, a helmeted head appeared and glanced down at them.

"Morning, Sergeant J" Came the tired voice of the young second lieutenant who commanded this platoon, a pleasant chap by the name of

Dunstable. "Morning, Dickie." The officer continued as he noticed Whittaker. "Are you still with us, then?"

"Certainly am, old boy." Whittaker confirmed. "I'm quite enjoying myself to be honest."

Dunstable grinned.

"Well, I've got a real treat for you then. Looks like the Jerries are going to try and take us from the flank. Numbers One and Three company have got a major assault building over on the right; looks as though the enemy are filtering round them and trying to get in between us and the chaps on our flank."

Jackson cleared his throat, and began adjusting the sights of his rifle.

"We've got a couple of dozen to our front too, Sir; over by those trashed vehicles. Could be setting up a fire support position, maybe?"

Dunstable pulled a face.

"Okay; you know the drill. Keep the buggers pinned down if you can, but watch the ammunition. Not sure if we'll be able to get much more. It's surprising how quickly you can get through it. "

The officer glanced back at Whittaker.

"If you *are* planning to get off, Dickie, you might want to think about going sooner rather than later."

Whittaker smiled in acknowledgement.

"Thanks; I'll have a think about it."

Whittaker nodded back.

"Righto, then. I'll get off back to my position now. Good shooting, everyone. I'll pop back later and see how you're getting on."

And with that, Dunstable disappeared again, back down the crawl trench and into the ditch. The sound of splashing feet gradually faded into the distance.

"You alright to do the Bren magazines again, Sir?"

Jackson was up in his fire position now, glancing back down at Whittaker.

"Absolutely." The pilot grinned. "I'd be honoured."

Whoosh-crump!

Another explosion shook the ground.

"I fucking hate Germans!" One of the guardsmen commented.

"Let's see if we can kill a few more of the bastards then." Jackson replied, then, drawing a huge breath, he bellowed out a fire control order.

"No.1 Section, four hundred, slightly left, burnt out trucks; enemy in trucks, rapiiiiiid… fire!"

TENNANT'S COMMAND POST – DUNKIRK HARBOUR
SATURDAY 1ST JUNE 1940 – 0815 HOURS

"Good Lord…" Tennant whispered, lowering his binoculars.

His theory about good news and bad news being equal in war was holding true; although today, it looked as if the bad news might have the better of it. Yesterday had been, rather surprisingly, the best day yet for the evacuation. Despite the slow start to the day, due mainly to the interference from enemy artillery and the poor sea condition along the beaches, things had improved as the day wore on, with the sea settling somewhat, just before the arrival of the substantial fleet of small craft despatched by Ramsay.

As a result of this development, and the continued use of the mole throughout the night, Tennant's staff estimated that in excess of 65,000 troops had been lifted during the previous twenty four hours. The bulk of the 2nd Corps of the BEF had gone, along with the remainder of GHQ, including Lord Gort himself. What was left was the Rear Guard, a not insignificant amount of waifs and strays, and of course, tens of thousands of Frenchmen who must now be evacuated hand in hand with the British, according to the latest orders.

But today, Tennant feared, was going to be a different story. Apart from the fact that the perimeter had shrunk due to the withdrawal of 2nd Corps the previous night, thereby allowing German artillery even closer to the beaches, Saturday morning over Dunkirk had dawned clear and bright. As a result, the Luftwaffe had appeared over the shattered town even as the darkness began to fade. For three and a half hours now, a relentless stream of German planes had rained explosive destruction on the packed ships around the harbour and mole, as well as those ships lying offshore. Even worse, the Stukas were back today. Tennant hated them. Their whining and screaming filled his mind constantly, adding to the cacophony of noise that pervaded the air, making it almost impossible to concentrate. Not only that, the sound of the Stukas rattled people. Everything seemed to take longer when the Stukas were above. Men were frozen in fear or else became indecisive and unable to apply simple logic. And of course, the Stukas were deadly accurate.

As Tennant stared out across the wide expanse of the Channel, his heart felt heavy as he watched the tragic sight of two Royal Navy destroyers on fire, one of them heeling dangerously over to starboard. In addition to the destroyers, there was a smaller vessel, a minesweeper by the looks, already slipping beneath the surface, a great plume of steam rising from her as she went down. Even without his binoculars Tennant could see the black smear on the water around the sinking ship. It wasn't oil; it was a mass of men. This was the grim reality of war at sea. Even for a hardened Naval man, this was a difficult scene to behold, not least of all because it made Tennant realise that since the last war, technology had introduced a new and terrible factor to war at sea; the aeroplane. Like it or not, aircraft had changed the dynamic. From now on, the Royal Navy would have to invest just as much time, effort and weaponry in its anti-aircraft defences as it did in its big guns and anti-submarine equipment. That was war for you.

"Captain Tennant, Sir?"

The Senior Naval Officer Ashore Dunkirk looked over as Lieutenant Drake, his young aide, emerged from the shelter of the nearby bunker.

"Yes, Mr Drake."

"Bad news, Sir, I'm afraid. We've had a message from Admiral Wake-Walker. He's transferring his flag; new ship to be confirmed. Apparently the Keith has been hit several times and she's starting to go down. She's being abandoned as we speak. The message also says that the Basilisk has taken some pretty serious damage too. There's a good chance she won't last."

Tennant absorbed the information silently. After a while he pointed out to sea.

"Any idea which ship that is that's going under? Looks like the Skipjack?"

Drake turned his gaze towards the Channel and took in the scene before him. Tennant watched as the lieutenant paled visibly.

"I'll go and ask, Sir." He said at last, a grave look on his youthful features.

Tennant nodded.

"Please do. And send an immediate signal back to Admiral Ramsay. Ask him to give the RAF a kick will you, please? It's not even nine o'clock and it looks like we've lost three ships already. If it carries on like this much longer then we'll be well and truly buggered."

THE REAR GUARD – BERGUES-FURNES CANAL, 6 MILES SOUTH-EAST OF DUNKIRK
SATURDAY 1ST JUNE 1940 – 1200 HOURS

"Leave him!" Jackson yelled at the RAF officer in the bottom of the trench. "Just keep filling those magazines!"

Whittaker, frozen in position by the shock, stared for several heartbeats at the blood-smeared face of the guardsman who had collapsed in a heap right in front of him. The man wasn't moving, moaning or giving any signs of life and, due to the huge amount of blood that covered the man's face from the eyes down, Whittaker assumed that he must have been hit in the face by something.

"Magazine!"

The voice of Guardsman Hawkins roared out as Whittaker heard the by now familiar metallic 'clink' as the Bren Gun fired its last round. Next came the sound of scrabbling, the click of a fresh magazine being rammed into place, the ratchet sound of the weapon being cocked, followed once more by the relentless 'rat-tat-tat' of automatic fire. An empty magazine was thrown, without ceremony, down into Whittaker's lap by the No.2 on the Bren Gun.

With a start, Whittaker jerked his gaze away from the badly injured soldier and returned to his endless task of re-filling the Bren Gun magazines. He grabbed the nearest bandolier and popped open the press-stud, removed the two five-round clips of ammunition and quickly dragged the individual rounds free from the metal chargers. Then, with tender, bleeding fingers, he slotted one round after another into the top of the curved magazine.

Several paces away down the trench, Jackson was screaming out a new fire-control order. This was Jackson's world and Whittaker was merely a visitor to this strange land, content to be subordinate not just to the sergeant, but to the guardsmen too. They were the professionals here; the men who had been trained for just such a situation and Whittaker simply did as he was told and did it as well as he could manage.

"Kendrick and Thompson, stop!" Jackson hollered towards the furthest two men in the long trench. "New target. Two hundred and fifty, half-right, derelict barn, enemy snipers in ruins; watch and shoot!"

"Everything alright, Sergeant Jackson?" Whittaker shouted as he forced yet more rounds into the magazine.

The platoon sergeant ducked below the parapet of the trench and dragged the bolt of his rifle open before reaching into his own pouch for a fresh clip of ammunition.

"The Jerries are trying to get right up to the bank across our whole frontage. Not sure if they're going to try and force a crossing or if they're just trying to pin us down while they push hard over on our right. There's a lot of fighting right along the canal as far as I can see."

Whittaker reached up and placed the filled Bren magazine on the parapet next to the No.2.

"Sounds bad?" Whittaker ventured.

"Could be… if the bastards get over the canal on our right. Just make sure you keep your head down, Sir. The fuckers have got our range."

Crack.

A bullet passed right overhead, missing the Bren Gun team by inches, confirming the validity of the sergeant's warning.

"Sergeant Jackson?"

Dunstable's voice sounded behind them and both the sergeant and Whittaker turned towards the crawl trench. The young platoon commander was there again, his head, shoulders and arms protruding through the cut away rat-run.

"Here you go..." The lieutenant said, tossing three bandoliers of ammunition down into the trench. "A present from the Company Sergeant Major. How are you doing?"

Jackson slammed his rifle bolt shut and locked it off.

"We're okay, Sir. The Jerries are weedling their way forward bit-by-bit, mind you. Not sure if they're just trying to keep us fixed here or if they're going to cross the canal."

Dunstable frowned.

"Just keep at them, Sergeant J. You've got to hold them. Whoever the unit was between us and the East Lancs, they've piled in apparently. I just spoke with Mr Langley from No.3 Company. The Jerries have got across on the right of the battalion and No.1 Company are having a hard time of it trying to shore that flank up. No.3 Company are in the same boat as us; same as No.2 Company."

Jackson nodded his understanding.

"Don't worry, Sir. As long as we've got ammunition we're not going anywhere!"

"Good man." Dunstable grinned.

Whoosh-crump! Whoosh-crump! Whoosh-crump!

The belt of mortar bombs exploded just yards away from the trench. Shrapnel whistled past the guardsmen as soil pattered down around them.

"Ah, fuck!" Hawkins swore.

"Hawkins? You alright?" Jackson looked up at the Bren gunner with alarm.

"Yeah..." Hawkins replied curtly, rubbing his eyes with his right fist. "Just got a load of dirt in my eyes. I'm okay."

Reassured, Jackson looked back at Dunstable.

"That's trench-mortar, that is; heavy rate of fire too. I reckon they're up to something."

"Probably." Dunstable agreed. "Just keep your eyes peeled and give the buggers hell!"

With those parting words, Dunstable shuffled backwards along the crawl trench and dropped back down into the drainage ditch.

No sooner had the young officer disappeared than the shout went up from the No.2 on the Bren Gun.

"Boats!"

"What?" Jackson threw his eyes back over the front of the parapet.

"Boats, Sergeant!" Guardsman Allen confirmed. "They're dragging a couple of rubber boats along the ditch behind the ruined barn! Looks like they're going to try a crossing!"

"Bollocks!" Jackson swore.

He looked down at Whittaker.

"Without sounding cheeky, Sir; do you know how to use a rifle?"

"Uum… it's been a while but I'm sure I can…"

"Good." Jackson snapped. "Because we're going to need every weapon we've got. Grab that rifle there, and a bandolier. Then get up here next to Kendrick, Sir, please? Shoot anything carrying a boat…"

TENNANT'S COMMAND POST – DUNKIRK HARBOUR
SATURDAY 1ST JUNE 1940 – 1750 HOURS

"That's a damn sight better, Sir." Exclaimed Drake, pointing up at the thick, grey cloud that now covered the sky above Dunkirk. "We haven't seen anything for over an hour now. Hopefully that'll keep the Luftwaffe away until nightfall."

Tennant snorted.

"Amen to that, Mr Drake."

The naval captain checked his wrist-watch.

"Almost six. Roll on nine. Darkness can't come soon enough."

Tennant stood there, fuming silently for a while. He was tired; very tired. Tired and under enormous pressure. And it had been a bad day. He wouldn't know how bad for a few hours yet, but even so, he had seen enough ships and small craft go beneath the surface today to understand that the evacuation fleet had suffered heavy losses; so heavy that they could not possibly sustain such losses indefinitely. And there still seemed to be an endless supply of troops to be taken off. Tennant really didn't know where the men were coming from. In fact, Tennant was becoming so worried that time would finally run out on him that he had, just that afternoon, made one of the most difficult decisions of the evacuation thus far. He had ordered that with the exception of dedicated hospital ships, the evacuation fleet was to stop taking stretcher cases on board its ships. As far as everybody was now concerned, it was standing room only for those wanting to get away from

Dunkirk. Besides, the reality was that if Britain was going to continue its war with Germany, she was going to need fit, able bodied, fighting men; not the maimed and the crippled. It was harsh, but it was the right thing, indeed the *only* thing to do. This was war.

He scanned the vista with his binoculars once more. The harbour was crammed with ships, still taking on men before making the dash across the Channel to Dover. Around the berthed vessels, the masts of numerous sunken craft punctuated the flat grey waters of Dunkirk harbour. Out to sea, departing ships were far off towards the horizon, many of them trailing huge plumes of smoke. Even those ships that hadn't been sunk had suffered heavily, Tennant reflected. It had certainly been a tough, hard day for the sailors. The only spark of light in an otherwise dark day was that, despite the best efforts of the Luftwaffe and the German artillery, the evacuation had continued throughout. Slowed considerably at times and interrupted momentarily on occasion, the flow of men out to the ships and boats had proceeded against all the odds. It was just possible that the day's sacrifices might have been worth it. Just possible. But it couldn't go on like this.

Tennant lowered his binoculars and turned to his aide once more.

"Mr Drake? Get a signal off to Dover for me would you, please? Tell Admiral Ramsay that it is now impossible to evacuate during the hours of daylight without suffering catastrophic losses to shipping. Therefore, with immediate effect, ships will only evacuate under cover of darkness. The last ship out of Dunkirk tonight will be 0300 hours, 2nd June. After that, the operation will come to a halt until tomorrow night."

Drake raised an eyebrow as he wrote the message down, glancing up at Tennant as if for confirmation. Tennant's face was impassive, his eyes red-rimmed and sunken with exhaustion.

"Get the signal off immediately please, Mr Drake."

Sunday 2nd June 1940
The Twenty Fourth Day

THE EAST MOLE – DUNKIRK HARBOUR
SUNDAY 2ND JUNE 1940 – 0300 HOURS

Jackson didn't consider himself a religious man, but if he'd been asked to describe a picture of hell, this was it. Behind him, half a mile away,

Dunkirk town and the quaysides of the main harbour still burned fiercely, the ancient port no more than a ruin; a pile of rubble that somehow contained enough combustible material still to feed the hungry flames. The garish light cast by the inferno played on the waters of the harbour, revealing the ghostly sight of numerous masts of sunken ships. Further back, towards the concrete pier, the beaches and the shattered town, the half-light gave just enough illumination to reveal to the retreating British soldiers the endless trail of dead bodies; human and animal, British and French, military and civilian. Dunkirk was, in every sense of the word, a slaughter house.

Jackson and his men had been on the move since just before midnight, having received the unbelievable news that they were to be saved after all. The French, it seemed, were staying put; manning a tight perimeter around the town itself by making use of the final, inner-canal line, while the remaining troops of the BEF's Rear Guard were pulled back to the harbour to await their deliverance. After an all day running battle and yet more casualties within his platoon, even Jackson had felt a sense of relief at the news. Not wanting to appear overly keen to abandon the fight however, he had ensured that the platoon's withdrawal had been as orderly as possible, and that they had brought all of their weaponry and equipment with them.

The Germans, thankfully, had taken something of a breather after their furious assaults of the previous thirty six hours, and so the men of the Rear Guard had been able to extract from their exposed positions under cover of darkness with little difficulty, but with much relief. Jackson's platoon, having started the campaign with thirty two, mustered just nineteen men now, including himself and Dunstable. And the RAF officer was still with them of course. Mustering well to the rear of their defensive positions, the remnants of the 2nd Battalion Coldstream Guards had rendezvoused behind the screen force from their own carrier platoon. In the darkness, as the platoons and companies reformed, it became apparent that the battles of the last few days had taken a terrible toll on the battalion.

Number Four Company had been relatively lucky, being able to muster some sixty five members, including all its officers. Numbers One and Three Companies however had been decimated. Not one officer was left in either of those rifle companies. Poor old Major McCorquadale, the popular commander of No.3 Company, was dead; Mr Langley, a well respected platoon commander, had been carted off to the rear, seriously wounded. The Signals Officer was dead also.

The list went on, as old comrades found each other in the dark and swapped the news of their exploits and hardships. Many of Jackson's friends from the Sergeants' Mess were dead, missing or wounded. Even Battalion

Headquarters had suffered its share of casualties from the relentless shelling and bombing. Thus it was that when the battalion began its rapid march back to the coast, through a dark, explosive filled landscape of chaos, a little over four hundred men from the original eight hundred were present in that long, snake-like column.

And here they stood, quietly agitated but pretending calmness as they queued, with the other battalions of the Rear Guard, on the perilously thin, exposed East Mole at the shattered harbour of Dunkirk. Every man had his rifle or Bren Gun, his helmet, webbing and small pack. The warrant officers and NCOs had made sure of it. As far as they were concerned, the regiment did not retreat, it only made tactical withdrawals, and so the whole business had been carried out with the appropriate level of discipline, and subject to the standard equipment checks that were a part of life for guardsmen.

"I hope they've got enough ships."

The sound of Whittaker's voice broke into Jackson's silent contemplation of the last few hours.

"There will be, Sir. Don't worry yourself." He answered the RAF officer confidently, although in truth, the same worry was beginning to niggle at his own mind.

"Just seems like the queue isn't moving very fast, that's all."

The RAF officer sounded exhausted, as if he could have fallen asleep where he was standing.

"It's always the way, Sir." Jackson reassured him. "Queues always seem to take hours to move anywhere, whether it's the queue for the NAAFI or the queue for the train, it always seems to take forever."

"Yes..." Whittaker allowed with a feint, tired chuckle. "I suppose..."

Whoosh-splosh.

Another German shell streaked down out of the darkness and landed in the harbour, some hundred yards away from the mole. It was just another in an endless stream that came whining in, every minute or so. Jackson watched the geyser of water rise in the semi-darkness and splash back down again.

"They don't give up, those bastards, do they?" He remarked casually.

"True; very true." Came a new, well-spoken voice. "But I wouldn't worry about it too much; they're not very accurate. Just being a bit of a nuisance, that's all."

Jackson peered at the tall figure that had appeared in front of them, having strolled nonchalantly along the mole from the direction of the embarkation point. Straining his eyes in the flickering light of distant flames, the sergeant suddenly realised that the newcomer was wearing a service dress jacket and Sam Browne, along with riding breeches and a steel helmet. Even in the half-light, it was obvious that the tall, elegant man was an immaculately turned out officer. As Jackson continued his study, he picked out, first the red collar tabs of an officer from the General Staff, and then, as one of the large fires in the harbour flared violently, the dignified features of Major General, The Honourable Harold Alexander. Shit; it was the Divisonal Commander.

"Platoon!" Jackson snapped sideways at his men.

Despite their fatigue, the line of guardsmen reacted instinctively and braced up, adopting the position of attention.

"Relax, gentlemen; please, relax." Alexander waved at them to stand easy. "I assume this must be the Coldstream, then?"

"It is, Sir, yes." Jackson continued, remaining in the position of attention despite Alexander's affable tone. "Number Sixteen Platoon, Number Four Company, Second Battalion, Sir."

"Mmm, Sixteen Platoon... is that young Langley's crew then?" The general asked.

"He's Fifteen Platoon, Sir." Jackson corrected.

Alexander was silent for a moment.

"Aah! Of Course he is; of course. So you'll have young Harry Dunstable?"

That's right, Sir." Jackson grinned, amazed that the Divisional Commander should know who the individual officers were in each platoon, let alone the companies.

Alexander, hands clasped comfortably behind his back, looked as if he were doing nothing more than conducting a routine unit visit during peace-time as he indulged Jackson with his small-talk.

"And how's the young fellow doing?" The general asked. "Have you licked him into shape yet?"

"He's doing just fine, Sir." Jackson assured Alexander. "He's a good officer; knows his stuff."

Alexander raised an eyebrow.

"Really? Well, that's excellent news. I know his father. I'll be able to pass on your good reports to him. Where is the young ragamuffin?"

Jackson pointed back up the line.

"I think you may have passed him, just up there, Sir; at the front of the platoon."

A shell screamed down and exploded on the main quayside a few hundred yards behind them, detonating with a terrifying thunderclap. Instinctively, many of the soldiers nearby ducked their heads. Alexander didn't move a muscle.

"Oh, right, well in that case I might pop back up there and have a quick chat with him; keep him on his toes, eh?"

"I'm sure he'll be delighted." Jackson responded, enjoying the light-hearted conversation.

"I'm sure he will!" Alexander winked, and made to walk back along the line. The general checked himself however, and turned back to face Jackson, Whittaker and the men round about them.

"Before I move on gentlemen, I must ask a small favour of you. As you will see by your watches, it is now gone 0300 hours. Those ships up there are full and they're just casting off. By the time they clear the harbour it will be getting on for dawn, which means that the Luftwaffe will be back. As you can imagine, I don't wish to risk your safety by having you stand out here in broad daylight while the enemy dive-bombs you; and to be honest, I can't really afford to get any more of the Navy's ships blown up or I'll be in serious trouble with the Admiralty. To that end, we're going to pause with the embarkation until it gets dark again tonight. Then I'll bring in a whole load more ships, and we can finally get you all away. So, I'm afraid I've had to ask your commanding officer if he would mind taking you back into the dunes by the old fort and establish a hasty defensive position there, just during the daylight hours. As soon as it's dark, I've asked him to bring you all straight back here. I hope that's alright, chaps?"

The men in front of Alexander had been marching and fighting non-stop for over three weeks. Almost half of their friends and colleagues were dead or wounded, and they hadn't had a proper meal for days. They were tired and they were being shelled continually, with half the German Army just a few miles way. Amazingly, the voices that responded to Alexander carried the ring of high-spirits, like a cricket team responding to a pep talk by its popular captain.

"No problem, Sir. Whatever you need us to do." Jackson beamed at the general.

"Good stuff." Alexander said. "Thank you for your patience. And well done for your efforts so far, gentlemen. I knew I could rely on the Coldstream to put on a good show. I shall see you all tomorrow evening, then."

And with that, the general sauntered back along the line again.

Whittaker, feeling a little out of place throughout the whole conversation, glanced left and right at the Coldstreamers standing either side of him.

"Did I just hear that correctly?" He asked, his voice half puzzled, half exasperated. "Have we got to spend another day here?"

Next to him, Guardsman Hawkins, leaning on his Bren Gun, blew his nose into the palm of his hand and casually flicked a huge gob of snot into the water below.

"Looks like it, Sir." The guardsman replied phlegmatically. "So we should be able to catch up on some sleep; providing the Frogs can hold the Jerries off, that is."

"Bloody hell…" Whittaker gasped as the reality sank in.

Next to him, Jackson hefted his Lee-Enfield over his shoulder and looked down at the Flight Lieutenant.

"Don't you worry, Sir. General Alex' knows what he's doing. They don't come any steadier than him."

At that, Jackson took a deep breath and threw his voice along the line of men.

"Alright Sixteen Platoon; make sure you've got all your kit; prepare to move back along the mole when we get the word."

HEADQUARTERS SS TOTENKOPF – SOUTH-WEST OF DUNKIRK
SUNDAY 2ND OF JUNE 1940 – 1100 HOURS

Merkal stepped out of the staff car and threw his gaze around the courtyard of the small chateau. It was filled with motorcycles and cars of various types, the collective paraphernalia of a divisional headquarters preparing to move. Rumour had it that fresh orders had come in for the next phase of the campaign and the bustle of activity around the building suggested that those orders were being disseminated at this very moment. Despatch riders exited the building and jumped on their machines before roaring off in a cloud of exhaust fumes, whilst groups of battalion level staff officers conferred in hushed tones in small groups around the yard.

Merkal however, had no idea why he had been summoned to Divisional Headquarters. His cryptic instructions had been to report to the Divisional Commander's Aide de Camp immediately, nothing more. With his curiosity aroused, the hauptsturmfuhrer turned to his driver.

"Park up, but don't go wandering off. I don't know how long I'll be. Just stay with the car."

With that brief instruction, Merkal turned away and headed for the main entrance of the chateau, which was in reality nothing more than a big farmhouse belonging to a reasonably wealthy farmer or landowner.

Before he reached the door however, Merkal came face to face with two men he recognised. Both of them were coming out of the building, chatting happily between themselves. Hauptsturmfuhrers Karl Bauer and Herman Kruger were both company commanders in one of the other battalions, and as they looked up and recognised Merkal, they waved a greeting.

"Josef!" Good to see you again, old friend, Bauer beamed at him.

Merkal stopped and shook hands with the two men.

"Likewise, good to see you both. Don't suppose you know where the Divisional Commander's ADC can be found, do you?"

Kruger brightened even more.

"Sure; we've just been with him in Eicke's office. He's got a desk on the first floor landing. Are you in to see the Divisional Commander too?"

Merkal frowned.

"I'm not sure; I just got a message to see his ADC. Why did you two have to go in and see Eicke?"

The two officers exchanged a quick look then lifted their hands almost simultaneously, unclenching their fists to reveal what they were carrying.

"We've both been good boys!" Bauer chuckled happily.

Merkal stared down at the small objects that both men carried in the palms of their hands. A pang of jealously and longing ran through him as he gawped in envy at the pair of Iron Crosses, Second Class. For a long while, he couldn't take his eyes off the medals.

"So you must be seeing Eicke too?" Kruger said, snapping Merkal out of his trance. "If the ADC wants you?"

Bauer nodded his agreement.

"Reckon so." He tapped Merkal good-naturedly on his upper arm. "Looks like you might be getting a present too, perhaps?"

"Yes, we heard about the scrap you had near Arras. Sounds like a rare old battle, that one. You must tell us all about it when things quieten down a bit."

Merkal's heart gave a small flutter. They were giving out Iron Crosses. He felt a small surge of excitement course through his veins.

"Yes…we must." He replied absently, his mind starting to wander. "When it's quieter; most definitely. Congratulations, gentlemen…"

As if in a dream, Merkal bade farewell to his fellow officers and began climbing the steps up to the doorway. As he entered the building, he barely acknowledged the field police NCO who greeted him, and completely ignored the remaining mass of people who moved around him at speed, caught up in their own urgent business. Quietly, fighting down the rising sense of exultation, Merkal ascended the wide stairs. An Iron Cross? So at last, somebody must have realised how deserving Merkal was after his life and death struggle with the British tanks near Wailly? Perhaps that Army general, Rommel was it, had nominated him for an award? Perhaps that Rommel fellow wasn't that bad after all?

He reached the landing and spotted the ADC immediately. A hauptsturmfuhrer like himself, the dapper looking blonde-haired officer glanced up from his paperwork as Merkal appeared in front of him.

"Ah, Merkal." The man gave a vague smile.

Merkal couldn't remember the man's name. He was one of the staff officers, not a combat soldier like Merkal. This lap-dog would never win an Iron Cross; not like Merkal and the others.

"Thank you for your promptness." The ADC continued. "The Divisional Commander is very busy, so this won't take long. Wait here please while I see if he's ready to see you?"

Without further elaboration, the hauptsturmfuhrer walked brusquely over to a nearby door, knocked twice, then entered the room beyond, closing the door behind him.

Left alone on the landing, Merkal looked into the full length mirror fixed to the wall and duly began adjusting his clothing, making himself presentable. Having done some minor preening, Merkal looked about him impatiently, trying to fight down the rising sense of excitement. He noticed the book laying open on the ADC's desk and, checking he wasn't being watched, sauntered over and glanced down. To his disappointment, the book was nothing more than a rough notepad. He spotted his own name, listed amongst a number of others; men of varying ranks from platoon commander to battalion commander. There was no clue as to the nature of his summons to be seen. He stepped away from the desk, clasping his hands behind his back, wringing them together as he tried to imagine what fine words the Divisional Commander might have for him before presenting a medal.

Was it possible to get the Iron Cross First Class in one go, Merkal wondered; or would he need to get the Second Class initially before proving himself again to move up a grade? These thoughts were still going round his head when the door to the room clicked open and the ADC appeared in the opening.

"Hauptsturmfuhrer Merkal." The ADC snapped loudly.

It was both an announcement to the person within the room and an order to Merkal. Immediately, his pulse beginning to race, Merkal stepped across the landing and cracked his heels to attention in the doorway as the ADC stood aside.

"Heil Hitler." Merkal's arm shot out in an immaculate Nazi salute.

There was a figure sitting in a high-backed chair behind a desk, the facial detail obscured by the glare of sunlight that shone through the window behind. Despite that, there was no mistaking the Bavarian drawl in the deep voice that growled the appropriate response back at him. Having exchanged formalities, the figure spoke again.

"Come over here."

Merkal strode forward, attempting to present himself as smartly as possible. He heard the ADC shut the door behind him. When he reached the desk, he clicked his heels together again, staring rigidly over the head of the figure in the chair. After a moment, the figure spoke again.

"Hauptsturmfuhrer Merkal?"

The company commander finally dropped his gaze to look directly at the man in the chair.

"Yes, Sir." He replied, looking straight into the eyes of SS Gruppenfuhrer Theodor Eicke; commander of the SS Division Totenkopf.

Eicke sat there like a huge, angry bull. His face was full, with a strong jaw-line, nose and brow; his eyes dark and shrewd. The gruppenfuhrer was munching on a large chunk of rye-bread, and a mug of steaming black coffee sat on the desk before him. Merkal felt a thrill of excitement run through him. This was his commander; good old 'Papa Eicke'. He wasn't like those aristocratic fools in the Army high command. Eicke had risen to greatness in the SS through his merit, his determination, and above all else, his loyalty to the cause. Now, Papa Eicke sat there in the leather arm chair, munching his bread thoughtfully as he studied Merkal with his hard, humourless expression.

"How goes your war, so far, Hauptsturmfuhrer?" Eicke grunted as he took another bite from the hunk of bread.

Merkal smiled enthusiastically.

"It is going well, thank you, Gruppenfuhrer. Hard work, but going well."

Eicke nodded his head vigorously.

"Hard work. Yes, indeed; it is very hard work." He swallowed the bread. "Bloody work too, eh? Dangerous, hard and very, very bloody."

Merkal simply smiled in response.

"It's been like that since those island-monkey bastards and their finely-perfumed French pals tried to jump us south of Arras. Ten days of hard slogging, eh?"

"Yes, Gruppenfuhrer." Merkal agreed.

Eicke took a swig of his coffee, swirled it around his mouth to free the crumbs from behind his teeth then gulped it down.

"And it got even worse when we had to cross the canal the other day." Eicke went on. "And your battalion in particular had a real battle on its hands. Lots of casualties; both ours *and* theirs."

Merkal smiled again, not sure what angle the Divisional Commander was taking with the conversation.

"Apart from the fact that they're a bunch of banana-sucking island-monkeys, those Tommies are quite good soldiers when they want to be, aren't they? Tough, resilient, and a proper pain in the arse."

Merkal laughed nervously.

"Yes, Sir; I suppose they are."

Eicke was staring at him intently now, and Merkal began to feel uneasy.

"Hauptsturmfuhrer Knochlein says they also have a tendency to keep fighting after waving white flags. He also says that some of them have been using 'dum-dum' bullets."

Merkal felt his stomach drop. Suddenly, he realised that today's interview was not going to involve the presentation of any medals.

"I believe those are the reasons that you and he decided to shoot a whole bunch of them at Le Paradis the other night?"

For a moment, Merkal thought he was going to feint.

"Er…" The hauptsturmfuhrer began, uncertainly, but Eicke went on, cutting him short.

"My legal officer from the divisional staff went to have a look for me. He said there were around a hundred of them, lined up against a wall in a meadow."

Eicke's voice remained steady, almost conversational. He got up and straightened his tunic.

"Does that sound about right, Hauptsturmfuhrer? About a hundred?"

Merkal's head was suddenly filled with a confusing array of options as he struggled to work out the most politic answer. In the end, he settled for something suitably non-committal.

"Yes, Sir… I'd say about that. About a hundred or so."

"Mmm…" Eicke murmured, turning towards the window.

The gruppenfuhrer stood there for a few moments, staring out of the window. Eventually, he turned back to face Merkal.

"I had a very irate staff officer from Corps Headquarters bothering me a couple of days ago; asking lots of awkward questions about the execution of prisoners of war. Fortunately, because of the new orders, I had a very good reason to stall him. Just as well, considering I didn't know anything about any Tommies getting executed."

He fixed Merkal with a meaningful look.

"Er…" Merkal began once more, but again, Eicke spoke over him.

"I have an officer preparing a report right now, explaining to Corps Headquarters that ninety seven enemy soldiers have been executed due to numerous instances of breaching the rules of war, including the misuse of white flags and Swastikas, and the use of dum-dum bullets, and several other suitable examples."

Merkal stayed silent. It was obvious now that this interview was to be a one-way conversation. Eicke glanced out of the window again as the sound of a roaring motorcycle engine caught his attention.

"In future, Hauptsturmfuhrer, the execution of prisoners is to be formally reported up the chain of command, *immediately*. In addition, I expect evidence to be… *acquired*; in order to justify the action taken. Is that clear, Hauptsturmfuhrer?"

"Yes, Gruppenfuhrer." Merkal croaked, his heart lurching with apprehension.

The Divisional Commander was quiet for a few moments, his eyes busy taking in the scene below in the courtyard. Eventually though, he began speaking once more.

"The powers-that-be will want answers over this, Merkal. However, we will shortly be launching into another hectic phase of the operation, and we don't have time to mess around with all this nonsense. So, to that end, I will speak to Corps Headquarters and… *make the problem go away.*"

Merkal cleared his throat.

"Right, Sir. Thank you, Sir."

Slowly, Eicke turned his head again and regarded Merkal with a stern glare.

"But do me a big favour, Merkal, will you? Next time, clean your own fucking mess up…"

MALO-LES-BAINS DUNES – ONE MILE FROM DUNKIRK HARBOUR
SUNDAY 2ND JUNE 1940 – 1500 HOURS

"Can you tell who's who?"

Dunstable squinted up at the blue sky as he lay on his back against the soft sand of the dunes in which the remaining men of the British Rear Guard had established a tiny defensive perimeter. Next to him, Whittaker gave a soft chuckle.

"Pretty much, old boy; the ones dropping the bombs are German!"

Dunstable also gave a tired laugh.

"I gathered that! I mean the ones higher up."

Whittaker squinted some more and shaded his eyes as he studied the tiny black dots that wheeled and manoeuvred in the expanse of sky, high above the waves of bombers. As Whittaker watched the distant aerial combat, he felt once more the horrible thrill in the pit of his stomach that one experienced when engaged in a dog fight with the enemy. Yet, as he stared upwards, the pilot noted how, from this angle at least, the whole business seemed so leisurely and dignified.

"No, not really." Whittaker admitted. "Truth be told; it's sometimes difficult to tell friend from foe when you're actually up there. Everything seems to happen so quickly."

"Really?" Dunstable asked, mildly surprised. "It looks so very sedate from down here."

"I can assure you, Harry, it's anything but sedate." Whittaker shook his head slowly. "One moment the sky can be empty... next moment you look over your shoulder and there's half a dozen Jerries on your tail. Then... Well, then it gets a bit bonkers to be honest. You sweat like merry hell, and everything seems to happen automatically. Before you know it your guns are empty or you're low on fuel and you've got to bottom out and run for it."

Dunstable looked sideways at his companion.

"Are the Jerries any good, then?"

"They are." Whittaker nodded. "They're *bloody* good in fact. And they've got loads of bloody planes too. Sometimes they seem to be everywhere at once."

Dunstable saw how serious the airman's face had gone.

"Have you ever been shot down?"

Whittaker paused for just a moment.

"Yes." He replied quietly, but made no attempt to elaborate.

Dunstable decided not to press the matter.

The Coldstream officer turned his eyes back to the aircraft in the distance and watched as a stick of bombs fell almost lazily towards the harbour. The black specs disappeared behind a dune and a moment later Dunstable heard a series of distant explosions. The bombing and shelling had become routine now and the men on the ground barely gave it a second thought. They could tell when something was coming close and unless they heard the tell tale sound that would give them just a couple of seconds warning, they went about their business without too much concern.

"I'm just going for a walk round the perimeter, Sir."

Dunstable looked to his right at the sound of Jackson's voice.

The sergeant was staring at him from the bottom of the dune, dressed as usual in full fighting order.

"The boys are all knackered, so I just thought I'd check on the sentries; make sure they're still awake, just in case the Frogs can't hold the canal-line."

Hearing the sergeant's words, Dunstable was reminded that much of the background noise was coming from the canal-line where the French were now holding the final defensive positions against the Germans. The fact that the French were now holding the enemy off whilst the remaining British sat on the beach awaiting evacuation made Dunstable feel slightly guilty, but he shrugged it off.

"Good idea." He replied to Jackson. "You're right. We'd best make sure we're ready for anything, in case the French don't manage to hold. I'll come with you."

He pushed himself upright with a tired groan.

"You'll have to excuse me for a moment or two." The officer apologised to Whittaker. "I'm just going to pop round and see how the men are doing."

The RAF officer nodded lazily.

"Keep your head down, old chap." He murmured.

Clambering to his feet and dusting himself off, Dunstable walked down the dune to meet up with Jackson. Together, they tramped off in the direction of their platoon's hastily dug shell-scrapes.

"How's the Pioneer Sergeant, Sir?" Jackson asked as they walked.

Dunstable chuckled at the sergeant's dry wit. Jackson had taken to referring to their RAF companion as the 'Pioneer Sergeant', due to the airman's two-week growth of facial hair. In the Coldstream Guards, only the Pioneer Sergeant was permitted to wear a beard.

"He's fine. Like all of us, he just wants to get the hell out of France now."

They walked a little further in silence.

"Do you know…" Dunstable smiled at Jackson as they ambled along. "When I was a boy I used to love lazing on the beach up on the Norfolk coast. But I have to say, I'm finding today rather tedious."

Jackson grunted.

"You and me both, Sir. I'm too on edge to relax. Keep checking my watch, but time seems to be standing still. Tonight can't come soon enough.

If the Jerries break through before dark it'll be a bloody business. I'm not going in any fucking prisoner of war camp, that's for sure."

Dunstable glanced at his platoon sergeant and saw from the man's grim expression that it was no idle boast. He was about to reply when the sound of

Whittaker's urgent call brought him to a dead halt. Jackson had stopped too, and together, the two men turned back towards the dune they had just left.

Whittaker was there; at the top of the dune, on his knees and waving madly to them. He was shouting at them as he gesticulated wildly in their direction.

"What's up with him?" Jackson grunted.

"… right over us…" The RAF officer's words came faintly to the two Coldstreamers as a breeze ran across their faces.

They watched as Whittaker suddenly threw himself face down in the sand, and then they heard it; the softest whisper, followed by a whine.

"Fuck…" Jackson managed to grunt, and then the world turned upside down.

The noise itself was unbelievable; like being right in the middle of a thunderclap. The flash and heat seemed almost incidental, but the blast wave, hitting Jackson like a brick wall, was the thing that threatened to overwhelm the big sergeant. He was vaguely aware that he couldn't breathe and that his lungs felt as if they were being squeezed tight inside his chest. At the same time, his view of the world lost its clarity and cohesion. Everything was upside down or sideways and he couldn't work out whether he was standing, sitting or lying down. He caught a glint of sunlight, the image of a pale face staring at him from behind a sand dune, and at that point he realised that he could only view the terrain from such a position if he were flying several yards above the ground. And then he hit the floor with a solid, heart-stopping thud.

For long, long moments, Jackson just laid there, his mouth full of salty sand, trying to remember how to breathe, his mind completely disorientated. There was a rushing noise in his ears, like the sound of rolling surf; yet he knew for sure that he wasn't that close to the sea.

"Sergeant Jackson!"

The first recognisable sound broke through the white noise and with a terrible rush of understanding, Jackson realised what had happened. With a jerk, his mind caught up and he instantly felt severe pain in his chest. Like a drowning man coming to the surface, the sergeant suddenly drew in a huge breath of air and began hyperventilating. As if in a trance, Jackson pushed himself up on his elbows, spitting sand as he went. Somewhere in the back of his mind, the inner guardsman was telling Jackson that, as the platoon sergeant, he needed to stand up and get a grip of himself. He was supposed to be in control, not scrabbling around on the floor in such an undignified manner. Shaking like jelly, he staggered to his feet, looking about him vacantly in search of his rifle.

"Sergeant Jackson? Harry!"

Again, that strange voice intruded on Jackson's thoughts as he scanned the sand about him. The ground appeared to be all churned up, he noticed absently. Then he saw the khaki body. Ignoring the growing number of voices that were now crowding in on his consciousness, Jackson tottered a few paces towards the figure in battle-dress that lay spread-eagled higher up the nearest dune. As he neared the figure, his mind took another leap forward and he recognised his platoon commander's ragged form, lying limp in the sand.

"Mr Dunstable?" Jackson croaked.

It hurt his throat when he spoke. He took several more steps towards the officer and noticed the shredded trousers, the bloody mess that had once been the lower part of the man's right leg.

"Mr Dunstable, Sir!"

Suddenly, Jackson's dislocation fell away as he stumbled the last few paces and collapsed to his knees next to the semi-conscious lieutenant.

"Mr Dunstable? Can you hear me, Sir?"

Jackson shook the young man by his shoulder. The officer's eye-lids fluttered briefly and he emitted a soft, child-like moan of despair.

"Jesus…" Jackson gasped. "Jesus fucking Christ!"

He fumbled in his pocket for a shell dressing, just as someone dropped down beside him.

"Sergeant Jackson? Are you alright?"

Jackson looked up and saw that it was the RAF officer. Another man joined him. It was Guardsman Hawkins. Like an ant-hill, the dunes round about were coming alive with people. Jackson saw Piggy Hogson appear over the top of a dune and start shouting at unseen people beyond it.

"Shit!" Hawkins was cursing as he took in Dunstable's shattered leg.

"Pull through." Jackson grunted at the guardsman.

Hawkins gawped back at him.

"Give me a pull-through; quickly man!" Jackson found his proper voice at last.

Hawkins, suddenly understanding, grabbed a nearby rifle and dragged his bayonet free of the scabbard at his waist. He pushed the point of the blade under the lip of the butt-trap and flicked the tiny brass door open. At any other time, Jackson would have reprimanded the guardsman severely for misuse of his bayonet, but on this occasion he had other things on his mind.

"Lift his leg up." Jackson snapped at Whittaker. "Carefully."

Without objection at Jackson's peremptory manner, Whittaker gingerly lifted the young officer's shredded limb, terrified lest it come away in his hand. As he lifted the bloody leg, Jackson began applying the shell dressing. Next to the airman, Hawkins yanked the pull-through from inside the butt-trap of the Lee-Enfield.

"Tie it round his thigh." Jackson ordered. "Use it as a tourniquet. Pull it tight. As tight as you can get it."

Normally used for cleaning the rifle's barrel, the long, thin rope was perfect for the task of arresting the bleeding, and Hawkins set about tying it around the upper part of Dunstable's injured limb. Jackson meanwhile, struggled to find the best place to tie off the dressing. The lower part of Dunstable's leg was covered in lacerations and tattered flesh, with bone clearly visible in at least two places.

"Davey? Are you alright, mate?"

Hogson had arrived beside them.

"I'm fine." Jackson was working steadily, his voice remarkably calm, as if in a trance of some kind. "Get me some more shell-dressings... And find out where the casualty clearing station is..."

Hogson was off in an instant. Jackson heard the lance sergeant's voice bellowing instructions to the remaining members of the platoon as he went.

"God Almighty..." Whittaker swallowed hard as he watched Jackson's bloody hands tie the bandage off around the dressing pad. "Is he going to live?"

"Yes." Jackson's reply was instant; categorical.

If it was humanly possibly, Jackson would make sure his platoon commander survived. They were world's apart, he and Dunstable, but over the last three weeks the pair of them had endured so much as a team; the two of them working hard to keep their platoon together as a disciplined and effective fighting force. There might be nearly ten years between them, but Jackson had developed a deep respect for the young lieutenant. Dunstable was *his* officer, and Jackson would not let him die.

Within less than a minute, more guardsmen arrived with spare shell-dressings.

"Get them on his leg." Jackson ordered. "All over. Cover the whole leg up."

The sergeant shuffled further up, beside Hawkins, and slipped his fingers underneath the pull-through that was now secured around Dunstable's upper-thigh.

"Not tight enough." He snapped, pulling on the improvised tourniquet. "Get me a stick or something metal; something long and thin."

There was a frenzy of activity around the injured officer now, as the men of No.16 Platoon fought to save their officer. Within seconds, Hawkins had found, of all things, a spanner from a discarded tool kit.

"Perfect." Jackson declared, snatching the tool from the soldier and slipping it under the pull-through.

With a grunt of effort, Jackson turned the spanner, using it as a windlass to tighten the cord around the injured man's thigh.

"Tuck it in." He croaked, struggling to hold the spanner in place as the pull-through went taught.

Hawkins, working quickly, hooked the end of the spanner over and under the cord to lock it in position.

"Davey? The nearest place is up in the town. This lad here, he's been there."

Jackson looked up and saw Hogson standing above him, the Company Commander's runner beside him.

"Show me where it is." Jackson demanded.

"I've sent for a stretcher…" Hogson continued.

"There's no time." Jackson replied. "I'll carry him."

"It'll be easier if…"

"I'll carry him!" Jackson cut the lance-sergeant short. "Give me a hand with him."

With that, Jackson pushed himself to his feet.

As he stood up, a sudden feeling of nausea washed over the sergeant and he had to steady himself, grasping Whittaker's shoulder in the process. Hogson watched his platoon sergeant stagger and his face became worried.

"Davey, you're not strong enough, mate…"

"I'll carry him." Jackson was having none of it.

He looked across at Hawkins.

"Hawkins! Grab my rifle; come with me."

He addressed the small crowd now.

"Get Mr Dunstable up and onto my shoulders."

Within moments it was done. Jackson, taking a deep breath and steadying himself, allowed the officer's dead weight to settle onto his shoulders as he held onto the injured lieutenant in a fireman's lift. Next to him, Hogson was holding Jackson's arm.

"Davey, mate? Are you sure?"

"I'm sure."

The sergeant jerked his head towards the crowd of men.

"Look after the platoon until I get back, Piggy. Get them back to their positions. You're in charge for the moment. Let the Company Commander know. Hawkins?"

"Here, Sergeant."

"Follow me." Jackson ordered. "And you, big lad." He waved a free arm at the company runner. "Show me where this dressing station is."

And with that, they were away.

Jackson was surprised at how light Dunstable was. Perhaps it was the adrenalin working, or maybe he was still in some kind of shock, but Jackson strode through the dunes behind the runner, his face set in a grimace of determination. Alongside him, Hawkins kept pace, watching his platoon sergeant for the first signs of exhaustion; ready to intervene if needed. The sergeant though was like an automaton; his face like stone, his legs stepping out resolutely; stride after stride through the soft sand.

After a while, they came out onto a hardened track of compressed gravel; some kind of slipway. It turned into tarmac and led onto the seafront of the burning suburbs of Dunkirk.

"You all right, Sergeant?" Hawkins queried.

"Fine." Came the curt reply.

Their route was a chaotic mess of burned out and abandoned vehicles, shell craters, rubble, dead horses and dead soldiers. A line of shattered cottages belched smoke still, even though the flames that had enveloped them were now dying away. None of this Jackson noticed, his implacable gaze remaining fixed on the back of the company runner. Wherever the man led, Jackson followed.

Every so often, the sergeant would pause briefly to shift the officer slightly on his shoulders. When the young man emitted that soft, child-like moan each time, Jackson would soothe him like a father by his sick child's bed. After more than ten minutes of navigating their way through the shattered town, Jackson began to struggle, his pace slowing and a constant growl of effort coming from deep in his throat.

"Let me carry him for a bit, Sergeant?" Hawkins offered again.

"It's just up here…" The runner called back over his shoulder.

"I'll do it…" Jackson gasped, the sweat pouring down his dirty, care-worn face.

Eventually, the trio of Coldstreamers came to a long line of abandoned ambulances that had been parked up on a driveway leading to a large red-brick building.

"This is it, Sergeant Jackson." The runner shouted back.

"Find me a doctor, Hawkins." The sergeant grunted, his footsteps becoming heavy and ponderous now.

Instantly, Hawkins raced forward up the drive, shouting out for the attention of a medical orderly. As he neared the large doorway, where the ornate wooden door stood wedged open, the guardsman noticed the line of badly wounded men lying to one side of the path. Some were clearly alive, whilst others lay perfectly still, no sign of life apparent. As Hawkins slowed, taking in the sight, one of the men, his face completely wrapped in bandages so that his face was hidden, turned his head slightly and spoke.

"If you're looking for a doctor," the soldier began, his voice muffled and distorted by the bloody bandages, "they're all inside. Those who are still here, that is."

Without replying, Hawkins turned away and entered the building. Inside, he found a sight of unimaginable horror. The great hallway of what had once been a grand building of some sort was completely covered with wounded men, The metallic stench of blood, mixed with the sickening odour of faeces, pervaded the stagnant air, making Hawkins gag. As he fought to stop his gorge rising, a medical orderly appeared in the hallway from a side door, carrying a water bottle. He glanced up at Hawkins with a weary, disinterested face.

"Is there a doctor here?" The Guardsman asked.

"Through there." The medical orderly nodded his head back towards the side door. "Why?"

At that point, Jackson, still carrying Dunstable and accompanied by the runner, burst through the doorway behind Hawkins.

"Where's the doctor?" The sergeant panted, his face bright red and wet with perspiration.

"In there." Hawkins pointed at the doorway as indicated by the medic.

Shifting Dunstable's weight on his shoulders, Jackson staggered forward, stepping clumsily over the numerous injured men on the floor. As he did so, a look of alarm crossed the medic's face.

"He's only taking those with a chance of survival." The orderly protested, taking a step towards Jackson as he advanced on the inner doorway. "We haven't got time to look at dying men."

"Get out of my way, you Chippy fucker!" Jackson snarled, baring his teeth at the medic.

Immediately, the medic stepped backwards out of the sergeant's way and Jackson barged through the door, closely followed by Hawkins.

They found themselves going down steps into a cellar, and Hawkins reached forward to grab the rear of Jackson's webbing lightly with two fingers, just in case the sergeant fell down the steep steps in the dim light. Within moments however, Jackson and Hawkins were in the basement of the big house. They stood there for a while, both Coldstreamers blinking in the semi-darkness. Around the subterranean room, several candles flickered weakly.

"What do you want?" A sharp, well spoken voice demanded from the shadows.

Jackson squinted at a dark figure that stepped forward into the half light of the candle. Although he couldn't see clearly enough to identify any badges of rank, the man's voice told Jackson all he needed to know.

"I want you to look at my platoon commander, Sir, please? He's been badly wounded."

The doctor stepped forward another pace and frowned at Jackson and Hawkins.

"Is he dying?"

Jackson fixed the officer with a serious look.

"I'd like you to make sure he doesn't, Sir…"

Silence. The doctor walked steadily over to Jackson and lifted Dunstable's head. With practiced speed, the medical officer checked Dunstable's carotid pulse and took a quick look at his eyes. Having done so, he walked around Jackson to take a look at the heavily bandaged leg. The doctor ran deft fingers across the numerous dressings before checking the tourniquet. After just a few moments, he flicked his gaze to Jackson, then to Hawkins, then back to the sergeant.

"I'm glad somebody round here knows basic first aid." He said drily. "Put him on this desk over here; quickly."

With a renewed sense of urgency, Jackson followed the doctor's directions and stumbled across to what had become a makeshift operating table. Carefully, assisted by Hawkins, the big sergeant lowered his platoon commander down onto the polished desk-top. Having settled the wounded officer, Jackson stepped back, groaning in relief at the sudden release of weight from his shoulders. The doctor, already taking a pair of scissors to Dunstable's trousers, glanced back up at the two guardsmen.

"You two can go now. Send one of my orderlies down; quick as you can."

Jackson took a deep breath.

"Right, Sir. Thank you, Sir."

And then he collapsed…

THE CASUALTY CLEARING STATION – MALO-LES-BAINS, DUNKIRK
SUNDAY 2ND JUNE 1940 – 1830 HOURS

"Sergeant? Are you alright?"

"What?"

At first, Jackson thought he was dreaming. Why else would he be lying down with that big dozy fucker, Hawkins, gawping at him like a doe-eyed child? It was with a certain sense of alarm that Jackson realised he wasn't dreaming at all. He jerked upright into a sitting position instantly and stared around with wide-eyes, desperately trying to make sense of where he was and who he was.

He was sitting on a wide lawn that had once been immaculately kept, but was now churned up by vehicles and feet, and strewn with bodies, stretchers, weapons and equipment, bandages and boots; all the detritus of war. Above him the blue sky played host to a bright, burning sun, spoilt only by the drifting black skeins of the smoke plume from the wrecked harbour. The sound of explosions and distant gunfire slowly intruded on Jackson's consciousness as he caught up with reality.

"Steady, Sergeant..." Hawkins put a gently restraining arm on the NCO's shoulder. "Not too fast. Don't want you passing out on us again!"

"What?" Jackson looked up sharply at the guardsman.

Hawkins gave a sheepish grin.

"You keeled over down in the cellar; once you put Mr Dunstable on the table. Must have been a rush of blood to the head or something..." He shrugged his shoulders. "I had to drag you up the stairs on my own. You weigh a bloody ton!"

Suddenly, everything came flooding back to Jackson.

"Mr Dunstable? Where is he?"

"He's inside, Sergeant; with Mr Whittaker."

"Who?"

"Mr Whittaker; that RAF bloke. He came after us to tell us we've got orders to be at the mole again at 2100 hours. He says we'd better get moving or the battalion will move off without us."

"Shit..." Jackson whispered. "Show me..."

The big sergeant struggled to his feet, shrugging off Hawkins' hand. He stood upright and cringed. A stab of pain ran through his head.

"Are you alright?" Hawkins asked, the concern obvious in his voice.

"Yes." Jackson snapped in irritation, then softened his tone. "Sorry... Yes, Hawkins. Thank you. I'm okay; just got a bit of a headache."

The guardsman gave a nervous laugh.

"I'm not surprised, Sergeant. That jerry bomb landed almost on top of you and Mr Dunstable. We all thought you were gonners. Mr Whittaker reckons it was the soft sand that saved you. He says it must have absorbed most of the blast."

Jackson creased his brow as the memories came flooding back into his mind. A bomb? Of course; that was it.

"Show me where the Platoon Commander is." He murmured.

Hawkins nodded and handed a steel helmet to his sergeant.

"These are yours, Sergeant." The guardsman said as he passed Jackson's small pack and rifle across after the helmet.

Muttering his appreciation, Jackson took the proffered items. Clipping on his small pack, he leaned forward and secured the hooks inside the brackets above his ammunition pouches. As he did so, another savage stab of pain went through his skull.

"Fucking hell, my head feels like it's been used as a football…"

The sergeant stood straight and grimaced as he took in the scene of devastation in the immediate area. He noticed that everything beyond about twenty paces seemed a little blurred. He blinked a couple of times and rubbed his eyes vigorously, but it made no difference. Hardly surprising, he reasoned. He was dog tired and probably had half the sand from the beach in his eyes.

"Come on then, Hawkins." He grunted. "Show me where he is."

They went inside the building and through the crowded hallway to a big room beyond. It looked as though it might once have been a big dining room or a ball-room of some kind, but now, like every other room in the building, it was jam-packed with wounded men. A smattering of medical staff moved quietly about the ranks of supine figures, tending to individuals where they were able. A low hum of pain-filled moaning filled the room. Here and there, men sobbed pathetically; completely distraught and overcome by their injuries and the apparent lack of effective medical treatment. As Jackson took in the scene, he noticed the man dressed in air force blue, crouching over somebody in the far corner.

"That's him, over there." Hawkins pointed.

Quickly, the two guardsmen threaded their way across the room to where Whittaker knelt beside Dunstable's unconscious figure.

"Ah, Sergeant J!" Whittaker looked up and smiled with genuine relief when he noticed Jackson appear beside him.

The sergeant nodded his greeting and stared down at Dunstable. The young lieutenant's leg had been re-dressed with clean dressings, although the pull-through cum tourniquet remained in its original place. The young officer appeared to be sleeping peacefully, although Jackson noticed with alarm that his face was as pale as a ghost's.

"How is he, Sir?"

Whittaker gave a reassuring smile.

"They reckon he'll live, at least. Thanks mainly to you and the boys. Your first aid managed to stop the majority of bleeding by all accounts. There's a good chance he may lose his leg though, I've been told."

Jackson didn't reply. He simply swallowed hard and licked his scabbed lips.

"But he *will* live?" The sergeant managed to ask at last.

"They're quite hopeful." Whittaker nodded. "Provided gangrene doesn't set in."

Jackson nodded slowly.

Whittaker stood and stretched his back off, glancing at Jackson as he did so.

"Are you alright?"

Jackson nodded again.

"Aye, Sir. I'm fine, thank you."

"We'd better get a move on. Your Company Commander told me to come and let you know that everyone's moving off shortly. The Navy are meant to be sending more destroyers in as soon as it gets dark. I saw that general again; the one from last night. He says that we'll be going out tonight for definite. There'll be no more ships after that."

At that comment, Jackson looked sharply at Whittaker, then at Hawkins.

"We need to find a stretcher." He said crisply.

"A stretcher?" Whittaker gave a bemused frown.

"For Mr Dunstable. We need to get him on a stretcher."

Whittaker shook his head, a sad look crossing his features.

"I'm afraid not, Sergeant. There's orders from above. No more wounded are to be evacuated. Standing room only. Only those who are fit to fight another day are to board the ships. No exceptions."

A look of distress filled Jackson's eyes; the closest to a normal human emotion that Whittaker had seen from the man since he'd first met him.

"I'm afraid Mr Dunstable will have to stay here for now." He continued more gently. "It's probably the best thing for him. The Germans will have their own doctors, I'm sure. He'll get all the treatment he needs sooner if he stays here. I'm sure he'll be fine."

Jackson didn't reply. He just kept staring from Whittaker to Dunstable and back again. For a brief moment, Whittaker thought he saw a tear in the corner of the sergeant's eye.

"Sergeant Jackson!"

Together, Jackson, Whittaker and Hawkins turned at the sound of the new voice and found themselves looking at Guardsman Matthews, one of the soldiers from their platoon, standing in the far doorway.

"Sergeant Hogson says to hurry up if you can; we've been told to form up by 1930 hours, ready to move. He says we're catching the last ships out of Dunkirk tonight, Sergeant."

Jackson looked back down at Dunstable for a long moment, before throwing his gaze back across the room towards Matthews.

"Alright, Matthews lad, get yourself back to the platoon. Tell Sergeant Hogson we're on the way…"

THE EAST MOLE – DUNKIRK HARBOUR
SUNDAY 2ND JUNE 1940 – 2330 HOURS

Side by side, Tennant and Alexander watched the soldiers file past. In the glare of the flames, the disciplined line of infantrymen, fully armed and equipped, shuffled steadily along the narrow walkway towards the last of the ships. Beyond the burning town and the dunes by the beach, the distant, steady rumble of artillery could be heard. It appeared to be the only effort the Germans were making for the present, having launched ferocious attacks throughout the day, most of which had been held, just, by the courageous stand of the French Rear Guard. The onslaught had slowed somewhat with the onset of darkness and so, as they stood there on the mole, both Tennant and Alexander felt somewhat like thieves in the night; about to sneak away under the enemy's nose, thereby denying them the spoils of victory.

Even so, both men were nervous. For a week now, both men had been expecting the enemy to break through and bring the entire campaign to a bloody and humiliating climax. Now, they stood there on the delicate remnants of the East Mole, daring to hope that the enemy would hold off just an hour or two longer. It was nerve wracking stuff.

"That's the last of 2nd Battalion Coldstream Guards, Sir."

The voice of a staff captain came to Alexander through the semi-darkness.

"Thank you, Gerald." The general responded. "Who've we got left?"

"If we've crunched the numbers correctly, Sir, it's just the 1st Battalion from the King's Shropshire Light Infantry."

"Excellent." Alexander murmured. "Make sure you check back along the mole for stragglers though, won't you?"

"Of course, Sir."

The shadowy figure of the captain disappeared into the gloom once more, pushing past the slow-moving column of men waiting for evacuation.

"I hardly dare breathe, General; I don't know about you!"

Alexander glanced sideways at Tennant and chuckled.

"Yes, I know what you mean, old boy. Rather trying on the nerves, isn't it? Still, can't be long now, if this is indeed the last battalion."

"What do you think the French will do?" Tennant asked quietly. "When we've gone?"

Alexander pulled a face.

"Goodness knows. To be honest, the only reason they've managed to get so many of their own men away is because we agreed to start taking them on a fifty-fifty basis with our own chaps. When you and your team leave, I've no idea how they're going to cope. They've been sending their own ships in, I know, but they don't seem to be very organised at all. Anyway, that's their worry; not ours. We've done what we were ordered to do."

"Yes…" Tennant's voice trailed off as he looked down the line of men. "Looks like the back of the queue coming up?"

Alexander followed his gaze.

"It does indeed."

Leaving his spot beside Tennant, Alexander wandered down the line of men for a few yards before halting again. Another figure was hurrying back up the mole towards him. Tennant sauntered after the general and stopped a couple of paces behind him so that he could listen.

"That's it, Sir."

Tennant recognised the staff captain's voice.

"There's no one else back down there. The commanding officer of the Shropshire's is at the rear of the line here with his adjutant. This is definitely the last unit, Sir."

Alexander murmured his thanks to the captain and instructed him to start gathering the remainder of his small headquarters staff together. Having done so, he turned back towards Tennant and glanced casually at his wrist watch.

"Well then," he remarked brightly, "that was easy enough, wasn't it?"

Tennant didn't reply. He simply took a deep breath and prayed that their luck would hold out just a little longer.

It seemed to take forever; for those last hundred men or so to shuffle along the pier and board the personnel ship. Tennant watched the ropes being cast off from the mole as the ship began to manoeuvre carefully out from the harbour, surrounded by the broken, sunken skeletons of so many doomed vessels. His heart thumped heavily in his chest; the tension almost unbearable. As the dark silhouette of the ship disappeared into the darkness beyond the harbour, Tennant sensed Alexander step close beside him.

"Well, I think that just about wraps it all up then. We may as well get off ourselves."

The Senior Naval Officer Ashore at Dunkirk glanced at the general and grinned.

"I think that would be a grand plan, Sir; just grand."

Tennant turned toward where several members of his shore party awaited further instructions.

"Mr Drake?" He called into the darkness.

"Yes, Sir?" The young officer's voice came back at him.

"Send an immediate signal to Admiral Ramsay, please? Tell him that the evacuation of the BEF is complete… and then tell him that we're returning to Dover."

FERRY SHIP ST HELIER – JUST OUT OF DUNKIRK HARBOUR
SUNDAY 2ND JUNE 1940 – 2355 HOURS

"Quiet!" Jackson's severe voice cut through the laughter and light-hearted banter that rang through the public deck of the civilian ferry. "Shut the fuck up and pin your ears back!"

The laughter subsided and a hush fell over the dozens of men who were crammed into this particular part of the ship. In truth, Jackson's sudden outburst had not been for the benefit of his own men, but for the many others, of differing units, who shared the space with them. His own men were obeying his earlier instructions regarding the maintenance of discipline, even once they were aboard ship.

"That Navy bloke up top reckons it's going to be a good few hours before we get back to England. In addition to that, the ship has to maintain blackout, so there's no going up top for a fag or any of that nonsense, and we can't exactly do anything useful while it's pitch black. To that end, keep the noise down and get some sleep. By my reckoning, we've got about four hours before it get's light enough to see properly down here. When it does, I'll give you all a kick. I want everyone clean shaven and weapons cleaned before we hit Dover. When we go back to England, we go back looking like soldiers; not like a rabble. Understand?"

There was an obedient murmur of assent from Jackson's platoon. From the dozens of others, there was stony silence.

Satisfied, Jackson sank down onto the deck floor.

"Alright then, get your heads down."

He let out a restless sigh.

"How's your headache?"

Whittaker's voice came quietly from the darkness nearby.

"It's fucking killing me." Jackson grumbled.

"You should get some sleep."

"No chance of that." Jackson muttered.

There was a pause.

"You should relax, Sergeant J." Whittaker soothed him. "We're safe now. We'll be home soon."

Jackson was silent for a moment.

"It's a disgrace." He said at last through clenched teeth.

"What is?" Whittaker asked in a bemused voice.

"This. This whole fucking disaster. It's a disgrace. Chased out of France with our tails between our legs, and everyone's fucking laughing and joking like they're on a day out to the fucking sea-side!"

Whittaker heard the anger and frustration in the sergeant's voice. The man's emotions were threatening to overwhelm him.

"It wasn't our fault though." Whittaker murmured. "We all did our best. You and the boys, and Mr Dunstable too; you did a marvellous job. You should be proud of yourselves."

"It was shit!"

Jackson sounded as if he could burst into tears he sounded that angry, even though he was keeping his voice low, keeping his frustration contained. The big sergeant was like a kettle boiling dry, Whittaker reflected. The man was so full of pent up emotion he was fit to burst.

"My dad fought the Jerries to a stand-still for four and a half years in the last war. And in less than three weeks, we've been spanked stupid, time after time, and sent bloody packing by the box-headed bastards! And you know why? Because we're shit! Because the British Army doesn't have any discipline anymore. It doesn't have any fighting spirit. It's too bloody busy singing stupid fucking songs about the fucking, bloody Siegfried Line!"

The sergeant's voice was breaking now. Whittaker sensed that the big NCO was holding on by a thread.

"You may be right, Sergeant J..." he kept his voice low and soothing, "but there's no point beating yourself up about it. What's done is done. Next time, it'll be different. You know what needs to be done now, don't you. You can train your chaps up and make sure that when you go back to France it's a different story next time round. I can tell you for nothing that the RAF has learned plenty of lessons too."

Jackson didn't respond for a moment. He was too busy thinking.

He thought about the Company Quarter Master Sergeant's head lying in the dixie of corned beef hash, about the terrifying scream of the Stukas, and the endless marching and digging in the searing heat. He thought about the poor teenage girl with no legs who Dunstable had shot by the roadside, and he thought of the thousands of ragged, terrified civilians caught up in the battles of the last three weeks. He thought of the desperate battle on the banks of the River Escaut and, just for a moment, he thought he could smell the breath of the German he'd wrestled in the dark, just before Hawkins had shot the man in the face. And then he thought of the carnage of Dunkirk; the noise and the smell, the hunger and the sense of uselessness. He remembered that awful moment when the bomb had nearly finished him off, and finally, he pictured young Mr Dunstable lying there at the casualty clearing station, skin as white as snow, his breathing shallow and delicate; like a child's. And as he thought about all those things, the tears began to pour down his cheeks, unseen in the darkness by those around him.

At last, through gritted teeth, the sergeant found his voice again.

"Oh, yes. I'll be fucking back alright…"

Tuesday 4th June 1940
The Twenty Sixth Day

CENTRAL COLLECTION CAMP – ALDERSHOT GARRISON, ENGLAND
TUESDAY 4TH JUNE 1940 – 0750 HOURS

By Army standards, the food had been excellent. For two days now, Moxon and Fellows had enjoyed some of the best meals of their Army service to date, along with endless hours laid on their beds, sleeping, sleeping, and sleeping some more. There had been baths too; hot baths and lovely fresh soap. In all their days as soldiers, the two drivers had never felt so contented. Despite that, the two men were beginning to feel restless as they wandered back from breakfast to the barrack block.

"What time did they say that parade was?" Moxon asked as they settled themselves on the steps of their billet.

"Nine bell." Fellows answered, offering his companion a cigarette.

The two men lit up and sat there in silent contemplation for a while.

"Suppose they've finally decided what to do with us, then?" Moxon commented at last.

Fellows nodded.

"Yeah; I heard one of the clerks say they've got posting orders and travel warrants for everyone. Looks like we'll be back with our own mob pretty soon."

Moxon pondered his friend's words for a while.

"Can't say I'm that thrilled about going back to the unit, to be honest."

"No." Fellows was nodding his agreement. "Can't say I'm in the mood for first-parading trucks and doing endless convoy runs again. Bit of a come-down after all the excitement to be honest."

Moxon was also nodding. After a while longer, he spoke again.

"I wonder what those Guards boys are up to? Do you think they got away?"

Fellows gave a grunt of laughter.

"If the Hangman had anything to do with it, I reckon they'll have been alright!"

"Christ Almighty, Stan!" Moxon laughed. "He was one nasty, mad bastard, that company sergeant major wasn't he?"

"He was that, mate." Fellows agreed. "A proper mad bastard!"

They sat in silence for a while.

"Tell you what, though, Stan." Moxon suddenly spoke. "I'm sort of missing those Guards lads in a funny kind of way."

Fellows looked sideways at his companion.

"Yeah, now you come to mention it Mickey, I am too. I got quite attached to them to be honest. They're a bit potty, and bloody strict, but a sensible kind of strict if you know what I mean?"

"I know what you mean, Stan. For all their strange ways, they knew how to look after each other, didn't they? We never got left to fend for ourselves did we? The Hangman was always there with something for us to eat, wasn't he? Always made sure we got our grub first before he had anything. Always made sure the sentry duty was shared out equal, like."

"Yeah…" Fellows mused. "Firm but fair, the Hangman was."

Again, the pair fell into silence. After a long while, fellows crushed out the dog-end of his fag.

"What you thinking about, Mickey?"

Moxon took a deep breath.

"I was thinking how much I felt like a soldier when I was with the Guards. I was thinking I quite liked it."

Fellows was eyeing his friend closely.

"I was thinking…" Moxon went on, "that I might see about transferring over to them."

Fellows allowed a slight smile to cross his features.

"Yeah; I was thinking something similar myself, Mickey."

HANGER 2 – ROYAL AIR FORCE BIGGIN HILL
TUESDAY 4TH MAY 1940 – 0800 HOURS

"Are you sure those guns are pointing the right way, Mac?"

Leading Air Craftsman McWilliams looked up from where he was busy working on the port battery of machine-guns. He stared down at the filthy, dishevelled figure of Flight Lieutenant Whittaker with steady, grey eyes, his face betraying not the slightest hint of surprise. For long moments, he ran his gaze over the officer, before finally muttering a nonchalant retort of his own.

"Have they run out of razor blades in the Officers' Mess, then, Sir?"

"I haven't had time for a shave; I've been too busy holding off the entire German Army with my friends from the Coldstream Guards."

McWilliams raised an eyebrow at Whittaker's reply.

"The Guards? I'm surprised they didn't throw you straight into the bloody Guardroom looking like that!"

Whittaker smiled.

McWilliams sat up straight and wiped his hands on a rag, then slid down from the wing and took a couple of steps towards the man he had given up for dead. Coming to a halt in front of Whittaker, McWilliams cocked his head to one side.

"I suppose you broke your plane again, did you?"

With a look of amused resignation, Whittaker nodded.

"I'm afraid I did, Mac; good and proper. Ended up having to burn the old girl to stop the Jerries from getting their hands on her."

McWilliams' expression changed to one of suspicion.

"Crash landed in one piece?" He quizzed the pilot.

"Glided down." Whittaker confirmed. "Ran out of fuel after a dogfight."

The armourer shook his head in mock disbelief.

"Ran out of fuel? What the bloody hell do they teach you lot at flying school?"

Whittaker looked down at the floor, smiling, knowing he wouldn't get the better of the cynical ground crewman.

"How did you get back?" McWilliams asked.

"Caught a boat from Dunkirk with the last of the Guards, just before midnight, the day before yesterday. Managed to find out where the squadron was refitting after making some enquiries at Dover, so hitch-hiked up here. How about you?"

McWilliams shrugged his shoulders.

"After the cock-up with the last operation, we got the word to move out via Paris in pretty short order. As soon as the planes came back, we were on our way. None stop to St Nazaire, then a boat back to Southampton. We've only been back here three days. They say we might be able to start trickling away on leave come the weekend."

Whittaker nodded, imagining the chaos that the squadron would have experienced. He had no doubt that they, like him, would have their own share of adventures to brag about. McWilliams took a good look at the pilot, taking in his filthy, torn uniform, the dirty face beneath the thick stubble, the tired, red-rimmed eyes, sunk back into their sockets.

"You look like shit, Sir."

"Thanks, Mac."

"Why don't you get yourself over the Mess, Sir; get yourself sorted out? The Squadron Leader will probably be at breakfast. I'm sure he'll enjoy taking the piss out of you as much as I do."

Whittaker nodded, smiling.

"Sounds like a good plan to me. Just hope they'll let me in."

He began to turn away.

"I'll see you later on, Mac; once I've had a bath, a shave, and about six weeks of sleep."

McWilliams watched the young officer shamble away towards the wide, open doorway of the hangar.

"Mr Whittaker, Sir?" He called.

Whittaker tottered to a halt and looked back towards the armourer.

"Good to have you back, Mr Whittaker, Sir." McWilliams smiled. "Bloody good to have you back."

HEADQUARTERS, PANZER GROUP GUDERIAN – SIGNY-LE-PETIT, NORTHERN FRANCE
TUESDAY 4TH JUNE 1940 – 1150 HOURS

Guderian watched them go; the collection of corps, divisional and regimental commanders who were all now a part of Guderian's newly formed panzer group. His new command comprised of no less than four panzer and two motorised infantry divisions; a potent force indeed. Although he had not been physically promoted, just to be given responsibility for such a large portion of Germany's elite forces was sufficient recognition for the energetic German general. He watched the commanders leave the room, laughing and joking with each other; indulging in the friendly, inter-unit rivalry that was common amongst fighting men. They were up for the challenge before them, of that there was no doubt. With the Allied armies in Northern France now dealt with, it was almost time to drive south and conquer the remainder of France, destroying her remaining seventy divisions in the process. Guderian felt his blood surging with excitement, just at the thought of it.

As the last commanders exited the conference room, Guderian's faithful chief of staff, Nehring, entered.

"Hello Walther." Guderian greeted the colonel brightly. "All well?"

"Yes, General; thank you. How were the formation commanders? They all seemed pretty boisterous?"

Guderian nodded proudly.

"They are, Walther; they are. Their tails are up. A few days rest has done them all the world of good. They're chomping at the bit to get going again, now."

Guderian settled himself on a chair and leaned back, stretching off.

"What about our equipment state though, Walther? Have we managed to improve it during the last few days? What's our tank strength looking like?"

Nehring glanced at his notebook.

"We're doing okay, Sir. We're back to sixty five percent availability already. If we stay put for another two days, we'll be up to seventy five percent easily. If we stay here another five days, we may even reach eighty five percent of our original strength. Beyond that, there's no way we can get back to a hundred percent unless we get new vehicles sent out from Germany, along with replacement crews."

Guderian nodded thoughtfully as he listened to the statistics.

"Good." He said after a while. "Eighty to eighty five percent will do fine. We fought the last week of the previous battle with between fifty to sixty percent. Besides, the best of the enemy's armoured units are gone. He has little armoured strength left by my reckoning. We must hope that he isn't able to concentrate his remaining armoured forces against us in the next few days, eh?"

Guderian mused on that for a few moments, then glanced back up at Nehring.

"Any other news?"

The colonel cleared his throat.

"Only that 18th Army has finally captured Dunkirk. A flash signal came in about an hour ago to say that all fighting has ceased and the enemy are surrendering en masse."

The general's eyes lit up.

"Aha! At last! That is good. Do you have any more details yet?"

"Only a few. It will take a while for the all the facts to come through, but the initial report suggests that well in excess of twenty thousand French prisoners have been taken."

Guderian frowned slightly. Twenty thousand? He had expected more than that.

"Twenty thousand Frenchmen?" He grunted. "What about the British?"

Nehring hesitated before he replied.

"The British... have gone, Sir."

"Gone?" Guderian asked quietly. "Gone where?"

Nehring drew in a deep breath.

"Back to England, General. They have evacuated their whole force; along with many Frenchmen too, it is believed."

"All of them?" Guderian queried his chief of staff. "Every Englander has gone?"

"Save the dead, General, there is not an Englishman left in Dunkirk."

The panzer general looked away, staring at the floor, his brow creasing in contemplation. This was not good. If the British Army had been captured, then Great Britain would have little chance of being able to continue the war. A quick end to the whole business would have been possible. But now? With her army safe, and the island of Britain protected by the sea, her navy and her air force, then Britain had every chance of fighting on. And in Guderian's considered opinion, knowing the British as he did, that was exactly what they would do. Fight on.

He raised his head and glanced back up at Nehring.

"That is not good, Walther; not good at all. Mark my words, this will come back to bite us on the arse..."

THE HOUSE OF COMMONS – LONDON
TUESDAY 4TH JUNE 1940 – 1200 HOURS

Churchill, having come to the end of the main part of his speech, paused briefly to gather his breath and glance down at his notes. Looking back up at the packed House, he saw the hundreds of faces gazing back at him. He had never seen the House of Commons so utterly silent, except when it was empty of course. The attention of the Members was absolute. Every man in the room was hanging on his every word. These men, so many of whom had spent a decade or more denouncing him as a war monger, were now his most attentive listeners; along with the British public of course. Above him, the microphones of the BBC hung down from the ceiling, recording his words for broadcast later that day. No barracking, no derisive laughter, no hoots of amusement or howls of indignation. Just silence. Absolute silence.

His gaze drifted along his own front bench momentarily. Lord Halifax was there, and it reminded Churchill that even within his own cabinet there were those who still remained unconvinced by Churchill's attitude to this war. But, Churchill reflected, none of them had been willing to step up to the mark when their country called. Not one of them. Only him. And he was the one that every pair of eyes in the room now watched, for they knew that the situation wasn't good.

And it wasn't good, that was a fact. But it wasn't disastrous. In fact, it was something of a miracle. Completely against every expectation, the Royal Navy had somehow managed to extract the British Expeditionary Force from Dunkirk, right under the noses of the Germans, along with thousands more Frenchmen. In all, more than three hundred and thirty thousand men had been brought back to Britain's shores over the last few days. Britain's Army was saved, and therefore she could carry on the fight against Germany. At a distance maybe, from this island fortress, but all the while re-arming, re-equipping, preparing for the re-match against the Nazi war-machine which must surely come at some point in the future. It might just be a matter of months, or it could even be a number of years, but Britain would fight on; if necessary, alone.

Churchill cleared his throat, fixed his eyes on the benches opposite, and continued his speech.

"Even though large tracts of Europe and many old and famous States have fallen, or may fall, into the grip of the Gestapo and all the odious apparatus of Nazi rule, we shall not flag or fail…"

Again he paused, just a heart beat, long enough to rake the entire House with his sweeping gaze. They were transfixed. Hardly any man present appeared to be drawing breath. Not one eye blinked. Churchill went on.

"We shall go on to the end. We shall fight in France, we shall fight on the seas and oceans..."

He allowed his voice to gather force, building in volume and pitch.

"...we shall fight with growing confidence and growing strength in the air..."

The entire audience seemed to sit up straighter as his voice increased in ferocity, but just as quickly, he dropped its pitch once more.

"...we shall defend our island, whatever the cost may be."

Churchill peered out at his audience over the rim of his reading glasses. Men were nodding now, seized by the appeal of his fighting talk. He had them. Doubters and pacifists, believers and fighters; they were in his palm now, and Churchill filled his voice with gravity as he delivered the killer sentence of his speech.

"We shall fight on the beaches, we shall fight on the landing-grounds, we shall fight in the fields and in the streets, we shall fight in the hills..."

Churchill allowed all of the drive, energy and self belief of the last decade to well up inside him as he launched the next words at his audience, bringing his voice to a crescendo once more; defying any man there to gainsay him.

"We shall never surrender!"

HISTORICAL NOTE

I must emphasise, that although this novel features many well known (and some lesser known) historical figures, it is after all a work of fiction. Most of the events in the novel did happen and are well recorded, as are the actions of the historical figures mentioned. Where the historical record is sufficiently detailed, I have 'dramatised' the event and put words into the mouths of the historical figures that are either recorded as having been said, or which, in my own opinion, would have been in keeping with the circumstance. Where there is a certain amount of doubt over an event or conversation, or a lack of clarity, I have done my best to steer an even and unbiased course through the murky waters of history. Where that was not possible, I have, quite simply, made up the events and invented characters in order to play safe.

No offence is implied or intended to any of those historical figures mentioned. They were all great men faced with great challenges and I would never attempt to judge them from a distance of more than seventy years and with the benefit of hindsight. For those who are interested, here are a few points of note.

The events of 8th, 9th and 10th of May for Winston Churchill and Neville Chamberlain were a whirlwind of political turmoil. Churchill stayed loyal to Chamberlain and tried to support him against the literal vote of no confidence in the Commons, but when it was clear that Chamberlain would go, Churchill accepted his destiny and calmly stepped up to the plate. I invented the late night meeting between Churchill and Brendan Bracken, but they were old allies and the discussion I invented for them is based on the real events that were going on behind the scenes at this time.

The assault on Eben Emael happened in a manner very similar to that described although there was no Machine Gun Nest South West. Corporal Braun and his squad are all fictional but their commanders, Koch and Witzig were both real and the pair of them were awarded the Knights Cross for their efforts. Witzig's glider did indeed suffer a premature release and landing, and he did manage to arrange a new aircraft to recover his stranded glider, therefore arriving at Eben Emael after the initial assault had begun; better late than never! As for the defenders, Major Jottrand was the real life garrison commander, but with the exception of Vermeulen, all the other officers mentioned are fictional. We know a little of what was happening inside Eben Emael once the garrison was cut off, and it is a well known fact that the fortress was essentially blind and ineffectual from a very early stage.

We will probably never know for sure the true state of mind of those trapped below the surface of the mighty fortress, but the accounts that are available show that there was a tremendous amount of consternation amongst the garrison and that morale deteriorated rapidly after the first day. I personally have no doubt that many of the Belgian soldiers and officers, including Jottrand and Vermeulen, fought bravely and to the best of their ability, but what is also not in doubt is that the fortress fell at around midday on the 11th May.

As for the Coldstream Guards, Dunstable, Jackson, Hawkins and Hogson from the 2nd Battalion, and the Hangman and his men from the 1st Battalion, are all fictional. Most of the other senior appointment holders mentioned from both battalions are historical figures. Jimmy Langley and Major McCorquadale were real people who fought gallantly throughout the campaign and you can find plenty of sources that will recount their amazing story. Likewise, Lieutenant Colonel Cazenove was indeed the Commanding Officer of the 1st Battalion. His family have continued to serve in the regiment long after the war. The visit to his battalion headquarters by Brooke is mentioned in the latter's war diary. Although I do not have the exact details of the visit or the conversation, Brooke stated that he wanted to show his face at the 1st Coldstream following the battalion's epic battle of a few days earlier where it sustained heavy casualties during the withdrawal from the Dyle. Having spent plenty of time hosting visitors to a Coldstream battalion headquarters myself, I essentially made the detail up to suit the event.

As for the stand of 2nd Coldstream and 3rd Grenadiers on the Escaut, I have followed a number of well documented accounts of this battle, many of which, as already mentioned in the foreword, have been drawn together skilfully by Dilip Sarkar in his excellent book. The fact is that the Grenadiers bore the brunt of the German assault and fought their opponents to a standstill. The Germans under Captain Ambrosius achieved an unbelievable feat of arms before being forced to withdraw. Lance Corporal Harry Nicholls, accompanied by Guardsman Percy Nash, did indeed launch a ferocious counter attack on 'Poplar Ridge' which resulted in Nicholls being awarded the Victoria Cross. Our friend Guardsman Slingsby, through whose eyes we see this amazing escapade, is fictional.

I couldn't let poor old Davey Jackson get left out however, so I invented a minor incursion in the Coldstream sector for him to deal with, in addition to one that really did happen back in 1940. Thus I was able to ensure that Jackson and Dunstable got plenty of action alongside their Grenadier comrades. The odious Captain Jack Tobin, like his fictional regiment the

Hallamshire Rifles, is a figment of my imagination, thankfully. Readers should not confuse Tobin's fictional regiment with any of the distinguished historical regiments that once bore the Hallamshire name.

Guderian and Rommel, along with Nehring and the unfortunate Lieutenant Most, are all real of course. Their parts in the campaign are more than familiar to anyone with knowledge of the period so it was relatively easy to write about their adventures. I have of course, put many of the words in their mouths, but they are all in keeping with contemporary accounts. In the case of Rommel, I arranged for him to have an impromptu run-in with the thoroughly unpleasant and fictional Hauptsturmfuhrer Merkal of the SS Totenkopf. The battles around Arras and Wailly on the 21st May were confused and vicious, and I hope that I have done justice to both the British and German combatants involved.

As for the massacre at Le Paradis, it is, I regret to say, a real historical event; one of several involving the SS during the campaign. Merkal is the only fictional SS officer in this passage. The others are reported to have been present at the discussion but it was Knochlein who, having survived the war, was identified as the culprit responsible for the atrocity. It emerged at the post-war trial of Hauptsturmfuhrer Knochlein that the conversation between the SS company commanders probably happened in a manner similar to that described (less Merkal's input, obviously) although Knochlein himself claimed to have not been present when the British soldiers were actually killed. Knochlein was subsequently found guilty of war crimes and executed in 1949. Hugh Sebag-Montefiore gives a blood-chillingly detailed account of this incident in his outstanding work, *Dunkirk: Fight to the last man.*

As for the French, there was no General Pierre Duval in charge near Dinant. The commander of the local division, the 18th, was I believe, General Camille Duffett, but I could not obtain sufficient detail of his headquarters and so I invented a fictional one. Likewise, the defenders of Blockhouse 75 are all fictional. The meeting between Churchill and the French hierarchy in Paris is based on Churchill's own description of the event.

Moving on to Dunkirk, Tennant is a real character; the highly competent architect of the evacuation on the French side of the Channel. He was so busy over the course of his week at Dunkirk that I have, through necessity been forced to package his achievements into just a few passages. I hope that in doing so I have been able to do him the justice he deserves. The discussions at BEF headquarters about the rear guard operation I have based on several accounts from people who were present. Whatever the true detail of that meeting, it was certainly a fraught one. The accounts by Brooke and Montgomery of Barker's emotional state are pretty ruthless. Personally, given what Barker and everyone else had been through, I find their opinions a little harsh. I imagine that by this point in the campaign, every British commander was feeling a little ragged.

Alexander is of course a very real character and would go on to great things. His imperturbability is almost legendary. Bill Slim recounts several vivid examples of this during the retreat from Burma in his classic *Defeat into Victory*. His discussions with the French commanders at Dunkirk have been the subject of much debate for over seventy years and will no doubt continue to be a point of friction between French and British commentators. I have therefore kept it simple in this novel. Whatever the claims and counter claims of who said what, the reality of the consequences is simple enough.

I regret that space did not allow me to go into more detail of the actions at sea during the evacuation. Had it not been for the supreme courage of the thousands of naval and civilian sailors involved, and the outstanding staff work by Ramsay, Wake-Walker, Tennant and their teams, then the BEF would never have got away, and history would be a very different story indeed. HMS Grenade wasn't the only unlucky ship at Dunkirk. As in the novel, she was catastrophically damaged during an air raid whilst embarking troops at the East Mole and subsequently sank with considerable loss of life. Many other vessels shared a similar fate.

Next, our friend 'Windy' Whittaker is entirely fictional, but I have based his adventures on the accounts of several pilots who fought over France during this period. His aircraft armourer, the long suffering McWilliams, is also fictional. The two unfortunate drivers from the RASC are fictional. Although both they and their corps suffer a certain amount of 'banter' during the novel from various other characters, it is worth mentioning that the RASC had a long and distinguished history. In fact, during the Dunkirk campaign, whilst the main fighting components were fixed in the north, it was often ad hoc groups of rear echelon troops who had the onerous task of 'plugging the gaps' in the rear as the panzer divisions ran amok and attempted to cut off the BEF from Dunkirk. My own father served in the RASC during his national service. His own experience of meeting guardsmen is what I used as my basis for developing Moxon's and Fellows' relationships with the Hangman.

Eicke, the commander of SS Division Totenkopf is a historical figure. Renowned for his brutal and ruthless nature, he was, by all accounts, idolised by his soldiers. Had he not been killed during the war on the Eastern Front, and given his division's reputation for committing atrocities, there is no doubt that he would have stood trial with other Nazis after the war. Given the fates of his fellow SS comrades who did stand trial, he would almost certainly have received a heavy sentence.

In summary, I should express my regret that I couldn't make the novel twice as big. I would have loved to do the French full justice for their defence of Lille and their stand in the Gembloux Gap, not to mention the hard fighting done by various Dutch and Belgian units, or the heroic stand of the French Rear Guard on the final Dunkirk perimeter. Also, the stand of many other distinguished units such as the Norfolk and Warwickshire Regiments would have featured more heavily if space had permitted. The fight at Cassel is certainly worthy of mention, as is the stand of the Rifle Brigade at Calais. The list could go on forever. I hope that in some small way the adventures of the characters within this novel reflect the outstanding service of all those units and individuals who took part in the campaign of May-June 1940.

If you are truly interested in this campaign, then my advice is to go for a drive around Belgium and France with a decent battlefield guide book and take a look at the ground over which this campaign was fought. Once you see the battlefields for yourself, along with the beaches of course, and reflect on the deeds that were done by the soldiers of all nationalities, then you will come away a humbler person.

Lest we forget…

ALSO BY ANDY JOHNSON

SEELÖWE NORD: THE GERMANS ARE COMING

ISBN: 978-1907294389

EXTRACT FROM PART 1: SEELÖWE

"Stand-by!" Captain Dullman shouted and slid down the ramp into the hold again. The company commander had been sitting on the main deck, staring through a small gap in the raised drop-ramp, trying to get a glimpse of the enemy shore.

"Twenty metres!" Dullman warned them. "Lots of smoke. Don't worry about it. Just run like fuck for the cliffs."

Halder had started praying aloud once more. Nuemark ignored him this time; he was too busy staring up at the drop-ramp, his fingers flexing repeatedly around the stock of his rifle, pre-occupied with his own private thoughts. From behind their squad came a harsh, boorish voice.

"Hey, Bachman. Don't you seize up on the ramp like you did on the net or I'll kick your arse into the water." It was the unpleasant Schmidt again, one of the privates in Second Squad.

Saltz turned to give the loud-mouthed private a blast, but Heyman, Schmidt's own squad sergeant, beat him to it.

"Shut the fuck up, Schmidt! Concentrate on your own job."

There was a loud, repeated, knocking sound on the wooden hull of the barge and Saltz realized with a start that it was the sound of bullets hitting the vessel's side.

"Oh, fuck." He breathed quietly to himself. "Oh, fuck, fuck, fucking fuck!"

There was a sudden judder that ran through the very structure of the boat and for a heartbeat, Saltz worried that they had been hit by something bigger and he waited, frozen in fear, expecting the side of the barge to suddenly implode as an enemy shell broke through in an explosive orgy of death. It didn't happen, and then a second later he heard a metallic squealing noise. He glanced upwards and saw the drop-ramp toppling forwards out of view. Christ almighty, this was it!

"Okay men," called Dullman over his shoulder, "let's go kill some fucking Tommies!"

There was the sound of a loud splash from above. The Navy marshal, who was crouching at the top of the exit-ramp, turned, gave the thumbs-up to Dullman, and slid down into the hold, out of the way. Saltz watched Dullman take a stride up the ramp and shout back over his shoulder.

"Gooo....!"

EXTRACT FROM PART 3: BREAKOUT

"Do you have any targets in mind at this stage, Alan?" Dill asked.

The Commander Home Forces exchanged a look with the Director of Military Intelligence. Without saying anything, Brooke jabbed his finger at the map, pointing directly at the town of Driffield. Maintaining the silence, the Director saw the indication, looked back at Brooke, and nodded firmly. Brooke turned back to Dill.

"Driffield." He said. "And everything in a three mile radius of the town. That's our first priority; followed by the road between Driffield and Bridlington. I know the town is probably still crammed with civilians, but the fact is that we have a German head of steam building up there. Driffield must be hit hard, and hit fast."

A sad smiled crossed Dill's features.

"I thought that would be the case." He said quietly. "As did Newall. Two entire bomber groups are receiving their orders as we speak. There is a lot of cloud up north at the moment, but it is expected to clear mid-morning. I know that the Air Striking Group is already making low level sweeps over the town but, unless the Prime Minister forbids it at our 0730 hours meeting, then at 1000 hours this morning, nearly one hundred bombers will flatten Driffield town."

Brooke and the Director accepted the information wordlessly. After a while, the Commander Home Forces broke the silence.

"War is a terrible business. And sometimes, we must do terrible things for the greater good. We can only pray that God understands our reasons for such actions."

Before the Chief of the Imperial General Staff could reply to that, there was an urgent knock on the door, and one of Brooke's staff entered.

"Sirs," he began without preamble, "there are two flash signals from Northern Command."

Brooke nodded curtly at the officer.

"Go on, Jamie."

The staff officer raised the first signal.

"The brigade at Beverley reports that Leaconfield aerodrome has been successfully cratered, and that they are under pressure on a broad front from large formations of enemy infantry and light armoured cars, backed by artillery and mortars. They are withdrawing quickly in order to prevent being enveloped on either flank."

He paused, looking up for Brooke's reaction. Brooke turned the information over in his mind quickly, before replying.

"What's the second message?"

The officer flicked to another piece of paper.

"Lead elements of 2nd Armoured Division are now in a screen five miles south-west of Driffield. They report a column of tanks moving south out of Driffield on the Beverley road."

Brooke flicked a worried glance at Dill, then the same at the Director.

"They're going for Hull, after all." The Director murmured.

Brooke turned back to the staff officer.

"Draft a reply to Northern Command. I'll be there in a moment to check it over. Tell them to get that brigade back into Hull immediately and to ensure the city is fortified. Also, tell them to find another brigade and get it over the Humber and into Hull, quickly."

Brooke paused a moment, his mind working rapidly.

"In fact," he went on, "tell them to make it the Guards Brigade from 1 Div, and tell them to appoint the commander of the Guards Brigade as the Hull Garrison Commander. I want that city held at all costs. Do it now."

Thus dismissed, the staff officer hurried off. Brooke took a deep breath, casting a serious look at Sir John Dill.

"Tell Newall and the Prime Minister that I fully support the new bombing strategy. Tell them to flatten Driffield by all means; and the sooner the better."

WHAT PEOPLE ARE SAYING ABOUT
SEELÖWE NORD: THE GERMANS ARE COMING

" **. . .a** thrilling, detailed and very cinematic novel from new author Andy Johnson.

The author, Andy Johnson, a former regimental sergeant major in the renowned Coldstream Guards, brings 24 years' worth of military experience to his writing, which crackles with the earthy dialogue and 'getting on with it' attitude of fighting men and machines with a job to do.

The novel sizzles with very cinematic action sequences that are character-driven, from both the British and German forces' points of view...

Seelöwe Nord is chockfull of gripping and all-too-human characters, ranging from Winston Churchill to the British and German soldiers fighting it out on the ground.

Seelöwe Nord bristles with knockout battle action, from close quarters fighting on land to breakneck sea engagements."

Lee Davis
www.inthenews.co.uk

"...can't put it down; a masterpiece"

R Atkinson – Essex

"I have finished the book and it is nothing short of brilliant!"

Serving infantry officer – British Army

"I've just finished the book... absolutely brilliant! I was completely engrossed and really taken in by the realism of it all. I'm a bit of a student of the Royal Navy in World War II and was particularly impressed with the writing on the naval side of things..."

Serving officer – British Army Staff College

Lightning Source UK Ltd.
Milton Keynes UK
UKOW052323030112

184706UK00001B/67/P